I0660588

Allyn Stanley Kellogg

Memorials of Elder John White

One of the first Settlers of Hartfor

Allyn Stanley Kellogg

Memorials of Elder John White
One of the first Settlers of Hartfor

ISBN/EAN: 9783337339548

Printed in Europe, USA, Canada, Australia, Japan

Cover: Foto ©Raphael Reischuk / pixelio.de

More available books at **www.hansebooks.com**

MEMORIALS

OF

ELDER JOHN WHITE,

ONE OF

𝕿𝖍𝖊 𝕱𝖎𝖗𝖘𝖙 𝕾𝖊𝖙𝖙𝖑𝖊𝖗𝖘 𝖔𝖋 𝕳𝖆𝖗𝖙𝖋𝖔𝖗𝖉, 𝕮𝖔𝖓𝖓.,

AND OF

HIS DESCENDANTS.

BY

▸ALLYN S. KELLOGG.

HARTFORD:
PRINTED FOR THE FAMILY,
BY CASE, LOCKWOOD AND COMPANY.
1860.

CONTENTS.

1

INTRODUCTION.

THIS volume of "Memorials" has been prepared with the design of preserving, in a convenient form, the most important facts which could be ascertained respecting ELDER JOHN WHITE and his descendants. It is presumed that those of his descendants now living, who bear the name of White, have a desire to learn the history of the families through which may be traced their descent from their first ancestor in this country. They may wish, also, to place in the hands of those who are to succeed them, a record, more enduring than tradition, which may perpetuate the memory of former generations, and of the times in which they lived.

PLAN AND ARRANGEMENT. A separate section is commonly given to each family named WHITE, the sections being numbered consecutively, through the volume. The generations are divided from each other, and the families in each generation are arranged in the order of seniority in the line of descent. The running titles of the left hand pages show to which generation the heads of the families belong, and those of the right hand pages, from which son of Elder John White they are descended.

The name of the head of a family, at the beginning of a section, is followed by a biographical notice, introducing the following particulars in the history of his life, so far as they could be ascertained: The place and date of his birth; dates of marriage and death, with age at death; occupation; principal residence; public offices held; and any other facts which seemed worthy of mention. The figures in parenthesis, after the name of his father, refer back to the section, in the preceding generation, in which an account of the father may be found. The names of the husband and wife are printed in small capitals. The account of the wife is intended to show her full name; dates of birth and death, with age at death; her residence before marriage; name of her father, and maiden name of her mother.

The remainder of the section, in smaller type, contains an account of the *family* of the person whose name stands at the beginning of the section. The names of his children are printed in italics, and are arranged and numbered in the order of birth, the date of birth, or of baptism, being uniformly given, if known. On the right side of the page, against the name of each son who had a family, is commonly placed a number in parenthesis, referring forward to the section of that number, in the next generation, in which an account of that son and of his family is given. If there is no reference number opposite a name, the history of the person named follows directly after the record of birth. Those who died in infancy, or unmarried, and frequently the males who left no sons to perpetuate the name of White, are noticed only in connection with this record of their birth.

In the second generation, a separate section is allotted to each daughter of Elder John White. In the later generations, the account which is given of a female who married, (unless she married a White,) and of her husband and family, follows the record of her birth. This account is designed to show the dates of her marriage and death, the name of her husband, his residence and occupation, date of his death, and his age at death. Also, the names of her children,—which are printed in common type, and are numbered consecutively,—with dates of birth, marriage, and death; the names of *their* wives and husbands, with dates of death of these, and their ages at death. Other facts respecting the married females and their families are sometimes introduced, particularly in the earlier generations. With a few exceptions, the lines of descent from the female members of the Family are traced no farther than to their children. If the names of grandchildren are mentioned, they are printed in italics.

The several marriages of a person who was more than once married, are designated by the numbers, "1st," "2d," &c., placed directly after the word "married," or after "m.," the abbreviation of married. The maiden surname of a married female is sometimes placed in a parenthesis, between her christian name and the surname she acquired by marriage. There are numerous references from one family to another, each family being designated by the number of the section in which an account of it is given.

The foregoing explanations will be more readily understood by referring to some section in the volume; as to section 10, page 37, containing an account of Ensign Daniel White and his family; or to section 14, page 42, of Captain Daniel White and family.

The biographical sketches are designed to present only the leading facts of each one's private history and public life. The titles by which men were commonly addressed in conversation, and which almost uniformly appear in connection with their names, on the public records, are here given to those belonging to the first six generations. The names of men who belong to the later generations are printed with their professional and honorary titles; but less care has been taken to specify the offices they have filled. If too much prominence seems to be given to titles and offices, it should be remembered that, in the case of many persons who lived in former times, we have no other means of judging of *character*, than the record of the public services to which they were called by those who knew them best. Many of those who moved in the more retired walks of life were, doubtless, worthy and useful citizens; but the materials for a notice of their lives have not been found.

Delineations of character have been but rarely attempted, since it would have been impossible to render equal justice to the memory of all. The virtues ascribed to many members of the Family, by their surviving kindred, and sometimes sketched with delicacy by the hand of affection, are a gratifying testimony that many individuals of the later generations have been not unworthy descendants of an honored ancestry.

SOURCES OF INFORMATION. The facts contained in this volume have been drawn from the records of the Colonies of Connecticut and Massachusetts, from the records of Probate Courts and the Registries of Deeds, from town and church records, from inscriptions on tombstones, from family records and oral statements, and from the replies to more than six hundred letters of inquiry. Besides the labors of those who have aided his researches, the compiler has visited about forty towns, and has personally examined more than sixty sets of public records. A few particulars have been taken from Goodwin's "Genealogical Notes," and other genealogical works, to which reference is occasionally made. Such works, however, have been chiefly useful as guides to the original sources of information, which have been consulted, if practicable, and by which the statements found in those works have been verified, or, as in a few cases, corrected.

DIFFICULTIES OF THE WORK. The difficulties attending the preparation of such Memorials need not be explained to those who have undertaken similar labors. But, as very few of those who will consult this volume are aware of these difficulties, it seems proper to state some of the reasons why it is impracticable to secure completeness and perfect accuracy.

The history of the first four or five generations is as complete as it could be made by a diligent searching of the public records, which are the principal sources of information respecting the early families. But the facts sought for were not all recorded. The early records of some towns and probate courts, and of many churches, are lost. Besides these defects, there are occasional discrepancies. The town record does not always agree with the church record. Still more frequently, one of these is found to differ from a family record, or from an inscription on a tombstone. In such cases, that name, or date, has been selected, which seemed to rest upon the highest authority. In a few instances, one of the different dates assigned to an event, or a date supplied by conjecture, has been placed in brackets, with a mark of interrogation.

The labor of perfecting the history of the later generations has been much increased by the general neglect of the public registration of families, for the last sixty or eighty years. During this period, the families of the race have become numerous, and have also been widely separated by emigration. A very large proportion of those who left the homes of their fathers, have been traced to their new homes, by following out the hints gathered from the descendants of their kindred who remained, from land and probate records, and from old family papers. It is believed that the families living in the present century are more fully represented on the following pages than is usual in works of this character.

Most of the members of the Family, who have been applied to for information, have responded promptly and intelligently. The indifference and carelessness of others have been the chief embarrassments experienced in the prosecution of the work, and the principal causes of its deficiencies and errors. Some persons have made no reply to letters of inquiry until several months had elapsed, while others have paid no attention to repeated applications. In a few instances, a ready promise has never been fulfilled. Letters have sometimes been filled with materials not asked for, and of no value, while definite inquiries that had been made were entirely neglected. Many families have no family records, and some errors doubtless occur in the statements given from memory. In more than one instance in which a person has named the wrong year, in giving the date of his birth, the error has been suspected by the compiler, and has been corrected by further correspondence.

These explanations are made in order that those persons who do not find the account of their own kindred as complete as they expected,

may understand that all reasonable effort has been made to secure full-
ness and accuracy. The compiler has carefully examined the records
within his reach, and the various manuscripts furnished him, and has
diligently sought for information from the sources to which he has been
referred. It has been his first and constant aim, to make this a *reliable*
book. But, for the errors and omissions of recorders and correspond-
ents, he is not responsible. Manifest errors in the spelling of names
have been corrected; but many peculiarities have been retained.
It is hardly possible to avoid making some mistakes in deciphering
and transcribing so many thousand names and dates, many of which
are found in manuscripts not remarkable for legibility. A few typo-
graphical errors are corrected in the Appendix, and perhaps others
have escaped detection. A list of corrections and additions is also
given, prepared from information received too late for use in its proper
place.

ABBREVIATIONS. Besides the abbreviations in common use, the
following are frequently employed in this volume: b. for born; bap.
for baptized; m. for married; pub. for published; unm. for unmarried;
wid. for widow; fam. for family; d. for died; æ. for aged; dau. for
daughter; prob. for probably; res. for resided; rem. for removed;
grad. for graduated; and Coll. for College. The names of towns are
frequently abbreviated, or are represented by their initial letters, when
the full name has been given just previously. It should be observed
that the same place may be designated by several different names.
"Middletown, Upper Houses," the home of Captain Nathaniel White,
was afterwards sometimes called "Upper Middletown," and is now the
town of "Cromwell." Those of his descendants who settled in "East
Middletown," afterwards the town of "Chatham," lived in that part of
Chatham which is now the town of "Portland." Similar changes have
occurred in the names of many other places mentioned in this book.

OLD STYLE AND NEW STYLE. Previous to 1753, the year, in
England and her colonies, commenced on the 25th of March. Thus,
the birth of Elizabeth, daughter of Captain Nathaniel White, recorded,
"March 7, 1654," was doubtless in the month which preceded April,
1655. The date is therefore printed, (page 27,) "March 7, 1655."
The New Style having been adopted in Catholic countries in 1582,
there arose the custom of sometimes using a *double date* for that part
of the year between the 1st of January and the 25th of March. Two
methods were in use: the one, expressing the year thus: "1645-6;"

or, " 1660 : 61," as in the second line of page 29 : the other, which was more common, placing the last figures of the date in the form of a fraction. Thus, the marriage of Daniel White, (page 49,) is recorded, " Jan. 19, 170⅘."

In this volume the year is intended to be conformed to the New Style. Some errors may have been made in doing this, as the practice of recorders was not uniform, particularly for a half century before the New Style was adopted. No correction has been made in the day of the month. To be strictly accurate, ten days must be added to dates before the first of March, 1700, and eleven days to dates between that time and the third of September, 1752. In some cases, however, events occurring previous to 1752 were recorded after that year, and according to New Style.

A few fac-similes of autographs are given, at the expense of individuals particularly interested in their insertion.

The Table of Heads of Families, following this Introduction, is arranged upon a plan not found in other works of this character. It offers a help for tracing out, and keeping in the memory, the line of one's ancestry, and for gaining a comprehensive view of the whole circle of kindred. This Table, and the copious Indexes at the close of the volume, afford all needful facilities to those who may consult these " Memorials."

This volume, in memory of Elder John White and his Descendants, is the fruit of a purpose long cherished by Mr. NORMAN WHITE, of New York, who became interested, many years since, in the history of his ancestors, and collected, from various sources, a large amount of information respecting different branches of the Family. The present completion of the design then formed is largely due to his continued interest and liberality. Besides contributing much to the value of the work, by the constant attention given to it in all its stages of progress, he has borne about one-third of the expense of preparing and publishing this volume, thus enabling it to be offered to other members of the Family at a price considerably less than its actual cost.

The biographical notices of Elder John White, and of his son, Captain Nathaniel White, were principally prepared by HENRY WHITE, Esq., of New Haven, Conn., who had also been long interested in collecting facts relating to his ancestors, and who has, in addition to liberal contributions, devoted much time to assisting in the preparation of this volume. A few of the briefer sketches were furnished by him, as well as the Extracts from English Records, in the Appendix, and most of the facts given respecting the descendants of Captain John White, of the fourth generation. He has also made many valuable suggestions, during the progress of the work.

The history of those early families that lived in Middletown, Conn., and the neighboring towns, was originally furnished by Mr. EBENEZER B. WHITE, of Portland, Conn., whose more recent indefatigable researches have left little to be hoped for, from any further examination of records in that vicinity. He has also aided in gathering the history of many families in other places, and has thrown light upon some obscure points, by his ingenious conjectures.

The memorials of so extensive a Family can not be prepared without the assistance of many of its members. The present work owes much of its completeness to the numerous descendants of John White who have collected the history of those branches of the Family to which they respectively belong, and have thus deserved the gratitude of all who may seek for information in these pages.

The compiler would also express his obligations to SYLVESTER JUDD, Esq., of Northampton, Mass., the veteran genealogist of the valley of the Connecticut; to Rev. LAVIUS HYDE, of Bolton, Conn.; to Mr. D. WILLIAMS PATTERSON, of West Winsted, Conn.; and to many other persons not connected with the Family, for varied assistance in the preparation of this work.

It is proper to acknowledge the liberality of those members of the Family who promptly subscribed for several copies of the Memorials, thereby encouraging and securing the publication of the book.

In conclusion, the compiler would express the hope that these "Memorials" may contribute to inspire the living with a reverence for their worthy ancestors, and to perpetuate the virtues which made them worthy of commemoration.

VERNON, CONN., *March*, 1860.

A TABLE OF HEADS OF FAMILIES.

This Table contains only the names of those men, surnamed White, of whose children some definite account is given in this volume.

Figures prefixed to a name show the number of the *Section* in which an account of the Family is given; and figures following the name show the *page* on which the section commences. The figures in the left-hand column refer back to the names of the *fathers* of the persons against whose names these figures stand. In a few instances, the same numbers serve both purposes of reference.

By means of this Table, lines of descent may be very readily traced, and degrees of affinity ascertained.

GENERATION VII.

Descendants of Nathaniel.

JOHN WHITE

AND HIS DESCENDANTS.

First Generation and Children.

1. ELDER JOHN WHITE was one of the first settlers of Cambridge in Massachusetts, of Hartford in Connecticut, and of Hadley in Massachusetts. Neither the time nor the place of his birth is known. From the ages of his children, and the time of his death, it may reasonably be inferred that he was born between the years 1595 and 1605. His connection with the Reverend Thomas Hooker and his church renders it probable that he had known and valued Hooker's ministry in England. Chelmsford,—the county-town of Essex County,—about thirty miles north-east of London, was the seat of Hooker's labors; and it has been plausibly conjectured, by historians, that the company who attached themselves to him were mostly from Chelmsford and its vicinity. An examination of the parish register of Chelmsford shows that the name of White was a common one in that town; but there is no satisfactory evidence connecting the subject of this sketch with any of the families named in the parish register. Some extracts from the public records at Chelmsford are given in the Appendix to this volume.

The first certain knowledge we have of John White is as a passenger in the ship Lyon, Captain Peirce, which sailed from England about the twenty-second of June, 1632, and arrived

3

at Boston, in Massachusetts, on Sunday, the sixteenth of
September following, after a voyage of eight weeks from the
Land's End; although the passengers had been twelve weeks
aboard. They had five days of east wind and fog, but no
disaster. There were one hundred and twenty-three passengers, of whom fifty were children, all in health. The names
of thirty-three adult male passengers are reported, including
the name of John White. He was doubtless accompanied by
his family, which then consisted of his wife and at least two
children. Many of the passengers belonged to the company
of the Reverend Thomas Hooker, who was prevented from
coming with them by the attempts of his enemies to arrest
him, but who came in the following year. About a month
before the arrival of the Lyon, that part of Mr. Hooker's
company which had come over before, and had located at
Braintree, removed to Cambridge, then called Newtown;
that township having been assigned to them, by the General
Court of Massachusetts, for their settlement. There, at Cambridge, our John White found his first home in this western
world. His homelot, with his dwelling house, was on the
street then called Cow-Yard Row. This homelot contained
about three-quarters of an acre of land, and was early allotted
to him, together with about thirty acres of farming lands.
On the 5th of August, 1638, three-quarters of an acre more,
near his homelot, was granted to him by the town, for a cow-
yard. "Gore Hall," the beautiful library building of Harvard
University, probably now graces this cow-yard. If not on the
identical site, it is, beyond a doubt, very near to it. The
location and quantity of his allotments of land indicate that,
in his contribution to the common stock of the settlement, he
was in a middle place; neither among the wealthier nor the
poorer class. It is a fair inference from this fact that his
condition in England, as to property, was an easy one, and
that no necessity of outward circumstances drove him from
his comfortable English home to the privations and perils of a
wilderness.

He was admitted a freeman of Massachusetts on the 4th of
March, 1638. In February, 1635, the town of Cambridge

made its first election of a board of seven men "to do the whole business of the town." These officers were afterwards called "Townsmen," and "Selectmen." John White was one of the number chosen. His associates were John Haynes, Simon Bradstreet, John Talcott, William Westwood, William Wadsworth, and probably James Olmsted; all of them prominent and influential men.

About this time, Mr. Hooker and his people began to feel straitened in their accommodations, and determined to find a new home, with more room for their friends whom they were still expecting from England, and for the full enjoyment of their religious privileges. They selected the valley of the Connecticut, and having obtained a reluctant consent from the government of Massachusetts, which appreciated their influence and enterprise, they began immediate preparations for removal. A new company, which arrived in 1635, with the Rev. Thomas Shepard for their minister, purchased the estates and improvements of Mr. Hooker's company, and continued the settlement of Cambridge. John White sold to Nicholas Danforth, on the 20th of October, 1635, his house and homelot, with most of his outlands; and on the 30th of May, 1636, another parcel of meadow and pasture. In this last deed, of May 30th, he describes himself, by anticipation, as "of the new towne upon Quinetacquet River," and the lands which he conveys, as "in Newtowne in the Massachusetts." On the 1st of March, 1642, he conveyed to Nathaniel Sparrowhawke a house and seven acres of land, on the south side of Charles River; probably the last parcel of his Cambridge "accommodation."

In June, 1636, the main body of the company, with whom, most probably, was our John White with his family, effected their removal to the Connecticut. A vivid idea of what he and his companions experienced in this migration is best obtained from the graphic but simple narrative of the historian, Trumbull:—"About the beginning of June, Mr. Hooker, Mr. Stone, and about a hundred men, women and children, took their departure from Cambridge, and travelled more than a hundred miles through a hideous and trackless wilderness to Hartford. They had no guide but their compass; made their way over mountains, through swamps, thickets, and rivers, which were not passable but with great difficulty. They had no cover but the heavens, nor any lodgings but those which simple nature afforded them. They drove with them a hundred and sixty head of cattle, and by the way subsisted on the milk of their cows. Mrs. Hooker was borne through the wilderness upon a litter. The people generally carried their packs, arms, and some utensils. They were nearly a fortnight on their journey. This adventure was the more remarkable, as many of this company were persons of figure, who had lived, in England, in honor, affluence, and delicacy, and were entire strangers to fatigue and danger."

In the Records of Hartford John White appears as one of the original proprietors. His allotments consisted—as nearly as can be determined from the records—of his house lot, containing about two acres, of about forty acres of meadow, about thirty-two acres of upland, ten acres of swamp, and one hundred and fifty acres of upland at Hockanum, east of the Great River. Of one hundred original proprietors, there were only eighteen whose share was larger than his. His homelot was on the east side of what is now called "Governor Street," formerly "Cole Street," and was about ten rods south of the Little River. The present name of this street was given to it from the circumstance that four of the original proprietors whose homelots were on this street, and within a stone's throw of each other, became Governors of Connecticut. John White's house was next to that of Governor Hopkins, and near to that of Governor Wyllys. The famous Charter Oak, already past its maturity, and beginning in its decay to construct the hollow which preserved the Charter of Connecticut from the grasp of its enemies, stood on the lot of Governor Wyllys; and its lengthening shadows, as the evening sun went down, rested on John White's dwelling.

At Hartford he was again called into public service. In 1642 he was chosen one of the selectmen of the town,—or "orderers," as these officers were at first called,—and again in 1646, in 1651, and in 1656. His name also appears frequently on the records of the Courts, as a juror, or as an arbitrator in the settlement of private differences.

Of his private life but little can be known. He was probably a farmer, gaining a support for his growing family by the practice of industry and frugality. The history of his children shows that they were trained to these virtues, and also that, amid the many cares resting upon him, he did not fail to secure for them a good education. He maintained a respectable standing as to property, and had some share in those early enterprises which encouraged the settlement of other towns. The records of Middletown show that on the 24th day of May, 1653, "John White Sen'' had granted to him thirty acres of upland, and joining to his homelot, being his proportion in Soheags fields." At the same time he was granted "his second and third divisions at Wongonk." The early records of Middletown are partially lost, and do not show the amount of his proprietary interest there, nor how long he retained it.

Soon after the death of the Reverend Mr. Hooker, in 1647, dissensions arose in the church at Hartford, between the Reverend Mr. Stone and Elder Goodwin. The exact points of difference between the parties are now somewhat obscure. It is supposed that Elder Goodwin and his supporters were zealously opposed to any relaxation of those requirements for a participation in church privileges, which they claimed that Mr. Hooker had taught and enforced. Several Councils were held upon the subject; but harmony was not restored. At length, the supporters of Elder Goodwin's views, among whom was John White, determined to found a new settlement on the Connecticut, above Springfield, where they might have room to follow out and enjoy their principles. On the 18th of April, 1659, sixty persons, from Hartford and Wethersfield, signed the agreement to remove to Hadley. The place of John White's name, as the fifth on the list, indicates that he was among the leaders of that important movement. At the same time, William Westwood, Richard Goodman, William Lewis, John White, and Nathaniel Dickinson were chosen to go and lay out homelots. The town record of Hadley commences with a record of these transactions, and, after mentioning the appointment of this committee, thus proceeds: "The plantation being begun by them and some others of the Ingagers, the rest of the Ingagers that remained at Hartford and Wethersfield, with those that were come up to Inhabit at the said plantation, did upon the ninth of. November, at Hartford, and about the said time at Wethersfield, and at the said plantation, chuse by vote William Westwood, Nathaniel Dickinson, Samuel Smith, Thomas Standley, John White, Richard Goodman, to order all publick occasions that conscerns the good of that plantation for the yeare Insueing." This is called on the margin of the record, "First choice of Townsmen;" though it is plain that this was a voluntary agreement among the proprietors of the new plantation, rather than a legal organization.

Thus were laid the foundations of Hadley. It was the frontier settlement of that day, looking out toward the north, west, and east, on the boundless forest and its savage Indian occupants. John White's share in the common enterprise was represented by £150, the largest share being represented by £200. His homelot was on the east side of Hadley Street, and is thus described in the town record: "One houselott containing Eight acres more or lesse as it lyes. Bounded by the land of Peter Tillton South, by the land granted to Thomas Standlye North, abutting West against the comon streete, and East against the woods; being in Bredth Sixteene rod and in length Eightie." A part of this homelot is now occupied by one of his descendants, having never been alienated from the family. He had also a large allotment of outlands. During his residence in Hadley, a large share of his time was given to the interests of the prosperous town. His name is very frequently found on the committees appointed to lay out lands for division among the proprietors, and on committees for laying out highways, or for doing other business incidental to a new settlement. After the town was legally organized, he was chosen one of the selectmen in 1662, in 1663, and in 1665. He also twice served the town, in 1664 and in 1669, as Representative—or Deputy, as it was then styled—to the General Court or Legislature of Massachusetts, sitting in good service to the churches. In 1676, and in 1677, he and his eldest son, Nathaniel, then of Middletown, were members of the council called to heal the difficulty which had long troubled the ancient church in Windsor; and the final recommendation of the council, with the autograph signatures of its members, may be seen in the archives of the State, at Hartford.

John White was married in England, a few years before he came to Massachusetts. The christian name of his wife was

mentioning the appointment of this committee, thus proceeds:
"The plantation being begun by them and some others of the
Ingagers, the rest of the Ingagers that remained at Hartford
and Wethersfield, with those that were come up to Inhabit
at the said plantation, did upon the ninth of. November,
at Hartford, and about the said time at Wethersfield, and at
the said plantation, chuse by vote William Westwood, Nathaniel
Dickinson, Samuel Smith, Thomas Standley, John White,
Richard Goodman, to order all publick occasions that conscerns
the good of that plantation for the yeare Insueing." This is
called on the margin of the record, "First choice of Townsmen;" though it is plain that this was a voluntary agreement
among the proprietors of the new plantation, rather than a
legal organization.

Thus were laid the foundations of Hadley. It was the
frontier settlement of that day, looking out toward the north,
west, and east, on the boundless forest and its savage Indian
occupants. John White's share in the common enterprise
was represented by £150, the largest share being represented
by £200. His homelot was on the east side of Hadley Street,
and is thus described in the town record: "One houselott
containing Eight acres more or lesse as it lyes. Bounded by
the land of Peter Tillton South, by the land granted to Thomas
Standlye North, abutting West against the comon streete,
and East against the woods; being in Bredth Sixteene rod and
in length Eightie." A part of this homelot is now occupied
by one of his descendants, having never been alienated from
the family. He had also a large allotment of outlands.
During his residence in Hadley, a large share of his time was
given to the interests of the prosperous town. His name is
very frequently found on the committees appointed to lay out
lands for division among the proprietors, and on committees
for laying out highways, or for doing other business incidental
to a new settlement. After the town was legally organized,
he was chosen one of the selectmen in 1662, in 1663, and in
1665. He also twice served the town, in 1664 and in 1669,
as Representative—or Deputy, as it was then styled—to the
General Court or Legislature of Massachusetts, sitting in

In the Rev. Dr. Parker's Historical Discourse in 1870, he says; —
"In March 1677, Mr. John White (he was one of the original withdrawers who went to Hadley, and returned to Hartford in 1671) was chosen and ordained to the

office of Ruling Elder, in the presence and with the approbation of the elders and messengers of some neighbor churches." "This holy man, having faithfully served the Lord in his place, and that also with good success through grace, (He was a good man, and God was with him,) fell asleep in Christ, and went to receive his reward, January, 1683." "   (p. 34.)

mentioning the appointment of this committee, thus proceeds: "The plantation being begun by them and some others of the Ingagers, the rest of the Ingagers that remained at Hartford and Wethersfield, with those that were come up to Inhabit at the said plantation, did upon the ninth of. November, at Hartford, and about the said time at Wethersfield, and at the said plantation, chuse by vote William Westwood, Nathaniel Dickinson, Samuel Smith, Thomas Standley, John White, Richard Goodman, to order all publick occasions that conscerns the good of that plantation for the yeare Insueing." This is called on the margin of the record, "First choice of Townsmen;" though it is plain that this was a voluntary agreement among the proprietors of the new plantation, rather than a legal organization.

Thus were laid the foundations of Hadley. It was the frontier settlement of that day, looking out toward the north, west, and east, on the boundless forest and its savage Indian occupants. John White's share in the common enterprise was represented by £150, the largest share being represented by £200. His homelot was on the east side of Hadley Street, and is thus described in the town record: "One houselott containing Eight acres more or lesse as it lyes. Bounded by the land of Peter Tillton South, by the land granted to Thomas Standlye North, abutting West against the comon streete, and East against the woods; being in Bredth Sixteene rod and in length Eightie." A part of this homelot is now occupied by one of his descendants, having never been alienated from the family. He had also a large allotment of outlands. During his residence in Hadley, a large share of his time was given to the interests of the prosperous town. His name is very frequently found on the committees appointed to lay out lands for division among the proprietors, and on committees for laying out highways, or for doing other business incidental to a new settlement. After the town was legally organized, he was chosen one of the selectmen in 1662, in 1663, and in 1665. He also twice served the town, in 1664 and in 1669, as Representative—or Deputy, as it was then styled—to the General Court or Legislature of Massachusetts, sitting in

Boston. The early records of the Church in Hadley are destroyed; but it is evidence of his good report among the brethren, that he was one of the "messengers" from Hadley when the Church at Northampton was gathered, in April, 1661.

After 1670 his name does not appear on the records of Hadley, and it was probably during this year that he returned to Hartford. Difficulties still existing in the old Church at Hartford resulted in another secession, and in the organization, on the 12th of February, 1670, of the South Church, under the ministry of the Reverend John Whiting. The same attachment for the ancient landmarks, in the constitution and discipline of the church, was the cause of this secession, and of that which, eleven years before, had founded Hadley. On his return to Hartford, John White connected himself with the South Church, and was chosen to the office of Elder in it. It is not improbable that he was called from Hadley to fill that office. The home of twenty-three years of the vigor of his life had doubtless retained a strong hold on his affections; and, as he felt the weight of advancing years, it may have needed only the attraction of a Church framed after his idea of the perfect scripture model, to win him back to its rest. If, now, this Church of his choice needed his help and services as an office-bearer, the call would become imperative.

After his return to Hartford, his name does not appear again upon the records, as holding civil office, or performing civil services. The office of Elder then exempted him who bore it from all duties of this kind. But as an arbitrator, referee, and council in ecclesiastical matters, he performed good service to the churches. In 1676, and in 1677, he and his eldest son, Nathaniel, then of Middletown, were members of the council called to heal the difficulty which had long troubled the ancient church in Windsor; and the final recommendation of the council, with the autograph signatures of its members, may be seen in the archives of the State, at Hartford.

John White was married in England, a few years before he came to Massachusetts. The christian name of his wife was

MARY; but nothing is known respecting her, except that she was living in March, 1666. She died before her husband, probably after his return to Hartford.

His will names the six following children, two or three of whom were born in England.

CHILDREN.

1. *Mary,*   b.   ; m. Jonathan Gilbert. . . . . (2)
2. *Nathaniel,* b. about 1629; m. 1st, Elizabeth ——; 2d, Mrs. Martha Mould. (3)
3. *John,*   b.   ; m. Sarah Bunce. . . . . (4)
4. *Daniel,*   b.   ; m. Sarah Crow. . . . . (5)
5. *Sarah,*   b.   ; m. Stephen Taylor and others. . . . . . (6)
6. *Jacob,*   b. Oct. 8, 1645; m. Elizabeth Bunce. . . . . (7)

The year of Nathaniel's birth is derived from his age at death, as given on his tombstone; the birth of Jacob is recorded at Hartford. The ages of the other children can not be exactly determined.

The life of John White was prolonged to a good old age, and in the winter of 1683–4 he rested from his labors. The exact time of his death is not known; but it must have occurred between the 17th of December, 1683, the date of his will, and the 23d of January, 1684, the date of the inventory of his estate. He lived to see all his children married, and to hold in his arms his children's children, to the third and fourth generations. Of his children, only three sons and one daughter survived him: two of these sons, with John, who died before him, were the heads of their tribes, and transmitted his name and principles to succeeding generations.

His will is recorded, and is on file, in the Probate Office at Hartford. The following is a copy of the original document, which is in the hand-writing of the principal witness.

The Last Will and Testament of Mr. John White, of Hartford.

"For as much as my time is Vncertaine, and I know not the day of my death, I Account it my dutie to make my last will and testament, which is as followeth.

I Resigne and give up my selfe, soul & bodie, to my soveraigne Lord & maker, my God and father in my Lord and saviour Jesus Christ: and to prevent trouble to those that shall survive mee, I do dispose of that portion of outward estate which the Lord hath in mercy blessed me with, in manner following (viz)

I give & bequeath to my son Nathanaell White thirtie pounds, and my best broad Cloath Coate, & I also give him my iron bound Chest in my Chamber, and my Cobirons in my parlour, & that part of my ox pasture which lyeth on the Left hand of the way as we go to Wethersfield I give to him & his heirs for ever, bounded upon the high way west, Henery Grimes land North, Mʳ Niccolls his Land South, the south meadow east.

I give to my son Daniell White twentie pounds.

I give to my son Jacob White & his heires for ever, that part of my ox pasture in Hartford which lyeth on the right hand of the way Leading to Wethersfield, bounded by the high way East, by Jonathan Bigaloes land South, by Henery Grimes his Land North, & Leuᵗ. Websters land West. I also give him my feather bed in the Chamber with a boolstar & pillow & the best blancket upon it, & the bed sted & Curtains belonging to it. I impower my Executor to give to my daughter Hixton according to his discretion as he shall see her need Calls ffor. And whereas fformerlie I intended to give one parcell of meadow land in great Ponset to Stephen Taylor, yet now being forced to pay a great summe of money ffor the Redemption of his house & homlott, I now see cause to dispose of that land for payment of that debt, and shall leave it to my Executor with the advise of the overseers, to give either to him or the rest of my daughter Hixtons Children as he shall see Cause.

I give to my grand Child, Stephen Taylor a flock bed & truckle bed sted at Nathanaell Whites at Hadly, and an old blancket upon my bed in my Chamber, and a linzy woolsie Coverlid at the feet of my bed in the parlour, and a peice of dutch searge now at the tailors to make me a pair of breeches & Jacket, I give to the said Stephen Taylor.

I give to Sarah White the daughter of my son Nathanaell five pounds.

I give to the Reverᵈ Mʳ John Whiting my honored pastor five pounds in silver.

My will is that due debts being discharged, and the above mentioned legacies payd, the remainder of my Estate shall be divided among my grand Children, (viz.) Jonathan Gilbert son of my daughter Mary, my son Nathaniells Children, my son Johns Children, my son Daniells Children & my Daughter Sarah Children, their sons to have as much more as their daughters, & if any of their sons shall dye before they Come to the age of one & twentie years then his or their portion to be divided equally among the survivors, and in like manner among the daughters, if any of them shall dye before the age of eighteen years. My will is that my wearing apparrell be divided amongst my sonns. My will also is that my Executor shall have four years time after my decease for the payment of the Legacies mentioned, only my will is that my moveable goods be payd to them that are readie to receive them presently, and I do give my said Executor full power to sell my land lying in the last out division in Hartford, being about Eightie acrees, and my share in the mill for the payment of the legacies as aforesaid, & what ever time or expences he shall be at, in managing these affaires, he shall fully satisfie him selfe out of the estate before division be made.

I do Constitute & ordaine my son Nathaniell White the sole Executor of this my Last will and testament; and I do desire my beloved friends Ensign

4

Nathaniell Stanly and Stephen Hosmer as overseers to assist in performance of this my last will, and I do give them twentie shillings apeice for their paines therein.

	his	
This was declared by	JOHN W WHITE senr	(L. S.)
John White senior to be	mark.	
his last will & Testament		
the seventeenth day of December,		
1683, in presence of		

> Caleb Watson,
> Mary Watson."

His will was made when the extreme feebleness of old age and disease forbade him to write his own name. The following is a fac-simile of his signature to the recommendation of the council already referred to, in the year 1677. The letter *h* was made with a downward stroke, as was common in former times.

The Inventory of his estate is dated Jan. 23, 1683, and amounts to £190. 9s. It contains nothing of particular interest, and is omitted. He had given away a part of his property during his lifetime.

The age and character of our John White, as well as the number of his descendants, justly entitle him to the appellation of Patriarch. The controlling power of religion over him is seen in his forsaking the comforts of his English home, and encountering the privations and perils of a wilderness, that he might help to maintain what he considered to be a true church, and might enjoy the pure worship of God and the teachings of his faithful ministers.

To the conscientiousness and zeal of the Puritan, he added the enterprise and daring of the Pioneer. Ever ready to forsake his old home and make for himself a new one, when the interests of truth and religion called, the Newtowne of Massachusetts was cheerfully exchanged for the Newtowne of Connecticut; and this last, again, for the frontier post of Hadley. And when he could serve the same cause with greater usefulness in his old home, we find him again at Hartford, with his harness on, and ready to labor, even in the feebleness of age.

His good sense and sound judgment are attested by the nature of the services which his fellow-citizens sought from him. Each of the three important towns in which he lived required his aid in the management of its prudential affairs. The capacity to discharge the duties of a townsman as well as those of a representative to the colonial legislature, was, in that day, an indispensable pre-requisite to the appointment.

The office of ruling elder in the church, which he held during the last ten or twelve years of his life, was one of great influence and importance. There was usually but one ruling elder in each church. His office was designed to relieve the teaching elder, or pastor, of a considerable part of the labor, responsibility, and anxiety attending the government and discipline of the church. It required a grave, discreet, and reliable man, one who had earned a good report of those without and those within the church. Such a one, in all respects furnished for his work, was our John White.

To be the descendant of one whose qualifications caused him to be called to these various duties in the state and in the church, and who appears to have discharged them well, is a matter of just pride. His descendants may safely and abundantly honor the ancestor in whose footsteps they may so safely walk.

Second Generation and Children.

2. MARY WHITE, daughter of Elder John, (1) was born in England, a few years before the family emigrated to Massachusetts. She died in Hartford, Conn., probably in the early part of the year 1650. She married, Jan. 29, 1646, JONATHAN GILBERT of Hartford, an early settler there. His name often occurs upon the public records, which show that he was a man of enterprise and influence. He sometimes represented the town in the General Court, was collector of the customs at Hartford, and was Marshal of the Colony;—the latter office corresponding to that of high-sheriff. He also rendered important service to the Colony in the difficulties with the Indians; acting as interpreter, and being often selected, on account of his bravery, as the leader in emergencies of danger and importance. He was extensively engaged in the trade and coasting business of the young colonies, and acquired great wealth, for that day. He died Dec. 10, 1682, in the 64th year of his age, leaving an estate of nearly £2500.

HER CHILDREN.

1. *Jonathan*, b. May 11, 1648. A part of his early life was spent in the West Indies. He afterwards settled as a merchant in Middletown, Conn., and m. June 22, 1679, Dorothy Stow of Middletown, dau. of Rev. Samuel and Hope Stow. Being dissatisfied with the legacy left him by his father, he petitioned the General Court for some further provision from his father's estate. A number of curious documents connected with this application are preserved among the State Papers, at Hartford. ("Private Controversies," Vol. II., pp. 129—137.) He d. Feb. 1, 1698, æ. 49. His widow d. July 14, 1698, æ. 40. He had, 1, Mary, b. May 18, 1680; 2. Jonathan, b. March 31, 1681, d. same day; 3. Mehetable, b. Feb. 8, 1682; 4. John, b. June 30, 1683; 5. Jonathan, b. Feb. 8, 1685, d. Feb. 27, 1685; 6. Jonathan, b. April 11, 1686 d. April 28, 1686; 7. Nathaniel, b. Dec. 27, 1689; 8. Ebenezer, d. March 21, 1718; 9. Sarah.

2. *Mary*, b. Dec. 15, 1649; probably d. young.

NOTE. After the death of his first wife, Jonathan Gilbert m. Mary Wells, by whom he had Sarah, b. July 25, 1651, and several other children. Mrs. Mary (Wells) Gilbert survived her husband, and d. July 3, 1700, æ. 74. A somewhat extended account of the "Gilbert Family" may be found in the N. E. Historical and Genealogical Register, Vol. IV., 1850.

3. Captain NATHANIEL WHITE, son of Elder John, (1) was born in England, about 1629, three years before his father came to New England. He was about seven years old when the family removed from Cambridge to Hartford.

In 1650 or 1651, when about twenty-one years old, he removed to Middletown, on the Connecticut River, being one of the original proprietors and first settlers of that town. His homelot was in that part of Middletown formerly called "Upper Houses," and afterwards "Upper Middletown," now constituting the town of Cromwell. His dwelling-house was in the lower part of the village, on the street that lies between the Middlesex turnpike and the Connecticut River.

He early acquired great influence, and was among the leading men of that section of the Colony. In civil life he was almost constantly employed in some of the various town offices, and also statedly represented the town in the Legislature—or General Court, as it was at first called—of the Colony. He was first chosen in 1659, when about thirty years of age, and from 1661 to 1710, a period of fifty years, he was chosen Deputy once every year, and often twice; the Legislature then meeting semi-annually, in May and October of each year, and a new election being held for each session. The only exception to his regular election was in the year 1688, when, in consequence of the usurpation of Sir Edmund Andross, there were no elections by the people. He was elected a representative from Middletown eighty-five times, and was eighty-one years old when last chosen. Very few instances can be found of so long an official life dependent on annual popular elections; probably no other, in which the same political community, by a majority of all its voters, has elected the same individual its representative in the Legislature of the State eighty-five times. Such facts as this have secured for Connecticut the appellation of the "land of steady habits."

In 1669 Nathaniel White was appointed by the Legislature a magistrate and commissioner for Middletown, and in 1684 for Middletown, Haddam, and the district of Meriden; and he held local courts for these places. In military life he rose through successive grades to the rank of Captain, the title of which office he carried with him through life. The following is a fac-simile of his signature as commissioner, in 1695.

It is evident from the nature of the public services he rendered, traces of which are found in the records of the town and of the Colony, that he was a man of ability and education, and that he deserved the great and long-continued confidence reposed in him by his fellow-citizens. The Rev. Dr. Field, in his address on the two-hundredth anniversary of the settlement of Middletown, says of him, that "he was a man of high religious character and sound judgment."

He died Aug. 27, 1711, "aged about 82," as the inscription on his monument informs us. His grave is in Middletown city, in the burying-ground near the river. In his will, which is dated Aug. 16, 1711, after some other bequests, he gives one-fourth of his undivided lands "to remain for the use of the Publick School already agreed upon in the Town of Middletown, forever." Respecting certain other provisions of his will, he makes this statement: "And the reason why I say my daughters shall have each of them one-third of what moveable household goods was in being when my former wife dyed, is because I intend what my now wife hath gained by her Industry, and what she brought with her to me, should be at her own dispose." The Inventory of his estate amounted to £927. 11s. 5d. He owned about 1500 acres of land, and was for a long time the second in property in the town.

He married, 1st, Elizabeth ———, who was the mother of his children. Her family name and her original residence have not been ascertained. Her grave-stone, which stands by that of her husband, and was probably erected after his death, says that she "died in the year 1690, aged about 65 years."[*]

He married, 2d, Mrs. MARTHA MOULD, widow of Hugh Mould of New London, Conn., and dau. of John Coit and Mary [Jenners?]. Two of her daughters had married sons of Captain White. She died April 14, 1730, "aged about 86." This is the age given on her grave-stone, at the Upper Houses. The town record says, "in ye 77th year of her age," which is doubtless an error.

CHILDREN;—BY THE FIRST MARRIAGE.

1. *Nathaniel*, b. July 7, 1652; m. Elizabeth Savage.   .   .   .   . (8)
2. *Elizabeth*, b. March 7, 1655; m. Sergt. John Clark of Middletown, and d. Dec. 25, 1711, æ. 56. He d. July 26, 1731. She had, 1. Nathaniel, b. April 18, 1676, m. Oct. 27, 1702, Sarah Graves of Hatfield, Mass.; (see Family 4;) 2. John, b. June 14, 1679, m. May 9, 1710, Sarah Goodwin of Hartford; 3. Daniel, b. Aug. 30, 1680, m. July 12, 1704, Elizabeth Whitmore, and d. March, 1725, æ. 44. His wid. m. 2d, Capt. Wm. Savage, and 3d, —— Williams, and d. Jan. 31, 1743, æ. 57; 4. Elizabeth, b. April 3, 1685, m. Ebenezer Selden of Hadley, Mass., who d. 1740: she was living in 1746; 5. Mary, b. April 3, 1691, d. in infancy; 6. Sarah, b. Sept. 8, 1692, m. Feb. 17, 1720, John Shepard; 7. White, a dau., b. Nov. 4, 1693, m. 1st, Joseph Cole of Wethersfield; m. 2d, March 22, 1744, Samuel Smith of Mid.; 8. Mary, b. May 4, 1695, m. James Thompson of Brimfield, Mass.
3. *John*, b. April 9, 1657; m. Mary ——.   .   .   .   .   . (9)
4. *Mary*, b. April 7, 1659; m. 1st, Jan. 16, 1678, Jacob Cornwell of Mid., who d. April 18, 1708, æ. 61. She m. 2d, April 13, 1710, John Bacon, sen., of Mid., who d. Nov. 4, 1732, æ. 70. She d. Nov. 15, 1732, æ. 73. By her first husband she had, 1. Mary, b. Nov. 2, 1679, m. May 30, 1698, Francis Whitmore of Mid.; 2. Jacob, b. Aug. 9; 1681, d. Nov. 9, 1681; 3. Jacob, b. Oct. 1, 1682, m. March 20, 1711, Edith Whitmore. He was buried July 5, 1767, æ. 84; 4. Nathaniel, b. Aug. 30, 1684; 5. Giles, b. Aug. 14, 1686; 6. Daniel, b. April 19, 1688; 7. Isaac, b. Sept. 22, 1690, m. July 29, 1714, Mary Burliss of Hartford; 8. Wait, b. Sept. 18, 1692, was a volunteer in the expedition to Canada, in 1709. He m. April 24, 1717, Mary Todd, and d. Jan. 8, 1742, æ. 49; 9. Elizabeth, b. July 21, 1697, m. March 26, 1724, Ebenezer Wetmore, who d. Jan. 11, 1743; 10. Timothy, b. Aug. 23, 1700, m. 1st, Nov. 23, 1726, Rebecca Wells; m. 2d, March 20, 1728, Susannah Hamlin.
5. *Daniel*, b. Feb. 23, 1662; m. Susannah Mould.   .   .   .   . (10)
6. *Sarah*, b. Jan. 22, 1664; m. John Smith of Haddam, Conn., probably a shipmaster. She d. before her father. She had, 1. Nathaniel, bap. at Mid., Jan. 5, 1696. An old memorandum, dated Feb. 8, 1787, says that he "went

---

[*] The will of Thomas Bunce, sen., without date, but probably made in 1682, mentions his "daughter, Elizabeth White," (see Family 7,) and also his "cousin, Elizabeth White." It is not improbable that in the latter case he refers to the wife of Capt. Nathaniel White; but no certain proof of this relationship has been discovered. In former times, the word *cousin* was frequently used instead of *nephew* or *niece*.

away a ship-carpenter, and was never heard of;" 2. Sarah, bap. May 8, 1698,
m. ——— Coleman of Glastenbury, Conn.; 3. Elizabeth, bap. Nov. 26, 1699,
m. Jeremiah Ludlum of Elizabethtown, N. J.; 4. Thankful, m. Jehiel Kelsey of Durham, Conn., who d. about 1757. · She d. Jan., 1787.

7. *Jacob*, b. May 10, 1665 ; m. 1st, Deborah Shepard; 2d, Rebecca Ranney. (11)
8. *Joseph*, b. Feb. 20, 1667 ; m. Mary Mould.   .   .   .   .   .   (12)

---

4. Sergeant JOHN WHITE, Jun., son of Elder John, (1)
settled in Hatfield, Mass. His homelot was on the east side
of the street, the fifth from the south end of the homelots, as
they were originally laid out. He was buried in Hatfield,
Sept. 15, 1665. His age is not known, but it was less than
35 years. The inventory of his estate, amounting to £313,
includes a house and homelot at Hatfield, and also at Hartford, Conn. It is probable that he resided at Hartford till
within a year or two of his death, and that his children were
born there.

He married SARAH BUNCE of Hartford, dau. of Thomas
and Sarah Bunce. After the death of her husband, the
widow Sarah White married Nicholas Worthington of Hatfield. She died June 20, 1676. Mr. Worthington again
married, and died Sept. 6, 1683. (An account of the descendants of Nicholas Worthington may be found in Goodwin's
" Genealogical Notes.")

CHILDREN.

1. *Sarah*, b.   ; m. Feb. 12, 1678, John Graves of Hatfield, who d. Dec.
   2, 1730. She had, 1. Sarah, b. Feb. 15, 1679, m. Oct. 27, 1702, Nathaniel
   Clark of Middletown, Conn.; (see Family 3 ;) 2. John, b. March 23, 1682,
   m. Jemima ———, and d. Aug., 1716, æ. 34 ; 3. Mary, b. Feb. 24, 1683, m.
   Jeremiah Wait ; 4. Thomas, b. July 4, 1685, d. 1689 ; 5. Abigail, b. Oct.
   29, 1687, m. ——— Wilcox ; 6. Martha, b. Nov. 4, 1689, m. 1716, John
   Crafts ; 7. Daniel, b. Oct. 13, 1690, d. young ; 8. Thomas, b. June 5, 1693 ;
   9. Daniel, b. Jan. 28, 1698, m. 1724, widow Thankful ———, and d. 1757,
   æ. 59 ; 10. Rebecca, b. May 4, 1700, m. Moses Nash of Hadley, afterwards
   of West Hartford, Conn., where she d. Oct. 6, 1743, æ. 43. He rem. to
   Wintonbury, (now Bloomfield,) Conn., and d. Jan. 26, 1760, æ. 63. (See
   "Nash Family," p. 46.)
2. *John*, b.   1663 ; m. Hannah Wells.   (13)

---

5. Lieutenant DANIEL WHITE, son of Elder John, (1) was
probably born in Hartford, Conn., as early as 1639. He
settled in Hatfield, Mass., about the year 1662, as appears

from the following entries on the town record of Hadley.
"Jan. 21: 1660: 61. This day Daniel White had a hundred
pound lot given him beyond the River, and his father John
White Ingages for him." Dec. 12, 1661, there was a renewal
of the grant to Daniel White, " provided he be resident on his
allotments in March next." His homelot was on the west
side of Hatfield Street, the fourth lot south of the Mill Lane,
or road leading westerly. Other lands were allotted to him,
and the records of Hatfield show that he was a farmer. He
was frequently called into the service of the town. Before
the division of Hadley, he was chosen a constable in 1666, and
one of the selectmen in 1670. The town of Hatfield was
incorporated in 1670, but the records of the town officers previous to 1677 are mostly lost. During the twenty years after
1678, Daniel White was eight times chosen one of the selectmen of Hatfield. He occasionally held other offices, and was
often appointed on committees for attending to various town
affairs which called for the exercise of discretion and sound
judgment. He was also active in the ecclesiastical affairs of
the town. The title of Lieutenant is first given him on the
records in Dec., 1692. The following is a fac-simile of his
autograph in 1701.

He died July 27, 1713, being probably not far from 75
years of age. By his will, dated July 11, 1713, he gave £4
to the church in Hatfield, and constituted his only surviving
son, Daniel, his executor. Previous to his death he had given
a part of his land to his son, Daniel, and to his daughter Hannah; but he left a large estate for those times. The inventory
amounted to £363, not including the homestead and some
other property, which was appraised in 1719, after the death
of his widow, at nearly £300.

He married, Nov. 1, 1661, SARAH CROW, daughter of
John Crow and Elizabeth Goodwin. Her father was an
early settler of Hartford and Hadley, and became one of
the largest landholders in the colony of Connecticut. Her

5

mother was the only child of Elder William and Susannah Goodwin. Elder Goodwin was a fellow-passenger with Elder John White, in the ship Lyon, and was one of the leaders in the settlement of Hadley. Sarah Crow was born at Hartford, March 1, 1647, and was but 14 years and 8 months old at the time of her marriage. She was one of seven daughters, who married into some of the best families in the valley of the Connecticut. A high authority in such matters has said, "Those Crow girls made smart women." Mrs. Sarah White died at Hatfield, June 26, 1719, æ. 72. Her inventory shows the following list of articles in her wardrobe. She was not only well supplied, but seems to have been a little extravagant, for that day, for one residing in a small town.

	£	s.	d.		£	s.	d.
8 Shifts, . . .	1	17	0	White waistcoat, . .	0	2	0
Damask Gown, . .	1	0	0	Damask Coat, . .	0	2	0
Silk Girdle, . .	0	1	0	Painted serge coat, .	0	15	0
Green ribbon girdle, .	0	1	6	Blue damask Mantua,	1	2	0
Linen Gloves, . .	0	2	0	Streaked under coat, .	0	8	0
Muff, ...	0	3	0	Silk prunella Mantua,	1	10	0
Head Linen, . .	1	10	0	Serge Hood & bluefacing,	1	10	0
Leather Gloves, .	0	3	6	Old serge Hood, . .	0	5	0
Pair blue Stockings,	0	1	6	Old reddish coat, .	0	4	0
Silk Gloves, .	0	9	0	Old black coat, .	0	2	0
Old blue Stockings, .	0	0	6	Pair of blue & red sleeves,	0	2	0
Lustring Hood, .	0	12	6	Old black Mantua, .	0	2	0
Alamode Hood, .	0	11	0	Blue Calico apron, .	0	1	6
Silk Handkerchief, .	0	5	0	2 do. 4s. & 4s. 6d.,	0	8	6
Painted do. . .	0	3	0	Garlix Apron, .	0	3	6
Cambric do. .	0	5	0	Yellow flannel Waistcoat,	0	5	0
2 Handk'fs 4s. & 3s.,	0	7	0	White Apron, . .	0	5	0
3 do. 5s., 3s. & 3s.,	0	11	0	Neck Handk'f, . .	0	4	0
Fan, . . .	0	1	6	Painted do. . .	0	1	6
Plain cloth Coat, .	0	10	0				
				Total, . . .	£16	8	0

Equal to $54.67.

The mantuas were gowns, or dresses; the coats were petticoats.

CHILDREN.

1. *Sarah,*   b. Oct. 15, 1662; m. 1st, March 31, 1680, Thomas Loomis of Hatfield, who d. Aug. 12, 1688. She m. 2d, Nov. 12, 1689, John Bissell of Windsor, Conn., who rem. to Lebanon. They were prob. both living in 1723. All her sons, except John Bissell, jun., lived in Lebanon. She had, by her 1st husband, 1. John, b. Jan. 1, 1681, m. Oct. 30, 1706, Martha Osborn; 2. Thomas, b. April 20, 1684, m. 1st, Jan. 8, 1713, Elizabeth Fowler, who d. July 18, 1742; m. 2d, Dec. 20, 1743, Hannah Hunt, who d. June

10, 1758, æ. 78. He d. April 30, 1765, æ. 81. By her 2d husband, 3. Sarah, b. Nov. 12, 1690, prob. m. Joseph Loomis; 4. John, (Capt.) b. Sept. 12, [10?] 1693, lived in Coventry, and d. about Dec., 1763, æ. 90. He m. 1st, Nov. 14, 1714, Sarah Fowler, who d. Aug. 25, 1751; m. 2d, Abigail ———; 5. Daniel, b. Jan. 4, 1698, d. Oct. 3, 1776, æ. 78. Perhaps he m. Feb. 15, 1747, Elizabeth Fitch; 6. Benjamin, b. March 22, 1701, d. Aug. 9, 1758, æ. 57. He m. 1st, July 17, 1728, Mary Wattle; m. 2d, Ann ———, who d. about Dec., 1778.

2. *Mary*, b. ; d. Sept. 5, 1664.

3. *Mary*, b. Aug. 5, 1665; m. 1st, ——— Wells; m. 2d, ——— Barnard. The Probate Records at Northampton show that her name was Wells in 1713, and Barnard in 1717. This is all that is known of her history.

4. *Elizabeth*, b. Nov. 13, 1667; m. July 2, 1688, Dea. Samuel Loomis of Windsor, Conn., who removed to Colchester, Conn., where he was chosen Deacon in 1702. She d. Feb. 18, [25?] 1736, æ. 68. He then m. Oct. 25, 1738, widow Elizabeth Church, who d. Aug. 10, 1751, æ. 78. He d. May 20, 1754, æ. nearly 88. She had, 1. Elizabeth, b. 1689, d. Aug. 6, 1689; 2. Samuel, b. Feb. 28, 1690, d. March 14, 1690; 3. Samuel, b. July 17, 1692, was Dea. at Colchester, and d. July 10, [June 26?] 1753, æ. 61. He m. Dec. 12, 1717, Elizabeth Holms, who d. May 27, 1760, æ. 67; 4. Isaac, b. Dec. 23, 1693, perhaps lived in Windsor, and m. April 26, 1716, Hannah Eggleston of W., who d. Nov. 6, 1752; 5. Jacob, b. Feb. 25, 1695, was Dea. at Colchester, and d. June 27, 1757, æ. 61. His wid., Hannah, prob. d. Aug. 26, 1766, æ. 74; 6. Azariah, b. May 2, 1700, d. Feb. 20, 1757, or, according to another entry, d. Feb. 9, 1758, æ. 56. He m. Dec. 25, 1723, Abigail Newton, who d. June 15, 1778; 7. Elizabeth, b. Nov. 13, 1702, m. Jan. 3, 1721, Daniel Worthington of Colchester. They had 18 children, of whom 13 were married. He d. March 1, 1784, æ. 85. She d. Dec. 3, 1789, æ. 87. (See Goodwin's "Genealogical Notes," p. 267;) 8. Sarah, b. March 7, 1705; 9. Caleb, b. Sept. 20, 1707, was living in Colchester in 1733; 10. Daniel, b. Feb. 20, 1709, d. in Col., March 28, 1784, æ. 75. He m. Oct. 7, 1731, Hannah Witherell, who d. March 1, 1779, æ. 75.

— 5. *Daniel*, b. July 4, 1671; m. Sarah Bissell and others. . . (14)

6. *Esther*, b. ; d. Feb., 1675.

7. *Hannah*, b. July 4, 1674; d. in infancy.

8. *John*, b. Nov. 16, 1676; d. Aug., 1677.

9. *Esther*, b. ; m. Dec. 7, 1696, Lieut. John Ellsworth of Windsor, Conn. He is called the first settler of Ellington, then a part of Windsor; although his family had not removed thither previous to his death, which occurred by accident. A stone was erected, bearing this inscription: "Lieut. John Ellsworth was killed here by the fall of a tree, Oct. 26th, 1720, aged 49 years and 19 days." The stone has been removed a short distance, and now stands by the road-side, about one mile southeast of the meeting-house. She d. Sept. 7, 1766, æ. about 89. She had, 1. John, (Capt.) b. Nov. 7, 1697, settled in East Windsor, and died Jan. 4, 1784, æ. 86. He m. Nov. [May?] 8, 1734, Ann Edwards of E. Windsor, who d. April 11, 1790, æ. 91; 2. Daniel, (Capt.) b. March 20, 1700; lived in Ellington, and d. Jan. 27, 1782, æ. 82. His widow, Mindwell, d. May 17, 1786, æ. 85; 3. Esther, b. March 9, 1702; m. Jan. 31, 1722, Capt. Samuel

Welles, 2d, of East Hartford, who d. March 2, 1760, æ. 66. She d. Nov. 3, 1791, æ. 89. Their dau., *Ruth*, m. Hon. Ebenezer White, (Family 65 ;) 4. Anna, b. April 27, 1705, m. Samuel Hunt of Northfield, Mass. ; 5. Martha, b. Feb. 27, 1709, m. Sept. 11, 1729, Nathaniel Stoughton of Windsor ; 6. Ann, b. 1712.——Guardians were appointed to both *Anna* and *Ann*, Jan. 1, 1723, and they both signed an agreement made by the heirs of their father, Jan. 14, 1736.

10. *Hannah*, b. Sept., 1679 ; m. Dea. Nathaniel Dickinson of Hatfield, Mass., who d. 1745. She had, 1. Jonathan, b. Nov. 7, 1699 ; 2. Martha, b. Dec. 25, 1701, m. March 2, 1727, Elnathan Graves ; 3. Obadiah, b. July 28, 1704, m. Mary ———; 4. Nathan, b. April, 1707, d. May 10, 1707 ; 5. Joshua, b. Feb. 7, 1709 ; 6. Elijah, b. Feb. 24, 1712, d. June 8, 1714 ; 7. Elijah, b. Sept. 20, 1714, d. May 28, 1715 ; 8. Joel, b. March 23, 1716 ; 9. Lucy, b. Sept. 9, 1718, d. Dec. 24, 1718.

11. *Mehitable*, b. March 14, 1683 ; m. Dec. 19, [18?] 1705, Jeremiah Bissell of Windsor, Conn., and had, 1. Rachel, b. Nov. 16, 1706 ; 2. Mabel, b. Jan. 16, 1708 ; 3. John, b. Sept. 1, 1709, m. Dec. 2, 1733, Hannah Watson, and d. July 15, 1737, æ. 28 ; 4. Sarah, b. July 4, 1711.

6. SARAH WHITE, daughter of Elder John, (1) was thrice married. She died at Hatfield, Mass., Aug. 10, 1702, after an eventful life.

She married, 1st, STEPHEN TAYLOR, who settled in Hatfield about 1662. He was buried there, Sept. 8, 1665, just one week before his brother-in-law, John White, jun.

She married, 2d, Oct. 15, 1666, BARNABAS HINSDALE of Hatfield, who was slain by the Indians, Sept. 18, 1675. He was one of the company under the command of Capt. Lathrop, which was surprised at "Bloody Brook," in Deerfield. A monument was erected in 1835, inscribed with the names of the ninety men who were then massacred.

She married, 3d, Feb., 1679, WALTER HICKSON of Hatfield, who died April 3, 1696.

HER CHILD ;—BY STEPHEN TAYLOR.

1. *Stephen*, b.   ; m. Nov. 27, 1700, Patience Brown, by whom he had four children, b. in Hatfield, 1701–1711. In 1713 he removed to Colchester, Conn., where he died, Jan. 3, 1719. His wife, and two of his children, Stephen and Mercy, survived him.

HER CHILDREN ;—BY BARNABAS HINSDALE.

2. *Barnabas*, b. Feb. 20, 1668 ; was admitted an inhabitant of Hartford in 1693, and d. there, Jan. 25, 1725, æ. 57. He m. Nov. 9, 1693, Martha Smith of Hartford, who d. about Dec., 1738, æ. 68. He had, 1. Barnabas, b. Aug. 28, 1694, settled in Tolland, Conn., where he d. Jan. 24, 1728, æ. 33. He m. June 17, 1725, Hannah Skinner ; 2. Martha, b. Feb. 17, 1696, m. Nov.

9, 1736, Thomas Bull of Harwinton, Conn., and d. April 15, 1761, æ. 65 ; 3. Jacob, b. July 4, [14 ?] 1698, lived in Harwinton. He m. July 8, 1731, Hannah Seymour ; 4. Sarah, b. July 22, 1700, m. Nathaniel White, (Family 22 ;) 5. Elizabeth, b Jan. 9, 1702, m. April 4, 1728, Jacob Benton of Harwinton ; 6. Mary, b. July 13, 1704, m. March 30, 1738, Joseph Skinner, jun.; 7. John, (Capt.) b. Aug. 13, 1706, lived in Kensington, (now Berlin,) Conn., and d. Dec. 2, 1792, æ. 86. He m. Nov. 8, 1733, Elizabeth Cole of Hartford, who d. July 1, 1784, æ. 73. His son, Rev. *Theodore*, grad. Yale Coll., 1762, was minister in Windsor, Conn , afterwards rem. to Hinsdale, Mass., the town being named in his honor, and d. there Dec. 29, 1818, æ. 80. *Elijah*, another son of Capt. John, had a dau. Elizabeth, who was the mother of Elijah Hinsdale Burritt, the astronomer, and of Elihu Burritt, the "learned blacksmith." *Lydia*, dau. of Capt. John, m. Samuel Hart of Berlin, and was the mother of Mrs. Emma Willard, and of Mrs. Almira Lincoln Phelps, each of them widely known as an instructress and authoress ; 8. Daniel, (Dea.) b May 15, 1708, lived in Hartford, and was buried Sept. 13, 1781, æ. 73. He m. Aug. 21, 1737, Katharine Curtiss of Wethersfield, Conn., who was buried April 12, 1778, æ. 68 ; 9. Amos, b. Aug. 24, 1710, was buried in Hartford, Jan. 1, 1792, æ. 81. He m. Experience ——, who d May 4, 1781, æ. 61. (The dates of births are taken from a copy of an ancient family record.)

3. *Sarah*, b.   ; m. Jan. 8, 1691, Dea. Samuel Hall, of East Middletown, Conn., who d. March 6, 1740, æ. 76. She d. between 1716 and 1722. She had, 1. Sarah, b. May 16, 1692, d. Dec. 16, 1712 ; 2. Elizabeth, b. Aug. 26, 1694 ; 3. Samuel, b. March 28, 1697, d. Feb. 22, 1713 ; 4. John, b. Aug. 19, 1699, d. Jan. 3, 1767 ; 5. Mercy, b. Nov. 13, 1704, d. Nov. 10, 1712 ; 6. Thomas, b. Oct. 15, 1707 ; 7. Isaac, b. May 2, 1709.

4. *Elizabeth*, b. Oct. 29, 1671 ; d. March 8, 1672.

5. *Isaac*, b. Sept. 15, 1673 ; was admitted an inhabitant of Hartford in 1697, and d. there about March 1, 1739, æ 65. He m. Jan. 6, 1715, Lydia Loomis, and had, 1, Lydia, b. Dec. 6, 1717 ; 2. Isaac, b. June 8, 1719 ; 3. Joseph, b. Aug 9, 1720, settled in Canaan, Conn.; 4. Jonathan, b. March 17, 1724, was probably the one of that name who was the first settler of Lenox, Mass., in 1750.

6. *Mary*, b. March 27, [1676?] The Hatfield record reads 1677 ; which is plainly an error. She is named in the will of her step-father, Walter Hickson, but nothing later is known of her.

HER CHILDREN ;—BY WALTER HICKSON.

7. *John*, b. Nov. 7, 1679 ; d. July 2, 1691, æ. 11.

8. *Elizabeth*, b. Jan. 26, 1681 ; probably d. young.

9. *Jacob*, b. Jan. 26, 1683. He was one of those taken captive by the Indians, at Deerfield, Feb. 29, 1704, and was slain by them at Cowas, N. H., on their journey to Canada. He was 21 years of age.

---

7. Ensign JACOB WHITE, youngest son of Elder John, (1) was born in Hartford, Conn., Oct. 8, 1645. He was less than fourteen years of age when his father removed to Hadley,

Mass., and probably accompanied the family thither. Soon
after reaching his majority, he returned to Hartford, and settled on his father's old homestead. He was admitted a freeman of the Colony in 1668. The nature of the various public
offices to which he was called, at Hartford, indicates that he
was a man of character and intelligence. In 1669 he was
chosen a land-surveyor for the town, and again in 1700. He
also served four times as Townsman, or Selectman, in the
years 1682, 1687, 1691, and 1696. In 1693 he was chosen
one of a committee to prepare an answer to a petition from
the inhabitants who lived east of the River. In military life
he reached the rank of Ensign. The exact time of his death
is not known, but it was probably in the early part of the year
1701, when he was 55 years of age. The inventory of his
estate was dated May 29, 1701, and amounted to £652. He
left no children surviving him.

He married, before 1683, ELIZABETH BUNCE of Hartford,
dau. of Thomas and Sarah Bunce, and sister of his brother
John's wife. She died at Hartford in 1716.

NOTE. On the Record of baptisms in the First Church in Middletown, under
the date of Nov. 2, 1679, is found this entry : "Eliz: White (daughter of Nathll &
Eliz: his wife ;) Mary (daughter of Jacob & Mary) White, are baptized." The
conjecture of a collaborator is doubtless correct, that this is an error of the re-
corder, for "Mary (daughter of Jacob & Mary) Cornwell." No record of the
baptism of Mary Cornwell is found, while the baptisms of the succeeding children
of this family are duly recorded.

Third Generation and Children.

8. Dea. NATHANIEL WHITE, son of Capt. Nathaniel, (3) was born at Middletown, Upper Houses, Conn., July 7, 1652. About the time of his marriage he removed to Hadley, Mass., where he settled upon the original homelot of his grandfather, Elder John White. He took the oath of allegiance in Hadley, February, 1679. The records show that there were but few larger landholders in the town. He gave a large part of his property to his children during his life time, so that the inventory of his estate, after his decease, was small. He left no will.

He was frequently called into the service of the town. In 1687 he was elected constable, and between the years 1684 and 1715 he was 9 or 10 times chosen one of the selectmen. He held the office of tything-man for several years after he was seventy-five years of age. The records of the Church in Hadley having been destroyed by fire, in 1766, it is not known when he was chosen to the office of Deacon. The title is first given him, in the town records, in 1697. He lived to a good old age, and died at Hadley, Feb. 15, 1742, æ. 89 years and 7 months.

He married, March 28, 1678, ELIZABETH SAVAGE of Middletown, dau. of John and Elizabeth Savage. She was born June 3, 1655, and died Jan. 30, 1742, æ. 86 years and 8 months. She died sixteen days before her husband, their married life having continued 63 years, 10 mos. and 2 days.

CHILDREN.

1. *Elizabeth*, b. Jan. 13, 1679; d. young.
2. *Nathaniel*, b. Nov. 4, 1680; m. Esther Strong.   .   .   .   (15)

3. *John,*   b. Nov. 28, 1682; m. Martha Church.   . . . . (16)
4. *Sarah,*   b.   ; probably d. young.
5. *Joseph,*   b. Feb. 28, 1687; m. Abigail Craft.   . . . (17)
6. *Daniel,*   b. March 1, 1690; m. Hannah Bagg.   . . . . (18)
7. *Jacob,*   b. Dec. 5, 1691; d. June, [1692?].
8. *Mary,*   b. Oct. 16, 1693; m. Jan. 28, 1719, Israel Dickinson of Hadley. She d. soon, without issue, and he m. Ruth Smith in 1724. He d. April, 1733.
9. *Elizabeth,* b. Nov. 8, 1695; m. Jan. [June?] 24, 1716, Dea. Samuel Montague of Sunderland, Mass. She d. 1753, æ. 57. He m. 2d, 1754, Mary, wid. of Jonathan Billing, and d. 1779, æ. 83. She had, 1. Samuel, b. 1720; 2. John, b. 1723, d. 1748, æ. 25; 3. Daniel, b. 1725; 4. Giles, b. 1727, d. 1732; 5. Richard, b. 1729; 6. Caleb, b. 1731; 7. Giles, b. 1733, d. 1734; 8. Elizabeth, b. 1735, d. 1743; 9. Nathaniel, b. 1739, killed at Lake George, 1757, æ. 18; 10. Ebenezer, b. 1741, d. 1743.
10. *William,* b. Aug. 15, 1698; m. 1st, Mrs. Mary Taylor; 2d, M. Warner. (19)
11. *Ebenezer,* b. April 9, 1701; m. Ruth Atherton.   . . . . (20)

---

9. JOHN WHITE, son of Capt. Nathaniel, (3) was born at Middletown, Upper Houses, April 9, 1657. He settled in the south part of Hartford, upon lands which had belonged to his grandfather, Elder John White, and frequently held some of the minor town offices. He survived all the other members of his father's family, and died about July, 1748, æ. 91 years. By his will, dated Nov. 7, 1747, he gave his homestead to his son Jacob, and a house and lands in Hartford to his son John. He also bequeathed to his children lands in Middletown, in New Hartford, and "in the five-mile, so called, on the east side of the Connecticut River, in Hartford," now constituting the town of Manchester. His estate was appraised at about £500.

He married MARY ———, who died before him.

CHILDREN.

1. *John,*   b. June 24, 1687; d. June 20, 1689.
2. *Mary,*   b. Aug. 14, 1689; d. Jan., 1694. (Hartford Record, Vol. I.)
3. *John,*   b. Feb. 8, 1691; m. Sarah Carter.   . . . . (21)
4. *A daughter,* b.   ; "John White's daughter" was buried Jan. 21, 1696. (Sexton's Record.)
5. *Nathaniel,* b. April 8, 1694; m. 1st, S. Hinsdale; 2d, Hannah ———. (22)
6. *Mary,*   b. May 4, 1696; d. young.
7. *Elizabeth,* b. June 11, 1698; m. Ebenezer Benton of Hartford, who d. about Jan., 1771. She survived her husband. She had a son, Ebenezer, jun., whose widow, Ruth, was living in 1764; a son, Asa; and prob. others.
8. *Jacob,* b. Sept. 22, 1700; lived on the homestead bequeathed to him by his

father. He d. unmarried, in 1776, æ. 75. His will is dated April 22, 1776. The inventory of his estate, dated May 21, amounts to nearly £900.

9. *Sarah*, b.　　　　　 ; m. Sept. 14, 1731, William Andrews, or Andruss. She was living in 1747.

10. *Ann*, b.　　　　　 ; m ——— Russ, and was living at the date of her father's will.

---

10. Ensign DANIEL WHITE, son of Capt. Nathaniel, (3) was born at Middletown, Upper Houses, Feb. 23, 1661. (So the town record: the grave-stone says, Feb. 27.) He lived in his native place, and was chosen a townsman, or selectman, of Middletown in 1690, and a constable in 1701. He died Dec. 18, 1739, æ. 78.

He married, March, 1683, SUSANNAH MOULD of New London, Conn., dau. of Hugh Mould, a noted ship-builder. Her mother, Martha Coit, was the dau. of John Coit, the first ship-wright in New London, and was the second wife of Capt. Nathaniel White, (Fam. 3.) Mrs. Susannah White was born April 2, 1663, and died Sept. 7, 1754, æ. 91.

CHILDREN.

1. *Daniel*, b. Dec. 8, 1683 ; m. Alice Cook. (23)
2. *Nathaniel*, b. Sept. 3, 1685 ; m. Mehitable Hurlburt. (24)
3. *Joseph*, b. ; d. Oct. 8, 1687.
4. *Joseph*, b. Oct. 8, 1688 ; m. Mary Hall and others. (25)
5. *Hugh*, b. Feb. 15, 1691 ; m. Mary Stone. (26)
6. *John*, b. Nov. 27, 1692 ; m. Susannah Alling. (27)
7. *Susannah*, b. Oct. [16?] 1694 ; (The town record gives Oct. 16, as the date of her birth ; the church record has Oct. 14, as the date of her baptism.) She m. Jan 2, 1718, Thomas Johnson, Esq., of Middletown, Up. H,. who d. Apr. 22, [24 ?] 1761, æ. 72. She d. Sept. 28, 1786, æ. 92. She had, 1. Thomas, b. Oct. 18, 1718. He was Dea., and d. Dec. 26, 1774, æ. 56; his wid., Mary, m. Ozias Willcox, and d. March, 1780 ; 2. Stephen, b. Feb. 14, 1720, lived in East Middletown, and d. Sept. 17, 1776, æ. 56 ; 3. Susannah, b. June 8, 1722 ; 4. Hepzibah, b. Nov. 21, 1724; 5. [Ruth ?] b. Sept. ——— ; 6. Daniel, b. April, 1729 ; was prob. a Capt. in the old French war, and d. at Schenectady, N. Y., June 18, 1756, æ. 27 ; 7. Amos, b. Jan. 27, 1731, m. Nov. 8, 1753, Mary Kirby ; he d. Sept. 19, 1758, "in the camp at Lake George," æ. 27 ; 8. Desire, b. July 5, 1735, m. June 17, 1756, Charles Burn ; 9. Thankful, twin with the last, m. May 6, 1755, Elisha Savage.
8. *Isaac*, b. Nov. 9, 1696 ; m. Sibbil Butler. (28)
9. *Jonathan*, bap. Mar. 30, 1701 ; d. May 7, 1702.
10. *Ruth*, b. Sept. 28, 1703 ; m. June 10, 1730, Jehiel Stone of North Guilford, Conn., (his 2d wife.) She d. March 28, 1774, æ. 70. He d. Oct. 18, 1780, æ. 76. She had, 1. Thomas, b. March 16, 1731, m. March 27, 1754,

Leah Norton of Guilford, who d. Jan. 28, 1772 æ. 42; 2. Sarah, b. Sept. 2, 1732, m. Daniel Norton, jun., of G., who rem. to New Durham; 3. Elihu, b. Aug. 16, 1734, m. Sept. 2, 1755, Thankful Hodgkiss of G.; he rem. to Branford in 1782, and thence to Litchfield; 4. Ruth, b. Mar. 23, 1736, m. Daniel Clarke of E. Haven; 5. Noah, b. June 23, 1738, d. Dec. 18, 1745; 6. William, b. Jan. 23, 1740, rem. to Harwinton, Conn., in 1782; 7. Aaron, b. Oct. 21, 1741, d. Jan. 7, 1821, æ. 79. He m. 1st, Sept. 22, 1760, Lois Dudley, of E. Guilford, who d. Apr. 18, 1797, æ. 52; m. 2d, Mrs. Abigail Coe, who d. Oct. 29, 1836, æ. 90; 8. Isaac, b. Feb. 25, 1743, d. Jan. 3, 1783, æ. 40. He m. Nov. 4, 1767, Parthena Dudley, sister of Lois; 9. John, b. Sept. 2, 1744, d. Feb. 15, 1754, æ. 9; 10. Noah, b. 1746; 11. John, b. [1749 ?], m. and rem. to Ohio.

11. *Rachel*, b. Feb. 3, 1705; m. April 16, 1729, William Chittenden, jun., of Guilford. She d. Oct. 15, 1752, æ. 47. He m. again, and d. Jan. 14, 1786, æ. 80. She had, 1. William, b. April 18, 1730, d. at sea, 1760, æ. 30. He m. Oct. 3, 1751, Elizabeth Fosdick of G., who d. Nov. 10, 1787, æ. 56; 2. Rachel, b. July 2, 1732, d. Sept. 22, 1751, æ. 19; 3. Jared, b. Aug. 20, 1734, d Feb. 12, 1824, æ. 89. He m. 1st, Aug. 17, 1757, Deborah Stone of G., who d. April 26, 1792, æ. 54; m. 2d, Sept. 12, 1793, Mrs. Elizabeth (Dudley) Ward, wid. of Luman Ward of G.; she d. Sept. 17, 1819, æ. 80; 4. Lucretia, b. Oct. 30, 1736, m. —— Ward; 5. Luther, b. Jan. 27, 1739, d. unm.; 6. Calvin, b. June 10, 1741, d. Sept. 19, 1742; 7. Rebecca, b. Aug. 13, 1743, d. Aug. 31, 1743; 8. Rebecca, b. Oct. 2, 1744, prob. d. young; 9. Miranda, b. Feb. 28, 1747, m. Nov. 10, 1773, Dea. Ambrose Leete of G., who d. Feb. 14, 1809, æ. 61; she d. Sept. 16, 1838, æ. 91; 10. Mary, b. Aug. 8, 1752, prob. d. unm.

---

11. JACOB WHITE, son of Capt. Nathaniel, (3) was born at Middletown, Upper Houses, May 10, 1665, and settled there. He was chosen constable in Middletown in 1694, and a select-man in 1715. He died March 29, 1738, æ. nearly 73.

He married, 1st, Feb. 4, 1692, DEBORAH SHEPARD, who died Feb. 8, 1721, æ. 51.

He married 2d, Dec. 16, 1729, Mrs. REBECCA (WILLETT) RANNEY, widow of Thomas Ranney of Middletown. The date of her death is not known.

CHILDREN;—BY THE FIRST MARRIAGE.

1. *Elizabeth*, b. Nov. 22, 1692; d. unm. March 24, 1755, æ. 62. She is styled "Mrs." on her grave-stone; a title of respect not unfrequently given to un-married ladies, in olden time.

NOTE. From the record of *baptisms* it appears that the four oldest children of this family were born one year earlier than the dates given in the town record.

2. *Deborah*, b. Feb. 26, 1694; m. Dec. 23, 1731, Willett Ranney of Mid., who d. Sept. 4, 1751, æ. 57. She had, 1. Deborah, b. May 28, 1733; 2. Elizabeth, b. March 17, 1735, m. April 17, 1755, Jonathan Savage.

3. *Rebecca*, b. Aug. 12, 1695; d. Feb. 12, 1697.

4. *Jacob,*   b. Jan.   29, 1697 ; m. Martha Savage.   .   .   .   (29)
5. *Hannah,* b. March 28, 1699 ; m. Jan. 2, 1728, Joseph Frarey of Mid. She
   had, 1. Samuel, b. Dec. 5, 1729, d. Oct. 23, 1741, æ. 11 ; 2. Joseph, b. April
   4, 1732, m. Dec. 22, 1762, Elizabeth Kirby ; 3. Eleazer, b. July 26, 1734, d.
   Nov., 1755, æ. 21, "in the camp at Lake George ;" 4. Jonathan, b. Jan. 26,
   1736 ; 5. Hannah, b. Jan. 9, 1738 ; 6. A child, b. Aug. 17, 1740, d. same
   day ; 7. Samuel, b. Aug. 8, 1742 ; 8. Sarah, b. Aug. 12, 1744.
6. *Thomas,* b. Aug. 14, 1701 ; m. 1st, Sarah Miller ; 2d, H. Woodward. (30)
7. *Samuel,* b. May   24, 1703 ; d. Aug., 1708, æ. 5.
8. *Rebecca,* bap. Sept. 14, 1707 ; prob. d. in infancy.
9. *Samuel,* b. Dec.   6, 1710 ; d. March 1, 1725, æ. 14.
10. *John,*   b. Oct.   19, 1712 ; m. Elizabeth Bordman.   .   .   (31)

---

12. JOSEPH WHITE, son of Capt. Nathaniel, (3) was born
at Middletown, Upper Houses, Feb. 20, 1667, and resided
there. He was a constable in 1698 and in 1721. He died
Feb. 28, 1725, æ. 58. The inventory of his estate amounts to
more than £800.

He married, April 3, 1693, MARY MOULD, sister of his
brother Daniel's wife, and dau. of Hugh Mould and Martha
Coit. She was born July 26, 1665, and died Aug. 11, 1730,
æ. 65.

CHILDREN.

1. *Martha,* b. Dec. 6, 1693 ; m. Jan. 24, 1717, Thomas Stow, jun., of Mid. She
   had, 1. Mary, b. Nov. 30, 1717 ; 2. Jerusha, b. Aug. 6, 1719, m. Oct. 14,
   1736, Joseph Stevens of Glastenbury, Conn. ; 3. Martha, b. May 6, 1721, m.
   Dec. 31, 1742, Jeremiah Ranney ; 4. Freelove, b. June 14, 1723 m. Nov. 13,
   1760, Gideon Warner ; 5. Hannah, b. Dec. 7, 1726, m. Oct. 6, 1748, Joseph
   Barns ; 6. Bethiah, b. Sept. 2, 1733, m. Aug. 8, 1757, Jonathan Steel.
2. *Sarah,* b. Feb. 27, 1696 ; m. March 5, 1719, Lieut. John Bacon, jun., of
   Mid., who d. 1783, æ. 88. She had, 1. Sarah, b. Jan. 31, 1720 ; 2. John, b.
   April 21, 1723, m. 1st, March 1, 1748, Rhoda Gould ; m. 2d, Mary Ely of
   Lyme ; 3. Jerusha, b. Oct. 25, 1724 ; 4. Mary, b. Jan. 12, 1727 ; 5. Joseph,
   b. May 14, 1728, m. 1st, Elizabeth Miller ; m. 2d, Rhoda Plumb ; 6. Martha,
   b. Sept. 14, 1729, m. June 27, 1748, Fenner Ward ; 7. Ebenezer, b. Feb. 4,
   1731 ; 8. Abigail, b. July 21, 1732, m. 1st, —— Plumb ; m. 2d, ——
   Hough ; 9. Sibbel, b. Feb. 19, 1734, d. April 24, 1734 ; 10. Sibbel, b. Aug.
   27, 1735, m. 1st, —— Knowles, of Chatham ; m. 2d, —— Norton ; 11.
   Dorcas, b. Nov. 25, 1736, m. —— Osborne, of Blanford, Mass.
3. *Mary,* b. Oct. 2, 1698 ; m. 1st, Dec. 28, 1721, Joseph Hollister, jun., of
   Glastenbury, who d. Oct. 8, 1746, æ. 49. She m. 2d, Jonathan Hale, Esq.,
   of Glastenbury, who d. July 2, 1772, æ. 76. She d. Jan. 18, 1780, æ. 81.
   By her first husband she had, 1, Mary, b. Sept. 23, 1722 ; m. —— Kilborn ;
   2. Anne, b. Nov. 13, 1726 ; 3. Abigail, b. April 13, 1728 ; 4. Joseph, b. Sept.
   5, 1732 ; 5. William, b. Jan. 24, 1737.
4. *Joseph,* b. Dec. 17 1700 ; d. Aug. 1, 1702.

5. *Jerusha*,   b. July 27, 1703 ; m. June 24, 1724, Ezra Carter of Mid., who rem.
to Marlboro, Conn. about 1733, and d. July 19, 1774.   She d. May 11, 1781,
æ. 77.   She had, 1. Ezra, b. March 14, 1725, d. Aug. 10, 1726 ; 2. Jerusha,
b. Jan. 11, 1727, m. April 26, 1752, Asa Foote of Marlboro, and d. May 15,
1770, æ. 43.   He d. May 11, 1799, æ. 72 ; 3. Margery, b. March 24, 1729,
d. 1818, æ. 89 ; 4. Ezra, b. Nov. 24, 1730, d. Jan. 21, 1737 ; 5. Mary, b.
Sept. 16, 1732, d. Jan. 29, 1737 ; 6. Eleazer, b. July 22, 1734, d. Jan. 26,
1737 ; 7. Ebenezer, b. July 24, 1736, d. Aug. 28, 1743 ; 8. Mary, b. Sept. 17,
1738, d. June 29, 1743 ; 9. Ezra, b. Nov. 2, 1740, m. 1st, Huldah Marvin
of Lyme ; m. 2d, Freedom Strong of Marlboro, who d. March 19, 1827, æ.
81.   He d. Sept. 28, 1829, æ. 89 ; 10. Eleazer, b. May 23, 1743, m. Eunice
Kellogg of Colchester, Conn., who d. Oct. 11, 1834, æ. 87.   He d. Dec. 23,
1829, æ. 86 ; 11. Mary, b. Aug. 9, 1745, d. March, 1812, æ. 66.

6. *Joseph*,   b. Aug. 17, 1705 ; d. April, 1706.
7. *Ebenezer*, b. May 22, 1707 ; m. Ann Hollister.   .   .   .   .   (32)

DESCENDANTS OF JOHN WHITE, JUNIOR.

13. Dea. JOHN WHITE, only son of Sergt. John, jun., (4)
was born about the year 1663.   He settled in Hatfield, Mass.,
as a farmer, on the homelot which had belonged to his father,
and for a period of 40 years took a leading part in the affairs
of that town.   Besides being frequently appointed to the
minor offices, he was 20 times chosen one of the selectmen of
the town, between the years 1689 and 1727.   For 7 or 8 years
his name was first on the list.   The title of Ensign is first
given him upon the records in 1707, and that of Deacon in
1713.   A fac-simile of his autograph in 1701 is here given.

In February, 1742, he sold his house and homelot to his son-
in-law, Daniel White, (Family 36,) who removed the same year
from Bolton, Conn., to Hatfield.   He probably lived with his
son-in-law for a few years, as he was still a resident of Hatfield,
Oct. 30, 1746.   But he seems to have removed, near the close
of his life, to the house of his son, Rev. David White, of Hardwick, Mass., where he died Nov. 13, 1750, æ. 87.

He married July 7, 1687, HANNAH WELLS of Hadley, dau.
of Thomas and Mary Wells.   She was born July 4, 1668, and
died Dec. 17, 1733, æ. 65.

CHILDREN.

1. *John,*   b. Sept. 26, 1689; m. 1st, Mrs. Sarah Barber; 2d, H. Meekins. (33)
2. *Mary,*   b. Jan. 3, 1692; died in infancy.
3. *Hannah,* b. March 26, 1695; m. July 14, 1720, John Hastings of Hatfield: (his 2d wife.) She had, 1. Silvanus, b. 1721; 2. John, b. 1722; 3. Oliver, b. Nov. 22, 1724; 4. Lemuel, b. Feb. 5, 1727; 5. Hannah, b. July 8, 1729; 6. Lydia, b. Aug. 19, 1732; 7. Mehitable, b. 1735.
4. *Mary,*   b.   1697; probably d. young.
5. *Jonathan,* b. Sept. 18, 1700; m. Esther ———, and others. .   (34)
6. *Sarah,*   b.   ; m. 1st, Jan. 11, 1722, Philip Smith of Hat., who d. April 13, 1728. She m. 2d, 1734, John Burk of Hat., who was drowned Nov., 1736. She m. 3d, Sept. 5, 1739, Daniel Griswold of Bolton, Conn. (See Family 14.) She had, by her first husband, 1. Simeon, b. ———, d. April 25, 1735; 2. Oliver, b. Jan. 18, 1727, d. April 19, 1728: by her second husband, 3. Ruth, b. Feb. 2, 1736, who was living in 1748.
7. *Elizabeth,* b.   ; m. Daniel White.   .   (Family 36)
8. *Martha,* b. March 14, 1708; m. Oct. 31, [Nov. 1?] 1732, Joseph Olmsted of Bolton, Conn., who rem. to Enfield, Conn., about 1742, and d. there about Nov., 1775. She was living in 1770. She had, 1. Joseph, b. Aug. 22, 1733, m. Aug. 2, 1764, Mabel Smith of E. Hartford, who d. Nov. 12, 1821, æ. 86; 2. Hannah, b. May 5, 1735, m. Benjamin Terry, jun., of Enfield, and d. Feb. 18, 1766, æ. 30; 3. Martha, b. March 1, 1737, m. Ephraim Terry; 4. John, bap. March 11, 1739, d. May 15, 1761, æ. 22; 5. David, bap. March 8, 1741, d. Feb. 25, 1787, æ. 46; 6. Elijah, b. May 1, 1743, m. Dec. 3, 1767, Sarah Terry; 7. Asa, b. Dec. 27, 1745, m. Nov. 24, 1785, Charlotte Dwight, and d. Nov. 5, 1803, æ. 58; 8. Simeon, b. Sept. 21, 1748, m. Feb. 7, 1771, Roxalana Abbe. She d. Feb. 20, 1847, æ. 96.
9. *David,*   b. July 1, 1710; m. Susanna Wells.   .   (35)
10. *Eunice,* b. Feb. 13, 1713; m. 1st, Oct. 31, [Nov. 1?] 1732, Timothy Olcott, jun., of Bolton, Conn., who d. Jan. 5, 1747, æ. 43. She m. 2d, Nov. 10, 1748, Daniel Morgan of Colchester, Conn.: (his 2d wife.) She d. March 23, 1757, æ. 44. He m. 3d and 4th wives. She had, by her first husband, 1. Bulkley, b. Oct. 28, 1733. He graduated at Yale College in 1758, was ordained pastor of the Congregational Church in Charlestown, N. H., May 28, 1761, and d. there June 16, 1792, æ. 58. He m. Martha Pomroy, dau. of Col. Seth Pomroy of Northampton, Mass.; 2. Simeon, b. Oct. 1, 1735. He graduated at Yale College in 1761, and settled as a lawyer in Charlestown, N. H. He was Chief Justice of the Court of Common Pleas, and of the Superior Court, of N. H., and was U. S. Senator, from 1801 to 1805. He d. Feb. 22, 1815, æ. 79. He m. Tryphena Terry, dau. of Benjamin Terry, jun., of Enfield, Conn. She d. Jan. 6, 1832, æ. 71; 3. Eunice, b. Aug. 15, 1737, m. Dec. 3, 1755, Judah Wells of Colchester, and d. Feb. 16, 1759, æ. 21; 4. Sarah, bap. Sept. 16, 1739, m. Joel Cooley of Charlestown, N. H., who d. Sept. 22, 1819, æ. 84. She d. Dec. 8, 1825, æ. 86. Their son, *Walter,* b. Jan. 28, 1775, m. Lucretia White; (see Family 72;) 5. Timothy, bap. Oct. 11, 1741, was a farmer in Chester, Vt. He m. the dau. of Col. Thomas Chandler of Chester; 6. Elias, b. Feb. 28, 1744,

was a farmer in Rockingham, Vt., where he d. Oct. 29, 1794, æ. 50. He m.
Sibbel Dutton of Rock., who d. Aug. 27, 1803, æ. 75; 7. Hannah, (posthumous,) bap. April 19, 1747, m. Jonathan Holten of Chester, Vt., and
rem. to Rockingham, where she died. He d. in Charlestown, N. H. (The
facts here given respecting the family of Timothy Olcott, jun., are taken
chiefly from an account of the "Descendants of Thomas Olcott," by Nathaniel Goodwin, Esq., published in 1845.) By her second husband, Daniel
Morgan, she had, 8. Mary, b. Feb. 25, 1750, m. May 19, 1773, Edmund
Clark; 9. Anna, b. April 10, 1752, m. Oct. 24, 1771, Elias Worthington,
who d. Sept. 23, 1811, æ. 62; 10. Daniel, b. Oct. 25, 1754.

DESCENDANTS OF LIEUT. DANIEL WHITE.

14. Capt. DANIEL WHITE, only surviving son of Lieut.
Daniel, (5) was born in Hatfield, Mass., July 4, 1671. He
first settled in Hatfield, but in 1704 or 1705 removed to
Windsor, Conn., where he was engaged in trade. It does not
appear that he held town offices, though he was sometimes
appointed on committees to manage important business. His
home was on the "north side of the rivulet;"—Farmington
River. He was Captain of the "troopers." He died June
22, 1726, æ. 55. The following is a fac-simile of his signature in 1709.

By his will, dated June 9, 1726, he made the following
disposition of his estate: To his wife, Elizabeth,—besides "her
dowry as the law allows,"—"my plate, or silver utensils, viz.
one silver tankard, two silver cups, and all my silver spoons:"
To his oldest son, Daniel, a house and certain lands in Hatfield; other lands there, to his youngest son, Oliver: "To my
son, Thomas White, my cloak. Also, I give and bequeath
and remitt to him all that he the said Thomas, oweth or is
indebted to me." This indebtedness was for his education,
and perhaps for lands in Bolton: To his son Joel, his house
and lot in Bolton, with his whole right in lands in that Township: To his sons Elisha, Simeon, and Seth, his lands in Hebron, to be equally divided between them: To his daughter

Sarah Griswold, £20, besides what had been given her before:
To his daughters Lucy and Elizabeth, £50 each. The remainder of his estate was to be equally divided among all his children. His estate was appraised at about £2000, of which
nearly £875 was in Hatfield. The currency of that day was
much depreciated, but this was a good estate, for those times.

He married, 1st, SARAH BISSELL of Windsor, dau. of Thomas
Bissell and Abigail Moore. Her grandfather, John Bissell, an
early settler in Windsor, and much occupied with public
affairs, died Oct. 3, 1677, æ. 86. She was born Jan. 8, 1672,
and died at Hatfield, July 18, 1703, æ. 31.

He married, 2d, July 6, 1704, ANN BISSELL of Windsor, a
cousin of his former wife. She was the dau. of John Bissell,
jun., and of [Isabel?] Mason. She was born April 28, 1675,
and died at Windsor, April 21, 1709, æ. 34.

He married, 3d, April 25, 1710, ELIZABETH BLISS of Norwich,
Conn., dau. of Samuel Bliss and Anna Elderkin. Soon after
the death of her husband, she returned to Norwich, where she
resided till her death, with the exception of a short time about
1746, when her residence was in Bolton. She was born Feb.
28, 1687, and died July 2, 1757, æ. 71.

CHILDREN ;—BY THE FIRST MARRIAGE.

1. *Sarah*, b.   1693; d. Feb. 24, 1693.
2. *Sarah*, b. Aug. 20, 1694; m. Sept. 5, 1716, Daniel Griswold, jun., of Windsor.
   They removed to Bolton in 1729, where she d. Feb. 1, 1738, æ. 43. He
   then m. 2d, Sept. 5, 1739, Mrs. Sarah Burk of Hatfield, wid. of John Burk,
   and dau. of Dea. John White. (See Family 13.) He and his wife, Sarah,
   were living in Harwinton, Conn., in 1760. He d. there, before 1777. The
   first wife, Sarah, had, 1. Sarah, b. Oct. 14, 1717, m. June 15, 1738, James
   Olcott of Bolton and New Hartford, brother of Timothy, jun.; (see Family
   13;) 2. Ann, b. March 20, 1719, m. June 26, [15?] 1739, Benjamin Smith ;
   3. Bathsheba, b. Dec. 2, 1720, m. June 16, 1740, Jabez Dart of B., and d.
   Feb. 1, 1746, æ. 25 ; 4. Mindwell, b. Feb. 12, 1722 ; 5. Daniel, b. May 26,
   1723, lived in B., and d. July 27, 1803, æ. 80. He m. 1st, June 28, 1744,
   Elizabeth Baldwin of Coventry, Conn. ; m. 2d, May 23, 1771, Mrs. Judith
   Shayler, widow of Ebenezer Shayler ; 6. Hannah, b. Feb. 8, 1726, d. Nov.
   4, 1757, æ. 31 ; 7. White, b. Oct. 22, 1727, settled in Harwinton, Conn.,
   and d. in the Revolutionary Army. He m. Feb. 14, 1751, Elizabeth Cheeney
   of Hartford ; 8. George, b. Jan. 1, 1730, d. in Bolton, April 26, 1813, æ. 83.
   He m. 1st, July 6, 1759, Sarah Jones of B., who d. April 6, 1763, æ. 27,
   [32?] ; m. 2d, Dec. 12, 1764, Susannah Cone of B., who d. June 16, 1815,
   æ. 79 ; 9. Seth, b. April 27, 1732, lived chiefly in New Hartford and Win-

chester, but d. in Colebrook, Conn., after 1801. He m. 1st, June 13, 1751, Susannah Shirtliff of Bolton; m. 2d, Ann ———, who d. in New Hartford, Sept. 16, 1774; m. 3d, Dec. 31, 1778, Mrs. Huldah (Priest?) Loomis, wid. of Simeon Loomis of Winchester; 10. A dau., b. June 12, 1736, d. same day, æ. 10 hours; 11. Reuben, b. Jan. 16, 1738.

3. *Daniel,* b. Sept. 5, 1698; m. 1st, Mary Dickinson; 2d, Eliz. White. (36)
4. *Thomas,* b. July 10, 1701; m. Martha Hunt. . . . . (37)

CHILDREN;—BY THE SECOND MARRIAGE.

5. *Joel,* b. April 6, 1705; m. Ruth ———, and others. . (38)
6. *Elisha,* b. Nov. 11, 1706; m. Ann Field. . . . . (39)
7. *Simeon,* b. March 11, 1708; m. Jerusha Wait. . . . (40)

CHILDREN;—BY THE THIRD MARRIAGE.

8. *Seth,* b. March 6, 1713. He settled in Providence, R. I., but removed to Plainfield, Conn., about ten years before his death, which occurred in Jan., 1758, in the 45th year of his age. By his will, dated Jan. 1, and proved Jan. 5, 1758, it appears that he left no children, as he gave all his property to his wife, Elizabeth, who was living in Sept., 1763. She was probably a widow at her marriage with Seth White, and was perhaps his second wife. From the inventory of his estate, which was small, it appears that he was a shoemaker.

9. *Lucy,* b. June 16, 1715; m. 1st, Joseph French of Norwich, afterwards of Coventry, where he d. Aug. 11, 1740, æ. 30 yrs. and 1 day. All his children were taken away within ten days of the same time. She m. 2d, April 23, 1741, Josiah Wolcott of Coventry, Andover Society, who rem. to Saybrook, Conn., about 1750, and lived there for several years; but the family disappears from Saybrook. (On the Coventry town record is this entry: "Josiah Wolcott and yͤ wedow Lucy French were married April 23, 1740." But this is pretty certainly an error for 1741.) She had, by her first husband, 1. Daniel, d. Aug. 7, 1740; 2. Lucy, d. Aug. 12, 1740; 3. Ezekiel, d. Aug. 10, 1740; 4. Tryphena, b. May 30, 1739, d. Aug. 2, 1740. By her second husband, 5. Lucy, b. Jan. 19, 1742; 6 Anna, b. March 19, 1744, d. March 26, 1744; 7. Anna, b. April 29, 1745, d. June 18, 1745; 8. Theodore, b. Nov. 4, 1746; 9. Anna, b. Jan. 15, 1749.

10. *Elizabeth,* b. May 18, 1717; m. Nov. 4, 1734, Samuel French of Norwich, who survived her, and d. about March, 1792. She had, 1, Elizabeth, b. Feb. 14, 1736; 2. Samuel, b. May 15, 1737, m. Nov. 23, 1758, Susanna Wallbridge of Nor.; 3. Eunice, b. July 24, 1739, m. May 24, 1759, Thomas Waterman; 4. Lucy, b. Aug. 9, 1741; 5. Daniel, b. Feb. 2, 1752, m. April 19, 1775, Desire Williams of Windham, Conn. These children were all living in April, 1793.

11. *Oliver,* b. March 26, 1720; m. Mary Beecraft. . . (41)

Fourth Generation and Children.

IN THE LINE OF DEA. NATHANIEL WHITE, OF HADLEY.

15. NATHANIEL WHITE, eldest son of Dea. Nathaniel, (8) was born in Hadley, Mass., Nov. 4, 1680. He settled in Hadley, but about 1727 removed to South Hadley, where he lived south of the meeting-house, on the west side of the street. In 1740 he was chosen one of the selectmen and assessors of Hadley, which then included the present town of South Hadley. He died May 28, 1762, æ. 81.

He married, May 10, 1709, ESTHER STRONG of Northampton, dau. of Samuel Strong and Esther Clap. She was born in Dorchester, Mass., April 30, 1685, and died Aug. 11, 1756, æ. 71.

CHILDREN.

1. *Nathaniel*, b. April 10, 1710; m. Martha Bascom.　.　.　(42)
2. *Samuel*, b. Oct. 22, 1711; d. Nov. 22, 1711.
3. *Timothy*, b. Aug. 9, 1712; d. Aug. 15, 1712.
4. *Submit*, b. Aug. 21, 1713; m. 1st, July 4, 1753, William Judd of Northampton, who d. May 6, 1755. She m. 2d, Dec. 4, 1760, Dea. John Clark of Southampton, Mass., who d. Aug. 21, 1766. By her first husband she had, 1. Eunice, b. Aug. 5, 1754, d. at S. Had., Feb. 22, 1760; 2. Submit, (posthumous,) bap. Nov. 2, 1755, m. Eber Eggleston of Westfield, Mass.
5. *Esther*, b. Dec. 4, 1715; m. Samuel Dickinson of Granby, Mass., who d. Feb. 10, 1750. She was living in S. Had., July, 1764. She had, 1. Hannah, b. Dec. 3, 1743, m. Waitstill Dickinson, who d. 1803; 2. Christian, b. Oct. 5, 1745, m. ——— Benton; 3. Samuel, b. May 15, 1747, m. Naomi ———, who d. 1813; 4. Eli, b. Nov. 10, 1749.
6. *Jonathan*, b. Jan. 29, 1717; m. 1st, Dorcas Alvord; 2d, Lydia Rugg. (43)
7. *Christian*, b. June 6, 1720; d. July 13, 1720.
8. *A child*, b. Jan. 2, 1722; d. same day.
9. *Christian*, b. May 9, 1723; d. Dec. 11, 1732, æ. 9.

7

10. *Samuel*, b. Oct.   1, 1725; d. Oct. 25, 1745, æ. 20.
11. *A child*, b. March 17, 1728; d. same day.

16. JOHN WHITE, son of Dea. Nathaniel, (8) was born in Hadley, Nov. 28, 1682, and resided there. The date of his death is not ascertained, but it was probably before 1766. His estate was settled in 1768.

He married, 1st, Jan. 5, 1715, MARTHA CHURCH of Hadley, born Sept. 23, 1694, dau. of Samuel Church, jun., and Abigail Harrison. The date of her death is not known.

He married, 2d, Feb. 27, 1722, ABIGAIL ATHERTON, who probably died May 10, 1766.

CHILDREN;—BY THE FIRST AND SECOND MARRIAGES.

1. *Martha*, b. March 18, 1716; m. Nov. 14, 1734, Henry Bartlett. She was a widow in 1768.
2. *Abigail*, b.   ; m. Feb. 16, [Jan. 19?] 1749, John Brooks of Hatfield. She was living in 1768, a widow.
3. *Ruth*, b.   ; m. 1st, Nov. 1, 1748, Daniel Rood ; m. 2d, 1764, Jacob Taylor of S. Had.
4. *Oliver*, b.   ; m. 1st, Eliz. Charter; 2d, Abigail Selden.   (44)
5. *John*, b.   ; m. Mary Emmons. .   .   .   .   . (45)
   No other children are named in the settlement of their father's estate.

17. Dea. JOSEPH WHITE, son of Dea. Nathaniel, (8) was born in Hadley, Feb. 28, 1687. He lived in Hadley and South Hadley, and was probably a deacon in the church in the latter place. In 1749 he was a selectman and assessor of Hadley, and occasionally held other offices. He had the military title of Captain. He died before 1770, the date not ascertained.

He married, Feb. 3, 1709, ABIGAIL CRAFT of Hadley, dau. of Thomas Craft (or Croft,) and Abigail Dickinson. She was born Sept. 29, 1688, and died Nov. 15, 1770, æ. 82.

CHILDREN.

1. *Moses*, b. Feb. 7, 1710; m. Lydia Bellows. .   .   .   . (46)
2. *Abigail*, b. Aug. 20, 1713; m. July 17, 1734, John Alvord, jun., of S. H., who d. July 8, 1758. She d. Nov. 19, 1757, æ. 44. She had, 1. Moses, b. Aug. 26, 1735; 2. Azariah, (Capt.) b. Jan. 20, 1738, lived in Springfield and S. Hadley, and d. Jan. 11, 1819, æ. 89. He m. 1st, Jan. 5, 1768, Abigail Nash, who d. March 31, 1782, æ. 42; m. 2d, March 5, 1789, Lucy Nash of Granby, Mass., who survived him, and m. John Stickney ; (see "Nash Family";) 3. Abigail, b. Sept. 23, 1739 ; 4. Jerusha, b. Sept. 27, 1741 ; 5. Dorcas, b. Nov. 4, 1743 ; 6. Rachel, b. April 15, 1747 ; 7. Phineas, b. June 26, 1750 ; 8. Luther, b. March 4, 1753, d. 1784, æ. 31 ; 9. Rebecca, b. April 14, 1756.

3. *Thomas*, b. July 20, 1715 ; m. Mindwell Alvord. . . . (47)
4. *Joseph*, b. Oct. 4, 1718 ; m. Editha Moody. . . . (48)
5. *Mary*, b. Oct. 15, 1721 ; d. July 8, 1726.
6. *Rebecca*, b. March 11, 1724 ; m. Jan. 17, 1745, Josiah Moody, of H. and S. H. She d. Sept. 15, 1751, æ. 27. He m. 2d and 3d wives. She had, 1. Eliphaz, b. Nov. 23, 1745, d. May 15, 1752 ; 2. Josiah, b. Aug. 7, 1748 ; 3. Rebecca, b. July 21, 1750, d. Sept. 6, 1758.
7. *Mary*, b. June 25, 1727 ; m. Dec. 11, 1744, William Eastman of Granby, and d. Nov. 19, 1752, æ. 25. He m. 2d, and d. July 20, 1793, æ. 74. She had, 1. Mary, b. Sept. 12, 1745 ; 2. Mercy, b. Dec. 31, 1746, d. Jan. 22, 1747 ; 3. Mercy, b. Feb. 17, 1748, d. Dec. 31, 1752 ; 4. William, b. Nov. 10, 1749 ; 5. Joseph, b. July 14, 1751, d. Feb. 26, 1752.
8. *Josiah*, b. 1729 ; m. Mary Smith. . . . . (49)

---

18. DANIEL WHITE, son of Dea. Nathaniel, (8) was born in Hadley, March 1, 1690. He settled in West Springfield, Mass., where he died Oct. 19, 1721, æ. 31.

He married, 1715, HANNAH BAGG of Springfield, dau. of John Bagg and Mercy Thomas. She died Dec. 11, 1764, æ. 72.

CHILDREN.

1. *Experience*, b. May 19, 1715 ; m. William Bliss, weaver, of Spr., who d. 1758, æ. 47. She had, 1. William, b. Sept. 18, 1745, d. in infancy ; 2. William, b. Nov. 22, 1746, settled in Belchertown, Mass., and d. Nov. 16, 1782, æ. 36. He m. Feb. 15, 1775, Eleanor Sikes ; 3. Gad, b. Feb. 6, 1748, m. 1770, Abiah Colton ; 4. Daniel, b. June 29, 1751, m. 1780, Mary Morgan, and d. Dec. 25, 1810, æ. 59 ; 5. Experience, b. Aug. 5, 1753, m. 1792, John Challomer ; 6. Elijah, b. March 6, 1756.
2. *Jacob*, b. Nov. 13, 1716 ; m. Amy Stebbins. . . . . (50)
3. *Daniel*, b. June 22, 1719 ; m. Priscilla Leonard. . . . (51)
4. *Preserved*, b. Aug. 31, 1721 ; m. 1st. R. Kilbourn ; 2d, S. Worthington. (52)

---

19. WILLIAM WHITE, son of Dea. Nathaniel, (8) was born in Hadley, Aug. 15, 1698. He lived there, and was one of the selectmen in 1750. He died May 30, 1774, æ. 75.

He married, 1st, March 22, 1728, Mrs. MARY TAYLOR of H., widow of John Taylor, and dau. of John Selden and Sarah Harrison. She was born Sept. 27, 1703, and died Aug. 10, 1735, æ. 32.

He married, 2d, June 2, 1737, MARTHA WARNER of H., dau. of Daniel Warner and Sarah Golding. She was born Oct. 25, 1706, and died Oct. 3, 1787, æ. 81.

CHILDREN;—BY THE FIRST MARRIAGE.

1. *Mary,* b. Feb. 2, 1729; m. Ebenezer Dodd, of New Haven and Guilford, Conn., who d. in Guil., May 19, 1782, æ. 76. She is said to have rem. to Vt., with her dau. Mary, and to have lived to old age. She had, 1. Sarah, m. Giles White; (see Family 53;) 2. Mary, m. Luman Ward of Guil. They were living in Georgia, Vt., Jan., 1792.

2. *Sarah,* b. Oct. 6, 1730; m. 1764, Thomas Chamberlain of Coos, N. H., and d. before 1788. Three of her children were living at that date, Jacob B., Sarah L., and Blanchard.

3. *William,* b. Oct. 4, 1732; m. 1st, Lydia Patterson; 2d, Mar. Chapin. (53)

4. *Daniel,* b. Aug. 10, 1734; d. Dec. 10, 1738.

CHILDREN;—BY THE SECOND MARRIAGE.

5. *Nathaniel,* b. Nov. 12, 1738; m. 1st, Sarah Stockwell; 2d, R. Shepard. (54)

6. *Daniel,* b. Sept. 1, 1740; m. Sarah Goodrich. . . . . (55)

7. *Martha,* b. Aug. 3, 1742; m. April 26, 1770, William Cooke of Hadley, and d. Oct. 14, 1816, æ. 74. He d. Oct. 20, 1817, æ. 84. She had, 1. Experience, b. Nov. 20, 1771; 2. Mary, b. Nov. 11, 1774, m. Stephen Cooke; 3. Martha, b. Sept. 18, 1777; 4. David White, b. July 26, 1779, m. 1799, Salome Cady; 5. William, b. Aug. 23, 1781.

8. *Ebenezer,* b. March 16, 1744; m. Abigail Porter. . . . . (56)

9. *John,* b. March 28, 1746; lived in H., and d. unm., May 22, 1819, æ. 73.

10. *David,* b. Feb. 18, 1748; m. Roxcellany Warner. . . . (57)

20. EBENEZER WHITE, youngest son of Dea. Nathaniel, (8) was born in Hadley, April 9, 1701. He remained with his father, and died March 23, 1733, æ. nearly 32.

He married, Oct. 28, 1730, RUTH ATHERTON. After the death of her husband, she continued in the family of his parents, and took care of them in their old age. For this kindness, her father-in-law gave her, by deed, a portion of the original homelot of Elder John White, which is still occupied by her descendants. She remained a widow, and died April 29, 1785, in the 85th year of her age.

CHILDREN.

1. *Rachel,* b. about 1731; d. in Hadley, unm., May 25, 1815, æ. 83.

2. *Ebenezer,* b. about 1733; m. Sarah Church. . . . . (58)

IN THE LINE OF JOHN WHITE, OF HARTFORD.

21. JOHN WHITE, son of John, (9) was born in Hartford, Conn., Feb. 8, 1691. He lived on the place owned, and afterwards bequeathed to him, by his father, on or near the road to Wethersfield. He was buried July 23, 1768, æ. 77.

He married, Dec. 2, 1714, SARAH CARTER. She was buried March 27, 1783, æ. 91.

CHILDREN.

1. *John,* b.   '; m. 1st, Honor Baxter; 2d, Abigail ———.   (59)
2. *A daughter,* b.   ; m. John Baxter of Wethersfield, who was living March 26, 1761. (See Hartford Land Records, Vol. X. p. 39.)

NOTE. Perhaps there were other children. Not a single birth in this family, or in those descended from it, has been found recorded at Hartford, and some errors may have been made in arranging the facts that have been gathered from the Land and Probate Records.

---

22. NATHANIEL WHITE, son of John, (9) was born in Hartford, April 8, 1694, and lived there, near his father. He died in 1747, æ. 53.

He married, 1st, July 29, 1725, SARAH HINSDALE, his second cousin, dau. of Barnabas Hinsdale and Martha Smith; (see in Fam. 6.) She was born about 1700, and died but a few years before her husband.

He married, 2d, HANNAH ———, who survived him.

CHILDREN ;—BY THE FIRST MARRIAGE.

1. *Elizabeth,* b. Aug. 28, 1726; m. May 13, 1756, Amos Benton of Harwinton, Conn., and d. Aug. 17, 1757, æ. 31. She had Amos, b. March 27, 1757.
2. *Martha,* b. April 24, 1729.
3. *Sarah,* b. July 4, 1731.
4. *Ann,* b. Dec. 30, 1733.
5. *Abigail,* b. Jan. 29, 1736. History of these four daughters not known.

IN THE LINE OF ENSIGN DANIEL WHITE, OF MIDDLETOWN.

23. DANIEL WHITE, eldest son of Ensign Daniel, (10) was born at Middletown, Upper Houses, Conn., Dec. 8, 1683. He lived there, and died Jan. 10, 1758, æ. 74. His son Jedediah was the executor of his will.

He married, Jan. 19, 1709, ALICE COOK of Guilford, Conn., dau. of Thomas Cook, jun., and Sarah Mason. She was born June 3, 1681, and died July 26, 1762, æ. 81.

CHILDREN.

1. *Jonathan,* b. Aug. 22, 1711 ; m. 1st, Tryphena Ely; 2d, Mrs. Editha Bliss. (60)
2. *Alice,* b. Feb. 25, 1714; m. Feb. 17, 1743, Nathaniel Eells of Mid., Up. H., who d. Sept. 9, 1776, æ. 69. She d. March 5, 1792, æ. 78. She had, 1. Martha, b. Dec. 12, 1743 ; 2. Mary, b. Jan. 18, 1746 ; 3. Nathaniel, b. Sept. 8, 1748, m. Huldah White, (see Family 72 ;) 4. Daniel, bap. Nov. 3, 1751, d. Aug. 1, 1752; 5. Theodotia, b. June 10, 1754 ; 6. Daniel, bap. Dec. 4, 1757.

3. *Sarah,*   b. April 22, 1716; m. March 16, 1738, Daniel Willcox of Mid., Up. H. She had, 1. Lois, b. June 14, 1738; 2. Sarah, b. Dec. 31, 1739; 3. Daniel, b. Nov. 17, 1741, m. 1st, Sept. 22, 1763, Susannah Porter; m. 2d, Nov. 7, 1771, Mercy Gypson; 4. David, b. Sept. 24, 1743, d. "at the Havannah," Oct. 1, 1762, æ. 19; 5. Hepzibah, b. Jan. 21, 1745, m. Sept. 22, 1763, David Bulkley; 6. Stephen, b. Oct. 19, 1746; 7. Huldah, b. May 24, 1748; 8. Josiah, b. March 31, 1750, m. Sept., 1773, [Huldah?] Treat; 9. Olive, b. Oct. 16, 1751; 10. Samuel, b. Sept. 12, 1753; 11. Isaac, b. Aug. 14, 1755; 12. Jacob b. June 21, 1758; 13. Patience, b. Jan. 4, 1760.

4. *Daniel,*   b. Oct. 29, 1718; d. March, 1740, æ. 21, "at Saltatadus."

5. *Abiah,*   b. April 22, 1721; m. July 10, 1753, Henry Johnson of Mid., Up. H.; his 2d wife. They prob. rem. to Williamstown, Mass., before 1770. She had, 1. Comfort, b. April 24, 1754; 2. Abigail, b. May 2, 1756; 3. Ozias, b. April 21, 1758; 4. Levi, b. April 26, 1760; 5. Henry, b. Oct. [28?] 1762; 6. Jesse, b. Oct. 3, 1763, [1765?]

6. *Susannah,* b.   ; m. July 2, [3?] 1752, Jacob Hall of Mid., who d. May 2, 1767. She had, 1. Lucy, b. July 23, 1753, d. Aug. 10, 1753; 2. Lucy, b. June 22, 1754, d. Oct. 30, 1754; 3. Jacob, b. Jan. 6, 1756; 4. Sarah, b. April 16, 1758, d. Nov. 2, 1759; 5. Calvin, b. April 22, 1760; 6. Alice, b. Feb. 26, 1763; 7. Susannah, b. June 4, 1765.

7. *Jedediah,* b. Jan. 23, 1730; m. Barbara Willcox. .   .   (61)

---

24. Capt. NATHANIEL WHITE, son of Ensign Daniel, (10) was born at Middletown, Upper Houses, Sept. 3, 1685. He settled as a farmer in East Middletown, afterwards called Chatham, in that part which is now the town of Portland. He and his wife were among those who united in forming the first Church in E. Middletown, Oct. 25, 1721. He was a selectman of Middletown in 1730, a constable in 1733, and also from 1735 to 1742. He died May 5, 1743, æ. 57. His son Noadiah was his executor.

He married, July 29, 1714, MEHITABLE HURLBURT, dau. of John Hurlburt and Mary Deming. [Demon?] She was born Nov. 23, 1690, and died Jan. 8, 1744, æ. 53.

CHILDREN.

1. *Nathaniel,* b. April 25, 1715; m. Mary Sage. .   .   (62)

2. *Mehitable,* b. Sept. 23, 1716; d. Dec. 25, 1716.

3. *Abigail,* b. Oct. 31, 1717; m. June 16, 1736, Daniel Churchill of E. Mid. She had, 1. Ruth, b. Oct. 20, 1736, m. Joseph White of Chatham, (East Hampton Society,) believed to be a lineal descendant of Peregrine White. Her son, *Joseph,* b. Sept. 26, 1762, d. July 3, 1832, was an eminent physician and surgeon in Cherry Valley, N. Y., as were also *his* sons, Delos and Menzo White; (see Francis's Lives of Eminent Physicians;) 2. Sarah, b. April 5, 1739, d. April 30, 1739; 3. Abigail, b. March 16, 1740, d. March 29, 1743; 4. Elisha, b. Aug. 24, 1742; 5. William, b. March 2, 1745, d. July 4,

1749 ; 6. Benjamin, b. Feb. 5, 1747 ; 7. Daniel, b. Oct. 2, 1750 ; 8. Abigail, b. May 2, 1753.

4. *Elijah,* b. Feb. 15, 1719 ; m. Abigail Hurlburt. . . . (63)
5. *Noadiah,* b. Feb. 26, 1720 ; m. Lois White. . . . . . (64)
6. *Mehitable,* b. July 22, 1721 ; d. March 15, 1743, æ. 21.
7. *Amos,* b. March 18, 1723 ; d. April 24, 1727.
8. *Sarah,* b. Oct. 24, 1724 ; m. Feb. 1, 1744, Dea. John Clark, jun., of Chatham, East Hampton Society. He was living in 1796. She had, 1. John, b. March 15, 1745 ; 2. Mehitable, b. Nov. 14, 1746, d. Nov. 1, 1747 ; 3. Sarah, b. Feb. 20, 1748 ; 4. Mehitable, b. April 8, 1750 ; 5. Daniel, b. Oct. 13, 1752 ; 6. Esther, b. Oct. 2, 1754 ; 7. Elijah, b. Nov. 1, 1756 ; 8. Desire, b. June 12, 1759, d. same day ; 9. David, b. May 23, 1760 ; 10. Lydia, b. April 10, 1763 ; 11. Moses, b. Nov. 23, 1766.
9. *John,* b. Jan. 14, 1727 ; d. July 14, 1727.
10. *A son,* b. March 21, 1728 ; d. April 4, 1728.

---

25. Dea. JOSEPH WHITE, son of Ensign Daniel, (10) was born at Middletown, Upper Houses, Oct. 8, 1688. He settled as a farmer in East Middletown, on lands which had belonged to his grandfather, and was a highly respected citizen. He was one of the selectmen of Middletown in 1729, 1735, 1744, 1745, and 1746, and was a justice of the peace. He was chosen a deacon of the Church in E. Middletown, now the First Church in Portland, Jan. 22, 1725. He died Dec. 14, 1770, æ. 82.

He married, 1st, June 18, 1717, MARY HALL of Guilford, Conn., dau. of Dea. Thomas Hall and Mary Hiland. She was born Nov. 5, 1693, and died Nov. 9, 1725, æ. 32.

He married, 2d, June 30, 1726, ABIGAIL BUTLER of Hartford, dau. of Thomas Butler. She was born Oct. 24, 1692, and died Dec. 28, 1751, æ. 59.

He married, 3d, Jan. 31, 1754, Mrs. LOIS BLISS of E. Mid., widow of Thomas Bliss. She was the dau. of Thomas Cadwell and Hannah Butler, was born in Hartford, Feb. 18, 1706, and died Jan., 1766, æ. 60.

CHILDREN ;—BY THE FIRST MARRIAGE.

1. *Joseph,* b. May 21, 1718 ; according to the family tradition, he d. in England, in early life, and unmarried.
2. *Mary,* b. June 16, 1722 ; m. Nov. 5, 1747, Aaron Clark of Chatham, East Hampton Society. She had, 1. Mary, b. Nov. 3, 1748, m. Sept. 25, 1766, Moses Cole of Chatham ; 2. Rachel, b. Jan. 9, 1751 ; 3. Aaron, b. March 30, 1753 ; 4. Lois, b. Dec. 19, 1756 ; 5. Ruth, b. July 19, 1759, d. April 11, 1761 ; 6. Ruth, b. March 18, 1762.

3. *Lois,*   b. Jan. 6, 1725; m. Noadiah White.   .   .   .   (Family 64)
       CHILDREN ;—BY THE SECOND MARRIAGE.
4. *Ebenezer,* b. July 24, 1727 ; m. Ruth Welles.   .   .   .   .   (65)
5. *Stephen,* b. Jan. 17, 1731 ; m. Honor Hubbard.   .   .   .   (66)

26. Hugh White, son of Ensign Daniel, (10) was born at Middletown, Upper Houses, Feb. 15, 1691. He resided there, and frequently held town offices, being chosen a constable in 1719 and 1725, and a selectman in 1729, '30, '36, '39, and '50. He died about the 1st of March, 1778, æ. 87.

He married, Aug. 13, 1717, Mary Stone of Guilford, dau. of Samuel Stone and Sarah Tainter. She was born Feb. 13, 1690, [1691 ?] and d. July 9, 1770, æ. 80.

CHILDREN.

1. *Timothy,*   b. March 15, 1719 ; m. Susanna ——. . . . . (67)
2. *Bathsheba,* b. April   5, 1721 ; m. 1st, Oct. 10, 1738, Gideon Sage of Mid., Up. H. She m. 2d, June 3, [30?] 1752, John Cotton, who prob. rem. to Litchfield, Conn., about 1765. She d. June 6, 1793, æ. 72. (Grave-stone, at Mid.) By her first husband she had, 1. Gideon, b. Jan. 20, 1739 ; he and his wife lived in New Framingham in 1764 ; 2. Giles, b. Feb. 24, 1742, m. 1st, Sept. 3, 1770, Esther Hall; m. 2d, Hannah ——, who d. Jan. 13, 1783 ; m. 3d, Oct. 9, 1783, Anna Wright ; 3. Olive, b. March 19, 1744 ; 4. Luther, b. April 2, 1746 ; 5. Milla, bap. July 10, 1748. By her second husband she had, 6. Eliakim, b. Sept. 1, 1753 ; 7. Millicent, b. Oct. 15, 1755, d. 1758 ; 8. Elizabeth, b. Sept. 23, 1757, d. 1758 ; 9. Samuel, b. March 9, 1760, m. March 11, 1784, Lucretia Hamlin ; 10. Timothy, b. April 9, 1762, d. Apr. 26 ; 11. Bathsheba, b. March 4, 1764.
3. *Aaron,* b. Oct. 25, 1723 ; m. Sarah Olmsted. . . . . (68)
4. *Rebecca,* b. May 16, 1726 ; m. 1st, July 31, 1746, William Powell; m. 2d, —— Baldwin. She is called Rebecca Baldwin in her father's will. By her first husband she had, 1. Rebecca, bap. July 27, 1746 ; 2. William, bap. April 22, 1750.
5. *Mary,* b. June 21, 1728 ; m. May 24, 1750, James Olmsted of East Hartford. She had, 1. James, b. 1751, m. Mary Bement ; 2. Mary, b. 1752, d. 1753 ; 3. Rachel, b. 1754, m. —— Woodruff ; 4. Mary, b. 1755, m. Benjamin Hyde of Lebanon, Conn. ; 5. Tryphena, b. 1758 ; 6. Timothy, b. 1759, m. Alice Olmsted ; 7. Thankful.
6. *Rachel,* b. Sept. 1, 1730 ; m. July 13, 1749, (so the church record ; but, July 15, 1750, town record,) Francis Whitmore of Mid., Up. H. She d. March 31, 1751, æ. 20, "by falling into the fire in a fit." He m. 2d, Sibbil White ; (see Family 28.)
7. *Hugh,*   b. Jan. 25, 1733 ; m. 1st, Mary Clark ; 2d, Mrs. Lois Davenport. (69)

27. Capt. John White, son of Ensign Daniel, (10) was born at Middletown, Upper Houses, Nov. 27, 1692. He was

a sea-captain. About 1720 he removed to New Haven, Conn., where he died, Jan. 15, 1783, æ. 90.

He married, Oct. 6, 1715, SUSANNA ALLING of New Haven, dau. of John Alling, Esq., and Susanna Coe. Her grandfather, Roger Alling, was Treasurer of the New Haven Colony. She died Oct. 18, 1776, æ. 82.

CHILDREN.

1. *Stephen*, b. Aug. 12, 1716; died in infancy.
2. *Stephen*, b. June 8, 1718; m. Mary Dyer. . . . . . (70)
3. *Mary*, b. April 22, 1720; m. March 1, 1744, Dea. Thomas Howell of New Haven, who d. May 18, 1797, æ. 78. She d. March 27, 1776, æ. 56. She had, 1. Hannah, bap. Jan. 6, 1745, m. July 29, 1767, Richard Cutler of N. H., and d. Dec. 9, 1827, æ. 83; 2. John, bap. May 3, 1747, d. June 22, 1770, [1776?]; 3. Mary, bap. April 15, 1750, d. in infancy; 4. Timothy, bap. Sept. 2, 1753, d. Sept. 24, 1782, æ. 29; 5. Thomas, bap. July 18, 1756, d. May 20, 1798, æ. 42; 6. Mary, bap. Aug. 17, 1760, d. May 6, 1798, æ. 38; 7. Susanna, bap. Dec. 4, 1763, d. Aug. 26, 1798, æ. 35.
4. *John*, b. May 19, 1722; m. Mary Dickerman. . . (71)
5. *Timothy*, b. Dec. 21, 1724; died without issue.
6. *Susanna*, b. March 5, 1727; m. 1st, Jan. 24, 1750, Ebenezer Bassett of North Haven, who grad. Yale Coll., 1746. She m. 2d, May 13, 1762, Charles Sabin of New Haven. She had, by her first husband, 1. Mary, b. Aug. 15, 1751, m. Stephen Trowbridge of New Haven; 2. Sarah, b. Feb. 8, 1756, m. Aug. 5, 1778, Samuel Barney of New Haven, and d. Dec. 8, 1845, æ. 89 y. 10 mo. By her second husband, 3. Charles, b. July 5, 1763; 4. Susanna, b. March 4, 1765, d. about 1798; 5. Hannah, b. about 1769, m. Eli Cooper of New Haven, and d. Aug. 23, 1828, æ. 59; 6. Sarah, twin with the last, m. Sabin Lake, and d. Oct. 11, 1826, æ. 57.
7. *Elisha*, b. Jan. 9, 1731; was a sea-captain, and died unmarried, Jan. 16, 1767, æ. 36.

28. Dea. ISAAC WHITE, youngest surviving son of Ensign Daniel, (10) was born at Middletown; Upper Houses, Nov. 9, 1696. He settled there, and held various town offices; was constable in 1735, and a selectman from 1746 to 1749. He was chosen a deacon of the church there, Jan. 15, 1749. He died June 26, [27?] 1768, æ. 71. (On the grave-stone, 1769; but the church record says, 1768, and his estate was settled in that year.)

He married, June 30, 1726, SIBBIL BUTLER, dau. of Thomas Butler of Hartford. She was born March 6, 1702, and died Nov. 7, 1781, æ. 79.

CHILDREN.

1. *Moses*, b. Aug. 22, 1727; m. Huldah Knowles. . (72)

8

2. *Martha*, b.   Oct.   27, 1728 ; d. unm., April 1, 1813, æ. 84. Called "Mrs."
    on her grave-stone.
3. *Sibbil*, b.   Aug.   14, 1731 ; m. April 18, 1753, Francis Whitmore of Mid.,
    Up. H. His first wife was her cousin, Rachel White : (see Family 26.)
    He d. Nov. 29, [Dec. 1?] 1757, æ. 31. She had, 1. Rachel, b. Dec. 22,
    1753, d. Jan. 31, 1755 ; 2. Mary, b. Nov. 26, 1755 ; 3. Sibbil, b. Oct. 12,
    1757, d. March 21, 1758.
4. *Elias*,   b.   May   5, 1734 ; m. Prudence Savage.   .   .   (73)
5. *Aaron*, b.   ; prob. d. young.
6. *Isaac*, b.   Jan.   16, 1741 ; d. Dec. 8, 1741.
7. *Ruth*,   bap. March 27, 1743 ; m. Dec. 26, 1764, Dr. John Osborne, of Middle-
    town city. He was eminent as a scholar and physician, was with the army
    at Ticonderoga, during the French wars, and practised medicine more than
    sixty years. He died in 1825, æ. 83. (See Rev. Dr. Field's Hist. Dis-
    course, pp. 92, 93.) She prob. d. in 1811, æ. 68. She had, 1. John Chevers,
    b. Sept. 15, 1766, was a physician, and d. 1819, æ. 52 ; 2. Ruth, b. July 14,
    1768 ; 3. Dolly, b. Dec. 6, 1770 ; 4. Samuel, b. Sept. 8, 1772, d. in infancy ;
    5. Samuel, b. Feb. 4, 1775, was a physician ; 6. Joseph ; 7. William Franklin.

IN THE LINE OF JACOB WHITE, OF MIDDLETOWN.

29. JACOB WHITE, Jun., son of Jacob, (11) was born at
Middletown, Upper Houses, Jan. 29, 1697, and died there,
June 20, 1734, æ. 37. His estate was appraised at £581.

He married, May 15, 1729, MARTHA SAVAGE. She probably
married, 2d, Nov. 15, 1739, Jonathan Riley of Hartford, and
3d, Capt. Samuel Parker of Coventry, Conn.

His only daughter,

Jerusha, b. April 28, 1733, d. July 25, 1736.

---

30. THOMAS WHITE, son of Jacob, (11) was born at Middletown, Upper Houses, Aug. 14, 1701. He settled as a
farmer in East Middletown, (Chatham,) but in 1731 removed
to the north part of the town of Lebanon, Conn., within the
present town of Andover. His farm lay on both sides of Hop
River, and was partly in the town of Coventry. About 1748
he removed to Coventry, east of the Skungamug River. The
time of his death is unknown, but it was probably after 1773.

He married, 1st, Dec. 23, 1725, SARAH MILLER, probably
dau. of William Miller of Glastenbury. She died Aug. 10,
1736. æ. 36. She was buried in Chatham.

He married, 2d; Feb. 3, 1737, HANNAH WOODWARD, probably born July 19, 1710, and dau. of Henry Woodward and Hannah Burrows.

CHILDREN;—BY THE FIRST MARRIAGE.

1. *Sarah,* b. Sept. 13, 1726 ; m. —— Benton ; was living in 1760.
2. *Thomas,* b. Feb. 7, 1728 ; d. in Coventry, unm., in 1760, æ. 32. His will is dated Jan. 2, 1760 ; his inventory, Feb. 11.
3. *Samuel,* b. Nov. 30, 1729 ; m. Mrs. Rachel Tilden. . - . . (74)
4. *Deborah,* b. May 19, 1732 ; m. Oct. 10, 1751, David Eaton of Tolland, and had, 1. Susanna, b. Sept. 26, 1752 ; 2. Stephen, b. Jan. 29, 1754 ; 3. Timothy, b. July 17, 1755, d. in infancy ; 4. Elisha, b. Jan. 8, 1757 ; 5. Timothy, b. Aug. 27, 1758 ; 6. Elijah, b. May 29, 1760.
5. *William,* b. Feb. 21, 1734 ; is named in the will of his brother Thomas. Perhaps he is the son who d. unm., in Nottingham, Maine.
6. *Jacob,* b. Jan. 20, 1736 ; m. Annar Lothrop. . . . (75)

CHILDREN;—BY THE SECOND MARRIAGE.

7. *Hannah,* b. April 5, 1738 ; prob. m. —— Parish, of Windham, Conn.
8. *Henry,* b. June 1, 1739 ; m. Sarah ——. . . . . (76)
9. *Lemuel,* b. June 12, 1741 ; perhaps the son who d. in Me. See No. 5, above.
10. *Elizabeth,* b. June 9, 1743 ; d. unm., in Torringford, Ct., Oct. 13, 1826, æ. 82.
11. *Silas,* b. May 18, 1745 ; m. 1st, Mary Birge ; 2d, Hannah Scoville. (77)
12. *Abigail,* b. Oct. 20, 1747.
13. *Joel,* b. Oct. 20, 1750 ; m. Sarah Osborn. . . . . (78)

---

31. JOHN WHITE, son of Jacob, (11) was born at Middletown, Upper Houses, Oct. 19, 1712. He lived there, and died Feb. 9, 1801, æ. 88.

He married, Oct. 21, 1736, ELIZABETH BORDMAN. She was probably the dau. of Samuel Bordman and Mehitable Cadwell, of Wethersfield, and born Dec. 22, 1713. She died Nov. 17, 1800, æ. 87.

CHILDREN.

1. *Jacob,* b. Nov. 7, 1737 ; m. Lucy Savage. . . . . (79)
2. *Jerusha,* b. June 23, 1739 ; d. unm., Oct. 12, [13?] 1796, æ. 57.
3. *John,* b. Sept. 28, 1741 ; d. Dec. 21, 1741.
4. *Sarah,* b. Jan. 16, 1743 ; m. John Collins of Mid., Up. H., and d. July 25, 1774, æ. 31. She had, 1. Freeman, bap. Aug. 9, 1767, m. Lucy White ; (see Family 79 ;) 2. Sarah, bap. July 23, 1769 ; 3. Elizur, bap. March 10, 1771, d. in infancy ; 4. Elizur, bap. March 14, 1773 ; 5. Deborah, bap. April 28, 1776.
5. *Deborah,* b. Dec. 23, 1744 ; m. May 13, 1766, David Blin, from Stepney, Conn., who d. at Mid., Up. H., May 6, 1772. She d. Aug. 18, 1782, æ. 37: [1781, grave-stone.] She had, 1. David, bap. June 22, 1766 ; 2. Jacob, bap. Feb. 25, 1768.
6. *Patience,* b. Dec. 14, 1746 ; m. Feb. 9, 1766, Thomas Sellew.
7. *Christian,* b. July 10, 1748 ; m. April 23, 1769, Eliakim Ufford of Chatham, and d. March 20, 1803, æ. 54. He then m. 2d, her sister, Rachel White.

She had, 1. Jerusha, bap. April 28, 1771, m. David Churchill of Chatham, and d. Oct. 16, 1805, æ. 34 ; 2. Patience, b. Feb. 10, 1773, d. Feb. 21, 1774.

8. *Mehitable,* b. Dec. 30, 1750 ; d. unm., Aug. 20, 1820, æ. 69.

9. *Rachel,* b. Jan. 21, 1753 ; m. May 1, 1803, Eliakim Ufford, (see above,) and d. May 10, 1809, æ. 56. He m. 3d, and d. May 24, 1811, æ. 63.

10. *Mabel,* b. Dec. 29, 1754 ; [1755, town rec.] m. Feb. 2, 1784, Elisha Tryon.

IN THE LINE OF JOSEPH WHITE, OF MIDDLETOWN.

32. EBENEZER WHITE, only surviving son of Joseph, (12) was born at Middletown, Upper Houses, May 22, 1707. He was a farmer there, and accumulated a large estate, which was appraised, after his decease, at £14,270, 2s. 6d. He died March 26, 1756, æ. 49.

He married, May 27, 1731, ANN HOLLISTER of Glastenbury, dau. of Joseph and Ann Hollister. She was born Jan. 16, 1707, and died June 16, 1787, æ. 80.

CHILDREN.

1. *Joseph,* b. Sept. 10, 1732 ; d. unm., Nov. 13, [14 ?] 1758, æ. 26.

2. *Anne,* b. June 25, 1735 ; m. Nov. 16, [17 ?] 1756, Abraham Plumb of Mid., who rem. to Canaan, Conn., in May, 1800, and d. there Sept. 8, 1810. She d. Feb. 24, 1814, æ. 79. She had, 1. Abraham, b. Oct. 5, 1759, was lost at sea, in early life ; 2. Joseph, b. May 6, 1762, rem. to Whitestown, N. Y., but d. in New Haven, Conn. ; 3. Frederick, b. Oct. 27, 1765 ; (b. June 30, 1764, says a Fam. Record : perhaps there were two of this name ;) was a physician in Canaan, and d. April 12, 1812, æ. 46. He m. Jan. 6, 1785, Anne Peet who d. Dec. 18, 1823, æ. 54. His son, *Ovid,* (d. 1856, æ. 69,) was also a physician in Canaan and Salisbury ; 4. William, b. Sept. 5, 1767, a mariner, m., and d. at Middletown ; 5. Anna, b. Dec. 5, 1769, m. 1st, Abner Kirby ; m. 2d, William Walter of New Haven ; 6. Isaac, b. Aug. 8, 1774, a mariner, m., and prob. d. at Windsor, Conn. ; 7. Amy, b. May 7, 1777, d. unm., in New Haven.

3. *Prudence,* b. Dec. 1, 1737 ; m. Feb. 6, 1765, Richard Hawley, prob. of Woodbury, Conn., and had a son, Richard, who went West about 1810.

4. *Mary,* b. July 11, 1740 ; m. Dec. 23, 1762, Gideon Hale of Glastenbury. She had, 1. Anna, b. Sept. 21, 1763, m. May 2, 1782, [1783 ?] Samuel Welles of G., and d. Jan. 11, 1816, æ. 52. He m. 2d, her sister, Hannah. *Gideon,* son of Anna, was for several years Comptroller of Conn. ; 2. Hannah, b. March 2, 1765, m. Oct. 6, 1816, Samuel Welles, (his 2d wife,) and d. Dec. 6, 1818, æ. 53. He d. Nov. 12, 1834, æ. 80 ; 3. Gideon, b. Feb. 28, 1767, m. May 18, 1803, Ann Case, and d. April 27, 1831, æ. 64 ; 4. Esther, b. March, 11, 1769, d. unm., Jan. 25, 1830, æ. 61 ; 5. Ebenezer, b. Jan. 22, 1771, m. Sarah Cornwall of Chatham, and d. June 25, 1843, æ. 72 ; 6. Reuben, b. Feb. 6, 1773, m. Wealthy Tracy of Towanda, Pa. ; 7. Elias White, b. April 11, 1775, grad. Yale Coll., 1794, was a lawyer at Lewiston, Pa., and d. Feb. 3, 1832, æ. 57. He m. Feb. 26, 1810, Jane Mulhallan ; 8. Amelia,

b. Aug. 16, 1777, m. Aaron Kinney of G., who d. April 24, 1815. She d. March 12, 1847, æ. 69 ; 9. Hezekiah, b. Oct. 14, 1779, m. Pamelia Coleman of G., and d. Feb. 25, 1832, æ. 52; 10. Mary, b. Jan. 25, 1782, m. Feb. 28, 1809, Solomon Cole of G.; 11. Nancy, b. April 11, 1785, d. unm., March 19, 1808, æ. 23.

5. *William*, b. Sept. 10, 1742 ; m. Mrs. Abigail Stow.   .   .   .   (80)

. *Esther*,   b. March 24, 1745 ; m. April 26, 1776, Samuel Ward of Stratford, Conn., who rem. to Cornwall, Conn.   She d. Sept. 9, 1796, æ. 51.   He d. May 8, 1808, æ. 57.   She had, 1. John, b. Jan. 21, 1778, m. June 20, 1803, Lucretia Rogers. He rem. to Sheffield, Mass:, and d. Sept. 9, 1852, æ. 74 ; 2. Prudence, b. Sept. 13, 1782, m. David Coe of Winchester, Conn., and d. Feb. 17, 1822, æ. 39; 3. Sarah, b. Nov. 2, 1784, m. Benjamin Johnson of Ohio, and d. Feb. 9, 1842, æ. 57 ; 4. Samuel, b. Dec. 12, 1786, d. in infancy ; 5. Anna, m. Joel Wright of Cornwall, and d. March 18, 1847 ; 6. Esther, b. Aug. 21, 1789, m. Reuben Hall of Winchester ;. both now living in Ohio.

7. *Elizur*, b. Feb. 19, 1750; m. Hannah Cooper.   .   .   .   (81)

<hr>

DESCENDANTS OF JOHN WHITE, JUNIOR.

33. JOHN WHITE, eldest son of Dea. John, (13) was born in Hatfield, Mass., Sept. 26, 1689.   He settled in West Springfield, Mass., and died there in 1759, æ. nearly 70.   His will was presented in Court, July 12, 1759.

He married, 1st, 1717, Mrs. SARAH BARBER, widow of Thomas Barber.   She was the dau. of Capt. Jonathan Ball of Springfield, and of Mrs. Susanna Worthington, the second wife of Nicholas Worthington, whose first wife was this John White's grandmother.   (See in Family 4.) Mrs. Sarah (Ball) White was born Aug. 6, 1685, and died Nov. 3, 1744, æ. 59.

He married, 2d, 1746, HANNAH MEEKINS of Hatfield, dau. of John Meekins.   She probably returned to H. in 1763.

CHILDREN ;—BY THE FIRST MARRIAGE.

1. *Sarah*, b. Dec. 26, 1718 ; m. Dec. 16, 1736, Samuel Bancroft, the first settler in Granville, Mass., who d. in 1788.   He held many town offices, and "may be regarded as having been the patriarch of Granville."   His descendants have been numerous in E. Granville, and characterized by "industry, intelligence and integrity."   (See Holland's Hist. West. Mass., Vol. II., p. 58.) In the will of her brother David, dated 1797, she is named as then living, and also the following children.   A part of these were bap. at W. Springfield.   1. Samuel, (bap. Apr. 30, 1738 ;) 2. Joel, (bap. Sep. 16, 1739 ;) 3. Lemuel, (prob. bap. Oct. 18, 1741 ;) 4. Sarah, (bap. May 27, 1744,) the widow of Nathan Parsons ; 5. John ; 6. Enoch ; 7. Sabra, the wife of Clark Cooley ; 8. Hannah, single ; 9. Ruth, the wife of Mr. Strickland.

2. *John*,   b. Aug.   3, 1722 ; d. in infancy.

3. *John*,   b. June   8, 1724 ; d. April 29, 1741, æ. 17.   He was the fifth *John*, in

the direct descent of that name. By his death the line of that name became
extinct.

4. *David,* b. May 9, 1728; lived in the Parish, now Town, of Agawam, in W.
Spr. In 1775 he was chosen a member of the "Committee of Correspondence, Inspection and Safety," in W. Springfield. He married, but died
without issue, about Nov., 1797, æ. 69. His wife's name has not been
ascertained.

34. Capt. JONATHAN WHITE, son of Dea. John, (13) was
born in Hatfield, Mass., Sept. 18, 1700. He lived there until
1731, when he removed to Hebron, Conn., and settled on a
farm which he bought of Elisha and Simeon White. He held
various town offices in both the towns in which he resided.
In 1750 and 1751 he was chosen town clerk and treasurer of
Hebron, and continued to hold the latter office till 1768.
About 1745 he was chosen a deacon of the church in Hebron.
He died March 28, 1776, æ. 75, leaving an estate of about
£575.

He married, 1st, ESTHER ———, who died in Hatfield,
March 25, 1727.

He married, 2d, ANNA ———, who died in Hebron, March
2, 1747.

He married, 3d, Oct. 6, 1747, Mrs. ANNA WRIGHT, who
died Sept. 30, 1777.

CHILD;—BY THE FIRST MARRIAGE.

1. *Asa,*   b. Jan. 16, 1724; d. Oct. 18, 1725.

CHILDREN;—BY THE SECOND MARRIAGE.

2. *Esther,* b. July 21, 1729; was living at the date of her father's will, as
were also her sisters. Their history is not known.
3. *Asa,*   b.   ; d. Sept. 22, 1742.
4. *Jonathan,* b. March 22, 1733; d. in Windham, Jan. 29, 1789, æ. 55, prob. unm.
5. *Anna,*   b. Feb. 5, 1735.
6. *Mary,*   b. Aug. 10, 1737.
7. *John,*   b. Dec. 29, 1739; d. Oct. 1, 1742.
8. *Hannah,* b. Nov. 30, 1741.
9. *Asa,*   b. Nov. 6, 1743; m. 1st, Mary Bingham; 2d, H. Cutler.   (82)
10. *John,* b. Oct. 2, 1745; d. Feb. 2, 1749.

35. Rev. DAVID WHITE, youngest son of Dea. John, (13)
was born in Hatfield, Mass., July 1, 1710. He graduated at
Yale College in 1730, and was ordained Pastor of the church
in Hardwick, Mass., Nov. 17, 1736. The church, consisting

of 12 members, was organized on that day. During the forty-seven years of his ministry there, he received 411 persons to full communion, and 77 under the half-way covenant. He baptized 1275 adults and infants, and married 316 couples. His salary was small, never more than $200 per annum; yet he gave his children a good education, his two sons having graduated at Harvard College. Allen's Biographical Dictionary says of him, that "he was esteemed and very useful." He died at Hardwick, Jan. 6, 1784, æ. 73.

He married SUSANNA [WELLS.] She was a granddaughter of the first Thomas Wells of Deerfield, Mass., and it is believed that her name was Wells. She was left an orphan at an early age, in Pennsylvania, and was brought up in the family of her uncle, the second Thomas Wells of Deerfield. She died about six months before her husband.

CHILDREN.

1. *Thomas Wells*, b. Aug. 12, 1739; m. Naomi Wright. . . . (83)
2. *Sarah*, b. May 29, 1741; m. Nov. 5, 1761, Rev. Lemuel Hedge of Warwick, Mass. He graduated at Harvard College in 1759, was ordained at Warwick, Dec. 3, 1760, and d. there Oct. 15, 1777, æ. 43. He was suspected of being a Tory, and the town forbade him to leave Warwick. (See Holland's Hist. West. Mass., Vol. II.) She died at Middlebury, Vt., in 1808, æ. 67. She had, 1. Lemuel, grad. Harvard College, 1784, was a teacher, and d. unm., in Washington, D. C., in 1801; 2. Levi, b. April 19, 1766, grad. Harv. Coll., 1792, was Tutor and Prof. there for 37 years. The degree of Doctor of Laws was conferred on him by Yale College, in 1823. He d. Jan. 3, 1844, æ. 77. He m. Jan. 15. 1801, Mary Kneeland of Cambridge, Mass., who d. Dec. 23, 1853, æ. 80; 3. Sarah, b. April 11, 1768, m. Feb. 23, 1788, Moses Fay. They settled in Barnard, Vt., but rem. to Rutland, Vt., about 1827, where they died. He d. Nov. 13, 1829. She d. April 8, 1831, æ. 63. Her son, *Edwin*, b. Sept. 22, 1794, m. Harriet P. White: (see in Fam. 144;) 4. Abraham, was a physician in Windsor, Vt., and d. unm.; 5. Samuel, settled in Windsor, Vt., rem. in 1810 to Montreal, C. E., and d. there about 1831. He was thrice married; 6. Susan, m. Col. Josiah Dunham, (U. S. A.,) and d. May, 1857. He grad. Dart. Coll., 1789, and was distinguished as a teacher; 7. Eleutheria, b. 1776, m. Hon. Daniel Chipman, LL. D., a lawyer, of Middlebury, Vt. He grad. Dart. Coll., 1788, was a Member of Congress, &c. She was living in 1858.
3. *Susanna*, b. Aug. 30, 1743; m. 1770, Jonathan Danforth of Hardwick, and d. Nov. 14, 1779, æ. 36. She had, 1. Samuel, rem. to Vt.; 2. Jonathan; 3. Pamelia; and perhaps others. Some of the children d. in early life.
4. *John*, b. June 11, 1745; grad. Harv. Coll., 1765, was clerk in an office in Worcester, Mass., where he d. 1796, æ. 51. He had the title of Major. He m. Sarah [Heney?] but left no children.

DESCENDANTS OF LIEUT. DANIEL WHITE.

36. Capt. DANIEL WHITE, eldest son of Capt. Daniel, (14) was born in Hatfield, Mass., Sept. 5, 1698. He removed with his father's family to Windsor, Conn., but returned to Hatfield as early as the time of his first marriage, and settled there as a farmer. In 1731 he removed to Bolton, Conn., where he resided till 1742.* In the spring of that year he bought, for £560, the house and homelot of his father-in-law, Dea. John White, and again settled in Hatfield. He took an active part in the public affairs of both the towns in which he resided. In Hatfield he was chosen constable in 1723, town clerk in 1729, and selectman and assessor in 1730. While residing in Bolton, he was 8 times chosen a selectman, from 1734 to 1741, and was almost constantly on the committee for laying out lands to the proprietors of the town. Upon his return to Hatfield he was again called to the office of a selectman, which he held for 17 years, between 1742 and 1763, making 26 years in which this office was conferred upon him by the people of both towns. He died in Hatfield, Dec. 15, 1786, æ. 88.

He married, 1st, Oct. 7, 1719, MARY DICKINSON of Hatfield, who died July 8, 1721.

He married, 2d, Jan. 19, 1726, ELIZABETH WHITE, dau. of Dea. John White. (Family 13.) She died July 4, 1770, æ. about 65.

CHILD;—BY THE FIRST MARRIAGE.

1. *Salmon*, b. June 23, 1721; d. in infancy.

CHILDREN;—BY THE SECOND MARRIAGE.

2. *Daniel*, b. Dec. 28, 1726; m. Submit Morton.   .   .   .   .   (84)
3. *Mary*, b. Aug. 30, 1729; m. Dr. Elijah Paine of Hat., afterwards of Williamsburg, Mass., where he was town clerk for several years. She d. April 19, 1804, æ. 74. He d. Jan. 14, 1814, æ. about 90. She had, 1. Mary, b. Jan. 7, 1753, d. April 1, 1756; 2. Elizabeth, b. Oct. 30, 1754, m. Asa Lud-

---

* Bolton attracted to it a large part of the near relatives of Daniel White and his wife. Four of his brothers lived there, with their families: Thomas, Joel, Elisha, and Oliver: also, his sister Sarah. His sister Lucy lived in Coventry, Andover Society, near the line of Bolton. Three sisters of his wife also lived in B.; Sarah, Martha, and Eunice. Her brother Jonathan lived in the adjoining town of Hebron.

The first settlements in Bolton were made in 1718, and the town was incorporated Oct., 1720. An entry in the Records of Lands, Vol. IV. p. 103, states that in Dec., 1761, the population of the town was 857; in the First Society, 561; in that part of the Second Society, (now Vernon,) which was in Bolton, 296. In 1850 the town of Bolton, (the former First Society,) had a population of 600.

den of W.; 3. Mary, b. Dec. 27, 1756, m. Dexter May of Goshen, Mass., and d. about 1843 ; 4. Hannah, b. Dec. 2, 1758, m. Isaac Little of W., who d. Aug., 1821. She d. March 14, 1839, æ. 80 ; 5. Elijah, b. Nov. 29, 1760, grad. Yale College, 1789, was a lawyer in Ashfield, Mass., and honored with various offices. He was a deacon for 30 years. He m. Martha Pomeroy of Northfield, who d. Jan., 1842, æ. 69. He d. Aug. 3, 1846, æ. 85. Three of his sons became ministers : 1. *Elijah*, b. Dec. 9, 1797, grad. Amh. Coll., 1823, was pastor at Claremont, N. H., and West Boylston, Mass., and d. Sept. 14, 1836, æ. 38 ; 2. *William P.*, (D. D.) b. Aug. 1, 1802, grad. Amh. Coll., 1827, is pastor at Holden, Mass ; 3. *John C.*, b. Jan. 29, 1806, is pastor at Gardner, Mass.; 6. Jerusha, b. Jan. 7, [17?] 1763, m. Elisha Wells of Williamsburg ; 7. Electa, b. Oct. 3, 1765, m. Jan. 11, 1787, Josiah Frost of Chesterfield, Mass. ; 8. John, b. Feb. 10, 1768, m. Lucy Curtis of W. He lived in Covington, N. Y., and d. Feb., 1858, æ. 90 ; 9. Seth, b. June 25, 1770, m. Sept. 20, 1793, Hannah Nash of W. He rem. to Brooksville, O., and d. July, 1814, æ. 44.

4. *Salmon*, bap. Oct. 31, 1731 ; m. Mary Wait. . (85)
5. *Elihu*, bap. April 21, 1734 ; m. Zeruiah Cole. . . . . . (86)
6. *Elizabeth*, bap. Sept. 5, 1736; m. Gen. Seth Murray of Hatfield, who d. Sept. 26, [28?] 1795, æ. 60. She d. Feb. 4, 1814, æ. 77. Her dau., Lucinda, b. Dec. 9, 1770, m. Nov. 10, 1790, Isaac Maltby, who grad. Yale Coll., 1786, and d. 1819. She d. about 1836, æ. 65.
7. *Hannah*, bap. Oct. 26, 1740 ; prob. d. young.

---

37. Rev. THOMAS WHITE, son of Capt. Daniel, (14) was born in Hatfield, Mass., July 10, 1701. A part of his childhood was spent in the family of his grandfather, in Hatfield. Perhaps he did not remove to Windsor until after his grandfather's death. He graduated at Yale College in 1720, in the same class with Pres. Jonathan Edwards, and taught the Grammar School in Northampton, Mass., for three years, commencing with 1721. About this time he was admitted to the church in that place, and probably pursued his theological studies, while teaching, with the Rev. Solomon Stoddard, the most noted divine in that vicinity. His first ministerial labors, of which any notice is found, were at Worcester, Mass., where he was elected pastor of the First Church, Aug. 24, 1724. The town, however, did not concur in the choice, but appointed a committee " to address Mr. White for his further assistance in the work of the Gospel." (Lincoln's History of Worcester, p. 167.) He removed soon after to Bolton, Conn., and was ordained the first pastor of the Church in that place, Oct. 26, 1725. During his ministry of more than 37 years, he received to the

9

church 310 persons, of whom·95 were from other churches. The number of persons baptized was 914. The Rev. George Colton, his immediate successor in the pastoral office, thus characterizes his life and ministry: "He was a sound, orthodox preacher, a friend of peace and order." He died Feb. 22, 1763, æ. 61. He resided a short distance east of the principal street, on the north side of the road leading to Andover. The house in which he dwelt was occupied by his successors in the ministry, till about the year 1845.

He married, June 17, 1725, MARTHA HUNT of Northampton, Mass., born April 18, 1699, dau. of Jonathan Hunt and Martha Williams. After the death of her husband, she married, 2d, Aug. 15, 1764, Col. Thomas Welles of Glastenbury, Conn., who died May 14, 1767, æ. 75. After his death, she lived with her eldest dau., in Somers, Conn., and died there, Feb. 17, 1784, æ. nearly 85.

CHILDREN.

1. *Martha*, b. March 20, 1726 ; m. July 25, 1744, Capt. Thomas Pitkin, jun., of Bolton and Somers. He was a justice of the peace, was town clerk of Bolton, and represented that town many times in the Legislature. She d. in Somers, June 4, 1802, æ. 76. He d. June 25, 1818, æ. 94. She had, (all b. in Bolton,) 1. Martha, b. Feb. 8, 1745, d. Nov. 1, 1754 ; 2. Thomas White, b. Sept. 25, 1747 ; 3. Samuel, b. Oct. 17, 1749, d. Jan. 23, 1751 ; 4. Samuel, b. Aug. 18, 1751, d. Aug. 4, 1772, æ. 21 ; 5. Elizabeth, b. June 19, 1753, m. Jan. 4, 1775, Eleazer Huntington ; 6. Martha, b. Sept. 8, 1755, m. March 5, 1778, Anderson Minor ; 7. Rebecca, b. Aug. 26, 1757, d. young ; 8. Paul, b. Oct. 11, 1759, m. ——— Lothrop, and d. Jan. 6, 1823, æ. 63 ; 9. Calvin, b. April 9, 1762, d. Oct. 18, 1822, æ. 60. He m. 1st, Sept. 29, 1785, Hannah Pease of Somers, who d. May 8, 1815. He m. 2d, June 5, 1818, Amelia Chapman of Tolland, who d. Nov. 2, 1822 ; 10. Lucy, b. Oct. 23, 1764, m. Nov. 27, 1788, Dea. Samuel Reynolds of Somers, Conn., and Longmeadow, Mass. She d. Feb., 1853, æ. 88 ; 11. Jerusha, b. Jan. 27, 1767, m. Sept. 7, 1786, Giles Pease of Somers, who d. Sept. 26, 1823, æ. 60. She d. Feb. 26, 1854, æ. 87.

2. *Sarah*, b. July 13, 1729 ; m. Sept. 20, 1750, Col. Samuel Chapman of Tolland, Conn., an officer in the French War and in the Revolution. He was a justice of the peace, was for about 30 years a representative from Tolland in the Legislature, and was a member of the Convention which ratified the Constitution of the U. S., in 1788. He d. Dec. 5, 1803, æ. 81. She d. April 10, 1800, æ. 71. She had, 1. Sarah, b. Oct. 9, 1751, d. Oct. 24, 1751 ; 2. Sarah White, b. Jan. 15, 1753, m. March 25, 1773, Ira West of T., and d. Aug. 1, 1792, æ. 39 ; 3. Samuel, b. April 20, 1755, d. July 15, 1756 ; 4. Samuel, (Capt.) b. Aug. 18, 1757, lived in Ellington, Conn., and d. March 13, 1839, æ. 81. He m. 1st, Oct. 24, 1782, Mary Carlton of T., who d. March 8,

1809 ; m. 2d, Nov. 12, 1812, Mrs. Sarah Chapin, wid. of Benj. C., of Chicopee, Mass. She d. July 28, 1827 ; 5. Eliakim, (Col.) b. July 31, 1760, d.
in Tol., April 16, 1838, æ. 77. He m. 1st, Nov. 24, 1785, Roxelaney Willes
of T., who d. Jan. 27, 1798 ; m. 2d, March 19, 1799, Nancy Willes of T.,
who d. Nov. 6, 1845, æ. 80.

---

38. Capt. JOEL WHITE, son of Capt. Daniel, (14) was born
in Windsor, Conn., April 6, 1705. He settled in Bolton,
Conn., as early as 1725, on lands which were soon after bequeathed to him by his father. He probably first lived on the
west side of the street, nearly opposite the burying-ground.
In February, 1747, he bought of Francis Smith the place on
the south-east corner of the main street and the road to Andover, "fronting near the meeting-house." This was his
home for more than forty years, and the large elms now standing there are said to have been planted by his own hands.
He was a merchant, engaged in an extensive business, and
was a large landholder. The records of Bolton show that he
bought lands there more than eighty times, and his name appears frequently upon the records of several other towns. At
the time of his death he owned over 500 acres of land, although
he had a few years previously given a farm to each of his four
surviving sons.

He was a justice of the peace, and took a prominent part in
the affairs of the town. In 1728 he was chosen town treasurer;
he was frequently constable and collector, and was eight times
chosen one of the selectmen, between the years 1738 and 1766.
He was often the moderator of the annual town meetings, and
from 1760 to 1781 was commonly the person selected for this
service. He was one of the first representatives from Bolton
to the Legislature, in October, 1750, and was frequently
re-elected, until October, 1774, when he had represented the
town at twenty-six sessions. Though advanced in life at the
time when the Colonies were struggling for independence, he
was an ardent and self-denying patriot. In 1777 he was twice
chosen a member of the "Committee of Correspondence, Inspection, and Safety," and was once its chairman. From his
will, and from the inventory of his estate, it appears that in
the early part of the War he loaned over £3,000 to the State

of Connecticut, and to the United States, a part of this sum being paid in the depreciated currency of those times. The nominal value of the "Public Securities" held by him at his death, with the interest that had accrued thereon, was about £5,000, or nearly equal to the appraised value of the remainder of his estate. These securities were divided among his heirs, who are supposed to have realized but a very small percentage upon their nominal value. His inventory amounts to a little more than £10,000. He died June 28, 1789, æ. 84. The following is a fac-simile of his autograph, from a signature in 1757.

The high social position of his family may be inferred from the fact that his five daughters married into families of great respectability: the husbands of four of them were graduates of Colleges.

He married, 1st, RUTH ———, who died Sept. 4, 1735, æ. 32. This is the date found in the town record. On the stone tablet inscribed to the memory of Joel White, Esq., and his four wives, the date is Sept. 15.

He married, 2d, Jan. 22, 1736, RUTH DART of Bolton, dau. of Daniel Dart, sen., and Elizabeth Douglass, and granddaughter of Richard Dart of New London. She was the youngest of eleven children, was born Aug. 26, 1711, and died Aug. 29, 1760, æ. 49.

He married, 3d, April 8, 1761, Mrs. EUNICE WOLCOTT, widow of Roger Wolcott, jun., Esq., of East Windsor, Conn., and dau. of John and Joanna Colton of Longmeadow, Mass. By her first husband, Ens. John Ely, 3d, of West Springfield, Mass., she was the mother of Justin Ely, who married Ruth White, dau. of her third husband. She was born Feb. 22, 1706, and died March 29, 1778, æ. 72. She was buried at West Springfield.

He married, 4th, 1778, Mrs. SARAH CONANT, widow of
[Shubael?] Conant, Esq., of Mansfield, Conn. It is supposed
that her family name was Avery, and that she was originally
of Groton, Conn. Her first husband was David Sluman of
Lebanon. Her second husband was Hon. Zebulon West of
Tolland. Her son, Dr. Jeremiah West, married Amelia Ely,
dau. of Capt. Joel White's third wife. Mrs. Sarah White died
Nov. 17, 1785, æ. 66. (Grave-stone, 1788: an error.)

CHILDREN;—BY THE FIRST MARRIAGE.

l. *Joel*,   b.   Dec. [28?] 1727 ; m. Anne Loomis.   .   .   .   .   (87)
    (On town record, b. Dec. 28; but on church record, bap. Dec. 10.)
2. *Ann*,   b.   Jan.   15,   1732 ; m. Dec. 28, 1749, Eleazer Steel of Tolland, and
    d. Feb. 20, 1751, æ. 19.   He m. 2d and 3d wives, and d. Feb. 26, 1799, æ. 72.
3. *Reuben*, b.   Aug. 22, 1735 ; d. Aug. 31, 1735.
    A family tradition says there was also an *Elijah*, who d. in infancy ; but no
    record is found of his birth or death.

CHILDREN ;—BY THE SECOND MARRIAGE.

4. *Lemuel*, b.   Nov.   6, 1736 ; m. Martha Loomis.   .   .   .   (88)
5. *Ruth*,   bap. Mar. 19, 1738 ; d. in infancy.
6. *Jerusha*, b. July 14, 1740 ; m. 1st, July 1, 1766, Rev. Samuel Clark. He
    grad. at the College of New Jersey, in 1751, settled as pastor of the Congre-
    gational church in Kensington, Conn., July 14, 1756, and d. there Nov. 6,
    1775, æ. 49. She m. 2d, April 26, 1787, Amos Hosford, Esq., of Berlin,
    Conn., who d. Nov. 13, 1822, æ. 85. She d. Dec. 13, 1827, æ. 87. She had,
    by her first husband, 1. Samuel, bap. May 20, 1770 ; 2. Jerusha, b. March 9,
    1774, m. Elisha Dunham of Berlin, and d. March 9, 1844; æ. 70; 3. Thomas,
    b. March 21, 1776, lived in Newington, Conn., and d. Dec. 25, 1814, æ. 38.
    He m. April 5, 1809, Alma Wells of N., who d. Jan. 24, 1824, æ. 43.
7. *Elijah*, b.   June 21, 1742 ; m. Eunice Day.   .   .   .   .   (89)
8. *Ruth*,   b.   Feb. 29, 1744 ; m. Nov. 9, 1762, Justin Ely, Esq. He grad. at
    Harvard College in 1759, and was a merchant in W. Springfield, Mass. He
    very frequently represented the town in the General Court of Mass., and was
    otherwise prominent in public affairs. She d. April 6, 1809, æ. 65. He m.
    again, and d. June 26, 1817, æ. 78. She had, 1. Theodore, b. Aug. 10, 1764,
    was for a few years a merchant in New York, but returned to W. Spr., where
    he d. Nov. 28, 1838, æ. 75. He m. Feb. 9, 1818, Hannah Chandler, who d.
    Aug. 12, 1829, æ. 48 ; 2. Anna, b. May 12, 1767, d. Jan. 6, 1776 ; 3. Justin,
    b. Sept. 22, 1772, grad. Harv. Coll., 1792, and was a merchant in W. Spr.,
    where he d. Aug. 26, 1850, æ. 78. He m. 1st, Jan. 25, 1803, Lucy Barron
    of Amherst, who d. Jan. 8, 1808, æ. 27. He m. 2d, March 1, 1809, Abigail
    Belden of Wethersfield, Conn., who is still living ; 4. Heman, b. April 24,
    1775, was associated with his eldest brother in business, in New York. He
    was the founder of Elyria, Lorain Co., Ohio, in 1817, and was Judge of the
    County Court. He d. Feb. 2, 1852, æ. 76. He m. 1st, Oct. 8, 1818, Celia
    Belden of Wethersfield, Conn., who d. Jan. 7, 1827, æ. 30. He m. 2d, Har-
    riet Salter, of Mansfield, Conn.

9. *Thomas*, b. Feb. 2, 1746; m. Ruth Talcott. . . . . . (90)
10. *Betty*, b. Dec. 17, 1747; m. 1st, Jan. 15, 1766, Rev. John Bliss. He grad. at
    Yale College in 1761, was ordained pastor of the church in Ellington, Conn.,
    Oct., 1764, was dismissed Dec., 1780, and d. in E., Feb. 13, 1790, æ. 53.
    She m. 2d, Sept. 15, 1790, Lemuel Pomeroy, Esq., of Southampton, Mass.,
    who d. Dec. 14, 1819, æ. 81. She went to live with her dau. in W. Spring-
    field, and d. there Jan. 17, 1836, æ. 88, having been blind for about 20 years.
    She was a woman of unusual energy and intelligence, and took a deep in-
    terest in public affairs. She had, by her first husband, 1. Betty, b. Nov. 30,
    1766, d. Sept. 7, 1769; 2. John, b. June 16, 1768, lived in Tolland, Conn.,
    and d. Aug. 23, 1850, æ. 82. He m. May 30, 1809, Sally Abbott of T.,
    who d. Feb. 18, 1853, æ. 72; 3. Betsey, b. April 9, 1770, m. Asahel Birge
    of Southampton, and d. Dec. 1, 1834, æ. 64; 4. Achsah, b. May 3, 1772, m.
    Lieut. Ruggles Kent of W. Springfield, and d. May 1, 1857, æ. 85; 5. Joel
    White, b. March 31, 1774, lived in Brattleboro, Vt., and d. Aug. 4, 1816, æ.
    42. He m. 1796, Lucy Hitchcock, who d. 1824, æ. 52; 6. Hosea, b. Feb.
    26, 1776, d. 1850, æ. 74. He m. 1st, April 26, 1798, Malah Rogers, who d.
    Sept. 29, 1821, æ. 43; m. 2d, Oct. 7. 1823, Tirzah Bagg; 7. Billy, b. Feb.
    27, 1778, d. May 25, 1781; 8. Daniel, b. Feb. 5, 1780, lives in Brattleboro,
    Vt. He m. 1st, April 23, 1807, Polly Miller of Marlboro, Vt.; m. 2d, Feb.
    26, 1820, Hannah Thurston; 9. William, b. May 11, 1783, d. July 25, 1786.
11. *Daniel*, b. Dec. 7, 1749; m. Sarah Hale. . . . . . (91)
12. *Ann*, b. Oct. 23, 1753; m. 1st, Sept. 16, 1772, Thomas Kimberly, Esq., of
    Glastenbury, Conn. He grad. at Yale College in 1766, was a lawyer, and
    d. Aug. 25, 1777, æ. 29. She m. 2d, April 15, 1778, Hon. Jonathan Brace.
    He grad. at Yale College in 1779, first settled in Vt., but returned to Glasten-
    bury in 1786, and rem. to Hartford in 1794. He was a Representative in
    Congress, 1798–1801, and for many years Judge of the Probate and County
    Courts. He d. Aug. 26, 1837, æ. 83. She d. Dec. 7, 1837, æ. 84. She
    had, by her first husband, 1. Thomas, b. July 7, 1773, d. Oct. 3, 1776; 2.
    Anson, b. Jan. 18, 1775, m. Sarah Ann Street. He was a merchant in
    Darien, Ga., and d. there Nov. 2, 1836, æ. 61; 3. Electa, b. Feb. 27, 1777, is
    living in Hartford. By her second husband, 4. Thomas Kimberly, b. Oct. 16,
    1779. He graduated at Yale College, 1801, became a lawyer, but soon
    entered largely into commercial business at Hartford, where he still resides.
    He was for many years Pres. of the Ætna Insurance Co., and has been
    mayor of the City. He m. 1st, 1807, Lucy M. Lee of Westfield, Mass.; m.
    2d, Mrs. Emily (Burt) Burnham of Longmeadow, Mass.; 5 Fanny, b.
    Sept. 23, 1781, m. 1813, Frederic Hall, LL. D., Prof. in Middlebury College,
    Vt., and afterwards in Trinity College, Conn. She d. Nov., 1826, æ. 45.
    He d. about 1843.

---

39. Capt. ELISHA WHITE, son of Capt. Daniel, (14) was
born in Windsor, Nov. 11, 1706. He settled early in Bolton,
but removed to East Guilford, (now Madison,) Conn., about
1744, and thence to the adjoining town of Killingworth, about
1749. He lived in that part of Killingworth which is now

Clinton, and was for a while engaged in mercantile business. He died there, probably about the year 1778.

He married, Aug. 31, 1732, ANN FIELD of Bolton, dau. of Ebenezer Field of E. Guilford, and Mary Dudley. She was born March 22, 1712, and died some years before her husband.

CHILDREN.

1. *Elisha*, b.   May 15, 1733; d. Aug. 3, 1742.
2. *Ann*,   b.   Sept. 19, 1735; d. Aug. 20, 1742.
3. *Chloe*, bap. Feb. 19, 1738; m. 1st, Capt. Walter Price Griswold of Killingworth, a ship-master in the foreign trade; m. 2d, Jonathan Boardman of Haddam, Higganum Society, Conn.; m. 3d, Capt. Daniel Hand of E. Guilford, who d. Oct. 16, 1816, æ. 84. She d. Nov. 28, 1821, æ. 84. She had, by her first husband, 1. Chloe, m. —— Young; 2. Sally, m. Jan. 25, 1789, David Hoyt of E. G., and rem. to Vt. He d. March 27, 1822. She d. Jan. 24, 1847; 3. Julia, m. George Bushnell, and settled in Hillsdale, Columbia Co., N. Y.; 4. Clarissa, m. —— Child of Middletown, Conn.; 5. Walter Price. By her second husband, 6. Samuel, resided at South Farms, (now the town of Morris,) in Litchfield, Conn. Perhaps she had other children.
4. *Dudley*, b. Jan. 8, 1741; m. Thankful Murray.   . . . .   (92)
5. *Ann*,   b.   ; m. Joseph Chatfield, and d. in Clinton.

---

40. SIMEON WHITE, son of Capt. Daniel, (14) was born in Windsor, Conn., March 11, 1708. He settled in Hatfield, Mass., where he died Sept. 6, 1779, æ. 71. He was constable in 1737, and surveyor in 1757 and 1760.

He married JERUSHA WAIT, who died in Williamsburg, Mass., Feb. 14, 1810, æ. 99 years and a few months. She retained her physical and mental powers, in a good degree, almost to the close of life.

CHILDREN.

1. *Simeon*, b.   1745; m. Hannah Hubbard   . . . .   (93)
2. *Asa*,   b.   1747; m. Zilpah Hayes.   . . . .   (94)
3. *Jerusha*, b.   1751; m. Jan. 6, 1789, Arnold Mayhew of Williamsburg, who d. April 6, 1830. She d. Dec. 1, 1839, æ. 88. She had, 1. Constant, b. April 15, 1790, d. Dec. 7, 1827, æ. 37. He m. Oct. 6, 1816, Roanna Phinney of W.; 2. Martha, b. Jan. 15, 1793, m. Sept. 15, 1816, Leavitt Thaxter, Esq., of Northampton, who rem. to Edgarton, Martha's Vineyard, Mass. He is a lawyer, has been in both Houses of the Legislature, a member of the Executive Council, and U. S. Collector at Martha's Vineyard.

---

41. OLIVER WHITE, youngest son of Capt. Daniel, (14) was born in Windsor, March 26, 1720. He settled in Bolton, where he resided in 1751, but removed to Saybrook, Conn.,

as early as 1762. It seems probable that he lived for a few years in some town not ascertained, and he may have had other children besides those named below. He died in Saybrook, Sept. 13, 1801, æ. 81.

He married, Feb. 21, 1745, MARY BEECRAFT. The time of her death is not known. The church records of Saybrook show that a "Mrs. Mary White" died there, May 11, 1802, æ. 65. Perhaps this was a second wife of Oliver White, and the mother of his younger children.

CHILDREN.

1. *George*,   b.   March 6, 1746; m. Mary Benton. .   .   .   .   (95)
2. *Tryphena*, b.   1747. The town record of Bolton says, b. Dec. 31, 1747; the church record, bap. Oct. 11, 1747.
3. *Mary*,   bap. May 20, 1750.
4. *Pierce*,   b.   July 27, 1762; Pearce, on record of baptism, at Saybrook.
5. *Joseph*,   b.   Sept. 2, 1764.

Fifth Generation and Children.

IN THE LINE OF DEA. NATHANIEL WHITE, OF HADLEY.

42. NATHANIEL WHITE, Jun., son of Nathaniel, (15) was born in Hadley, Mass., April 10, 1710. He settled as a farmer in South Hadley, and died there, March 23, 1787, æ. 77. "He was an eminently pious man."

He married, Nov. 24, 1741, MARTHA BASCOM of Northampton, dau. of Thomas Bascom of N., and Hannah Catlin of Deerfield. She was born Sept. 16, 1713, and died Dec. 6, 1796, æ. 83.

CHILDREN.

1. *Timothy,* b.   1743; d. unmarried, Feb. 21, 1789, æ. 46.
2. *Samuel,* b. Oct. 3, 1747; m. Mary Collins.   .   .   .   .   (96)
3. *Nathaniel,* b. Nov. 28, 1749; m. Huldah Clark.   .   .   .   .   .   (97)
4. *Christian,* b.   1751; d. unmarried, May 5, 1801, æ. 50.
5. *Ezekiel,* b.   1754; was a physician in S. Hadley; was also a teacher and composer of music. He d. unm., Nov. 3, 1789, æ. 35.
6. *Ebenezer,* b. May 6, 1756; m. Ruth Lyman.   .   .   .   .   (98)
7. *Ezra,* b.   1758; d. unm., April 7, 1790, æ. 32.   .

---

43. JONATHAN WHITE, son of Nathaniel, (15) was born in Hadley, Jan. 29, 1717. He was a farmer at the "Fall Woods," in South Hadley, where he died Aug. 2, 1789, æ. 72.

He married, 1st, DORCAS ALVORD, who died Nov. 24, 1744, æ. 24.

He married, 2d, Feb. 6, 1745, LYDIA RUGG, dau. of Samuel Rugg. She was born Jan. 1, 1723, and died Nov. 18, 1802, æ. 80.

CHILD ;—BY THE FIRST MARRIAGE.

1. *Enoch,* b. Nov. 8, 1744; d. Nov. 15, 1744.

10

CHILDREN;—BY THE SECOND MARRIAGE.

2. *Enoch,*   b. Feb.,   1747; m. Susannah Goodman,   .   .   .   (99)
3. *Phineas,* b.   1748; d. while a student at Yale College, Sept. 5, 1769, in his 22d year. His monument is in the cemetery at New Haven.
4. *Thankful,* b. Sept. 21, 1752; m. Aaron White.   .   .   .   (Family 102)
5. *Esther,* b.   ; m. Enos Goodman of S. Hadley, and had, 1. Cynthia, b. Aug. 25, 1775; 2. Erastus, b. Aug. 15, 1777; 3. Phineas, b. May 12, 1780; 4. Enos, b. July 16, 1782; 5. Cleopas, b. Dec. 8, 1784; 6. Esther, b. July 23, 1787; 7. Thomas, b. Aug. 22, 1789; 8. Tryphosa, b. April 15, 1792; 9. Sophia, b. Dec. 17, 1794.
6. *Lydia,* b.   1759; m. Darius Smith of S. H., who rem. to Susquehannah, N. Y. He d. Aug. 11, 1820, æ. 74. She d. March, 1837, æ. 78. She had, 1. Darius, b. Oct. 21, 1781, m. Hannah Elmer of Amherst; 2. Bernice, b. Feb. 27, 1783, m. Emily Smith of Granby; 3. Lydia; 4. Prudence; 5 & 6. Twins, both d. in infancy; 7. Sylvester, b. Nov., 1789, d. Oct., 1855, æ. 66; m. Sarah Kirby of Bainbridge, N. Y.; 8. Emma, b. Oct. 17, 1791, m. Oct. 13, 1824, Austin Brainerd of S. H.; 9. Louisa, bap. Sept., 1793, m. Ambrose Bennett, and lives in Masonville, N. Y.; 10. Tamesin White, m. Robert Foster, now of Masonville; 11. Hazor, bap. April, 1797, m. Elizabeth Wells; 12. Mary, bap. May, 1799, m. Simeon Cook; 13. Tirzah, m. Quartus Brown.
7. *Phebe,* b.   ; m. Gad Alvord of Granby, Mass. She had, 1. Sewall; 2. Theodosia; 3. Gaius, bap. May 18, 1788; 4. Mary, bap. June 6, 1790; 5. Alvin; 6. Clarissa; 7. Electa; 8. Alanson; 9. Amanda; and others who d. young.

---

44. OLIVER WHITE, son of John, (16) was born in Hadley, and lived there, south of Ralph's Lane. He died June 28, 1789, æ. probably about 65.

He married, 1st, Feb. 17, 1752, ELIZABETH CHARTER, who died June 29, 1752.

He married, 2d, 1755, (pub. Jan. 18,) ABIGAIL SELDEN, who survived him.

CHILD;—BY THE FIRST MARRIAGE.

1. *A son,* b. June 6, 1752; d. Aug. 15, 1752.

CHILDREN;—BY THE SECOND MARRIAGE.

2. *Oliver,* b. Dec. 19, 1755; m. ———— ————, ...   (100)
3. *Elizabeth,* b. Nov. 29, 1757; m. Phineas Clark of Easthampton, Mass., who d. Feb. 15, 1817, æ. 57. She d. March 25, 1847, æ. 89. She had, 1. Submit, b. Oct. 7, 1781, m. Jonathan Parsons; 2. Elihu, b. July 6, 1783, was living in Lee, Mass., 1855; 3. Sylvester, b. Feb. 9, 1785, d. in the State of N. Y.; 4. Salome, b. Sept. 17, 1786, m. Rufus Smith, of S. Hadley and Worthington; 5. Lucinda, b. June 10, 1788, m. Justin Cook, jun.; 6. Silence, b. March 10, 1790, m. Dea. Asa Marble; 7. Paulina, b. Jan. 5, 1792; 8. Elizabeth, b. Oct. 5, 1793, m. Dea. Elisha King; 9. Erastus, b. July 19, 1795;

10. Lydia, b. Feb., 1797, m. Medad King, jun. ; 11. Amanda, b. July 19, 1799, m. Morris Parsons ; 12. Persis, b. April 1, 1802, d. June 26, 1803.

4. *Moses*, b. Dec. 3, 1759 ; m. Chloe Peck. . . . . . (101)

5. *Jerusha*, b. March 5, 1762 ; m. Aug., 1781, Seth Kellogg.

6. *Eunice*, b. March 18, 1764 ; m. March 2, 1784, George Wells. They rem. to N. Y., or Vt., about 1800.

7. *Elihu*, b. March 8, 1766 ; d. March 27, 1766.

8. *Esther*, b. April 2, 1768 ; m. Jan. 1, 1789, William Ingram, who rem. to N. Y. The following chil. were bap. in Hadley ; 1. Oliver, and 2. Experience, bap. Sept. 30, 1792 ; 3. Quartus, bap. Nov. 24, 1793 ; 4. Charles, bap. Jan. 29, 1797.

9. *Abigail*, b. Sept. 24, 1770 ; m. Feb. 11, 1789, Green Wells of Mapletown, and rem. to Vt., or N. Y.

45. JOHN WHITE, Jun., son of John, (16) was born in Hadley, but probably removed to some place not ascertained. He is supposed to be the one who had the following family, in Hadley.

He married, 1759, (published Aug. 18,) MARY EMMONS of Hadley.

CHILDREN.

1. *Mary*, b. May 20, 1764.
2. *Elisha*, bap. Oct. 5, 1766.

46. MOSES WHITE, son of Dea. Joseph, (17) was born in Hadley, Feb. 7, 1710. He was a trader in South Hadley, and died there, probably in 1783, æ. 73.

He married, July 29, [1738?] LYDIA BELLOWS.

CHILDREN.

1. *Lydia*, ⎰ b. March 30, 1739 ; d. April 19, 1739.
2. *A child*, ⎱ Twins, d. on the day of birth.
3. *Elizabeth*, b. 1741 ; m. Reuben Judd of S. Hadley, and d. May 9, 1765, æ. 24. He m. again twice, and d. March 7, 1815, æ. 81. She had, 1. Achsah, b. Oct. 8, 1759, m. 1778, Thomas Wells, and d. Jan., 1847, æ. 87 ; 2. Reuben, b. Jan. 10, 1761, m. Nov. 27, 1791, Rachel Smead, and d. Oct., 1835, æ. 74 ; 3. Lydia, b. June 10, 1762, m. Eli Day, and d. May 8, 1812, æ. 50 ; 4. Elizabeth, b. Jan. 10, 1764, d. 1767.

47. THOMAS WHITE, son of Dea. Joseph, (17) was born in Hadley, July 20, 1715. He settled in South Hadley, where he died July 18, 1795, æ. 80. (On grave-stone, æ. 78.)

He married MINDWELL ALVORD, who died Aug. 25, 1764, æ. 59. (Grave-stone.)

CHILDREN.

1. *Joel*,   b.   ; d. 1771. He prob. m. Anna ——, who survived
him. Anna White and Thomas White, 2d, were appointed administrators
on the estate of Joel White, Oct. 1, 1771.

2. *Mindwell*, b.   1739; m. 1st, —— Looman; m. 2d, Lieut. Thomas
White, 2d, of S. Hadley, who came from Lancaster, Mass. She d. Oct. 10,
1768, æ. 29. He m. again, and d. Feb. 20, 1814, æ. 75. She had, by her
first husband, 1. Eunice, b. 1761, m. Frederick Loomer, and d. April 25, 1804,
æ. 43. By her second husband, 2. Lucy, b. 1767, m. Oliver Taylor, jun., of
S. H., and d. Jan. 18, 1845, æ. 77. He d. March 5, 1848, æ. 81.

3. *Abigail*, b.   ; m. Caleb Ely, of S. H. and Norwich, Mass. Her
dau. Abigail, m. Justus Wright. J. W. and wife both d. in Billerica, Mass.

4. *Aaron*, b. May 29, 1744; m. Thankful White. .   .   .   .   (102)

5. *Job*,   b. about 1752; m. 1st, Charity Chapin; 2d, Mindwell Clapp. (103)

6. *Mary*,   b. July 1, 1754; m. Dec. 3, 1780, Perez Smith of S. H., who d. June
12, 1822, æ. 74. She d. March 10, 1835, æ. 80. She had, 1. Pliny, b. June 12,
1781, was a physician at Masonville, N. Y., and d. April 7, 1854, æ. 72. He
m. Hannah Smith of Granby; 2. Perez, b. April 13, 1783, m. Hannah Lyman of Hadley; 3. Rodney, b. March 24, 1785, m. Sarah Hall of Norwich,
Mass., and d. Oct. 19, 1839, æ. 54; 4. Eliel, b. Feb. 6, 1787, m. Sabra Booth
of E. Windsor, Conn., who d. in Vernon, Conn., March 16, 1858, æ. 67; 5.
Mary, b. Jan. 17, 1789, d. Aug. 26, 1791; 6. Norman, b. June 9, 1791, was a
lawyer at New Salem, Mass., and d. Aug. 27, 1852, æ. 61. He m. Elizabeth
Harwood of N. Brookfield, Mass.; 7. Joel White, b. Aug. 25, 1793, lives in
Ellington, Conn. He m. Elizabeth Booth of E. Windsor, who d. May 12,
1859, æ. 71; 8. Hervey, b. June 16, 1797, m. Lucinda Abbee of Kingston,
N. Y., and d. May 18, 1843, æ. 46.

7. *Simeon*, b.   ; m. 1st, Roxa Pomeroy; 2d, Mrs. Urania Stebbins. (104)

---

48. JOSEPH WHITE, son of Dea. Joseph, (17) was born in
Hadley, Oct. 4, 1718. He settled in South Hadley, and died
there, Nov., 1795, æ. 77.

He married, Oct. 23, 1746, EDITHA MOODY of S. H., probably dau. of Ebenezer Moody and Editha Kellogg. She died
July, 1793.

CHILDREN.

1. *Editha*, b. Jan. 27, 1748; m. —— Chamberlain.

2. *David*, b. Oct. 14, 1749; d. unm., Sept., 1811, æ. 62.

3. *Moses*, b. April 10, 1751; m. Abigail ——.   .   .   .   .   (105)

4. *Rebecca*, b. Jan. 14, 1753; m. Eleazer Goodman, and rem. to the vicinity of
Lake George, N. Y.

5. *Joseph*, b. Dec. 13, 1754; m. Sally Yeomans.   .   .   (106)

6. *Lois*,   b. Oct. 20, 1756.

7. *Miriam*, b. Aug. 2, 1758; m. Samuel Alvord of S. H., who d. July 9, 1814,
æ. 62. She d. Feb. 25, 1844, æ. 85. She had, 1. Calvin, b. Aug. 3, 1779;
2. Orange, b. Feb. 25, 1781; 3. Julius, b. June 6, 1783, d. Oct. 9, 1785; 4.
Miriam, b. May 25, 1785, m. Levi White; (Fam. 224;) 5. Samuel, b. Sept.

11, 1787, m. Dec. 23, 1810, Sophia Day of S. H.; 6. Cyrus, b. Sept. 25, 1789; 7. Luther, b. Dec. 25, 1791; 8. Editha, b. Feb. 3, 1794; 9. Sophia, b. Nov. 24, 1796, d. Oct. 12, 1803; 10. Fidelia, b. Dec. 10, 1799.

3. *Reuben*, b. Oct. 1, 1761; m. Mabel White. . . . . (107)

49. Dea. JOSIAH WHITE, son of Dea. Joseph, (17) was born about 1729. He settled in South Hadley, where he died, March 29, 1809, æ. 80. He is called "Major" on the Probate Records.

He married, March 16, 1749, MARY SMITH of S. H., dau. of Samuel and Lydia Smith. She was born March 3, 1732, [1733?] and died Sept. 21, 1818, æ. 85, or 86.

CHILDREN.

1. *Maria*, b. Aug. 13, 1749; d. unm., Aug. 29, 1772, æ. 23.
2. *Mary*, b. Feb. 13, 1752; m. Phineas Smith.
3. *Irene*, b. March 30, 1755; d. Sept. 12, 1757.
4. *Josiah*, b. Feb. 22, 1759; d. Feb. 12, 1760.
5. *Josiah*, b. March 30, 1761; m. Mabel Mitchell. . . (108)
6. *Irene*, b. Feb. 26, 1763; d. Oct. 2, 1775, æ. 12.
7. *Keziah*, b. March 30, 1766; m. Dec. 31, 1799, Joel Clark of S. H., and d. Nov. 28, 1810, æ. 44. Their son, Joel Chapin, d. Sept., 1815, æ. 13.
8. *Eldad*, b. March 31, 1768; m. Hannah Day. . . . (109)
9. *Medad*, b. Sept. 5, 1771; d. Oct. 10, 1771.
10. *Medad*, b. Nov. 25, 1774; d. Sept. 26, 1775.

50. Lieut. JACOB WHITE, son of Daniel, (18) was born in West Springfield, Mass., Nov. 13, 1716. He was a saddler in Springfield, and also owned one-third part of the iron-works there. He died Jan. 10, 1762, æ. 45.

He married, Feb. 2, 1745, AMY STEBBINS, dau. of John Stebbins of Springfield. She was born Aug. 6, 1724, and died Oct. 7, 1760, æ. 36.

CHILDREN.

1. *Amy*, b. July 25, 1745; is probably the one of that name who m. Dr. Chauncey Brewer, of W. Springfield and Springfield. He grad. Yale College, 1762, was justice of the peace, a delegate from W. S. to the 1st, 2d, and 3d Provincial Congresses of Mass., and was a deacon of the First Church in Springfield. He d. in 1830, æ. 87. She d. May, [1821?] æ. 76. She had, 1. Lucy, b. April 17, 1771, d. unm., March 16, 1801, æ. 30; 2. Daniel Chauncey, b. Dec. 27, 1772, d unm., Sept. 26, 1848, æ. 76; 3. Sarah, b. Aug. 21, 1774, m. Thomas Dikeman, and d. Feb. 26, 1832, æ. 57; 4. Sophia, b. Aug. 24, 1776, d. unm., Dec. 29, 1846, æ. 70; 5. Henry, b. March 14, 1779, m. Lucy Pynchon; 6. Martin, b. Jan. 20, 1781, d. unm., Oct. 24, 1846, æ. 65; 7. Betsey, b. Nov. 28, 1782; 8. Katherine, b. Feb. 19, 1785, d. Nov.

19, 1786 ; 9. Eunice, b. Jan. 13, 1788, m. J. Ladd of Ohio ; 10. James, b.
Dec. 8, 1789, m. Harriet Adams of Mansfield, Conn., and d. July 20, 1856,
æ. 66 ; 11. Francis, b. June 16, 1793, m. Mrs. Myra Hinsdale. (See
" Chauncey Memorials," p. 201.)

2. *Jacob*, b. July 11, 1747. The will of his father provided that he should
"have a liberal education." But his name is not found upon the Catalogue
of any New England College, and his history is unknown.

3. *Luther*, b. Sept. 11, 1749 ; m. ——— ———.   .   .   (110)
4. *Lucy*, b. Dec.   7, 1751 ; d. Nov. 8, 1753.
5. *Lucy*, b. March 1, 1754 ; d. Dec. 5, 1757.
6. *Calvin*, b. July   19, 1756.
7. *Paul*, b. July 29, 1759 ; perhaps d. in S., May 18, 1812, æ. 53.

---

51. Sergeant DANIEL WHITE, son of Daniel, (18) was born
in West Springfield, June 22, 1719. He was a house carpenter there, but lived for nearly half a century in a log-cabin,
which was standing in 1840. He was a man of athletic frame,
and somewhat eccentric in character. He died at the house
of his son Pliny, Jan. 7, 1805, æ. 85.

He married, July 29, 1747, PRISCILLA LEONARD, dau. of
John and Sarah Leonard of W. S. She was born June 21,
1725, and died July 20, 1800, æ. 75.

CHILDREN.

1. *Horace*, b. April 26, 1749 ; m. Mercy Cooley.   .   .   .   (111)
2. *Daniel*, b. Nov. 2, 1752 ; [Nov. 8?] m. Hannah Lamb.   .   . (112)
3. *Pliny*, b. Oct. 12, 1761 ; m. Lydia Granger.   .   .   .   (113)
4. *Edward*, b. July 27, 1764 ; m. Hannah Bedortha.   .   .   . (114)

---

52. PRESERVED WHITE, son of Daniel, (18) was born in
West Springfield, Aug. 31, 1721. He settled in Springfield,
and died July 16, 1802, æ. 81. In 1743 he was called a
weaver.

He married, 1st, 1740, (pub. Nov. 29,) RACHEL KILBOURN,
dau. of John Kilbourn and Mercy Day. She was born July
8, 1721, and died June, 1777, æ. 56.

He married, 2d, Feb. 29, 1784, Mrs. SARAH WORTHINGTON,
who died Jan. 16, 1797.

CHILDREN;—BY THE FIRST MARRIAGE.

1. *Rachel*, b. April 18, 1742 ; m. Jan. 1, 1767, Ambrose Collins of S., and had,
    1. Lucy, b. July 14, 1769 ; 2. Cynthia, b. Dec. 14, 1771 ; 3. Nancy, b. Aug.
    22, 1773 ; 4. John, b. July 14, 1776.
2. *Preserved*, b. Nov. 25, 1743 ; [Nov. 23?] m. Mary Terry.   .   . (115)
3. *David*,   b. Jan. 30, 1747 ; m. 1st, Lydia Ely ; 2d, Sarah Pynchon. (116)

4. *Hannah*, b. Aug. 21, 1750; [Aug. 20?] m. July 9, 1780, William Stephenson of Springfield, said to have rem. to Thetford, Vt.

5. *Lewis*, b. Feb. 25, 1753; d. Sept. 11, 1754.

6. *Persia*, b. Aug. 29, 1755.

7. *Zervia*, b. March 19, 1758; m. Dec. 7, 1780, Stoughton Bliss of East Windsor, Conn., who d. May 7, 1835, æ. 77. She had, 1. Jonathan, b. Oct. 6, 1781, d. Nov. 16, 1823, æ. 42; 2. Lucy, b. Jan. 21, 1785, m. Nov., 1820, Jonathan Blake of Springfield, and d. June 16, 1827; [1824?]; 3. Nancy, b. April 28, 1787; 4. William, b. Jan. 3, 1790, d. Sept. 8, 1828; 5. Pelatiah, b. April 15, 1792; 6. Reuben, b. Jan. 28, 1795, d. Dec. 31, 1796; 7. Reuben, b. Feb. 23, 1799.

8. *Lewis*, b. June 20, 1760; m. Susannah King. . . . (117)

9. *Walter*, b. June 13, 1765; m. Sabina Keep. . . . . (118)

---

53. WILLIAM WHITE, Jun., son of William, (19) was born in Hadley, Mass., Oct. 4, 1732. He lived in Hinsdale, N. H., in Northfield and Springfield, Mass., and died in Hadley, Dec. [30?] 1810, æ. 78.

He married, 1st, April, 1757, LYDIA PATTERSON of Northfield, born in 1737, and dau. of Elizur Patterson and Lydia Moore.

He married, 2d, Nov. 14, 1765, MARTHA CHAPIN of Spr.

CHILDREN ;—BY THE FIRST MARRIAGE.

1. *Giles*, b. ; m. his cousin, Sarah Dodd of Guilford, Conn.; (see Fam. 19.) They were living in Guilford, April, 1786, but rem. to Halifax, Vt., and thence to Cobleskill, Schoharie Co., N. Y., where they were living Sept. 15, 1797.

2. *Sarah*, b.

3. *Mary*, b.

CHILDREN ;—BY THE SECOND MARRIAGE.

4. *William*, b.

5. *Samuel*, b.

6. *Gad*, b. ; m. Flavia ———. . . . . . (119)

There were other children, whose names have not been ascertained.

---

54. NATHANIEL WHITE, son of William, (19) was born in Hadley, Nov. 12, 1738. He lived there, on the "Bay road," and kept a public house. He was a selectman in 1784. He died March 12, 1821, æ. 82.

He married, 1st, Nov. 5, 1761, SARAH STOCKWELL of Springfield, dau. of Abel Stockwell. She was born March 10, 1742, and died March 4, 1802, æ. 60.

He married, 2d, REBECCA SHEPARD of Hartford, Conn., who survived him.

CHILDREN;—BY THE FIRST MARRIAGE.

1. *Jarib*, b. April 27, 1763; m. Ruth Sherman. . . . . . (120)
2. *Sarah*, b. March 27, 1765; m. Nov. 16, 1791, Orange Hart Warren of Williamsburg, Mass., who d. May, 1830. She d. Dec., 1828, æ. 63. She had, 1. Horace, b. Oct. 28, 1792, m. Clarissa ——, and d. 1846, æ. 54; 2. Zenas, b. July 8, 1794; 3. Pliny, b. April 30, 1796, d. Sept. 9, 1857, æ. 61. His wife, Mary, d. June, 1847; 4. Rowena, b. March 31, 1798, d. Dec. 6, 1821, æ. 23; 5. Louisa, b. July 21, 1800, d. Sept. 28, 1805; 6. Sarah, b. July 15, 1802, d. Aug., 1830, æ. 28; 7. Nathaniel White, b. May 26, 1804, d. Oct. 4, 1810; 8. Marah, b. July 23, 1807, d. July, 1828, æ. 21.
3. *Lydia*, b. March 27, 1765; (twin with Sarah,) m. Jan. 8, 1800, Benjamin Burr of S. Hadley, and d. Feb. 28, 1834, æ. 69. She had, 1. Nancy, b. Nov. 10, 1801, m. Dec. 6, 1821, William A. Miller; 2. Lydia, b. March 31, 1804, m. Feb. 28, 1822, Gordon B. Miller of Ludlow, Mass.; 3. Benjamin, b. April 15, 1806, d. Oct. 16, 1807; 4. Maria, b. Jan. 9, 1809.
4. *Mabel*, b. Sept. 1, 1767; m. Reuben White. . . . (Family 107)
5. *Lois*, b. July 20, 1770; [July 22?] m. Jan. 16, 1794, Cotton Mather Warren of Williamsburg, who d. Nov. 10, 1837. She d. July 19, 1842, æ. 72. She had, 1, Harriet, b. Oct. 5, 1794, m. Feb. 26, 1824, Silas Sikes; 2. Sophia, b. Sept. 14, 1796, m. Dec. 23, 1813, Samuel Seeley; 3. Ansel, b. Sept. 3, 1798, d. Sept. 7, 1800; 4. Mather, b. Oct. 14, 1800, m. Oct. 28, 1823, A. M. Fairfield; 5. Charles, b. Sept. 22, 1802, d. Sept. 20, 1805; 6. Juliana, b. Sept. 21, 1804, m. Nov. 20, 1836, Charles Bridgman; 7. Lois, b. Dec. 24, 1806, d. 1814; 8. George, b. Feb. 21, 1809, m. Nov. 19, 1832, Lovina Dickenson; 9. Lucinda, b. Aug. 11, 1812, m. May 5, 1836, Hiram Bryant.
6. *Tirzah*, b. Aug. 13, 1772; m. Nov. 8, 1797, Phineas Thompson of Palmer, Mass. She had several children; one of them, Eliza, bap. at Hadley, June 22, 1800.

---

55. Capt. DANIEL WHITE, son of William, (19) was born in Hadley, Sept. 1, 1740. His name appears in a list of soldiers in the old French War, in 1759. He settled as a farmer in Hadley, where he was frequently called into the service of the town. He was seven times chosen one of the selectmen, between the years 1779 and 1799. In 1778 and 1783 he was a member of the "Committee of Correspondence, Inspection, and Safety." He died Nov. 17, 1815, æ. 75.

He married, June 11, 1772, SARAH GOODRICH, dau. of Aaron Goodrich. She was born Oct. 10, 1747, and died in 1837, æ. 90.

CHILDREN.

1. *Zenas*, b. Oct. 10, 1773; was a farmer in H., and d. unm., Sept. 16, 1844, æ. 71.
2. *Judith*, b. March 27, 1775; the 2d wife of Eli Graves; see the next name.
3. *Bethene*, b. Feb. 14, 1777; m. Jan. 10, 1798, Eli Graves. She d. Aug. 12, 1802, æ. 25, and he m. 2d, March 10, 1806, her elder sister, Judith White,

who d. June 2, 1837, æ. 62. He d. Feb. 28, 1850. The children of E. G. were,—by his first wife, Bethene, 1. John Judd, b. Oct. 26, 1798, m. April 21, 1824, his cousin, Maria Cook; 2. Fidelia Goodrich, b. July 21, 1800, d. April 10, 1807; 3. Bethene White, b. Aug. 1, 1802, d. Dec. 7, 1802: By his second wife, Judith, 4. Emily, b. Dec. 15, 1806, m. Jan. 7, 1840, Andrew Warner; 5. Julia, b. May 1, 1809; 6. Daniel Hezekiah, b. Feb. 3, 1811, m. July 2, 1843, Lucretia Nash, and d. Nov. 21, 1853, æ. 42; 7. Jane, b. Sept. 9, 1812, d. Jan. 14, 1826; 8. Fidelia Ursula, b. Jan. 24, 1815; 9. Sarah Ann Goodrich, b. Jan. 26, 1821, d. Feb. 12, 1845, æ. 24.

4. *Sarah*, b. Jan. 26, 1779; m. Jan. 22, 1799, John Cook, jun., of Hadley, who d. April 6, 1856, æ. 80. She was living in 1858. Has had, 1. Maria, b. Oct. 19, 1799, m. April 21, 1824, John J. Graves; (see above;) 2. Zenas, b. Sept. 1, 1801, m. Lucy Russell; 3. Ephraim, b. Sept. 30, 1803, d. Sept. 19, 1804; 4. Ephraim, b. June 14, 1805, m. Phebe English; 5. Roswell Wells, b. June 7, 1807, m. May 19, 1835, Harriet A. Nash of Greenfield; 6. Elizabeth Smith, b. April 28, 1810, m. Norman Hamilton; 7. Horace, b. March 8, 1812, d. Oct. 29, 1820; 8. Sarah Porter, b. June 7, 1814, d. Sept. 16, 1838, æ. 24; 9. Silas Wright, b. Dec. 8, 1816, m. Mary Cook; 10. John Dudley, b. Feb. 28, 1821; 11. Emily White, b. March 28, 1824, d. Aug. 22, 1831.

5. *Permelia*, b. Nov. 2, 1780; m. Jan. 23, 1805, Roswell Wells of Hadley, who rem. before 1820 to Waterbury, Vt., where some of their children are supposed to be living. She d. about 1853.

6. *Grace Grant*, b. Oct. 18, 1782; m. Nov. 28, 1802, Stephen Montague of Hadley, who d. May 18, 1851. She was living in 1858. Has had, 1. Sarah Goodrich, b. Sept. 9, 1803, d. unm., Dec. 2, 1839, æ. 36; 2. Sophronia, b. May 15, 1807, d. April 10, 1827, æ. 20; 3. Mary, b. Feb. 2, 1809, d. May 8, 1848, æ. 39; 4. Daniel Nathaniel, b. June 9, 1811, m. May, 1840, Mary Pierce; 5. Henry, b. July 30, 1813, m. Oct. 19, 1836, Abigail Kingsley; 6. Susan Grant, b. Feb. 12, 1817, m. Jan. 18, 1838, Elijah Ayres; 7. Stephen Stone, b. Dec. 8, 1818, m. 1st, Sept. 24, 1841, Mary C. Kellogg, of Amherst, who d. April, 1842; m. 2d, Oct. 2, 1844, Lucy W. Kellogg, sister of Mary C.; 8. Harriet Maria, b. Nov. 30, 1820, m. Nov. 30, 1842, Edmund Bartlett; 9. Sabra Ward, b. Dec. 28, 1822, m. Aug. 28, 1855, Martin F. Cook; 10. Pamela White, b. March 9, 1825.

7. *Silva*, b. April 20, 1785; m. Aug. 8, 1813, John Baker of Westhampton, Mass., who is dead. She is said to be living in Michigan. She has, 1. John; 2. Mary.

8. *Daniel*, b. Nov. 6, 1789; m. Dorcas Barrows.   .   .   .   (121)

56. EBENEZER WHITE, son of William, (19) was born in Hadley, March 16, 1744. He settled in Pittsfield, Mass., and died there, May 15, 1794, æ. 50.

He married, March 13, 1766, ABIGAIL PORTER, dau. of Abraham Porter of Hartford, Conn.

CHILDREN.

1. *Esther*, b. April 24, 1767; m. Josiah Ward of P., and d. Nov., 1836, æ. 69. She had, 1. Samuel, b. Nov. 14, 1789, d. Jan. 9, 1814, æ. 24; 2. William White,

11

b. March 24, 1793, lives in P.; 3. Abigail Porter, b. March 12, 1795, d. Oct.
  30, 1816, æ. 21; 4. Hannah, b. June 26, 1797.
2. *William Porter*, b. Oct. 10, 1769; m. Elizabeth Allen.   .   .   .   (122)
3. *Lydia*, b. May 24, 1772; m. Maj. Butler Goodrich, who is still living in Pittsfield, (1859.)   She d. April 12, 1842, æ. 70.   She had, 1. Ebenezer White,
  b. May 21, 1793, d. Sept. 12, 1819, æ. 26; 2. Caleb, b. Aug. 27, 1795;
  3. Edward, b. Jan. 17, 1797; 4. William, b. Feb. 14, 1799; 5. Elizabeth,
  b. Dec. 11, 1801; 6. Daniel, b. Jan. 12, 1804; 7. Huldah, b. Feb. 10, 1806;
  8. Butler, b. June 22, 1808, d. at Princeton, N. J., Feb. 12, 1836, æ. 27;
  9. George Washington, b. June 25, 1810; 10. Abigail Porter, b. Nov. 28,
  1812; 11. Lydia Maria, b. Jan. 3, 1816.
4. *Enoch*, b. March 19, 1775; m. Sally Lanckton.   (123)
5. *Polly*, b. July   28, 1777; d. July 8, 1779.
6. *David*, b. April 19, 1780; d. in S. America, May 1, 1807, æ. 27.
7. *Polly*, b. Nov.   20, 1782; d. unm., June 1, 1847, æ. 64.
8. *Abigail*, b. Nov. 19, 1786; d. May 11, 1803; æ. 16.

---

57. Lieut. DAVID WHITE, son of William, (19) was born in
Hadley, Feb. 18, 1748, and lived there. He was a Lieut. in
the Expedition to Canada, early in 1776. He died about
1778, æ. 30. His inventory is dated May 5, 1778.

He married, Dec. 17, 1772, ROXCELLANY WARNER, who survived him, and married, 2d, May 20, 1779, Joseph Crafts of
Whately, Mass.

CHILDREN.

1. *Cotton*, bap. July 10, 1774; m. 1st, Demis Dickinson; 2d, Eliz. Bancroft. (124)
2. *Luther*, bap. Sept. 10, 1775; m., and had two sons before he left Hadley. He
  died at the South.

---

58. EBENEZER WHITE, only son of Ebenezer, (20) was born
in Hadley, about 1733. He lived on the original White place,
and died Oct. 11, 1817, æ. 84.

He married SARAH CHURCH of Amherst, dau. of Samuel
Church. She was born Aug. 17, 1736, and died about 1802,
æ. about 66.

CHILDREN.

1. *Sarah*, b.   1770; m. Nov., 1787, John Sumner, of Hadley and Belchertown.   She d. Aug., 1803, æ. 33.   He d. July, 1804.   She had, 1. Susan,
  b. July, 1790, d. Dec., 1811, æ. 21; 2. Margaret, b. March 29, 1792, m. Nov.
  19, 1816, Addi Wallis of H.; 3. Samuel, b. May, 1794, d. Aug., 1800; 4.
  John, bap. Aug. 27, 1795, d. 1795.
2. *Jonathan*, b. Oct. 29, 1774; m. 1st, Lydia Atwood; 2d, Phebe Rider.   (125)
3. *Elijah*, b. June 28, 1778; m. Lucy Pierce.   .   .   .   .   (126)

IN THE LINE OF JOHN WHITE, OF HARTFORD.

59. JOHN WHITE, son of John, (21) lived in Hartford, and died there, at an advanced age, between 1808 and 1814.

He married, 1st, Dec. 7, 1752, HONOR BAXTER of Wethersfield, born March 2, 1729, dau. of Timothy Baxter and Sarah Kilbourn.

He married, 2d, ABIGAIL ———, who survived him, and was living in 1815. She was perhaps the Abigail Gilbert who married John White, Dec. 15, 1765. (Middletown Church Record.) This A. G. was probably the dau. of Ezekiel Gilbert, jun., and Elizabeth Blake, and born July 4, 1745.

CHILDREN;—BY THE FIRST MARRIAGE.

1. *John,*   b. about 1753 ; m. Anna Waters.   .   .   .   .   .   (127)
2. *Nathaniel,* b.   ; m. Sarah Steele.   .   .   .   .   .   (128)
3. *Sarah,*   b.   ; m. Jonathan Chapman of Hartford, a joiner.
4. *Anna,*   b.   ; m. James Sarvant of Hartford, a tailor.
5. *Honor,*   b.   ; m. ——— Barnard, a farmer.

See Note to Family 21.

IN THE LINE OF ENSIGN DANIEL WHITE, OF MIDDLETOWN.

60. Dea. JONATHAN WHITE, son of Daniel, (23) was born in Upper Middletown, Conn., Aug. 22, 1711. He settled in West Springfield, Mass., where he was an honored and influential citizen. He was a house-joiner, and was employed to help build the first Indian meeting-house at Stockbridge, Mass., but he also engaged in farming, and in other kinds of business. He was often called into the service of the town; was a selectman for seven years, 1774 to 79, and 1782; a delegate to the Provincial Congress in 1775, and also a member of the "Committee of Inspection and Safety;" and a representative to the General Court, in 1787. He was chosen a deacon of the Church in W. Springfield, March 1, 1759, and retired from the office in 1782. "He retained his vigor to old age, and regularly walked one mile to church, after entering his ninetieth year." The following is the inscription on his gravestone: "In Memory of Dea. Jon^a. White, who, after a long course of eminent Piety, diffusive Benevolence, exemplary Virtue, and extensive Usefulness in Church and State, calmly fell asleep, 12th Oct., 1805, Æt. 95."

He married, 1st, April 5, 1739, TRYPHENA ELY, dau. of Samuel Ely of Springfield. She was born April 7, 1712, and died Dec. 30, 1754, æ. 42.

He married, 2d, Dec. 20, 1759, Mrs. EDITHA BLISS, widow of Pelatiah Bliss, and dau. of Ebenezer Day. She was born Aug. 20, 1715, and died Feb. 4, 1797, æ. 81.

CHILDREN ;—BY THE FIRST MARRIAGE.

1. *Samuel*, b. April 5, 1740; d. July 4, 1748.
2. *Tryphena*, b. Oct. 6, 1742; m. Nov. 22, 1781, Dr. Timothy Horton of W. S., who d. Oct. 5, 1795, æ. 69. In 1812 she emigrated with her brother Aaron to Camillus, N. Y., and was uncommonly vigorous till near the close of life. She d. without issue, May 14, 1835, æ. 92.
3. *Sarah*, b. Dec. 23, 1744; d Aug. 30, 1746.
4. *Aaron*, b. Sept. 4, 1747; m. Lucy Kellogg. . . . . . (129)
5. *Joseph*, b. Dec. 24? 1749; m. 1st, Sarah Leonard; 2d, Phebe Clapp. (130)
6. *Elijah*, b. May 31, 1752; d. Dec. 30, [3?] 1773, æ. 21.

61. JEDEDIAH WHITE, son of Daniel, (23) was born in Upper Middletown, Jan. 23, 1730. He lived there for several years after his marriage, but soon after the close of the Revolutionary War removed to New Durham, Greene Co., N. Y. In Feb., 1798, he removed to Paris, (now Marshall,) Oneida Co., N. Y., where he died Nov. 9, 1822, æ. nearly 93.

He married, Dec. 4, 1760, BARBARA WILLCOX. She died March 8, 1812, æ. 71.

CHILDREN.

1. *Alice*, b. Sept. 24, 1761 ; d. unm., Dec. 20, 1848, æ. 87.
2. *Rachel*, b. Oct. 24, 1762; m. Apr. 20, 1786, Levi North of Berlin, Conn., and d. Jan. 31, 1839, æ. 76. He d. Oct. 2, 1846, æ. 86. She had, 1. Patty, b. Dec. 7, 1787, m. 1833, Chester Bronson of Salisbury, Herkimer Co., N. Y., who d. May 18, 1857 ; 2. Jedediah, b. June 22, 1789, m. March 10, 1813, Betsey Bulkley of Rocky Hill, Conn., and d. Jan. 30, 1835, æ. 45 ; 3. Lucy, b. Oct. 2, 1790, m. 1822, Rev. Thomas W. Duncan, now of Roxbury, N. H. ; 4. Sarah, b. Sept. 30, 1792 ; 5. Bulah, b. Sept. 8, 1794 ; 6. Rachel, b. March 26, 1796 ; 7. Edmund, b. Oct. 10, 1797, lives in Berlin. He m. 1st, April 7, 1825, Clarinda Boardman of Mid., who d. Dec. 4, 1826, æ. 25 ; m. 2d, July 7, 1828, Maria M. Wilcox of Mid., who d. March 30, 1847, æ. 46 ; m. 3d, May 7, 1851, Mrs. Almira (Kelsey) Wilcox of Berlin ; 8. Marilla, b. April 1, 1799 ; 9. Olive, b. Oct. 15, 1800, m. 1st, 1819, Thomas H. Skinner of Haddam, Conn., who d. Dec., 1826 ; m. 2d, Jacob Chapman, now of Lyndon, Vt. ; 10. Norris, b. July 29, 1802, res. in Elmira, N. Y. He m. 1st, 1826, Mercy Alger of Hartwick, N. Y. ; has a 2d wife ; 11. Julia, b. March 26, 1804, m. Nov., 1830, Titus Penfield of Berlin ; 12. Levi, b. Aug. 18, 1807, m. May 19, 1833, Ann Taylor of Wethersfield.

3. *Daniel*, b. Jan., 1764 ; m. Sally Merriam. . (131)
4. *Lois*, b. ; d. in infancy.
5. *John*, b. 1768 ; m. Nancy Ann Landon. . . . . (132)
6. *Martha*, b. ; m. Theodore Monross. Both d. in Clinton, N. Y.
7. *Sarah*, b. March 27, 1771 ; m. Sept. 8, 1795, Eli Page of Freehold, Greene Co., N. Y., a farmer. They rem. in 1799 to Marshall, Oneida Co. She d. Aug. 24, 1846, æ. 75. He d. May 15, 1858. She had, 1. Ebenezer, b. June 30, 1796, d. Sept. 17, 1797 ; 2. Pamela, b. Feb. 25, 1798, d. June 14, 1813, æ. 15 ; 3. Albert, b. March 31, 1800, m. Dec. 29, 1824, Caroline Taylor ; 4. Daniel, b. May 17, 1802, m. Sept. 7, 1826, Clarissa Hinman ; 5. Louisa, b. Nov. 13, 1804, m. Dec. 17, 1828, John Sergeant ; 6. Elvira, b. March 19, 1807, m. Jan. 28, 1835, Edward Peck ; 7. Eli, b. Feb. 25, 1809, m. March 1, 1832, Drusilla Hay ; 8. Benjamin, b. Nov. 22, 1813, m. Feb. 28, 1839, Jemima Holmes ; 9. Herman L., b. Aug. 27, 1818, m. Sept. 10, 1843, Maria Camp.
8. *Susannah*, b. ; d. unm., in Canaan, Conn.
9. *Lois*, bap. May 30, 1773 ; m. Hart Norton. Both d. in the State of N. Y.
10. *Polly*, b. ; m. ——— Whitney, and d. in N. Y.
11. *Rebecca*, b. ; d. unm., in N. Y.
12. *Abigail*, b. ; d. unm., June 8, 1805.

---

62. NATHANIEL WHITE, son of Capt. Nathaniel, (24) was born in East Middletown, afterwards called Chatham, April 25, 1715. He was a farmer there, and died Feb. 11, 1767, æ. 52.

He married, May 17, 1737, MARY SAGE, dau. of Timothy and Margaret Sage. She was born March 31, 1716, and died Jan. 31, 1767, æ. 50.

CHILDREN.

1. *Mary*, b. ; d. 1739.
2. *Mary*, bap. Jan. 6, 1740 ; d. in infancy.
3. *Margaret*, b. July 5, 1741 ; m. John Bartlett, of Chatham, and d. April 24, 1775, æ. 33.
4. *Mehitable*, bap. July 22, 1744.
5. *Nathaniel*, b. Nov. 8, 1745 ; d. April 27, 1751.
6. *John*, b. Mar. 23, 1748 ; m. Elizabeth ———. . . . (133)
7. *Mary*, b. July 23, 1750 ; m. Feb. 27, 1772, Darius Adams, and soon after rem. from Chatham.
8. *Nathaniel*, b. Aug. 14, 1754 ; m. Abigail Miller. . . (134)

63. Capt. ELIJAH WHITE, son of Capt. Nathaniel, (24) was born in East Middletown, Feb. 15, 1719. He settled in East Haddam, Conn., and was probably engaged in trade, as he owned a store and wharf there. He died May 18, 1778, æ. 59. His will is dated Dec. 12, 1776.

He married, July 9, **1741**, ABIGAIL HURLBURT. (May 6, 1741, a family record.) She is called the "dau. of David and Mary Hurlburt," upon the Mid. Record. But this is probably an error, as in 1763 his wife was "Abigail, the dau. of Ebenezer Hurlburt." She was born March 1, 1722, was living at the date of her husband's will, and probably survived him.

CHILDREN.

1. *Amos*, b. March 6, 1742; d. March 17, 1742.
2. *Rachel*, b. Feb. 14, 1744; [Feb. 15?] m. Aug. 30, 1761, Samuel Phillips Lord of E. Haddam, an eminent merchant. She d. June 23, 1807, æ. 63. He d. July 21, 1811, æ. 77. She had, 1. Hope, b. April 30, 1762, m. 1st, 1796, Capt. Selden Chapman, of Hartford and E. Had., who d. June, 1809. She m. 2d, 1814, Col. Richard Ely Selden, of Hadlyme, Conn. She d. July 17, 1843, æ. 81. Col. S. d. 1848; 2. Abigail, b. Feb. 25, 1764, d. July 11, 1775, æ. 11; 3. Samuel Phillips, b. Feb. 9, 1766, d. unm., in Brooklyn, O., Aug. 4, 1826, æ. 60; 4. George, b. May 3, 1768; was a merchant in E. Had., and d. Oct. 5, 1827, æ. 59. He m. May 9, 1802, Ann Randall of Westchester, N. Y., now d. ; 5. Rachel, b. Oct. 6, 1770, m. Nov. 15, 1796, Joel Foote of Marlboro, Conn., and d. Oct. 6, 1843, æ. 73. He d. July 12, 1846, æ. 83; 6. Sophia, b. June 28, 1773, m. 1802, Josiah Barber, of Hebron, Conn., and Brooklyn, O., and d. May 27, 1827, æ. 54. He d. Dec., 1843, æ. 71; 7. Abigail, b. Aug. 13, 1775, m. April 28, 1805, George Randall of New York, who d. Jan. 29, 1814, æ. 39. She lives in Cleveland, O.; 8. William, b. May 4, 1778, d. July 4, 1804, æ. 26. He m. April 20, 1802, Jerusha Cornwall of Chatham, who m. 2d, Chevers Brainerd of E. Had.; 9. Richard, b. Aug. 13, 1780, was a merchant and manufacturer at Cleveland, O., and d. Jan. 24, 1857, æ. 76. He m. Sept. 30, 1811, Ann Atwood, of E. Had. ; 10. Epaphras, b. May 15, 1784, d. Oct. 18, 1801.
3. *Amos*, b. Nov. 20, 1745; m. Sarah Griswold.   .   .   .   .   (135)
   (This birth is so recorded at Middletown : a fam. record says, Nov. 28.)
4. *Elijah*, b. Feb. 28, 1748; m. Elizabeth Arnold.   .   .   .   (136)
5. *Daniel*, b. April 13, 1750; d. March 6, 1751.
6. *Abigail*, b. March 6, 1752; d. Oct. 3, 1758, æ. 6.
7. *Daniel*, b. Feb. 26, 1754; d. Sept. 27, 1756.
8. *Daniel Hurlburt*, b. July 16, 1757; m. Hannah Brainard.   .   (137)

---

64. Capt. NOADIAH WHITE, son of Capt. Nathaniel, (24) was born in East Middletown, Feb. 26, 1720. He settled there as a farmer, and held the office of constable in 1757 and 1761. When advanced in life, he removed, with most of his family, to the State of New York, and died there, at Middlefield, Otsego Co., Feb., 1811, æ. 91.

He married, Jan. 19, 1744, LOIS WHITE, his cousin, dau. of

Dea. Joseph White of Chatham. (Fam. 25.) She was born Jan. 6, 1725, and died in Chatham, Aug. 31, 1795, æ. 70.

CHILDREN.

1. *Noadiah,* b. Nov. 18, 1744; d. Feb. 9, 1745.
2. *Noadiah,* b. Dec. 18, 1745; m. Mercy Mayo. . . (138)
3. *Lois,* b. Sept. 13, 1748; d. July 8, 1757.
4. *Joseph,* b. March 18, 1752; (March 29, N. S.;) m. Hannah Gates. (139)
5. *Mehitable,* b. June 21, 1754; m. April 15, 1779, Gen. Seth Overton of Chatham. He was a Justice of the Quorum, 1806–1818. She d. Aug. 20, 1828, æ. 74. He d. Aug. 17, 1852, æ. 94. She had, 1. Seth, b. March 5, 1780; 2. Prudence, b. Feb. 6, 1783; 3. Charlotte, b. March 10, 1785; 4. Augustine, b. March 24, 1787; 5. Oliver, b. Aug. 22, 1789, was a lawyer in Bellefontaine, Ohio, and d. 1825, æ. 36.
6. *Abijah,* b. Nov. 18, 1756; d. Sept., 1758.
7. *Lois,* b. Jan. 14, 1759; d. unm., at Canajoharie, N. Y., about 1840, æ. 80.
8. *Samuel,* b. March, 1761; d. April 8, 1762.
9. *Abijah,* b. Jan. 18, 1763; m. Hannah Hall. . . . . (140)
10. *Samuel,* b. Feb. 11, 1767; m. Cynthia Allis. . . . . (141)
11. *Sarah,* b. Dec. 25, 1768; was living at Middlefield, N. Y., 1858.

---

65. Hon. EBENEZER WHITE, son of Dea. Joseph, (25) was born in East Middletown, July 24, 1727. He was a farmer there, on his father's homestead, and was highly esteemed for his ability and integrity. He represented the town of Chatham at thirty-two sessions of the Legislature, between the years 1769 and 1791, and in the Convention which ratified the Constitution of the United States, in 1788. From 1786 to 1796 he was an Associate Judge of the County Court. He succeeded his father as deacon of the First Church in Chatham, April 21, 1768. He died July 29, 1817, æ. 90. (July 27, on the grave-stone: an error.)

He married, Sept., 1753, RUTH WELLES of East Hartford, dau. of Capt. Samuel Welles, 2d, and Esther Ellsworth. (See in Fam. 5.) She was born Dec. 17, 1727, and died Nov. 23, 1780, æ. 53.

CHILDREN.

1. *David,* b. Sept. 7, 1754; m. 1st, Mary A. Stocking; 2d, Mary Prior. (142)
2. *Abigail,* b. 1757; d. Oct. 20, 1759.
3. *Abigail,* b Aug. 8, 1760; m. May 4, 1786, Rev. Cyprian Strong, D. D.; (his 2d wife.) He graduated at Yale College in 1763, was ordained Pastor of the First Church in Chatham, Aug. 19, 1767, and d. Nov. 17, 1811, æ. 67. (See Sprague's "Annals of the American Pulpit," Vol. II.) Mrs. Abigail Strong d. May 2, 1796, æ. 35. She had,

1. Elnathan, b. March 25, 1787; was a merchant in Hardwick, Vt., and a deacon in the Congregational Church there. He d. June 19, 1847, æ. 60. He m. Oct. 17, 1820, Jane Chamberlain, dau. of Gen. C., of Peacham, Vt., and had, 1. *Harriet Ellsworth*, b. Sept. 21, 1821, m. Nov. 27, 1841, Rev. John H. Worcester of St. Johnsbury, Vt., and d. March, 1842, æ. 20; 2. *William Chamberlain*, b. Aug. 18, 1823, grad. Dart. Coll.; lives at Newton, Mass. He m. July, 1850, Margarette Breck of Brighton, Mass.; 3. *Charles Cyprian*, b. May 10, 1825, d. May, 1827; 4. *Jane Chamberlain*, b. Dec. 1, 1827, m. 1852, Rev. John O. Means, now of Roxbury, Mass.; 5. *Elnathan*, b. May 2, 1832, grad. Dart. Coll., and at Andover Theo. Sem. He m. 1856, Lizzie Mitchel of Roxbury, Mass.

2. Erastus, b. May 6, 1789; is a farmer at Portland, and has held various public offices. He m. Apr. 22, 1818, Mary Lewis, of Chatham, and has, 1. *Charles Cyprian*, b. Nov. 19, 1819, m. April, 1845, Julia Talcott of Hartford; 2. *Mary Amelia*, b. Aug. 16, 1822; 3. *John Ellsworth*, b. Aug. 28, 1824.

3. Amelia, b. Nov. 10, 1790; m. Feb. 3, 1817, Dr. Aaron Smith of Hardwick, Vt. Has had, 1. *Amelia Ann*, b. Nov. 12, 1817, d. Sept. 16, 1833, æ. 15; 2. *Eliza Abigail*, b. April 25, 1819, d. April 24, 1837, æ. 18; 3. *Laura Esther*, b. Sept. 21, 1822, m. Dec. 30, 1841, Rev. John King Lord, son of Pres. Lord of Dartmouth College. He d. at Cincinnati, O., July 10, 1849, æ. 30. She is now principal of a school at Montpelier, Vt.; 4. *Charles Strong*, b. July 24, 1824, grad. Brown Univ., and studied theology. He m. July 24, 1854, Lucy A. Maynard of Walton, N. Y., who d. Feb. 2, 1857, æ. 29.

4. Charles Wells, b. Nov. 10, 1792; d. March 8, 1793.

5. Charles, b. Feb. 5, 1794; d. in N. Y. city, Oct. 26, 1813, æ. 19.

4. *Esther*, b. March 26, 1763; lived with her brother Daniel, and d. unm., July 14, 1845, æ. 82.

5. *Daniel*, b. Oct. 24, 1765; m. Abigail Hills. .   .   .   .   .   (143)

6. *Ruth*, b. Nov. 11, 1767; m. April 29, 1789, Rev. Elijah Gridley. He grad. Yale Coll., 1788, was minister at Mansfield, Conn., was settled in 1797 at Granby, Mass., and d. there, June 10, 1834, æ. 74. She d. May 13, 1851, æ. 83. She had, 1. Harry White, b. May 29, 1791, rem. to Ottawa, Ill. He m. Oct. 19, 1815, Lucy D. Dickinson of Granby; 2. Ralph Wells, b. April 5, 1793, grad. Yale Coll., 1814, was pastor at Williamstown, Mass., 1816 to 1834, and rem. to Ottawa, Ill. He was afterwards pastor at Jacksonville, Ill., until his death. He d. at Ottawa, Feb. 2, 1840, æ. 47. He m. 1816, Eliza Barnes of New Haven, Conn., who d. Jan. 19, 1841, æ. 46; 3. Laura White, b. Jan. 5, 1797, m. Jan. 5, 1819, Hon. William Bowdoin, a lawyer, of South Hadley Falls, Mass., and d. April 21, 1822, æ. 25. He d. June 23, 1856; 4. Addison, b. Dec. 18, 1801, lives in Granby. He m. 1st, Jan. 11, 1827, Sibbil Ayres of G., who d. Nov. 14, 1845, æ. 37. He m. 2d, March 2, 1847, Mrs. Maria Burnham of Lisbon, Conn.

---

66. Lieut. STEPHEN WHITE, son of Dea. Joseph, (25) was born in East Middletown, Jan. 17, 1731, and was a farmer there, on a part of his father's homestead. He was chosen

constable in the town of Middletown, from 1763 to 1766, and held offices in Chatham, after that town was organized. He died Nov. 23, 1774, æ. 43.

He married, Feb. 10, 1757, HONOR HUBBARD of Glastenbury. After his death, she married, 2d, Jan. 12, 1780, Capt. Thomas Wadsworth of E. Hartford, who died 1783, æ. 67. She was born Jan. 1, 1734, and died Jan. 31, 1789, æ. 55.

CHILDREN.

1. *Prudence*, b. Aug. 23, 1757; m. Samuel Wadsworth of E. Hartford, who d. 1798, æ. 52. She d. 1822, æ. 65. She had, 1. Molly, bap. 1782, d.; 2. Mabel, b. 1783; 3. Samuel, b. 1784, m. 1805, Hannah Roberts, and d. 1822; 4. Oliver, b. 1790, was lost at sea, about 1806; 5. Hezekiah, b. 1792, m. 1st, Maria Jones, who d. 1835, æ. 33; m. 2d, 1837, Mrs. Heppy (Hills) Forbes; 6. Charles, b. March, 1794, is a minister at Richfield Springs, N. Y.; 7. Titus, b. 1796, d. 1848; 8. Polly, b. 1799.
2. *Honor*, b. June 27, 1759; m. Dec. 24, 1779, Noah Sage of Chatham, and d. Nov. 2, 1812, æ. 53. He d. Sept. 9, 1822, æ. 75. She had, 1. Henry, b. 1780, d. Jan. 26, 1797, æ. 16; 2. Harriet, b. 1781, m. Feb. 17, 1801, Dr. Isaac Conkling, who d. Feb. 26, 1824, æ. 44. She d. Aug. 17, 1855, æ. 74.
3. *Josiah*, b. Sept. 5, 1761; m. Hannah Hills, and others.   .   . (144)
4. *George*, b. Sept. 18, 1763; m. 1st, Mabel Hills; 2d, Hannah T. Starr. (145)
5. *Ann*, b. Sept. 21, 1765; d. May 2, 1775.
6. *Molly*, b. Sept. 22, 1767; d. May 27, 1775.

67. TIMOTHY WHITE, son of Hugh, (26) was born in Upper Middletown, March 15, 1719. He was a resident of Haddam in 1748, and of East Haddam in 1751, and was probably engaged in trade. He died in E. H., Oct. 16, 1757, æ. 38.

He married SUSANNAH ———. Her history is not known.

CHILDREN.

1. *Hannah*, b.   ; m. June 10, 1762, Benjamin Reed of E. Haddam, and had, 1. Mary, b. June 11, 1763; 2. Benjamin, b. Feb. 20, 1765; 3. Joseph, b. Jan. 2, 1767.
2. *Susannah*, b. Oct. 5, 1749; m. Oct. 28, 1772, John Spencer of E. H., and had, 1. John, b. Oct. 17, 1773; 2. Molly, b. July 23, 1775; 3. Oliver, b. Aug. 25, 1777; 4. Samuel White, b. Oct. 8, 1779; 5. Susannah, b. Sept. 12, 1781.
3. *Mary*, b.   ; d. Aug. 22, 1752.
4. *Mary*, b. Dec. 15, 1752; m. James Clark, 2d, of Haddam.
5. *Timothy*, bap. Mar. 2, 1755; m. 1st, Mehitable Smith; 2d, Ursula Sloper. (146)
6. *Samuel*, b. Aug. 16, 1757; lived in Hartford, and d. in early life.

68. AARON WHITE, son of Hugh, (26) was born in Upper Middletown, Oct. 25, 1723. He settled there, and died Jan. 19, 1802, æ. 78.

He married, April 6, 1749, SARAH OLMSTED of East Hartford, dau. of James Olmsted and Mary Butler. She died March 18, 1814, æ. 90.

CHILDREN.

1. *Aaron,* bap. May 26, 1754; d. unm., in the West Indies, Feb. 5, 1782, æ. 28.
2. *Sarah,* bap. Sept. 12, 1756; m. March 4, 1779, Gideon Savage.
3. *Rebecca,* bap. March 11, 1759; m. Feb. 7, 1786, Nathaniel Loomis of Ashford, Conn. Her son Samuel was bap. at Up. Mid., Jan. 27, 1788, the parents "belonging to Whitesboro," N. Y.
4. *Samuel,* b. July 3, 1762; m. Anna Merrow. . . . (147)
5. *Chloe,* bap. May 5, 1765; m. —— Olcott.
6. *Lydia,* bap. Dec. 20, 1767; m. James Cary.
   The members of this family are all dead.

---

69. Hon. HUGH WHITE, youngest son of Hugh, (26) was born in Upper Middletown, Jan. 25, 1733. He settled there, and was one of the selectmen of Middletown from 1779 to 1783. He was a commissary in the army, during a part of the Revolutionary War. Soon after the close of the War, he became the Pioneer of the settlements in Central New York. In May, 1784, he left Middletown, with four sons who had arrived at manhood, a daughter, and daughter-in-law, and founded a settlement at *Sedaghquate,* a few miles from the present city of Utica. In the January following he took thither his wife and the remainder of his family. Several of his relatives, with others from Middletown and its vicinity, quickly followed; and the new settlement, under the name of "Whitestown," soon became widely known as the place in which the emigration from New England centered. The hardships and perils encountered by these early settlers can scarcely be conceived of, by those who now visit that thickly-peopled region. The whole country was in the wildness of nature. The nearest mill was at Palatine, forty miles distant. The hostility of the Indian Tribes had hitherto rendered the settlement of that region impossible, and at the close of the War the whole central and western portions of the State were without civilized inhabitants. It was therefore necessary that the Pioneer of the new settlement should conciliate the favor of the Indians. In his intercourse with them he was frank and decided. On one occasion, an Indian Chief demanded of Mr.

White, as a test of his professed confidence, that he would permit him to take to his wigwam a little grand-daughter, then playing about the house. The Chief promised to keep the child safely, and to bring her home again the next day. The child was entrusted to him; but it was not until the approach of night, when fears of treachery had almost overcome her mother, that she was returned, finely arrayed in Indian dress, with many ornaments. This incident is said to have contributed much toward establishing a lasting friendship between the new settlers and the neighboring Indians. (See Lectures of Wm. Tracy, Esq.; also, Historical Collections of New York, p. 379.)

In 1788 the town of "Whitestown" was organized. It included in its limits all the State of New York lying westward of a line passing through Utica, and reaching from the southern boundary of the State to the St. Lawrence River. This territory had 6000 inhabitants in 1792, and Judge White lived to see it containing a population of over 300,000. At the organization of Herkimer County, Mr. White was appointed a Judge. He afterwards held the same office in the new County of Oneida. He died April 16, 1812, æ. 79. The following is a fac-simile of his autograph.

He married, 1st, Aug. 23, 1753, MARY CLARK of Middletown, dau. of Daniel and Mary Clark. She was born Feb. 10, 1734, and died about the year 1774.

He married, 2d, Mrs. LOIS DAVENPORT of New Hartford, Conn., widow of Rev. Ebenezer Davenport of Greenwich, Conn., and dau. of Jonathan Marsh and Elizabeth Loomis. She died at Whitestown, April 13, 1829, æ. 86.

CHILDREN;—BY THE FIRST MARRIAGE.

1. *Molly*, bap. Mar. 31, 1754; "was drowned in a well," May 6, 1758.
2. *Rachel*, bap. Dec. 7, 1755; d. Dec. 16, 1755.

3. *Rachel*, b.   Jan. 2, 1757; m. John Allen, and lived to an advanced age. She had, John, Moses, Rachel, and several others.

4. *Daniel Clark*, b. Mar. 2, 1759; m. Esther Paine.   .   .   .   . (148)

5. *Joseph*, b. Jan. 16, 1761; m. 1st, Lucy Bulkley;2d, Mrs. Sybil Willis. (149)

6. *Hugh*, b. Jan. 16, 1763; m. 1st, Tryphena Lawrence; 2d, S. Smith. (150)

7. *Ansel*, b. Jan. 11, 1765; m. Anna Root.   .   .   .   .   . (151)

8. *Philo*, b. June 25, 1767; m. Esther Holt.   .   .   .   . . . (152)

9. *Aurelia*, b. Jan. 20, 1770; [July 22?] m. 1788, Parsons Wetmore of Whites-town, a farmer, who rem. to Warren Co., Pa., in 1815, afterwards to Steuben-ville, O., and in 1827 to Rochester, N. Y. She d. July 16, 1846, æ. 76. He d. Sept. 23, 1852, æ. 84. She had, 1. Betsey, b. March 3, 1789, m. Feb. 19, 1817, Dyer Fitch, and d. May 30, 1818, æ. 29; 2. Lois, b. March 20, 1790, d. Aug. 9, 1808, æ. 18; 3. Lansing, b. Aug. 28, 1792, d. Nov. 15, 1857, æ. 65. He was a lawyer in Warren, Pa., and for more than forty years a prominent citizen. He was County Judge, an Elder in the Presbyterian Church, and filled other important positions. He m. Nov. 22, 1816, Caroline Ditmars; 4. Parsons, b. Aug. 1, 1794, was a silversmith. He spent about 15 yrs. in various places in Mexico, and, returning homeward about 1832, d. in Steu-benville, O., unm., æ. about 37; 5. Aurelia White, b. Sept. 30, 1797, m. Sept. 22, 1819, Dyer Fitch, (his 2d wife;) they now reside in Robinson, Crawford Co., Ill.; 6. Melancton Clark, b. Feb. 1, 1801, m. 1826, Octavia Parker; is a farmer near Rochester, N. Y.; 7. Daniel White, b. Aug. 11, 1803, m., and res. in Buffalo, N. Y.; 8. Leonard, b. July 19, 1805, m. 1829, Sophronia Barber, who d. about 1840; 9. Angeline, b. Sept. 8, 1807, m. 1833, Abraham DeKroyft of Rochester; 10. Mary Louise, b. Feb. 8, 1810, m. 1832, George S. Williams of Buffalo; 11. Zephaniah Davenport, b. Oct. 18, 1812, d. Sept., 1823, æ. 11; 12. Viscount Stone, b. May 12, 1816, d. Aug. 16, 1840, æ. 24.

10. *Mary Stone*, b. March 8, 1772; [Nov. 23?] m. June, 1792, John Young, the founder of Youngstown, Ohio. He was a surveyor, and much engaged on public works. They returned to Whitestown in 1803. He d. April 26, 1825, æ. 52. She d. Sept. 23, 1839, æ. 67. She had, 1. Mary, b. Aug. 20, 1793, d. in infancy; 2. John J., b. Oct. 27, 1794, is a Captain, U. S. Navy, and res. in Baltimore, Md. He m. Sept. 26, 1816, Cornelia Ensor of Bal., who d.; 3. George White, b. Nov. 16, 1796, was a Civil Engineer, and was drowned at Baker's Falls, June 23, 1828; 4. William Clark, b. Nov. 25, 1799, is a Civil Engineer, and has been President of the Hudson River and Panama Rail Roads. He res. in Buffalo. He m. June 19, 1827, Catherine Willard of Albany; 5. Mary Foster, b. Feb. 8, 1802, m. May 20, 1820, John L. Curtenius, Esq., of Buffalo, a lawyer; 6. Charles Clark, b. July 25, 1804, grad. Union Coll., 1826, was a lawyer in New York, now res. in Aurora, Cayuga Co., N. Y. He m. 1st, April 17, 1833, Elizabeth Huntington of Rome, N. Y.; m. 2d, Aug. 5, 1836, Harriet Huntington of Rome; m. 3d, Mrs. Mary B. Morgan, wid. of John Morgan, Esq., of Aurora; 7. Jane Maria, b. Feb. 10, 1806, m. Jan. 23, 1832, Rev. Washington Roosevelt, now of Pelham, N. Y.; 8. Jeremiah Smith, b. Sept. 10, 1809, grad. at Andover Theol. Sem. in 1839, and was pastor at Dover, N. H. He now resides at Fall River, Mass. He m. 1st, April 14, 1840, Harriet F. Merland of An-dover, Mass., who d. June, 1850; m. 2d, a sister of his first wife.

70. Rev. STEPHEN WHITE, son of Capt. John, (27) was born in Upper Middletown, June 8, 1718. He graduated at Yale College in 1736, and was ordained pastor of the Congregational Church in Windham, Conn., Dec. 24, 1740, as the successor of President Clap of Yale College. He died Jan. 9, 1794, æ. 75, having ministered to the same people more than 53 years.

Allen's American Biographical Dictionary says of him, "He was a scholar, a christian, and an able and judicious divine." Rev. Elijah Waterman, his successor in the ministry at Windham, in his published Centennial Sermon thus describes him: "Mr. White possessed good natural abilities, improved by early education. In his station he was a workman that needeth not to be ashamed; and the manuscript sermons left behind him are a testimony of real piety and faithfulness. He was constitutionally modest, and, unless with his acquaintances, reserved in conversation. In his domestic relations he was tender and indulgent; and the same affectionate temper he manifested towards his church and people." A fac-simile of his autograph is given, from a signature in 1742.

Stephen White,

He married, Sept. 2, 1741, MARY DYER of Windham, dau. of Col. Thomas Dyer and Lydia Backus. She was born Jan. 31, 1719, and died May 27, 1802, æ. 83.

CHILDREN.

1. *Hannah*, b. Dec. 20, 1742; d. at New Haven, Sept. 8, 1748.
2. *Mary*, b. Dec. 23, 1743; d. unm., March 11, 1828, æ. 84.
3. *Lydia*, b. April 28, 1745; m. Nov. 23, 1767, Vine Elderkin of Windham, who d. Aug. 15, 1800, æ. 55. She d. Oct. 2, 1818, æ. 73. She had, 1. Harriet, b. Oct. 4, 1768, m. Dr. James Jackson of Manlius, N. Y., and d. Sept., 1809, æ. 41; 2. Bela, b. Feb. 3, 1770, m., and lived in Penn., d. 1851; 3. Mary Ann, b. Dec. 18, 1771, m. 1st, Feb. 1, 1796, Henry Clark of Manlius, N. Y.; m. 2d, Dr. James Jackson; (his 2d wife, see above,) d. July, 1858; 4. Stephen Whitehead, b. Sept. 12, 1773, d. 1856; 5. Juliana, b. Jan. 20, 1776, m. Nov. 14, 1795, Timothy Staniford of Windham, d. Oct. 27, 1844; 6. Lucy, b. Nov. 27, 1778, m. —— Strong, d. 1819; 7. Charlotte, b. March 23, 1781, m. Charles Moseley.
4. *Susanna*, b. Oct. 21, 1746; d. unm., April 5, 1837, æ. 90.
5. *Eunice*, b. Jan. 7, 1749; m. 1st, May 15, 1771, Stephen Whitehead Hubbard. He grad. Yale Coll., 1766, and d. Sept. 1, 1771, æ. 24. She m. 2d, Capt. Joseph Bradley of N. H., and d. without issue, Dec. 31, 1799, æ. 51.

6. *Twin* }
7. *sons,* } b. March 6, 1750; both d. the same day.

8. *Hannah,* b. Feb. 22, 1751; d. unm., Dec. 19, 1793, æ. 42.
9. *John,* b. Oct. 3, 1752; grad. Yale College, 1774, settled in Windham, and d. there, unm., July 17, 1810, æ. 58.
10. *Elisha,* b. Sept. 16, 1754; m. Lois Webb. . . . . (153)
11. *Sarah,* b. Nov. 10, 1757; d. unm., Dec. 28, 1836, æ. 79.
12. *Huldah,* b. April 17, 1760; m. July 18, 1784, Dr. John Barker. He grad. Yale College, 1777, was a physician in Newbern, N. C., 1785 to 1788, rem. to Windham, Conn., in 1788, to New Haven in 1795, and d. there, Feb. 24, 1813, æ. 55. She d. Sept. 19, 1848, æ. 88. She had, 1. Julia, b. Nov. 25, 1786, d. unm., June 22, 1855, æ. 68 ; 2. A daughter, b. July 2, 1788, "was washed out of her mother's arms, in a storm at sea," July 23, 1788 ; 3. John, b. March 17, 1791, d. at sea, unm., Aug. 26, 1820, æ. 29 ; 4. Charlotte, b. May 13, 1795, d. June 24, 1803 ; 5. Charles, b. July 4, 1799, d. unm., in N. Y. city, Sept. 4, 1822, æ. 23 ; 6. William. b. June 8, 1802, m. Clarissa Cutler, and d. in N. Carolina, Oct. 25, 1833, æ. 31 ; 7. George W., b. Feb. 9, 1805, m. Sarah Phelps, and d. in Waverly, Ill., Nov. 22, 1843, æ. 38.
13. *Dyer,* b. May 20, 1762; m. Susanna Whittelsey and others. . . (154)

---

71. Dea. JOHN WHITE, son of Capt. John, (27) was born in New Haven, May 19, 1722. He settled as a farmer in Woodbridge, Conn., then the Society of Amity, in the town of Milford, but removed to New Haven, where he died, Nov. 24, 1797, æ. 75.

He married, Dec. 27, 1744, MARY DICKERMAN of New Haven, dau. of Isaac Dickerman and Mary Atwater.

CHILDREN.

1. *Sybil,* b. Oct. 15, 1745; m. 1st, Elisha Sanford of Woodbridge ; m. 2d, Dea. Asa Goodyear of Hamden. She had, by her first husband, 1. Rachel, m. Zeri Downes ; 2. Elisha, m. Margaret Tolles ; 3. Esther, m. Jared Sperry ; 4. Huldah, d. ; 5. Sybil, m. —— Sperry ; 6. Amos, m. —— Atwater ; 7. Lucretia; 8. Lucy, m. —— Sperry.
2. *Timothy,* b. Oct. 21, 1747; m. 1st, —— ——; 2d, Mercy Clark. . (155)
3. *Hannah,* b. Nov. 13, 1749; m. Robert Townsend of New Haven, and d. Sept. 20, 1803, æ. 54. He d. Nov. 19, 1806, æ. 59. She had, 1. Amos, m. Sarah Howe ; 2. Polly, m. Amos Benedict ; 3. Larmon, m. 1st, Hannah Gunn ; m. 2d, Clarissa S. Byington. He d. May, 1858, æ. 81 ; 4. Betsey, d. ; 5. Eli, m. Abigail Trowbridge ; 6. Hannah, m. Feb. 4, 1807, Asa Bradley ; 7. Nancy, m. Augustus Maltby ; 8. William, m. Harriet Ford.
4. *Mary,* bap. Jan. 5, 1752; d. in infancy.
5. *Amos,* bap. Mar. 10, 1755; prob. d. young.
6. *John,* bap. July 11, 1756; m. Anna Bostwick. . . . . (156)
7. *Mary,* bap. Feb. 11, 1759; m. Timothy Gorham of N. H., and d. without issue.
8. *Elisha,* bap. Jan. 21, 1761; d. unm., æ. about 20.

9. *Susanna*, b.   1763; m. Jonathan Brigden of N. H., and d. in 1846,
    æ. 83. She had, 1. John, m. Harriet Augur; 2. Betsey, m. John Sabin;
    3. Polly, m. John Tomlinson; 4. Grace, m. Alfred Clarke; 5. Daniel, d.;
    6. Harriet, m. —— Pitner; 7. Asenath, m. Lewis Kimberly.
10. *Isaac*, b.   ; d. about 1780. This is inserted on the authority
    of a tradition which is somewhat obscure.
11. *Rebecca*, b.   1772; m. Merrit Carrington of N. H., and d. in 1844, æ.
    72. She had, 1. Mary, m. Enos A. Prescott; 2. John, d.; 3. Rebecca, m.
    Roger S. Prescott.

---

72. Moses White, eldest son of Dea. Isaac, (28) was born
in Upper Middletown, Conn., Aug. 22, 1727. He was a hatter by trade, and spent the greater part of his life in his native
place, but sometimes resided in other towns. He was living
in Guilford, 1752 to 1755, in Chatham in 1783, and is said to
have been living in Killingworth, just before he removed, in his
old age, to Newport, New Hampshire, to a house near that of
his son James. He died about 1812, æ. about 85. "He died
very suddenly, while standing, conversing with his son."

He married, Oct. 12, 1749, Huldah Knowles, of Hartford.
She is said to have lived to old age, with her son James, and
with her youngest daughter.

CHILDREN.

1. *Huldah*, b. Feb. 10, 1751 ; m. Feb. 22, 1776, Nathaniel Eells, (see in Fam. 23.)
    She d. in Skaneateles, N. Y., having had, Nathaniel, Huldah, Richard, Syl-
    vester, Clarissa, Susan, and Horace.
2. *Isaac*, b. Oct. 14, 1752 ; m. Thankful Clark. .   .   .   . (157)
3. *Ruth*, b. .   1754; m. June 29, 1778, Joseph Runney of Up. Mid., and d.
    Jan. 20, 1824, æ. 69. He d. Jan. 30, 1835, æ. 83. She had, 1. Henry, b.
    Sept. 10, 1778, d. June 16, 1801, æ. 22; 2. Rebecca, b. Sept. 24, 1780, m.
    1st, John Edwards ; m. 2d, May 15, 1810, Capt. Thomas White ; (Fam.
    178 ;) 3. Mary, b. April 3, 1783 ; 4. Moses, b. Dec. 22, 1785, d. Feb. 7, 1812,
    æ. 26 ; 5. Joseph, b. Nov. 27, 1788, d. Feb. 14, 1806, æ. 17 ; 6. Calvin, b.
    April 15, 1791, d. Aug. 16, 1818, æ. 27 ; 7. Norman, b. April 22, 1793, d.
    Oct. 9, 1825, æ. 32; 8. Harvey, b. April 14, 1795, d. in Charleston, S. C.,
    Aug. 23, 1819, æ. 24.
4. *Moses*, b.   1757; m. Melitta Porter. .   .   .   . (158)
5. *Roderick*, bap. Mar. 18, 1759; "he went to sea during the War, and was
    never heard from."
6. *James*, bap. Feb. 1, 1761 ; m. Tirzah Taylor. .   .   . (159)
7. *Calvin*, b. Dec. 17, 1762; m. 1st, P. Camp; 2d, J. Mardenbrough. (160)
    (The fam. rec. says, b. Dec. 17, 1763 ; but a Calvin was bap. Dec. 19, 1762.)
8. *Roxana*, bap. Sept. 30, 1764; m. Stephen Root, a farmer, of Southington, Ct.
9. *Elisha*, bap. Sept. 21, 1766; m. Honor Sumner. .   .   . (161)
10. *A child*, b. Feb.,   1769; d. day of birth ; buried Feb. 9.

11. *Lucretia*, b. Mar. 5, 1773; m. Nov. 17, 1797, Walter Cooley, (see in Fam. 13.)
He was living in Charlestown, N. H., in 1858. She d. Jan. 3, 1849, æ 75.
She had, 1. Sally, b. June 13, 1799, d. Sept. 19, 1803; 2. Simeon Olcott, b.
Dec. 12, 1801, m. April 11, 1824, Harriet Lovell of Rockingham, Vt.;
3. Sally L., b. June 14, 1804, m. Elias Cady of Hartland, Vt., and d. Dec.
19, 1836, æ. 32. He d. Feb. 28, 1849.

73. ELIAS WHITE, son of Dea. Isaac, (28) was born in
Upper Middletown, May 5, 1734. He lived in his native place,
and died there, Jan. 27, 1800, æ. 65.

He married, Nov. 13, 1760, PRUDENCE SAVAGE of Up. Mid.,
dau. of Joseph and Prudence Savage. She was born July 3,
1737, and died at Whitestown, N. Y.

CHILDREN.

1. *Sibbil*, b. Oct. 28, 1761; m. Nov. 28, 1782, Leveret Bishop of Guilford, Conn.,
a ship-carpenter.
2. *Mary Savage*, b. June 8, 1763; m. May 16, 1782, William Cheney Gaylord, a
mason, who d. Nov. 29, 1825, æ. 66. She d. at Rochester, N. Y., March 15,
1828, æ. 64. She had, (bap. at Up. Mid.,) 1. Mary, bap. Nov. 6, 1785, m.
Paul Abbott, and d. Sept. 2, 1809, æ. 26; 2. Sally, bap. Nov. 6, 1785;
3. Vester, [Sylvester?] bap. Nov. 26, 1786; 4. Lucy, bap. Feb. 10, 1788;
5. Nancy, bap. Feb. 14, 1790, m. Seth Dowd of Mid. and d. at Utica, N. Y.;
6. Milly, bap. Feb. 26, 1792, m. 1st, —— Clark; m. 2d, an Episcopal
clergyman in Western N. Y.; 7. Cynthia, bap. Mar. 23, 1800, m. William
McKee, of Up. Mid., now of Brooklyn, N. Y.; 8. Amanda, m. —— Smith,
now of Oswego, N. Y.
3. *Reuben*, b. Mar. 10, 1765; d. about June, 1783, "in prison at New York,"
(Dr. Field's Hist. Disc., p. 75.)
4. *Edmund*, b. Oct. 15, 1766; Aug. 24, d. 1782, æ. 15. It is said that he was
taken sick on board a man-of-war, but d. at home.
5. *Comfort*, bap. Nov. 6, 1768; was a ship-carpenter, and d. unm., at Dema-
rara, S. A.
6. *Joseph*, b.   ; m. Matty Hasgill.   .   .   .   . (162)
7. *Prudence*, bap. Jan. 31, 1773; m. Dea. Joseph Blake of Whitestown, N. Y.,
and d. about 1825. She had, 1. Emily; 2. Edmund, d.; 3. Lucy.
8. *Elias*, b.   ; m. —— ——.   .   .   .   . (163)
9. *Isaac*, b.   June 22, 1780; m. Priscilla Plumb.   .   .   .   . (164)

IN THE LINE OF JACOB WHITE, OF MIDDLETOWN.

74. SAMUEL WHITE, son of Thomas, (30) was born in East
Middletown, Conn., Nov. 30, 1729. He settled in North Coventry, Conn., and died there, about May, 1785, æ. 55.

He married, March 14, 1756, Mrs. RACHEL TILDEN of Coventry, widow of Joshua Tilden. She died about Aug., or Sept., 1790.

CHILDREN.

1. *Samuel,*   b. Nov. 5, 1757; m. Rachel Porter.   .   (165)
2. *Lemuel,*   b. Dec. 30, 1758; m. Anna Brigham.   .   .   .   (166)
3. *Experience,* b. April 2, 1760; m. James Dunham, of N. Cov., and d. about 1818. He d. March 23, 1855, æ. 91. She had, 1. Sophia, m. Horace Thompson of Mansfield, Conn.; 2. Samuel, m. and d.; 3. William, d.; 4. Alpheus; 5. Mason, d. unm.; 6. Ebenezer; 7. Timothy.
4. *Timothy,* b. March 8, 1764; m. Margaret Gurley.   .   .   .   (167)

75. JACOB WHITE, son of Thomas, (30) was born in Lebanon, (Andover Society,) Conn., Jan. 20, 1736. He was a cooper, and lived in Tolland, Conn., until about 1780, when he removed to Torrington, Conn., where he died Feb. 15, [10?] 1788, æ. 52.

He married, Nov. 5, 1761, ANNAR LOTHROP of Coventry. She died in Burke, Vt., Oct. 26, 1822, æ. 80. Her death was caused by her clothes taking fire.

CHILDREN.

1. *Dan,*   b. Sept. 22, 1762; m. Rowena Wilson.   .   (168)
2. *Thomas,* b. Nov. 28, 1764; m. Jedidah Baldwin.   .   .   .   (169)
3. *Jacob,*   b. Aug. 28, 1768; m., and had four sons. He lived in Romulus, N. Y., till about 1826, when he rem. to Michigan.
4. *Lucinda,* b. Sept. 19, 1771; d. in Burke, Vt.
5. *Anna,* b. May 8, 1774; m. 1st, May 26, 1793, Jabez Beardsley, who d. Aug. 1, 1813; m. 2d, John Vanduzee of W. Sandlake, N. Y., who d. in Bath, Rensselaer Co., N. Y. She is still living, at W. Sandlake. She had, by her first husband, 1. Edwin, b. Aug. 20, 1794, d. Aug. 1, 1813; 2. Edwy, b. Aug. 13, 1806, d. Aug. 5, 1807; 3. Chloe Ann, b. Jan. 1, 1809, d. Jan. 18, 1829, æ. 20; 4. William Henry, b. Sept. 20, 1812, d. Sept. 7, 1814.
6. *Elam,* b. April 14, 1778; was twice married.   .   .   .   (170)

76. HENRY WHITE, son of Thomas, (30) was born in Andover, Conn., in the town of Lebanon, June 1, 1739. He settled in Gilsum, N. H., but removed to Tunbridge, or the adjoining town of Royalton, Vt., where he was living in 1798. He and his wife were among the members of the church that was gathered in Gilsum in 1772.

He married SARAH ———.

CHILDREN.

1. *Henry.*   3. *Silas.*
2. *Olive.*   4. *Thomas,* bap. about 1785.

     These were baptized at Gilsum; no dates on the Church Record.   .

13

77. SILAS WHITE, son of Thomas, (30) was born in Andover, Conn., May 18, 1745. He was a carpenter, and settled in Torrington, (Torringford Society,) Conn., where he died in the fall of 1802, æ. 57. He was for three years a revolutionary soldier.

He married, 1st, 1770, MARY BIRGE of Torrington, dau. of John Birge and Mary Kellogg. She was born Oct. 31, 1752, and died April 20, 1790, æ. 37.

He married, 2d, HANNAH SCOVILLE. After his death, she removed to the State of New York, with her son.

CHILDREN;—BY THE FIRST MARRIAGE.

1. *Silas,* b.　　　　　 1772; m. Elizabeth Plumb.　.　.　.　(171)
2. *Roswell,* b. Jan. 27, 1778; m. 1st, Abi Northway; 2d, Mary Sawyer. (172)
3. *A child,* b.　　　　 ; d. Dec. 12, 1782.
4. *Chauncey,* b. Sept. 11, 1783; m. 1st, Betsey Plumb; 2d, Mrs. M. Taylor. (173)
5. *Brainard,* b. May　5, 1786; m. Eliza Stedman.　.　.　.　(174)
6. *A child,* b.　　　　 ; d. June 19, 1789.
7. *Orrin,* b.　　　　 ; d. in childhood.
8. *A child,* b.　　　　 ; d. Feb. 14, 1795.
9. *A child,* b.　　　　 ; d. Feb. 19, 1795. There were 4 daughters by the first marriage; probably the children who d. young, names not recorded.

CHILDREN ;—BY THE SECOND MARRIAGE.

10. *Lester,* b. about 1796; rem. to the State of N. Y.
11. *Orrin,* b.　　　　 ; perhaps the *Origin,* who d. July 15, 1804, æ. 6.
12. *Percy,* b.
13. *A daughter,* b.　　　　 ; d. young. Order of this family uncertain.

---

78. JOEL WHITE, son of Thomas, (30) was born in North Coventry, Conn., Oct. 20, 1750. He settled in Blanford, Mass., but in 1803 removed with his family to Russia, Herkimer Co., N. Y., where he died May 3, 1826, æ. 75. He was a wheelwright.

He married SARAH OSBORN of Blanford. She was born April 7, 1757, and died May 19, 1840, æ. 83.

CHILDREN.

1. *Gershom,* b. May 28, 1775; m. Sally Parks.　.　.　(175)
2. *Thomas,* b. May 28, 1777; d. Sept. 8, 1781.
3. *Joel,* b. Feb. 28, 1779; m. Isabel Stewart.　.　(176)
4. *Sally,* b. Oct. 23, 1780; d. Sept. 17, 1781.
5. *Sally,* b. July 17, 1782; d. Sept. 22, 1794, æ. 12.
6. *Elizabeth,* b. Dec.　9, 1784; d. Sept. 25, 1794, æ. 9.
7. *Silas,* b. Nov. 13, 1786; d. Sept. 18, 1794, æ. 7.
8. *Clarissa,* b. Dec. 15, 1788; m. Philander McMaster of Russia, who d. She

lives in R.   She has had, 1. Rufus, m. —— Stephens ; 2. Sally, m. Johnson Fanning of R. ; 3. Orrilla Pauline, m. —— Phillips ; 4. Margaret, m.
1839, —— Coventry, and d. 1842 ; 5. Joel, m. —— Macomber, and
rem. west ; 6. Mary ; 7. Betsey, m. John Clark of R. ; 8. Caroline, m. ——
Coventry, her sister's husband ; 9. John, lives in R. ; 10. Harriet.

9. *Hannah,*   b. Dec. 19, 1790 ; d. Sept. 25, 1794.
10. *Orrilla,*   b. June 9, 1793 ; m. Gilbert Gardner of Russia, now of Gouverneur, N. Y.   She has had, 1. Sally ; 2. Joel.
11. *Polly Anna,* b. Dec. 2, 1795 ; d. unm., March 18, 1825, æ. 29.
12. *Corintha,*   b. Jan. 2, 1798 ; m. 1818, Sidney Gardner of Russia, and d.
March 1, 1842, æ. 44.   He is d. She had, 1. Permelia ; 2. Lucinda ;
3. Orrilla ; 4. Emily ; 5. Harriet ; 6. Franklin.

---

79. JACOB WHITE, son of John, (31) was born in Upper
Middletown, Conn., Nov. 7, 1737.   He settled there, and died
Jan. 5, 1789, æ. 51.   (So the Church record: on grave-stone,
1788.)

He married, Nov. 25, 1760, LUCY SAVAGE, (Lucia, on the
town record.)   She was the dau. of Joseph and Prudence
Savage of Up. Mid.; was born July 16, 1741, and died Aug.
20, 1812, æ 71.

CHILDREN.

1. *Elizabeth,* bap. Nov. 29, 1761 ; d. unm., Sept., 1846, æ. 84.
2. *Lucy,*   bap. May 1, 1763 ; d. May 28, 1763.
3. *Martha,*   bap. Oct. 14, 1764 ; d. May 26, 1783, æ. 18.
4. *John,*   b.   ; m. Ruth Ranney. .   (177)
5. *Lucy,*   bap. July 19, 1767 ; d. May 28, 1773.
6. *Jacob,*   bap. April 7, 1771 ; was drowned, Aug. 29, 1819, æ. 48. Was unm.
7. *Thomas,*   b. June 10, 1773 ; m. 1st, Katharine Keith ; 2d, R. Edwards. (178)
8. *Catharine,* b.   1775 ; d. unm., April 8, 1807, æ. 32.
9. *Lucy,*   b.   ; m. Nov. 27, 1794, Freeman Collins of Up.
Mid.; her cousin ; (see Fam. 31.)   He d. March 11, 1809, æ. 42.   She had,
1. Freeman, bap. Sept. 18, 1796 ; 2. Lucy, bap. May 13, 1798, d. Dec. 17,
1814, æ. 17 ; 3. Ezekiel, bap. Oct. 12, 1800, was "killed at a cider mill,"
Sept. 5, 1805 ; 4. George Henry, bap. June 3, 1804, d. Jan. 6, 1816, æ. 12.
10. *Lemuel,*   b. Dec. 20, 1776 ; m. Abigail Bartlett and others.   .   (179)
11. *Luther,*   bap. July 18, 1779 ; d. in youth, in the West Indies.
12. *Alexander,* b. Mar. 6, 1782 ; m. Abigail Beadle.   .   .   .   (180)
13. *Asa,*   bap. Aug. 15, 1784 ; m. Mehitable White.   .   .   (181)

IN THE LINE OF JOSEPH WHITE, OF MIDDLETOWN.

80. WILLIAM WHITE, son of Ebenezer, (32) was born in
Upper Middletown, Sept. 10, 1742.   He was much in the
service of the town, being chosen a constable of Middletown

in 1769, 1771, and from 1778 to 1785, and a selectman in 1786 and 1787. He died May 11, 1790, æ. 47.

He married, Feb. 5, 1785, Mrs. ABIGAIL STOW, widow of Jonathan Stow, and dau. of John Eells. After his death, she married, 3d, March 21, 1793, Capt. William Sage of Up. Mid., who died Nov. 8, 1833, æ. 85. She died Jan. 19, 1831, æ. 80.

CHILDREN.

1. *William*, b. Jan. 19, 1786; d. at New London, Conn., on his return from sea, Nov. 21, 1803, æ. 17. He was buried at New London.
2. *Joseph*, b. March 14, 1788; m. Esther C. Morell. . . (182)

81. ELIZUR WHITE, son of Ebenezer, (32) was born in Upper Middletown, Feb. 19, 1750. He was a merchant in Middletown city, but removed to Canaan, Conn., and afterwards, with his sons Elizur and Joseph, to Granville, Washington Co., N. Y., where he died.

He married HANNAH COOPER, dau. of Lamberton Cooper of Middletown. She died about 1830.

CHILDREN.

1. *Elizur*, b. July 1, 1770; m. Hannah Savage. . . . (183)
2. *Joseph*, bap. Feb. 6, 1774; rem. to Granville, and d. there unm., about 1813, æ. 39.
3. *Hannah*, bap. Jan. 28, 1776; m. Joseph Ballery, rem. to Grand Isle, Vt., and d. several years since.
4. *William*, b. 1777; m. 1st, Grace Savage; 2d, Fanny Stocking. (184)
5. *Elizabeth*, bap. Jan. 18, 1778; m. Col. Nathaniel Frank of Granville. She had, 1. Shipman, d.; 2. Hannah, lives in Ill.; 3. Nathaniel, lives in Iowa; 4. Elizur, d.; 5. Andrew, lives in Ill.; 6. Joseph, d.; 7. Eliza Ann.
6. *Ebenezer*, b. 1781; m. Elizabeth Sage. . . . (185)

DESCENDANTS OF JOHN WHITE, JUNIOR.

82. ASA WHITE, son of Capt. Jonathan, (34) was born in Hebron, Conn., Nov. 6, 1743. He was a farmer there, but about 1783 removed to Windham, Conn., where he died about May, 1820, æ. 75. His will, dated June 5, 1819, names all his eight children.

He married, 1st, May 8, 1765, MARY BINGHAM of Windham, who died March 25, 1804.

He married, 2d, April 7, 1805, HANNAH CUTLER, who survived him.

CHILDREN ;—BY THE FIRST MARRIAGE.

1. *John,*   b. Feb. 5, 1766 ; m. Chloe Smith.   .   .   .   .   (186)
2. *Mary,*   b. July 3, 1768 ; m. April 2, 1789, Timothy Warner Hebard of Windham, and d. Nov., 1843, æ. 75. She had, 1. Henry, b. Oct. 22, 1790, lives in Ithica, N. Y. ; 2. Lydia, b. Oct. 12, 1795 ; 3. Jeremiah, b. May 16, 1800, d. 1832.
3. *Asa,*   b. Aug. 26, 1770 ; prob. d. num.
4. *Hannah,* b. March 23, 1773 ; m. Feb. 11, 1796, Joseph Morse. They soon rem. to the State of N. Y., where he was a farmer. He d. March 30, 1834, æ. 65. She d. without issue, April 26, 1858, æ. 85.
5. *Mehitable,* b. Aug., 1775 ; m. June, 1796, Benjamin Simms of Canterbury, Conn., who d. April 26, 1813, æ. 39. She d. April 18, 1820, æ. 44. She had, 1. John, b. 1798, m. 1823, Julia Treby of New London, Conn., and was lost at sea, Jan., 1825 ; 2. Hannah M., b. Dec. 31, 1800, m. 1831, Charles Droz of New York, who d. 1842 ; 3. Ralph, b. Sept., 1802, is a merchant in Newville, Herkimer Co., N. Y. He m. June, 1824, Amanda Wilcox ; 4. Mary, b. Aug. 4, 1805, m. Jan., 1830, Isaac L. Moore of West Winfield, Herkimer Co., N. Y. ; 5. Nelson, b. Jan., 1807, m. Margaret Monk.
6. *Jeremiah,* b. June 8, 1780 ; m. Sally Bottom and others.   .   .   (187)
7. *Sarah,*   b. Nov. 10, 1782 ; m. —— Herrick, and d. about 1825, leaving children.
8. *Ralph,*   b. March 19, 1785 ; m. and had three children.

---

83. THOMAS WELLS WHITE, son of Rev. David, (35) was born in Hardwick, Mass., Aug. 12, 1739. He graduated at Harvard College in 1759, and settled as a merchant in Hardwick. About 1776 he removed to Barnard, Vt., and was the first town clerk of Barnard, from 1778 to 1785. In the fall of 1799 he removed to Ohio, and the next spring settled in Roxbury, now Waterford, Washington Co. He lived there with his son David, and his daughter Susanna, and died Sept. 3, 1815, æ. 76.

He married, NAOMI WRIGHT of Northfield, Mass., who died in Barnard, Vt., in 1799. She was perhaps the dau. of Phineas Wright, and born in 1746.

CHILDREN.

1. *David,*   b. Dec. 4, 1765 ; m. Patta Cheadle and others.   .   (188)
2. *Thomas,* b. July 26, 1767 ; m. Joanna Samson.   .   .   .   (189)
3. *Theodosia,* b. Aug. 19, 1769 ; m. Stephen Ellis of Barnard, and had two sons, Stephen and David.
4. *Naomi,*   b. Sept. 13, 1771 ; m. 1792, John Cheadle. They went to Ohio with her father, and settled in Windsor, Morgan Co., where she d. Feb., 1816, æ. 44. He d. Sept. 9, 1823, æ. 51. She had, 1. Electa, b. May, 1793, m. 1814, James Davis, and d. Nov., 1850, æ. 57 ; 2. Pamelia, b. July, 1795, m. Jacob Nulton, now of Greene Co., Ill. ; 3. John, b. Nov. 23, 1797 ; 4. Rial,

b. Sept., 1801, m. 1819, Mary Tuft, and lives in Morgan Co. ; 5. Gilman, h. March, 1807, m. March, 1828, Susannah Rockey, and lives in Fulton Co., O.

5. *Rhoda*, b. Oct. 17, 1773; m. Jonathan Fay of Barnard, and rem. to Salina, N. Y. They are both dead. She had, 1. Roxanna ; 2. Austin, d. about 1847 ; 3. Marietta.

6. *Sally*, b. Feb. 11, 1776; m. George Clapp of Barnard, and had several children. The family rem. to the State of N. Y.

7. *Susanna*, b. Dec. 28, [1778?] ; m. Charles Swift, a farmer. They rem. to Ohio in 1800, and settled in Waterford. She d. Oct. 28, 1825, æ. 46. He m. again thrice, and d. June 26, 1855, æ. 79. She had, 1. Whitfield, b. Oct. 19, 1799, d. Aug. 27, 1818, æ. 18 ; 2. Phebe, b. Oct. 6, 1801, m. 1st, Isaac Ross ; 2d, Charles Davis, and d. July 7, 1829, æ. 27 ; 3. Fanny, b. June 18, 1806, d. Sept. 27, 1823, æ. 17 ; 4. Charles, b. Aug. 27, 1807, m. July 21, 1831, Amy Andrews. He and his brothers are farmers in Waterford ; 5. Ira, b. May 20, 1811, d. ; 6. Eunice, d. ; 7. Guy, b. April 14, 1813, m. 1836, Mary Hinkley ; 8. Lyman, b. Dec. 13, 1815, m. Nov. 27, 1839, Sibil Webster ; 9. Mary, b. Oct. 3, 1817, m. Daniel Emerson, and d. ; 10. Rufus, b. May 19, 1820, m. Dec. 10, 1846, Elizabeth Balderson.

8. *John*,   ⎱ b.   1783; m. Laura Rising.   .   .   .   .   .   (190)
9. *Fanny*, ⎰ Twins.   m. 1817, Nathaniel Ripley of Weybridge, Vt., and d. March 22, 1824, æ. 41.

10. *Olcott*, b. Jan. 9, 1786; m. Electa Abernethy.   .   .   (191)
11. *Samuel*, b.   1789; m. Eunice Emerson.   .   .   . (192)

DESCENDANTS OF LIEUT. DANIEL WHITE.

84. DANIEL WHITE, son of Capt. Daniel, (36) was born in Hatfield, Mass., Dec. 28, 1726. He settled there ; was constable in 1757, and perhaps held other offices. In 1777 he was a member of the "Committee of Correspondence, Inspection, and Safety." He died Aug. 13, 1805, æ. 78.

He married, 1754, SUBMIT MORTON of Hatfield. She died July 21, 1798, æ. 71.

CHILDREN.

1. *Sarah*, b. March 6, 1755 ; m. March 24, 1780, Lt. Samuel Smith of Hat., who d. Oct. 26, 1834, æ. 83. She d. Dec. 7, 1843, æ. 88. She had, 1. Sarah, b. Dec. 23, 1780; 2. Clarissa, b. Aug. 16, 1783 ; 3. Fanny, b. June 17, 1787, m. William Dickinson, and d. Feb., 1853, æ. 65 ; 4. Samuel, b. Dec. 20, 1792; 5. Asenath, b. April 19, 1794 ; 6. William, b. Sept. 5, 1797, d. 1798.

2. *Lucy*, b. Aug. 23, 1757 ; m. Jan. 26, 1779, Elijah Smith of Hat., who d. Nov. 30, 1829, æ. 73. She d. June 9, 1839, æ. 81. She had, 1. Charles, b. Feb. 21, 1782, d. young ; 2. Erastus, b. Jan. 14, 1784, d. Jan., 1858, æ. 74 ; 3. Mary ; 4. Charles, b. Jan. 17, 1787, d. June, 1857, æ. 70 ; 5. Lucy, b. April 28, 1789 ; 6. Elijah, b. Aug. 7, 1791, d. unm.

3. *Hannah*, b. June 8, 1759 ; m. June 22, 1780, Elisha Hubbard, of Hatfield and Williamsburg. He kept a public house in W., and was town clerk. He d.

May 17, 1843, æ. 84. She d. March 27, 1824, æ. 64. She had, 1. Lucinda, b. Aug. 27, 1780, lives in W. ; 2. Sally, b. Oct. 10, 1782, d. Oct. 11 ; 3. Jeremiah, b. Oct. 10, 1783, d. Nov. 25, 1786 ; 4. Jeremiah, b. Nov. 24, 1786, d. May 18, 1850, æ. 63. He m. Feb. 25, 1813, Huldah Nash of W., now living there ; 5. Elisha, b. Sept. 29, 1789, grad. at Williams College, 1811, settled as a lawyer in W., and several times represented the town in the Legislature. He d. unm., Aug. 30, 1853, æ. 64 ; 6. Erastus, b. Feb. 27, 1792, m. 1818, Wealthy Amanda Mayhew, who d. Feb. 3, 1849, æ. 51. He d. Sept. 14, 1850, æ. 58 ; 7. Hannah, b. July 4, 1794, d. æ. 7 ; 8. Lucretia, b. Dec. 25, 1796, m. Jan. 5, 1815, Walker Price of W. ; 9. Sally, b. Sept. 7, 1799, m. 1818, Moses Putney ; lived in Monroe Co., N. Y. She d. 1838, æ. 39. He d. 1840 ; 10. Hannah, b. Oct., 1800.

4. *Eunice*, b. Oct. 10, 1761 ; m. March 1, 1789, Amasa Wells of Hat., who d. June 12, 1816, æ. 54. She d. April 28, 1824, æ. 62. She had, 1. Horace, b. June 8, 1789, m. Dolly Taylor ; 2. Cephas, b. June 21, 1791, m. Betsey Edwards, 3. Barnabas, b. May 20, 1793, m. 1st, Sophia Parsons ; 2d, Mrs. Coney ; 3d, Louisa Woods ; 4. Hannah, b. Aug. 26, 1795, m. Jan. 28, 1823, Joseph Smith of Hat. ; (see in Fam. 86 ;) 5. Elisha, b. April 29, 1797, m. Jan. 14, 1823, Louisa Field of Conway, Mass.

5. *Submit*, b. March 28, 1764 ; m. Feb. 19, 1783, Nathan Bliss of Hat., who d. 1813. She d. Aug. 8, 1840, æ. 76. She had, 1. Charlotte, b. Aug. 17, 1783 ; 2. Harriet, b. May 12, 1785 ; 3. Martha, [Matilda?] b. 1787 ; 4. Nancy, bap. Dec. 6, 1789 ; 5. Pamela, b. April 8, 1792 ; 6. Sylvester, bap. Jan. 20, 1799.

6. *Daniel*, b. March 17, 1766 ; he was a physician ; lived several years in Whitestown, N. Y., but returned to Hatfield, and d. there, without issue, Jan. 26, 1848, æ. nearly 82. He m. 1st, March 8, 1796, Lucy Allis of Somers, Conn., who d. Jan. 7, 1814, æ. 47. He m. 2d, Sept. 27, 1815, [1814?] Lucy Burt, dau. of Nathaniel B. of Longmeadow, Mass. She was b. Sept. 30, 1773, and d. Dec. 15, 1833, æ. 60. He. m. 3d, Sept. 2, 1834, Mrs. Elizabeth (Bancroft) White, widow of Cotton White. (Fam. 124.) She was b. in Westfield, Mass., Nov. 8, 1787, and d. May 20, 1843, æ. 55. He m. 4th, Aug. 30, 1843, Mrs. Sarah Burt, widow of Moses Burt, and dau. of Ebenezer Fitch of Hatfield. She was b. March 5, 1779, and was living in Hat.1858.

7. *Elijah*, b. April 26, 1768 ; m. Mary Smith. . . . . . (193)

8. *John*, b. Feb. 27, 1775 ; was baptized and died the same day.

---

85. Dea. SALMON WHITE, son of Capt. Daniel, (36) was born in Bolton, Conn., where he was baptized Oct. 31, 1731. He settled in that part of Hatfield, Mass., which became the town of Whately. In 1764 he was chosen a constable in Hatfield. He was moderator of the first town meeting of Whately, May 6, 1771, and was then chosen to the several offices of town clerk, treasurer, assessor, and selectman. He continued active in public affairs for a long time, and was a member of the third Provincial Congress, in Massachusetts. He was

chosen a deacon of the Church in Whately, April 16, 1773.
He died June 21, 1815, æ. nearly 84.

He married MARY WAIT, who died June 22, 1821, æ. 90, or
91. She was perhaps the dau. of Joseph and Mary Wait of
Hatfield, who was born Oct. 17, 1730: but the identity is not
certainly ascertained.

CHILDREN.

1. *Salmon*, b. Sept. 22, 1760; m. 1st, Lydia Amsden; 2d. Mrs. Anna Allis. (194)
2. *John*, b. Jan. 9, 1762; m. Elizabeth Brown. .   .   .   .   (195)
3. *Mary*, b. Jan. 24, 1764; m. March 24, 1785, Ebenezer Arms, jun., of Greenfield, Mass., who d. July 6, 1812, æ. 52. She d. in Prattsburg, Steuben Co.,
   N. Y., Dec. 26, 1837, æ. 73. She had, 1. Elizabeth, b. Dec. 8, 1787; m. 1st,
   James Gould, of Gill, Mass.; m. 2d, Josiah Allis of Prattsburg, N. Y. She
   is a widow, and lives in Fredonia, N. Y.; 2. Chester, b. Sept. 13, 1789, is a
   farmer in Greenfield, Mass. He m. Dec. 10, 1816, Rebecca Goodman;
   3. Mary, b. Jan. 12, 1791, m. Rev. William Goodale, now of Auburn, N. Y.,
   and d. Sept. 14, 1850, æ. 59; 4. Harriet, b. Sept. 3, 1792, m. Gen. Thomas
   Gilbert, of Amherst, Mass., and d. Feb. 13, 1837, æ. 44; 5. Eroe, b. June
   21, 1794, m. Jan. 1, 1822, Eurotas Hastings, (see below,) and d. Nov. 24,
   1853, æ. 59. He d. May 22, 1858, æ. 68; 6. A dau., b. June 8, 1798, d. same
   day; 7. Ebenezer White, b. Dec. 30, 1799, d. Aug. 29, 1802; 8. Sophia, b.
   Sept. 8, 1802, m. Jan. 1, 1840, William A. Van Vranken of Geneva, N. Y.;
   9. Ebenezer White, b. March 29, 1805, grad. Yale Coll., 1828, and is a lawyer in Aurora, Cayuga Co., N. Y. He m. Nov. 12, 1835, Lydia Avery of
   Aurora; 10. Roger Newton, b. Oct. 19, 1806, m. Lucretia Jane Taylor of
   Lansingburgh, N. Y., and d. in Philadelphia, Pa., Nov. 16, 1852, æ. 46.
4. *Elizabeth*, b. Feb. 18, 1766; m. Oct. 31, 1787, Perez Hastings of Hatfield, who
   d. March 11, 1822, æ. 67. She d., having had, 1. Elizabeth, b. Nov. 15, 1788,
   m. June, 1814, Horace Hastings, a merchant in Geneva, N. Y. She d. Aug.
   15, 1837, æ. 48; 2. Eurotas, b. May 15, 1790, was a banker at Buffalo, N. Y.,
   and d. May 22, 1858, æ. 68. He m. Jan. 1, 1822, Eroe Arms of Greenfield;
   his cousin; (see above.) She d. Nov. 24, 1853, æ. 59; 3. Electa, b. Jan. 15,
   1792, m. July 4, 1816, Dr. David Field, of Geneva, N. Y., who d. Feb. 14,
   1855, æ. 72; 4. Perez, b. May 29, 1794, was a merchant in Geneva, N. Y.,
   and d. April 26, 1852, æ. 58. He m. May, 1822, Eunice Hastings.
5. *Mercy*, b. March 3, 1768; m. Nov. 14, 1798, Asahel Wright, jun., of Deerfield,
   Mass., who d. April 10, 1828, æ. 60. She d. Aug. 25, 1842, æ. 74. She
   had, 1. Miranda, b. Sept. 10, 1799, m. Oct. 17, 1821, J. A. Saxton of D., and d.
   Nov. 28, 1844, æ. 45; 2. Luke, b. Nov. 27, 1801, lives in D. He m. Nov.
   21, 1832, Mary Ann Stebbins; 3. Lucy, twin with Luke, d. 1805; 4. George,
   b. Nov. 25, 1803, lives in D. He m. Nov. 27, 1834, Martha Hawks; 5. Lucy,
   b. Sept. 17, 1805, m. June 26, 1825, Isaac Gere of Williamsburg, Mass.,
   now of Oxford, Butler Co., Ohio; 6. Mary White, b. Dec. 17, 1810, d. Apr.
   4, 1814.
6. *Judith*, b. Dec. 29, 1770; was for more than twenty years a highly successful
   teacher in Whately. She d. unm., April 18, 1824, æ. 53.
7. *Thomas*, b. April 12, 1773; m. Hannah Harwood. .   .   .   .   (196)

8. *Electa*, b. Sept. 22, 1775; m. Nov. 27, 1800, Josiah Allis of East Whately, (see Fam. 174;) a farmer, and has held various offices. She d. April, 1859, æ. 83. He survives her. She had, 1. Salmon White, b. Nov. 27, 1801; is a hotel proprietor at New Haven, Conn. He m. 1824, Emily Stockbridge of Whately; 2. Josiah, b. July 17, 1803, is a farmer in E. W. He m. April 13, 1826, Eliza White; (see Fam. 197;) 3. Lydia, b. Dec. 1, 1805; res. in E. W.; 4. Judith, b. Nov. 8, 1807, m. 1833, Dr. Myron Harwood of Whately.

---

86. Lieut. ELIHU WHITE, son of Capt. Daniel, (36) was born in Bolton, Conn., in 1734. He settled in Hatfield, Mass., where he took a prominent part in public affairs, especially during the Revolutionary War. He was a selectman in 1771, 1778, 1779 and 1782. In May, 1775, Elihu White and John Dickinson were chosen to represent the town of Hatfield in the Provincial Congress to be held at Watertown, on the 31st of May. From 1776 to 1780 he was a member of the Committee of Correspondence, Inspection, and Safety. He died Dec. 23, 1793, æ. 60.

He married ZERUIAH COLE, dau. of Ebenezer Cole of Hatfield. She married, 2d, Feb. 19, 1795, Capt. Perez Graves of Hatfield, who died Dec. 17, 1809. She was born Nov. 30, 1741, and died Dec. 13, 1820, æ. 79.

CHILDREN.

1. *Electa*, b. June 4, 1764; m. June 26, 1783, Benjamin Morton of H., and d. without issue, about 1835.
2. *Ebenezer*, b. Feb. 28, 1766; m. Mary Dickinson. . . (197)
3. *Elihu*, b. Dec. 17, 1767; m. Sarah Smith. . . . . (198)
4. *Lois*, b. Oct. 14, 1769; m. Feb. 19, 1789, Joseph Smith, 2d, of H., and d. Oct. 10, 1829, æ. 60. He d. Jan. 2, 1836, æ. 77. She had, 1. Austin, b. Oct. 8, 1790; 2. Joseph, b. April 1, 1792, m. Jan. 28, 1823, Hannah Wells; (see in Fam. 84;) 3. Elihu White, b. April 11, 1794, d. unm., Aug. 17, 1829, æ. 35; 4. Sophia, b. Aug. 27, 1796; 5. Harriet, b. 1800; 6. Miranda, b. Feb. 12, 1803, d.; 7. Louisa, d.
5. *Anna*, b. Dec. 14, 1771; m. Dec. 30, 1790, Elias Lyman of Hartford, Vt., one of the earliest cotton manufacturers in that State. He d. Nov. 22, 1830, æ. 62. She d. Feb. 11, 1844, æ. 72. She had, 1. Lewis, b. Dec. 17, 1791, m. March 1, 1821, Mary Blake Bruce of Boston, Mass., and d. Jan. 29, 1837, æ. 45; 2. Fanny, b. Aug. 26, 1793, m. Oct. 14, 1812, Charles Dodd of Hartford, Conn., and d. Feb. 26, 1816, æ. 22; 3. Normand, b. Feb. 23, 1795, is a merchant in Hartford, Conn. He m. Dec. 27, 1824, Elizabeth Walker of Providence, R. I.; 4. Wyllys, b. May 5, 1797, res. in Burlington, Vt. He m. Sarah B. Marsh of Woodstock, Vt., now deceased; 5. Anna, b. Nov. 18, 1798, m. 1st, June 19, 1822, Charles Dodd of Hartford, Conn., (his 2d wife; see above.) He d. May 21, 1844, æ. 56. She m. 2d, April 18, 1855, Dr.

14

James Spaulding of Montpelier, Vt., and d. Dec. 11, 1856, æ. 58. He d. March 15, 1858; 6. Elias, b. July 8, 1800, res. in Burlington. He m. Cornelia Hall of Troy, N. Y.; 7. Horace, b. March 16, 1802, d. Aug. 20, 1814, æ. 12; 8. Theodore, b. Oct. 27, 1803, d. æ. 18 hours; 9. Clementine, b. Sept. 19, 1804, m. Joseph F. Tilden, now of Galesburg, Ill.; 10. George, b. April 6, 1806, res. in Hartford, Vt. He m. Dec. 30, 1828, Minerva Briggs of Rochester, Vt.; 11. Charles, b. Oct. 5, 1808, m. Maria Spaulding of Montpelier, where he res.; 12. Simeon, b. Aug. 16, 1810, m. Lucinda Hall of Troy, N. Y., and d. in Montpelier, Oct. 1, 1855, æ. 45. She res. in Burlington; 13. Hannah, b. July 7, 1813, m. George S. Kendrick of Lebanon, N. H., and d. March 14, 1857, æ. 43; 14. Jane, b. Aug. 7, 1816, m. Harvey King of Montpelier, and d. April 11, 1852, æ. 35.

6. *Patty*, b. Dec. 14, 1773; m. 1st, March 24, 1795, Elihu Robbins of Hat., who d. June 12, 1801, æ. 30; m. 2d, Elisha Clapp of Deerfield, Mass., who is d. She d. about 1856, having had, by her first husband, 1. A son, b. Oct. 26, 1795, d. in infancy; 2. Electa Morton, b. Nov. 1, 1796; 3. Mary Hatton, b. Jan. 13, 1799; 4. Nancy White, b. March 3, 1801, m. May 18, 1824, Gerizim Morgan of Northfield, Mass.

7. *Betsey*, b. Jan. 28, 1776; [Jan. 27?] m. June, 1798, Wyllys J. Cadwell of Montpelier, Vt., who d. March 8, 1823, æ. 44. She d. Sept. 30, 1849, æ. 73. She had, 1, William W., b. May 12, 1799, lives in M. He m. Dec. 14, 1836, Elizabeth Oaks, who d. March 13, 1851; 2. Eliza, b. Feb. 27, 1801, d. Aug. 28, 1802; 3. Maria, b. Feb. 14, 1803, m. Sept. 10, 1827, Constant W. Storrs; 4. Almira, b. Feb. 10, 1805, m. Feb. 21, 1827, Epaphroditus Ransom; 5. Betsey, b. Dec. 14, 1806; 6. Julia Ann, b. Jan. 30, 1809, m. Oct. 16, 1833, Levi Spaulding, and d. at Derby, Vt., April 7, 1854, æ. 45; 7. Lucy Ann, b. March 1, 1811, m. April 16, 1834, George P. Riker, who d. Aug. 1, 1851; 8. Elia Ann, b. July 28, 1813, m. Dec. 7, 1832, Joseph Hutchins.

8. *Nabby*, b. April 30, 1778; m. Aug., 1804, Isaac Freeman of Montpelier, who d. without issue, about 1848.

9. *Jonathan Cole*, b. Feb. 17, 1780; m. Cynthia Parkhurst.   .   .   (199)

---

87. JOEL WHITE, Jun., son of Capt. Joel, (38) was born in Bolton, Conn., December, 1727. He first settled as a farmer in Coventry, Andover Society, but returned to Bolton about 1784. He died Dec. 27, 1809, æ. 82, having been blind for a few years previous to his death.

He married ANNE LOOMIS of Bolton, dau. of Jabez and Mary Loomis. She was born May 22, 1734, and died June 18, 1807, æ. 73.

He had only one child,

Jabez Loomis, b. Dec. 29, 1763; m. Elizabeth Wales.   .   .   .   .   (200)
     This birth is recorded on the town records of Coventry.

88. LEMUEL WHITE, son of Capt. Joel, (38) was born in Bolton, Nov. 6, 1736. It is believed that he was the one of that name who graduated at Yale College in 1759. He settled in East Hartford, Conn., and was probably a merchant. He occasionally held civil offices. He died May 4, 1780, æ. 43. His inventory shows that he had acquired a good estate, and that he had loaned nearly $2,000, for carrying on the War, to the United States and the State of Connecticut.

He married, June 12, 1760, MARTHA LOOMIS of Bolton, dau. of Matthew Loomis and Martha Perkins. She married, 2d, Timothy Cheney, Esq., of Manchester, who died Sept. 27, 1795, æ. 65. She was born March 2, 1740, and died Jan. 28, 1803, æ. 63.

CHILDREN.

1. *Perseus,* } b. Apr. 26, 1761 ; d. May 4, 1761.
2. *Pericles,* } Twins.   d. June 19, 1775, æ. 14.
3. *Lemuel,* b. Nov. 1, 1762 ; m. 1st, Mary Buckland ; 2d, Mary Wells. (201)
4. *Martha,* b. Feb. 9, 1764 ; m. Silas Chapman of East Hartford. She d. without issue, about 1812. He m. again, and died.
5. *Clarissa,* b. Aug. 11, 1766 ; was brought up in the family of her aunt Ely, at W. Springfield : (see Fam. 38.) She m. Nov. 4, 1793, Oliver P. Dickinson of Pittsfield, Mass., and d. Dec. 15, [7?] 1847, æ. 81. He d. Dec., 1850, æ. 80. She had, (all living in 1858,) 1. Clarissa White, b. April 12, 1797, m. 1st, May 15, 1821, Noah F. Willis of P., who d. June 16, 1825. She m. 2d, June 13, 1832, Titus Goodman of P., who rem. in 1848 to Dayton, Ohio. He d. July 31, 1857 ; 2. Martha Chapman, b. Jan. 22, 1800, m. Otis Peck of P. ; 3. Elizabeth Lathrop, b. Feb. 15, 1802, m. April 15, 1830, Levi Fisk Claflen of Westhampton, Mass., now of Dayton, Ohio ; 4. Israel, b. July 9, 1805, is a bookseller at La Fayette, Ind. He m. Jan. 11, 1841, Lucia Hawley of Norfolk, Conn., who d. June 18, 1857, æ. 50.
6. *Betsey,* b. May 4, 1768 ; m. John Olcott, merchant, of Manchester, who d. June, 1833, æ. 65. She d. June 23, 1847, æ. 79, having had, 1. Solomon, d. unm. ; 2. George, d. unm. ; 3. John T., m. 1st, Mrs. Almina (Ingraham) Sage of Vernon, wid. of George Sage. She d. May 5, 1847, æ. 45. He m. 2d, Mrs. Hanover ; 4. Elizabeth ; 5. William.
7. *William,* b. July 18, 1769 ; supposed to have died at sea, unm.
8. *John J.,* b. April 28, 1771 ; m. 1st, E. Shelton ; 2d, C. L. Woodbridge. (202)
9. *Solomon,* b. March 21, 1773 ; d. 1793, æ. 20.
10. *Anne,*   b. Oct. 7, 1775 ; d. Aug. 11, 1776, æ. 10 mos. ; (1777, on gravestone.)
11. *Anne,*   b. Nov. 2, 1778 ; m. Col. Lebbeus P. Tinker, merchant, of Vernon. He was for a long time town clerk of V., post-master, and justice of the peace. She d. without issue, Feb. 10, 1852, æ. 73. He d. April 29, 1852, æ. 81 yrs. 8 mos.

89. ELIJAH WHITE, Esq., son of Capt. Joel, (38) was born in Bolton, June 21, 1742. (So the town record; a family record says, June 25.) He was a merchant in that place, engaged in a very extensive and successful business. He took an active part in public affairs, particularly during the Revolution. He was probably the Lieut. Elijah White who marched to New York, with a company of thirty-seven men, in 1776. He was a selectman in 1777, 1778, and 1781, was town clerk from 1784 to 1789, was eleven times chosen one of the representatives to the Legislature, between 1785 and 1807, and was for a long time a justice of the peace. He died April 27, 1818, æ. 76. The following is a fac-simile of his autograph.

He married, Nov. 7, 1770, EUNICE DAY of West Springfield, Mass., dau. of Col. Benjamin Day and Eunice Morgan. She was born June 1, 1745, and died May 24, 1826, æ. 81.

CHILDREN.

1. *Elijah*, b. Nov. 14, 1771; d. July 15, 1777.
2. *Elihu*, b. July 27, 1773; m. Sarah Trumbull. . . . (203)
3. *Henry*, b. April 18, 1775; d. July 28, 1777.
4. *Sophia*, b. Aug. 9, 1777; d. unm., Sept 15, 1801, æ. 24.
5. *Eunice*, b. July 6, 1779; m. March 7, 1821, Eliphalet Averill, a merchant, of Hartford; (his 2d wife.) She had one child, which d. in infancy. He d. March 8, 1842, æ. 65. She d. Jan. 19, 1845, æ. 65.
6. *Randolph*, b. Jan. 30, 1782; d. June 20, 1783.
7. *Elijah*, b. Aug. 15, 1784; m. 1st, Electa Fox; 2d, Delia Sheldon. (204)
8. *Julius*, b. April 21, 1787; m. Lydia Day. . . . . . (205)

---

90. THOMAS WHITE, son of Capt. Joel, (38) was born in Bolton, Feb. 2, 1746, and was a farmer there. He died Nov. 25, 1800, æ. 54.

He married, July 7, 1773, RUTH TALCOTT of Glastenbury, Conn., dau. of Dea. Elizur Talcott and Ruth Wright. She was born May 11, 1753, and died June 4, 1821, æ. 68.

CHILDREN.

1. *Ruth*, b. July 10, 1774; m. 1st, Nov. 29, 1792, Matthew Loomis, jun., of B.
   She m. 2d, Nov. 28, 1808, Richard Skinner of B.   She d. Sept. 21, 1836,
   æ. 62.   She had, by her first husband, 1. Russell, b. Nov. 27, 1793, was for
   many years a sea-captain.   His 1st wife, Sally, d. April 7, 1834, æ. 31.   His
   2d wife, Maria, d. June 26, 1844, æ. 39; 2. Chester, b. July 17, 1795.

2. *Amelia*, b. April 14, 1776; m. March 23, 1796, Nathan Strong of B.   They
   rem. to Berlin, Vt., and d. there.   She d. about 1848.   She had, 1. Theodore, b. April 30, 1797; 2. Amelia, b. Feb. 4, 1800; 3. Julia White, b. Oct.
   23, 1804; 4. Nathan Halsey, b. Nov. 18, 1807; 5. Lovina, b. Sept. 28, 1809.

3. *Thomas*, b. Oct. 27, 1778; m. Dorothy Hammond　　.　　.　　.　　. (206)

4. *Polly*,　b. March 20, 1782; m. May 11, 1802, Asa Talcott of Glastenbury, and
   d. April 14, 1808, æ. 26.   He m. again, and lives in G.   She had, 1. Amelia,
   b. March 25, 1803, m. Nov. 7, 1847, Maj. David Hills of Hartford, who d.
   Oct. 18, 1856.   She lives in G.; 2. Southmayd Stillman, b. Aug. 7, 1804,
   lives in Mendon, Ill.; 3. Polly, b. Jan. 7, 1806, m. March 26, 1848, Henry
   Seymour of Hartford; 4. Asa, b. Aug. 7, 1807, m. March 30, 1831, Maria
   Grossman of G., and lives in Jacksonville, Ill.

5. *George*,　b. July 14, 1784; d. in Georgia, unm.

6. *Theodore*, b. June 25, 1787; d. March 29, 1797.

7. *Asa*,　　b. April 13, 1791; m. Eunice Scoville.　.　　　.　　. (207)

8. *Julia*,　　b. Jan. 30, 1795; d. Feb. 26, 1795.

---

91. Capt. DANIEL WHITE, youngest son of Capt. Joel, (38) was born in Bolton, Dec. 7, 1749. He settled in Coventry, Andover Society, upon the farm next south of that occupied by his half-brother, Joel. He was well educated, intelligent, and highly esteemed. He frequently held town offices; was five times chosen one of the selectmen of Coventry, and was a representative from that town at seven sessions of the Legislature, between 1787 and 1804. He died Sept. 1, 1816, æ. 66. The following is a fac-simile of his autograph in 1782.

He married, Jan. 1, 1772, SARAH HALE of Glastenbury, Ct., dau. of Capt. Jonathan Hale, who died in the army, at Jamaica Plain, Mass., March 7, 1776, æ. 58, and of Elizabeth Welles. She was born Aug. 19, 1749, and died Dec. 30, 1812, æ. 63.

CHILDREN.

1. *Daniel*, b. July 14, 1773; m. Eunice Stanley.　　.　　.　　.　　. (208)

2. *Sarah*,　b. Feb. 20, 1775; lived chiefly with her brother Daniel, and d. unm.,
   Oct. 1, 1844, æ. 69.

3. *Samuel*, b. Feb. 23, 1777; m. Wealthy Pomeroy. .   .   (209)

4. *Jerusha*, b. Jan. 27, 1779; d. unm., Sept. 23, 1800, æ. 21.

5. *Fanny*, b. Feb. 5, 1781; m. Oct. 17, 1802, Flavel Bingham of Andover. They rem. to Utica, N. Y., where she d. July 11, 1804, æ. 23. He d. Aug. 13, 1804, æ. 23. Their only child, Flavel White, b. Nov. 8, 1803, was removed to Andover, after the death of his parents, and was brought up in the family of his maternal grandfather. He graduated at Union College, 1829, and settled as a lawyer in Cleveland, Ohio, where he now resides. He has been Mayor of the City, and Judge of the Probate Court. He m. May 27, 1835, Emeline Day, of Catskill, N. Y.

6. *Electa*, b. Feb. 20, 1783; m. May 18, 1808, Rev. Richard Williams. He was b. in Lebanon, Conn., April 17, 1780, grad. at Yale College, 1802, was pastor of the church in Brookfield, Conn., 1807 to 1811, in Cairo, Greene Co., N. Y., 1812 to 1816, and in Penn Yan, N. Y., 1820 to 1825. He also labored as a missionary in Central N. Y., and was for several years engaged in Bible distribution. He d. in Union Springs, Cayuga Co., N. Y., Nov. 15, 1844, æ. 64. Mrs. Electa Williams d. in the same place, March, 25, 1851, æ. 68. She had, 1. Samuel White, b. April 1, 1809, res. in Norwich, Chenango Co., N. Y. He m. Jan. 26, 1834, Mary Marsh; 2. Sophia, b. Aug. 10, 1810, m. Sept. 12, 1833, Joshua Davis, now a farmer in Wheatland, Mich.; (P. O., Hudson, Lenawee Co.;) 3. Justin, b. May 1, 1813, is a merchant at Seneca Falls, N. Y.; 4. Electa, b. Jan. 15, 1816, m. Aug. 13, 1844, Benjamin P. Davis, a teacher, now of West Whiteland, Chester Co., Penn.; 5. Caroline Cornelia, b. Jan. 16, 1818, m. Sept. 22, 1842, William Anthony, now of Santa Cruz, Cal.; 6. Charles Cornelius, twin with the last, lives at Seneca Falls, N. Y. He m. Oct., 1850, E. Minerva Everts; 7. Elizabeth, b. Aug. 27, 1820, m. Sept. 14, 1854, Joseph Ruffner, a farmer, of Santa Cruz, Cal.; 8. Harriet Aurelia, b. April 12, 1825, m. May 7, 1850, Isaac W. Allen, now a merchant at Seneca Falls; 9. Richard, b. July 28, 1828, lives in Santa Cruz, Cal. He m. Dec. 30, 1857, Isabella Pollard.

7. *Calvin*, b. March 16, 1786; d. unm., April 29, 1809, æ. 23.

---

92. DUDLEY WHITE, son of Capt. Elisha, (39) was born in Bolton, Conn., Jan. 8, 1741. He lived in Killingworth, (now Clinton,) Conn., was a goldsmith, and also practiced various other kinds of handicraft. He died March 27, 1811, æ. 70.

He married THANKFUL MURRAY of East Guilford, (now Madison.) She died May 20, 1826, æ. 84.

CHILDREN.

1. *William*, b. July 19, 1760; m. Juliana Pierson. .   .   .   (210)

2. *Elisha*, b. Dec. 2, 1762; m. Abigail Bates.   .   .   .   . (211)

3. *Submit*, b. March 2, 1766; d. in childhood, of small pox.

4. *Anne*, b. July 17, 1768; m. Aug. 25, 1791, Joy Ward, and is said to have rem. to Genessee Co., N. Y.

5. *Benjamin*, b. May 7, 1772; m. 1st, Mary Scranton; 2d, Polly Franklin. (212)

6. *Chloe*, b. Aug. 12, 1775; d. in Clinton, unm., April 30, 1857, æ. 81.

7. *Submit,*   b. Dec. 5, 1777 ; lives in Clinton, unm.
8. *Sarah,*   b. May 26, 1780 ; prob. d. young.
9. *John,*   b. Oct. 22, 1784 ; a farmer, lives in Clinton, unm.

---

93. SIMEON WHITE, Jun., son of Simeon, (40) was born in Hatfield, Mass., about 1745. He settled in Williamsburg, near the line of Whately. He was town clerk in 1773, and held various town offices. About 1812 he went to live with his son George, in Rutland, Jefferson Co., N. Y., and died there, Aug. 20, 1820, æ. 75.

He married, Aug. 2, 1770, HANNAH HUBBARD of Hatfield, dau. of Elisha Hubbard and Lucy Stearns. She was born Feb. 2, 1750, and died Feb. 17, 1786, æ. 36.

CHILDREN.

1. *Charles,* b. Oct. 10, 1770 ; m. —— ——.   .   .   .   .   (213)
2. *Henry,* b. March 9, 1772 ; m. Almira Tinker.   .   .   .   (214)
3. *William,* b. Jan. 25, 1774 ; was clerk for his uncle Asa. He afterwards lived in Sunderland and Vergennes, Vt., and d. about 1830 to 1835. He m., and had a family.
4. *George,* b. Oct. 10, 1775 ; m. Lydia Williams.   .   .   .   .   (215)
5. *Frederick,* b.   ; m. Mary B. Whiting.   .   .   .   (216)
6. *Hannah,* b. March 9, 1779 ; m. Amos White.   .   .   (Family 271)
7. *John,* b.   ; lived at Chatham, C. W., and was a large landholder. He d. unm., in 1852.
8. *Solomon,* b.   ; m. Lucy Lee.   .   .   (217)

---

94. Hon. ASA WHITE, son of Simeon, (40) was born in Hatfield, Mass., about 1747. He removed to Williamsburg about 1781, and resided there till his death, excepting a few years, from 1812 to 1816, when he lived in Chesterfield. He was a merchant in Williamsburg for more than 30 years, and acquired a large estate. He was town clerk for several years after 1790, was a Justice of the Peace, and of the Quorum, and an officer of the Hampshire Co. Missionary Society. He is said to have been of commanding personal appearance, courteous and dignified in manner, and much relied upon for his intelligence and sound judgment. He died Sept. 15, 1829, æ. 82.

He married, Jan. 20, 1785, ZILPAH HAYES, of Granby, Conn. She died April 2, 1833, æ. 72.

CHILDREN.

1. *Clarissa*, b. Dec. 2, 1785; d. Aug. 11, 1796.
2. *Asa*,   b. Oct. 29, 1787; was a merchant in New York. He d. unm., in 1844, æ. 56.
3. *Mary*,   b. April 27, 1790; d. unm., Feb. 18, 1814, æ. 23.
4. *John Johnson*, b. April 3, 1793; m. Catharine A. Waide.   .   .   (218)
5. *Chester*, b. Sept. 18, 1797; m. Clarissa W. Spencer.   .   .   . (219)
6. *Joel*,   b. Aug. 23, 1798; d. same day.
7. *Zilphia*, b. Feb. 8, 1800; m. 1837, Phineas Hubbard, a merchant in Stanstead, C. E., who d. Dec. 27, 1846. She has Ellen W., b. 1839 : one child d. in infancy.
8. *Addison Hayes*, b. Aug. 23, 1803 ; m. 1st, M. J. Brown ; 2d, C. Taylor. (220)

---

95. GEORGE WHITE, son of Oliver, (41) was born in Bolton, Conn., March 6, 1746. He settled in Tolland, and is said to have worked at the iron-works then in operation in the east part of Rockville, near the line of Tolland. He entered the Revolutionary army, and was for some time held a prisoner by the British, in New York. Upon gaining his release he started for home, but was able to proceed no farther than East Hartford, where he died, "of the small-pox, on the night after the 16th of January, 1777." His age was nearly 31 years.

He married MARY BENTON of Tolland. She married, 2d, Azariah Grant of East Windsor. She was born Sept. 15, 1741, and died at Winsted, Conn., Dec. 3, 1800, æ. 59.

CHILDREN.

1. *Mary*, b.   1766 ; m. Sept. 3, 1786, William Cogswell of Coventry, afterwards of Tolland. He d. March 23, 1842, æ. 77. She d. in Vernon, Sept. 16, 1847, æ. 81. She had, 1. Harry, b. Dec. 27, 1787, d. Jan., 1856, æ. 68. He m. 1st, Lovina Dimock of T., who d. Sept. 29, 1821 ; m. 2d, her sister, Miranda Dimock, who d. 1854 ; 2. Mary, b. June 8, 1790, m. Ebenezer West of T., and d. Aug. 28, 1847, æ. 57. He d. 1855 ; 3. Charles, b. Sept. 18, 1793, d. July 1, 1797 ; 4. Lucius, b. June 26, 1796, d. Jan. 22, 1797 ; 5. Lucia, b. Sept. 9, 1797, m. Novatus Chapman of T., now of Rockville; 6. William White, b. Feb. 15, 1801, d. March 10, 1801 ; 7. William Thompson, b. Dec. 31, 1803, is a joiner at Rockville. He m. Maria McKinney of Ellington ; 8. George White, b. Dec. 18, 1809, d. July 24, 1812.
2. *Oliver*,   b. about 1772 ; m. Lucy Wood.   .   .   .   .   .   . (221)
3. *Elizabeth*, b.   ; m. Ira Drake, and lived in Bethany, Wayne Co., Penn. She d. æ. about 80, having had, Sophia, Ira, Elizabeth, Warren, and others.
4. *Daniel*, b. Dec. 11, 1774 ; m. Clarissa Cleveland.   .   .   .   . (222)
5. *George*, b. Jan. 17, 1777 ; m. Mary Alfred.   .   .   .   .   . (223)

Sixth Generation and Children.

IN THE LINE OF DEA. NATHANIEL WHITE, OF HADLEY.

96. SAMUEL WHITE, son of Nathaniel, jun., (42) was born Oct. 3, 1747. He settled in South Hadley, Mass., and died there, Jan. 22, 1817, æ. 69.

He married, Sept., [Oct.?] 1771, MARY COLLINS. She was born Dec. 14, 1748, and died May 31, 1831, æ. 82.

CHILDREN.

1. *Sarah,* b. Sept. 8, 1772; m. Marcus Cole of Conway, Mass., and d. Sept., 1846, æ. 74. She had Horace, and others.
2. *Luther,* b. July 9, 1774; m. Dec., 1800, Elizabeth Walden of Wilbraham, Mass. He was drowned in the Conn. River, Oct. 20, 1804, æ. 30. His widow d. æ. 80. He had, 1. Elisha Walden, d. Oct., 1803; 2. Luthera.
3. *Electa,* b. Oct., 1776; d. Dec., 1777.
4. *Electa,* b. Sept. 13, 1778; m. Josiah Thompson, and d. Aug. 25, 1822, æ. 44. He d. Oct. 25, 1822, æ. 43. She had, 1. Milton; 2. Luther; 3. Almira; 4. Erasmus Darwin.
5. *Mary,* b. Jan. 2, 1781; [Jan. 19?] d. unm., May 8, 1830, æ. 49.
6. *Lucretia,* b. April 27, 1783; d. unm., Oct. 10, 1847, æ. 64.
7. *Jerusha,* b. Sept. 28, 1785; d. unm., Oct. 10, 1812, æ. 27.
8. *Clarine,* b. April 3, 1789; m. April 4, 1815, Elijah Dickinson of Hadley, who d. March 22, 1848, æ. 64. She d. March 4, 1855, æ. 66. She had, 1. Elijah Walden, b. Feb. 29, 1816, m. Nov. 12, 1839, Mary A. Crossett; 2. Jerusha, b. Feb. 15, 1819, m. Nov. 25, 1847, Warren S. Judd; 3. Alphonso, b. Nov. 3, 1821, m. Jan. 20, 1853, Abby Alcie Field; 4. Samuel Collins, b. Dec. 11, 1824, m. 1st, May 16, 1846, Rachel S. Parsons, who d. He m. a 2d wife; 5. Emeline, b. Nov. 5, 1826, d. Sept. 1, 1847, æ. 20; 6. Luther White, b. Nov. 30, 1830.

---

97. NATHANIEL WHITE, son of Nathaniel, jun., (42) was born in South Hadley, Mass., Nov. 28, 1749. He was a farmer there until about 1794, when he removed to Easthampton,

15

Mass. He was a revolutionary soldier; was in the battle of Bunker Hill, and was present at Burgoyne's surrender. He taught common and singing schools, twenty-six seasons. He died Oct. 15, 1828, æ. 79.

He married, May 14, 1778, HULDAH CLARK, dau. of Eliakim Clark and Martha Bascom. She was born Feb. 5, 1748, and died Feb. 20, 1826, æ. 78. She was the fifth in descent from the "Most Worshipful William Clarke, Esq.," who died in Northampton, July 19, 1690, æ. 81.

CHILDREN.

1. *Levi,*　b. Feb. 14, 1779 ; m. Miriam Alvord.　.　.　.　.　(224)
2. *Huldah,* b. Jan. 20, 1781 ; m. Asahel Parsons, jun., of Easthampton, who d. July 4, 1836, æ. 63. She d. without issue, April 29, 1842, æ. 61.
3. *Clark,*　b. Dec. 16, 1782 ; m. 1st, May 17, 1827, Sarah Kingsley, dau. of Samuel K. of Westhampton. She d. Jan. 4, 1836, æ. 53, and he m. 2d, Sept. 14, 1836, Irene Parsons, b. Sept. 11, 1788, dau. of David P. of Westhampton. He d. without issue, Nov. 23, 1842, æ. 60.
4. *Jemima,*　b. Sept. 14, 1784 ; m. Jan. 1, 1836, Julius Phelps, who d. Jan. 13, 1858, æ. 78.
5. *Nathaniel,* b. Aug. 23, 1786 ; d. unm., at Pittsfield, Mass., Oct., 1830, æ. 44. He was the sixth *Nathaniel,* in the direct line of that name, which became extinct by his death.
6. *Theodosia,* b. July 29, 1788 ; m. April 10, 1828, John Hannum, who d. Oct. 23, 1852, æ. 72.
7. *Ezekiel,*　b. Jan. 12, 1791 ; m. 1st, Rachel Janes ; 2d, M. H. Bates.　(225)

---

98. EBENEZER WHITE, son of Nathaniel, jun., (42) was born in South Hadley, May 6, 1756. He settled first in his native place, but removed to Ludlow, Mass., where he died, March 29, 1829, æ. 73.

He married, Sept. 26, 1793, RUTH LYMAN, dau. of Benjamin Lyman of Easthampton. She was born Dec. 9, 1765, and died March 11, 1839, æ. 73.

CHILDREN.

1. *Ezra,*　b. Aug. 4, 1794 ; m. Mary Wight.　　　　(226)
2. *Lyman,*　b. April 16, 1796 ; m. Anna Granger.　.　.　(227)
3. *Martha,*　b. Nov. 5, 1797 ; d. Oct. 17, [16?] 1803.
4. *Ruth,*　b. Sept. 15, 1799 ; m. Elihu Dwight of Belchertown, Mass., who d. She d. Oct. 22, 1828, æ. 29, having had, 1. Justus ; 2. Nathaniel ; 3. Elihu.
5. *Christian,* b. July 24, 1801 ; m. William Town, a joiner, of Granby, Mass., now of Whitehall, N. Y.
6. *Hannah,*　b. July 17, 1803 ; m. Solon Lyon of Ludlow, a farmer, and has, 1. Josiah ; 2. Lucy ; 3. Solon ; 4. Ruth ; 5. Christian ; 6. Ebenezer ; 7. Charlotte.

7. *Ralph,* b. Aug. 20, 1805; m. 1st, Ruth Lyon; 2d, Julia Bliss. . (228)
8. *Martha,* b. Oct. 23, 1807; m. Addison Everett of Middlefield, Mass., now of
   Princeton, Ill. She has had, Lucas, Carlos, Edward, Ellen, Luna, Milo,
   and three others who d. young.
9. *Ebenezer,* b. Dec. 13, 1810; [1811?] m. 1st, Louisa Wright; 2d, E. Crouch. (229)

---

99. Dea. ENOCH WHITE, son of Jonathan, (43) was born
in South Hadley, February, 1747. He succeeded his father
in the possession of the homestead, at Fall Woods, and was a
thrifty farmer. He was a Lieut. in the Revolutionary Army.
He served the town of South Hadley as selectman, and as a
member of the Legislature, and was a deacon of the church in
that town. He died Jan. 10, 1813, æ. nearly 66.

He married SUSANNAH GOODMAN of South Hadley, dau. of
Thomas Goodman and Rebecca Shepherd. She died Aug.
30, 1822, æ. 75. (Grave-stone and church record.)

CHILDREN.

1. *Phineas,* b. Oct. 30, 1770; m. Esther Stevens. . . . (230)
2. *Tamesin,* b. Nov. 20, 1771; d. unm., Oct. 28, 1794, æ. 23.
3. *Tirzah,* b. June 1, 1773; m. Nov. 8, 1798, Luther Clapp, who d. Aug. 11,
   1811, æ. 39. She d. without issue, Aug. 31, 1811, æ. 38.
4. *Mary,* b. Sept. 21, 1777; m. Feb. 11, 1802, Bohan Clark of Easthampton, a
   merchant and mill-owner. They rem. to Northampton in 1818, where he
   d. July 13, 1846. She resides in Northampton. She has had, 1. Enoch
   White, b. Nov. 16, 1802; resided chiefly in Providence, R. I., and Philadelphia, Pa., and, with his brothers, belonged to the well-known banking house
   of "E. W. Clark & Co." He d. in Phila., Aug. 3, 1855, æ. 52. He m. Feb.
   1, 1826, Sarah Crawford Dodge, of Providence, R. I.; 2. Tamesin Susannah, b. Oct. 6, 1804; 3. Bohan Asahel, b. March 17, 1807; was drowned in
   Boston Harbor, June 12, 1832, æ. 25; 4. Mary Ann, b. Dec. 11, 1808, m.
   June 24, 1835, Watson Loud of Westhampton, Mass., now of Romeo,
   Mich.; 5. Joseph Washington, b. Sept. 16, 1810; resides in Dedham, Mass.
   He m. Nov. 12, 1834, Eleanor A. Jackson, of Prov., R. I.; 6. Luther Clapp,
   b. July 4, 1814; resides in New York. He m. 1st, Sept. 12, 1839, Julia C.
   Dikeman, who d. Aug. 15, 1841, æ. 22. He m. 2d, Aug. 10, 1843, Julia
   Crawford of Putney, Vt.
5. *Enoch,* b. June 1, 1781; m. Martha Lamb. . . (231)

---

100. OLIVER WHITE, Jun., son of Oliver, (44) was born
in Hadley, Dec. 19, 1755. He is said to have removed to
Vt., or N. Y., about 1800. The name of his wife is not
known. He had,—

1. *Eunice;*   2. *Anne.* Both bap. at Hadley, Feb. 6, 1795.

101. Moses White, son of Oliver, (44) was born in Hadley, Dec. 3, 1759. He lived on the place of his father, and died Nov. 10, 1823, æ. 64.

He married, Jan. 17, 1788, Chloe Peck of Hadley.

CHILDREN.

1. *David,* b. Sept. 24, 1788; m. 1st, Mary Bumps; 2d, C. D. Bragg.   (232)
2. *Cynthia,* b. Jan. 14, 1792; m. Dec. 15, 1814, Jonathan Smith of Hadley.
3. *Elihu,* b. Sept. 22, 1794; m. Ruth Rider.   .   .   .   .   .   (233)

102. Aaron White, son of Thomas, (47) was born May 29, 1744. He lived in South Hadley, and died Feb. 8, 1810, æ. 65.

He married, March 6, 1770, Thankful White, dau. of Jonathan White. (Fam. 43.) She was born Sept. 21, 1752, and died July 7, 1820, æ. 67.

CHILDREN.

1. *A daughter,* b. Feb. 23, 1771; d. Feb. 25, 1771.
2. *Noadiah,* b. Feb. 28, 1772; m. Rachel Trueby, who d. July 3, 1820. He d. Aug. 11, 1849, æ. 77. His dau., Elizabeth, prob. m. Jan. 3, 1822, Alvin Judd. He had three other children.
3. *Jonathan,* b. Dec. 8, 1774; m. and had a family; is dead.
4. *Aaron,* b. Feb. 19, 1776; m. and d.; left a family.
5. *Rhoda,* b. June 16, 1779; d. unm., Aug. 3, 1827, æ. 48.
6. *Justus,* b. Feb. 26, 1789; m. 1st, Cynthia Brewster; 2d, E. Strong. (234)
7. *Horace,* b. Sept. 10, 1792; m. Jan. 17, 1821, Jerusha Skinner of Enfield, Mass., and died.

103. Job White, son of Thomas, (47) was born in South Hadley, about 1752. He lived principally in Northampton, where he was for many years keeper of the jail. He died Feb. 12, 1807, æ. 54.

He married, 1st, Charity Chapin of Springfield, dau. of Benoni and Esther Chapin. She was born Jan. 21, 1757, and died about 1784, æ. 27.

He married, 2d, Oct. 6, 1785, Mindwell Clapp. She was born Feb. 23, 1750, and died about 1824.

CHILDREN;—BY THE FIRST MARRIAGE.

1. *Charity,* b. Feb. 25, 1776; d. in infancy.
2. *Charity,* b. June 27, 1779; m. Sept. 16, 1798, Nichols Goddard of Rutland, Vt., a silversmith and clock-maker. He d. Sept. 29, 1823, æ. 50. She d. at Claremont, N. H., Nov. 10, 1857, æ. 78. She had, 1, Evelina Pamela, b. Dec. 31, 1799, m. March 11, 1818, Simeon Ide, of Windsor, Vt., now of

Claremont, N. H. She d. May 25, 1857, æ. 57. Messrs. Ide, Dutton, N. W.
and E. L. Goddard, are associated as the "Claremont Manufacturing
Co.," in the manufacture of paper and books ; 2. Edward, b. Dec. 28, 1801,
d. Sept. 14, 1803 ; 3. Harriet Martha, b. Jan. 2, 1804, m. Dec. 20, 1830,
Ormond Dutton of Keene, N. H., now of Boston, Mass.; 4. Nichols White,
b. Dec. 17, 1806 ; res. in Claremont. He m. May 19, 1836, Sarah Matilda
Brewer, of Haverhill, N. H. ; 5. Edward Lewis, b. June 9, 1809 ; res. in
Claremont. He m. 1st, July 4, 1833, Elizabeth Worth, who d. May 7, 1852,
æ. 39 ; m. 2d, June 13, 1855, Elizabeth P. Marsh ; 6. Nathan Chapin, b.
Sept. 22, 1811 ; is a merchant in Boston ; res. in Jamaica Plain, Mass.
He m. Sept. 22, 1846, Martha Brewer ; 7. Charlotte Mary, b. April 29,
1814, d. unm., Nov. 18, 1837, æ. 23.
3. *A child*, b.   ; d. in infancy.
4. *Pamela*, bap. Oct., 1783 ; d. in infancy.

CHILDREN ;—BY THE SECOND MARRIAGE.

5. *Lewis*,   b.   1786 ; d. Jan. 19, [24?] 1804, æ. 17.
6. *Chester*, b. Feb. 19, 1788 ; m. Eunice Edwards.   .   .   .   (235)
7. *Polly*,   b.   1789 ; m. 1828, James Ostrander ; they now live with
         the Shakers, at Niskayuna, Schenectady Co., N. Y.
8. *Job*,   b. Dec. 27, 1790 ; m. Margaret Stebbins.   .   .   .   (236)
9. *Charlotte*, b. Sept. 10, 1792 ; m. March 20, 1820, Curtiss Hubbell, who d. Oct. .
         16, 1854. She lives in Buffalo, N. Y. She has had, 1. Edward Lewis, b.
         1822, d. 1823 ; 2. Adaline Curtiss, b. Nov. 30, 1824 ; 3. Martha Ann, b.
         1827, d. 1828 ; 4. Selim Booth, b. Jan. 14, 1830, m. Feb. 11, 1858, Lois
         Heath ; 5. William Chester, b. Aug. 18, 1836.

---

104. SIMEON WHITE, son of Thomas, (47) was born in South
Hadley. He lived there, and died Oct. 7, 1822.

He married, 1st, March, 1785, ROXA POMEROY. [Roxana?].
She died July 29, 1804, æ. 38.

He married, 2d, Mrs. URANIA STEBBINS of Longmeadow,
widow of Zadock Stebbins, and dau. of Jonathan Burt. She
was born May 1, 1762, and died Dec. 8, 1819, æ. 57.

CHILDREN ;—BY THE FIRST MARRIAGE.

1. *Roxa*, b. May 9, 1787 ; m. Nov. 10, 1808, Ephraim Smith, jun., and d. Jan. 22,
         1820, æ. 32. She had, 1. Edmund ; 2. Andrew. E. S., jun., has a 4th wife.
2. *Quartus*, b. April 28, 1789 ; m. Persis Stebbins.   .   .   .   (237)
3. *Calvin*, b. Aug. 26, 1791 ; m. Patty Smith ; has several children.
4. *Polly*,   b. Oct. 25, 1794 ; d. April, 1811, æ. 16.

---

105. MOSES WHITE, son of Joseph, (48) was born in South
Hadley, April 10, 1751. He lived there, and died Sept. 15,
1777, æ. 26.

He married ABIGAIL ———.

CHILDREN.

1. *Lois,*   b. Nov. 30, 1775 ; m. Nov. 8, 1802, Elam Brooks of Hartford, Vt.
2. *Abigail,* b. July 13, 1777 ; m. Jan. 9, 1800, Frederic Miller.

---

106. Lieut. JOSEPH WHITE, son of Joseph, (48) was born in South Hadley, Dec. 13, 1754. He was a farmer there, and also kept a public house. He died July 30, 1829, æ. 74.

He married, Dec. 14, 1788, SALLY YEOMANS of Colchester, Conn. She was born July 6, 1759, and died Aug. 9, 1840, æ. 81.

CHILDREN.

1. *Sarah,* b. Oct. 14, 1789 ; m. 1st, March 14, 1814, Andrew Henry of S. H., who
    d. Feb. 3, 1821, æ. 33. She m. 2d, Sept. 17, 1828, Dr. William F. Sellon
    of Amherst, who d. Dec. 31, 1842, æ. 56. She d. in N. Y. city, Dec. 14,
    1855, æ. 66. By her first husband she had, 1. Sarah Ann, b. Sept. 30, 1815,
    m. Sept. 16, 1834, Isaac C. Pray of New York ; 2. Helen Amanda, b. Aug.
    9, 1820 ; resides with her sister.
2. *Joseph Austin,* b. April 27, 1791 ; d. unm., Feb. 25, 1816, æ. 24.
3. *Theodore,* b. May 17, 1795 ; d. unm., Jan. 28, 1823, æ. 27.
4. *Amanda,* b. July 10, 1797 ; m. 1st, Nov., 1825, William Lyman of S. H., who
    d. Oct. 26, 1837 ; m. 2d, Oct. 2, 1843, Cyrus White. (Fam. 240.) She had,
    by her first husband, 1. Theodore White, b. Sept. 26, 1826 ; is a physician.
    He m. Sept. 11, 1850, Elizabeth Scrugham, of S. H., who d. Jan. 25, 1853,
    æ. 25 ; 2. Joseph Austin, b. Nov. 14, 1828 ; 3. Mary Amanda, b. Oct. 16,
    1831, d. May 16, 1848, æ. 16 ; 4. William Wirt, b. April 30, 1834.
5. *Augustus,* b. Jan. 17, 1802 ; d. Sept. 25, 1803.

---

107. REUBEN WHITE, son of Joseph, (48) was born in South Hadley, Oct. 1, 1761. In 1818 he removed from South Hadley to Belchertown, Mass., where he died, Feb. 27, 1856, æ. 94.

He married, May 18, 1797, MABEL WHITE, dau. of Nathaniel White. (Fam. 54.) She was born Sept. 1, 1767, and died Sept. 20, 1855, æ. 88.

CHILDREN.

1. *Emily,* b. Dec. 21, 1798 ; m. Nov. 9, 1826, Capt. Simeon Pepper of Belcher-
    town. He and his sons are carriage makers. She d. Dec. 26, 1840, æ. 42,
    having had, 1. Sarah Emily, b. Dec. 11, 1828, d. May 30, 1829 ; 2. Simeon
    Wait, b. Dec. 30, 1830, m. Julia Joanna Hinkley of B. ; 3. Hervey White,
    b. Jan. 6, 1835, m. Sarah Eliza Griggs of B. ; 4. Emily White, b. Sept. 18,
    1837, d. April 11, 1839.
2. *Moses,* b. Aug. 10, 1800 ; lives in Belchertown. He m. Feb. 10, 1848, Jane N.
    Snow, b. Dec. 19, 1819, dau. of Zenas and Asenath Snow, of Lebanon, N. H.
3. *Hervey,* b. July 27, 1802 ; d. unm., May 5, 1833, æ. 30.
4. *David,* b. May 27, 1804 ; d. Jan. 10, 1814.

5. *Mabel*, b. July 13, 1806; [July 19?] m. April 10, 1833, John Parker of B., a painter. She has had, 1. Joseph Edson, b. May 11, 1835, d. same day; 2. John Henry, b. Feb. 13, 1837 ; 3. Charles Gilbert, b. Feb. 7, 1839, d. June 22, 1841 ; 4. Edwin White, b. April 27, 1843, d. Aug. 24, 1845 ; 5. Harriet Elizabeth, b. Oct. 4, 1846, d. March 16, 1858.

6. *Reuben Augustus*, b. Feb. 19, 1809 ; m. Emeline M. Snow.   .   (238)

---

108. Dea. JOSIAH WHITE, Jun., son of Dea. Josiah, (49) was born in South Hadley, March 30, 1761. He was a farmer in that place, and died Feb. 26, 1829, æ. 68.

He married, Nov. 22, 1787, MABEL MITCHELL of S. H., dau. of David and Mary Mitchell. She was born May 8, 1765, and died Feb. 2, 1840, æ. 74.

CHILDREN.

1. *Maria*, b. Aug. 27, 1788; m. 1808, Dr. Otis Goodman of S. H., and d. Feb. 19, 1853, æ. 64. She had, 1. Josiah White, b. Nov. 12, 1809; lives in W. Roxbury, Mass. He m. 1st, Abigail Moody ; m. 2d, Dorcas Judd ; 2. Edmund Otis, b. April 28, 1813 ; res. in Cincinnati, O. He m. —— Holmes.; 3. Helen Maria, b. May 15, 1817, m. Dr. William Pierson of Dayton, O. ; 4. Henry Martyn, b. Aug. 11, 1823, m. Elizabeth Fuller, and d. Aug. [Sept?] 9, 1852, æ. 29 ; 5. Harvey, b. June 5, 1832, d. Sept. 1, 1837.

2. *Mabel*, b. Nov. 23, 1789 ; d. unm., Oct. 27, 1837, æ. 48.

3. *A son*, b. March 2, 1791 ; d. same day.

4. *Mary*, b. Jan. 26, 1792 ; m. Nov. 17, 1841, Augustus White of South Hadley ; (son of Lieut. Thomas White ; see in Fam. 47.)

5. *A son*, b. Nov. 12, 1793 ; d. same day.

6. *Harriet*, b. Oct. 2, 1794 ; m. Dec. 7, 1820, Dea. Alonzo Bardwell of South Hadley Falls. She has had, 1. Alonzo Smith, b. Dec. 16, 1822, d. Nov. 24, 1855, æ. 33 ; 2. Harriet White, b. March 5, 1825, m. James Benton ; 3. Charles Addison, b. Oct. 7, 1826 ; 4. Carlos, b. March 2, 1829 ; 5. Edwin, b. Oct. 4, 1830, d. Oct. 8, 1838 ; 6. George, b. May 12, 1832, d. Oct. 2, 1833 ; 7. Joseph, b. March 9, 1835 ; 8. Mabel White, b. April 25, 1837 ; 9. Spencer, b. May 31, 1839, d. May 24, 1840.

7. *Josiah*, b. March 25, 1796 ; d. Feb. 1, 1797.

8. *Clarissa.* b. Dec. 14, 1797 ; m. Dec. 2, 1819, Henry Collins of S. H., and d. Jan. 28, 1840, æ. 42. She had, 1. Henry, d. ; 2. Wolcott Edgar, b. Jan. 8, 1822, m. Sabrina Wilcutt ; 3. Cornelia White, b. Aug. 8, 1824 ; m. Asa A. Howland of Conway ; 4. Henry Augustus, b. Aug., 1826, m. 1st, Juliette Bliss of Wilbraham ; m. 2d, Mary Graves of Springfield.

9. *Sumner*, b. Sept. 28, 1799 ; d. April 13, 1800.

10. *Semanthe*, b. May 15, 1801 ; m. May, 1825, Reuben R. Eastman of Granby. Has had, 1. Sarah Shepherd, d. July 14, 1851, æ. 25 ; 2. Mary White, d. June 11, 1853, æ. 24 ; 3. Frances ; 4. Semanthe White, m. Rev. Prescott Fay of Lancaster, N. H. ; 5. Maria ; 6. Jane, d. Sept. 24, 1834 ; 7. William, d.

11. *Josiah*, b. Oct. 19, 1802 ; d. Jan. 28, 1803.

12. *Samuel Wolcott*, b. Oct. 27, 1804 ; d. Sept. 6, 1808.

13. *Cornelia Mitchell*, b. Oct. 25, 1806 ; d. Sept. 8, 1808.

109. ELDAD WHITE, son of Dea. Josiah, (49) was born in South Hadley, March 31, 1768. He died there, April 11, 1823, æ. 55.

He married, March 31, 1789, HANNAH DAY of S. H., dau. of Ezra Day. She was born May 7, 1769, and died March 15, 1851, æ. 82.

CHILDREN.

1. *Horace,* b. April 8, 1790; d. unm., Oct. 27, 1821, æ. 31.
2. *Heman,* b. April 17, 1792; m. 1st, Clarissa Smith; 2d, Sarah Kelley.   (239)
3. *Cyrus,* b. Oct. 21, 1794; m. Elvira White, and others.   .   .   (240)
4. *Eldad,* b. May 9, 1797; lived in S. H., and d. March 7, 1843, æ. 45. He m. Julia Day, who is still living. His only child, Cornelia, b. Dec. 26, 1818, d. unm., Aug. 7, 1840, æ. 21.
5. *Medad,* b. June 8, 1800; m. Lucy Snow.   .   .   .   .   .   (241)
6. *Keziah,* b. Oct. 15, 1802; m. Jan. 20, 1824, Sedgwick White of S. H.; (a grandson of Lieut. Thomas White; see in Fam. 47.) She d. Feb. 25, 1837, æ. 34. He m. again. She had, 1. Horace, b. Nov. 6, 1824, d. Jan. 22, 1828; 2. A son, b. April 29, 1826, d. same day; 3. Maria, b. June 6, 1827, d. Oct. 7, 1839; 4. Sophia, b. June 8, 1830, d. May 20, 1831; 5. Amanda, b. April 4, 1832, m. Oct. 6, 1853, Joseph Thompson of Rockville, Conn.; 6. Josiah, b. March 25, 1834, d. Aug. 10, 1835.
7. *Irene,* b. June 20, 1804; m. May, 1824, Daniel Paine of S. H., now of Amherst, and d. Oct. 18, 1834, æ. 30. He has a 3d wife. She had, 1. Eliza, b. March 4, 1825; was for several years Principal of the Female Seminary at Du Quoin, Ill. She m. Aug. 23, 1858, Nathan S. Weeks of Du Quoin; 2. Edward Elliot, b. July 3, 1827, d. Dec. 22, 1829; 3. Elliot Edward, b. July 10, 1829, d. Feb. 5, 1832; 4. Melissa, b. Sept. 9, 1831, d. Aug. 19, 1847, æ. 16.

---

110. LUTHER WHITE, son of Lieut. Jacob, (50) was born in Springfield, Mass., Sept. 11, 1749. He probably died there about 1795, leaving a son,

Luther, b. about 1780. Feb. 10, 1796, Aaron Bartlett was appointed guardian to Luther, aged about 16 years, son of Luther White, deceased.

---

111. Lieut. HORACE WHITE, son of Sergt. Daniel, (51) was born in West Springfield, Mass., April 26, 1749. He was a blacksmith in that town, and died Dec. 3, 1834, æ. 85.

He married, Dec. 3, 1772, MERCY COOLEY, dau. of Capt. Abel Cooley of West Springfield. She was born Jan. 29, 1750, and died July 17, 1834, æ. 84.

CHILDREN.

1. *Rufus,* b. May 10, 1773; d. March 1, 1783.
2. *Sewall,* b. May 6, 1776; m. Fanny Granger.   .   .   .   (242)

3. *Sarah*, b. March 24, 1779 ; m. Jan. 28, 1802, Capt. Benjamin Ashley of W. S., and d. Nov. 24, 1855, æ. 76. He d. 1856, æ. 82. She had, 1. Daniel, b. Jan. 6, 1804 ; 2. Edwin, b. Nov. 26, 1807, d. Nov. 13, 1808 ; 3. Edwin, b. June 1, 1811.

4. *Homer*, b. Dec. 16, 1782 ; d. Dec. 20, 1794, æ. 12.

5. *Priscilla*, b. July 22, 1786 ; lives in W. S.

6. *Mercy*, b. March 5, 1790 ; d. Dec. 13, 1794.

112. DANIEL WHITE, son of Sergt. Daniel, (51) was born in West Springfield, Nov. 2, [8 ?] 1752. He was a revolutionary soldier, and was in the expedition to Canada, in 1775, when Montgomery was killed. He settled in W. S., and died there, Sept, 15, 1814, æ. 62.

He married HANNAH LAMB, dau. of Samuel Lamb. She died Aug. 22, 1841, æ. 83.

CHILDREN.

1. *Gordon*, b. May 9, 1783 ; m. Nabby M. Hubbard.   .   .   .   (243)

2. *Hannah*, b. Feb. 10, 1785 ; m. Feb. 8, 1809, Amasa Smith of W. S., who d. May 3, 1839, æ. 52. She has had, 1. Phebe Worthington, b. Jan. 19, 1810, d. 1811 ; 2. Abigail Woodmancy, b. Nov. 21, 1811, m. Dec. 20, 1837, Rufus Leonard of W. S. ; 3. Hannah Minerva, b. Jan. 7, 1814, m. Oct. 26, 1854, Hambleton P. Cady ; 4. Elmer White, b. March 16, 1816, m. April 15, 1840, Sophia Burbank, and d. Aug. 2, 1853, æ. 37 ; 5. Newton Belknap, b. April 26, 1818, d. Sept. 20, 1839, æ. 21 ; 6. Ursula Priscilla, b. Feb. 8, 1822, m. March 14, 1844, Alfred Flower, jun., of W. S.

3. *Clara*, b. Dec. 13, 1789 ; d. Nov., 1790, æ. 11 mos.

4. *Emily*, b. July 12, 1795 ; m. 1817, Dr. Charles Culver, jun., of W. S., who d. Oct., 1854, æ. 67. She had, 1. Sarah Ervilla, m. George Cady, and d. Sept., 1854 ; 2. Charles, m. ; 3. Amelia Jane, m. Dr. James Hillman of Lyons, Wayne Co., N. Y.

5. *Theodosia*, b. Aug. 26, 1798 ; m. 1st, Nov., 1823, Samuel Palmer, who d. Nov. 29, 1829, æ. 37 ; m. 2d, July 10, 1841, Horace Palmer, who d. July 13, 1848, æ. 50. She had, by her first husband, 1. Samuel, m. Azubah Hendrick ; 2. Francis ; 3. Loren, m. Mary Leonard. By her second husband, 4. Mary, b. Jan. 5, 1843.

113. PLINY WHITE, son of Sergt. Daniel, (51) was born in West Springfield, Oct. 12, 1761. He was a farmer there, and died Oct. 8, 1808, æ. 47.

He married, July 14, [13 ?] 1793, LYDIA GRANGER, dau. of Daniel and Lydia Granger. She was born March 22, 1770, and died Aug. 27, 1843, æ. 73.

He had one child,

Daniel Granger, b. May 28, 1796 ; m. Harriet Day.   .   .   .   (244)

114. EDWARD WHITE, son of Sergt. Daniel, (51) was born in West Springfield, July 27, 1764. He was a farmer, and died Dec. 14, 1799, æ. 35.

He married HANNAH BEDORTHA. She married, 2d, Jan. 17, 1804, Capt. Mulford Eldredge, who died July 12, 1854, æ. 91. She died Jan. 18, 1855, æ. 90.

He had one child,

Edward Corbett, b. June 29, 1785; m. Mrs. Lucy Bagg.   .   .   .   (245)

---

115. PRESERVED WHITE, Jun., son of Preserved, (52) was born in Springfield, Nov. 25, [23?] 1743. He lived there, and died June 8, 1823, æ. 79.

He married, Aug. 20, 1767, MARY TERRY of Springfield, dau. of Samuel and Sarah Terry. She was born Feb. 27, 1746, [1745?] and died Nov. 4, 1804, æ. 58, or 59.

CHILDREN.

1. *Roderick*, b. May   14, 1768; [May 20?] d. June 19, 1777, æ. 9.
2. *Martin*,   b. June   4, 1770; m. Lucy Collins.   .   .   .   .   (246)
3. *Luther*,   b. April   7, 1772; d. Aug. 12, 1775, æ. 3.
4. *Mary*,   b. March 21, 1774; m. Oct. 10, 1799, Luther Burt of Longmeadow, who d. Jan. 28, 1847, æ. 74. She was living in L. in 1858. She has had, 1. Mary, b. Aug. 31, 1800, m. Oct. 13, 1829, Nathaniel Bliss of L., who d. July 14, 1845, æ. 50; 2. Anna, b. June 21, 1802, m. Dec., 1830, Henry B. Coomes of L.; 3. Rhoda, b. June 6, 1804; 4. Hezekiah, b. April 11, 1806, m. Dec., 1835, Lucretia Morgan of Springfield; 5. Lucius Colton, b. March 5, 1808, m. 1st, Harriet Scarl of Springfield, who d. Aug., 1840; m. 2d, Nov., 1840, Mrs. Nancy A. Lathrop, wid. of Lyman L.; 6. Augustine, b. July 4, 1810, m. Asenath Hamblet; 7. Luther White, b. July 4, 1812, m. Mercy Amidon of Belchertown, who d. May 22, 1845. He d. March 25, 1847, æ. 34; 8. John, b. Jan. 30, 1815, m. Francinai Kibbee of Somers, Conn.; 9. Richard Storrs, b. Oct. 26, 1817, m. Maria A. Boardman of Hartford, Conn.; 10. Delia Bliss, b. July 7, 1820, is a teacher.
5. *Luther*,   b. July   7, 1776; m. Abigail Stebbins.   .   .   (247)
6. *Roderick*, b. June 26, 1778; d. July 25, 1778.
7. *Rachel*,   b. July 29, 1779; m. April, 1803, Noah Torrey, now of New York Mills, Oneida Co., N. Y. She had several children, and d. May 11, 1827, æ. 47.
8. *Hannah*, b. July 21, 1781; d. July 9, 1782.
9. *Roderick*, b. Feb. 24, 1784; m. Delight Bement.   .   .   .   (248)
10. *Hannah*, b. Feb. 20, 1786; m. Dec. 13, [14?] 1809, Charles Burnham of Springfield. She d. Oct. 16, 1812, æ. 26, and he m. 2d, May 23, 1813, her sister, Persis White. He d. 1850. The children of C. B. were,—by his first wife, Hannah,—1. Charles, b. March 20, 1811, res. in S. He m. Sept. 19, 1838, Olivia Sarah Bliss, b. Aug. 22, 1810, dau. of John Bliss of Tolland, Conn.;

(see in Fam. 38 :) By his second wife, Persis,—2. Hannah White, b. May 23, 1815, m. April 16, 1837, Eleazer L. Hatch ; 3. George, b. March 11, 1817, m. Feb. 13, 1843, Anna Hemple ; 4. Nancy, b. Jan. 5, 1819 ; 5. James Henry, b. March 10, 1821, m. Aug. 3, 1841, Maria De Witt, and d. March 14, 1843, æ. 22 ; 6. Franklin White, b. July 2, 1823, m. 1853, Martha Kimball ; 7. William Stanford, b. Aug. 8, 1825, d. Dec. 11, 1845, æ. 20 ; 8. Edward Goodwin, b. June 2, 1827, m. Sept., 1853, Mary Ferree ; 9. Simeon Colton, b. June 13, 1835.

11. *Walter*,   b. June 20, 1787 ; d. same day.
12. *Preserved*, b. April 27, 1789 ; m. 1st, Sarah Chaffee ; 2d, Lucinda Rice. (249)
13. *Persis*,   b. April 30, 1792 ; was the second wife of Charles Burnham ; see number 10 in this family. She res. in Philadelphia.

---

116. DAVID WHITE, son of Preserved, (52) was born in Springfield, Jan. 30, 1747. He was a joiner, and lived in Springfield and Longmeadow. He died in Longmeadow, Oct. 2, 1823, æ. 76.

He married, 1st, Jan. 30, 1777, LYDIA ELY of Longmeadow, dau. of Nathaniel Ely, 2d, and Mary Esterbrook. She was born June 2, 1748, and died Feb. 19, 1781, æ. 32.

He married, 2d, Dec. 5, 1782, SARAH PYNCHON of Springfield, dau. of William Pynchon and Sarah Harris. She was born Oct. 5, 1751, and died July 26, 1826, æ. 74.

CHILDREN ;—BY THE FIRST MARRIAGE.

1. *Sarah*, b. Nov. 23, 1778 ; d. unm., Jan. 28, 1850, æ. 71.
2. *David*, b. Oct.   2, 1780 ; d. Jan. 30, 1781.

CHILDREN ;—BY THE SECOND MARRIAGE.

3. *David*,   b. Jan. 30, 1786 ; m. Clarissa Hall.   .   .   .   (250)
4. *William*, b. June 25, 1789 ; m. Lois Cooley.   .   .   .   .   (251)
5. *Lydia*,   b. Sept. 15, 1791 ; m. May 25, 1819, Daniel Gates of L.   She has, 1. Sarah Pynchon, b. Oct. 8, 1822, m. Elisha Kingsbury of Warehouse Point, Conn. ; 2. Lydia Ely, twin with Sarah P., m. William T. Clement of Shelburne Falls, Mass.; 3. Francis, b. Aug. 21, 1825, m. Feb. 1, 1858, Lois Spencer of Somers, Conn.

---

117. Dr. LEWIS WHITE, son of Preserved, (52) was born in Springfield, June 20, 1760. He was a practising physician for more than 50 years, and a skillful surgeon. He resided chiefly in Wilbraham and Longmeadow, and died in the latter place, Jan. 24, 1844, æ. 83.

He married, Sept. 20, 1787, SUSANNAH KING of Wilbraham, dau. of Parmenas and Hannah King. She was born Nov. 7, 1756, and died Jan. 13, 1840, æ. 83.

CHILDREN.

1. *Lewis*,　b. Aug. 21, 1788; d. at Sacketts Harbor, N. Y., June 4, 1818, æ. 29.

2. *Susannah*, b. Aug. 3, 1790; m. Joseph Ashley of L., and d. Aug. 24, 1855, æ. 65. She had, 1. Lewis, lives in Anna, Ill.; 2. Ann Eliza; 3. Persis; 4. Franklin; 5. Harriet, d. Feb., 1856; 6. Esther, b. Jan. 4, 1828, d. Sept. 20, 1855, æ. 27; 7. Joseph Franklin.

3. *Henry*, b. Jan. 4, 1792; grad. at Bangor Theol. Seminary, 1823, and was ordained pastor of the Congregational Church of Brooks and Jackson, Maine, Oct. 19, 1825. He was pastor at Loudon Village, N. H., 1835 to 1838, and for some time previous to his death labored in St. Albans, Me. He was the author of a volume upon the Early History of New England. He d. without issue, Dec. 7, 1858, æ. 67. He m. Jan. 25, 1827, Esther Sewall, b. March 29, 1802, in Bath, Me.

4. *Persis*, b. June 22, 1795; m. March 5, 1816, Orren Taylor.

5. *Sylvia*, b. Feb. 13, 1797; d. Oct. 9, 1803.

---

118. Dea. WALTER WHITE, son of Preserved, (52) was born in Springfield, June 13, 1765. He settled in Longmeadow, and died there, July 14, 1819, æ. 54.

He married, March 22, 1792, SABINA KEEP, dau. of Samuel Keep and Sabina Cooley. She was born Nov. 20, 1769, and died May 9, 1835, æ. 65.

CHILDREN.

1. *Franklin*, b. Jan. 14, 1793; d. April 23, 1813, æ. 20.

2. *Walter*, b. March 31, 1795; grad. at Amherst College, 1825, is a preacher, and resides in Galesburg, Illinois. He has added to his name that of his elder brother, Franklin.

3. *Cynthia*, b. March 13, 1797; m. Dec. 3, 1819, Dea. Eli Pease of Blanford, Mass., and has, 1. Franklin W., b. March 9, 1822, lives in Pittsfield, Mass. He m. July 29, 1845, Alice P. Dewey; 2. Mary C., b. March 18, 1825; 3. Delia S., b. Nov. 17, 1828; 4. William E., b. Jan. 1, 1831; 5. Maria E., b. Jan. 16, 1834.

4. *Sabina*, b. Nov. 19, 1800; m. Jan. 10, 1826, Dr. Bela B. Jones of Southampton, Mass., now of Hudson, Mich.: (his 2d wife.) She has had, 1. William, b. Oct. 11, 1826, m. 1st, Catharine Bennett of Mich., who d. July, 1853; m. 2d, Mary Norton of Jordan, N. Y.; 2. Amelia Danforth, b. July 2, 1828, m. Sept. 6, 1852, Rev. George I. Stearns of Windham, Conn. He grad. Amherst Coll., 1849; 3. Henry White, b. Oct. 17, 1830, grad. Amh. Coll., 1857, is a student in E. Windsor Theol. Sem., Conn.; 4. Charles Storrs, b. Jan. 19, 1833, lives in Buffalo, N. Y. He m. Oct., 1856, Susan Hayward of Springfield; 5. Sabina White, b. June 1, 1835, d. Jan. 1, 1844.

5. *John*, b. Sept. 22, 1804; d. at New Haven, Conn., April 19, 1822, æ. 17.

6. *Eliza*, b. Nov. 1, 1807; lives in Blanford.

7. *Samuel*, b. Sept. 8, 1810; d. unm., Aug. 25, 1833, æ. 23.

119. GAD WHITE, son of William, (53) probably lived for several years in Springfield. The following children of Gad and FLAVIA White are recorded there.

1. *Porter Welles*, b. Dec. 6, 1808.
2. *Angeline*, b. July 31, 1811.

---

120. JARIB WHITE, son of Nathaniel, (54) was born in Hadley, Mass., April 27, 1763. He was a farmer in Amherst, and lived about three miles south of the center of the town. He died Feb. 2, 1821, æ. 57.

He married, Feb. 24, 1794, RUTH SHERMAN, dau. of Thomas Sherman of Bridgewater, Mass. She was born July 10, 1763. The time of her death is not ascertained.

CHILDREN.

1. *Jay*, b. June 8, 1795; was a merchant in Amherst, and d. April 1, 1825, æ. 29. He m. June 29, 1823, Caroline Wood of West Brookfield, Mass., who m. 2d, . Rev. D. G. Sprague, now of Orange, N. J. His only child, Caroline Amelia, b. Aug. 30, 1824, m. May 20, 1857, J. H. Denison, of Cincinnati, Ohio.
2. *Orra*, b. March 8, 1796; m. June 1, 1821, Rev. Edward Hitchcock, D. D., LL. D. He was pastor of the Cong. Church in Conway, 1821 to 1825, was a Professor in Amherst College from 1825 to 1845, when he was chosen President of the College. In 1854 he resigned the Presidency, and is now Professor of Natural Theology and Geology. She has had, 1. Edward, b. May 9, 1822, d. March 15, 1824 ; 2. Mary, b. July 13, 1824 ; 3. Catharine, b. March 16, 1826, m. March 9, 1851, Rev. Henry Martyn Storrs, now of Cincinnati, O. He grad. Amh. Coll., 1846; 4. Edward, b. May 23, 1828, grad. Amh. Coll., 1849, m. Nov. 30, 1853, Mary L. Judson of Bridgeport, Conn.; 5. A son, b. March 23, 1832, d. same day; 6. Jane Elizabeth, b. March 6, 1833 ; 7. Charles Henry, b. Aug. 23, 1836, grad. Amh. Coll., 1856 ; 8. Emily, b. Nov. 9, 1838.
3. *Bela*, b. Feb. 23, 1798 ; resides near Omaha City, Nebraska. He m. 1st, Feb. 1, 1832, Julia Ann Stratton; m. 2d, Harriet Hoppin. His son, William Stratton, d. March 7, 1841.
4. *Perez*, b. Aug. 14, 1799 ; d. July 31, 1800.
5. *Mabel*, b. May 8, 1801 ; d. Aug. 16, 1803.
6. *Rebecca*, b. Feb. 13, 1803 ; d. Aug. 19, 1803.
7. *George*, b. July 5, 1806 ; grad. Amh. Coll., 1825, was a physician, and d. unm., in Carlinville, Macoupin Co., Ill., Sept. 1, 1834, æ. 28.

---

121. DANIEL WHITE, son of Capt. Daniel, (55) was born in Hadley, Nov. 6, 1789, and is a farmer there.

He married, Sept. 25, 1816, DORCAS BARROWS, born Sept. 29, 1790, dau. of Eleazer Barrows of Barre, Mass.

CHILDREN.

1. *Sarah Jane*, b. Oct. 2, 1817 ; m. April 22, 1840, Enos Foster Cook of H., now of Amherst. She has had, 1. Henry A., b. Dec. 8, 1840 ; 2. A child, b. Feb. 9, 1844, d. Feb. 19; 3. William E., b. April 18, 1845, d. Aug. 31, 1848; 4. A child, b. March 16, 1847, d. March 18; 5. Martha Jane, b. Jan. 16, 1850, d. Dec. 29, 1856 ; 6. Mary A., b. June 20, 1853, d. Sept. 27 ; 7. William Foster, b. July 1, 1855 ; 8. A child, b. Feb. 18, 1858.
2. *Daniel Sherman*, b. Aug. 25, 1819 ; d. Sept. 20, 1819.
3. *Pamela Wells*, b. March 3, 1824 ; d. Aug. 25, 1832, æ. 8.
4. *George*,   b. Dec.   2, 1825 ; m. Elizabeth S. Judd.   . (252)
5. *Daniel Sherman*, b. Aug. 10, 1827 ; m. Elizabeth W. Powers.   . (253)
6. *Charles*,   b. July   3, 1831 ; is a physician in Chicago, Ill.
7. *John Baker*,   b. Dec.   4, 1833 ; is a druggist in New York.

122. WILLIAM PORTER WHITE, son of Ebenezer, (56) was born in Pittsfield, Mass., Oct. 10, 1769. He graduated at Dartmouth College in 1790, engaged in mercantile pursuits, and settled in Boston. In 1797 he went to England, and thence to India, in October of that year, leaving in London his wife, whose health was insufficient for the voyage, and his infant son. He spent most of his life in foreign countries, and died in Buenos Ayres, South America, in 1842, æ. 72.

He married ELIZABETH ALLEN, dau. of Rev. Thomas Allen of Pittsfield. She was born Feb. 8, 1775, and died in London, Feb. 2, 1798, æ. 23. She was interred in the burying-ground of the "New Chapel." A commemorative discourse, preached by her father, was published.

Their only son,

Allen, b. in London, 1797, baptized there, Sept., 1797, grad. at Dart. College, 1816. After leaving College he joined his father, abroad. He is married, and has been for many years a teacher in Buenos Ayres, S. A.

123. ENOCH WHITE, son of Ebenezer, (56) was born in Pittsfield, March 19, 1775. He lived mostly in that town, but removed to Quincy, Ill., where he died, Feb. 23, 1854, æ. 79.

He married, Jan. 2, 1800, SALLY LANCKTON. She was born June 22, 1779, and died in Quincy, May 1, 1846, æ. 67.

CHILDREN.

1. *Ebenezer*, b. Nov. 2, 1803 ; m. 1st, Cynthia P. Clark ; 2d, S. A. Gage. (254)
2. *Abigail*, b. Aug. 27, 1805 ; d. Feb. 29, 1806.
3. *David*,   b. March 23, 1807 ; graduated at Union College in 1831, and at

Princeton Theol. Seminary in 1835. He devoted himself to the missionary work in West Africa, and reached Cape Palmas, Dec. 25, 1836. He was soon attacked with the acclimating fever, and died Jan. 23, 1837, æ. 28. He m. Oct. 11, 1836, Helen Maria Wells of Newburgh, N. Y., who also died of fever, Jan. 27, 1837. (See Missionary Herald, Sept., 1837, pages 364–368.)

4. *William Henry*, b. Feb. 19, 1809 ; d. Sept. 19, 1811.

5. *James Porter*, b. Jan. 23, 1811 ; m. 1st, Jan. 22, 1832, Lucetia A. Phelps of West Martinsburgh, N. Y., who d. Aug. 25, 1836. He m. 2d, Nov. 4, 1838, Helen Maria Dapine of New York. He d. in N. Y. city, Dec. 14, 1841, æ. 31, leaving one dau., Sarah Jane, who is m. and living in the State of N. Y.

6. *John William Henry*, b. Feb. 25, 1813 ; m. 1st, M. D. Van Hise ; 2d, —— ——. (255)

7. *Sarah Jane*, b. March 27, 1815 ; m. April 7, 1836, Allen Comstock of Lenox, Mass., now of Quincy, Ill. She has had, 1. David White ; 2. Virginia W. ; 3. Henry Allen ; 4. Henry Cooke ; 5. George Allen ; 6. Helen Maria ; 7. Helen Wells ; 8. Frank Russell.

8. *Frederick*, b. July 1, 1817 ; d. April 7, 1818.

9. *Henry Strong*, b. Aug. 17, 1819 ; m. Feb. 27, 1845, Susan Mead of Quincy, Ill. He d. there, Feb. 6, 1846, æ. 26.

10. *William Phillips*, b. June 2, 1822 ; d. Jan. 4, 1823, [1824?]

---

124. COTTON WHITE, son of Lieut. David, (57) was born in Hadley, in 1774. He lived in Hatfield and Hadley, and died in the latter place, May 19, 1826, æ. 52.

He married, 1st, Oct. 9, 1799, DEMIS DICKINSON, who died Dec. 20, 1801.

He married, 2d, Feb. 19, 1807, ELIZABETH BANCROFT of Westfield, Mass., who married for her 2d husband, Dr. Daniel White. (See Fam. 84.) She was born Nov. 8, 1787, and died May 20, 1843, æ. 55.

CHILD ;—BY THE FIRST MARRIAGE.

1. *Sarah*, b. Aug. 20, 1800 ; said to have m. —— Taylor, and died.

CHILDREN ;—BY THE SECOND MARRIAGE.

2. *David*, b. July 5, 1809 ; his history not ascertained.

3. *Elizabeth*, b. April, 1816 ; m. Rev. Mr. McKee of New York.

---

125. JONATHAN WHITE, son of Ebenezer, (58) was born in Hadley, Oct. 29, 1774, and died there, April 13, 1846, æ. 71.

He married, 1st, May 30, 1799, LYDIA ATWOOD, who died about 1811.

He married, 2d, PHEBE RIDER, dau. of Isaac Rider of Middlebury, Mass. She died May 15, 1856, æ. 69.

CHILDREN;—BY THE FIRST MARRIAGE.

1. *Thankful*, b.
2. *Pamela*,   b.   ; m. Charles Warner of H. Has had, Giles, John, Charles, Jonathan, Charlotte D., b. Jan. 31, 1830, d. April 13, 1853, æ. 23; and others.
3. *Sarah*,   b.   .
4. *Ruth*,   b.   ; m. Nov. 22, 1824, Samuel Dunakin, and has several children.
5. *Lydia*,   b.   ; m. John Miller; has John, and others.

CHILDREN;—BY THE SECOND MARRIAGE.

6. *Susan*,   b.   ; m. Nov. 28, 1833, James Wilbur of Hatfield; has a family; one son, Jonathan, d. Oct. 20, 1853, æ. 7 mos.
7. *Olive*,   b.   ; m. —— Stacey, of Davenport, Iowa.
8. *Phebe*,   b.   ; m. 1st, Sept., 1841, Samuel Hager of Enfield, Mass., who d. Nov. 4, 1849; m. 2d, June 25, 1857, Stoddard Meekins of Hadley. By her first husband she had, 1. Edward Augustus, b. June 10, 1842; 2. Eleazer W., b. Sept. 22, 1843, d. Jan. 5, 1846; 3. Mary Isabella, b. Jan. 22, 1848: 4. Justina, b. Jan. 23, 1850.
9. *Jonathan*, b. Dec. 21, 1817; m. 1st, Amanda G. Hodge; 2d, L. Church. (256)
10. *Emeline*, b.   ; m. Levi Ramsdell of Westfield; has a son, Albert.
11. *Elijah*,   b. June 23, 1821; d. July 2, 1821.

---

126. ELIJAH WHITE, son of Ebenezer, (58) was born in Hadley, June 28, 1778. He lived there, and died Nov. 24, 1856, æ. 78.

He married, Dec. 24, 1799, LUCY PIERCE of Hadley, dau. of Josiah Pierce, jun. She was born April 26, 1778, and died Oct. 18, 1855, æ. 77.

CHILDREN.

1. *Josiah*, b. Aug. 1, 1800; m. Hannah Cushing.   .   .   .   .   (257)
2. *Samuel Sumner*, b. May 10, 1803; m. Lucretia A. Rowe.   .   .   .   (258)
3. *Ebenezer*, b. Sept. 11, 1805; m. Mary Ann Coon.   .   .   .   .   (259)
4. *Delia*,   b. Jan. 20, 1808; m. March 28, 1827, Isaac Stall, who d. April, 1841. She lives in Northampton. She has had, 1. Margaret Elizabeth; 2. Fanny Washington; 3. Samuel, d. æ. 20; 4. Mary Ann; 5. June; 6. Ellen; 7. Frederick Elijah; 8. Harriet, d. æ. 3.
5. *Margaret Smith*, b. March 20, 1811; m. April, 1828, Lewis Tower. Has had, 1. Lucy Fairfield, d. 1853, æ. 22; 2. Pamela; 3. Charles; 4. Lewis Clark; 5. Julia, d. æ. 1.

IN THE LINE OF JOHN WHITE, OF HARTFORD.

127. JOHN WHITE, Jun., son of John, (59) was born in Hartford, Conn., about 1753. He lived there, and died Jan. 31, 1827, æ. 73. (Grave-stone.)

He married ANNA WATERS, who died June 10, 1826, æ. 71. (Grave-stone.)

CHILDREN.

1. *John,* b.   ; m. Anna Sarvant.   .   .   . (260)
2. *Anna,* b.   ; m. William Merritt.
3. *Ruth,* b.   ; m. Orrin Smith.
4. *Lucy,* b.   ; m. Charles Weeks.
5. *Laura,* b.   ; m. 1st, Isaac Palmer ; 2d, James McLean.
6. *A child,* b.   ; buried July 27, 1782. (Sexton's record.)
     None of these are living, except Lucy and Charles Weeks, and James McLean. See Note to Family 21.

---

128. NATHANIEL WHITE, son of John, (59) was born in Hartford, and died there in 1827. (Administrator appointed Oct. 19.)

He married SARAH STEELE of Hartford, dau. of Timothy Steele and Sarah Seymour. She is probably "the wife of Nathaniel White," who was buried Nov. 12, 1794, æ. 28. (Sexton's record.)

CHILDREN.

1. *Sarah,* b.   ; m. Horace Meacham of Albany, N. Y., a maker of musical instruments. Both d. She had, 1. Roswell Steele, m. and lives in Albany ; 2. Mary Ann, m. ; 3. Elizabeth, m. ; 4. Martha, m. ; 5. Sarah, m. ; 6. John H., m., is a minister.
2. *Nathaniel,* b.   ; m. Elizabeth Marcellus.   .   .   . (261)
3. *Rufus,* b.   ; was living in Hartford in 1826 ; d. unm.

IN THE LINE OF ENSIGN DANIEL WHITE, OF MIDDLETOWN.

129. AARON WHITE, son of Dea. Jonathan, (60) was born in West Springfield, Mass., Sept. 4, 1747, and was a farmer and miller there. He was chosen a selectman of that town in 1781, and was for ten years the town clerk and treasurer. In 1812 he removed to Camillus, Onondaga Co., N. Y., and died there, Nov. 28, 1833, æ. 86.

He married, Aug. 23, 1785, LUCY KELLOGG of W. S., dau. of Joseph and Martha Kellogg. She was born Jan. 19, 1760, and died March 3, 1848, æ. 88.

CHILDREN.

1. *Lucy,* b. July 22, 1786 ; m. 1808, Walter Hitchcock, a blacksmith, of W. S. They rem. to Onondaga, N. Y., in 1816, and now res. at Cedar Falls, Iowa. She has had, 1. Luther White, b. Dec. 1, 1808, m. and lives in Mo. ; 2. Cornelius, b. Nov. 2, 1810, m ; 3. Samuel, b. Aug. 19, 1813, m., lives at Wil-

17

mington, Ill.; 4. Francis, b. Sept. 26, 1815, m.; 5. Walter, b. April 4, 1818, m., lives at Cedar Falls, Iowa; 6. Eliza Jane, b. May 16, 1820, d.; 7. Aaron Ely, b. Feb. 16, 1823, m; 8. Charles, b. May 5, 1826, lives at Cedar Falls, Iowa; 9. Lucy, b. July 10, 1828, m. Bryan Fisher of Wilmington, Ill.

2. *Samuel Kellogg*, b. May 4, 1789; m. Mary M. Hoffman.   .   .   .   (262)
3. *Aaron*,   b. Aug. 15, 1791; m. Lucretia Hughes.   .   .   .   (263)
4. *Jonathan*,   b. Jan. 6, 1794; m. Mrs. Marietta White.   .   (264)
5. *William Ely*, b. June 22, 1796; m. Emily Seymour.   .   .   .   (265)
6. *Amelia*,   b. Oct. 25, 1799; d. Oct. 23, 1800.
7. *Eliza*,   b. Sept. 14, 1801; m. May 6, 1841, Elkanah C. Austin of Onondaga, N. Y., a farmer. She has, 1. Charles Comstock, b. April 14, 1842; 2. Aaron White, b. March 29, 1845.
8. *Arthur*,   b. Feb. 10, 1804; m. Amanda M. Hollister.   .   (266)

---

130. JOSEPH WHITE, Esq., son of Dea. Jonathan, (60) was born in West Springfield, Dec. 24, [17?] 1749. He settled there as a farmer, and was also a surveyor. He was a soldier in the Revolutionary War, and was for many years a selectman in West Springfield. In 1806 he removed to Camillus, Onondaga Co., N. Y.; was a pioneer in the eastern part of that town, and was for several years a magistrate. In 1816 he received an injury, from the fall of a tree, which deprived him of the use of his limbs. He died Dec. 21, 1830, æ. 81.

He married, 1st, April 3, 1775, SARAH LEONARD of West Springfield, dau. of Dea. John and Ann Leonard. She was born May 8, 1752, (N. S.) and died Nov. 27, 1788, æ. 36.

He married, 2d, Dec. 7, 1791, PHEBE CLAPP of Easthampton. She was born Dec. 26, 1752, and died July 21, 1830, æ. 77.

CHILDREN;—BY THE FIRST MARRIAGE.

1. *Harold*, b. April 18, 1779; d. March 12, 1786.
2. *Amia*, b. Aug. 30, 1780; m. 1st, Oct. 3, [4?] 1798, Selden Leonard of W. S., a farmer. They rem. in 1806 to Camillus, N. Y., where he d. July 27. She m. 2d, 1811, Ebenezer Healy, farmer, of Sennett, Cayuga Co., N. Y., who d. Sept. 22, 1857, æ. 90. She had, by her first husband, 1. Joseph Warren, b. Aug. 5, 1800, res. in Victory, Cayuga Co., N. Y. He m. Feb. 22, 1827, • Lydia Green; 2. Frances, b. June 18, 1804, m. Sept., 1826, Rev. Jireh D. Cole, and d. Oct. 22, 1857, æ. 53. By her 2d husband, 3. George, b. Aug. 19, 1812; he is a civil engineer, and res. at Sennett, N. Y. He m. Oct. 6, 1841, Theodosia Polhemus.
3. *Elijah*, b. March 10, 1782; was a farmer and clothier in Camillus, N. Y., and also a practical surveyor. He d. unm., Aug. 8, 1836, æ. 54.
4. *Tryphena Ely*, b. March 25, 1784; m. Nov. 28, 1813, Frederick Kellogg, a farmer, of Brutus, Cayuga Co., N. Y., and d. Jan. 27, 1816, æ. 31. He d.

Oct. 16, 1832, æ. 66. Her only son, Charles White, b. May 21, 1815, is a merchant in New York. He m. Demmis D. Comstock of Fort Ann, N. Y.

5. *Harold*, b. May 2, 1786; m. Marietta Morley. . . . . (267)

---

131. DANIEL WHITE, son of Jedediah, (61) was born in Upper Middletown, Conn., January, 1764. He served in the army of the Revolution, and was held a prisoner by the British, in New York, at the close of the war. After the war he settled as a farmer in New Durham, Greene Co., N. Y., where his children were born. About the year 1816 he removed to Lenox, Madison Co., N. Y., and died there, April 13, 1837, æ. 73.

He married, Aug., 1793, SALLY MERRIAM of Richmond, Mass. She died Jan. 27, 1856, æ. 84.

CHILDREN.

1. *Ruth*, b. Sept., 1795.
2. *Lucia*, b. April 27, 1797; m. Jan. 14, 1818, William Page of Augusta, Oneida Co., N. Y.
3. *Abraham M.*, b. July, 1800; m. Dolly Gleason. . . . (268)
4. *Daniel*, b. Sept., 1803; m. Ann Hubbard. . . . . (269)
5. *Eli E.*, b. March, 1808; is a farmer in Lenox.

---

132. JOHN WHITE, son of Jedediah, (61) was born in Upper Middletown, Conn., about 1768. He was a farmer in Oneida Co., N. Y. and afterwards in Wayne County. He died Sept. 29, 1827, æ. 59.

He married, Jan. 1, 1805, NANCY ANN LANDON of Oneida Co., dau. of William and Ann Landon. She was born Dec. 6, 1776, and died Dec. 24, 1854, æ. 78.

CHILDREN.

1. *Josiah W.*, b. Dec. 25, 1805; m. Sabra R. Trumbull. . (270)
2. *Nancy B.*, b. Sept. 18, 1807; d. May 20, 1809.
3. *Mary*, b. Oct. 25, 1809; d. July 27, 1811.
4. *John*, b. Dec. 29, 1811; is a merchant in Sodus, Wayne Co., N. Y.; has been post-master, and has held town offices. He m. Feb. 23, 1841, Harriet H. Landon, b. April 17, 1818.
5. *William*, b. Jan. 22, 1815; d. Oct. 4, 1815.
6. *Daniel*, b. Jan. 9, 1817; is a farmer at Allegan, Mich. He m. Oct. 28, 1852, Phebe Parsons.

---

133. JOHN WHITE, son of Nathaniel, (62) was born in Chatham, Conn., March 23, 1748. He settled there as a farmer,

but is said to have "removed to the West," about 1784, and to
have died May 20, 1825, æ. 77.

He married ELIZABETH ———.

CHILDREN.

1. *Amos*, b.   Feb.   7, 1774; bap. Feb. 27, and died next day.
2. *Asahel*, bap. Aug. 20, 1775.
3. *Molly*, bap. Sept. 28, 1777.
4. *Amos*, bap. Oct. 24, 1779.
5. *Lucy*, bap. July 14, 1782. History of these children not ascertained.

---

134. NATHANIEL WHITE, son of Nathaniel, (62) was born
in Chatham, Aug. 14, 1754.   He was living there in 1779,
but is said to have "removed to the West."   The later history
of this family is unknown.

He married, Oct. 19, 1775, ABIGAIL MILLER of Chatham.

CHILDREN.

1. *Elijah*, b. Sept. 16, 1777.
2. *Deborah*, b. Aug. 14, 1779.

---

135. AMOS WHITE, son of Capt. Elijah, (63) was born in
Chatham, Nov. 20, 1745.   He settled in East Haddam, Conn.,
and was engaged in foreign trade.   He died in Meriden,
Conn., Aug. 21, 1825, æ. 79.

He married, April 8, 1767, SARAH GRISWOLD of E. Haddam,
dau. of Caleb Griswold.   She was born May 11, 1749, and
died Feb. 15, 1791, æ. 41.

CHILDREN.

1. *Abigail*, b. Oct. 16, 1769; m. 1st, April 28, 1793, Sylvanus Lindsley, of E.
   Haddam, a druggist. He d. Aug. 14, 1811, and she m. 2d, about May,
   1822, Samuel Tibballs of Meriden, who d. July 14, 1829. She d. in Brooklyn, O., Sept. 19, 1831, æ. 62. She had, by her first husband, 1, George
   White, b. March 5, 1794, rem. to Eastern Tenn. ; 2. Edward Johnson, b.
   Dec. 14, 1796, was a clerk in Tenn., and d. unm., Sept., 1823, æ. 26 ;
   3. Sylvester Brainard, b. Dec. 17, 1798, was a farmer in Brooklyn, O., and
   d. in 1834, æ. 36. He m. 1830, Hannah Andrews of Meriden, Conn., who
   m. 2d, Lester Pasco, of Hartford, Conn., and d. April 7, 1857, æ. 47 ; 4. Abby
   Ann, b. Aug. 2, 1802, m. May 20, 1821, Edwin Foote, a farmer of Brooklyn,
   O., and d. March 21, 1837, æ. 34. He d. Oct. 31, 1853, æ. 54 ; 5. Sarah
   White, b. Dec. 15, 1803, m. July 2, 1829, Diodate Clark, a farmer, of Brooklyn, O., where they now reside.
2. *Amos*,   b. Oct. 13, 1772; m. Hannah White.   .   (271)
3. *William*, b. Aug. 17, 1774; d. July 27, 1775.
4. *Sarah*,   b. May 31, 1776; m. Oct. 4, 1801, Sylvester Pratt, a ship-master, of
   E. Haddam, who d. Dec. 10, 1823, æ. 46. She d. Feb. 20, 1840, æ. 63.

She had, 1. Richard S., b. Oct. 23, 1805, is a merchant and manufacturer in E. H. He m. April 25, 1836, Mary Bulkeley of Chatham ; 2. Sarah White, b. Dec. 11, 1809, m. Aug. 4, 1833, Lester Pasco of E. H., and d. April 30, 1835, æ. 25.

5. *William*, b. Oct. 16, 1778 ; d. July 19, 1783.
6. *George*, b. Feb. 11, 1781 ; d. April 27, 1782.
7. *Elizabeth*, b. May 29, 1784 ; [1783, town rec.] ; m. Sept. 11, 1808, Eleazer Scovil of Meriden, and d. July 24, 1849, æ. 66. She had, 1. Elizabeth White, m. May 9, 1832, Henry T. Wilcox, a grocer, of Meriden ; 2. Frances A., b. May 31, 1811, m. Feb., 1854, Benjamin Radcliff, a farmer, and resides near Circleville, O. ; 3. George W., b. Feb. 11, 1813, m. Mary Burnes of Pittsburgh, Penn. He was lost on the Ohio River, Nov., 1849 ; 4. Lyman E., b. Nov. 30, 1815, is a farmer in Williamsport, O. He m. March, 1847, Rebecca Alkiah ; 5. Jane J., b. June 25, 1817, m. 1836, John F. Towner of Baltimore, Md., a merchant ; 6. A child, b. and d. Jan., 1819 ; 7. Roxanna G., b. Sept. 25, 1821, m. Linus Baldwin of Meriden.
8. *Charles*, b. Aug. 8, 1785 ; was a sea-faring man, and d. unm., Nov. 27, 1824, æ. 39.
9. *George*, b. Sept. 28, 1787 ; is a dry goods merchant in New York.
10. *Sophia*, b. July 16, 1790 ; d. Nov. 23, 1790.

---

136. Col. ELIJAH WHITE, son of Capt. Elijah, (63) was born in East Haddam, Conn., Feb. 28, 1748. He is said to have resided there for a few years, and to have been a sea-captain, his vessel sailing from New Bedford, Mass. He removed to Washington, Berkshire Co., Mass., where he was living in 1778, and thence to Granville, Washington Co., N. Y., and is supposed to have been a merchant there. He died in Granville, Dec., 1804, æ. 56.

He married, May 9, 1767, ELIZABETH ARNOLD. She was born Nov. 15, 1746, and died in Granville, July 31, 1820, æ. 73.

CHILDREN.

1. *Elijah*, b. June 12, 1767 ; m. 1st, Olive Cone ; 2d, Mrs. M. Standish. (272)
2. *Wilson*, b. March 15, 1769 ; d. Oct. 13, 1769.
3. *Wilson*, b. June 30, 1770 ; m. 1st, Rebecca Town ; 2d, Mary Stebbins. (273)
4. *Elizabeth*, b. Aug. 24, 1772 ; m. William Jones, of Sherburne, Chenango Co., N. Y.
5. *Rachel*, b. Jan. 1, 1775 ; perhaps m. ——— Gould.
6. *Clara*, b. April 6, 1777 ; m. Moses Chandler, a farmer, and resided near Warsaw, Wyoming Co. N. Y.
7. *Lydia*, b. March 30, 1780 ; m. April 12, 1798, James Bowen of Hartford, N. Y., a carpenter and farmer. She is now a widow. Her only dau., Lydia, m. Zachariah Sill of Hartford.
8. *Laura*, b. Oct. 13, 1782 ; [1783?] m. Jan. 7, 1802, Amos Palmer, jun., of Granville, and d. Dec. 6, 1850, æ. 68. He d. June 16, 1856, æ. 81. She

had, 1. Clarissa, b. Oct. 11, 1802, d. Feb. 17, 1825, æ. 22 ; 2. Hannah, b. March 16, 1804, m. Nov. 20, 1823, Eli Stone ; 3. Anna Mason, b. Jan. 8, 1806 ; 4. Eliza Delia, b. Jan. 25, 1808, m. Nov. 8, 1829, Dennis Scranton ; 5. Amos, b. Jan. 26, 1810, m. 1st, Sept. 9, 1835, Lydia Felch ; m. 2d, July 27, 1837, Ruth Barker ; 6. Abijah, b. Oct. 3, 1812, m. 1st, Dec. 3, 1843, Charlotte L. Sterling ; m. 2d, March 23, 1848, Laura Emily Briggs ; 7. Nathan, b. Dec. 14, 1814, m. Nov. 22, 1837, Amelia Canda; 8. Henry Wolcott, b. Dec. 11, 1816, m. 1st, Lorain Bartlett ; m. 2d, March 20, 1856, Sally Ann Sweet; 9. Mary White, b. March 3, 1819, m. May 24, 1838, Milo Dibble ; 10. William Edwin, b. Dec. 31, 1820, lives in Cleveland, O. ; 11. Charles White, b. Feb. 2, 1823, lives in Cleveland, O. He m. June, 1850, Martha Otis ; 12. Sarah Jane Smith, b. June 14, 1825, m. May, 1849, Daniel Wooden.

9. *Alfred*, b. July   16, 1785 ; m. Huldah Symonds, and had several children.
10. *Sophia*, b. July   11, 1787 ; m. Abner Mitchel, and lived in Penn.
11. *Charles*, b. March 17, 1791 ; m. Sarah L. Johnson.   .   .   .   (274)

---

137. DANIEL HURLBURT WHITE, son of Capt. Elijah, (63) was born in East Haddam, July 16, 1757. He removed to Granville, Washington Co., N. Y., about 1788, and died there, Feb. 24, 1805, æ. 47. He was a silversmith.

He married, Aug. 31, 1780, HANNAH BRAINARD of East Haddam, dau. of Daniel Brainard and Esther Gates. She was born Aug. 25, 1761, and died at Brutus, N. Y., May 3, 1826, æ. 64.

CHILDREN.

1. *Gideon Brainard*, b. Feb. 2, 1781 ; d. Oct. 6, 1795, æ. 14. (This family is recorded at East Haddam. The eldest child was born in Guilford, Conn.; the five youngest in Granville, N. Y.)
2. *William*,   b. Oct. 11, 1783 ; m. Electa Everts.   .   .   .   .   (275)
3. *Hope Lord*, b. Aug. 10, 1786 ; m. 1st, Oct. 12, 1806, John Walker, who d. in Auburn, N. Y., about 1815 ; m. 2d, 1817, Aaron B. Sheldon, a farmer, who d. Feb., 1826 ; m. 3d, 1836, David Thomas, a farmer of Skaneateles, N. Y., where they now reside.
4. *Coral Case*, b. Feb. 25, 1789 ; m. Esther B. Johnson.   .   .   (276)
5. *Fanny*,   b. Sept. 24, 1790 ; d. Jan. 4, 1796.
6. *Jeremiah Gates Brainard*, b. Dec. 22, 1795 ; m. Lois A. Richardson.   (277)
7. *Fanny Fidelia*, b. May 27, 1798 ; m. Nov. 11, 1823, John Olmsted of Auburn, N. Y., a cabinet-maker. She d. without issue, Dec. 8, 1842, æ. 44.
8. *Hannah Adelia*, b. June 24, 1801 ; m. March 27, 1826, David Bonta, now of Syracuse, N. Y. She d. Aug. 17, 1842, æ. 41, having had, 1. Derrick Hurlburt, b. Jan. 21, 1827 ; 2. F. Fidelia, b. July 24, 1829 ; 3. John Olmsted, b. Aug. 15, 1831 ; 4. Hope Ann, b. June 15, 1833 ; 5. Catharine T., b. Aug. 27, 1835 ; 6. Margaret M., b. Dec. 1, 1839 ; 7. Mary S., b. Jan. 16, 1841.

138. NOADIAH WHITE, Jun., son of Capt. Noadiah, (64) was born in Chatham, Conn., Dec. 18, 1745. He was a farmer there, but in 1805 removed to Hartford, Vt., where he lived with his eldest son. He died in 1816, æ. 71.

He married, Jan. 30, 1772, MERCY MAYO of Chatham. She was born April 27, 1742, and died in 1816, æ. 74.

CHILDREN.

1. *Noadiah,* b. Oct. 22, 1772; d. Dec. 16, 1776.
2. *Eunice,* b. April 2, 1775; lived with her brother Amos, and d. unm., Feb., 1814, æ. 38.
3. *Noadiah,* bap. June 8, 1777; m. Wealthy Hazen. . . . (278)
4. *Rebecca,* bap. July 11, 1779; m. Oct. 5, 1804, Joseph Wells of Chatham, and d. July 31, 1814, æ. 35. He d. April 18, 1823. She had, 1. Eunice, b. Aug. 7, 1805; 2. Thomas, b. June 16, 1807, rem. to Ohio; 3. Hannah, b. Sept. 23, 1809, m. Philip H. Sellew.
5. *Richard,* b. Jan. 8, 1782; is unm., and lives in Ontario, Wayne Co., N. Y.
6. *Amos,* b. June 3, 1785; m. Sally White. . . . . . (279)

---

139. JOSEPH WHITE, son of Capt. Noadiah, (64) was born in Chatham, March 29, 1752. (N. S.) He was a farmer in that town, but removed to Middlefield, Otsego Co., N. Y., where he died, July 31, 1835, æ. 83. His children were all born in Chatham.

He married, March 29, 1791, HANNAH GATES of East Haddam, dau. of Timothy Gates and Hannah Percival. She was born March 29, 1762, and died April 25, 1835, æ. 73.

CHILDREN.

1. *Gustavus,* b. April 25, 1792; d. unm., at Middlefield, June 25, 1853, æ. 61.
2. *Laura,* b. May 30, 1794; m. March 16, 1815, James J. Rice, who d. at Salina, N. Y., April 2, 1838, æ. 46. She d. Dec. 20, 1853, æ. 59. She had, 1. Emily, b. June 19, 1816, d. Feb. 19, 1839, æ. 22; 2. Augusta, b. Feb. 25, 1819, d. July 11, 1837, æ. 18; 3. Juliet, b. April 28, 1821, d. April 28, 1838, æ. 17; 4. A son, d. in infancy; 5. De Witt C., b. May 5, 1823, is a physician in Marysville, Cal. He m. March 23, 1854, Lydia C. Mitchell; 6. Celestia, b. Nov. 16, 1825, d. Jan. 3, 1826; 7. Charlotte F., b. Dec. 30, 1826, m. Aug. 18, 1852, Mark Brummagim, a banker in San Francisco, Cal.; 8. Euclid E., b. Dec. 6, 1829, a druggist in Marysville, Cal.; 9. Cynthia A., b. March 15, 1832, m. April 26, 1857, Charles Wood of Marysville; 10. Joseph G., b. Aug. 15, 1835, resides in Middlefield, N. Y.; is a civil engineer.
3. *Caroline,* b. March 10, 1796; m. Feb. 15, 1820, Ebenezer S. Rice of Salina, N. Y., who d. June, 1845. She resides in S. She has had, 1. Maria Gates, b. May 13, 1821, d. Nov. 17, 1839, æ. 18; 2. Edwin White, b. Sept. 5, 1822, d. March, 1849, æ. 26; 3. Lucien Percival, b. Sept. 30, 1824, a machinist at

Adrian, Mich. ; 4. Evelin Hart, b. Nov. 10, 1826, d. Sept. 1, 1828 ; 5. Oth-
man Sawyer, b. Jan. 20, 1829, d. Dec. 16, 1838 ; 6. Oscar Derobayne, b.
April 7, 1831, d. 1855, æ. 24 ; 7. Franklin Elliot, b. Jan. 13, 1841.
4. *Statira*, b. March 25, 1798 ; lives in Middlefield.
5. *Joseph*, b. May 9, 1800 ; m. Marietta Roseboom.   (280)
6. *Hannah Esther*, b. March 10, 1803 ; lives in Middlefield.

---

140. ABIJAH WHITE, son of Capt. Noadiah, (64) was born
in Chatham, Jan. 18, 1763. He removed to the State of
N. Y., and died in Canajoharie, Jan. 24, 1842, æ. 79.

He married, Feb. 1, 1789, HANNAH HALL of Chatham.
She was born Feb. 1, 1769, and died March 6, 1841, æ. 72.

CHILDREN.

1. *Lester*, b. Dec. 12, 1789 ; d. Oct. 2, 1790.
2. *Sally*, b. July 11, 1791 ; m. Amos White.   (Family 279)
3. *Polly*, b. Nov. 10, 1793 ; m. Bushnel Hibbard of Canajoharie, a merchant, who
    d. June, 1830. She has had several children, of whom Charles and Rufus
    reside in Canajoharie, and have families.
4. *Augustus*, b. May 4, 1796 ; d. Nov. 3, 1796.
5. *Abijah L.*, b. Aug. 25, 1797 ; m. Sally Jones.   (281)
6. *Nancy*,   b. Aug. 25, 1800 ; m. James Durham, for some years a clerk in one
    of the Departments at Washington, D. C. She d. in W., July, 1851, leav-
    ing a family.
7. *Lucinda*,   b. March 27, 1802 ; m. George Geortner, a farmer, of Canajoharie.
    She has five daughters, and one son, now living.
8. *Amos H.*, b. Aug. 24, 1804 ; m. Jane Ann Paff.   (282)
9. *Laura*,   b. March 1, 1807 ; m. Willard R. Wheeler, merchant, who d. May
    18, 1844, æ. 43. She resides at Ames Village, Canajoharie.
10. *Jane Ann*, b. March 12, 1810 ; m. Clinton Wetmore. They rem. to Missouri,
    where she d. May 2, 1844, æ. 34.

---

141. SAMUEL WHITE, son of Capt. Noadiah, (64) was born
in Chatham, Conn., Feb. 11, 1767. He was living in Thetford, Vt., at the time of his marriage, but after a few years
removed to N. Y., and died in Georgetown, Madison Co., May
10, 1843, æ. 76.

He married, Jan. 21, 1798, CYNTHIA ALLIS of Somers,
Conn., dau. of Samuel Allis and Olive Makepeace. She was
born April 27, 1773, and died Aug. 27, 1849, æ. 76.

CHILDREN.

1. *Backus*, b. Dec. 17, 1798 ; m. Ann Maria Powers.   (283)
2. *Marinda*, b. Jan. 9, 1801 ; m. Jan. 4, 1827, Edward Smith, a farmer, of De
    Ruyter, Madison Co., and has had, 1. Charles W., b. Sept. 20, 1827 ; 2. Ze-
    lotes A., b. May 20, 1829, d. Aug. 24, 1830 ; 3. Henry C., b. Oct. 6, 1831,
    d. Sept. 17, 1832 ; 4. Samuel E., b. May 25, 1836.

3. *Cynthia*, b. July 25, 1803 ; m. Jan. 20, 1822, Dwight Gardner of De Ruyter, a
farmer. She has, 1. Lucinda, b. Feb. 5, 1823, m. Jan. 13, 1842, Wilson
Lamb ; 2. Harriet, b. April 1, 1825, m. Sept. 15, 1857, Henry P. Hart;
3. Susan, b. Aug. 17, 1827, m. Jan. 27, 1859, John H. Fuller ; 4. Marinda,
b. Feb. 19, 1830, m. March 8, 1849, Warren I. Alvord ; 5. Esther, b. Dec.
15, 1832, m. July 7, 1857, Mason M. Marsh ; 6. Cynthia Alice, b. April 20,
1835 ; 7. Dwight F., b. March 5, 1838 ; 8. Austin A., b. April 17, 1841.
4. *Austin A.*, b. July 19, 1805 ; m. Polly M. Powers.   .   .   .   (284)

---

142. DAVID WHITE, Esq., son of Hon. Ebenezer, (65) was
born in Chatham, Conn., Sept. 7, 1754. He inherited a part
of his father's homestead, and settled there as a farmer, in the
present town of Portland. In connection with his brother Daniel, he also carried on the business of ship-building, for several
years. He was a justice of the peace. He died Sept. 18, 1833,
æ. 79.

He married, 1st, Dec. 29, 1774, MARY ANN STOCKING of
Upper Middletown. She died Dec. 4, 1797, æ. 45.

He married, 2d, Oct. 15, 1798, Mrs. MARY PRIOR, widow of
Allen Prior of Windsor, and dau. of Dr. Joseph Wells, of Berlin, and of Mary Hart. She died Dec. 15, 1838, æ. 79.

CHILDREN ;—BY THE FIRST MARRIAGE.

1. *Sally*, b. Nov. 24, 1777 ; m. Feb. 14, 1802, Edmund Ward, master-carpenter
for her father. They settled in Fairfield, Herkimer Co., N. Y., where he
was a farmer. He d. Jan. 12, 1824, æ. 62. She d. Dec. 18, 1824, æ. 47.
She had, 1. Henrietta, b. Sept. 3, 1802, m. March 10, 1828, Ebenezer Butler
White: (Fam. 287 ;) 2. Sally Gould, b. Dec. 24, 1804, m. Alden B. Cooper
of Fairfield, N. Y. She d. in Portland, Conn., Oct. 29, 1849, æ. 45 ; 3. Sidney David, b. July 28, 1807, m. Feb. 24, 1830, Nancy Mariette Priest of
Fairfield ; 4. William Edmund, b. Oct. 11, 1810, d. Aug. 13, 1831, æ. 21 ;
5. Mortimer, b. Jan. 6, 1812, rem. to Texas.
2. *David*, b. July 9, 1779 ; m. Abigail Ames.   .   .   .   .   (285)
3. *Anna*, b. Sept. 18, 1781 ; m. June 21, 1801, Silas Shepard of Herkimer, N. Y.
She has had, 1. Lucy, m. —— Hyzer of Steuben, N. Y.; 2. Ralph W.,
lives in Freedom, Ohio. He m. 1st, Mary Shepard of Chatham, Conn. ;
m. 2d, Julia A——; 3. Sally, m. John Hartman of Herkimer, and d. ;
4. Charles, is a physician at Grand Rapids, Mich. He m. —— Doolittle
of Herkimer ; 5. David Daniel, m. and d.

CHILDREN ;—BY THE SECOND MARRIAGE.

4. *Mary Ann*, b. July 27, 1799 ; d. Nov. 6, 1810, æ. 11.
5. *James Wells*, b. April 27, 1802 ; m. 1st, Fanny Hall ; 2d, M. B. Lewis. (286)

---

143. Col. DANIEL WHITE, son of Hon. Ebenezer, (65) was
born in Chatham, Oct. 24, 1765. He was a farmer there, on

18

the homestead of his father and grandfather. In 1814 he served, for a few months, with the rank of Major, in the defence of New London, Conn. He was a selectman of Chatham, and held other town offices. Individual trusts were also frequently committed to his charge. He died Dec. 25, 1845, æ. 80.

He married, Jan. 24, 1791, ABIGAIL HILLS of East Hartford, dau. of Jonathan Hills and Mabel Stanley. She was born July 23, 1772, and died Feb. 22, 1838, æ. 65.

He had one son,

Ebenezer Butler, b. Nov. 15, 1804; m. Henrietta Ward.   (287)

---

144. JOSIAH WHITE, son of Lieut. Stephen, (66) was born in Chatham, Sept. 5, 1761. He settled there as a farmer, but for a few years. previous to 1812, lived in other places, being engaged in merchandizing. In 1812 he removed to Verona, Oneida Co., N. Y., and in 1825 to Floyd, in the same county. While there, he held the offices of post-master and sheriff. He returned to Verona, where he died, Sept. 17, 1831, æ. 70.

He married, 1st, April 25, 1780, HANNAH HILLS of Glastenbury, Conn., dau of Samuel and Eunice Hills. She was born Jan. 7, 1762, and died Sept. 5, [21?] 1792, æ. 30.

He married, 2d, 1795, REBECCA HILLS of East Hartford, Conn., dau. of Jonathan Hills and Mabel Stanley. She was born Nov. 16, 1766.

He married, 3d, Feb. 13, 1809, ELISABETH PORTER of East Hartford, born Jan. 1, 1786, dau. of Job and Margaret Porter. She now resides in Selma, Ala.

CHILDREN;—BY THE FIRST MARRIAGE.

1. *Stephen*, b.   1781; d. Aug. 23, 1781.
2. *Stephen*, b. Feb. 22, 1783; m. Mary Lavinia Cossitt. .   .   . (288)
3. *Henry*, b. Aug. 11, 1785; grad. at Williams College in 1812, and was a teacher, in Utica, N. Y., 1813–1816. He then went to the South for the benefit of his health, and spent most of his subsequent life in Alabama and the adjoining States. His health not permitting him to settle in the ministry, he labored chiefly with destitute churches in those States, and sometimes as a missionary among the Cherokee Indians, preaching to them through an interpreter. He was a part of the time engaged in teaching, and for a few years previous to his death "employed his unwearied exertions in establishing and endowing a Female Seminary at Claiborne, Ala., which he had the satisfaction to see in full and successful operation." He d. unm., March 13, 1829, æ. 43.
4. *William Czar*, b. Nov. 25, 1787; m. Betsey House.   .   . (289)

5. *Eveline,* b. Sept. 1, 1789; m. 1st, April, 1813, Benjamin B. Smith of Glastenbury, Conn., a cabinet-maker. They rem. to Verona, N. Y. She m. 2d, Jan. 27, 1825, Hibbard Pride, a farmer, of Busti, Chautauque Co., N. Y., where they now reside. She has, by her first husband, 1. William Henry, b. June 1, 1815, lives in Elk, Saginaw Co, Mich. He m. Jan. 5, 1837, Financy Markress, who d. Sept. 22, 1855, æ. 38; 2. Elmina Fidelia, b. April 13, 1817, m. June 20, 1842, Cyrus Spicer, now of Busti.

CHILD;—BY THE SECOND MARRIAGE.

6. *Walter,* b. Nov. 20, 1795; d. unm., Feb. 11, 1821, æ. 25.

CHILDREN;—BY THE THIRD MARRIAGE.

7. *Harriet Porter,* b. Jan. 18, 1810; m. July 1, 1829, Edwin Fay, Esq. (See in Fam. 35.) He grad. at Harvard College in 1817, is a lawyer by profession, but has spent most of his life in teaching. He is now a planter at Rocky Mount, Autauga Co., Ala. She has had, 1. Harriet Eleutheria, b. June 9, 1830, d. Aug. 31, 1831; 2. Edwin Hedge, b. March 17, 1732, grad. Harv. Coll., 1852, and is a teacher in La.; 3. Sarah Elisabeth White, b. Feb. 6, 1835, m. Samuel P. Stoddard of Selma; 4. Eleutheria Olivia, b. Jan. 15, 1838, d. Aug. 6, 1857, æ. 19; 5. William Henry, b. March 1, 1841; 6. Josiah Dunham, b. Nov. 1, 1844.

8. *Olivia Hubbard,* b. May 6, 1812; m. 1st, March 17, 1831, Edmund Olmsted, a farmer, of Floyd, N. Y., who d. Jan. 5, 1832; m. 2d, Dec. 21, 1842, Rev. James M. McKee, a Presbyterian clergyman, now of Orion, Pike Co., Ala. She has had, by her second husband, 1. Edwin Leroy, b. Nov. 3, 1843; 2. Harvey Lloyd, b. March 10, 1846; 3. Caroline Louisa, b. Dec. 13, 1848; 4. John McPherson, b. March 5, 1851; 5. William Henry, b. June 18, 1853, d. in infancy.

9. *Elisabeth Adeline,* b. Nov. 27, 1814; m. Oct. 31, 1839, Amos H. Lloyd of Selma, Ala., a merchant tailor.

10. *Caroline Amanda,* b. April 1, 1821; was a music-teacher, and d. unm., Aug. 30, 1845, æ. 24.

---

145. GEORGE WHITE, Esq., son of Lieut. Stephen, (66) was born in Chatham, Sept. 18, 1763. He was a farmer there; was a justice of the peace, and a representative from that town, in the Legislature, in 1821. He died June 1, 1848, æ. 84.

He married, 1st, MABEL HILLS of East Hartford, dau. of Jonathan Hills and Mabel Stanley. She was born Nov. 16, 1766, and died Dec. 6, 1817, æ. 51.

He married, 2d, 1818, HANNAH T. STARR of Middletown. She resides in Portland.

CHILDREN;—BY THE SECOND MARRIAGE.

1. *George J.,* b. May 20, 1819; m. Esther Myrick. . . . (290)
2. *Stephen H.,* b. Dec. 15, 1820; m. 1st, Sarah Risley; 2d, A. W. Ufford. (291)
3. *Esther,* b. Jan. 13, 1823; d. Jan. 15, 1823.
4. *William S.,* b. Mar. 26, 1824; m. Emily Strickland. . . (292)
5. *Hannah E.,* b. Aug. 20, 1826.
6. *Elizabeth,* b. Nov., 1829.

146. TIMOTHY WHITE, son of Timothy, (67) was probably born in East Haddam, Conn., about 1754. He was a blacksmith, and was living in Hartford in 1776, but resided chiefly in Upper Middletown, where he died, April 27, 1824, æ. 70.

He married, 1st, Aug. 20, 1778, MEHITABLE SMITH, of Haddam, dau. of Abner Smith. She died Sept. 1, 1794, æ. 38.

He married, 2d, URSULA SLOPER of Southington, Conn. She died many years since.

CHILDREN;—BY THE FIRST MARRIAGE.

1. *Samuel,* b. March 10, 1780; m. 1st, Elizabeth Smith; 2d, Mrs. C. Hill. (293)
2. *Sally,* b. Feb. 4, 1782; m. Oct. 25, [26?] 1800, John McIntyre of Hartford, and d. July 13, 1849, æ. 67. He d. Aug. 20, 1859, æ. 80. She had, 1. Mary, b. March 26, 1802, m. John Church; 2. Adaline, b. Jan. 27, 1803, m. James Lovett; 3. Sarah, b. March 19, 1805, m. June 21, 1826, Charles Loomis of Petersburg, Va.; 4. Julia Ann, b. Sept., 1807; 5. Rebecca, b. Aug. 22, 1808; 6. Katharine, b. Feb. 21, 1811, m. David Stebbins of New York, and d. Nov., 1848, æ. 37; 7. Harriet, b. Feb. 27, 1814, m. Wiley Jackson of Richmond, Va.; 8. Fanny, b. April 7, 1816; 9. Clarissa, b. July 4, 1818; 10. John Sanford, b. Aug. 22, 1822, res. in Hartford. He m. March 5, 1854, Harriet Colton; 11. George Henry, b. July 29, 1824; 12. James Lovett, b. April 30, 1825, d. Nov. 11, 1831.
3. *Mehitable,* b. Sept. 10, 1784; m. Asa White.   . . (Family 181)
4. *Susanna,* b. Dec. 8, 1786; d. March 8, 1787.
5. *Timothy,* b. Dec. 26, 1787; m. Roxy Sage.   . . . (294)
6. *Heman,* b. Nov. 19, 1789; d. at the Island of St. Bartholomew, W. I., Oct. 25, 1809, æ. nearly 20.
7. *Luther,* b. April 2, 1792; d. Oct. 15, [14?] 1803, æ. 11.
8. *Benjamin,* b. Aug. 9, 1794; m. Sally Cook.   . . (295)

CHILD;—BY THE SECOND MARRIAGE.

9. *Orville,* b. May 4, 1797; d. Nov. 17, 1797.

---

147. SAMUEL WHITE, son of Aaron, (68) was born July 3, 1762. He removed from Upper Middletown, Conn., to Oneida Co., N. Y., and lived in Holland Patent, in the town of Trenton, where he died, March, 1833, æ. 70.

He married, Oct. 3, 1787, ANNA MERROW of East Hartford, Conn., dau. of Elisha Merrow. She was born Nov. 19, 1764, and died Feb. 2, 1851, æ. 86.

CHILDREN.

1. *Aaron,* b. Nov. 2, 1788; m. Rhoda Bagg.   . . . . (296)
2. *Nancy,* b. Dec. 18, 1789; m. Samuel Guiteau, who is dead. She has three children, and resides in Trenton.
3. *Elizabeth,* b. Nov. 25, 1791; m. Dr. David Perry.

4. *Walter*, b. July 5, 1793; d. in Schoolcraft, Mich., unm., Oct. 17, 1846, æ. 53.

5. *Sophia*, b. Mar. 22, 1795; d. unm., Mar. 9, 1842, æ. 47.

6. *Laura*, b. Mar. 15, 1797; m. Daniel Buck, who is dead. She has five children; the family are in Ohio.

---

148. Col. DANIEL CLARK WHITE, son of Hon. Hugh, (69) was born in Upper Middletown, Conn., March 2, 1759. He accompanied his father to Whitestown, N. Y., upon its first settlement, and was a brewer and inn-keeper there. He died June 4, 1800, æ. 41.

He married ESTHER PAINE of Middletown, dau. of Moses and Esther Paine. She was born May 27, 1760, and died Feb. 19, 1839, æ. 78.

CHILDREN.

1. *Andrew*, b. about 1782; d. unm., May 6, 1838, æ. about 56.

2. *Esther*, b. March 15, 1785. She was the first white child born in Whitestown. She m. Sept. 21, 1810, Hon. Henry Randolph Storrs. He grad. Yale Coll., 1804, and became an eminent lawyer; was first Judge of Oneida Co. Court, and a Member of Congress from 1817 to 1821, and 1823 to 1831. He d. July 29, 1837, æ. 49. Mrs. Storrs now res. in Gardiner, Me. She has had, 1. Henry Lemuel, b. July 1, 1811, was an Episcopal clergyman, and d. at Yonkers, N. Y., May 16, 1852, æ. 41; 2. Fortune Kingsley, b. Feb. 15, 1813, d. unm., at San Francisco, Cal., Dec. 12, 1853, æ. 40; 3. Eliza, b. Oct. 21, 1814, d. Aug. 28, 1837, æ. 22; 4. William Champion, b. Sept. 5, 1816, is a lawyer in Rochester, N. Y.; 5. Peyton Randolph, b. April 17, 1818, d. at Milwaukee, Wis., June 13, 1855, æ. 37.

3. *Fortune Clark*, b. July 10, 1787; m. Experience Patten. (297)

---

149. JOSEPH WHITE, son of Hon. Hugh, (69) was born at Upper Middletown, Conn., Jan. 16, 1761. He was one of the company that first settled Whitestown, N. Y., and was a farmer there. He died June 17, 1827, æ. 66.

He married, 1st, April 4, 1782, LUCY BULKLEY of Wethersfield, Conn., dau. of Benjamin Bulkley. She died Nov. 20, 1810, æ. 59.

He married, 2d, Mrs. SYBIL WILLIS, who died in 1832.

CHILDREN;—BY THE FIRST MARRIAGE.

1. *Susan*, b. Feb. 6, 1783; was the child taken home by the Indian Chief; (see p. 87.) She m. Nathaniel Eells of Whitestown, who d. about 1825. She d. 1850, æ. 67. She had a son Calvin.

2. *Lucy*, b. July 22, 1784; m. 1st, 1805, Ornan Clark of Farmington, Conn., a

farmer, who d. Feb. 14, 1815, æ. 38. She m. 2d, May, 1816, Jesse Stanley
of New Britain, Conn., a farmer, who d. Aug. 19, 1827, æ. 48. She is living
in Farmington. She had, by her first husband, 1. Henry White, b. Feb.,
1807, m. 1832, Emily Stanley, and res. in Cleveland, O.; 2. Sarah, b. July
19, 1809, m. Feb. 3, 1831, Oren Stanley North.of New Britain; 3. Mervin,
b. 1812, m. Caroline Guptill, and d. June 27, 1854, æ. 42. By her second
husband, 4. A son, b. March 20, 1818, d. in infancy; 5. Almira, twin with
the last, m. June 15, 1843, George S. Coe of Brooklyn, N. Y., cashier of the
Am. Exchange Bank, New York; 6. Margaret, b. Nov. 26, 1820, m. Dec.
31, 1844, John E. Cowles of Farmington; 7. Oliver Cromwell, b. Feb. 23,
1823, m. Oct. 13, 1847, Charlotte Hine of New Milford, Conn., and res. in
New Britain.

3. *Huldah*, b. April 19, 1786; d. in infancy.
4. *Henry*, b. Feb. 8, 1788; m. Julia Bidwell. .   .   .   (298)
5. *Abigail*, b. Aug. 26, 1789; m. Samuel Wilcox, a farmer in Whitestown, and
   has had, 1. Julia Ann, b. Sept. 21, 1814; 2. Lucy Bulkley, b. Dec. 9, 1816;
   3. George Chauncey, b. Dec. 29, 1818; 4. Susan Eells, b. March 5, 1823;
   5. Henry White, b. Feb. 14, 1826; 6. Edward Lindsley, b. Nov. 6, 1829;
   7. Samuel, b. Sept. 6, 1832.
6. *Bulkley*, b. March 10, 1791; d. in infancy.
7. *Bulkley*, b. May 2, 1793; d. in infancy.
8. *Joseph*, b. Dec. 10, 1794; m. —— ——.   .   .   .   .   (299)
9. *Thomas Bulkley*, b. Feb. 3, 1797; m. and had a family. He lived in Mich.
   for a few years. He was a soldier in the Mexican war, and d. in Texas, or
   Mexico, about 1850.
10. *Eliza*, b. Nov. 7, 1798; m. Reuben Wilcox of Whitestown, had four chil-
    dren, and d. about 1825.
11. *Mary*, b.   1800; m. Henry Cooley of Auburn, N. Y., and d. with-
    out issue, in 1836.

---

150. HUGH WHITE, Jun., son of Hon. Hugh, (69) was born
at Upper Middletown, Conn., Jan. 16, 1763. He was for
three years a soldier in the Revolutionary Army, and was for
a while on board of a privateer. He went with his father to
Whitestown, N. Y., and was a farmer there. A few years
previous to his death, he removed to Shrewsbury, N. J., where
he died, April 7, 1827, æ. 64.

He married, 1st, about 1787, TRYPHENA LAWRENCE of Canaan, Conn., dau. of Jonas Lawrence and Tryphena Lawrence.
She was born July 4, 1768, and died March 30, 1800, æ. 31.

He married, 2d, March 5, 1801, SUSAN SMITH of Whitestown, who died July 21, 1805.

CHILDREN;—BY THE FIRST MARRIAGE.

1. *Robert*, b. Nov. 27, 1788. He lived many years in preferred retirement, in Missouri, and died at a time and place unknown, leaving, it is said, six children.
2. *Canvass*, b. Sept. 8, 1790; m. Louisa Loomis.   .   .   .   (300)

3. *Charlotte*, b. Oct. 15, 1792; m. Esek Walcott, and rem. to Walnut Hills, Miss., where she d. Jan., 1831, æ. 38. He d. about 1837. She had, 1. Charlotte; 2. Edward, d.; 3. Ann; 4. Louisa.

4. *Tryphena*, b. Sept. 30, 1794; d. Feb. 10, 1801, æ. 6.

5. *Sophia*, b. Jan. 6, 1796; m. 1816, John Duston, now of Kingston, Mo. She has Anna Maria, and other children.

6. *Hugh*, b. Dec. 25, 1798; m. Maria M. Mansfield. . (301)

CHILD ;—BY THE SECOND MARRIAGE.

7. *Susan*, b. July 17, 1802; m. 1820, Joseph S. Porter of Utica, now of Alleghany, N. Y.

---

151. ANSEL WHITE, son of Hon. Hugh, (69) was born at Upper Middletown, Conn., Jan. 11, 1765. He accompanied his father to Whitestown, N. Y., and settled there as a farmer. He died Feb. 21, 1858, æ. 93.

He married, about Jan., 1791, ANNA ROOT. She was born July 7, 1770, and died Nov. 2, 1854, æ. 84.

CHILDREN.

1. *Ebenezer*, b. Jan. 7, 1792; d. unm., Oct. 18, 1851, æ. 59.

2. *Lavinia*, b. Sept. 15, 1793; m. Nov. 4, 1816, Nathan S. Roberts, a civil engineer, and resided in Canastota, Madison Co., N. Y. He d. about Nov., 1850. She d. about April 15, 1858, æ. 64. She had, 1. DeWitt Clinton, b. July 28, 1817, res. in Canastota. He m. 1st, Sept. 14, 1842, Caroline Cummins, who d. He m. 2d, May 25, 1847, Helen Ward; 2. Mary Jane, b. Dec. 7, 1819, m. July 2, 1839, S. Spencer, Esq., and d. April 14, 1840, æ. 20; 3. Albert Backus, b. March 20, 1822; 4. Lavinia Catherine, b. Feb. 26, 1825, m. Aug. 16, 1847, Addison G. Williams, now of Buffalo, a civil engineer; 5. Frances Josephine, b. June 27, 1827, m. June 27, 1849, William B. Fisk of Syracuse; 6. Nathan Smith, b. Feb. 3, 1833.

3. *Aurelia*, b. April 16, 1795; m. —— Graves, and d. about April, 1828, æ. 33.

4. *Fanny*, b. Feb. 19, 1797; m. 1st, —— Sprague; m. 2d, John Robinson of Whitestown. She had, by her first husband, 1. Lydia Ann, m. Fay Hutchins, of Chittenango, N. Y.: by her second husband, 2. Catherine.

5. *Halsey*, b. June 26, 1800; is a farmer in Tully, Mo.

6. *Sally*, b. Sept. 21, 1802; d. unm., Nov. 4, 1852, æ. 50.

7. *Catherine*, b. Sept. 11, 1807; m. June 16, 1832, John Crouse, a merchant in Syracuse, N. Y., and has, 1. John J., b. Aug. 16, 1834 ; 2. D. Edgar, b. June 11, 1843.

8. *Ansel*, b. June 19, 1808; went to the West.

9. *John*, b. July 17, 1810; went to Missouri.

10. *Lydia Ann*, b. Aug. 5, 1812; d. Aug. 15, 1814.

---

152. PHILO WHITE, son of Hon. Hugh, (69) was born at Upper Middletown, Conn., June 25, 1767. He was a farmer in Whitestown, N. Y., and was also at one time engaged in

merchandizing, at that place and at Tioga Point. He died
April 12, 1849, æ. 82.

He married, 1788, ESTHER HOLT of Whitestown, dau. of
Isaac Holt. She died February, 1841, æ. 75.

CHILDREN.

1. *Jonas,* b. Sept. 10, 1789; m. Mary Lewis.   (302)
2. *Charlotte,* b.   1791; d. 1793.
3. *Harriet,* b. Sept. 6, 1792; m. 1st, Nov., 1811, Lewis J. Dauby of Whitestown,
   who d. 1817.   She m. 2d, March 31, 1822, James Goodrich of W.   She has
   had, by her first husband, 1. Helen, b. Nov. 14, 1812, d. Oct. 7, 1813; 2. Helen,
   b. Dec. 8, 1816, m. July 9, 1840, S. Wright Crittenden of Rochester, N. Y.,
   and d. Aug. 17, 1842, æ. 25. By her second husband, 3. Cordelia, b. March
   2, 1823, m. March 7, 1842, James L. Smith of W., now of Tabor, Fremont
   Co., Iowa; 4. Henrietta, b. March 6, 1825, m. April 24, 1849, Daniel S.
   Frost of Knowlesville, Orleans Co., N. Y., who d. Sept. 15, 1850; she res.
   in W.; 5. Gustavus, b. July 29, 1826, m. 1850, Jane P. Thompson of
   Whitesville, Racine Co., Wis., where he resides; 6. Edmond Curran, b.
   Aug. 26, 1828, lives in Whitestown. He m. Sept. 6, 1849, Harriet E. Curtiss of Sauquoit, Oneida Co.; 7. Dwight, b. July 31, 1831, lives in Milwaukee, Wis. He m. Sept. 8, 1857, Alzina A. Johnson of Watertown, Wis.
4. *Hiram,* b. April 11, 1794; m. Aminta Thruston. .   .   .   .   (303)
5. *Philo,* b. June 23, 1796; m. Nancy R. Hampton. .   .   .   .   (304)
6. *Charles,* b. Sept.,   1799; was a jeweller in Mobile, Ala., where "he frequently filled responsible municipal posts." He d. unm., Oct., 1848, æ. 49.
7. *Esther,* b.   1802; m. 1826, David O. Macomber of Utica, now of the
   city of New York.
8. *Lois,* b.   1805; m. 1828, George Manchester of Utica, N. Y.
   They resided in Boston, Mass., where she d. without issue, about 1851. He
   d. about 1852.
9. *Julia Ann,* b. July 13, 1808; m. Jan. 1, 1827, Sidney R. Kennedy, of Brookfield, Madison Co., now of Auburn, N. Y. She has had, 1. Cornelia, b. Sept.
   9, 1829, m. May, 1849, Joseph Perkins of Phelps, Ontario Co., N. Y.;
   2. Harriet White, b. Oct. 3, 1831, m. Sept., 1852, Theodore H. Cone of Auburn; 3. Norman Hulbert, b. June 6, 1833; res. in Auburn. He m. Feb.,
   1857, Mary Jane Van Tuyl; 4. Esther Elizabeth, b. June 9, 1835, m. Aug.,
   1855, Peter Petrie of Phelps, N. Y.; 5. Arthur Sidney, b. Oct. 31, 1837, is
   in the U. S. Navy; 6. Isaac Eugene, b. May 24, 1840, lives at Clifton
   Springs, N. Y.; 7. Charles White, b. Aug. 1, 1844, d. Jan. 22, 1846.

---

153. ELISHA WHITE, son of Rev. Stephen, (70) was born
in Windham, Conn., Sept. 16, 1754. He was a farmer in that
town, and died there, Feb. 3, 1835, æ. 80.

He married, Nov. 4, 1779, LOIS WEBB of Windham, dau. of
Samuel Webb and Deborah Davidson. She was born Feb. 16,
1754, and died Jan. 22, 1835, æ. 81.

CHILDREN.

1. *Harry*, b. Feb. 14, 1781 ; d. Aug. 23, 1782.
2. *Samuel*, b. Sept. 22, 1782 ; d. July 31, 1796, æ. 13.
3. *Thomas*, b. Sept. 23, 1784 ; sailed from New York, for New Orleans, Dec., 1814, in a vessel which was never heard from. He was unmarried.
4. *Oliver Dyer*, b. Feb. 17, 1787 ; d. Jan. 31, 1788.
5. *Dyer*, b. Dec. 6, 1788 ; d. unm., at Warren, Ohio, Sept. 12, 1852, æ. 63.
6. *Elisha*, b. Aug. 9, 1791 ; m. Lydia Dyer.   .   .   .   .   . (305)
7. *Mira*, b. Mar. 25, 1794 ; m. May 5, 1834, John Champion, formerly of Leb-anon, Conn., afterwards of Ypsilanti, Mich. He d. March 9, 1853, æ. 71. She resides in Ypsilanti, and has, 1. Charles Rockwell, b. Aug. 19, 1835 ; 2. Henry Crane, b. Dec. 28, 1836.
8. *Charles*, b. June 20, 1797 ; res. in Warren, Trumbull Co., O.

---

154. Hon. DYER WHITE, son of Rev. Stephen, (70) was born in Windham, Conn., May 20, 1762. After studying law with the Hon. Charles Chauncey, he commenced the practice of his profession in New Haven, Conn., in 1785, and resided there during the remainder of his life. He possessed to a great degree the esteem and confidence of his fellow-citizens, and was much resorted to, as a judicious adviser, a safe legal counsellor, and a kind and efficient friend. He held the office of Clerk of the Superior Court for New Haven County, for twenty years, and was one of the Judges of the County Court, or Court of Common Pleas, for the same County, for seven-teen years. By his sound judgment and consistent piety, he was enabled to do much useful service for the community in which he lived, and for the Church of Christ with which he was connected. He died Nov. 2, 1841, æ. 79. The following is a fac-simile of his autograph.

He married, 1st, March 18, 1791, SUSANNA WHITTELSEY of New Haven, dau. of Rev. Chauncey Whittelsey, pastor of the First Congregational Church in New Haven, and of Martha Newton. She was born Sept. 25, 1766, and died Oct. 2, 1796, æ. 30.

He married, 2d, March 11, 1801, HANNAH WETMORE of Mid-

19

dletown, dau. of Seth Wetmore and Mary Wright. She was born May 28, 1773, and died June 20, 1830, æ. 57.

He married, 3d, Oct. 24, 1832, Mrs. EUNICE BASSETT, widow of Rev. Amos Bassett, D. D., of Hebron, Conn., and dau. of Ralph Pomeroy of Hartford. She was born Nov. 25, 1776, and is still living.

CHILD ;—BY THE FIRST MARRIAGE.

1. *Harriet*, b. Dec. 28, 1793; d. Sept. 11, 1795.

CHILDREN ;—BY THE SECOND MARRIAGE.

2. *A son*, b. Jan. 9, 1802; d. the same day.
3. *Henry*, b. March 5, 1803; m. Martha Sherman. . . (306)

---

155. Capt. TIMOTHY WHITE, son of Dea. John, (71) was born Oct. 21, 1747. He was a sea-captain, and resided in New Haven, where he died, May 31, 1803, æ. 55. The name of his first wife is not ascertained.

He married, 2d, MERCY CLARK of Woodbridge, Conn. She died April 12, 1838, æ. 85.

CHILD ;—BY THE FIRST MARRIAGE.

1. *Isaac*, b. April 28, 1769; d. unm., at Hispaniola, W. I., July 27, 1795, æ. 26.

CHILDREN ;—BY THE SECOND MARRIAGE.

2. *Mary*, b. April 14, 1773; m. 1st, Benjamin English, jun., of New Haven; m. 2d, Chauncey Johnson of Seymour, Conn.
3. *Huldah*, b. Oct. 7, 1775; m. Eldad Gilbert of New Haven, and d. Jan. 4, 1840, æ. 64. He d. Dec. 19, 1841. She had, 1. Eunice; 2. Isaac, d.; and two children who d. in infancy.
4. *Amos*, b. Oct. 31, 1777; m. Polly Kimberly. . . . (307)
5. *Jared*, b. April 15, 1780; d. unm., in Augusta, Ga., Sept. 3, 1803, æ. 23.
6. *Almira*, b. July 30, 1782; m. Feb. 5, 1804, Joseph N. Clark of New Haven, and is now living, a widow.
7. *Aaron Clark*, b. Oct. 19, 1784; m. Clarissa S. Warland. (308)
8. *Hannah*, b. Feb. 9, 1787; d. Aug. 22, 1795, æ. 8.
9. *Timothy*, b. March 17, 1789; d. at Staten Island, N. Y., of yellow fever, Sept. 25, 1806, æ. 17. (Oct. 10, 1806, on grave-stone.)

---

156. Lieut. JOHN WHITE, son of Dea. John, (71) was born in 1756. He settled in Derby, Conn., and died Feb. 18, 1830, æ. 74. He was a Revolutionary soldier.

He married, May 25, 1778, ANNA BOSTWICK of Derby. She died June 4, 1831, æ. 73.

CHILDREN.

1. *Elisha*, b. Nov. 14, 1779; m. Ethelinda Canfield. . . . . (309)
2. *John*, b. Dec. 29, 1780; m. Martha Hotchkiss. . . . . (310)

3. *Anna,* b. May 30, 1783 ; m. Nathan Tomlinson of Oxford, Conn., had two children, and d. Aug., 1815, æ. 32.
4. *Sally,* b. April 5, 1785 ; m. David Sanford of Bethany, and d. Feb., 1836, æ. 50. She left no children.
5. *Daniel,* b. Nov. 11, 1787 ; m. Sally Sharp. . . . (311)
6. *Isaac,* b. Sept. 2, 1789 ; m. Ann Gilbert. . . . . (312)
7. *Maria,* b. Oct. 10, 1791 ; m. Alling Brown of New Haven, and d. Aug. 4, 1855, æ. 63. She had five children, all of whom d. young.
8. *Polly,* b. Oct. 11, 1793 ; m. John Jenks of Amenia, Dutchess Co., N. Y. She is living, a widow. She has had, 1. Frederick, m., lives in Sharon, Conn. ; 2. Marietta, d. unm. ; 3. Jane ; 4. Ann Maria ; 5. Emily, m. —— Dutton ; lives in Norfolk, Conn.
9. *Rebecca,* b. Aug. 23, 1795 ; m. Medad Keeney of Seymour, Conn., and d. May, 1826, æ. 30, leaving two sons and two daughters.
10. *Susan,* b. Sept. 17, 1797 ; m. Isaac Johnson of Derby, and d. April, 1850, æ. 52. He is dead. She had three children.
11. *Amanda,* b. Oct. 2, 1799 ; m. Samuel Spencer of Derby, who is dead. She d. in 1855, leaving two children, who are m.
12. *Raymond B.,* b. Aug. 31, 1801 ; m. Harriet Warner. . (313)
13. *Amos,* b. Dec. 22, 1803 ; has been twice married. . (314)

---

157. ISAAC WHITE, son of Moses, (72) was born in Guilford, Conn., Oct. 14, 1752. He lived for several years in Southington, Conn., from whence he removed, about 1791, to Herkimer Co., N. Y., and resided a few miles east of Utica. About 1815 he removed to Springville, Erie Co., N. Y., where he died, Jan. 13, 1821, [1822?] æ. 68.

He married, Dec. 7, 1775, THANKFUL CLARK of Southington, dau. of Col. Joel Clark, who died in New York in 1776, while a prisoner of war. She was born Jan. 1, 1760, and died June 27, 1836, æ. 76.

CHILDREN.

1. *Nancy,* b. Jan. 31, 1779 ; m. Sylvanus Munson, and d. Aug. 13, 1849, æ. 70. She rem. to Ohio or Indiana, and had a large family ; Sophia, Sally, and others.
2. *Truman,* b. Nov. 8, 1780 ; m. Betsey Tuthill. (315)
3. *Francis,* b. July 22, 1782 ; m. Emma Rushmore. . . (316)
4. *Moses,* b. June 30, 1784 ; m. Mary Tuthill and others. . . (317)
5. *Isaac,* b. April 27, 1786 ; was a carpenter. He d. of yellow fever, in N. Y. city, Aug. 21, 1807, æ. 21. (Grave-stone, in Trinity Church-yard. Aug. 24, a family record.)
6. *Roderick,* b. Dec. 8, 1788 ; m. Lucy Blakeslee. . . . . (318)
7. *Polly,* b. Dec. 22, 1790 ; m. Dec. 16, 1812, Samuel Reed Watson, a farmer, of Newport, Herkimer Co., N. Y. She has had, 1. Albert Clark, b. Oct. 11, 1814, d. Oct. 15, 1837, æ. 23 ; 2. Ruth, b. Jan. 6, 1816, m. Jan. 1, 1835,

Daniel Bowen, and d. Oct. 12, 1838, æ. 22 ; 3. Lydia, b. July 15, 1820, d.
Oct. 4, 1839, æ. 19 ; 4. George Francis, b. Oct. 21, 1830, lives in Buffalo,
N. Y.

8. *Henry,*   b. Nov. 8, 1792 ; d. May, 1793, æ. 6 mos.
9. *Joel,*   b. July 2, 1794 ; is a farmer in Westfield, Medina Co., Ohio. He
m. 1822, Phebe Blakeslee of Paris, N. Y.
10. *Albert,*   b. May 19, 1797 ; m. —— ——.   .   .   .   .   (319)
11. *Thankful,* b. Sept. 29, 1799 ; m. Sept. 5, 1818, Henry Edmonds, and d. July
24, 1838, æ. 37. She had, 1. Amanda Malvinia, b. May 16, 1819, d. April
19, 1841, æ. 22 ; 2. Sylvania, b. Jan. 13, 1821, m. Aug. 31, 1843, Joel Willard ; 3. Frederick Henry, b. Jan. 13, 1823 ; 4. Thankful W., b. Jan. 9,
1827, m. Jan. 31, 1850, William C. Day of Mohawk, Herkimer Co., N. Y. ;
5. Mary M., b. Oct. 21, 1829, d. July 15, 1838 ; 6. Orrilla, b. June 12, 1832,
m. Dec. 31, 1853, James H. Buchanan ; 7. Albert M., b. Jan. 23, 1835 ;
8. Byron W., b. July 17, 1838, was drowned July 17, 1845, æ. 7.
12. *Almer,*   b. March 14, 1802 ; m. Ruth Ann Tefft and others.   .   (320)
13. *Frederick,* b. Oct. 24, 1804 ; lived in Cincinnati, O. He m. Malvina ——.

---

158. MOSES WHITE, Jun., son of Moses, (72) was born
about the year 1757. He resided in Southington, Conn.
According to the family tradition, "he joined the American
Army during the Revolutionary War, marched to Canada,
and was there taken prisoner by the British. He was treated
very humanely by Gen. Guy Carleton, who liberated him."
His daughter states that "he left Southington, Jan. 22, 1783,
and sailed from New Haven. He was taken prisoner, and
carried to Tortola, W. I., where he was set at liberty. He
then went to St. Thomas, thence to Santa Cruz, and thence to
Cape Francis, Hispaniola, where he died, about the last of
November, 1783, aged 26 years."

He married, Nov. 15, 1779, MELITTA PORTER, dau. of Joshua
Porter. She married, 2d, Oct. 25, 1786, Dr. Perez Mann of
Burlington, Conn., and died Nov. 19, 1789.

CHILDREN.

1. *Porter,*   b. June 12, 1780 ; d. Sept. 12, 1782.
2. *Laurinda P.,* b. April 22, 1782 ; m. May 17, 1801, John Miles of Cheshire,
Conn., a farmer, who d. July 11, 1853, æ. 75. She is living in Cheshire.
She has had, 1. Roderick, b. Aug. 3, 1802, m. May 29, 1828, Zeruiah Clark
of Southington, who d. Feb. 16, 1831, æ. 22. He d. in Cheshire ; 2. Fidelia, b.
Feb. 9, 1804, m. George Gridley of S. ; 3. Ralzy, b. Jan. 28, 1806, d. March 3,
1807 ; 4. Almeron, b. June 1, 1808, lives in Meriden. He m. Sept. 12, 1833,
Caroline Laurence ; 5. John, b. April 5, 1810, d. Jan. 25, 1818 ; 6. Laurinda,
b. Jan. 7, 1812, d. ; 7. Alvinza, b. Sept. 23, 1813, d. Feb. 9, 1815 ; 8. Gertrude K., b. Feb. 1, 1817, m. Edwin B. Payne of Cheshire ; 9. John, b. Nov.

28, 1818, lives in Meriden. He m. Nov. 21, 1842, Abigail Sanderson of Cheshire ; 10. A son, b. Feb. 8, 1825, d. Feb. 11, 1825.

159. Capt. JAMES WHITE, son of Moses, (72) was baptized at Upper Middletown, Conn., Feb. 1, 1761. In early life he settled in Newport, N. H., as a hatter. He also kept a public house for several years. He died of spotted fever, in 1813, æ. 52. His wife and two daughters were taken away by the same epidemic.

He married, about 1782, TIRZAH TAYLOR of Cornish, N. H., dau. of Capt. Joseph Taylor and —— Sumner. She died in 1813.

CHILDREN.

1. *James,* b. Feb., 1784 ; m. Grace Wilcox. . . . (321)
2. *Experience,* b. Sept. 20, 1788 ; m. Asa McGregory of Newport, a farmer. They afterwards rem. to Canada West, where he d. about 1833. She d. in Ohio, a few years later. She had, 1. Florilla, d. in Newport, æ. 5 ; 2. Carlos ; 3. Arlin Ann ; 4. Philander White ; 5. Henrietta ; 6. Milton.
3. *Calvin,* b. ; m. Hannah Fields. . . . (322)
4. *Huldah,* b. ; m. Ruel Durkee of Hanover, N. H., a farmer, and had, 1. Betsey ; 2. Clarence ; 3. Grace.
5. *Betsey,* b. ; d. in 1813.
6. *Fanny,* b. ; m. Laomy McGregory of Newport, now of Whitefield, a carpenter. She has, 1. Melinda ; 2. Joel ; 3. Martha ; 4. Mary.
7. *Melinda,* b. ; d. in 1816.
8. *Sophia,* b. ; d. in 1813.
9. *Philander,* b. ; d. in 1816, at the house of his brother Calvin.
10. *Elisha,* b. Feb. 26, 1807 ; m. Lucinda S. Bennett. . . (323)
11. *Orpha Emeline,* b. Sept. 21, 1808 ; m. Elias Powers of Croydon, N. H., a farmer. She has, 1. Albina H., b. Nov. 24, 1834, m. Jan., 1856, Lydia Stocker of Springfield, N. H. ; 2. Myra A., b. Nov. 7, 1836, m. Sept. 28, 1858, Stephen H. Bickford of Nashua, N. H. ; 3. Abijah, b. Sept. 28, 1839 ; 4. Elias F., b. Feb. 18, 1844 ; 5. Wilbur H., b. Jan. 22, 1849.

160. Rev. CALVIN WHITE, son of Moses, (72) was born in Upper Middletown, Conn., Dec. 17, 1762. He graduated at Yale College in 1786, studied theology, and was ordained a Congregational minister in 1789. He was installed pastor of the Presbyterian Church in Hanover, Morris Co., N. J., June 29, 1791, and was dismissed, at his own request, Nov. 17, 1795. He soon after entered the ministry of the Protestant Episcopal Church, laboring for a short time at Stamford, Conn., and for many years at Derby, Conn. In 1821 he adopted the Roman

Catholic faith, but did not enter the priesthood. "He was a devoted and accomplished scholar, and one of the few who loved and thoroughly mastered the Hebrew tongue. In politics he was a tory, and when speaking of the Revolutionary War, never failed to call it the 'rebellion.' He never voted in his life." He died in Derby, March 21, 1853, æ. 90. The following fac-simile of his autograph is copied from the signature to a letter written when he was eighty-eight years old.

He married, 1st, Feb. 28, 1792, PHEBE CAMP of Newark, N. J., dau. of Capt. Nathaniel and Rachel Camp. Capt. Camp was an American officer during the War of the Revolution. She was born June 18, 1770, and died Nov. 23, 1826, æ. 56.

He married, 2d, 1827, JANE MARDENBROUGH, who is still living.

CHILDREN;—BY THE FIRST MARRIAGE.

1. *Robert,*　b. Dec. 1, 1792; m. Hannah Gibbs. . . . . (324)
2. *Sarah,*　b. April 19, 1794; d. unm., Sept. 2, 1856, æ. 62. She d. at Shrewsbury, N. J., of fever, having contracted the disease by attendance upon her brother Chandler.
3. *Richard Mansfield,* b. May 26, 1797 ; m. Ann Eliza Tousey. . . (325)
4. *Moses,*　b. April 11, 1799 ; m. Margaret Palmer. . . . (326)
5. *Carleton,* b. Feb. 20, 1801 ; m. Judith C. Miller. . . (327)
6. *A son,*　b. 　　; d. in infancy.
7. *Chandler,* b. June 14, 1806 ; m. Anna Matilda Miller. (328)
8. *Mardenbrough,* b. March 6, 1810 ; m. Clarissa Jones. (329)
9. *George Berkeley,* b. July 7, 1814 ; m. Clara Miller. . . (330)

---

161. ELISHA WHITE, son of Moses, (72) was born in Upper Middletown, Sept. 13, 1766. He was a hatter, and settled in Claremont, N. H., but removed to Weybridge, Vt., in 1799, and was a farmer there until his death, April 3, 1802, æ. 35.

He married, Dec. 30, 1790, HONOR SUMNER of Claremont, dau. of Col. Benjamin Sumner and Prudence Hubbard. She was born Feb. 18, 1772, and died in Claridon, Ohio, April 21, 1854, æ. 82.

CHILDREN.

1. *Polly,*   b. Dec. 19, 1791; d. unm., at E. Claridon, O., Sept. 7, 1858, æ. 66. Her death was caused by her clothes taking fire.

2. *Maria,*   b. June 4, 1793; m. Jan. 11, 1819, James N. Willard of North Hartland, Vt., a merchant. She has, 1. James Nutting, b. June 5, 1821, a merchant in N. Hartland. He m. Feb. 27, 1844, Mary G. Thayer of Thetford, Vt.; 2. Eluthera Maria, b. May 23, 1823, d. June 10; 3. Phineas K., b. Aug. 21, 1825, m.; 4. Louisa Maria, b. March 29, 1828, d. Sept. 18, 1829; 5. Allen H., b. Jan. 24, 1830, m.; 6. Daniel Spaulding, b. Aug. 16, 1833; 7. George Elisha, b. April 19, 1837.

3. *Honor,*   b. March 14, 1795; m. 1st, Aug. 26, 1811, Joseph Brackett, and resided in Weybridge; m. 2d, May 9, 1821, Chester Wells, a farmer, of Claridon, Geauga Co., O. She has had, by her first husband, 1. Marion P., b. Sept. 5, 1812, m. July 4, 1834, Orrin P. Gager of Claridon; 2. Helen Maria, b. Jan. 28, 1815, m. Oct. 18, 1838, Marcus Hitchcock of C. By her second husband, 3. Honor Melissa, b. May 3, 1822; 4. Edgar C., b. July 3, 1824; 5. Marcia Ann, b. Nov. 9, 1826, m. Sept. 10, 1850, Lester C. Treat of C., and d. Aug. 12, 1857, æ. 30; 6. Caroline Matilda, b. May 5, 1830, d. July 8, 1844, æ. 14.

4. *Roderick,*   b. May 22, 1797; formerly a farmer in E. Claridon, O., now carries on the business of tanning, at Chagrin Falls, Cuyahoga Co., O.

5. *Eluthera,*   b. June 29, 1799; m. March 2, 1820, Benjamin B. Gorton, a paper maker. They rem. to O. in 1822, and now res. in Claridon. She has had, 1. William B., b. Dec. 5, 1820, d. Sept. 4, 1822; 2. Helen M., b. Oct. 23, 1823, d. Jan. 23, 1824; 3. William Benjamin, b. April 1, 1825, m. Oct., 1848, Lucinda Roberts of Warren, O.; 4. Helen Maria, b. June 23, 1827, m. Sept., 1849, Dennis Freeman of C.; 5. Roderick White, b. Aug. 23, 1829; 6. Jane E., b. June 9, 1831, m. Feb. 20, 1851, James M. Hathaway, now of Farmington, Wis.; 7. Mary Ann, b. July 19, 1833; 8. Laura Amanda, b. Aug. 21, 1835, m. May 15, 1859, Albert L. Jenks, now of Dresbach City, Min.; 9. Melissa A., b. June 20, 1842.

6. *George Elisha,* b. June 2, 1801; m. Mrs. Martha R. Christie.   .   (331)

---

162. JOSEPH WHITE, son of Elias, (73) was born in Upper Middletown, about 1771. He removed to Granville, Washington, Co., N. Y., was a farmer there, and died about 1830. He married, Oct. 18, 1795, MATTY HASGILL.

CHILDREN.

1. *Lucy,*   bap. Nov. 20, 1796; bap. at Upper Middletown.
2. *Betsey,* b.   ; probably b. in Granville.
3. *Sarah,* b.   .   Perhaps there were other children.

---

163. ELIAS WHITE, son of Elias, (73) was born in Upper Middletown. He settled in Cornwall, Conn., about 1800, and resided there till his death. Name of his wife not known.

1. *Comfort;* lives in Sheffield, Mass.
2. *Edwin.*
3. *Elias.*
4. *Edward Rogers;* lives in Cornwall. Perhaps further particulars may be given after family 331, in the Seventh Generation.

---

164. Capt. Isaac White, son of Elias, (73) was born in Upper Middletown, June 22, 1780. He resided there, was a mariner, and at the time of his death was master of a vessel. He died in New London, Oct. 29, 1821, æ. 41.

He married, Oct. 28, 1808, Priscilla Plumb, dau. of Reuben and Priscilla Plumb of Middletown. She was born Oct. 22, 1787, and died in the winter of 1823.

CHILDREN.

1. *Henry Champlin,* b. Nov. 14, 1809; m. Mary F. Browning.   (332)
2. *Mary Ann,*   b. March 13, 1813; m. John Cook of Buffalo, N. Y., and has one dau., Ruth Anne, b. about 1843.
3. *Isaac,*   b. June 29, 1814; m. Sarah Ann Girard.   . (333)
4. *Harriet Plumb,* b. June 22, 1816; m. Lyman Strong of Oswego, N. Y., and has one son, Henry White.
5. *Jane,*   b. May 30, 1818; m. Richard Chappel, now of St. Peters, Minnesota. She has Henry, and two others.

IN THE LINE OF JACOB WHITE, OF MIDDLETOWN.

165. Samuel White, Jun., son of Samuel, (74) was born in North Coventry, Conn., Nov. 5, 1757. He resided there, and died about Feb., 1807, æ. 49.

He married Rachel Porter of N. Coventry, dau. of Dea. Jonathan Porter, jun., and Lois Richardson. She was born May 28, 1761, and died May, 1815, æ. 54.

CHILDREN.

1. *Marcia,* b.   ; m. Amos Avery of N. Cov., and d. March, 1838, having had, 1. Marilla, m. Clark Steer, and d. in Vernon, Nov., 1847; 2. Munroe; 3. Francis; 4. Martha Amelia, d.; 5. Franklin; 6. John Maffit; 7. Harriet, d.; 8. Columbus; 9. Lewis.
2. *Samuel,* b. May, 1782; m. Lydia Jewett.   .   .   . (334)
3. *Leonard,* b. March, 1788; d. Sept., 1808, æ. 20. He was killed by the discharge of a pistol, at a military review.
4. *Mary,* b. Feb. 27, 1790; m. Dec. 30, 1814, Zolvah Brown of N. Cov., a farmer. She has had, 1. Mary Kingsbury, b. Sept. 27, 1816, m. May 11, 1840, Joseph D. Barrows of Mansfield, Conn.; 2. George Oliver, b. Aug. 7, 1820, d. unm., Nov. 3, 1848, æ. 28; 3. Emeline Francis, b. May 7, 1824,

m. Milo Loomis of N. Cov. ; 4. Catharine Porter, b. July 22, 1825, m. Nathaniel W. French ; 5. Walter Clark, b. Oct. 14, 1831, m. Sarah Ann Clark.

5. *Walter*, b.   ; m. Betsey Hinkley of Tolland, dau. of Ichabod Hinkley. He lived for some time in Rochester, N. Y., but rem. to Wisconsin, where he d. without issue, about April, 1855.

6. *Rachel*, b.   ; lives in Colchester, Conn.

7. *Jonathan Porter*, b.   ; m. Abigail Scripture.   .   .   .   (335)

8. *Laura*, b.   ; m. 1st, Urial Andrus of N. Cov., who d. in 1826, æ. 31 ; m. 2d, James Bennett of Bolton. She has had, by her first husband, 1. Urial; 2. Royal George, m. Harriet M. Neff; 3. Walter Scott W. By her second husband, 4. James ; 5. Henry Payson, d. ; 6. William Harrison, d.

9. *Adotia*, b. March 28, 1800 ; m. Dec. 2, 1820, Isaac Keeney, jun., of Bolton. She has, 1. Samuel White, b. Dec. 14, 1823 ; 2. Julia Ann, b. March 28, 1826, m. Dec., 1847, John N. King of South Windsor ; 3. Mary Ann, b. Jan. 26, 1829, m. Jan., 1855, John H. Thompson of Bolton.

10. *Emily*, b.   ; m. Dr. Stebbins, now of Detroit, Mich., and has, 1. Dwight ; 2. Edward ; 3. Theodore.

---

166. LEMUEL WHITE, son of Samuel, (74) was born in North Coventry, Dec. 30, 1758. He lived there for some years, but removed to Batavia, N. Y., where he died, Aug. 7, 1850, æ. 91.

He married, May 17, 1781, ANNA BRIGHAM of Coventry, dau. of Uriah Brigham and Anne Richardson. She was born Oct. 14, 1759, and died Feb. 11, 1845, æ. 85.

CHILDREN.

1. *Percy*, b. Jan. 14, 1782; d. Sept. 20, 1798, æ. 16.
2. *Brigham*, b. July 1, 1783; m., and d. June 27, 1839, æ. 56.
3. *Grace*, b. Dec. 15, 1786; lives in Middlebury, Vt.
4. *Laura*, b. April 16, 1788; m. Reuben Ross, now of Middlebury, Vt.
5. *Chester*, b. Feb. 1, 1790; d. Feb. 10, 1790.
6. *Chester*, b. Feb. 14, 1793; m. Lucy Topliff.   .   .   .   (336)
7. *Lemuel*, b. April 9, 1796; m. Eliza Matthews.   .   .   .   (337)
8. *Lucy*, b. June 9, 1802; d. Nov. 15, 1820, æ. 18.

---

167. TIMOTHY WHITE, son of Samuel, (74) was born in North Coventry, March 8, 1764. He is said to have removed to Springfield, Otsego Co., N. Y., and to have died there.

He married, Nov. 11, 1790, MARGARET GURLEY, of Mansfield, Conn. She is reported to be still living, with her son, Ulysses, who is said to be a banker in the State of New York ; but his residence has not been ascertained.

---

168. DAN WHITE, Esq., son of Jacob, (75) was born in Tolland, Conn., Sept. 22, 1762. He was a Revolutionary

20

soldier, and was held a prisoner in New York, more than four months, in 1782. He was a farmer, and for some years after his marriage lived in Torrington and Norfolk, Conn., but removed in 1800 to Burke, Caledonia Co., Vt., where he erected the first framed house, and was the first justice of the peace. He was also engaged in merchandizing there. In 1806 he removed to Littleton, N. H., and afterwards to Danville, Vt., where he died, Feb. 2, 1823, æ. 60.

He married, April 6, 1786, ROWENA WILSON of Torrington, dau. of Noah Wilson. She was born Nov. 26, 1766, and died Aug. 23, 1821, æ. 54.

CHILDREN.

1. *Calvin,*   b. July 6, 1786; m. Mary Burns. .   .   .   . (338)
2. *Erastus Wilson,* b. Sept. 27, 1793 ; m. Lydia K. Remick.   .   . (339)
3. *Laura,*   b. Oct. 26, 1803 ; m. about 1829, Sidney Robinson of Quebec, Canada, who d. the following year. She now resides in Wilbraham, Mass.

---

169. THOMAS WHITE, son of Jacob, (75) was born in Tolland, Conn., Nov. 28, 1764. He was a cooper, and lived in Torrington, Conn., where he died, Sept. 6, 1845, æ. 81.

He married, Dec. 21, 1797, JEDIDAH BALDWIN of Goshen, Conn., dau. of Asahel Baldwin and Patience Bronson. She died Jan. 28, 1848, æ. 79.

CHILDREN.

1. *Hiram Jacob,* b. July 26, 1802 ; m. Henrietta S. Clark. .   .   . (340)
2. *Anna Eliza,* b. Oct. 30, 1803 ; m. March 22, 1824, William Parmele of Goshen, Conn., a farmer, who rem. in 1826 to Ohio, and d. in Bath, Summit Co., Oct. 13, 1848, æ. 47. She res. in Bath, and has had, 1. Mary S., b. Sept. 30, 1825, d. in Torrington, Conn., Sept. 20, 1847, æ. 22 ; 2. Hiram White, b. May 6, 1829 ; 3. Erastus, b. Aug. 6, 1831, m. Oct. 21, 1852, Eliza J. Watkins.
3. *Eleanor,*   b. Oct. 6, 1810 ; lives in Bath, Ohio.

---

170. ELAM WHITE, son of Jacob, (75) was born in Tolland, April 14, 1778. He settled as a farmer in Burke, Caledonia Co., Vt., and died there, Sept. 21, 1851, æ. 73.

He married, 1st, May 12, 1803, WEALTHY COE, dau. of Amasa Coe. She died Oct. 12, 1823, æ. 38.

He married, 2d, ESTHER ——, who died Dec. 28, 1851, æ. 69.

CHILDREN;—BY THE FIRST MARRIAGE.

1. *Florrilla,* b. March 22, 1804 ; m. Nov. 8, 1825, Charles C. Newell of East

Burke, Vt., and d. April 27, 1854, æ. 50. She had, 1. Florrilla, b. April 18, 1828, m. Jan. 7, 1851, Dr. James D. Folsom of Lancaster, N. H.; 2. Amasa W., b. Feb. 28, 1830, m. Sept. 2, 1851, Hannah E. Spencer; 3. Amelia, b. Dec. 30, 1834, m. May 18, 1858, Rev. H. N. Burton of Newbury, Vt.; 4. Elam W., b. April 5, 1838; 5. Harriet, b. Nov. 19, 1840; 6. Oliver W., b. Feb. 11, 1843.

2. *Ransom Coe*, b. Oct. 2, 1806; m. Hannah B. Walter. (341)
3. *Osman*, b. Nov. 1, 1808; m. Frinda Smith. . . . . (342)
4. *Emily*, b. April 3, 1811; m. Nov. 22, 1831, Almon Smith, of Brighton, Vt., and d. in Albany, Vt., Jan. 22, 1854, æ. 42. She had, 1. Eleanor, m. Eli Harly, who d.; 2. Volney; 3. Adny; 4. Almon; 5. Osman.
5. *Roenza*, b. Dec. 29, 1812; m. Nov. 22, 1836, Abner H. Eggleston of Burke, and has had, Myron, Charles, Craig, Marietta, Celia, and two others who d. young.
6. *Elam*, b. Feb. 2, 1817; d. June 28, 1823, æ. 6.
7. *Wealthy*, b. April 18, 1819; m. Sept. 30, 1851, Henry Gage of Burke. She has had, Calista, and two children that d. young.
8. *Caroline*, b. June 25, 1823; m. April 26, 1849, John C. Page of Burke, and has, 1. Elam Cutler; 2. Flora Emma; 3. A dau.

CHILD;—BY THE SECOND MARRIAGE.

9. *Mary*, b. March 8, 1830; d. Dec. 28, 1846, æ. 16.

---

171. SILAS WHITE, Jun., son of Silas, (77) was born in Torrington, Conn., about 1772. He died there, Feb. 11, 1828, æ. 55.

He married, 1797, ELIZABETH PLUMB of Litchfield, who died Nov. 9, 1846, æ. 67.

CHILDREN.

1. *Ransom*, b. 1799; d. unm., Feb. 19, 1820, æ. 21.
2. *David*, b. 1801; m. 1828, Almira Goodale of Glastenbury, and d. without issue, Nov. 20, 1829, æ. 29.
3. *Fanny*, b. 1803; m. 1827, Hermon Northrop of Salisbury, Conn., now of Unionville.
4. *Harriet*, b. 1805; d. unm., Nov. 10, 1829, æ. 24.
5. *Sally*, b. 1808; m. 1829, Thomas L. Day; they live in Guilford, Chenango Co., N. Y. She has, 1. William W.; 2. Helen A.

---

172. ROSWELL WHITE, son of Silas, (77) was born in Torrington, Conn., Jan. 27, 1778. He was a carpenter, and settled in Granville, Mass., about 1805. In 1826 he removed to Rochester, N. Y., and in 1842 to Hartland, Niagara Co., N. Y., where he died, Nov. 5, 1844, æ. 66.

He married, 1st, April 18, 1799, ABI NORTHWAY of Torringford, dau. of James Northway and Polly Fuller. She was born June 20, 1781, and died May 18, 1810, æ. 29.

He married, 2d, Feb. 20, 1812, MARY SAWYER of Granville,

Mass., dau. of Jacob Sawyer and Mary Rathbone. She was born in Hartland, Conn., May 11, 1781, and died in Spencer, O., March 8, 1850, æ. 68.

CHILDREN ;—BY THE FIRST MARRIAGE.

1. *Roswell Osmond,* b. April 30, 1800; was a comb manufacturer in Rochester, N. Y. He m. 1826, Lucy Murdock of Rochester, and d. without issue, July 14, 1828, æ. 28.

2. *Mary Birge,*   b. March 22, 1802; m. June, 1828, Carmi Coburn of Rochester, a carpenter. She d. in Rogersville, Pa., July 3, 1832, æ. 30. She had one son, James White, b. March 6, 1830, m., and lives in Allegan, Mich.

3. *James Northway,* b. Sept.   1, 1804; a comb manufacturer in Rochester, N. Y. He m. 1827, Ann Raymond, and d. without issue, July 28, 1829, æ. 25.

4. 5. & 6. *Sons ;* all d. in infancy, before their mother.

CHILDREN ;—BY THE SECOND MARRIAGE.

7. *Nelson,*   b. Jan. 20, 1813 ;. m. Emily Penfield.   .   .   (343)
8. *Orrin Chauncey,* b. March 16, 1814; m. Mary E. Shedd. .   .   (344)
9. *John Birge,*   b. Oct. 30, 1817; m. Hannah Luce. .   .   .   (345)
10. *Abi N.,*   b. April 28, 1819 ; d. unm., Feb. 27, 1850, æ. 30.
11. *Adelia Elvira,* b. Aug. 11, 1824; m. Jan. 2, 1851, Martin M. Grandy of Spencer, O., a farmer. She has, 1. Mary L., b. Nov. 25, 1856 ; 2. Martin Julian, b. March 20, 1859.

---

173. CHAUNCEY WHITE, son of Silas, (77) was born in Torrington, Conn., Sept. 11, 1783.   He resides in Westmoreland, Oneida Co., N. Y.

He married, 1st, March 5, 1804, BETSEY PLUMB of Litchfield, Conn., dau. of Ebenezer and Betsey Plumb. She died May 22, 1822, æ. 41.

He married, 2d, Dec. 10, 1823, Mrs. MELINDA TAYLOR.

CHILDREN ;—BY THE FIRST MARRIAGE.

1. *Charles Plumb,* b. Aug. 5, 1809; m. Mercy Wilcox.   .   .   .   (346)
2. *Jane Eliza,*   b. Dec. 27, 1815 ; m. Sept. 24, 1834, Harvey Coe of Granville, Mass., now of Bloomingdale, Du Page Co., Ill. She has, 1. Harriet Jane, b. Nov. 9, 1835, m. May 17, 1857, Lorin Barnes of Bloomingdale, who grad. Yale Coll., 1849 ; 2. Urania Eliza, b. Dec. 6, 1838, grad. Rockford Fem. Sem., Ill., 1859 ; 3. Curtiss H., b. Aug. 11, 1841 ; 4. Adella B., b. Nov. 9, 1846 ; 5. Edgar D., b. March 23, 1848 ; 6. Wilbur E., b. Dec. 10, 1855.
3. *Orrin,*   b.   ; d. æ. 4 years.

CHILD ;—BY THE SECOND MARRIAGE.

4. *Harriet Elizabeth,* b. Sept.,   1826 ; d. May 25, 1844, æ. 17.

---

174. BRAINARD WHITE, son of Silas, (77) was born in Torrington, Conn., May 5, 1786.   He died in Winsted, Conn., April 17, 1833, æ. 47.

He married, Nov. 12, 1807, ELIZA STEDMAN of New Hartford, Conn., dau. of Justus and Elizabeth Stedman. She now lives with her son, in Canastota, N. Y.

CHILDREN.

1. *Elijah Brainard*, b. Aug. 29, 1808 ; m. Mary Camp.   .   (347)
2. *Edwin Riley,*   b. Oct. 15, 1810 ; m. Julia Westlake.   .   . (348)
3. *A child,*   b.   ; d. Aug. 28, 1812.
4. *Nathan Curtis,*   b. Sept. 24, 1820 ; m. 1st, J. C. Stanton; m. 2d, D. Dana. (349)

175. GERSHOM WHITE, son of Joel, (78) was born in Blanford, Mass., May 28, 1775. He was a joiner, and settled in Russia, Herkimer Co., N. Y. He died in Gouverneur, St. Lawrence Co., while on a journey, April 15, 1833, æ. 58.

He married, 1804, SALLY PARKS of Russell, Mass. After her husband's death, she returned to Russell.

CHILDREN.

1. *Emily,*   b.   ; m. William Walters of Russia, N. Y., and rem. to Ohio.
2. *Roland P.,* b.   1816 ; was a merchant in Russell, Mass. He m., and d. in W. Springfield, Mass., July 11, 1853, æ. 37.
3. *Harriet,*   b.   ; is married.

176. JOEL WHITE, Jun., son of Joel, (78) was born in Blanford, Mass., Feb. 28, 1779. He was a farmer in Russia, N. Y., till 1818, when he removed to Edwards, St. Lawrence Co., where he and his wife still reside.

He married, Feb., 1805, ISABEL STEWART of Blanford, born April 18, 1784.

CHILDREN.

1. *William,*   b. Nov. 9, 1805 ; m. Margaret Morgan and others.   .   (350)
2. *Betsey Ann,* b. July 23, 1808 ; m. Jan., 1826, Constant Wells of Pitcairn, St. L. Co., and d. Nov., 1844, æ. 36. She had, 1. William N.; 2. Edwin M.; 3. Isabel, d. 1846, æ. 17; 4. Dexter ; 5. Constant ; 6. Joel ; 7. Albert.
3. *Albert,*   b. April 16, 1811 ; m. 1st, Lucy Sloper ; 2d, M. C. Mitchell. (351)
4. *Arlina,*   b. May 9, 1818 ; m. 1st, Oct., 1838, Warren W. Wright of Potsdam, St. L. Co., who d. May, 1848. She m. 2d, Jan., 1854, Charles Carr of Edwards. She d. Feb. 17, 1857, æ. 38. She had, by her first husband, 1. Dexter J.; 2. Warren M. By her second husband, 3. Harriet ; 4. Arlina.
5. *Frederic,*   b. April 21, 1823 ; m. Nancy Snow.   .   .   .   (352)

177. JOHN WHITE, son of Jacob, (79) was born in Upper Middletown, Conn., and resided there. He was drowned at sea, March 19, 1799, æ. about 33.

He married, March 31, 1790, RUTH RANNEY, born Feb. 22, 1772, dau. of Ebenezer Ranney.

CHILDREN.

1. *John,* b. June 26, 1790; m. 1st, Emily Savage; 2d, Mrs. S. Jones. (353)
2. *Jacob,* b. April 27, 1792; m. Susan Sage. .   .   .   .   . (354)
3. *Harriet,* b. Jan. 12, 1795; m. 1st, Sept. 30, 1816, William Keith of Up. Mid.,
      who d. July 11, 1818, æ. 33. She m. 2d, Dec. 21, [19?] 1827, Miles Mer-
      win, jun., of Durham, Conn., and d. June 5, 1858, æ. 63. She had, by her
      first husband, 1. Harriet Stocking, b. Dec. 22, 1817. By her second hus-
      band, 2. Wealthy Sage, b. Nov. 24, 1828, m. Dec. 5, 1858, John Ives of
      Meriden, Conn.; 3. Caroline Ellen, b. June 28, 1831; 4. Phebe Camp, b. Oct.
      24, 1832, m. April 24, 1853, Gershom Birdsey, 2d, of Meriden, Conn.;
      5. Margaret, b. July 10, 1836; 6. Maria White, b. Sept. 25, 1839.
4. *Alma,* b. July 18, 1797; m. Dec. 6, 1821, George Ranney of Up. Mid., who
      d. May 16, 1842, æ. 47. She had, 1. William K., b. Nov. 1, 1822; 2. Almira
      R., b. Nov. 1, 1824; 3. Samuel R., b. Nov. 6, 1827.
5. *Luther,* b. Jan. 11, 1799; m. Maria Hayden.   .   .   (355)

178. Capt. THOMAS WHITE, son of Jacob, (79) was born in
Upper Middletown, Conn., June 10, 1773. He resided in that
place, and was a ship-master. He died Sept. 13, 1849, æ. 76.

He married, 1st, Sept. 8, 1803, KATHARINE KEITH, dau. of
William Keith of Up. Mid. She was born Jan. 20, 1779, and
died Aug. 19, 1807, æ. 27.

He married, 2d, May 15, 1810, Mrs. REBECCA EDWARDS,
widow of John Edwards, and dau. of Joseph Ranney and Ruth
White. (See in Fam. 72.) She was born Sept. 24, 1780.

CHILD;—BY THE .FIRST MARRIAGE.

1. *Sarah Maria,* b. July 26, 1804; d. unm., Aug. 26, 1849, æ. 45.

CHILDREN;—BY THE SECOND MARRIAGE.

2. *Catharine L.,* b. July 9, 1811; d. unm., Oct. 15, 1833, æ. 22.
3. *Ruth,*   b. June 6, 1813; m. Sept. 19, 1839, Edmund Beaumont of Up.
      Mid., and d. Sept. 10, 1856, æ. 43. She had, 1. William, b. Jan., 1855, d.
      æ. 3 days; 2. Thomas, b. Sept. 3, 1856.   .
4. *Clarissa,*   b. July,   1815; d. Aug. 8, 1815, æ. 5 weeks.
5. *Augusta,*   b. Jan. 1, 1821.

179. LEMUEL WHITE, son of Jacob, (79) was born in Upper
Middletown, Conn., Dec. 20, 1776. He settled in Middletown, Westfield Society, and died there, Aug. 5, 1847, æ. 70.

He married, 1st, Feb. 14, 1799, ABIGAIL BARTLETT, dau. of
James Bartlett. She died May 23, 1818, æ. 43.

He married, 2d, March, 1819, SARAH DOWD, dau. of Richard
Dowd. She died Nov. 9, 1822, æ. 34.

He married, 3d, May 6, 1823, ANNA JOHNSON, dau. of Aaron
Johnson. She died July 29, 1845, æ. 51.

CHILDREN;—BY THE FIRST MARRIAGE.

1. *Noah B.*, b. April 11, 1800; d. Feb. 25, 1804.
2. *Lemuel*, b. April 11, 1802; m. Almira Iligby. . . . . (356)
3. *Abigail*, b. Oct. 27, 1804; m. Alanson Andrus of Canton, Conn., and has had, 1. John R., b. Aug. 30, 1826; 2. Joseph, b. Nov. 7, 1828; 3. Catherine, b. June 27, 1833, d. Jan. 14, 1840.
4. *Catherine*, b. May 3, 1807; m. John Chandler of Canton, and d. Sept. 25, 1838, æ. 31.
5. *Noah B.*, b. Aug. 19, 1809; d. May 20, 1810.

CHILD;—BY THE SECOND MARRIAGE.

6. *Sarah Ann*, b. March 26, 1820; m. Harvey Lounsbury of Greenwich, Conn., and has, 1. Amelia; 2. Charles; 3. Marion; 4. A child.

CHILDREN;—BY THE THIRD MARRIAGE.

7. *Harriet L.*, b. March 2, 1824; d. Feb. 15, 1845, æ. 21.
8. *Lois P.*, b. Dec. 21, 1825; m. 1848, Ichabod M. Roberts, and lived on the homestead in Westfield. She d. Nov., 1850, æ. 25, leaving one son, George P., b. Jan., 1849.
9. *Emeline B.*, b. Oct. 29, 1827; d. Sept. 17, 1830.
10. *Aaron J.*, b. Sept. 7, 1829; m. Jane Chapman. . . . (357)
11. *Maria E.*, b. Oct. 17, 1831; d. March 20, 1845, æ. 13.
12. *Isaac S.*, b. Sept. 18, 1833; lives in Marion city, Iowa.
13. *Henry H.*, b. July 23, 1835; lives in Rockford, Ill.
14. *Lucy S.*, b. June 3, 1837.
15. *John L.*, b. Feb. 10, 1842.

---

180. ALEXANDER WHITE, son of Jacob, (79) was born in Upper Middletown, March 6, 1782. He removed to Wethersfield, Conn., and died Feb. 21, 1834, æ. 52.

He married, 1806, ABIGAIL BEADLE. She was born Aug. 4, 1786, and died April 4, 1844, æ. 57.

CHILDREN.

1. *Sarah Saloma*, b. June 24, 1808; d. unm., Aug. 24, 1827, æ. 19.
2. *Abigail*, b. Dec. 13, 1810; m. May 1, 1846, William Johnson of New York, and d. Aug. 14, 1850, æ. 39. She had, 1. William, b. May, 1847; 2. Albert, b. May, 1849.
3. *Alexander*, b. Feb. 23, 1813; d. unm., Aug. 20, 1836, æ. 23.
4. *Maria Warner*, b. Feb. 7, 1815; m. March, 1834, Norman Eddy of New Britain, Conn. She has had, 1. Albert, b. Dec., 1834, m. Oct., 1856, Jane Hurlburt of Plainville; 2. Martha Elizabeth, b. Jan. 16, 1839; 3. Alice Maria, b. July 6, 1847, d. Oct., 1854, æ. 7; 4. Arthur, b. Nov. 16, 1857.
5. *Elizabeth*, b. Feb. 4, 1818; m. May 16, 1838, Edwin W. Moseley, and has, 1. Clementine Elizabeth, b. March 26, 1842; 2. Arabella, b. May 24, 1857.
6. *Jerusha Deming*, b. March 4, 1822; m. Nov. 4, 1840, Lorenzo Wood of Somers, Conn. She has had, 1. Julia Maria, b. April 8, 1842; 2. Albert O., b. Jan. 5, 1848, d. Sept. 6, 1849; 3. Frederick Lorenzo, b. Sept. 29, 1854.
7. *John Jacob*, b. Oct. 20, 1825.

181. Capt. Asa White, youngest son of Jacob, (79) was born in Upper Middletown, where he was baptized Aug. 15, 1784. He was a sea-captain, and was lost in the brig Nestor, of which he was master, about 1826, æ. 41.

He married, Dec. 5, 1805, Mehitable White of Upper Middletown, dau. of Timothy White. (See Fam. 146.) She was born Sept. 10, 1784, and died in Hartford, Oct. 18, 1841, æ. 57.

CHILDREN.

1. *Asa,* b. 1806; d. Jan. 30, 1816, æ. 9.
2. *Clarissa,* b. 1810; d. July, 1818, æ. 7.
3. *Louisa,* b. Jan. 16, 1812; m. Jan. 2, 1843, Dr. Warren Thrall of Glastenbury.
4. *Lucy Collins,* b. 1816; m. May 3, 1849, John Baker, jun., now of Collinsville, Conn., and has Mortimer, b. Sept. 3, 1850.
5. *Asa Glover,* b. 1817; d. Sept. 5, 1823, æ. 6.

IN THE LINE OF JOSEPH WHITE, OF MIDDLETOWN.

182. Joseph White, son of William, (80) was born in Upper Middletown, March 14, 1788. He resides in Otis, Mass.

He married Esther C. Morell, who died Sept. 19, 1855, æ. 63.

CHILDREN.

1. *William Morell,* b. April 20, 1815; d. March 14, 1817.
2. *Jane Maria,* b. Jan. 1, 1818; d. Nov. 9, 1853, æ. 34.
3. *Mary Morell,* b. Dec. 19, 1820; d. Oct. 2, 1830, æ. 9.
4. *William Morell,* b. July 29, 1822; m. Emily F. Cooley.   .   (358)
5. *Helen Mar,* b. Aug. 30, 1823; m. April, 1844, Dr. Hablam C. Champlain of Owego, N. Y., and has, 1. Anise C., b. 1848; 2. Jane F., b. 1851.
6. *Frederic Augustus,* b. Dec. 12, 1825; lives in Sacramento City, Cal.
7. *Frances Henrietta,* b. Oct. 6, 1827; m. March 27, 1854, Hilliard M. Miller of Coloma, El Dorado Co., Cal.
8. *Mary Clarissa,* b. Sept. 17, 1831; d. Aug. 5, 1855, æ. 24.
9. *Harriet Catherine,* b. Dec. 17, 1833.
10. *Georgiana Caroline,* b. July 4, 1836.

183. Elizur White, Jun., son of Elizur, (81) was born in Upper Middletown, July 1, 1770. He removed with his father to Granville, Washington Co., N. Y., and died there, Jan. 28, 1839, æ. 68.

He married, May 4, 1795, Hannah Savage of Up. Mid. She was born Jan. 26, 1773, and died July 20, 1851, æ. 78.

He had one daughter,

Sally, b. May 25, 1796; m. Feb. 4, 1813, Benjamin Leavens of Mobile, Ala. She
d. in Mobile, May 3, 1839, æ. 43. He d. March 27, 1851. She had, 1. Emily
White, b. Aug. 10, 1815, m. Sept. 28, 1840, Samuel H. St John of New
York; 2. Benjamin Franklin, b. July 11, 1817, d. Jan. 17, 1850, æ. 32;
3. James Bayley, b. Nov. 9, 1819, d. Sept. 17, 1821; 4. James Bayley, b.
June 1, 1823, d. March 9, 1824; 5. Edward, b. April 25, 1825, d. Dec. 9,
1854, æ. 29; 6. Frederick, b. March 2, 1830; 7. Joshua B., b. Sept. 1, 1835,
d. April 25, 1836.

---

184. WILLIAM WHITE, son of Elizur, (81) was born about
1777. He settled in Upper Middletown, and died there, Dec.
5, 1827, æ. 50.

He married, 1st, Jan. 20, 1805, GRACE SAVAGE of Up. Mid.,
dau. of Capt. Abijah Savage. She died May 14, 1806.

He married, 2d, July 6, 1808, FANNY STOCKING, dau. of
William Stocking of Upper Middletown. She was born Nov.,
1785, and died Feb. 20, 1859, æ. 73.

CHILDREN;—BY THE SECOND MARRIAGE.

1. *Catharine Chauncey*, b. June 10, 1810; m. Jan. 6, 1830, Charles Kirby of Up.
Mid., and has, 1. Sarah Goodrich, b. Oct. 19, 1831; 2 Fanny Elizabeth, b.
Sept. 12, 1833; 3. Catharine White, b. Nov. 14, 1835.
2. *Nancy A.*, b. May 7, 1813; d. unm., April 27, 1856, æ. 42.
3. *Elizabeth*, b.   1816; d. Nov. 1, 1817, æ. 1 yr. 7 mos.

185. Capt. EBENEZER WHITE, son of Elizur, (81) was born
about 1781, and resided in Upper Middletown. He was lost
at sea, Sept. 16, 1810, by the capsizing of a brig of which he
was commander. His age was 29 years.

He married, Dec. 28, 1806, ELIZABETH SAGE of Upper Middletown, dau. of Epaphras Sage and Elizabeth Wells. She
married, 2d, 1817, Ashbel Post, and 3d, 1824, Dea. Josiah
Beckwith of Hartford, who died in 1827. She was born March
14, 1785, and died in Cromwell, April 14, 1859, æ. 74.

CHILDREN.

1. *Elizabeth Wells*, b. April 23, 1807; m. Dec. 4, 1833, Stephen S. Holmes of
Springfield, Mass. She has had, 1. Emily Leavens, bap. Sept. 18, 1836;
2. Elizabeth, b. July, 1850, d. Dec. 5, 1858.
2. *Hannah Cooper*, b. Jan. 31, 1809; m. Aug. 18, 1833, Henry Lyman Eastman.
He resided in Savannah, Ga., and d. Feb. 14, 1840, æ. 28. She res. in Cromwell, and has had, 1. Sarah Elizabeth, b. Nov. 24, 1834, d. Nov. 7, 1840;
2. Henry White, b. April 7, 1837, d. Nov. 18, 1840; 3. Georgia Ann, b. May
3, 1839.
3. *Ebenezer*, b.   1811; (posthumous;) d. Oct. 30, 1812, æ. 1 yr. 5 mos.

21

DESCENDANTS OF JOHN WHITE, JUNIOR.

186. Capt. John White, son of Asa, (82) was born in He-bron, Conn., Feb. 5, 1766. About 1788 he settled in Rome, Oneida Co., N. Y., and was a farmer there. In 1834 he removed to Potsdam, St. Lawrence Co., N. Y., where he died, May, 1838, æ. 72.

He married, May 15, 1788, Chloe Smith of Windham, Conn., dau. of Benjamin and Lydia Smith. She was born Aug., 1767, and died Sept., 1842, æ. 75.

CHILDREN.

1. *Dan,*   b. Oct. 21, 1789; m. Polly Jones.   .   .   .   (359)
2. *Gurdon,*   b. June 24, 1791; m. Betsey Jones.   .   .   .   (360)
3. *Benjamin,* b.   1792; d. æ. 4 years.
4. *Ralph,*   b.   1794; d. at Honey Creek, Ind., in 1824, æ. 30.
5. *Asa,*   b. Oct. 13, 1796; m. Electa Slayton.   .   .   .   (361)
6. *Mary,*   b. Oct. 26, 1797; m. April 13, 1820, Tilness Hawley, a farmer. She d. in Martinsburgh, N. Y., Dec. 16, 1824, æ. 27. She had, 1. Mary, b. Feb. 9, 1821, m. May 24, 1842, George H. Perry; 2. Frances, b. March 1, 1823, m. July, 1844, Henry S. Husted.
7. *Harry,*   b. Feb. 23, 1801; m. Deborah T. Jenne.   .   .   .   (362)
8. *David,*   b. Jan. 30, 1803; m. 1st, C. Seymour; 2d, L. L. Barnum. (363)
9. *Sally,*   b. March 3, 1806; m. June 1, 1831, Palmer Husted, a farmer, and has Frances Chloe, b. Oct. 12, 1835.
10. *Joseph,* b.   1808; m. Philena Topliff.   .   .   (364)

---

187. Jeremiah White, son of Asa, (82) was born in Hebron, Conn., June 8, 1780. He lived for some time in Windham, afterwards in Chaplin, but now resides in Ashford, Conn.

He married, 1st, Oct. 1, 1801, Sally Bottom of Windham, dau. of Asa Bottom. She died Aug., ——, æ. 37.

He married, 2d, Elizabeth Bottom, a sister of his former wife. She died May, ——, æ. 29.

He married, 3d, Mrs. Alice (Utley) Hartson, widow of John Hartson. She died May, ——, æ. 40.

He married, 4th, Anna Parkhurst of Chaplin, dau. of Stephen Parkhurst. She is now living.

CHILDREN ;—BY THE FIRST MARRIAGE.

1. *Malinda,*   b. May 21, 1803; d. May, 1813, æ. 10.
2. *Joseph M.,* b Sept. 14, 1806; m., and lives in Tioga Co., Pa. He and his married brothers have families, but the particulars have not been furnished.
3. *John E.,*   b. May 26, 1809; m., and lives in Tioga Co., Pa.
4. *Mary Ann,* b. May 2, 1811; m. 1st, 1844, William H. Merritt of Ashland,

Mass., who d. March 25, 1850, æ. 35. She m. 2d, 1857, Amos B. Davis of E. Medway, Mass. She has, by her first husband, 1. William Franklin, b. Feb. 26, 1846 ; 2. Mary Louisa, b. Feb. 20, 1850.

5. *Sarah*,　　b.　　　　1813 ; d. Oct., 1813, æ. 4 mos.

　　　　　CHILDREN ;—BY THE SECOND MARRIAGE.

6. *Sumner P.*, b. July 19, 1814 ; m., and lives in Charlestown, Mass.

7. *Sophronia*, b.　　　　; d. Nov.,　　æ. 7.

　　　　　CHILDREN ;—BY THE THIRD MARRIAGE.

8. *George*,　　b. May　6, 1819 ; m., and lives in Tioga Co., Pa.

9. *Truman*,　　b. Nov. 25, 1820 ; d. 1848, æ. 18.

10. *Earl*,　　b. Sept. 10, 1822 ; m., and lives in Chicago, Ill

11. *Angeline*,　　b. June 23, 1824 ; m. Charles G. Coffin, 3d, of Nantucket, Mass., and has 6 children.

12. *Sophronia*, b. June 22, 1826 ; m., and lives in Wisconsin.

13. *Charles*,　　b. July 15, 1828 ; lives in Hartford.

14. *Henry*,　　b. May　3, 1831 ; lives in Ashford.

　　　　　CHILDREN ;—BY THE FOURTH MARRIAGE.

15. *Lester*,　　b. May　2, 1832 ; lives in Ashford, and is married

16. *Eliza Ann*, b. Oct. 23, 1833 ; d. 1854, æ. 21.

17. *Sarah A.*, b. May 27, 1835.

18. *Lucian*,　　b. July 19, 1838.　　　　The dates furnished by this family can not be harmonized, and a part of them are omitted.

---

188. Dea. DAVID WHITE, son of Thomas Wells, (83) was born in Hardwick, Mass., Dec. 4, 1765. He removed with his father to Barnard, Vt., where he lived till the fall of 1799, when he removed, with his father and two brothers, to Washington Co., Ohio. He settled on a farm in the township of Roxbury, now Waterford ; was for many years a deacon of the Presbyterian Church in that place, and a highly useful citizen. He died Nov. 13, 1840, æ. 75, and was buried in the grave-yard of the family, on his farm, where also rest the remains of his three wives, his father, and several other relatives.

He married, 1st, 1792, PATTA CHEADLE of Barnard, Vt., dau. of Asa Cheadle and Patta Paddock. She died May 16, 1800, æ. 25.

He married, 2d, REBECCA PORTER, who died July 14, 1806, æ. 28.

He married, 3d, Mrs. CATHARINE (HARRIS) BRIGGS, who died Jan. 18, 1835, æ. 61.

　　　　　CHILDREN ;—BY THE FIRST MARRIAGE.

1. *Anna*, b. Sept. 22, 1792 ; m. April 18, 1813, Charles Slocum Cory, of Waterford, O., a merchant, now a farmer : has been a justice of the peace. She

has had, 1. Maria White, b. Feb. 7, 1814; 2. Leander David, b. Oct. 1, 1815, d. Nov. 6, 1852, æ 37; 3. Martha White, b. May 8, 1817, d. May 21, 1854, æ. 37; 4. Charles Slocum, b. Sept. 2, 1819, m. June 10, 1852, Lillis Henry; 5. Thomas Wells, b. Oct. 24, 1821, m. Sept. 4, 1854, Martha Jane Barclay; 6. Asa, b. Dec. 1, 1823; 7. Julia, b. March 9, 1826, m. May 9, 1854, John Chadwick; 8. William Benton, b. Oct. 27, 1835, m. Jan. 10, 1858, Eliza Biggum.

2. *Ruth,* b. Dec. 31, 1793; m. 1st, John Greenman, who d. She m. 2d, June 27, 1833, Dr. Isaac Baker of Bloomington, McLean Co., Ill., where he has held county offices. She d. Nov. 21, 1848, æ. 56, having had, by her first husband, 1. Lydia E., b. May 31, 1810, d. 1837, æ. 27; 2. William D., b. Nov. 26, 1811, m. and d.; 3. Mary D., b. March 29, 1814, m. —— Paul, and d. 1835, æ. 21; 4. Esek E., b. Jan. 23, 1816, m.; 5. David White, b. Nov. 9, 1817, d.; 6. John, b. Feb. 11, 1820; 7. Jeremiah, b. March 23, 1822, m., and d. 1854, æ. 32; 8. Adaline, b. May 11, 1824, m.; 9. Amanda M., b. Feb. 18, 1827, m.; 10. Parmenia, b. May 14, 1829, d. 1829; 11. Emily C. W., b. Sept. 16, 1830, m. By her second husband she has, 12. Julia A., b. July 17, 1834; 13. Laura A., b. July 10, 1839.

3. *David,* b.   1796; d. in infancy, at Barnard, Vt.
4. *Asa,* b. July 20, 1797; m. Cynthia Keyes.   .   .   .   (365)
5. *Wells,* b. April,   1799; m. Sarah Evans.   .   .   .   .   (366)

CHILDREN;—BY THE SECOND MARRIAGE.

6. *David,* b. July 4, 1804; m. Nancy Ann Miller.   .   .   (367)
7. *Rebecca,* b. April 22, 1806.

CHILDREN;—BY THE THIRD MARRIAGE.

8. *Harris,* b. Nov. 17, 1808; m. Frances Steel.   .   .   .   .   (368)
9. *Henry,* b. Nov. 12, 1811; m. 1st, Lovisa Coleman; 2d, E. Hinkley. (369)
10. *Hiram,* b. Aug. 11, 1813; d. July 27, 1832, æ. 19.

---

189. THOMAS WHITE, Esq., son of Thomas Wells, (83) was born in Hardwick, Mass., July 26, 1767. He removed from Barnard, Vt., to Ohio, in 1799, with his father and brothers, and settled in Waterford, on a farm adjoining that of his brother David. He was for about twenty years a justice of the peace. He died Feb. 6, 1848, æ. 80.

He married, 1794, JOANNA SAMSON, born in 1775. She resides in Windsor, Morgan Co., O., with her youngest daughter.

CHILDREN.

1. *Samson Keyes,* b. Aug. 21, 1796; m. Rhoda Richmond.   (370)
2. *Elias,* b. Nov. 29, 1798; m. Sarah Olney.   .   .   .   (371)
3. *Rebecca,* b. March 7, 1801; d. Oct. 17, 1801.
4. *Rebecca,* b. Nov. 11, 1802; m. 1st, Jan. 4, 1821, Rufus Lawrence of Waterford, O., who d. 1827; m. 2d, Oct. 15, 1834, Dea. Benjamin Hart of Harmar, Washington Co., O., and d. Sept. 19, 1856, æ. 54. She had, by her first husband, 1. Lydia Minerva, b. July 9, 1822, m. Simeon Hart;

2. Henderson, b. May 31, 1825, m. ——— Fleming ; 3. Sarah White, (posthumous,) b. Jan. 13, 1828, m. May 17, 1853, William Gray Hayward. By her second husband, 4. William, d. ; 5. Frances Adelia.

5. *Polly*, b. Nov. 2, 1806; d. Dec. 7, 1806.

6. *Mary*, b. July 17, 1808; m. Aug. 29, 1825, Samuel Miller Evans, now of Marion, Linn Co., Iowa. She has had, 1. Mary Dodge, b. March 18, 1827, m. Addison E. White ; (see Fam. 365 ;) 2. Joanna White, b. Oct. 26, 1828, m. Nov. 28, 1850, George E. Keyes ; 3. William Thomas, b. Sept. 6, 1830; 4. Lydia Pierpoint, b. June 11, 1832, m. Jan. 1, 1852, John Clinton Shrader; 5. Minerva Lawrence, b. Feb. 25, 1835, m. Oct. 9, 1855, Thompson Sharp; 6. Elizabeth M., b. Jan. 19, 1837, m. March 1, 1857, Willis Wellington Gray; 7. Erastus Brown, b. Feb. 9, 1839; 8. Samuel Hamilton. b. Feb. 24, 1841 ; 9. Elias Henry, b. Jan. 1, 1843 ; 10. Sarah Green, b. Jan. 1, 1845 ; 11. Prudence Ann, b. Aug. 23, 1847 ; 12. George Everet, b. Sept. 23, 1850, d. Oct. 9, 1853 ; 13. Jesse White, twin with the last ; 14. Charles Warren, b. Aug. 17, 1853, d. Nov. 20, 1855.

7. *Joanna*, b. April 12, 1814 ; m. Dec. 29, 1831, Henry Olney of Windsor, O., and has had, 1. Harriet Newel, b. Dec. 9, 1832, m. Dec. 22, 1855, John Havener; 2. John White, b. Jan. 8, 1835, d. Aug. 27, 1854, æ. 19 ; 3. Sylvanus, b. Feb 10, 1837, d. May 25, 1837 ; 4. Elizabeth Nixon, b. April 15, 1838, m. Aug. 12, 1858, Joseph Smith ; 5. Jesse Blackmer, b. May 13, 1841, d. May 25, 1841 ; 6. Anna Slack, b. July 4, 1842, d. Sept. 7, 1854, æ. 12 ; 7. Mary Evans, b. March 30, 1845 ; 8. Willard Davis, b. Jan. 21, 1848 ; 9. Louisana, b. Dec. 31, 1851 ; 10. Franklin, b. Dec. 9, 1854 ; 11. Alice Cornelia, b. Sept. 21, 1856.

8. *Augustus Stone*, b. May 5, 1818 ; m. Locia Webster. (372)

---

190. JOHN WHITE, son of Thomas Wells, (83) was born in Barnard, Vt., in 1783. He was a clothier in Rupert, Vt., and died October, 1829, æ. 46.

He married LAURA RISING of Rupert. After the death of her husband, she removed to the West, with her parents. The present residence of the family has not been ascertained.

CHILDREN.

1. *Olcott.*
2. *Laura.*   There were two other children, names not known.

---

191. OLCOTT WHITE, son of Thomas Wells, (83) was born in Barnard, Vt., Jan. 9, 1786. He lived for some years in Middlebury, Vt., but removed to Ohio about 1820, and resides in Zanesville, Muskingum Co. He was formerly a clothier and a calico-stamper, but is now a bookseller and bookbinder.

He married, Dec. 5, 1811, ELECTA ABERNETHY, born in Stockbridge, Mass., May 25, 1791, dau. of James Palmer Abernethy and Thankful Wright.

CHILDREN.

1. *John Wright*, b. Oct. 19, 1814 ; m. Catherine Springer.   .   .   (373)
2. *Fanny*,   b. Feb. 19, 1816 ; m. Oct. 3, 1834, John Alexander Dutre of
   Zanesville, a tailor, and has, 1. Charles William, b. Oct. 23, 1835 ; 2. James
   Milo, b. Nov. 30, 1837 ; 3. Thomas White, b. Dec. 19, 1839 ; 4. Eveline, b.
   Aug. 3, 1842 ; 5. Ann, b. Jan. 26, 1846 ; 6. Martha, b. Feb. 28, 1849.
3. *Laura*,   b. July 8, 1819 ; m. Dec. 22, 1852, Henry Elliott, a bookbinder and
   bookseller in Zanesville.
4. *Horatio*, b. Nov. 5, 1823 ; m. Susan Clossman.   .   .   .   .   (374)
5. *Caroline*, b. Sept. 20, 1831 ; d. unm., Dec. 6, 1856, æ. 25.

---

192. SAMUEL WHITE, youngest son of Thomas Wells, (83)
was born in Barnard, Vt., Nov. 30, 1789. He removed to Ohio,
with his father, in 1799, and afterwards settled as a farmer in
Windsor, Morgan Co., where he died, Oct. 12, 1823, æ. 34.

He married EUNICE EMERSON of Barnard, Vt., dau. of Asa
Emerson and Eunice Foster.   She was born March 14, 1791,
and died in Windsor, Aug. 29, 1839, æ. 48.

CHILDREN.

1. *Mary*,   b. Sept. 10, 1810 ; m. May 21, 1830, Lorenzo Andrews of Center,
   Morgan Co., O., a farmer. She has had, 1. Laura, b. 1831 ; 2. Hiram B.,
   b. 1833, m. Hannah Lewis ; 3. Pedee Ann ; 4. Christopher ; 5. Lydia, m. ;
   6. Ellen Matilda ; 7. Joanna ; 8. Melissa ; 9. Curtis.
2. *Susanna*, b. May   22, 1812 ; m. 1831, William Hook of Windsor, a farmer,
   and has had, 1. Henry, b. Feb. 26, 1832, m. Angeline Smith ; 2. John, b.
   Sept. 6, 1833 ; 3. William Bernard, b. July 7, 1835 ; 4. Martha, b. March
   30, 1837, m. 1858, David Brooks ; 5. Susanna, b. Jan. 14, 1840, d. Jan. 10,
   1844 ; 6. Rachel Jane, b. March 1, 1843 ; 7. Charles Cory, b. April 4, 1845 ;
   8. Isaac, b. July 3, 1847 ; 9. Lydia, b. Nov. 26, 1849.
3. *Roxana*, b. March 14, 1814 ; m. Jan. 1, 1853, Richard Kitchen of Cincinnati,
   O., a farmer.
4. *Lydia*,   b. March 2, 1816 ; m. Jan. 18, 1835, David Stokely of Roseville,
   ' Muskingum Co., O., and has, 1. Rufus ; 2. Edwin ; 3. Benjamin Olney.
5. *Abigail*, b. May   6, 1818 ; m. April 1, 1847, John Green, Esq., of Anamosa,
   Jones Co., Iowa, a lawyer. He d. Aug. 14, 1853, æ. 36. She has had,
   1. Laura Roxana, b. July 13, 1848 ; 2. Philip Melancthon, b. May 18, 1851 ;
   3. Merle D'Aubigne, twin with the last, d. Oct. 3, 1852.
6. *Asa Gates*, b. June 24, 1820 ; m. 1st, A. F. Davidson ; 2d, A. E. Stone. (376)

DESCENDANTS OF LIEUT. DANIEL WHITE.

193. ELIJAH WHITE, son of Daniel, (84) was born in Hatfield, Mass., April 26, 1768.   He settled there, and died Feb.
18, 1831, æ. 62.

He married, April 19, 1792, MARY SMITH, 3d, of Hatfield.
She was born Nov. 7, 1769, and died Dec. 1, 1853, æ. 84.

CHILDREN.

1. *John,*   b. Aug. 22, 1792 ; m. 1st, Sophia White ; 2d, Elizabeth Drake. (376)
2. *Betsey,* ⎱ b. Nov. 3, 1794.
3. *Electa,* ⎰   Twins.   m. July 28, 1819, Stearns Hubbard of Hatfield,
    and d. May 23, 1857, æ. 62, having had six children.   Her dau., Ruth, m.
    Dec. 30, 1840, Israel W. Billings.
4. *Mary,*   b. Dec. 13, 1795 ; m. March 2, 1820, George Wait, and d. Nov.
    6, 1827, æ. 32.
5. *Submit,*   b. Aug. 7, 1798 ; m. Feb. 7, 1824, Sylvester Bliss of Whitestown,
    N. Y.   She has had, 1. Jason S., b. Feb. 18, 1825, m. May 24, 1848, Ma-
    rietta Phelps of Westmoreland, N. Y. ; 2. George W., b. Jan. 15, 1829.
6. *George,*   b. Dec. 28, 1799 ; m. Delia Sheldon.   .   .   .   .   (377)
7. *Daniel,*   b. Nov. 2, 1801 ; m. Lucy Elvira Rice. .   .   .   (378)
8. *Quartus,* b. Dec. 26, 1803 ; d. Sept. 3, 1805.
9. *Lucy Ann,* b. Jan. 22, 1806 ; m. Oct. 15, [16?] 1834, Salmon D. Bardwell of
    Hatfield, now of Margaretta, O.   She has, 1. Sarah Ann L., b. July 2, 1835,
    m. May 11, 1859, William Graves of Margaretta ; 2. Maria L., b. Feb. 19,
    1838.
10. *Louisa,*   b. Sept. 25, 1808 ; m. April 17, 1833, Seth Bardwell, of Hatfield,
    now of Groton, Erie Co., O.   She has had, 1. Pamela, b. July 11, 1834, m.
    Feb. 20, 1851, Ralph Ramsdale of Oxford, O. ; 2. Dwight L., b. June 13,
    1836, d. April 1, 1843 ; 3. Sophia A., b. June 7, 1839, m. Dec. 27, 1855,
    David Compton of Margaretta ; 4. Mary W., b. July 7, 1842 ; 5. Seth E.,
    b. Dec. 6, 1844 ; 6. Alma L., b. Sept. 4, 1847 ; 7. Charles F., b. Jan. 9, 1851.
11. *Quartus,* b. Feb. 1, 1811 ; m. Julia Ann Wilkee.   .   .   .   (379)

---

194. SALMON WHITE, Jun., son of Dea. Salmon, (85) was
born in Whately, Mass., Sept. 22, 1760.   He was a farmer in
that place, and died May 1, 1822, æ. 61.

He married, 1st, LYDIA AMSDEN of Deerfield, Mass.   She
died Feb. 22, 1799, æ. 33.

He married, 2d, Nov. 27, 1799, Mrs. ANNA ALLIS of Whately,
widow of Josiah Allis, who died April 17, 1794, æ. 40.   She
was the dau. of Elisha Hubbard and Lucy Stearns ; was born
in Hatfield, Dec. 26, 1755, and died June 21, 1839, æ. 83.*

CHILDREN ;—BY THE FIRST MARRIAGE.

1. *Justus,* b.   1787 ; m. Rhoda Frary. .   .   .   .   (380)
2. *Harriet,* b. March 4, 1790 ; m. Nov. 12, 1811, Moses Arms, jun., of Greenfield,
   Mass., who d. April 13, 1823, æ. 38.   She is living with her dau. in Ill.   She

---

* The manner in which families are sometimes connected by numerous marriages,
is illustrated by the case of Mrs. Anna Allis and her relatives.   Her son, Elijah Allis,
m. Electa White, a sister of her second husband, Salmon White, jun. ; (see Fam. 85 :)
her son, Jere Allis, m. Mary White, a daughter of her second husband ; (see Fam. 194 :)
and her grandson, Josiah Allis, m. Eliza White, a daughter of her second husband's
cousin ; (see Fam. 197.)   Her brother, Elisha Hubbard, m. Hannah White, a cousin of
Salmon White, junior ; (see Fam. 84 ;) and her sister, Hannah Hubbard, m. Simeon
White, jun., a cousin of Salmon White, senior ; (Family 93.)

has, 1. George, res. in Mt. Pleasant, Iowa; 2. Moses, res. in Cal.; 3. Harriet, m. —— Dame, and res. in Ill.

3. *Mary*,   b. June 3, 1793; m. Oct. 1, 1814, Jere Allis, now of Oxford, Chenango Co., N. Y. She has had, 1. Edward P., b. Dec. 31, 1815, d. Aug. 16, 1821; 2. Elisha, b. Aug. 26, 1819, d. Aug. 25, 1821; 3. Mary A., b. Aug. 4, 1821, m. May 9, 1843, Rev. H. Callahan, a Presbyterian minister in Oxford; 4. Edward P., b. May 12, 1824, res. in Milwaukee, Wis. He m. Sept. 12, 1848, Margaret Watson; 5. Lucy Jane, b. Sept. 19, 1828, m. June 30, 1852, Joseph T. Gilbert, a merchant in New York.

4. *A child*, b. April 19, 1798; d. same day.

195. Dea. JOHN WHITE, son of Dea. Salmon, (85) was born in Whately, Jan. 9, 1762. He was a farmer there, and was chosen a deacon of the church in Whately, in March, 1810. He was a justice of the peace, was frequently chosen a selectman, and represented the town in the Legislature. He died April 2, 1836, æ. 74.

He married, Feb. 7, 1796, ELIZABETH BROWN of Worcester, Mass., dau. of Samuel Brown and Elizabeth Adams. She died March 26, 1853, æ. 83.

CHILDREN.

1. *Luke Brown*, b. May 8, 1797; m. Mary Wells.   .   .   .   (381)
2. *Elizabeth Mary*, b. Jan. 23, 1799; m. Sept. 23, 1819, John Bardwell Morton of Hatfield, now of Whately, and d. Oct. 24, 1858, æ. 59. She had, 1. Elizabeth Mary, b. Feb. 16, 1821, m. Aug. 23, 1843, Rev. John A. McKinstry, now of Harwinton, Conn. He grad. Amherst Coll., 1838; 2. Harriet Arms, b. Jan. 8, 1823, d. Jan. 2, 1844, æ. 21; 3. John White, b. Jan. 21, 1826, m. March 24, 1858, Henrietta A. Kingsley of Williamsburg; 4. Eurotas, b. July 6, 1828; 5. Elvira White, b. June 7, 1835; 6. Judith White, b. Dec. 3, 1839.
3. *Judith*, b. Nov. 17, 1800; d. Aug. 27, 1810, æ. 9.
4. *Maria*, b. Oct. 31, 1802; m. Eurotas Morton, now of Ypsilanti, Mich., and has, 1. Eunice White; 2. Martha Baldwin, m. 1858, William A. Heartt of Wahjamega, Tuscola Co., Mich; 3. Maria Elizabeth.
5. *John*, b. Aug. 2, 1804; m. Cornelia White.   .   .   .   (382)
6. *Elvira*, b. Oct.,   1806; m. Levi Bush of Westfield, Mass., and has, 1. Elizabeth White; 2. Harriet Morton.
7. *Eunice*, b. Feb. 14, 1809; d. Aug. 9, 1817, æ. 8.
8. *Samuel Brooks*, b. Jan. 9, 1811; m. Experience P. Wells.   .   (383)
9. *Judith*, b. May 8, 1813; d. May 4, 1837, æ. 24.
10. *Eunice*, b. Dec. 24, 1819; d. Dec. 30, 1824, æ. 5.

196. THOMAS WHITE, Esq., son of Dea. Salmon, (85) was born in Whately, April 12, 1773. About 1798 he removed to Ashfield, where he was a blacksmith and a farmer. He was

a justice of the peace, was a selectman for about twenty-five years, and several times represented the town in the Legislature. He was much employed in the settlement of estates, and in the public business of the town and county. He died Aug. 17, 1848, æ. 75.

He married, Aug. 30, 1795, HANNAH HARWOOD, dau. of Nathan Harwood of Windsor, Mass. She was born Nov. 17, 1771, and died May 10, 1848, æ. 76. A brief memorial of her "rare virtues and acquirements" was printed for distribution among the friends of the family.

CHILDREN.

1. *Horace,* b. July 17, 1796; d. July 30, 1796.
2. *Amanda,* b. Aug. 20, 1797; m. July 8, 1823, Rev. William M. Ferry, who grad. Union College, 1820, and has been for many years a missionary on the Island of Mackinaw, Mich. She has, 1. William M., b. July 8, 1824, m. Oct. 25, 1851, Jeannette Hollister; 2. Thomas W., b. June 1, 1826; 3. Amanda H., b. Sept. 20, 1828; 4. Noah H., b. April 30, 1831; 5. Hannah E., b. April 16, 1834; 6 & 7. Edward P. and Mary L., twins, b. April 16, 1837.
3. *Hannah,* b. March 4, 1800; has been a teacher for many years, and now has the superintendence of the classes of teachers sent to the West by the National Board of Popular Education.
4. *Morris E.,*   b. April 27, 1803; m. 1st, L. C. Payson; 2d, P. Rowe. (384)
5. *Thomas Wait,*   b. Nov. 15, 1805; m. Caroline Norton.   .   . (385)
6. *Luke A.,*   b. Oct. 17, 1808; m. Clarissa J. Perkins.   . (386)
7. *Nathan Harwood,* b. April 13, 1811; m. Sarah B. Britton.   .   . (387)
8. *Mary A.,*   b. Sept. 18, 1813; has been for more than twenty years a teacher in Mich. and Ill.

---

197. EBENEZER WHITE, son of Lieut. Elihu, (86) was born in Hatfield, Mass., Feb. 28, 1766. He was a farmer in that place, and died Jan. 6, 1826, æ. 60.

He married, Jan. 10, 1793, MARY DICKINSON, dau. of Elijah Dickinson. She was born Jan. 17, 1772, and died May 11, 1850, æ. 78.

CHILDREN.

1. *Sophia,* b. Dec. 6, 1793; m. John White.   .   .   . (Family 376)
2. *Mary,* b. May 5, 1799; m. 1st, Dec. 21, 1826, Dr. Chester Johnson of Hadley, who d. April 7, 1829, æ. 31. She m. 2d, Feb., 1835, Medad Vinton of Amherst; is now living in Iowa. She had, by her first husband, Charles Dickinson, b. April 3, 1828.
3. *Eliza,* b. May 22, 1801; m. April 13, 1826, Josiah Allis, of East Whately; (see in Fam. 85.) She has had, 1. Justin Wright Clark, b. March 31, 1827; 2. Silas Dickinson White, b. Dec. 11, 1828; 3. Mary Eliza White, b. Sept.

22

29, 1830 ; 4. Lewis Edward Sikes, b. July 14, 1832 ; 5. Edmond Bridges, b. July 31, 1834, d. Feb. 17, 1835; 6. Edmond Bridges, b. Dec. 11, 1635, grad. Yale College, 1859.

4. *Julianna*, b. July 8, 1804 ; m. April 11, 1832, Elijah Hubbard of Hatfield, and d. Oct. 11, 1840, æ. 36. He d. Oct. 11, 1854, æ. 56. She had, 1. Horace White, b. March 11, 1833 ; 2. Marshall Ney, b. March 22, 1836 ; 3. Charles Edward, b. Oct., 1838, d. April 12, 1839 ; 4. Charles Edward, b. Feb. 8, 1840.

5. *Harriet*, b. July 31, 1806 ; [July 15?] d. March 8, 1809.

6. *Charlotte*, b. Oct. 9, 1808 ; m. May 25, 1831, Charles Morris Billings of Hatfield, and has had, 1. Frederick Dickinson, b. July 25, 1832 ; 2. Arthur White, b. July 25, 1834 ; 3. Martha Dickinson, b. July 7, 1836 ; 4. Charles Morris, b. July 20, 1839 ; 5. Joseph, b. Aug. 12, 1842 ; 6. David, b. July 6, 1849, d. Jan. 16, 1851 ; 7. Harriet Charlotte, b. Feb. 5, 1853.

7. *Silas Dickinson*, b. Dec. 25, 1810 ; m. Mrs. Amanda Clapp.   .   . (388)

8. *Horace*,   b. March 6, 1815 ; d. unm., Dec. 24, 1844, æ. 29.

---

198. ELIHU WHITE, Jun., son of Lieut. Elihu, (86) was born in Hatfield, Dec. 17, 1767. He resided there, and died June 26, 1816, æ. 48.

He married, July 5, 1792, SARAH SMITH of Hatfield.

CHILDREN.

1. *Lemira*, b.   ; m. Seth Kingsley. Both are dead.
2. *Moses*, b. Oct. 24, 1794 ; d. Dec. 8, 1811, æ. 17.
3. *Theda*, b. April 4, 1798.
4. *Prescott*, b. Sept. 15, 1801 ; m. Caroline Townsley of Walpole, N. H., and died.
5. *Sarah*, b. April 6, 1806 ; m. Sept. 3, 1834, Alexander H. Harman.
6. *Edward*, b. March 18, 1810 ; m. Jerusha King, and died.

---

199. JONATHAN COLE WHITE, son of Lieut. Elihu, (86) was born in Hatfield, Feb. 17, 1780. He settled in Hartford, Vt., where he died, Aug. 17, 1844, æ. 64. He was a hatter.

He married CYNTHIA PARKHURST, who died Nov. 16, 1828, æ. 43. His only child,

Caroline, b. about 1805, m. Sidney Barlow of Burlington, Vt., and d. without issue, two years after marriage, æ. about 27.

---

200. JABEZ LOOMIS WHITE, Esq., only son of Joel, jun., (87) was born in Andover, Conn., Dec. 29, 1763. He settled as a farmer in Bolton, where he frequently held town offices. He was for a long time a justice of the peace, and once a representative to the Legislature. He died Sept. 1, 1844, æ. 81.

He married, Nov. 13, 1783, ELIZABETH WALES, dau. of Timothy Wales of Hebron, Conn. She died Aug. 25, 1845, æ. 82.

CHILDREN.

1. *Anna L.*, b. Feb. 5, 1784 ; m. March, 1803, Roswell Bailey of Lebanon. He grad. Yale Coll., 1801, was a merchant and teacher, and d. 1850. She d. in Bolton, April 20, 1858, æ. 74. She had, 1. Roswell White, b. Feb., 1805, is a farmer in Bolton. He m. March 20, 1826, Elizabeth C. Stowel of Plainfield, Conn. ; 2. Elizabeth Ann Loomis, b. April 7, 1811, m. April 9, 1829, Benjamin Hoxie, who d. Aug. 26, 1856.

2. *Elizabeth*, b. Sept. 14, 1785 ; m. Nov. 11, 1806, Aaron Cook of Ashford, a blacksmith. He d. Jan. 16, 1838. She res. in Manchester, and has, 1. Julia W., b. Sept. 1, 1807, m. June 7, 1827, Dr. William C. Williams of Manchester, who d. Oct. 6, 1857 ; 2. Aaron, b. Dec. 7, 1808, res. in Manchester. He m. June 29, 1837, Mabel Lyman of Manchester.

3. *Sarah*,   b. April 5, 1787 ; m. March 12, 1812, Samuel Williams, a blacksmith. He res. in Bolton. She d. Aug. 23, 1849, æ. 62. She had, 1. Samuel White, b. Feb. 22, 1813, res. in Bolton. He m. Oct. 2, 1839, Cornelia Badger of Bolton ; 2. William, b. Sept. 6, 1815, res. in Buffalo, N. Y. He m. Oct. 9, 1838, Lovisa K. Stedman of Hartford ; 3. Jabez Loomis, b. Dec. 18, 1819, m. Oct., 1849, Wealthy T. Sherman of Lebanon ; 4. Sarah Ann, b. Oct. 31, 1821, m. 1st, May 12, 1840, Sylvester T. Skinner of Bolton, who d. Feb. 16, 1853 ; m. 2d, June, 1858, Elbridge Belden of Bristol, Conn. ; 5. Harriet Wales, b. April 28, 1823, m. Nov. 2, 1841, Eli Baker Francis of Bolton ; 6. Elizabeth White, b. Oct. 18, 1825, m. Oct. 26, 1858, Charles O. Morse of Bristol, Conn. ; 7. Clarissa White, b. July 1, 1827, d. Sept. 28, 1852, æ. 25 ; 8. Mary Loomis, b. Oct. 12, 1829, m. June 19, 1855, Isaac W. Hakes of Norwich ; 9. Julia Sophronia, b. Oct. 12, 1833.

4. *Roxanna*, b. Feb. 6, 1789 ; d. Feb. 22, 1797, æ. 8.

5. *Clarissa*, b. Nov. 5, 1790 ; m. 1st, Oct. 31, 1811, Elijah Alvord of Bolton, who d. Nov. 19, 1820, æ. 31. She m. 2d, Nov. 10, 1825, Hon. Benjamin Ruggles of St. Clairsville, Ohio, U. S. Senator from 1818 to 1833. He d. Sept., 1857. By her first husband she had one dau., Eleanor Kellogg, b. Sept. 3, 1812, m. C. C. Carroll, M. D., afterwards a lawyer in St. Clairsville. He d.

6. *Jabez Loomis*, b. June 18, 1792 ; m. Emily Hammond.   .   .   (389)

7. *Sophronia*,   b. Dec. 1, 1794 ; m. Nov. 24, 1819, Chester Strickland of B., a farmer, who d. April 28, 1842, æ. 45. She has one dau., Julia Ann, b. Dec. 31, 1821, m. Jan. 26, 1843, Arnold Martin, now of B.

8. *Joel Wales*, b. April 24, 1795 ; m. 1st, Sarah Fox; 2d, E. M. Moseley. (390)

9. *Royal Stiles*, b. Aug. 26, 1799 ; res. in Bolton, and has been a merchant. He has held town offices, has been a justice of the peace, and has twice represented the town in the Legislature.

10. *Thomas Jefferson*, b. March 31, 1802 ; m. Phebe Ann Farmer.   .   (391)

11. *George Clinton*, b. Nov. 28, 1804 ; m. Mrs. Elizabeth B. Morgan.   (392)

---

201. Capt. LEMUEL WHITE, son of Lemuel, (88) was born in East Hartford, Conn., Nov. 1, 1762. He was a sea-captain, in the China trade, and afterwards a merchant at East Hartford, where he was post-master, and a justice of the peace. He died Dec. 8, 1843, æ. 81.

He married, 1st, June 1, 1789, MARY BUCKLAND of East

Hartford, dau. of Capt. Stephen Buckland. She was born April 18, 1769, and died May 12, 1790, æ. 21.

He married, 2d, June 25, 1793, MARY WELLS of East Hartford, dau. of John Wells and Jerusha Pitkin. She was born Feb. 13, 1765, and died Sept. 1, 1845, æ. 80.

CHILD ;—BY THE FIRST MARRIAGE.

1. *Buckland,*   b. May   1, 1790 ; d. Oct. 26, 1806, æ. 16.

CHILDREN ;—BY THE SECOND MARRIAGE.

2. *Wells,*   b. March 19, 1794 ; d. Oct. 30, 1794.
3. *James Wells,* b. Sept. 21, 1800 ; m. Catharine R. Garner.   .   .   (393)
4. *Mary,*   b. Dec. 31, 1802 ; resides in Rockville, Conn.

---

202. JOHN J. WHITE, son of Lemuel, (88) was born in East Hartford, April 28, 1771. He was for many years a teacher in Hartford, and in other places. He is supposed to have died of the cholera, while traveling, in the summer of 1832, æ. 61. He probably died at Philadelphia.

He married, 1st, July 20, 1794, ELIZABETH SHELTON. She was born April 4, 1776, and died Feb. 15, 1804, æ. 28.

He married, 2d, Feb. 12, 1815, CHARLOTTE LUCRETIA WOODBRIDGE of Hartford, dau. of Joseph and Lucy Woodbridge. She was born Aug. 7, 1789, and died June 3, 1852, æ. 63.

CHILDREN ;—BY THE FIRST MARRIAGE.

1. *Charles Shelton,* b. June 12, 1795 ; d. unm., Sept. 3, 1821, æ. 26.
2. *Susan Shelton,* b. Aug. 28, 1796 ; d. Feb. 1, 1804, æ. 7.
3. *Martha Cheney,* b. Sept. 18, 1799 ; m. Jan. 21, 1821, Rev. Sturges Gilbert, an Episcopal clergyman at Great Barrington, Mass., who d. at Cherry Valley, N. Y., Aug. 3, 1847. She lives in C. V., and has had, 1. Martha Elizabeth, b. Nov. 18, 1821, d. 1840, æ. 19 ; 2. Marcus Aurelius, b. July 27, 1823 ; 3. Charles Marcellus, b. Dec. 26, 1824, d. Dec. 1, 1856, æ. 32 ; 4. Caroline Amelia, b. Jan. 6, 1828, m. 1st, April 15, 1846, George E. Foote of New York, who d. Nov. 19, 1849 ; m. 2d, June 30, 1857, Charles W. Robb, Esq., of Pittsburg, Pa. ; 5. Fanny Cornelia, b. Dec. 29, 1829, m. June 18, 1851, Dr. George W. Merritt of C. V. ; 6. Julia Maria, b. Aug. 25, 1832.

CHILDREN ;—BY THE SECOND MARRIAGE.

4. *Elizabeth Ann,* b. March 3, 1816 ; m. July 15, 1848, Edmund Perry, Esq., a lawyer, of Flemington, N. J., and has, 1. Samuel Edmund, b. May 7, 1849 ; 2. Auguste Belmont, b. March 14, 1853 ; 3. A daughter, b. March, 1859.
5. *Sheldon Woodbridge,* b. June   2, 1817 ; d. June 4, 1817.
6. *Joseph Woodbridge,* b. Aug. 7, 1818 ; m. Mary E. Dollen.   .   .   (394)
7. *Julia,*   b. March 26, 1820 ; m. Jan. 21, 1841, John S. Dobson of Vernon, a manufacturer, and has Emma Sophia, b. Nov. 3, 1841.
8. *William H.,*   b. Jan. 8, 1822 ; m. Eliza Dollen.   .   .   (395)
9. *Emma Woodbridge,* b. May 20, 1824 ; d. Nov. 15, 1838, æ. 14.

203. ELIHU WHITE, son of Elijah, Esq., (89) was born in Bolton, Conn., July 27, 1773. After a few years residence in Hartford, Conn., he removed to New York, and established a type-foundry there in 1810. He was a man of great ingenuity, and made valuable improvements in the art of type-making. He was also for several years a bookseller and publisher. In his business relations, as well as in private life, he was highly esteemed for his intelligence and uprightness. He died Nov. 7, 1836, æ. 63. The following is a fac-simile of his autograph.

He married SARAH TRUMBULL of Hartford, dau. of Hon. John Trumbull, Judge of the Supreme Court of Conn., and author of "M'Fingal." Her mother was Sarah Hubbard. Mrs. Sarah White was born September, 1784, and died June 10, 1816, æ. 31.

CHILDREN.

1. *John Trumbull*, b. Nov. 5, 1809; m. Sarah G. Carroll. . . . (396)
2. *Julia*, b. Sept. 22, 1811; m. April 23, 1832, Rt. Rev. Alfred Lee, D. D. He graduated at Harvard College in 1827, first studied law, but in 1837 entered the ministry of the Protestant Episcopal Church, and in 1841 was chosen Bishop of the Diocese of Delaware. He resides at Wilmington, Del. She has had, 1. Benjamin, b. Sept. 26, 1833, grad. at the University of Penn. in 1852, and at the N. Y. Medical College in 1856; is a physician in New York. He m. April 5, 1859, Emma Hale White; (see Family 404;) 2. Leighton, b. Sept. 20, 1837, d. Feb. 13, 1853, æ. 15; 3. Clementina Smith, b. April 10, 1846; 4. Elizabeth Leighton, b. April 8, 1849, d. Nov. 12, 1850; 5. Julia Trumbull, twin with the last; 6. Alfred, b. March 25, 1852; 7. Edmund, b. March 9, 1855, d. Dec. 9, 1857.
3. *Charles*, b. Sept. 21, 1813; d. in Penn., unm., Sept. 1, 1848, æ. 35.
4. *Sarah T.*, b. Nov. 27, 1815; d. July 22, 1816.

---

204. ELIJAH WHITE, Jun., son of Elijah, Esq., (89.) was born in Bolton, Aug. 15, 1784. He was a merchant and farmer in that place, until 1831, when he removed to White

Pigeon, St. Joseph Co., Mich., where he became a large landholder. In 1853 he removed to Davenport, Iowa, and thence in Oct., 1854, to Winterset, Madison Co., Iowa, where he died, Nov. 16, 1854, æ. 70.

He married, 1st, Sept. 14, 1818, ELECTA Fox of Bolton, dau. of Jacob Fox. She was born Oct. 22, 1790, and died June 14, 1835, æ. 44.

He married, 2d, Oct. 12, 1835, DELIA SHELDON of Rupert, Vt., born Aug. 9, 1801, dau. of Increase Sheldon and Hannah King. She resides at Winterset, Iowa.

CHILDREN ;—BY THE FIRST MARRIAGE.

1. *Benjamin Day,*   b. Oct. 11, 1819; m. Julia M. Sheldon.   .   (397)
2. *Charles James Fox,* b. Jan. 16, 1821; d. unm., Dec. 24, 1855, at Michigan Bluff, Cal. He was killed by an accident in a mining tunnel.
3. *John,*   b. Aug. 16, 1822; d. March 22, 1833, æ. 10.
4. *A son,*   }
5. *A daughter,* } b. Aug. 11, 1823; twins : both d. Aug. 12, 1823.
6. *Henry Dwight,* b. Oct. 13, 1824; lost on Lake Superior, in the wreck of the steamer "Superior," Oct. 30, 1856, æ. 32. He was unmarried.
7. *Samuel,*   b. Feb. 15, 1826; lives at Campo Seco, Calaveras Co., Cal.
8. *Electa Jane,*   b. Sept. 8, 1827; m. Sept., 1845, Erasmus D. Smith of Adell, Dallas Co., Iowa, and has Clarence.
9. *William,*   b. April 6, 1829; lives in Lockport, N. Y.
10. *Mary,*   b. Sept. 1, 1830; d. at Detroit, Mich., Aug. 9, 1831, æ. 11 mos.
11. *Frederick Ely,* b. Oct. 18, 1832; lives in Campo Seco, Cal.

CHILDREN ;—BY THE SECOND MARRIAGE.

12. *Mary,*   b. Sept. 14, 1836; d. May 24, 1856, æ. 19.
13. *John Trumbull,* b. Jan. 23, 1839; lives in Winterset.
14. *Robert Clark,* b. Sept. 5, 1841; d. Aug. 25, 1842.
15. *Julia Sophia,* b. March 18, 1843.
16. *Francis Sheldon,* b. Feb. 17, 1845; d. Dec. 28, 1854.

---

205. JULIUS WHITE, son of Elijah, Esq., (89) was born in Bolton, April 21, 1787. He died in East Hartford, Aug. 15, 1830, æ. 43.

He married, May 11, 1819, LYDIA DAY of West Springfield, Mass., dau. of Heman Day and Lois Ely. She was born May 5, 1793, and died June 12, 1839, æ. 46.

CHILDREN.

1. *Henry,* b. April 19, 1821; m. Eliza Hazen.   .   .   .   .   (398)
2. *Sophia,* b. Aug. 12, 1823; m. Aug. 17, 1842, J. Henry Efner, now of W. Springfield, and has had, 1. Henry White, b. Oct. 26, 1844 ; 2. Robert, b. Feb. 1, 1846, d. Dec. 31, 1851 ; 3. Alice, b. Nov. 4, 1854.

206. THOMAS WHITE, Jun., son of Thomas, (90) was born in Bolton, Oct. 27, 1778. He was a farmer in that town until 1834, when he removed to Portage Co., Ohio. He there lived principally in the town of Franklin, where he died, Aug. 18, 1850, æ. 71.

He married, May 16, 1802, DOROTHY HAMMOND of Bolton, dau. of Nathaniel Hammond and Eleanor Olmsted. She was born June 15, 1783, and died March 3, 1848, æ. 64.

CHILDREN.

1. *Edwin Hammond,* b. March 14, 1803; res. at Franklin Mills, Ohio.
2. *Elizur Talcott,* b. Aug. 30, 1806; d. Sept. 23, 1806.
3. *Horace Freeman,* b. Feb. 29, 1808; res. at Franklin Mills.
4. *Maria D.,* b. Dec. 20, 1811; res. at Franklin Mills.
5. *Nathaniel Olmsted,* b. Jan. 25, 1815; res. at Franklin Mills.
6. *Walter Pitkin,* b. April 21, 1817; d. June 6, 1827, æ. 10.
7. *Eleanor,* b. Oct. 7, 1822; res. at Franklin Mills.

207. ASA WHITE, son of Thomas, (90) was born in Bolton, April 13, 1791. He was a farmer there, and died April 2, 1855, æ. 64.

He married, Dec. 31, 1812, EUNICE SCOVILLE of Bolton, born Dec. 23, 1793, dau. of Henry Scoville.

CHILDREN.

1. *William Wright,* b. Aug. 16, 1813; m. 1st, H. E. Lyman; 2d, L. Segur. (399)
2. *Eunice Scoville,* b. Jan. 23, 1815.
3. *Julia Talcott,* b. May 19, 1817; m. Sept. 4, 1843, Chauncey Goodrich of Bristol, Conn., and has, 1. Julia Ann; 2. Ellen.
4. *Theodore Hale,* b. Sept. 19, 1819; m. Priscilla King. . . (400)
. 5. *Edward Elijah,*⎱ b. Sept. 16, 1820; m. Charlotte A. Wells. . . (401)
6. *Edmund Elizur,*⎰ Twins. d. Jan. 29, 1840, æ. 19.
7. *Catherine Cornelia,* b. Nov. 25, 1824; m. Dec. 3, 1848, Harvey Merchant of New Haven: has had, 1. Dwight Edmund, b. Jan., 1850; 2. Elsie, d. æ. 1 yr.
8. *Lavius Parmelee,* b. June 27, 1827; lives in Bolton.
9. *Sarah Lavinia,* b. July 8, 1829; m. Oct. 31, 1848, Brewster Bishop of B.
10. *Lydia Charlotte,* b. Aug. 3, 1831; m. May 2, 1853, Jonathan W. Pond of Bristol.
11. *Henry Asa,* . b. June 8, 1834; m. Sarah J. Hamlin. . . (402)
12. *John,* b. Nov. 1, 1838.

208. DANIEL WHITE, Esq., son of Capt. Daniel, (91) was born in Andover, Conn., July 14, 1773. He was a farmer in that place until 1844, when he removed to Rockville, Conn., where he died, March 29, 1847, æ. 73. He had the military

rank of Captain, and was a justice of the peace. He frequently held town offices, and several times represented the town of Coventry in the Legislature. Being highly esteemed for his integrity and sound judgment, he was much employed in the settlement of estates, and was very frequently selected as an arbitrator to whom private differences were referred. The following is a fac-simile of his autograph.

Daniel White

He married, Feb. 19, 1800, Eunice Stanley of Coventry, dau. of Moses Stanley and Eunice Strong. She was born April 25, 1773, and died Aug. 10, 1847, æ. 74.

CHILDREN.

1. *Eliza*, b. June 10, 1801; m. Jan. 9, 1822, Dea. Allyn Kellogg of Vernon, Conn., a farmer. She has had, 1. Allyn Stanley, b. Oct. 15, 1824, grad. at Williams College in 1846, and at Yale Theological Seminary in 1850 : has preached several years ; is now residing in Vernon ; 2. Martin, b. March 15, 1828, grad. at Yale College in 1850, and at Union Theological Seminary, N. Y., in 1854 ; is now minister of the Congregational Church in Grass Valley, Nevada Co., Cal. ; 3. A daughter, b. June 27, 1832, d. July 4, æ. 7 days.
2. *Stanley*, b. Sept. 18, 1802 ; m. 1st, Rosanna Reed ; 2d, Anna R. Rose. (403)
3. *Norman*, b. Aug. 8, 1805 ; m. Mary A. Dodge.   .   .   .   .   (404)
4. *Fanny*, b. April 3, 1810 ; resides in Rockville.

---

209. Dr. Samuel White, son of Capt. Daniel, (91) was born in Andover, Conn., Feb. 23, 1777. He was a physician and surgeon of great eminence, in Hudson, N. Y., and was for many years proprietor of a private hospital for the treatment of the insane. He was Professor of Surgery in the Berkshire Medical College at Pittsfield, Mass., and President of the N. Y. State Medical Society. He was several times chosen Mayor of the city of Hudson, and was an Elder in the Presbyterian Church in that place. He died Feb. 10, 1845, æ. 68.

He married, Jan 1, 1799, Wealthy Pomeroy of North Coventry, Conn., dau. of Eleazer Pomeroy and Sybil Kingsbury. She was born Oct. 14, 1778, and died Oct. 31, 1854, æ. 76.

CHILDREN.

1. *Emeline*, b. Oct. 17, 1799 ; m. Feb. 28, 1820, Frederick J. Barnard of Albany,
   N. Y., a lumber merchant, and d. June 18, 1833, æ. 33. She had, 1. Samuel White, b. 1820, m. Nov., 1855, Cordelia Chapman of Lyons, N. Y. ;
   2. Frances, b. 1822, m. Henry Hawley of Albany ; 3. Sarah, b. 1824, m.
   1853, Thomas Stamps of Va., who d. 1855. She d. Oct., 1856, æ. 32 ;
   4. Anna Hale, b. 1826 ; 5. Benjamin Stanton, b. 1828, grad. Williams College, 1848 ; 6. Frederick Joseph, b. 1831, d. 1856, æ. 25.
2. *Samuel Pomeroy*, b. Nov. 8, 1801 ; m. Caroline M. Jenkins.   .   .   (405)
3. *Jane Augusta*,   b. Jan. 26, 1804 ; d. unm., Sept. 9, 1832, æ. 28.
4. *Frances Mary*,   b. Dec. 26, 1805 ; m. May 9, 1826, Rev. William Chester,
   D. D., of Hudson, N. Y., now of Philadelphia, Pa. He grad. Union College, 1815, and has been for twenty-eight years Associate Secretary of the
   Board of Education of the Presbyterian Church. She has had, 1. Elizabeth,
   b. March 12, 1829 ; 2. John, b. April 23, 1832, grad. College of N. J., 1851,
   and at the Med. Coll. of the Univ. of Penn. ; is now a theological student.
   He m. Oct. 2, 1855, Rachel Annie Alward of Columbia, Penn. ; 3. Charles
   Chauncey, d. in infancy.
5. *George Hale*, b. Oct. 24, 1808 ; was a physician in Hudson and in New York,
   and d. without issue, April 11, 1857, æ. 48. He m. Sept. 3, 1840, Lucy
   C. Huntington of New York, b. April 11, 1822, dau. of Joseph Huntington
   and Julia Dodge.
6. *John Chester*, b. Feb. 21, 1811 ; m. Lavinia Maxwell.   .   .   .   (406)
7. *Sarah*,   b. Feb. 2, 1813 ; d. unm., Aug. 21, 1843, æ. 30.
8. *Elizabeth*,   b. May 10, 1814 ; m. July 1, 1847, Ambrose S. Russell, Esq.,
   a lawyer, now of Hudson. She has, 1. Florence, b. April 19, 1848 ; 2. Jane
   Frances, b. Nov. 12, 1850 ; 3. John R., b. Nov. 10, 1852 ; 4. William Averell,
   b. Dec. 5, 1854 ; 5. Frederick Barnard, b. Dec. 2, 1857.
9. *Henry Kirke*, b. July 28, 1816 ; resides in New York.
10. *Anna Hale*, b. Jan. 11, 1820 ; m. Nov. 10, 1841, Charles T. Leake of New
    York, and has had, 1. William, b. April 28, 1847, d. in infancy ; 2. Cathe-
    rine Quintard, b. March 22, 1848 ; 3. Frances Chester, b. Sept. 4, 1850 ;
    4. Charles Pomeroy, b. Feb. 13, 1853 ; 5. Henry Delavan, b. Aug. 14,
    1855.

---

210. WILLIAM WHITE, son of Dudley, (92) was born in Killingworth, Conn., July 19, 1760. He was a goldsmith, and
resided in that place until Sept., 1821, when he removed to
Twinsburg, Summit Co., O., where he died, Jan. 6, 1839, æ. 78.

He married, 1790, JULIANA PIERSON of Killingworth. She
was born July 6, 1767, and died Aug. 13, 1836, æ. 69.

CHILDREN.

1. *A child*, b.   ; d. unnamed, in infancy.
2. *Julia*,   b. July,   1795 ; d. Oct., 1821, æ. 26, while on the way to Ohio.
3. *Hanford*, b. July 3, 1797 ; m. 1st, Hepzibah Pratt ; 2d, Mary Herrick.   (407)
4. *Polly*,   b. Dec.,   1798 ; d. Jan., 1817, æ. 18.

23

5. *Fanny*, b. May 19, 1801; m. 1st, June 27, 1821, James H. Kelsey of Twins-
     burg, who d. June 18, 1833, æ. 32; m. 2d, Oct. 13, 1839, Moses Eggleston
     ·of Aurora, Portage Co., Ohio. By her first husband, she had one son, Oscar
     O., lives in Twinsburg.
6. *Philena*, b. Aug. 3, 1806; res. in Twinsburg.
7. *William*, b. March, 1808; d. Oct., 1821, æ. 13, on the way to Ohio.

211. ELISHA WHITE, son of Dudley, (92) was born in Killingworth, Conn., Dec. 2, 1762. He removed to Haddam, and
died there about 1824. Was a mariner.

He married, Sept. 9, 1789, ABIGAIL BATES of Haddam, dau.
of Samuel Bates. She was born Nov. 20, 1769, and was
living in 1858.

CHILDREN.

1. *Sylvia*,   b. Sept. 25, 1792; m. Sept. 10, 1818, Horace Arnold of Haddam.
2. *Sarah*,   b. July 15, 1794; d. Oct. 14, 1807, æ. 13.
3. *Elizabeth*,   b. April 13, 1796; m. Edmond Doan of Winthrop, Conn.
4. *William*,   b. Feb. 18, 1799; m. Laura Dickinson.   .   .   .   (408)
5. *Charlotte*,   b. July 13, 1800; d. March 2, 1807.
6. *Stephen*,   b. March 2, 1802; drowned in Conn. River, Oct. 25, 1839, æ. 37.
7. *Reuben*,   b. July 3, 1804.
8. *Abby Ann*,   b. May 31, 1806.
9. *Dudley*,   b. Sept. 7, 1807; m. Ann Gilbert of Lyme ; has one child.
10. *Elisha*,   b. June 4, 1809; d. at sea, unm., Feb. 12, 1834, æ. 24.

212. BENJAMIN WHITE, son of Dudley, (92) was born in
Killingworth, Conn., May 7, 1772. He settled in Woodbury,
Conn., as a farmer, but removed to Fairfield, Herkimer Co.,
N. Y., and from thence to Russia, in the same county, where
he died, Jan. 26, 1838, æ. 65.

He married, 1st, MARY SCRANTON of Madison, Conn., dau. of
Josiah Scranton and Abigail Blatchley. She died in Woodbury, May, 1797, æ. 25.

He married, 2d, March 3, 1799, POLLY FRANKLIN of Woodbury, dau. of Samuel Franklin. She was born April 14, 1777,
and died at Albany, N. Y., Nov. 13, 1838, æ. 61.

CHILD;—BY THE FIRST MARRIAGE.

1. *Lyman*,   b. Nov. 7, 1796; m. Lydia Salisbury.   .   .   .   (409)

CHILDREN;—BY THE SECOND MARRIAGE.

2. *Amarilla*, b. Jan. 17, 1800; m. May, 1822, James C. Wilson, a farmer, now of
     Wakeman, Huron Co., O., and has 5 children.
3. *Harlow*,   b. Dec. 14, 1802; m. Levina Talcott.   .   .   .   .   (410)

4. *Alfred*, ⎫ b. Dec. 12, 1803 ; m. Florilla Stevens. . . . . (411)
5. *Alpha*, ⎭ Twins. m. Dec. 9, 1830, Linus E. Ford, a hatter, now of Dereham, C. W. : has had six children, three of whom died.
6. *Fanny*, b. Nov. 3, 1806 ; m. March 12, 1828, John B. Fenner, a farmer in Fairfield, and has had four children.
7. *Polly*, b. Nov. 7, 1808 ; m. Jan. 21, 1826, George Harris of Albany : has had thirteen children, seven of whom are dead.
8. *Charles*, b. July 17, 1810 ; m. Jane M. Carter. . . . . (412)
9. *Sally*, b Feb. 8, 1812 ; m. Jan. 2, 1832, Job Borden, now of Mohawk, Herkimer Co., N. Y. Has had two children, one of them died.

213. CHARLES WHITE, son of Simeon, jun., (93) was born in Hatfield, Mass., Oct. 10, 1770. He was a house-builder, and resided in New York, where he died, March 6, 1855, æ. 84. He married, May 17, 1806, MARY JAY, who died in 1842.

CHILDREN.

1. *Ann Matilda*, b. July 7, 1807 ; m. Dec. 17, 1827, Dr. Henry Villers of New York, and d. July 6, 1856, æ 49. She had seven children, of whom only three are now living : 1. Mary Virginia, b. Oct. 10, 1828, m. Aug. 31, 1846, John W. Orr, a wood-engraver, of New York ; 2. Joseph Jay, b. 1836 ; 3. Laura M., b. 1841.
There were four other children of Charles White, all of whom d. in infancy.

214. HENRY WHITE, son of Simeon, jun., (93) was born March 9, 1772. He resided chiefly in Athens, Greene Co., N. Y., where he was engaged in merchandizing. He died May 31, 1843. [May 10, 1844?]
He married, Feb. 1, 1795, ALMIRA TINKER of East Haddam, Conn., dau. of Capt. Jehial Tinker. She died May 3, 1850.

CHILDREN.

1. *Julia Hubbard*, b.   ; m. Patrick Stephenson of Coxsackie, Greene Co., N. Y., a merchant. He d. about 1854. She has five children : one dau. m. Rev. Alexander Mead, of Newark, N. J., and one dau. m. Rev. Levi Weed.
2. *Eliza*, b.   ; d. in infancy.
3. *Eliza A.*, b.   ; res. in Redwood, N. Y.
4. *Almira*, b. Nov. 28, 1807 ; m. Albert L. White. . (Family 418)
5. *Tempy Jane*, b.   ; d. young.
6. *Henry*, b.   ; m. Mary E. Akin. . . . (413)
7. *Clarissa Matilda*, b.   ; m. 1845, Rev. Sylvander Curtis, a Lutheran minister, now of Clermont, Columbia Co., N. Y. She has two sons.
8. *Tempy Jane*, b.   ; m. Jan. 23, 1838, George Smith of Watertown, N. Y. She has three sons.

215. Hon. GEORGE WHITE, son of Simeon, jun., (93) was born Oct. 10, 1775. He was a farmer, and settled in Rutland, Jefferson Co., N. Y. During the last war with Great Britain, he held a commission as Major, and was in the battle of Sack-etts Harbor. He was a member of the N. Y. Legislature in 1824, and was a Judge of the County Court. He died March 9, 1853, æ. 77.

He married, March 28, 1798, LYDIA WILLIAMS of Trenton, N. Y., dau. of Roger Williams and Hannah Howard. She was born Oct. 13, 1782, and died April 5, 1841, æ. 58.

CHILDREN.

1. *Stephen*,   b. April 17, 1799 ; m. Calista Keyes.   .   .   .   (414)
2. *Lyman*,   b. Sept. 14, 1800 ; m. Abby M. Fisk.   .   .   .   (415)
3. *Hannah*,   b. April 1, 1802 ; m. Jan. 7, 1827, Col. Elias Sage of Cham-pion, N. Y , and d. Oct. 25, 1844, æ. 42.
4. *Frederick W.*, b. May   6, 1806 ; m. Elvira P. Foster.   .   .   (416)
5. *William H.*,   b. Dec. 13, 1808 ; m. Abby M. Harrison.   .   .   (417)
6. *Albert L.*,   b. Oct. 11, 1810 ; m. Almira White.   .   .   .   (418)
7. *Eliza C.*,   b. Aug. 30, 1812 ; m. Jan. 23, 1838, Hiram Holcomb of Water-town, N. Y., and d. Dec. 11, 1844, æ. 32. She had one dau., Elizabeth.
8. *Edwin C.*,   b. May 18, 1816 ; m. Laura J. Wilson.   .   .   (419)
9. *Lucy A.*,   b. July 27, 1826 ; m. Nelson Tuttle of Chicago, Ill., and d. May 6, 1852, æ. 25. She had, 1. Mary Louisa ; 2. Lucy A.

216. FREDERICK WHITE, son of Simeon, jun., (93) was born in 1777. He was a banker and merchant at Buffalo, N. Y. He died in Rutland, at the residence of his brother, George White, Oct. 1, 1831, æ. 54 yrs. 7 mos.

He married MARY B. WHITING of Utica, N. Y., who is dead. He had one son,

Alexander, b. Aug. 27, 1812 ; residence not ascertained.

217. SOLOMON WHITE, son of Simeon, jun., (93) resided at New Haven, Oswego Co., N. Y., and died July 17, 1857.

He married LUCY LEE of Watertown, N. Y. His son,

Solomon, is said to be living at New Haven. Perhaps there were other children.

218. Hon. JOHN JOHNSON WHITE, son of Hon. Asa, (94) was born in Williamsburg, Mass., April 3, 1793. He gradu-ated at Williams College in 1810, and spent three or four years in teaching, in Richmond and Winchester, Ky., and in

New Orleans. He then studied law, and in 1817 settled in Gallatin, Sumner Co., Tenn., where he has ever since resided. His practice has been extensive and profitable during the whole of his professional career, extending now to a period of forty-two years, and is, at this time, confined mainly to the Chancery and Supreme Courts of the State. In several important cases, in which a judge of the Supreme Court has been disqualified to act, Mr. White has been appointed a special judge, to act in connection with the regular judges of the Court. In 1820 he was one of the presidential electors of Tennessee. In 1834 he was chosen a member of the Convention for revising the Constitution of the State, and took a leading part in the business and debates of that body.

He has been for about fifteen years past an Elder in the Presbyterian Church at Gallatin. He is also President of the Sumner Co. Bible Society, and a Director of the Theological Seminary at Danville, Ky.

A more extended notice of Mr. White's life and public services may be found in Livingston's "Portraits and Memoirs of Eminent Americans," Vol. IV.

He married, March 17, 1829, CATHARINE ANN WAIDE of Elizabethtown, Ky. She was born March 14, 1810, and was the dau. of Col. Daniel Waide, and of Martha McDougal, whose father, Rev. Alexander McDougal, died in Hardin Co., Kentucky, in 1841, at the advanced age of 104 years.

Mr. White's adopted daughter, Catharine M., is the wife of Charles A. R. Thompson, a merchant in Nashville, Tenn.

---

219. CHESTER WHITE, Esq., son of Hon. Asa, (94) was born in Williamsburg, Mass., Sept. 18, 1797. He graduated at Yale College in 1825, studied law, and spent a few years in Tennessee, in the practice of his profession. He subsequently resided in Augusta, Ga., and in Alabama, being chiefly engaged in teaching. About 1836, he engaged in mercantile pursuits, in Penn Yan, N. Y., and in 1839 removed to Racine, Wis., where he has been Mayor of the city, and still resides.

He married, Oct. 4, 1847, CLARISSA W. SPENCER of Stanstead, C. E., dau. of William Spencer. She died Sept. 23, 1854.

CHILDREN.

1. *Ellen Maria,*   b. July 27, 1848.
2. *Stella Hayes,*   b. Aug.   2, 1851.
3. *William Chester,* b. March 12, 1853.
4. *John Jay,*   b. Sept. 7, 1854.

---

220. ADDISON HAYES WHITE, Esq., son of Hon. Asa, (94) was born in Williamsburg, Mass., Aug. 23, 1803. He graduated at Yale College in 1823, studied law, and practiced for several years in Tennessee, residing principally in Covington, Tipton Co., of which city he was chosen Mayor. In 1839 he returned to the old homestead in Williamsburg, where he still resides, engaged in farming, and in the practice of his profession.

He married, 1st, Feb. 27, 1833, MATILDA J. BROWN of Tipton Co., Tenn., dau. of Rev. Samuel Brown. She died Dec. 10, 1837, æ. 25.

He married, 2d, April 30, 1840, CLARISSA TAYLOR, born Sept. 24, 1811, dau. of Ariel Taylor of Williamsburg.

He has one son, by the second marriage,

Addison, b. Oct. 21, 1843.

---

221. OLIVER WHITE, son of George, (95) was born in Tolland, Conn., about 1772. He settled in Winsted, Conn., but early removed to Dyberry, Wayne Co., Pa., where he died about 1855, æ. 82.

He married LUCY WOOD.

CHILDREN.

1. *Oliver,*   b. Nov. 12, 1796; m. Pamelia Bacon.   .   . (420)
2. *Ralph,*   b.   1803; d. Dec. 27, 1809, æ. 6.
3. *Daniel,*   b.   ; m. Nancy ———.   .   .   .   . (421)
4. *Lucy,*   b.   ; m. Halsey Burr, and has had, 1. Eliza, b. July 19, 1819; 2. Dency, b. April 10, 1821, d. May 26, 1848; 3. Matilda, b. July 28, 1822; 4. Jehiel, b. Aug. 24, 1824; 5. Lucy, b. July 5, 1827; 6. Mary, b. June 13, 1829; 7. James A., b. June 27, 1831; 8. Nancy, b. July 7, 1833; 9. George H., b. Aug. 7, 1837; 10. Abby M., b. June 2, 1839; 11. Carlos, b. Dec. 29, 1841.
5. *Charlotte,* b.   ; lives in Bethany, Pa.
6. *Maria,*   b.   ; m. Nov. 25, 1838, Alonzo R. Bishop of Winchester, Conn., now of Bethany, Pa.

7. *Rietta,* b. ; m. March 8, 1837, William Weaver, of Winchester, Ct.
8. *Eliza,* b. ; m. Jonas Stanton : has several children.

---

222. DANIEL WHITE, son of George, (95) was born in Tolland, Conn., Dec. 11, 1774. He settled in Winsted, Conn., in 1797, and has chiefly resided there.

He married, July 4, 1799, CLARISSA CLEVELAND of Winsted, dau. of Rufus Cleveland and Mary Chamberlain. She was born Feb. 6, 1782, and died June 12, 1822, æ. 40.

CHILDREN.

1. *Emily,* b. Feb. 9, 1801 ; m. Feb. 23, 1825, Hezekiah Goodwin Butler, and lives in Prompton, Wayne Co., Pa. She has had, 1. Alphonso E., d. Feb. 2, 1851 ; 2. Samuel ; 3. Edward Payson ; 4. Mary Elizabeth.
2. *Lavinia,* b. Aug. 20, 1803 ; m. Oct. 4, 1835, Gideon Hall of Winsted, a farmer, who held various offices. He d. Feb. 23, 1850, æ. 75. She has one dau., Jane Catharine, b. Oct. 20, 1845.
3. *Mary Cleveland,* b. Jan. 31, 1805 ; m. April 18, 1833, Edward Adams Rugg of New Marlboro, Mass., now a farmer in Winchester, Conn. She has had, 1. Harlan Page, b. July 16, 1838 ; 2. Urania, b. Oct. 17, 1839 ; 3. Mary, b. June 23, 1841 ; 4. Edward, b. Aug. 11, 1843 ; 5. Elizabeth, b. Nov. 30, 1845 ; 6. Arthur, b. June 19, 1847, d. March 24, 1848.
4. *Harriet,* b. Jan. 28, 1807 ; m. Dec. 26, 1846, Oren Kellogg, a farmer in Colebrook, Conn.
5. *Horace Cleveland,* b. Feb. 22, 1809 ; m. Susan A. Wolcott. . . (422)
6. *Urania Clarissa,* b. July 20, 1811 ; was a student in Oberlin College, and went to the vicinity of Lake Superior, as a teacher. "She died at the Mission House, La Pointe, Lake Superior," Aug. 5, 1839, æ. 28.
7. *Philenda Miller,* b. June 11, 1814 ; m. Sept. 6, 1835, Elizur G. Perry, a joiner. They last resided in Ion, Alamakee Co., Iowa, where she d. Nov. 6, 1857, æ. 43. He d. Oct. 6, 1858. She had, 1. Jennett, b. Feb. 7, 1836, m. June 19, 1858, George Perry ; 2. Edwin R., b. March 14, 1838 ; 3. Philo, b. April 7, 1840 ; 4. Lavinia Hall, b. Oct. 12, 1843, d. May 31, 1844 ; 5. Frederick Kellogg, b. Jan. 1, 1845 ; 6. Lavinia, b. June 11, 1850 ; 7. Philenda, b. Jan. 24, 1852 ; 8. Martha, b. May 6, 1854, d. Aug. 31, 1855. .
8. *Jennett,* b. April 6, 1816 ; d. July 26, 1816.
9. *Pembroke,* b. Sept. 18, 1819 ; is now living in Ion, Alamakee Co., Iowa.

---

223. GEORGE WHITE, son of George, (95) was born in Tolland, Jan. 17, 1777, the day after his father's death. He is a joiner, and about 1801 settled in Hartford, Conn., where he still resides.

He married, June 2, 1803, MARY ALFRED of Hartford, who died Dec. 3, 1837, æ. 63.

CHILDREN.

1. *Mary Benton,*   b. March 19, 1805 ; m. Oct. 30, 1839, Russell Arnold of Hartford, a joiner, and has, 1. George White ; 2. Mary Jane.
2. *George Caldwell,* b. Aug. 11, 1807 ; m. Sarah Dunn.   .   .   .   (423)
3. *Sarah Jane,*   } b. Dec. 18, 1813 ; m. Feb. 21, 1844, Henry Kennedy of E.
                          Hartford, now keeper of the jail in Hartford.
4. *Sophia Julia,* }   Twins.
5. *Laura Catharine,* b. July 22, 1815 ; m. July 21, 1834, Albertus Green Olmsted of E. Hartford, who d. in California, May 18, 1850. She d. in Hartford, Sept. 18, 1856, æ. 41. Her dau., Eveline Jenette, m. J. Hinman Warren of Oswego, N. Y.

Seventh Generation and Children.

DESCENDANTS OF CAPT. NATHANIEL WHITE.

224. LEVI WHITE, son of Nathaniel, (97) was born in South Hadley, Mass., Feb. 14, 1779. He was a painter, and resided in Easthampton, Mass., where he died, Aug. 26, 1852, æ. 73.

He married, March 13, 1806, MIRIAM ALVORD of South Hadley, dau. of Samuel Alvord and Miriam White: (see Fam. 48.) She was born May 25, 1785, and survives her husband.

CHILDREN.

1. *Julius*, b. July 16, 1808; res. in Southampton, Mass., and is a house painter. He m. 1st, Nov. 27, 1835, Elizabeth Sheldon of S., dau. of Schuyler Sheldon. She d. June 17, 1847. He m. 2d, Oct. 17, 1849, Mrs. Almira Barron, wid. of Jehiel Barron, and dau. of Benjamin Munson.
2. *Cecil*, b. June 8, 1810; d. Sept. 18, 1810.
3. *Edson*, b. Nov. 27, 1811; is a farmer and painter in Easthampton. He m. Feb. 1, 1855, Mrs. Frances White, widow of his brother Lysander.
4. *Lucena*, b. Nov. 17, 1814; m. May 18, 1843, Julius Pomeroy of Easthampton, and d. Dec. 4, 1858, æ. 44. She had, 1. Herbert White, b. Aug. 27, 1844; 2. Ella Lucena, b. Dec. 15, 1849; 3. Miriam White, b. Oct. 6, 1852.
5. *Lysander*, b. April 27, 1818; was a painter, and lived in Easthampton. He m. Nov. 5, 1839, Frances Parsons, b. Dec. 21, 1817, dau. of Joel Parsons. He d. without issue, May 8, 1852, æ. 34. She m. 2d, his brother, Edson White.
6. *Amanda*, b. June 1, 1821; m. Augustine Munson, and has one dau., Lyander, b. Aug. 22, 1852.

---

225. EZEKIEL WHITE, son of Nathaniel, (97) was born in South Hadley, Jan. 12, 1791. He was a painter, and resided in Easthampton, where he died, June 14, 1858, æ. 67.

He married, 1st, Nov. 30, 1826, RACHEL JANES of Easthampton, dau. of Lieut. Jonathan Janes and Rachel Clark. She was born Nov. 20, 1797, and died Jan. 22, 1842, æ. 44.

24

He married, 2d, June 22, 1843, MELINDA H. BATES of Cummington, Mass., born June 14, 1805, dau. of Levi Bates and Lovina Hersey.

CHILDREN;—BY THE FIRST MARRIAGE.

1. *Jonathan Janes*, b. Sept. 16, 1827.
2. *Mary Lucina*, b. Sept. 6, 1831.

---

226. EZRA WHITE, son of Ebenezer, (98) was born in South Hadley, Aug. 4, 1794. He resides in Wilbraham, Mass., where he has been a shoemaker and shoe dealer.

He married, Jan. 15, 1818, MARY WIGHT of Chester, Vt., born Nov. 4, 1792, dau. of Ephraim Wight and Patience Cleaveland.

CHILDREN.

1. *Charlotte*, b. Aug. 11, 1819; m. June 10, 1840, Rev. Alanson Latham, a Methodist minister, now of Holmes Hole, Mass. She has had, 1. Charlotte W., b. Nov. 13, 1842; 2. Alanson W., b. July 15, 1845; 3. Caroline Augusta, b. July 30, 1847; 4. Francis E., b. Sept. 7, 1849; 5. Julia Elizabeth, b. May 26, 1853, d. May 17, 1854; 6. Benjamin Franklin, b. May 17, 1855; 7. Augustus Blair, b. Sept. 9, 1857.
2. *Lorenzo*, b. May 9, 1821; m. Elizabeth Babcock.   .   .   .   (424)
3. *Ephraim*, b. Feb. 22, 1823; d. May 30, 1823.
4. *Francis*, b. July 22, 1826; d. June 8, 1846, æ. 20.
5. *Wilbur Fisk*, b. June 17, 1831; d. Sept. 26, 1846, æ. 15.

---

227. LYMAN WHITE, son of Ebenezer, (98) was born in South Hadley, April 16, 1796. He is a shoemaker, and has resided chiefly in South Hadley, Worthington, and Hinsdale, Mass., but removed in 1859 to Chester, Morris Co., N. J. He was a deacon of the Congregational Churches in Worthington and Hinsdale.

He married, Nov. 19, 1815, ANNAH GRANGER of Worthington, born Dec. 19, 1794, dau. of Luther and Ruth Granger.

CHILDREN.

1. *Luther*, b. Sept. 14, 1816; m. Mrs. Amanda Delvan.   .   (425)
2. *Edwin*, b. Feb. 17, 1818; m. Jerusha C. Stebbins.   .   .   .   (426)
3. *Samuel*, b. Sept. 22, 1819; is a teacher and farmer; res. in Chester, N. J. He m. May 22, 1844, Caroline S. Woodhull of Chester, b. Aug. 5, 1810, dau. of John and Mary Woodhull.
4. *James*, b. July 9, 1821; m. Juliet Washburn.   (427)
5. *Lyman*, b. Dec. 6, 1822; d. July 6, 1823.
6. *Julia A.*, b. Sept. 28, 1824.
7. *Clarissa*, b. April 18, 1830; d. Dec. 19, 1854, æ. 24.
8. *Emerancy*, b. Nov. 27, 1833; d. Oct. 20, 1847.

228. RALPH WHITE, son of Ebenezer, (98) was born in South Hadley, Aug. 20, 1805. He is a shoe dealer; has resided chiefly in South Hadley, Ludlow, and Chicopee, Mass., but removed in 1857 to Excelsior, Minnesota.

He married, 1st, March 31, 1828, RUTH LYON of Ludlow, Mass., born June 10, 1806.

He married, 2d, Feb. 22, 1859, JULIA BLISS of Ludlow, dau. of Charles Bliss.

CHILDREN;—BY THE FIRST MARRIAGE.

1. *Cordelia R.*, b. Jan.   1, 1829 ; d. Jan. 5, 1834.
2. *Deborah B.*, b. Nov.   9, 1830 ; m. July 31, 1853, George W. Leach, and has,
   1. Ella, b. Nov. 24, 1854 ; 2. Carrie Ostella, b. July 9, 1856 ; 3. Eugene Watts, b. Sept. 15, 1857.
3. *Philena*,   b. Jan.   1, 1833 ; m. Sept. 14, 1855, George M. Powers, and has Orianna, b. Jan. 6, 1858.
4. *Lyman A.*,   b. March 5, 1835.
5. *Samuel*,   b. Aug.   1, 1837.
6. *George W.*,   b. June 20, 1840.
7. *Cordelia O.*,   b. Jan. 19, 1843.

229. EBENEZER WHITE, son of Ebenezer, (98) was born in South Hadley, Dec. 13, 1810. He is a mason, and resided in Chicopee, Mass., but removed in 1854 to Princeton, Bureau Co., Ill. Has been mayor of Princeton.

He married, 1st, Aug. 12, 1832, LOUISA WRIGHT of Ludlow, Mass., dau. of Elam Wright. She died Oct. 5, 1839, æ. 25.

He married, 2d, EMILY CROUCH of Brimfield, Mass., dau. of Ephraim Crouch.

CHILDREN;—BY THE FIRST MARRIAGE.

1. *Helen V.*,   b. July 24, 1833; m. Sept., 1857, Romanus Hodgman, a merchant in Galva, Ill.
2. *Isabella M.*, b. Jan.   1, 1835 ; m. Nov. 19, 1856, James H. Wolcott of Springfield, Mass.
3. *Victoria*,   b. Sept. 1, 1837.
4. *Louisa M.*,   b. July 15, 1839.

CHILDREN ;—BY THE SECOND MARRIAGE.

5. *Harriet J.*,   b. Feb. 28, 1844 ; d. Jan. 4, 1845.
6. *Lizzie J.*,   b. Aug. 21, 1847 ; d. March 19, 1849.
7. *Emma Viola*, b. April 29, 1851.

230. Hon. PHINEAS WHITE, son. of Dea. Enoch, (99) was born in South Hadley, Mass., Oct. 30, 1770. He graduated at Dartmouth College in 1797, and studied law with the Hon,

Charles Marsh of Woodstock, Vt., and Judge Samuel Porter of Dummerston, Vt. In 1800 he commenced the practice of his profession in Putney, Vt., where he resided through life. He was called to many positions of honor and responsibility. He was post-master of Putney from 1802 to 1809, was for several years State's Attorney for the County of Windham, was Judge of the Probate Court, and from 1818 to 1820 was Chief Judge of the County Court. In 1820 he was elected a Representative to Congress, and served one term. In 1836 he was a member of the Convention for revising the Constitution of Vermont, and from 1838 to 1840 was a Senator in the State Legislature, having previously been several times a Representative from the town of Putney. He belonged to the Masonic Order and was Grand Master of the Grand Lodge of Vermont.

After his election to Congress, he almost wholly abandoned his law business, engaging extensively, and with good success, in farming. The Colleges of the State, and various benevolent institutions, shared largely in his counsels and liberality. He was one of the Trustees of Middlebury College, and was for several years President of the Vt. Bible Society, and of the Vt. Colonization Society. He was also an active member of the Congregational Church in Putney, with which he and his wife united in 1815. He died July 6, 1847, æ. 76.

He married, July 5, 1801, ESTHER STEVENS of Plainfield, Conn., dau. of Nehemiah Stevens and Hepzibah Kellum. She was born Jan., 1777, and died Sept. 25, 1858, æ. 81.

CHILDREN.

1. *Susan Esther*, b. May 23, 1802; m. June 3, 1823, Hon. William D. Williamson of Bangor, Me., and d. without issue, March 9, 1824, æ. 22.
2. *Tirzah Maria*, b. April 2, 1804; m. Nov. 25, 1828, James Crawford, Esq., of Putney, a lawyer. She d. in Putney, Nov. 15, 1837, æ. 33. He rem. to Dubuque, Iowa, and d. Nov., 1846, æ. 48. She had, 1. Phineas White, b. Sept. 21, 1829, grad. Ill. Coll., 1849, and is a lawyer in Dubuque. He m. Nov. 30, 1852, Harriet Connel of Dubuque; 2. Theophilus, b. Oct., 1831, d. May 8, 1853, æ. 21 ; 3. William Henry, b. Feb., 1834, is a merchant in Muscatine, Iowa. He m. Sept., 1853, Cornelia Ann Smith of Hopkinton, Iowa ; 4. Susan Esther White, b. Sept. 8, 1835 ; 5 & 6. James and John, twins, b. Oct., 1837; James d. æ. 9 mos.; John is an engineer, now in Cal.
3. *Frances Mary*, b. Feb. 14, 1806; m. Sept. 2, 1834, John Kimball, Esq., of Claremont, N. H. He grad. Dart. Coll., 1822, and is a lawyer. In 1839 he rem. to the homestead of his father-in-law, and now resides there. She has had, 1. Charles White, b. 1836, lives with his father and is a farmer ;

2. Hellen S., b. Dec. 5, 1838, d. Sept. 5, 1839 ; 3. John Dudley, b. Aug. 23, 1842, d. Jan. 5, 1853, æ. 10.
4. *Helen Rebecca*, b. Sept. 25, 1808 ; d. Oct. 26, 1815, æ. 7.
5. *Phineas Enoch*, b. Nov. 18, 1810 ; d. Sept. 23, 1825, æ. 15.
6. *Enoch Stevens*, b. Dec. 30, 1812 ; d. March 20, 1814.
7. *Abby Lydia*, b. June 20, 1814 ; m. June 20, 1832, Rev. William H. Williams of Tuscaloosa, Ala., now of Keokuk, Iowa, and has had, 1. George Bethune, b. Sept. 3, 1833, m. Oct. 31, 1854, Mary Emma Nelson, dau. of Rev. David Nelson, D D., of Quincy, Ill., and d. Nov. 18, 1857, æ. 24 ; 2. Emily Maria, b. Dec. 12, 1835, d. Aug. 6, 1839 ; 3. William White, b. Jan. 2, 1838, grad. Williams College, 1859 ; 4. Abby Maria, b. Nov. 26, 1839 ; 5. Charles Fitch, b. Nov. 5, 1841, is a member of Williams College ; 6 & 7. Frances Stevens and Helen Scott, twins, b. Sept. 23, 1843 ; Helen S. d. April 23, 1846 ; 8. Theodore Sturtevant, b. Jan. 3, 1846 ; 9. Louis Edward, b. June 7, 1850 ; 10. Frederic Arthur, b. Oct. 19, 1856.
8. *William Wallace*, b. Aug. 31, 1816 ; m. Frances A. Atherton.   (428)

---

231. ENOCH WHITE, Jun., son of Dea. Enoch, (99) was born in South Hadley, June 1, 1781. He resided there, and died Aug. 5, 1827, æ. 46.

He married, Nov. 7, 1805, MARTHA LAMB of Belchertown, dau. of Daniel Lamb. She was born Aug. 23, 1783, and died in Lapeer, Mich., May 12, 1847, æ. 63.

CHILDREN.

1. *Jonathan Ripley*, b. Sept. 10, 1806 ; m. Louisa Dexter.   .   .   (429)
2. *Adaline Maria*, b. Sept. 8, 1808 ; m. Nicholas Poss, a farmer in Lapeer, and d. Nov. 29, 1849, æ. 41. She had, 1. Tirza White, b. May 24, 1838 ; 2. Elizabeth, b. Aug. 4, 1841 ; 3. Jonathan White, b. Feb. 17, 1846.
3. *Phineas*, b. May 1, 1810 ; m. Fidelia Day.   .   .   .   (430)
4. *Enoch J.*, b. March 2, 1814 ; m. Elizabeth W. Gaylord.   .   .   (431)
5. *George*, b. Jan. 19, 1816 ; d. [June?] 1816.
6. *Tirzah C.*, b. April 20, 1817 ; d. at Lapeer, Sept. 23, 1835, æ. 18.
7. *Martha L.*, b. June 3, 1819 ; m. July 3, 1836, Asahel W. Abbott of Leverett, Mass., who rem. to Lapeer. She has had, 1. Louisa, b. Aug. 30, 1837, d. March 17, 1848 ; 2. Austin, b. Aug. 11, 1840 ; 3. Julia B., b. May 12, 1843 ; 4. Martha A., b. Dec. 4, 1847, d. March 30, 1848 ; 5. Antha M., b. June 6, 1849, d. Dec. 29, 1856 ; 6. Fidelia E., b. Dec. 8, 1852 ; 7. Lucy H., b. Nov. 17, 1856, d. July 19, 1858.
8. *Henry K.*, b. Oct. 24, 1820 ; is a surveyor ; now at Puget Sound, Washington Territory.
9. *Theodore Austin*, b.   ; d. at Lapeer, June 29, 1838.

---

232. DAVID WHITE, son of Moses, (101) was born in Hadley, Sept. 24, 1788, and died there, April 18, 1851, æ. 62.

He married, 1st, Jan. 15, 1815, MARY BUMPS of Pelham, who died in 1836, æ. 44.

He married, 2d, Sept., 1836, CELINDA D. BRAGG, born July 4, 1805, dau. of Abial Bragg of Enfield, Mass.

CHILDREN;—BY THE FIRST MARRIAGE.

1. *Cynthia*, b.   ; m. 1st, Stephen Atwood, who d., and she m. again. She has had by her first husband, 1. June ; 2. Charles ; 3. Henry, d. Nov. 1854 ; 4. Mary.
2. *Zenas*,   b.   ; m., and lives in Wisconsin.
3. *Oliver*,   b.   ; m. Sophia S. Pattrill.   .   .   (432)
4. *Sarah Ann*,   b. April 22, 1822 ; m. Oct. 18, 1843, Lyman Stocking of Cabotville, Mass., and has had, 1. George, b. July 22, 1844 ; 2. James H., b June 28, 1848, d. June 14, 1849 ; 3. Franklin, b. Feb. 2, 1851, d. Jan. 23, 1854 ; 4. Mariette, b. May 24, 1856.
5. *James Porter*, b.   ; m. Caroline A. Judson.   .   .   (433)
6. *Reuben*,   b. Feb.,   1830 ; m. Harriet ——.   .   .   (434)
7. *Sylvester*, b. Nov. 28, 1832.
8. *Harvey*,   b. June 2, 1836.

CHILDREN ;—BY THE SECOND MARRIAGE.

9. *Albert Rensselaer*, b. Dec.,   1837.
10. *Mary Bumps*,   b. March 26, 1843.

---

233. ELIHU WHITE, son of Moses, (101) was born in Hadley, Sept. 22, 1794, and died there, Sept. 5, 1850, æ. 56.

He married, March 21, 1820, RUTH RIDER, born Feb. 27, 1797, dau. of Isaac Rider of Enfield, Mass.

CHILDREN.

1. *Eliza Ann*,   b.   ; d. æ. 1 yr. 3 mos.
2. *George Smith*, b.   .
3. *Henry*,   b. Feb ,   1824 ; d. unm., Jan. 12, 1854, æ. 30.
4. *Eliza Ann*,   b. June 11, 1826 ; m. June 3, 1846, Lewis H. Wilder, and lives in Iowa. She has had, 1. Isabel, b. Sept., 1849 ; 2. Laura Elizabeth, b. Sept., 1853, d. Feb., 1857, æ. 3.
5. *Moses*, b.   ; lives in Hadley. He m. Sept., 1848, Jane Berditt.
6. *David*, b.   ; m. Anna B. Warren.   .   .   .   (435)
7. *Elijah*, b. Jan. 3, 1830 ; m. Lucy W. Fitch.   .   .   .   (436)

---

234. JUSTUS WHITE, son of Aaron, (102) was born in South Hadley, Feb. 26, 1789, and resides there.

He married, 1st, Jan. 4, 1821, CYNTHIA BREWSTER. She was born July 26, 1789, and died Nov. 3, 1829, æ. 40.

He married, 2d, July 7, 1830, EUNICE STRONG of Northampton, born July 6, 1785.

CHILDREN ;—BY THE FIRST MARRIAGE.

1. *Henry Lewis*, b. Oct. 19, 1821.
2. *Edwin Clark*, b. Aug. 20, 1823 ; m. 1847, Honora O'Brien.
3. *Sarah Ann*,   b. June 6, 1825.
4. *Ellen Amanda*, b. Nov. 24, 1827 ; m. Feb. 17, 1847, Luther Walcott of Southampton.

235. CHESTER WHITE, son of Job, (103) was born Feb. 19, 1788, and died Nov. 11, 1852, æ. 64.

He married EUNICE EDWARDS of Northampton, dau. of Benjamin Alvord Edwards. She was born Oct. 2, 1790, and died Dec. 5, 1845, æ. 55.

CHILDREN.

1. *Lewis Clapp,*   b. Oct. 9, 1809; m. Mary Ann Smith.   .   .   (437)
2. *James Edwards,* b. Jan. 14, 1812; m. Jane Ann Phisty. .   .   (438)
3. *Chester R.,*   b. Feb. 14, 1814; res. principally in Springfield, Mass.; is proprietor of the "Island House," Bellows Falls, Vt.

236. JOB WHITE, son of Job, (103) was born Dec. 27, 1790. He is a painter, and lives in Waterloo, Seneca Co., N. Y.

He married, March 29, 1817, MARGARET STEBBINS, born June 2, 1797, dau. of William and Margaret Stebbins.

CHILDREN.

1. *Charlotte S.,*   b. Feb. 7, 1819; m. Dec. 31, 1846, Erastus T. Judd, and d. without issue, Jan. 29, 1853, æ. 34.
2. *William Chester,* b. Sept. 10, 1821 ; m. Catharine Bramhall.   .   (439)
3. *Mary N.,*   b. March 24, 1824 ; m. Nov. 23, 1843, C. Lorenzo Judd, now of Port Byron, N. Y. She has had, 1. Clarissa Stacy, d. æ. 7 ; 2. Mary Alice.
4. *Samuel,*   ' b. July 27, 1825; d. March 5, 1828.
5. *Caroline E.,*   b.   1828; d. 1828.
6. *Samuel,*   b.   1829; d. 1840.
7. *Caroline Ely,*   b. March 16, 1832.
8. *Margaret A.,*   b.   1834; d. 1839.
9. *Eunice E.,*   b.   1836; d. 1840.

237. QUARTUS WHITE, son of Simeon, (104) was born in South Hadley, April 28, 1789. The births of his children are recorded there.

He married PERSIS STEBBINS.

CHILDREN.

1. *Emeline,*   b. March 2, 1810; m. March 24, 1832, Francis W. Kellogg.
2. *Francis Stebbins,* b. April 6, 1811.
3. *Albert Colton,*   b. Aug. 21, 1815.

238. REUBEN AUGUSTUS WHITE, son of Reuben, (107) was born in South Hadley, Feb. 19, 1809. He has been a carriage-maker and carpenter ; is now a hotel-keeper in Belchertown.

He married, May 7, 1834, EMELINE M. SNOW, born April 30, 1814, dau. of Zenas and Asenath Snow, of Lebanon, N. H.

CHILDREN.

1. *William Augustus,* b. March 7, 1835 ; is a carpenter in Springfield.
2. *Reuben Austin,*   b. Sept. 24, 1836.

3. *Sarah Jane,*   b. Sept. 30, 1838.
4. *Susan Maria,*   b. Sept. 8, 1840.
5. *Mabel Asenath,* b. Oct. 25, 1842.
6. *Aaron John,*   b. Nov. 23, 1844.
7. *Henry Kirke,*   b. Feb.   6, 1851 ; d. Sept. 3, 1852.
8. *George Henry,* b. April, 13, 1856.

---

239. HEMAN WHITE, son of Eldad, (109) was born in South Hadley, April 17, 1792, and resides there.

He married, 1st, Feb. 1, 1814, CLARISSA SMITH of South Hadley, dau. of Selah Smith. She was born April 9, 1796, and died Jan. 4, 1830, æ. 33.

He married, 2d, April 2, 1839, SARAH KELLEY of Granville, Mass., born April 24, 1803, dau. of Martin Kelley.

CHILDREN ;—BY THE FIRST MARRIAGE.

1. *Mary,*   b. Sept. 3, 1815; d. Nov. 16, 1831, æ. 16.
2. *Heman,*   b. Aug. 20, 1817 ; d. Sept. 8, 1818.
3. *Heman,*   b. July 2, 1820; m. Clara N. Bartlett.   .   .   (440)
4. *Clarissa,* b. Jan. 10, 1822 ; d. May 11, 1842, æ. 20.
5. *Rebecca,* b. Dec. 3, 1823 ; d. Aug. 21, 1828.

CHILD ;—BY THE SECOND MARRIAGE.

6. *Clarissa,* b. June 5, 1843 ; d. Sept. 29, 1844.

---

240. CYRUS WHITE, son of Eldad, (109) was born in South Hadley, Oct. 21, 1794, and is a farmer there.

He married, 1st, June 12, 1816, ELVIRA WHITE of Monson, Mass., dau. of Asa White and Margaret Dodge: (not descended from Elder John White.) She was born Oct. 28, 1794, and died May 12, 1826, æ. 31.

He married, 2d, March 29, 1827, REBECCA WHITE of South Hadley, dau. of Joel White and Dorcas Nash, and granddaughter of Lieut. Thomas White, 2d: (see in Family 47.) She was born May 15, 1805, and died July 5, 1843, æ. 38.

He married, 3d, Oct. 2, 1843, Mrs. AMANDA LYMAN of S. H., widow of William Lyman, and dau. of Lieut. Joseph White: (see Family 106.) She was born July 10, 1797.

CHILDREN ;—BY THE FIRST MARRIAGE.

1. *Edwin,* b. May 21, 1817 ; m. Harriet Allen.   .   .   .   .   (441)
2. *Cyrus,* b. Jan. 3, 1819 ; res. in South Hadley. He m. Nov. 27, 1845, Celestia E. Spaulding, dau. of Timothy Spaulding.
3. *Elvira,* b. Oct. 28, 1821 ; d. April 25, 1843, æ. 21.
4. *Irene,* b. Oct. 6, 1823 ; d. Feb. 15, 1848, æ. 24.
5. *Abigail,* b. May 10, 1826 ; d. May 20, 1826.

CHILDREN ;—BY THE SECOND MARRIAGE.

6. *Rebecca*, b. May 5, 1828; m. Dec. 8, 1858, Calvin P. Langdon of Somers, Conn., a farmer.

7. *William*, b. June 30, 1829; is a farmer in Chicopee, Mass. He m. April 21, 1852, Amanda Preston of S. H., dau. of Gardner Preston.

8. *Henry*, b. May 2, 1832.

9. *George*, b. July 19, 1834.

10. *Josiah*, b. Nov. 11, 1835.

11. *Augustus*, b. Dec. 7, 1839; d. Dec. 28, 1839.

12. *Joseph*, b. July 8, 1841 ; d. April 1, 1842.

13. *A son*, b. May 7, 1843; d. June 2, 1843.

---

241. MEDAD WHITE, son of Eldad, (109) was born in South Hadley, June 8, 1800, and died there, April 21, [18?] 1850, æ. 50.

He married, April, 1824, LUCY SNOW, who died Dec. 30, 1849, æ. 45.

CHILDREN.

1. *Sarah*, b. Dec. 15, 1824; m. Nov. 16, 1842, Job Williams, who d. Their dau., Lucy Ann, d. Sept. 2, 1844, æ. 11 mo.

2. *Anson*, b. Jan. 31, 1828; d. Sept. 9, 1829.

3. *Helen*, b. Jan. 7, 1831 ; d. unm., Dec. 22, 1852, æ. 22.

4. *Jane*, b. Aug. 24, 1835 ; m. ———— Ridley, of West Haven, Conn.

---

242. SEWALL WHITE, son of Lieut. Horace, (111) was born in West Springfield, Mass., May 6, 1776. He has been a merchant in that town, and still resides there.

He married, June 22, 1804, FANNY GRANGER, who died Sept. 4, 1837, æ. 55. She was killed by the falling of a chimney, on the corner of Cliff and Beekman streets, New York. (Date of marriage, from his family record : June 28, on town record.)

CHILDREN.

1. *Julia Ann*, b. June 23, 1805.

2. *Horace Homer*, b. Jan. 1, 1810; m. Mary Jane Loring. . . (442)

3. *Charles*, b. Nov. 14, 1811 ; m. Louise Bradley. . . (443)

4. *Joseph Addison*, b. Oct. 17, 1815; d. without issue, in Mobile, Ala., Nov. 18, 1841, æ. 26. He m. Aug. 31, 1836, Louisa Foster of Great Barrington, Mass. She d. at Barbourville, Ala., July 27, 1842, æ. 27.

5. *Sarah*, b. Dec. 11, 1817; m. Jan. 12, 1843, Hon. De Witt Clinton Ballou, of Warsaw, Mo., a Judge of the Circuit Court of Mo. She has had, 1. Clinton Osage, d. ; 2. Horace, d. ; 3. William, d. ; 4. Charles ; 5. Maria Louise.

6. *William Cowper*, b. June 30, 1821 ; is a jeweller in Springfield. He m. June

25

9, 1852, Chloc M. Bradley of W. S., dau. of Ezra Bradley.   She was b.
Sept. 3, 1822, and d. April 25, 1854, æ. 31.

---

243. GORDON WHITE, son of Daniel, (112) was born in
West Springfield, May 9, 1783. He was a farmer there, in
the Society of Feeding Hills, in the present town of Agawam.
He died Nov. 11, 1850, æ. 67.

He married NABBY M. HUBBARD, dau. of Jesse Hubbard
and Eunice Coe. She was born in Middletown, Conn., Aug.
6, 1793, and survives her husband.

CHILDREN.

1. *Clarissa,*   b. May   5, 1814 ; d. May 15, 1817.
2. *Emily,*   b. Feb.   1, 1817 ; m. Jan. 4, 1838, George W. Cowles of
   Westfield, a joiner, and has, 1. James M., b. Nov. 5, 1838 ; 2. Jane E., b.
   Aug. 25, 1842.
3. *Daniel H.,*   b. March 21, 1819 ; m. Thankful Leonard and others.   (444)
4. *Hannah Lamb,* b. Oct.   29, 1828 ; m. Feb. 4, 1851, Henry C. Smith of Feeding
   Hills, a farmer, and has had, 1. Frances E., b. Nov. 4, 1855, d. March 21,
   1856 ; 2. Laura J., b. Oct. 30, 1858.

---

244. DANIEL GRANGER WHITE, son of Pliny, (113) was
born in West Springfield, May 28, 1796. He resided there,
and died Aug. 4, 1859, æ. 63.

He married, March 22, 1830, HARRIET DAY of W. S., born
Oct. 30, 1797, dau. of Heman Day and Lois Ely.

CHILDREN.

1. *Fanny,*   b. Dec. 5, 1832.
2. *Harriet,*   b. Aug. 12, 1834.
3. *Daniel Granger,* b. June 12, 1838.

---

245. Capt. EDWARD CORBETT WHITE, son of Edward, (114)
was born in West Springfield, June 29, 1785, and died there,
Aug. 5, 1823, æ. 38. He was a captain in the War of 1812.

He married Mrs. LUCY BAGG, who died July 17, 1843.
His only child,

Chauncey Edward, b. Nov. 20, 1819, is a printer in Chicago, Ill.   He m. Margaret
   Foot, dau. of Noah Foot of Springfield.

---

246. MARTIN WHITE, son of Preserved, jun., (115) was born
in Springfield, June 4, 1770. He was a carpenter in that
place, and died Nov. 20, 1836, æ. 66.

He married, June 15, 1791, LUCY COLLINS of Springfield. She died in Longmeadow.

CHILDREN.

1. *Theodore*, b. Feb.   1, 1794.
2. *Harvey*,   b. May   29, 1796; d. Sept., 1809, æ. 13.
3. *Deniah*,   b. July   9, 1798; d. March 7, 1804.
4. *Jared*,   b. Sept.   9, 1800; m. Electa Loomis. .   (445)
5. *Benjamin Stedman*, b. Nov. 14, 1802.
6. *Deniah*,   b. March 14, 1805; d. unm., July 15, 1835, æ. 30.
7. *Albert*,   b. Jan.   31, 1807; d. young.

---

247. LUTHER WHITE, son of Preserved, jun., (115) was born in Springfield, July 7, 1776.   He was an armorer there, and died April 13, 1850, æ. 73.   .

He married, Oct. 30, 1799, ABIGAIL STEBBINS of Springfield, dau. of Lemuel and Rhoda Stebbins.   She was born Feb. 12, 1780, and died Dec. 9, 1850, æ. 70.

CHILDREN.

1. *Norman Stebbins*, b. Aug. 14, 1800; d. June 25, 1803.
2. *Amelia*,   b. Feb. 16, 1802; m. Alvah Smith, and res. at Delaware, Ohio. She has had, Franklin, and others.
3. *Caroline*,   Twins.   d. day of birth.
4. *Norman Stebbins*, b. Oct. 26, 1803; m. Susan Noyes. .   .   .   (446)
5. *Roland*,   b. April 7, 1806; d. June 17, 1806.
6. *Alfred*,   b. June   9, 1807; m. Emily Cady.   .   .   . (447)
7. *Luther*,   b. July 14, 1810; a photographic artist in Montpelier, Vt.
8. *Franklin*,   b. May   17, 1813; a photographic artist in Lancaster, N. H.

---

248. RODERICK WHITE, son of Preserved, jun., (115) was born in Springfield, Feb. 24, 1784.   He was for many years a bookseller and publisher in Hartford, Conn.; now resides in Enfield, Conn.

He married, Oct. 29, 1808, DELIGHT BEMENT of Enfield, born Aug. 5, 1784, dau. of Dennis Bement and Lydia Adams.

CHILDREN.

1. *Roderick Adams*, b. Oct. 24, 1809; m. Elizabeth W. Hungerford.   .   (448)
2. *Mary A.*,   b.   ; m. June 6, 1838, Luke B. Case, a merchant in New York, who d. Oct. 28, 1857. She has had, 1. Adrian E., b. July 29, 1841, d. May 19, 1855; 2. Caroline G., b. May 13, 1843, d. April 30, 1844; 3. Frank D., b. March 15, 1849; 4. Joseph W., b. March 11, 1852.
3. *Delia B.*,   b.   ; res. in Enfield.
4. *Caroline E.*,   b.   ; is a teacher in Brooklyn, N. Y.

249. PRESERVED WHITE, son of Preserved, jun., (115) was born in Springfield, April 27, 1789. He was an armorer in that place, and died Sept. 10, 1832, æ. 43.

He married, 1st, SARAH CHAFFEE of Wilbraham, dau. of Calvin and Sarah Chaffee. She died July 30, 1822.

He married, 2d, July 13, 1823, LUCINDA RICE of Ludlow, born Dec. 22, 1794, dau. of Jeduthan Rice. She now resides in Hartford.

CHILDREN;—BY THE FIRST MARRIAGE.

1. *Preserved Merritt*,   b. Oct.   10, 1816 ; m. Catharine Finlay.   (449)
2. *Sarah Chaffee*,   b. July   16, 1819 ; d. Sept. 8, 1822.

CHILDREN;—BY THE SECOND MARRIAGE.

3. *Albert Milton*,   b. June   18, 1824 ; is a farmer in Hartford.   He m. April
       1, 1846, Laurinda Cutler of Brookline, Vt., b. March, 1828.
4. *Lewis*,   b. Dec.   22, 1825 ; m. Mary Wakefield.   .   (450)
5. *Lyman*,   b. Feb.   18, 1827 ; m. Julia Ann Bush.   . . (451)
6. *Le Roy Sunderland*, b. May   14, 1828 ; m Sarah Jane Lancey.   .   (452)
7. *Sarah Ann*,   b. March 24, 1830 ; m. March 7, 1854, George A. Wash-
       burn of Hartford, and has, 1. George Arthur, b. March 18, 1855 ; 2. Albert
       Lyman, b. July 4, 1857.
8. *William Wirt*,   b. March 9, 1832 ; m. Mary Jane Washburn.   (453)

---

250. DAVID WHITE, Jun., son of David, (116) was born in Longmeadow, Mass., Jan. 30, 1786. He is a farmer, and resided in Longmeadow until 1846, when he removed to Elba, Genesee Co., N. Y. In 1849 he removed to Gaines, Orleans Co., N. Y., where he now resides.

He married, Nov. 17, 1813, CLARISSA HALL of L., dau. of George and Lura Hall. She was born July, 1785, and died Dec. 20, 1846, æ. 61.

CHILDREN.

1. *George Hall*,   b. March 30, 1815 ; m. Eliza Morgan.   .   (454)
2. *Gurdon*,   b. May   25, 1819 ; d. Feb. 24, 1820.
3. *Joseph Pynchon*, b. June 14, 1822 ; m. Ruth L. Morgan.   . (455)

---

251. WILLIAM WHITE, son of David, (116) was born in Longmeadow, June 25, 1789, and resides there. He was post-master from 1820 to 1855, town clerk from 1820 to 1852, and town treasurer from 1824 to 1856.

He married, Nov. 12, 1820, LOIS COOLEY of L., born Feb. 18, 1798, dau. of Calvin Cooley and Eunice Warriner.

CHILDREN.

1. *Mary Cooley,*   b. Sept. 23, 1821; m. Sept. 3, 1851, Rev. Theodore A. Leete of Windsor, Conn., who grad. Yale Coll., 1839. She has, 1. Ella Louisa, b. March 28, 1853; 2. William White, b. Oct. 11, 1854; 3. Theodore Woolsey, b. Nov. 4, 1856.
2. *William Pynchon,*   b. Feb. 24, 1824; m. Mary A. James. .   .   (456)
3. *Jeannette Chittenden,* b. Dec. 27, 1827; d. April 3, 1858, æ. 30.
4. *James Cooley,*   b. Feb. 9, 1838.

---

252. GEORGE WHITE, son of Daniel, (121) was born in Hadley, Dec. 2, 1825, and is a farmer in that place.

He married, March 14, 1851, ELIZABETH S. JUDD of South Hadley, born Sept. 12, 1831, dau. of William Judd. He has,

Ellen Jane, b. Dec. 10, 1855.

---

253. DANIEL SHERMAN WHITE, son of Daniel, (121) was born in Hadley, Aug. 10, 1827, and is a farmer there.

He married, Feb. 24, 1854, ELIZABETH W. POWERS of New Salem, Mass., born April 23, 1835, dau. of Chester Powers. He has one son,

Edward Sherman, b. Jan. 27, 1858.

---

254. EBENEZER WHITE, son of Enoch, (123) was born in Pittsfield, Mass., Nov. 2, 1803. He removed to Quincy, Ill.

He married, 1st, 1822, CYNTHIA P. CLARK of Northampton, Mass. She died in Quincy, April 5, 1838.

He married, 2d, Sept. 27, 1838, SALLY ANN GAGE of Quincy.

CHILDREN ;—BY THE FIRST MARRIAGE.

1. *Elizabeth,*   b. March 21, 1824; m. William McGaine of Keokuk, Iowa, and has had three children.
2. *Catharine Eugenia,* b. July 28, 1832; m. Thomas J. Rice of Keokuk, Iowa: has three children.

CHILD ;—BY THE SECOND MARRIAGE.

3. *William Gage,* b.   .

---

255. JOHN WILLIAM HENRY WHITE, son of Enoch, (123) was born in Pittsfield, Mass., Feb. 25, 1813. He resides in New York.

He married, 1st, MARGARET S. VAN HISE of Pittsfield, dau. of Benjamin Van Hise. She died in N. Y. city, Jan. 19, 1843.

He married, 2d, —— ——.

CHILDREN ;—BY THE FIRST MARRIAGE.

1. *Henry Childs,*   b. June 22, 1830; lives in New York. He m. Margaret
    ———, and has one son, b. Sept., 1851.
2. *Richard Benjamin,* b. Oct. 28, 1831.
3. *William Porter,*   b. Dec. 2, 1834; lives in Hightstown, N. J. He m. Jan.
    16, 1856, Jane D. Reed of Monroe, N. J., dau. of William and Sarah P.
    Reed.
4. *Mary Jane,*   b. May 21, 1836.
5. *Helen Lucretia,* b. July 24, 1838 ; d. Feb., 1842.
6. *James,*   b. March, 1840.
7. *Melissa Margaret,* b. Sept. 3, 1841.
    These births are recorded at Pittsfield.

256. JONATHAN WHITE, Jun., son of Jonathan, (125) was
born in Hadley, Dec. 21, 1817. He lives in Hadley, on a
part of the original homelot of Elder John White.

He married, 1st, Sept. 3, 1840, AMANDA G. HODGE, dau. of
Charles Hodge. She died March 28, 1846, æ. 25.

He married, 2d, March 17, 1847, LUCY CHURCH of South
Hadley, born Jan. 20, 1821, dau. of Pliny Church.

CHILDREN ;—BY THE FIRST MARRIAGE.

1. *Francis William,* b. July 18, 1841.
2. *Charles,*   b. Jan. 28, 1844.
3. *A son,*   b. March 28, 1846; d. April 11, 1846.

CHILDREN ;—BY THE SECOND MARRIAGE.

4. *Ellen Amanda,*   b. Dec. 28, 1847.
5. *Rufus Pliny,*   b. Nov. 9, 1849.
6. *Albert Jonathan,* b. June 16, 1851.

257. JOSIAH WHITE, son of Elijah, (126) was born in Hadley, Aug. 1, 1800. He lives in Dover, Wisconsin.

He married HANNAH CUSHING of Chesterfield, Mass.

CHILDREN.

1. *Amaryllis Cassandra,* b. April 27, 1820; m. Alonzo Kellogg of Hadley, who
    d. Dec. 18, 1844, æ. 23. She d. May 7, 1846, æ. 26, having had, 1. George ;
    2. Francis H., b. April 3, 1843, d. April 27, 1844.
2. *Harriet,*   b.   ; m. David Murray of Portsmouth, O.
3. *Adaline,*   b.   ; m. ——— Fayer ; lives in Wis.
4. *Mary,*   b.   .
5. *Susan,*   b. Feb. 16, 1829; d. March 17, 1848, æ. 19.
6. *Josiah,*   b. May 9, 1831; rem. West. He m. Cholora Pease of Somers,
    Conn. Has two children.
7. *Sarah,*   b.   .
8. *Rheuminah,* b.   .
9. *Abna Christianna,* b. Aug., 1838 ; d. Oct. 10, 1843.

258. SAMUEL SUMNER WHITE, son of Elijah, (126) was born in Hadley, May 10, 1803, and lives in that town.

He married, Oct. 2, 1827, LUCRETIA AUSTIN ROWE, born Aug. 10, 1810, dau. of Abel Rowe of Montague, Mass.

CHILDREN.

1. *Elijah,* b. May 10, 1831 ; d. July 31, 1838, æ. 7.
2. *Mary Julia,* b. April 12, 1839 ; d. July, 1842, æ. 3.
3. *Julia,* b. April 19, 1842 ; d. Oct. 11, 1844, æ. 2.

259. EBENEZER WHITE, son of Elijah, (126) was born in Hadley, Sept. 11, 1805. He lives in Dover, Wis.

He married, 1829, MARY ANN COON.

CHILDREN.

1. *Delia.*   3. *Charles.*   5. *Harriet.*
2. *Henry.*   4. *William.*   6. *Adaline.*

IN THE LINE OF JOHN WHITE, OF HARTFORD.

260. JOHN WHITE, son of John, jun., (127) was born in Hartford, Conn., and lived there, on the road to Wethersfield. He died several years since.

He married ANNA SARVANT, who died Feb. 29, 1856, æ. 76.

CHILDREN.

1. *Frances,* b. 1804 ; m. William Butler of H., who d. April, 1846. She has had, 1. Julia, b. 1831, d. 1839 ; 2. Edward, b. 1832 ; 3. Lucy, b. 1833, m. Anson Thrasher of Wethersfield ; 4. Martha A., b. Nov. 13, 1837, m. Oct. 29, 1857, Frederick Mudge of H. ; 5. Mary, twin with last, d. æ. 8 mos. ; 6. Emily, b. Oct., 1842.
2. *John,* b. ; m. Sarah Hurlburt. . . . (457)

261. NATHANIEL WHITE, Jun., son of Nathaniel, (128) was born in Hartford, Conn., in 1792. He learned the trade of a bookbinder, in Albany, N. Y., and remained in the same establishment forty-one years, till his death, Aug., 1849, æ. 57.

He married, Feb., 1816, ELIZABETH MARCELLUS, dau. of Gilbert and Sarah Marcellus. She was born in Albany, in 1797, and died June 19, 1846, æ. 49.

CHILDREN.

1. *Sarah,* b. Feb., 1817 ; d. in infancy.
2. *Walter,* b. Nov., 1819 ; d. in infancy.
3. *Caroline Augusta,* b. Sept. 3, 1824 ; grad. Albany Female Academy, 1841, and became a teacher : is more recently an authoress, having written a memoir of her first husband, and other works. She m. 1st, Aug. 28, 1843, Rev.

Henry B. Soule of Utica, N. Y., for several years a Universalist minister in Hartford, Conn. He d. Jan. 29, 1852. She m. 2d, July 10, 1855, A. B. Holcomb of Granby, Coun., now of Boonsboro, Boone Co., Iowa. By her first husband she had, 1. Sarah Freeman Packard, b. July 29, 1844 ; 2. Henry Channing, b. Feb. 28, 1846 ; 3. Frank, b. Oct. 30, 1847 ; 4. Eugene, b. June 2, 1849 ; 5. Lizzie, b. Jan. 14, 1851. By her second husband, 6. Sumner White, b. Aug. 29, 1857.

4. *Sarah Marion,* b. June 9, 1826 ; m. 1st, March, 1844, Leverett Dyer, who d. March, 1845 ; m. 2d, Feb., 1846, James L. Hyatt of Albany, a lumber merchant.

5. *Mary Steele,*   b. Aug,   1828 ; d. in infancy.

6. *Kate Weed,*   b. Feb. 22, 1834 ; d. unm., Sept. 16, 1858, æ. 24.

IN THE LINE OF ENSIGN DANIEL WHITE, OF MIDDLETOWN.

262. SAMUEL KELLOGG WHITE, son of Aaron, (129) was born in West Springfield, Mass., May 4, 1789. He is a merchant, and now resides in Cumberland, Md.

He married, Jan. 8, 1822, MARY M. HOFFMAN of Baltimore, Maryland.

CHILDREN.

1. *Mary Lucy,*   b. Feb. 7, 1823.
2. *Charlotte Eliza,*   b. April 16, 1824.
3. *Louisa Catherine,* b.   ; m. John H. Carter of Cincinnati, O.
4. *Samuel Hoffman,* b. April 29, 1828 ; lives at Napoleon, Ark.
5. *Julian,*   b. May 12, 1830 ; a merchant in Cincinnati, O.
6. *Arthur,*   b. Feb. 20, 1832 ; a physician at Lockport, Ind.
7. *Henry Kirke,*   b.   ; lives in St. Louis, Mo.
8. *Emma,*   b.   .

263. AARON WHITE, Jun., son of Aaron, (129) was born in West Springfield, Mass., Aug. 15, 1791. He was a farmer in Camillus, N. Y., and in other places. He died at Bellevue, Mich., April 18, 1856, æ. 64.

He married, 1816, LUCRETIA HUGHES of Camillus, dau. of Henry and Sally Hughes. She died March 22, 1857.

CHILDREN.

1. *Tryphena,*   b. Jan. 19, 1817 ; m. Noble Blossom, and d. in 1837, æ. 20.
2. *William Henry,* b. Nov. 5, 1819 ; m. Margaret Hitchcock. .   . (458)
3. *Maria,*   b. Nov. 7, 1822 ; m. Oct. 10, 1842, A. B. Green, and has had, 1. Oscar F., b. July 18, 1843 ; 2. Franklin, b. 1849, d. 1852 ; 3. Cornelia, b. July 21, 1850.
4. *Amelia Jane,*   b. Sept. 21, 1824 ; m. Oct. 8, 1841, Charles M. Nichols of Battle Creek, Mich., an iron-founder. She has, 1. Amelia Jane, b. July 26, 1844 ; 2. Mary Louisa, b. March 23, 1847 ; 3. Frank Eugene, b. May 28, 1852.

5. *Aaron,*　　　　　b. Aug. 5, 1827 ; m. Laura J. Beman.　　　　　(459)
6. *Charles Augustus,* b. March 12, 1830 ; is a farmer in Bellevue.
7. *Eleanor,*　　　　　b.　　　　1832; m. Oct. 12, 1854, Philip Jenks, and has,
　　1. Victory E., b. March 5, 1856 ; 2. Amos A., b. May 22, 1858.
8. *Samuel Kellogg,* b. April 11, 1835; m. Ann Redfern.　.　.　(460)
9. *George,*　　　　　b. Sept. 16, 1838 ; a farmer in Bellevue.

264. JONATHAN WHITE, son of Aaron, (129) was born in West Springfield, Mass., Jan. 6, 1794. He is a farmer in Camillus, Onondaga Co., N. Y., and has been for about thirty years an elder in the Presbyterian Church in that place.

He married, April 11, 1838, Mrs. MARIETTA WHITE, widow of Harold White, (Family 267,) and dau. of David Morley and Hannah Griswold. She was born Feb. 13, 1793, and died March 14, 1855, æ. 62.

He has one son,

Jonathan Bliss, b Jan. 23, 1839.

265. WILLIAM ELY WHITE, son of Aaron, (129) was born in West Springfield, Mass., June 22, 1796. He is a merchant, and resides in Aurora, Dearborn Co., Ind.

He married, Feb. 28, 1821, EMILY SEYMOUR.

CHILDREN.

1. *Frederick William,* b. May 22, 1823 ; d. in infancy.
2. *Cornelia Ann,*　　b. April 9, 1830 ; d. 1845, æ. 15.
3. *Elisa Maria,*　　　b.　　　　　; m. Henry Andrews of Cincinnati, Ohio,
　　a merchant, and has one son, William.

266. ARTHUR WHITE, son of Aaron, (129) was born in West Springfield, Mass., Feb. 10, 1804. He is a farmer in Camillus, N. Y.

He married, Feb. 17, 1834, AMANDA M. HOLLISTER of Camillus, born Dec. 27, 1815, dau. of Asahel and Catherine Hollister.

CHILDREN.

1. *Marian Amelia,* b. April 29, 1837.
2. *Helen Adelia,*　　b. Sept. 7, 1839.
3. *Catherine Louisa,* b. Sept. 13, 1842.

267. HAROLD WHITE, son of Joseph, Esq., (130) was born in West Springfield, Mass., May 2, 1786. He was a farmer and clothier in Camillus, N. Y., and for several years previous to his death was a magistrate. He died Sept. 10, 1832, æ. 46.

26

He married, Oct. 25, 1827, MARIETTA MORLEY of West Springfield, dau. of David Morley and Hannah Griswold. She married, 2d, Jonathan White: (Family 264.) She was born Feb. 13, 1793, and died March 14, 1855, æ. 62.

CHILDREN.

1. *George Clinton*, b. Aug. 27, 1828 ; m. Evaline A. Comstock.   . (461)
2. *Phebe Clapp*, b. Feb. 2, 1830; d. May 20, 1845, æ. 15.
3. *Harold Morley*, b. Oct. 8, 1832 ; grad. Union Coll., 1856, and is a lawyer in Syracuse, N. Y.

---

268. ABRAM WHITE, son of Daniel, (131) was born in Durham, Greene Co., N. Y., July 13, 1800. He is a farmer in Lenox, Madison Co., N. Y.

He married, Nov. 17, 1825, DOLLY GLEASON of Lenox, dau. of Barzillai and Mary Gleason. She was born April 8, 1801, and died Oct. 15, 1837, æ. 36.

CHILDREN.

1. *Sally,* b. Jan. 26, 1827.
2. *Polly,* b. April 25, 1829 ; d. Oct. 12, 1834.
3. *Daniel Symond*, b. May 11, 1831 ; a farmer in Lenox. He m. Nov. 8, 1855, Harriet Adams of Lenox, b. March 22, 1828, dau. of Minard and Caroline Adams. He has Ella Francis, b. Feb. 18, 1859.
4. *Ruth,* b. March 16, 1833.
5. *Jannette,* b. May 6, 1835 ; m. Sept. 11, 1852, Charles Judd of Sullivan, N. Y., and has Lilian, b. July 18, 1858.
6. *Lucia,* b. Oct. 15, 1837 ; m. July 3, 1856, Charles H. Grey of Sullivan, and has, 1. Charles, b. March 18, 1857 ; 2. Relland, b. April 16, 1852.

---

269. DANIEL WHITE, Jun., son of Daniel, (131) was born in Durham, N. Y., Sept. 1, 1802. He is a farmer in Sullivan, Madison Co., N. Y.

He married, May 27, 1836, ANNA HUBBARD of Sullivan, born Jan. 18, 1811, dau. of Enos and Anna Hubbard.

Has one son,

John Merriman, b. Feb. 27, 1837.

---

270. JOSIAH W. WHITE, son of John, (132) was born Dec. 25, 1805. He was a farmer in Sodus, Wayne Co., N. Y., and afterwards in Otsego, Allegan Co., Mich., where he died, March 4, 1856, æ. 50.

He married, March 24, 1836, SABRA R. TRUMBULL of Conn., born Nov. 27, 1818.

CHILDREN.

1. *William H.*, b. July 16, 1840.
2. *John T.*, b. July 13, 1844.

---

271. AMOS WHITE, Jun., son of Amos, (135) was born in East Haddam, Conn., Oct. 13, 1772. In 1799 he settled in Meriden, Conn., as a merchant, and was chosen a representative from that town in 1808. He removed from Meriden in 1846, and now resides at Elizabethtown, N. J.

He married, March 17, 1799, HANNAH WHITE of Williamsburg, Mass., dau. of Simeon White, jun.: (see Family 93.) She was born March 9, 1779, and died Dec. 18, 1853, æ. 74.

CHILDREN.

1. *Eliza Ann*, b. Nov. 3, 1800; m. Nov. 7, 1824, George Webb of Windham, Conn., now of New York. She has Sarah E., b. July 31, 1825.
2. *Frederick Augustus*, b. May 18, 1802; d. unm., at Sacramento, Cal., Dec. 20, 1849, æ. 47.
3. *Sarah Griswold*, b. Feb. 10, 1805; m. Dec., 1825, Remmick K. Clark of Meriden, Conn. She d. without issue, June 7, 1844, æ. 39.
4. *Hannah Hubbard*, b. March 9, 1807; d. Dec. 13, 1807.
5. *William Henry*, b. Aug. 15, 1815; m. Mary King. . (462)

---

272. ELIJAH WHITE, Jun., son of Col. Elijah, (136) was born June 12, 1767. He was a very active, energetic, and successful business man, conducting a general mercantile business, simultaneously, at Granville, Sandy Hill, and Plattsburgh, N. Y., at the same time being extensively engaged in various manufactures. He resided in Granville, but in 1825 removed to Plattsburgh, where he died, Oct. 24, 1839, æ. 72.

He married, 1st, Oct. 30, 1794, OLIVE CONE. She was born April 16, 1768, and died May 1, 1804, æ. 36.

He married, 2d, Dec. 6, 1804, Mrs. MARY STANDISH, widow of Dr. Zachariah Standish, and dau. of Matthew Scott and Mercy Ashley. She was born March 24, 1778, and died July 31, 1824, æ. 46.

CHILDREN;—BY THE FIRST MARRIAGE.

1. *George W.*, b. May 5, 1795; d. unm., June 18, 1837, æ. 42.
2. *Olive*, b. Feb. 6, 1797; d. March 28, 1805, æ. 8.
3. *Pamilia*, b. March 29, 1799; m. Sept. 8, 1819, Robert Sackrider, a merchant, who d. Sept. 9, 1826, æ. 34. She d. Feb. 26, 1856, æ. 57. She had, 1. Mary White, b. Oct. 17, 1820, d. Aug. 12, 1842, æ. 21; 2. Cornelia Mer-

ritt, b. June 6, 1822, m. ——— Pease, of Detroit, Mich.; 3. Elijah White,
b. Aug. 7, 1825, is a druggist in Cleveland, Ohio.

4. *Minerva,*   b. March 22, 1801; d. unm., June 16, 1832, æ. 31.

5. *Delia,*   b. April 25, 1803; d. March 6, 1805.

CHILDREN;—BY THE SECOND MARRIAGE.

6. *Charles Scott,* b. Nov. 6, 1805; d. June 17, 1826, æ. 20.

7. *Mary Emilia,* b. June 10, 1807; m. Dec. 23, 1830, George Moore, Esq., of
Plattsburgh, a lawyer, and d. Nov. 10, 1851, æ. 44. She had, 1. Samuel,
b. Oct. 3, 1831; 2. John White, b. July 27, 1834; 3. Mary Emilia, b. Feb.
26, 1839; 4. Sarah Jane, b. Sept. 11, 1842.

8. *Olive Delia,*   b. July 24, 1809; m. Norman Sackrider, now of Ogdensburgh,
N. Y. She d. July 3, 1833, æ. 24. She had, 1. Delia, d. young; 2. Charles,
a merchant in Nashua, N. H.

9. *Harriet Elizabeth,* b. May 8, 1811; m. Amos Shepard Hutchinson, a merchant in Cleveland, O., now of New York. She d. Oct. 22, 1847, æ. 36,
having had, 1. Mary, b. 1840; 2. Amos Shepard, b. 1842; and others, who
d. young.

10. *Frances Caroline,* b. Sept. 12, 1813; d. June 25, 1829, æ. 15.

11. *Edward Griffin,* b. July 26, 1815; d. unm., at Cleveland, O., July 19, 1849,
æ. 34.

12. *John Elijah,*   b. Sept. 5, 1817; m. Emma L. W. Shaw.   .   (463)

13. *Catharine Maria,* b. May 16, 1819; m. Samuel Richards Hutchinson, a merchant, of Cleveland, O., now of St. Louis, Mo. She d. Jan. 26, 1855, æ. 35,
having had, 1. Samuel, d. æ. 7; 2. Jane White, b. 1840; 3. Edward, b. 1849.

14. *Jane Ann,*   b. Feb. 26, 1821; m. Heman Monroe Cady, now of Green
Bay, Wis. She has had, 1. Leslie, b. 1844; 2. Lewis, b. 1850; and others,
who d. young.

---

273. WILSON WHITE, son of Col. Elijah, (136) was born in
East Haddam, Conn., June 30, 1770. He settled as a farmer
in Granville, Washington Co., N. Y., and died there, Feb. 7,
1823, æ. 52.

He married, 1st, REBECCA TOWN of Belchertown, Mass., dau.
of Israel Town and Naomy Stebbins. She was born Sept. 9,
1772, and died Oct. 30, 1800, æ. 28.

He married, 2d, Oct., 1801, MARY STEBBINS of Belchertown, Mass., dau. of Capt. Gideon Stebbins and Mary Hinsdale. She was born Feb. 24, 1776, and died Aug. 22, 1819,
æ. 43.

CHILDREN;—BY THE FIRST MARRIAGE.

1. *A child,* b.   ; d. in infancy.

2. *A child,* b.   ; d. in infancy.

3. *Nelson,* b. July 20, 1798; d. unm., in Western N. Y., about 1830.

4. *Naomia,* b. April 2, 1800; m. Sept., 1820, Joseph Bascom of Benson, Vt.
She d. Oct. 22, 1822, æ. 22, leaving one dau., Harriet Naomia, m. Willice
Warner of Vermontville, Eaton Co., Mich.

CHILDREN;—BY THE SECOND MARRIAGE.

5. *Gideon Stebbins*, b. April 12, 1803 ; m. Mary E. Jarnagin.   .   .   (464)
6. *Elijah*,   b. April 3, 1805 ; m. Margaret Smith, and others.   (465)
7. *Josiah A.*,   b. June 13, 1807 ; m. J. A. Warren, and another.   (466)
8. *Mary Rebecca*, b. Jan. 29, 1810 ; m. Jan. 2, 1828, Joseph Townson of Hartford, N. Y., now a farmer in Brooklyn, Jackson Co., Mich. She, has,
   1. George E., b. Oct. 29, 1830, lives in Hamilton, Gratiot Co., Mich. He
   m. April 3, 1858, Mary Southworth ; 2. Mary, b. May 29, 1835, d. Sept. 5,
   1836 ; 3. Mary E., b. Dec. 10, 1837; 4. Joseph N., b. May 13, 1841 ; 5. Harriet C., b. Nov. 24, 1844.

---

274. CHARLES WHITE, son of Col. Elijah, (136) was born in
Granville, N. Y., March 17, 1791. He was a merchant at
Sandy Hill, Washington Co., N. Y., and died there, May 2,
1857, æ. 66.

He married, Nov. 20, 1817, SARAH L. JOHNSON of Sandy
Hill, dau. of Luther Johnson and Anna Dean.

CHILDREN.

1. *Charlotte P.*, b. Sept. 27, 1819 ; m. Oct. 15, 1845, John M. Niles of Spencer-
   town, Columbia Co., N. Y., and has Henry White, b. Jan. 24, 1853.
2. *Caroline E.*, b. Aug. 4, 1821.
3. *Charles A.*, b. Dec. 14, 1823; m. Deborah Burch.   .   .   .   (467)
4. *James H.*,   b. Aug. 15, 1826 ; was for several years connected with the N. Y.
   and Erie R. R., and d. Dec. 12, 1852, æ. 26.
5. *Frances E.*   7. *Mary E. Moore.*   9. *Harriet A.*
6. *Sarah A.*   8. *Delia J.*

275. WILLIAM WHITE, son of Daniel Hurlburt, (137) was
born in East Haddam, Conn., Oct. 11, 1783, and died at
Elbridge, N. Y., Oct. 8, 1824, æ. 41. He was a hatter.

He married ELECTA EVERTS, who died Jan. 30, 1825, æ. 39.

CHILDREN.

1. *Juliaett*, b.   1807; m. 1826, Horace Moses, a merchant in Marcellus,
   N. Y., who d. Jan. 2, 1840. She d. Aug. 22, 1852, æ. 45, having had one
   son, Horace M., b. about 1830.
2. *Millicent*, b. Aug., 1809 ; m. —— Gillespie: res. in Livingston Co., Mich.
3. *Daniel Brainard*, b. Aug., 1812 ; is a hatter ; lives in Orange, N. J.
4. *Milo Everts*,   b. Oct., 1814 ; m. Janette Paddock.   .   .   (468)
5. *Catharine Jemima*, b. Aug. 3, 1820 ; d. May 8, 1834, æ. 13.
6. *William*,   b. April 3, 1822 ; d. April 18, 1825.

---

276. CORAL CASE WHITE, son of Daniel Hurlburt, (137)
was born in Granville, Washington Co., N. Y., Feb. 25, 1789.
He is a farmer, and resides in Ledyard, Cayuga Co., N. Y.

He married, Feb. 17, 1811, ESTHER B. JOHNSON, dau. of
Gurdon Johnson.

CHILDREN.

1. *Fidelia Anna,*   b. Nov. 20, 1811; m. June 5, 1834, Frederick D. Morgan, a farmer in Ledyard, and has one son, Coral White, b. Nov. 6, 1835.

2. *Statira Johnson,*   b. Oct. 20, 1817; m. Nov. 23, 1836, Sanford Gifford, a
farmer, and has had, 1. Abby Fidelia, b Nov. 10, 1838; 2. Ann Eliza, b.
.Oct. 7, 1840; 3. Frances Adell, b. Aug. 17, 1846, d. Oct. 26, 1848.

3. *Jeremiah Brainard,* b. March 11, 1821; d. July 15, 1825.

4. *Coral Case,*   b. Jan. 21, 1823; m. Cornelia Morgan. .   .   (469)

5. *Adell H.,*   b. June 3, 1826; lives with her parents.

---

277. JEREMIAH GATES BRAINARD WHITE, son of Daniel
Hurlburt, (137) was born in Granville, N. Y., Dec. 22, 1795.
He is a hatter, and resides in Marcellus, Onondaga Co., N. Y.

He married, Oct. 10, 1822, LOIS A. RICHARDSON, born at
Cazenovia, N. Y., June 21, 1802, dau. of Ephraim Richardson and Lois Porter.

CHILDREN.

1. *Helen Louisa,*   b. Nov. 12, 1824; m. Aug. 21, 1843, Charles A. Brown of
Cazenovia, N. Y., a stove dealer. She has, 1. George Henry, b. Dec. 2,
1848; 2. Francis E., b. Aug. 6, 1855.

2. *William Brainard,* b. April 14, 1826; is a stove dealer at Marcellus.

3. *Henry Gates,*   b. Sept. 19, 1830; d. July 22, 1854, æ. 23.

4. *George Andrew,*   b. April 10, 1836; d. March 31, 1841, æ. 5.

5. *Mary Jane,*   b. June 4, 1838; d. Oct. 10, 1838.

---

278. NOADIAH WHITE, son of Noadiah, Jun., (138) was
born in Chatham, Conn., in 1777. He settled in Hartford,
Vt., as a tanner and shoemaker, but after a few years became
a farmer in that town. In 1832 he removed to Garrettsville,
in the township of Hiram, Portage Co., Ohio, where he died
in 1839, æ. 62.

He married, Dec., 1799, WEALTHY HAZEN of Hartford, Vt.,
born in 1783, dau. of Col. Joshua and Mercy Hazen. She
lives with her eldest daughter.

CHILDREN.

1. *Eunice P.,*   b. April 24, 1803; m. 1843, Rev. George C. Baker. They
live in Garrettsville, on the homestead of her father.

2. *Wade,*   b. Aug. 21, 1805; m. Emily Hunt. .   .   .   (470)

3. *Willard Stanley,* b. Dec. 4, 1807; m. 1st, M. Newton; 2d, E. Dean. (471)

4. *Joshua Hazen,*   b. March 26, 1810; m. 1st, H. Beman; 2d, S. Daily. (472)

5. *John D.,*   b. Oct. 15, 1812; m. Charlotte Hunt.   .   .   (473)

6. *Noadiah Wells,* b. May 19, 1815; rem. to Wisconsin, and d. in 1844, æ. 29.

7. *Wealthy S.,*   b. 1817; m. 1846, Rev. Waitstill B. Orvis, a grad.
of Oberlin College, for some time an editor in Ravenna, O., now laboring in
Mo. She has, 1. Clarkson Finney, b. 1847; 2. Gurney Mahan, b. 1849.

8. *Richard W.,*　b.　　　　1820; m. Elizabeth Heath.　.　.　(474)
9. *Amos,*　　　b.　　　　1823; m. Laura Hunt.　.　.　.　(475)
10. *Charles A.,*　b.,　　　　1825; m. 1853, Lucinda Landfear.

279. AMOS WHITE, son of Noadiah, Jun., (138) was born in Chatham, Conn., June 3, 1785. In 1811 he settled as a farmer in Williamson, Wayne Co., N. Y., where he now resides.

He married, Jan. 1, 1811, SALLY WHITE, born July 11, 1791, dau. of Abijah White. (See Family 140.)

CHILDREN.

1. *Sylvester,* b. Dec. 18, 1813 ; m. Roxana Rice.　　.　　(476)
2. *Abijah,*　b. Dec. 3, 1818 ; m. Mariette Snyder.　.　.　.　.　(477)
3. *Amos,*　b. June 27, 1834 ; lives in Williamson. Other children died young.

280. Dr. JOSEPH WHITE, son of Joseph, (139) was born in Chatham, Conn., May 9, 1800. He resides in Canajoharie, Montgomery Co., N. Y., and is a physician.

He married, March 20, 1845, MARIETTA ROSEBOOM, born March 29, 1813, dau. of Abraham Roseboom and Ruth Johnson.

CHILDREN.

1. *John Roseboom,* b. March 25, 1846.
2. *Sarah Elizabeth,* b. Oct. 27, 1849.
3. *Joseph Henry,* b. Aug. 29, 1855.

281. ABIJAH L. WHITE, son of Abijah, (140) was born Aug. 25, 1797, and died June 3, 1843, æ. 45.
He married SALLY JONES.

CHILDREN.

1. *Willard,* b.　　　; a farmer in Cherry Valley, N. Y.: has a family.
2. *Augustus,* b.　　　; a farmer in Canajoharie : has a family.
　There were other children, names not reported.

282. AMOS H. WHITE, son of Abijah, (140) was born Aug. 24, 1804, and died July 16, 1853, æ. 49.
He married JANE ANN PAFF.

CHILDREN.

1. *George,* b.　　　; lives near Cazenovia, N. Y.
2. *Amos,* b.　　　; lives in New York city.
3. *Mary,* b.　　　; m. —— Davidson of N. Y. city.

283. BACKUS WHITE, son of Samuel, (141) was born Dec. 17, 1798, and is a farmer in De Ruyter, Madison Co., N. Y.

He married, Jan. 9, 1831, ANN MARIA POWERS, born in Prescott, Mass., July 10, 1808, dau. of Dr. Isaac Powers and Anna Mellon.

CHILDREN.

1. *Alverson Backus*, b. Oct.   1, 1832; m. Jan. 5, 1859, Emily A. Allen.
2. *Mary A.*,   b. March 24, 1835.
3. *Colister P.*,   b. Sept. 30, 1837.

---

284. AUSTIN A. WHITE, son of Samuel, (141) was born July 19, 1805. He is a farmer in Georgetown, Madison Co., N. Y.

He married, Feb. 21, 1829, POLLY M. POWERS, born in Prescott, Mass., Dec. 14, 1810, dau. of Dr. Isaac Powers and Anna Mellon.

CHILDREN.

1. *Ann Maria*,   b. Dec. 25, 1829; m. Sept. 13, 1849, James H. Snow, and d. Aug. 10, 1852, æ. 22.
2. *Addison Samuel*, b. Jan. 6, 1832; was a tanner at Fabius, Onondaga Co., N. Y., and d. Sept. 30, 1858, æ. 26.
3. *Zelotes Allis*,   b. Nov. 7, 1834; m. Oct. 5, 1858, Cynthia S. Burgess.
4. *Sarah Eliza*,   b. May 28, 1846.

---

285. DAVID WHITE, Jun., son of David, Esq., (142) was born in that part of Chatham which is now the town of Portland, Conn., July 9, 1779. He was a farmer and merchant in that place, and died Oct. 27, 1836, æ. 57.

He married, May 17, 1801, ABIGAIL AMES, dau. of Nicholas Ames and Abigail Robinson. She died Dec. 19, 1839, æ. 61.

CHILDREN.

1. *Harriet*, b. Dec. 27, 1801; m. Dec. 4, 1823, Edward Savage of Cromwell, Conn., a farmer, and manufacturer of fire-arms. She has had, 1. Josiah, b. Oct. 5, 1824, grad. Yale Coll., 1846, and d. in Cal., Nov. 1, 1849, æ. 25; 2. Mary Griswold, b. Oct. 24, 1828; 3. Harriet White, b. April 25, 1831, m. June 10, 1857, James A. Wheelock, now of Middletown; 4. Edward Benjamin, b. Oct. 6, 1836.
2. *Maria*,   b. March 10, 1804.
3. *Evelyn*,   b. July 13, 1806; m. Frances E. Penfield. .   .   .   (478)
4. *Theodosia*, b. Feb. 11, 1809; m. Nov. 17, 1840, Philip H. Sellew of Portland.

---

286. JAMES WELLS WHITE, son of David, Esq., (142) was born in Portland, then a part of Chatham, April 27, 1802. He is a farmer there, on his father's homestead.

He married, 1st, Jan. 20, 1825, FANNY HALL of Portland, dau. of Samuel Hall and Ruth Bates. She died Nov. 8, 1825.

He married, 2d, Dec. 24, 1827, MARGARET B. LEWIS of Portland, dau. of Abel Lewis and Mary Cruttenden.

CHILDREN ;—BY THE SECOND MARRIAGE.

1. *Fanny H.*, b. Dec. 8, 1828 ; m. Feb. 22, 1857, A. B. Reynolds of Chicago, Ill.
2. *Alfred*,   b. Dec. 24, 1830.
3. *Cornelia*, b. May 26, 1833 ; m. Oct. 18, 1853, John L. Patterson of New York, and has, 1. Alexander John Lumsden, b. Aug. 21, 1854 ; 2. Margaret White, b. Sept. 5, 1856.
4. *Mary*,   b. May 25, 1840.

287. EBENEZER BUTLER WHITE, son of Col. Daniel, (143) was born in Chatham, Nov. 15, 1804. He is a farmer there, in the present town of Portland, on the homestead of his father and grandfather. He has held town offices, and is deputy and county surveyor.

He married, March 10, 1828, HENRIETTA WARD of Fairfield, N. Y., born Sept. 3, 1802, dau. of Edmund Ward and Sally White. (See Family 142.)

CHILDREN.

1. *Martha*, b. Jan. 26, 1829.
2. *Ward*, b. May 25, 1832 ; d. Sept. 13, 1847, æ. 15

288. STEPHEN WHITE, son of Josiah, (144) was born in Chatham, Conn., Feb. 22, 1783. He was a merchant, at first in connection with his father, in Glastenbury, Conn., and Middlebury, Vt., and from 1810 to 1826 in Granby, Conn. He was a church-warden of the Episcopal Church in Granby, and held various town offices. In 1826 he removed to Union Village, Rensselaer Co., N. Y., and in 1831 to Verona, Oneida Co., N. Y., where he settled as a farmer. After 1836 he resided in the village of New London, in that town, where he died, Nov. 25, 1841, æ. 58.

He married, Jan. 21, 1810, MARY LAVINIA COSSITT of Granby, Conn., dau. of Asa Cossitt, Esq., and of Mary, dau. of Rev. Samuel Cole of Claremont, N. H. She resides in Rome, N. Y.

CHILDREN.

1. *Henry Cole*, b. March 15, 1812 ; engaged in mercantile pursuits in Verona, New London, and Rome. He d. in Rome, unm., June 16, 1855, æ. 43.
2. *George Cossitt*, b. Aug. 10, 1816 ; m. Sarah Maria Cossitt. . . (479)
3. *Mary Lavinia*, b. May 23, 1826 ; resides in Rome.

289. WILLIAM CZAR WHITE, son of Josiah, (144) was born in Chatham, Conn., Nov. 25, 1787. He was a farmer, and

27

last resided in the township of Sheridan, Mich., where he died, Sept. 18, 1838, æ. 50. Was a deacon.

He married, Nov. 25, 1806, BETSEY HOUSE of Glastenbury, Conn., born Jan. 13, 1789, dau. of Matthew and Lois House. She resides in Sheridan.

CHILDREN.

1. *Hannah,*   b. Jan.   20, 1808 ; d. Oct. 8, 1823, æ. 15.+
2. *Henrietta H.,*   b. Sept. 24, 1809 ; m. Dec., 1830, Oliver Barnes, a farmer, of Berea, O., and d. Aug., 1844, æ. 35. She had, 1. Marilla, b. April, 1832 ; 2. William, b. July, 1834 ; 3. Mary, b. Jan., 1836.
3. *Lois H.,*   b. Aug. 16, 1811 ; m. Aug., 1831, Henry G. Spencer of Strongsville, O., and d. Aug. 31, 1843, æ. 32. He d. Sept. 30, 1844. She had, 1. Celia I., b. Oct. 17, 1833 ; 2. Harriet, b. Sept. 18, 1838.
4. *Mary H.,*   b. April 16, 1815 ; m. Jan. 21, 1841, Phinelson W. Marsh of Albion, Mich., a builder and mill-wright. She has, 1. Harriet L., b. Dec. 4, 1842 ; 2. William S., b. July 2, 1848.
5. *Harriet E.,*   b. July   17, 1817 ; m. June 6, 1837, John C. Strong of Strongsville, O. She d. Jan. 17, 1853, æ. 35, leaving one son.
6. *Matthew H.,*   b. Aug. 24, 1819 ; m. Victoria Lyman.   .   .   . (480)
7. *Harry Hamlin,* b. March 16, 1821 ; d. Sept. 16, 1847, æ. 26.
8. *John F.,*   b. Dec.   23, 1823 ; is a farmer on the homestead.
9. *George H.,*   b. Jan.   17, 1827 ; d. July 28, 1828.
10. *Hannah H.,*   b. April 15, 1828 ; m. May, 1850, Warner H. Strong of Strongsville, O., and has one son, b. Aug., 1852.

---

290. GEORGE J. WHITE, son of George, Esq., (145) was born in Portland, Conn., May 20, 1819. He is a farmer there, on a part of the family homestead.

He married, Oct. 15, 1845, ESTHER MYRICK of Portland, dau. of Alfred Myrick and Mary Coleman.

CHILDREN.

1. *George William Myrick,* b. Oct. 10, 1846.
2. *Frederick H.,*   b. Aug. 12, 1848.
3. *Catherine E. Teresa,*   b. Feb.   6, 1853.
4. *Mary Elizabeth,*   b. Oct. 21, 1856 ; d. Feb. 12, 1857.

---

291. STEPHEN H. WHITE, son of George, Esq., (145) was born in Portland, Dec. 15, 1820. He resides there, and is a farmer and carpenter.

He married, 1st, Nov. 24, 1844, SARAH RISLEY of Glastenbury, dau. of Harlow Risley and Sarah Hubbard. She died Oct. 14, 1846, æ. 20.

He married, 2d, Nov. 13, 1850, ALMIRA W. UFFORD of Portland, dau. of Russell Ufford and Charity Cone.

CHILDREN;—BY THE SECOND MARRIAGE.

1. *Sarah A.,*   b. Dec. 15, 1851.
2. *Annie Maria*, b. March 23, 1859.

---

292. WILLIAM STARR WHITE, son of George, Esq., (145) was born in Portland, March 26, 1824, and is a farmer and carpenter in that place.

He married, June 2, 1847, EMILY STRICKLAND of Portland, dau. of Ammial Strickland and Susan Penfield.

He has one child,

Jane E., b. March 15, 1848.

---

293. SAMUEL WHITE, son of Timothy, (146) was born in Upper Middletown, March 10, 1780. He lived in that place, except a few years in Sharon, till about 1837, when he removed to Cheshire, Conn., where he now resides.

He married, 1st, Jan. 3, 1802, BETSEY SMITH of Haddam, dau. of Henry and Susan Smith. She was born April 13, 1784, and died Feb. 15, 1837, [1836 ?] æ. 52.

He married, 2d, Sept. 3, [Aug. 27 ?] 1837, Mrs. CONCURRENCE (AUSTIN) HILL of Cheshire, widow of Jonas Hill.

CHILDREN;—BY THE FIRST MARRIAGE.

1. *Abner,*   b. May 1, 1803; d. unm., Nov. 5, 1834, æ. 31.
2. *Susan B.,* b. March 1, 1805; m. Nov. 22, 1826, Ira Brainerd, and d. Feb. 3, 1855, æ. 50. She had, 1. Nancy ; 2. Levi ; 3 Susan ; 4. Henry.
3. *Luther,*   b. April 5, 1807; m. Emily Phelps. .   .   .   .   (481)
4. *Betsey,*   b. Jan. 28, 1809; m. Nov. 13, 1828, Luther Sage of Cromwell, and has had, 1. Elizabeth Ann, b. Sept 2, 1829 ; 2. Charles L., b. Nov. 9, 1831 ; 3. Emily B., b. Dec. 11, 1833, d. April 8, 1838 ; 4. Francis Augustus, b. March 5, 1838 ; 5. Sarah Almira, b. Oct. 18, 1841 ; 6. Georgianna, b. Feb. 18, 1846 ; d. June 22, 1848.
5. *Heman,*   b. March 5, 1811 ; m. 1st, C. Atwood ; 2d, C. C. Mallory. (482)
6. *Samuel,* ⸗ b. May 8, 1813 ; m. Almira Brooks.   .   .   .   (483)
7. *Eliza,*   b. April 2, 1815; m. 1836, Elbridge G. Hall of Wallingford, Conn., now a merchant in San Francisco, Cal. She d. in Cincinnati, O., April 1, 1847, æ. 32.
8. *Mariette,* b. Nov. 6, 1817 ; m. July 6, 1835, William G. Atwater of Cheshire, now of Meriden, a mechanic. She d. March 28, 1852, æ. 34. She had, 1. Caroline E., b. Sept. 13, 1836 ; 2. George A., b. Jan. 26, 1842 ; 3. Ellen A., b. April 30, 1846.
9. *Almira,*   b. Nov. 22, 1819; m. Dec. 7, 1842, Garry J. Mix of Wallingford, Conn., a manufacturer. She has, 1. Ann Eliza, b. Feb. 25, 1846; 2. Frances A., b. Dec. 21, 1847.
10. *Henry S.,* b. July 17, 1822; m. Susan M. Couch. .   .   . (484)

11. *Timothy,*   b. Nov.   2, 1824 ; m. Caroline E. Cowles. .   .   .   .   (485)
12. *Flora Ann,* b. July 14, 1827 ; m. Sept. 18, 1853, Russell J. Ives of Meriden,
    a merchant, and d. Nov. 11, 1857, æ. 30.   She had, 1. Edwin R., b. July 12,
    1855 ; 2. Flora A., b. Jan. 9, 1857.
13. *Benjamin,* b. Dec. 12, 1829 ; d. Jan. 14, 1838, æ. 8.

---

294. Capt. TIMOTHY WHITE, son of Timothy, (146) was
born in Upper Middletown, now Cromwell, Dec. 26, 1787.
He resided there, and was a sea-captain.   He died Aug. 22,
1858, æ. 70.

He married, March 5, 1811, ROXY SAGE of Upper Middletown, dau. of Solomon Sage.   She was born Feb. 17, 1790,
and died Aug. 24, 1857, æ. 67.

CHILDREN.

1. *William Henry,* b. Jan. 14, 1812 ; lives in Middletown.
2. *Timothy Sage,*   b. Dec. 11, 1816 ; d. Feb. 1, 1819.
3. *Jerusha Savage,* b. Jan. 30, 1818 ; m. April 4, 1843, Alfred Harris of Goshen,
   Orange Co., N. Y.   She has, 1. Alfred White, b. Jan. 19, 1844 ; 2. Luther,
   b. Oct. 13, 1845 ; 3. Laura Harriet, b. Aug. 23, 1847 ; 4. Ellen Maria, b.
   Feb. 19, 1849.
4. *Laura Sage,*   b. Sept. 17, 1820 ; lives in Cromwell.

---

295. BENJAMIN WHITE, son of Timothy, (146) was born in
Upper Middletown, Aug. 9, 1794.   He lived in the city of
Middletown, and died May 14, 1828, æ. 33.

He married, April 25, 1819, SALLY COOK.

CHILDREN.

1. *Martha Birdsey,* b. April 26, 1820 ; m. Norman W. Pomeroy of Meriden.
2. *Sina Cook,*   b. March 19, 1822.
3. *Silvia Antoinette,* b. July 19, 1824.
4. *Lavinia Maria,* b. Oct.   3, 1827.

---

296. AARON WHITE, son of Samuel, (147) was born Nov.
2, 1788.   He is a farmer in Holland Patent, Oneida Co., N. Y.
He married RHODA BAGG of Lanesboro, Mass.

CHILDREN.

1. *Charles Merrow,* b.   ; a farmer in Holland Patent.
2. *Martha,*   b.   .

---

297. Hon. FORTUNE CLARK WHITE, son of Col. Daniel Clark,
(148) was born in Whitestown, N. Y., July 10, 1787, and has
resided chiefly in that place.   He is a lawyer, and for five
years from about 1837 was First Judge of Oneida County
Court.   He has been a Brigadier General of the N. Y. State

Militia, and has twice been a member of the Legislature. In 1826 the honorary degree of Master of Arts was conferred on him by Hamilton College.

He married, Aug. 3, 1815, EXPERIENCE PATTEN of Hartford, Conn., dau. of Nathaniel Patten and Lucinda Hitchcock. She died June 23, 1851.

CHILDREN.

1. *Nathaniel Patten*, b. May 21, 1816 ; is a dentist at Port Huron, St. Clair Co. Mich.
2. *Lucinda Patten*, b. July 31, 1817 ; d. 1832, æ. 15.
3. *Junius*, b. Dec. 20, 1818 ; d. 1819.
4. *Edgar*, b. Oct. 3, 1820 ; m. Adelia Jones. . . . (486)
5. *James Hillhouse*, b. April 28, 1822 ; m. A. M. Wetmore, and another. (487)
6. *Henry Randolph*, b. April 23, 1824 ; m. Sarah Bruce Clark. . . (488)
7. *Frances Amelia*, b. Jan. 11, 1826 ; m. Sept. 1, 1846, George Dickinson Hill, a merchant in Ann Arbor, Mich., and has had, 1. George White, b. Aug. 4, 1847 ; 2. Florence, b. Sept. 11, 1849, d. April 21, 1852 ; 3. Susan Esther, b. April 2, 1852 ; 4. Henry Rowland, b. Nov. 19, 1853.

---

298. HENRY WHITE, son of Joseph, (149) was born in Whitestown, N. Y., Feb. 8, 1788. He is engaged in farming in that place, but resides in Utica. From 1822 to 1838 he was Superintendent of the Utica and Schenectady Packet Boat Company.

He married, Feb. 7, 1815, JULIA BIDWELL of Farmington, Conn., dau. of Titus Bidwell and Nancy Langdon. She was born Nov. 25, 1797, and died July 27, 1841, æ. 43.

CHILDREN.

1. *Edward Bidwell*, b. Dec. 4, 1815 ; d. Aug. 17, 1828, æ. 12.
2. *Harriet Maria*, b. Jan. 2, 1818 ; m. Aug. 31, 1837, E. G. Peckham of Lockport, N. Y., and has, 1. Edward B.; 2. Julia B.; 3. Fanny; 4. Charles.
3. *Jane Amelia*, b. March 26, 1824 ; m. Sept. 26, 1844, Henry Seymour Lansing, proprietor of a "Foreign Express." She now resides in Paris, France, and has, 1. Henry White; 2. Arthur Livingston.
4. *Emily*, b. ; d. in infancy.
5. *Abby*, b. ; d. in infancy.
6. *Sarah Eliza*, b. Sept. 28, 1829 ; m. Feb. 25, 1848, Henry Malsom of Albany, N. Y., and d. July 17, 1856, æ. 26. She had, 1. Anna; 2. Julia.

---

299. JOSEPH WHITE, son of Joseph, (149) was born in Whitestown, N. Y., Dec. 10, 1794. He removed to the West, and was for some time a hatter in St. Louis, Mo., but is said to be now residing with his son-in-law, in New Orleans, La. Name of his wife not ascertained.

CHILDREN.

1. *A daughter* ; m. ——— Twichell of New Orleans.
2. *A son;* said to be living in California.   Perhaps there are other children.

300. CANVASS WHITE, son of Hugh, Jun., (150) was born in Whitestown, N. Y., Sept. 8, 1790. He served one campaign on the frontier, in the war of 1812, as Lieutenant in a corps of volunteers, and was at the sortie of Fort Erie. He was one of the earliest and ablest Engineers on the Erie Canal, and while engaged on this, resided principally in Troy, N. Y. He subsequently resided in Reading and Bethlehem, Pa., and in Princeton, N. J., while engaged on the Union, Lehigh, and the Delaware and Raritan Canals. He died at St. Augustine, Florida, whither he had gone in pursuit of health, Dec. 18, 1834, æ. 44.

He married, 1820, LOUISA LOOMIS of Lowville, Lewis Co., N. Y. She now resides with her daughter, in Bethlehem, Pa.

CHILDREN.

1. *Charles L.*, b.   1821 ; res. in Mauch Chunk, Carbon Co., Pa.; an agent on the Lehigh Valley R. R.   He m. Ellen Till of Easton, Pa., and has one daughter.
2. *Cornelia P.*, b. Nov., 1832 ; m. Aug., 1852, R. Henry Barnes of Summit Hill, Carbon Co., Pa., who d. Oct., 1856.   She has, 1. Edward ; 2. Henry.
3. *Susan L.*, b. Oct.,   1833 ; d. in Jersey City, N. J., June 29, 1853, æ. 19. Other children died in infancy.

301. Hon. HUGH WHITE, son of Hugh, jun., (150) was born in Whitestown, N. Y., Dec. 25, 1798. He graduated at Hamilton College in 1823, and fitted for the Bar in the office of Col. Charles G. Haines of New York city, but soon turned his attention to other business pursuits, and engaged in agriculture, extensive manufacturing, and contracting on public works. In 1825 he settled in Chittenango, Madison Co., N. Y., and in 1830 removed to Waterford, Saratoga Co., where he now resides, near the village of Cohoes. He has taken an active interest in public affairs, and in 1844 was chosen a Representative to Congress. He served in Congress for three terms, from 1845 to 1851, having been twice re-elected.

He married, April 10, 1828, MARIA MILLS MANSFIELD of Kent, Conn., born Feb. 5, 1808, dau. of William P. Mansfield and Sally Mills.

CHILDREN.

1. *Florilla,*   b. July 31, 1830; d. June 23, 1851, æ. 21.
2. *William Punderson,* b. June,   1832; d. July, 1832, æ. 3 weeks.
3. *William Mansfield,* b. July 8, 1833; a farmer in Ossian, Livingston Co., N. Y.
4. *Isabel,*   b. March 22, 1837; m. Jan. 3, 1855, William W. Niles, Esq. He grad. Dartmouth Coll., 1845, and is a lawyer in New York. She has Robert Lossing, b. July 2, 1857.
5. *Sarah,*   b. Dec. 24, 1840; d. Dec. 3, 1844.
6. *Charlotte,* b. Jan. 6, 1843.
7. *Maria,*   b. March 7, 1849; d. Sept., 1849.

---

302. JONAS WHITE, son of Philo, (152) was born in Whitestown, N. Y., Sept. 10, 1789, and is a farmer in that place.

He married, July 25, 1813, MARY LEWIS of Whitestown, born Jan. 22, 1790, dau. of John and Anna Lewis.

CHILDREN.

1. *Jonas Autle,*   b. July 25, 1815; m. Almira H. Foote.   .   .   (489)
2. *Morris Pratt,* ⎫ b. April 26, 1817; m. Julia A. Jones.   .   .   .   (490)
3. *Mary,*   ⎭   Twins.   m. John F. Gray of Racine, Wis., who d. July 14, 1854, æ. 50. She now res. in Whitestown.
4. *Lewis,*   b. April 30, 1819; m. Ambrosia Lamb.   .   (491)
5. *Philo,*   b. April 24, 1821; is a jeweler in San Francisco, Cal.
6. *George Manchester,* b. July 30, 1825; m. Submit Bliss.   .   .   (492)
7. *Cynthia Ann,*   b. Sept. 5, 1827; d. April 1, 1842, æ. 14.
8. *Louisa,*   b. Feb. 19, 1830; d. July 31, 1831.
9. *Charles,*   b. May 27, 1832; is a farmer in Whitestown.

---

303. HIRAM WHITE, son of Philo, (152) was born in Whitestown, April 11, 1794. He was formerly a hatter, but has been for some years past a merchant and farmer in Illinois.

He married, about 1823, AMINTA THRUSTON of Petersburg, Va., who died about 1851, æ. about 53.

CHILDREN.

1. *Catharine,* b. about 1824; m. about 1846, a Baptist minister in North Carolina, who d. She m. again.
2. *Maria,*   b. about 1827; m. about 1845, —— Pender, of Tarboro', N. C.
3. *Indiana,*   b. about 1829; m. 1853, William Henry Stratton of New York.

---

304. Hon. PHILO WHITE, LL. D., son of Philo, (152) was born in Whitestown, N. Y., June 23, 1796. After spending a few years in a printing office in Utica, he removed to North Carolina, and in 1820 located at Salisbury, Rowan County. Here he became the editor of the " Western Carolinian," which he continued to conduct until 1830, when he was appointed

United States Navy Agent for the Pacific Station. Returning home in 1834, he established the "North Carolina Standard," at Raleigh, and was elected State Printer. From 1837 to 1844 he was a Purser in the U. S. Navy, and was attached to the squadron in the Pacific.

Mr. White removed to Wisconsin at an early period of its territorial existence, and ultimately fixed his residence at Racine. He was the editor of several newspapers, at different periods. In 1847 he was chosen a member of the Council of the Territorial Legislature, and in the following year was elected to the Senate of the State Legislature. Here he took a prominent part in promoting various measures of public utility. As chairman of the Committee on Education and School Lands, he shared largely in devising and framing the present system of public instruction in that State. At a later period, he was active in the founding of Racine College, under the auspices of the Protestant Episcopal Church of that Diocese, and was one of its Trustees. In 1856 the College conferred upon Mr. White the honorary degree of Doctor of Laws. In 1852 he was chosen one of the presidential electors of Wisconsin. He has also been a Brigadier General of the State Militia.

In 1849 Mr. White was appointed U. S. Consul to the Hanseatic Republic of Hamburg, and resided there for one or two years. In July, 1853, he was appointed Charge d'Affaires to the Republic of Ecuador, S. A., and in 1855 was raised to the grade of Minister Resident in that country. He continued in this office until September, 1858, and has now returned to take up his residence in Whitestown, his native place.

For a more extended notice of Mr. White's public career, the reader is referred to Livingston's "Portraits and Memoirs of Eminent Americans," Vol. IV., from which most of the facts in the foregoing sketch have been taken.

He married, May 9, 1822, NANCY R. HAMPTON of Salisbury, N. C., born Sept., 1802, dau. of William and Mary Hampton.

CHILDREN.

1. *Mary*, b. July 20, 1824 ; m. Aug., 1844, Hon. John W. Ellis of Salisbury, and d., Oct. 19, 1844, æ. 20. Mr. Ellis is a lawyer, has been for nine years a Judge of the Superior Courts, and is now Governor of the State.
2. *Esther*, b. Nov. 9, 1830 ; d. April 24, 1832.

305. ELISHA WHITE, Jun., son of Elisha, (153) was born in Windham, Conn., Aug. 9, 1791. He resided there, and died Jan. 26, 1821, æ. 29.

He married, Sept. 10, 1815, LYDIA DYER of Windham, dau. of Col. Thomas Dyer and Elizabeth Ripley. She died May 9, 1817, æ. 26.

He left one child,

Mary Lydia, b. April 6, 1816; m. Isaac Allen Stoddard of Windham, and d. Nov. 14, 1839, æ. 23.

---

306. HENRY WHITE, Esq., son of Hon. Dyer, (154) was born in New Haven, Conn., March 5, 1803. He graduated at Yale College in 1821, and was a Tutor in the College from 1823 to 1825. He is a lawyer in New Haven, has been much occupied with the settlement of estates, and the care of trust funds, and is a deacon in the First Congregational Church.

He married, Jan. 7, 1830, MARTHA SHERMAN of New Haven, born Feb. 13, 1807, dau. of Roger Sherman and Susanna Staples, and grand-daughter of Roger Sherman, the Signer of the Declaration of Independence.

CHILDREN.

1. *Henry Dyer*,   b. Sept. 24, 1830; grad. at Yale College in 1851, and is a lawyer in New Haven.
2. *Charles Atwood*,   b. Nov. 11, 1833; grad. at Yale College in 1854, and lives in New York.
3. *Willard Wetmore*, b. Feb. 7, 1835; lives in New York.
4. *Roger Sherman*,   b. Dec. 26, 1837; grad. at Yale College in 1859.
5. *Thomas Howell*,   b. Feb. 4, 1840.
6. *Oliver Sherman*,   b. Nov. 2, 1842.
7. *George Edward*,   b. March 17, 1845.

---

307. Capt. AMOS WHITE, son of Capt. Timothy, (155) was born in New Haven, Oct. 31, 1777. He resided there, and was a sea-captain.

He married POLLY KIMBERLY, dau. of Asahel Kimberly of West Haven.

CHILDREN.

1. *Amelia*, b. 1803; m. John Warland of New Haven, and is now living, a widow. Her dau., Clarissa, b. Oct. 8, 1829, m. June 4, 1850, Nathan S. Starr.
2. *Mary*, b. 1805; m. John Smith, and d. about 1844, leaving two children.

308. Capt. AARON CLARK WHITE, son of Capt. Timothy, (155) was born in New Haven, Oct. 19, 1784. He was a sea-captain, and resided in New Haven, where he died, Feb. 6, 1849, æ. 64.

He married, Jan. 22, 1811, CLARISSA S. WARLAND of New Haven, dau. of William Warland. She died Jan. 25, 1830.

CHILDREN.

1. *William,*   b. Feb. 10, 1813; d. March 9, 1813.
2. *Clarissa S.,*   b. Oct. 17, 1815; d. Oct. 19, 1815.
3. *Aaron Raymond,* b. May   4, 1819; m. Oct. 20, 1858, Maria A. Braman of Litchfield, Conn.
4. *Caroline A.,*   b. March 27, 1817; d. July 1, 1841, æ. 24.
5. *Henry H.,*   b. April 19, 1821; m. Nannie Gerard.   .   . (493)
6. *William W.,*   b. Nov. 4, 1823; m. Sept. 15, 1857, Elizabeth S. Black.
7. *Mary W.,*   b. Oct. 10, 1827; m. Nov. 3, 1849, Jeremiah J. Atwater of New Haven.

309. ELISHA WHITE, son of Lieut. John, (156) was born in Derby, Conn., Nov. 14, 1779. He died at sea, April, 1805, æ. 25.

He married ETHELINDA CANFIELD of Derby. His son,

Abram Canfield, b.   ; lives in Ohio.

310. JOHN WHITE, Jun., son of Lieut. John, (156) was born in Derby, Dec. 29, 1780. . He was a carpenter and mill-wright, and resided principally in that part of Derby now called Seymour, but, removed, a few years before his death, to Bethany. He died Nov. 7, 1852, æ. 72.

He married, Feb. 9, 1802, MARTHA HOTCHKISS of Bethany, born May 9, 1781, dau. of Isaac and Elizabeth Hotchkiss. She lives with her youngest son.

CHILDREN.

1. *Joel,*   b. April 8, 1803; m. Emma French.   .   .   . (494)
2. *Elisha,*   b. April 5, 1805; m. Emeline Chapman. .   .   . (495)
3. *John Edwin,* b. Dec. 6, 1813; was a farmer, and d. without issue, March 8, 1836, æ. 22. He m. Jan., 1835, E. Ann Davis of Seymour, now the wife of John J. Sperry of Bethany.
4. *William C.,* b. Nov. 15, 1817; m. Harriet Prince.   .   . (496)

311. DANIEL WHITE, son of Lieut. John, (156) was born in Derby, Nov. 11, 1787, and resides there, at Humphreysville, in the present town of Seymour. He has held various town offices in Derby. Is a carpenter.

He married, Jan., 1809, SALLY THORP.

CHILDREN.

1. *Isaac*, b. Sept. 25, 1811; m. Grace Keeney. . . . (496a)
2. *Mary Ann*, b. Jan. 12, 1814; m. Walter R. Clark of Seymour, who d. She res. in Bridgeport, and has, 1. Julia, m. George Perkins of B.; 2. Minnie.
3. *Juliet*, b. June 22, 1816; m. Heman Childs, of Derby; and has, Evelyn, Irene, Sarah Jane, John, Edward, William, and one other.
4. *Sarah Jane*, b. Nov. 7, 1818; d. unm., May 31, 1842, æ. 23.
5. *Harriet Eliza*, b. March 19, 1821; m. Charles Hyde, a carpenter, now of Seymour, and d. Feb. 18, 1849, æ. 28. She had, Hannah, and two d. young.
6. *George Bostwick*, b. May 1, 1823; lives in Seymour.
7. *Henry Kirke*, b. May 7, 1825; m. Eliza Brown of Monroe, and d. June 26, 1853, æ. 28.
8. *Nathan Francis*, b. Nov. 16, 1827; resides in Troy, N. Y.
9. *Henrietta*, b. July 3, 1830; m. David Holbrook.
10. *Augustus*,) b. June 1, 1832; a painter; lives in Wolcottville, Conn.
11. *Augusta*,) Twins. m. Simon Lathrop of Wolcottville, and has, Harriet, Lillie, and Nellie.
12. *Margaret*, b. Nov. 13, 1834.
13. *John Edwin*, b. June 13, 1836; d. æ. 4 mos.

312. ISAAC WHITE, son of Lieut. John, (156) was born in Derby, Sept. 2, 1789. He lives in Seymour.
He married ANN GILBERT of Litchfield.

CHILDREN.

1. *Betsey Ann*, b. ; m. —— Beecher, and d.
2. *Walter*, b. ; lives in Seymour.
3. *Amos*, b. ; lives in Seymour.
4. *John*, b. ; m. and lives in Waterbury.

313. RAYMOND B. WHITE, son of Lieut. John, (156) was born in Derby, Aug. 31, 1801. Is a carpenter in Plymouth, Ct. He married HARRIET WARNER of Plymouth.

CHILDREN.

1. *James Warner*, b. ; m. Louisa Stone; res. in Plymouth.
2. *Edward*, b. 1824; m. Mary A. Sweet. . . . (497)
3. *Oscar Leeds*, b. March 14, 1826; m. Martha Taylor; res. in New Haven.
4. *William*, b. Nov. 14, 1829; lives in Winsted; is a carpenter.
5. *George*, b. Sept. 8, 1833; m. Lovina A. Downes. . . (498)
6. *Ann Maria*, b. March 12, 1836.

314. AMOS WHITE, son of Lieut. John, (156) was born in Derby, Conn., Dec. 22, 1804. He resides in Rochester, N. Y., and is a shoe manufacturer.

He married, 1st, Dec. 3, 1829, HANNAH MARIA COOK of Rochester, dau. of Lewis C. Cook and Hannah Miller. She was born Oct. 14, 1804, and died Oct. 13, 1849, æ. 45.

He married, 2d, Dec. 14, 1851, JANE GOLDFINCH YATMAN
of Rochester, born Jan. 30, 1826, dau. of John G. Yatman
and Margaret Huber.

CHILDREN;—BY THE FIRST MARRIAGE.

1. *Edward Francis,* b. Sept. 1, 1830 ; lives in Milwaukee, Wis.   He m. June 15,
   1854, Margaret Miller of Penn Yan, Yates Co., N. Y.
2. *George,*   b. Feb. 22, 1834 ; is a jeweler in Newark, Wayne Co., N. Y.

---

315. TRUMAN WHITE, son of Isaac, (157) was born in Southington, Conn., Nov. 8, 1780.   He was for a while engaged in
merchandizing, but about 1812 settled as a farmer in Springville, Erie Co., N. Y.   He now resides with his son, in Buffalo,
N. Y.

He married, May 27, 1804, BETSEY TUTHILL of Trenton,
Oneida Co., N. Y., dau. of Daniel Tuthill and Elizabeth Davis.
She was born in Southold, L. I., July 28, 1784, and died in
Buffalo, June 29, 1852, æ. 68.

CHILDREN.

1. *Charlotte,* b. June 4, 1805 ; m. Oct. 21, 1822, William Riley Burt of Palermo,
   N. Y., a farmer, who d. Sept. 20, 1850, æ. 51.   She has had, 1. Hannah
   Permelia, b. March 11, 1824, d. April 15, 1825 ; 2. Hubbard Tuthill, b.
   Aug. 1, 1825, m. May 6, 1852, Cornelia C. Ball, and d. April 18, 1853, æ. 24.
   She d. June 15, 1854 ; 3. Harriet, b. Nov. 4, 1827, m. Nov. 1, 1849, Riley
   Harding ; 4. William Riley, b. May 2, 1831, d. June 1, 1834 ; 5. Charles, b.
   Sept. 20, 1833, d. April 2, 1853, æ. 19 ; 6. William Clark, b. Sept. 22, 1837 ;
   7. Jane Elizabeth, b. Oct. 17, 1839, m. Aug. 12, 1855, Peter White ; 8. Lorenzo White, b. July 12, 1842 ; 9 Mary Jackson, b. March 3, 1844.
2. *Daniel D. Tompkins,* b. March 22, 1807 ; m. Alma Wilbur.   .   . (499)
3. *Harriet,*   b. Feb. 29, 1809 ; m. 1829, Harry H. Mattison, a merchant, now of Buffalo, and d. Aug. 27, 1849, æ. 40.   She had, Helen, Carlos, Edwin, and two others, who d. young.
4. *Jane Clark,*   b. March 13, 1812 ; m. July, 1834, Levi Austin Tooley,
   a farmer in Oswego Co., N. Y.   She has had, 1. Charlotte E., b. April 21,
   1836, d. April 30, 1852, æ. 16 ; 2. Oscar P., b. May 29, 1838, d. Jan. 6,
   1840 ; 3. Harriet L., b. May 8, 1841, d. March 19, 1857, æ. 16 ; 4. Marion M.,
   b. Jan. 2, 1844, d. May 30, 1848 ; 5. Francis Eugene, b. Feb. 25, 1851.
5. *Joel Clark,* b. Jan. 31, 1817 ; m. 1st, M. E. Lake ; 2d, M. A. DeForest. (500)
6. *Hubbard Tuthill,* b. June 7, 1819 ; m. Catharine Trumbull. .   . (501)
7. *Vincent,*   b. Nov. 18, 1821 ; d. æ. 5 yrs.
8. *William Riley,*   b. June 1, 1824 ; d. æ. 14 mos.
9. *Charles Burt,*   b. Aug. 30, 1826 ; m. Mariette Canada. .   .   . (502)
10. *Baldwin T.,*   b. Jan. 15, 1828 ; m. Louisa Mace.   .   . (503)

---

316. FRANCIS WHITE, son of Isaac, (157) was born July 22,
1782.   He settled in Springville, Erie Co., N. Y., and died
Jan. 7, 1858, æ. 75.

He married EMMA RUSHMORE, dau. of Jacob Rushmore and Emma Green.

CHILDREN.

1. *Isaac,* b. Feb. 7, 1810 ; m. Anna Smith. . . (504)
2. *Jacob,* b. Feb. 6, 1812 ; m. Alvira Tarbox. . . . . (505)
3. *Roderick,* b. June 23, 1814 ; m. Sarah Nichols. . . . . (506)
4. *Francis,* b. Aug. 15, 1817 ; lives in Springville. He m. Augusta Perigo, of Maine.
5. *Justus,* b. Aug. 6, 1827 ; m. Mary J. Hill. . . . . . (507)

317. MOSES WHITE, son of Isaac, (157) was born June 30, 1784. He is a goldsmith, and now resides near River Falls, Pierce Co., Wis.

He married, 1st, MARY TUTHILL, who died in 1816.

He married, 2d, SALLY CHENY, who died in 1854.

He married, 3d, Mrs. MARY C. LEONARD, widow of David Leonard.

CHILDREN ;—BY THE FIRST MARRIAGE.

1. *Daniel,* b. ; is a merchant in Illinois.
2. *Almira,* b. ; m. Judson Warner, a farmer near River Falls.

CHILDREN ;—BY THE SECOND MARRIAGE.

3. *Hiram W.,* b. ; m. Rose Ann Stewart. . . . (508)
4. *Frederick,* b. ; res. at Scales Mound, Jo Daviess Co., Ill.
5. *Nancy,* b. ; m. Harris Gleason, Esq., a lawyer, of Scales Mound, Ill.
6. *Wells H.,* b. ; is m., and res. in Dubuque, Iowa.
7. *John,* b. ; is a farmer near Dubuque.
8. *Eunice,* b. ; m. Lyman Carpenter of Pierce Co., Wis.
9. *Polly,* b. .

Several of the married children have families.

318. RODERICK WHITE, son of Isaac, (157) was born in Southington, Conn., Dec. 8, 1788. He settled in that part of Paris, Oneida Co., N. Y., which is now the town of Kirkland, where he still resides.

He married, July 5, 1816, LUCY BLAKESLEE of Paris, born Sept. 1, 1798.

CHILDREN.

1. *Leonard,* b. May 30, 1817 ; m. Clarissa Cone. . . . (509)
2. *Moses Clark,* b. July 24, 1819 ; m. 1st, Jane I. Atwater; 2d, Mary Seely. (510)
3. *Lois,* b. Feb. 27, 1822 ; m. Dec. 24, 1844, George M. Tooley, now a farmer in Palermo, Oswego Co., N. Y. She has had, 1. Jennett Lucretia, b. Sept. 27, 1845, d. Aug. 15, 1848 ; 2. Lucy Jane, b. July 14, 1847 ; 3. Martha Elizabeth, b. Nov. 17, 1849 ; 4. Laura Maria, b. April 26, 1853, d. Oct. 18, 1853 ; 5. Mary Louisa, b. Nov. 2, 1854 ; 6. George Addison, b. Nov. 4, 1857.

4. *Aaron*,   b. Sept. 18, 1824; is Professor of Mathematics in Oneida Conference Seminary, Cazenovia, N. Y.

5. *Joseph*,   b. April 10, 1827; m. Susan E. Beebe.   .   .   .   **(511)**

6. *Martha*,   b. April 16, 1829; m. Aug. 1, 1857, Alva H. Long of Cazenovia, a teacher.

7. *Jennette*, b. July 6, 1831; m. Nov. 2, 1853, Franklin B. Lohnes, a farmer, of Floyd, N. Y., now of Canada, and has Jenny, b. Aug. 11, 1858.

8. *Eli*,   b. Nov. 15, 1833; d. March 17, 1840, æ. 6.

9. *Phebe*,   b. July 1, 1836.

10. *Laura*,   b. Dec. 23, 1838.

11. *Sampson*, b. Feb. 2, 1845.

---

319. ALBERT WHITE, son of Isaac, (157) was born May 19, 1797. He is said to be living in Mansfield, Ohio. He has a family; one son a physician. Particulars not received.

---

320. ALMER WHITE, son of Isaac, (157) was born March 14, 1802. He is a farmer in Springville, Erie Co., N. Y.

He married, 1st, April 25, 1827, RUTH ANN TEFFT of Oriskany, N. Y., who died Jan. 3, 1842.

He married, 2d, June 30, 1842, REBECCA ELLINWOOD, who died May 16, 1845.

He married, 3d, July 22, 1846, CORNELIA ELLINWOOD, sister of his second wife.

CHILDREN;—BY THE FIRST MARRIAGE.

1. *William*,   b. April 5, 1828; m. Cordelia Hammond.   .   **(512)**

2. *Calista A.*, b. Jan. 21, 1831; d. May 10, 1846, æ. 15.

3. *Maria A.*, b. March 27, 1833.

4. *Mary Ann*, b. May 26, 1835; m. May 25, 1853, John R. Bensley of Wayne Station, Du Page Co., Ill. She has, 1. Seward Russell, b. Oct. 22, 1855; 2. Maria Vestina, b. July 15, 1857.

5. *Alma*,   b. Sept. 26, 1837; d. April 5, 1840.

6. *Louisa*,   b. Sept. 26, 1839.

CHILDREN;—BY THE SECOND MARRIAGE.

7. *Seth B.*,   b. March 22, 1843; d. June 18, 1843.

8. *Cornelia E.*, b. Aug. 22, 1844; d. Aug. 25, 1845.

CHILDREN;—BY THE THIRD MARRIAGE.

9. *Harriet R.*, b. Aug. 2, 1848.   11. *Helen O.*,   b. Sept. 25, 1852.

10. *Edward E.*, b. March 29, 1850.   12. *Frank G.*,   b. April 21, 1854.

---

321. JAMES WHITE, Jun., son of Capt. James, (159) was born in Newport, N. H., Feb., 1784, [1785?] and was a farmer there. The time and place of his death are not ascertained.

He married, 1805, GRACE WILCOX of Newport, dau. of Dea. Jesse Wilcox and Thankful Stevens. She was born Feb. 10, 1782, and died Nov. 9, 1819, æ. 37.

CHILDREN.

1. *Caroline*, b. Feb. 14, 1806; m. Aug. 17, 1835, Jonathan Edwards Rowell, a farmer in Claremont, N. H., who d. Jan. 31, 1855, æ. 48. She has had, 1. George Edwards, b. May 16, 1841; 2. Henry Louis, b. Aug. 26, 1843; 3. Ellen Maria, b. July 23, 1845; d. Nov. 9, 1855, æ. 10.
2. *Meroa*, b. Dec. 16, 1808; m. John L. Manning of Goffstown, N. H., a carpenter.
3. *Harriet Annesley*, b. May 18, 1810; m. Dec. 30, 1835, Rev. John L. Smith of Brookfield, Vt., and has had, 1. Ceylon Chase, b. Dec. 31, 1836, d. Dec. 29, 1837; 2. Ceylon Pomeroy, b. March 8, 1839; 3. Hiland Howell, b. March 11, 1842; 4. John Rowland, b. July 18, 1846; 5. Martha Matilda, b. Jan. 15, 1849.
4. *Alverse L.*, b. July 31, 1811; m. Mary Colo. . . . (513)
5. *James E.*, b. Aug. 31, 1813; went to Oregon about 1849.

322. CALVIN WHITE, son of Capt. James, (159) was born in Newport, N. H. He is a farmer in Dalton, N. H.

He married HANNAH FIELDS of Newport.

CHILDREN.

1. *James.*
2. *Emeline.*
3. *Philander.*
4. *John.*
5. *Eliza.*

323. ELISHA WHITE, son of Capt. James, (159) was born in Newport, N. H., Feb. 26, 1807. He is a farmer; has lived chiefly in Brownington, Vt., where his children were born, but now resides in West Charleston, Vt.

He married LUCINDA S. BENNETT, who was born in Randolph, Vt., Feb. 14, 1819.

CHILDREN.

1. *Homer H.*, b. Dec. 7, 1838; is a merchant in Texas.
2. *James E.*, b. Feb. 7, 1843.
3. *Laura L.*, b. Oct. 9, 1845.
4. *Elisha J.*, b. Oct. 26, 1848.
5. *Harry B.*, b. Nov. 17, 1852.
6. *Frank H.*, b. Sept. 24, 1858.

324. ROBERT WHITE, son of Rev. Calvin, (160) was born in Hanover, N. J., Dec. 1, 1792. After 1827 he wrote his name, "Robert White, Jr." He was a merchant in New York, and also for a short time resided in Birmingham, England. In 1833 he retired from business, and became a farmer at Shrewsbury, N. J., where he died, Jan. 12, 1856, æ. 63.

He married, April 9, 1818, HANNAH GIBBS, born July 7, 1795, dau. of Abel and Elizabeth Gibbs.

CHILDREN.

1. *Abel*, b. Oct. 18, 1819; d. Aug., 1820.
2. *Phebe Corlies*, b. Oct. 12, 1821; m. May 9, 1844, George C. Baker, a bookseller

in New York, and lives in Flushing, L. I.   She has had, 1. Hannah White,
b. Feb. 17, 1846; 2. Mary Baker, b. April 20, 1849; 3. George Dobel, b.
March 6, 1851, d. Aug. 26, 1852; 4. Sarah H., b. March 2, 1853; 5. Robert
Haydock, b. July 3, 1855.

3. *Robert Cornell*, b. Nov. 1, 1823; m. Hannah D. Baker.   .   .   .   (514)
4. *Rachel Camp*, b. Jan. 26, 1826; m. Nov. 4, 1847, Joseph Baker, of New York,
a merchant, and has, 1. Margaret Corlies, b. Oct. 16, 1848; 2. Anna, b. Oct.
8, 1852; 3. Robert White, b. June 25, 1855.
5. *Anna*,   b. Jan. 21, 1831; joined the Society of Shakers at New Lebanon,
N. Y., in 1849, and now resides there.
6. *John Corlies*, b. Jan. 5, 1835; was adopted by his mother's uncle, after whom
he was named; is now a student in Harvard College.

---

325. RICHARD MANSFIELD WHITE, son of Rev. Calvin, (160)
was born in Bloomfield, N. J., May 26, 1797.   In 1815 he
was appointed "a Cadet in the service of the United States,"
at West Point, but resigned the appointment, and, entering
commercial life, became a shipping and commission merchant
in New York.   He was afterwards secretary and financial
manager of the Allaire Iron Works.   He took a leading part
in the movement which resulted in the establishment of the
first Episcopal Sunday Schools in New York and Brooklyn.
In 1827 he removed from New York to Brooklyn, L. I., and
in 1845 to Orange, N. J., where he died, Jan. 19, 1849, æ. 51.

He married, May 25, 1820, ANN ELIZA TOUSEY, of Newtown,
Conn., dau. of Donald Grant Tousey and Lucretia Beers.
She was born Aug. 5, 1802, and died in Brooklyn, June 8,
1842, æ. 40.

CHILDREN.

1. *Richard Grant*, b. May 23, 1821; m. Alexina B. Maese.   .   .   (515)
2. *Marian*,   b. Sept. 6, 1823; m. Nov. 3, 1847, Edward Williams of
Orange, N. J., and has had, 1. Edward Grant, b. Oct. 22, 1848, d. Aug. 30,
1849; 2. James Austin, b. June 3, 1850; 3. George Herbert, b. May 13,
1853; 4. Ann Eliza, b. March 23, 1855; 5. Marion, b. Aug. 30, 1857.
3. *Ann Eliza*,   b. Nov. 15, 1831; d. April 23, 1849, æ. 17.
4. *Charles McIlvaine*, b. Feb. 15, 1834; d. April, 1842, æ. 8.
5. *Augusta*,   b. Aug. 8, 1838.

---

326. MOSES WHITE, son of Rev. Calvin, (160) was born in
Stamford, Conn., April 11, 1799.   He was for several years a
merchant in New York, New Orleans, and Cincinnati, and
afterwards lived for twelve years in Derby, Conn.   He now
resides in Mt. Vernon, Knox Co., Ohio.

He married, July 8, 1833, MARGARET PALMER, of Stonington, Conn., born Feb. 6, 1814, dau. of Dudley and Marietta Palmer.

CHILDREN.

1. *Carleton,*   b. May 11, 1834 ; m. Nov. 11, 1857, Lizzie H. Dunn.
2. *Clement,*   b. Nov. 3, 1836 ; d. Sept. 26, 1838.
3. *Moses,*   b. Aug. 16, 1839 ; d. Aug. 9, 1843.
4. *Eliza Lloyd,* b. May 16, 1846.

327. CARLETON WHITE, son of Rev. Calvin, (160) was born in Stamford, Conn., Feb. 20, 1801. He was formerly a sea-captain, in the "Black Ball" line of Liverpool packets. He now resides in New Haven, Conn.

He married, Aug. 12, 1829, JUDITH C. MILLER, born in New York, Aug. 12, 1807, dau. of John Miller and Phebe Pine.

328. CHANDLER WHITE, son of Rev. Calvin, (160) was born in Derby, Conn., June 14, 1806. He was a merchant in New York, and for a few years in New Orleans. In 1854 he was chosen a director and vice-president of the "New York, London and Newfoundland Telegraph Company," and was active in promoting its plans for securing telegraphic communication between the two continents. He died at his residence, near Fort Hamilton, L. I., of yellow fever, Aug. 7, 1856, æ. 50. He had no children.

He married, Oct. 10, 1831, ANNA MATILDA MILLER, of Brooklyn, L. I.

329. MARDENBROUGH WHITE, son of Rev. Calvin, (160) was born in Derby, Conn., March 6, 1810. He has been a merchant in Mt. Vernon, O., and is now a farmer in Gambier, Knox Co., O.

He married, March 31, 1834, CLARISSA JONES, of Providence, R. I.

CHILDREN.

1. *Sarah,* b. Jan. 18, 1836 ; m. Sept. 26, 1854, Rev. Edward C. Benson of Gambier, and has, 1. Elden ; 2. Joseph Baker ; 3. Harry Copeland, b. Dec. 8, 1857.
2. *Anna Matilda,* b. Dec. 21, 1839.
3. *Clarissa Jones,* b. Jan. 10, 1842.
4. *Margaret Palmer,* b. Feb. 6, 1844.
5. *Henry Kirke,* b. Feb. 27, 1847.
6. *Mardenbrough,* b. July 20, 1850 ; d. Aug. 21, 1850. .

29

330. GEORGE BERKELEY WHITE, son of Rev. Calvin, (160) was born in Derby, Conn., July 7, 1814. He is a merchant in Mt. Vernon, Ohio.

He married, Oct. 10, 1839, CLARA MILLER of Mt. Vernon, dau. of Judge Eli Miller.

CHILDREN.

1. *Ellen,*	b. Oct. 12, 1840.	6. *Clara,*	b. Jan. 14, 1851.
2. *Frances,*	b. Oct. 4, 1842.	7. *Miller,*	b. April 4, 1853;
3. *Calvin,*	b. March 17, 1844.		d. Nov. 5, 1855.
4. *Thomas Ewing,*	b. April, 1846.	8. *Harriet,*	b. Dec. 26, 1855.
5. *George,*	b. Feb. 5, 1848.	9. *Maria Butler,*	b. April 9, 1858.

331. GEORGE ELISHA WHITE, son of Elisha, (161) was born in Weybridge, Vt., June 2, 1801. He was a surveyor and civil engineer; resided principally in East Claridon and Chagrin Falls, Ohio, but removed in 1851 to Salineville, Columbiana Co., Ohio, where he died, Jan. 25, 1852, æ. 50. He was a justice of the peace, and was post-master at East Claridon and at Chagrin Falls.

He married, March 20, 1851, Mrs. MARTHA (RUSSEL) CHRISTIE, of Salineville. She now resides at Chagrin Falls.

He had one daughter,

Martha Ophelia, b. Jan. 17, 1852.

331a. COMFORT WHITE, son of Elias, jun.,* (163) was born in Cornwall, Conn., Jan. 3, 1802. He is a farmer in Canton, Conn. Formerly lived in Sheffield, Mass.

He married, 1st, Dec. 3, 1826, LAURA NORTON of Cornwall, dau. of Theodore Norton and Mary Judd. She died Sept. 13, 1836.

He married, 2d, May 31, 1837, MIRANDA ROOD of North Canaan, Conn.

CHILDREN;—BY THE FIRST MARRIAGE.

1. *Mary Eliza,* b. July 26, 1829; m. Feb. 15, 1355, Walker S. Millard, and has,
     1. Laura Miranda, b. Dec. 31, 1855; 2. Emma Amanda, b. July 22, 1857.
2. *Augustus Frederick,* b. March 6, 1832; m. April, 1858, Harriet Watts.
3. *Julia Maria,*   b. Feb. 21, 1834.
4. *Edward Rogers,* } b. May 14, 1836; d. March 3, 1837.
5. *Edwin Norton,*   }   Twins.

CHILD;—BY THE SECOND MARRIAGE.

6. *Augusta Rogers,* . b. Oct. 22, 1849.

---

* For a corrected account of the family of Elias White, jun., (163) see Appendix.

331*b*. EDWARD ROGERS WHITE, son of Elias, jun., (163) was born in Cornwall, Conn., Feb. 14, 1804, and is a farmer there. He has held town offices, and in 1845 represented that town in the Legislature.

He married, 1827, ABIGAIL BALDWIN of Cornwall, dau. of Henry Baldwin and Jane Shipman.

CHILDREN.

1. *Edward Henry*, b. May 19, 1828 ; m. Nov. 10, 1856, Rebecca A. L. Todd of Cornwall, and d. Dec. 16, 1858, æ. 30.
2. *Cynthia Jane*, b. Aug. 8, 1830; d. Dec. 27, 1858, æ. 28.

331*c*. EDWIN WHITE, son of Elias, jun., (163) was born in Cornwall, Conn., Sept. 21, 1806. He is a farmer there, has held civil offices, and was a representative in 1842 and 1843.

He married, Sept. 13, 1837, LAURA WHEDON of Winchester, dau. of Stephen Whedon and Abigail Drake.

CHILDREN.

1. *Frances Abigail*, b. Aug. 19, 1838.   3. *Edwin Augustine*, b. Dec. 27, 1854.
2. *Laura Isabella*, b. May 21, 1848.   4. *Cynthia Josephine*, b. Sept. 3, 1858.

331*d*. ELIAS WHITE, son of Elias, jun., (163) was born in Cornwall, Conn., April 16, 1809. He resides at Poughkeepsie, N. Y., and is engaged in a railroad office. Has been a justice of the peace.

He married, 1st, April 25, 1833, CYNTHIA ANN HAGEMAN of Poughkeepsie, dau. of Peter Hageman and Phebe Bogardus. She died March 2, 1850.

He married, 2d, Oct. 10, 1853, ELIZABETH ANN BROWER, dau. of John and Maria Brower.

CHILD ;—BY THE FIRST MARRIAGE.

1. *Sarah Elizabeth*, b. May 26, 1839 ; m. May 16, 1859, Benjamin Lee of Fishkill, N. Y.

CHILDREN ;—BY THE SECOND MARRIAGE.

2. *Casper Brower*, ⎰ b. Sept. 26, 1854.
3. *Mary Frances*, ⎱   Twins.   d. Sept. 15, 1859.

332. HENRY CHAMPLIN WHITE, son of Capt. Isaac, (164) was born in Upper Middletown, Nov. 14, 1809. He resides in Hartford, Conn.

He married, Aug. 19, 1834, MARY FREELAND BROWNING of Brimfield, Mass., born Nov. 3, 1815, dau. of James Browning and Lucinda Smith.

CHILDREN.

1. *Samuel Howes,* b. April 21, 1836 ; m. Cecilia A. Stillman.   .   (516)
2. *Isaac,*   b. Aug. 26, 1839.
3. *Henry C.,*   b. March 4, 1844.

333. ISAAC WHITE, son of Capt. Isaac, (164) was born in Upper Middletown, June 29, 1814. He resides in Utica, N. Y.

He married, May 10, 1838, SARAH ANN GIRARD, dau. of Luther Girard and Lydia Blaisdell.

CHILDREN.

1. *Henry Champlin,*   b. Feb. 17, 1839.
2. *Sarah Elisabeth,*   b. Feb. 5, 1841.
3. *Arthur,*   b. June 26, 1843.
4. *Harriett Antoinette,* b. Sept. 14, 1845.
5. *Mary Jane,*   b. Nov. 14, 1847.
6. *Frances Louise,*   b. June 20, 1850.
7. *Caroline Amelia,*   b. June 19, 1852.
8. *Priscilla Agnes,*   b. March 21, 1854.
9. *Ella Lydia,*   b. Oct. 13, 1856.

IN THE LINE OF JACOB WHITE, OF MIDDLETOWN.

334. SAMUEL WHITE, son of Samuel, Jun., (165) was born in North Coventry, Conn., May, 1782. He lived in Buffalo, N. Y., and died there, March, 1854, æ. 72.

He married LYDIA JEWETT of N. Coventry, dau. of Ichabod Jewett. She is dead.

CHILDREN.

1. *Jennette.*   Record of this family not furnished.
2. *Leonard.*
3. *Ichabod J.* These sons are hardware dealers and edge-tool makers, Buffalo.

335. JONATHAN PORTER WHITE, son of Samuel, Jun., (165) was born in North Coventry. He was killed by the explosion of a powder-mill, in Mansfield, Conn., Nov. 10, 1825.

He married ABIGAIL SCRIPTURE of Mansfield. She is now the wife of Dr. Adrastus Doolittle of New York.

CHILDREN.

1. *Samuel Porter,*   b. Dec. 3, 1820 ; is a carpenter in N. Y. city. He m. 1851, Caroline Adams, and has had, 1. Caroline, d. ; 2. Abigail A., d. ; 3. William M., d.
2. *Charles Fayette,*   b.   ; d. 1858, in Cook Co., Ill. ; left a family.
3. *Norman Brigham,* b.   ; m. Eveline Gilbert.   .   (517)
4. *James Albert,*   b.   ; is a R. R. Conductor ; lives in Brooklyn, L. I. He m. Letitia Reeves of Greenport, L. I., who d. July, 1858, leaving two children.

336. CHESTER WHITE, son of Lemuel, (166) was born Feb. 14, 1793. He is a farmer in Batavia, Genesee Co., N. Y.

He married, Jan. 1, 1816, LUCY TOPLIFF of South Coventry, Conn. She died Feb. 5, 1851.

CHILDREN.

1. *Harrison*, b. Sept. 21, 1816; m. Sarah Dunn.   .   (518)
2. *Mary*,   b. Oct. 28, 1818; lives in Batavia.
3. *Emily*,   b. Jan. 4, 1822; m. Oct. 23, 1845, George Terry of Batavia, and
     has, 1. Harriet; 2. Jenny; 3. John; 4. Cleveland.
4. *Jerome*,   b. Feb. 15, 1824; d. July 5, 1825.
5. *Lemuel*,   b. March 15, 1826; went to Cal. in 1854.
6. *Maria*,   b. Aug. 22, 1828; m. Chester Mann of B., and d. Feb. 17, 1858,
     æ. 29. She had, 1. Harrison; 2. Jenny; 3. Jerome; 4. Ellen.
7. *Laura*,   b. Sept. 21, 1830; m. May 25, 1851, Henry Hammond of B., and
     has, 1. Jay; 2. Emma? 3. Charles.
8. *Ann*,   b. Jan. 15, 1833.
9. *Eliza*,   b. July 26, 1836.
10. *Kirke*,   b. Nov. 24, 1838.

---

337. LEMUEL WHITE, Jun., son of Lemuel, (166) was born April 9, 1795. He was a harness-maker in Buffalo, N. Y., where he died, May 5, 1840, æ. 44.

He married, Nov. 6, 1817, ELIZA MATHEWS of New York, born May 2, 1797, dau. of James Mathews and Mary Clark.

CHILDREN.

1. *William Chester*, b. March 21, 1819; m. 1844, Elizabeth Burgess, a native of
     London; has had three children.
2. *Ann Maria*, b.   ; m. Alexander McKay, a merchant; had two
     children.
3. *Eliza*, b.   1824; m. Nov. 18, 1846, Andrew J. Trumbull, a merchant.
4. *John B.*, b. March 29, 1831; m. 1853, Louisa Sawin of Buffalo; has three
     children.
5. *Walton Otis*, b. Aug. 11, 1834.   Two other children died in infancy.

---

338. CALVIN WHITE, son of Dan, Esq., (168) was born in Torrington, Conn., July 6, 1786. He removed with his father to Vermont, and died in Waterford, Feb. 11, 1810, æ. 23.

He married, 1809, MARY BURNS, dau. of Capt. Burns, of Whitefield, N. H. She died in 1813. His only child,

Rowena, b. 1810; m. 1831, Samuel Huntoon, now of Holland, Orleans Co., Vt.
     She has, 1. Calvin, b. 1832; 2. Paran, b. 1833; 3. Samuel Alden, b. 1835;
     4. Mary Elizabeth, b. 1838, d. 1854; 5. Moses, b. 1847; 6. John, b. 1849;
     7. A child.

339. ERASTUS WILSON WHITE, son of Dan, Esq., (168) was born in Norfolk, Conn., Sept. 27, 1793. In 1815 he engaged in mercantile pursuits in Quebec, Canada, and in 1834 removed to Morristown, St. Lawrence Co., N. Y., where he now resides. He has held the offices of town clerk, post-master, and justice of the peace.

He married, 1817, LYDIA K. REMICK, born in 1796, dau. of David Remick of Stanstead, C. E.

CHILDREN.

1. *Laura Ann,*   b. March 17, 1820; m. 1838, Hon. Dunbar Ross of Quebec, late Solicitor General for Lower Canada, and now a member of the Provincial Parliament. She has, 1. Dunbar, b. 1840; 2. George, b. 1854; 3. Frances Hincks, b. 1856.
2. *Sophia,*   b.   1823; d. 1824.
3. *William Wilson,* b.   1824; d. 1847, æ. 23.
4. *Sophia Amelia,* b.   1826; d. 1828.
5. *George,*   b.   1829; drowned in Morristown, 1849, æ. 20.
6. *Burns Erastus,* b. Sept. 27, 1830; res. in Morristown. He m. Sept. 22, 1858, Mary Catharine Ames of Lisbon, N. Y., b. Oct. 2, 1837, dau. of Joseph P. Ames.
7. *Charles Augustus,* b.   1832; d. 1833.
8. *Emma Augusta,* b.   1835; d. 1836.

---

340. HIRAM JACOB WHITE, son of Thomas, (169) was born in Torrington, Conn., July 26, 1802. He is a merchant in Boston, Mass.

He married, Aug. 14, 1828, HENRIETTA SOPHIA CLARK of Waterbury, Conn., dau. of Cyrus and Nancy Clark. She died Aug. 22, 1835, æ. 26.

CHILDREN.

1. *Martha Louisa,* b. April 11, 1829; m. Charles G. Merriman of New Haven, Conn., a merchant.
2. *William Henry,* b. Dec.   5, 1833; d. Dec. 22, 1835.

341. RANSOM COE WHITE, son of Elam, (170) was born in Burke, Vt., Oct. 2, 1806. He resides in East Haven, Vt.

He married, June 30, 1829, HANNAH B. WALTER of East Haven, born July 22, 1809.

CHILDREN.

1. *Alonzo,*   b. Nov. 2, 1830; m. Huldah L. Hosford.   .   .   (519)
2. *Alanson,* b. Feb. 27, 1832; m. Oct. 23, 1855, Arminda A. Powers of Burke.
3. *Hilamon,* b. Aug. 2, 1833; d. Jan. 28, 1852, æ. 18.
4. *Elam II.,* b. Jan. 26, 1840.
5. *Harriet Eliza,* b. June 5, 1846.

342. OSMAN WHITE, son of Elam, (170) was born in Burke, Vt., Nov. 1, 1808, and resides there.

He married, March 18, 1835, FRINDA SMITH, born in Hinsdale, N. H., March 27, 1813.

CHILDREN.

1. *Twin* } b. Oct. 17, 1836; d. same day.
2. *children,* }
3. *Melvin,* ' b. Aug. 12, 1838.

343. NELSON WHITE, son of Roswell, (172) was born in Granville, Mass., Jan. 20, 1813. He is a carpenter; is now a farmer in Spencer, Medina Co., Ohio.

He married, Oct. 3, 1839, EMILY PENFIELD, of Penfield, Monroe Co., N. Y.

CHILDREN.

1. *Edward Nelson,* b. Feb. 12, 1842.
2. *Augusta Beulah,* b. March 7, 1850.

344. ORRIN CHAUNCEY WHITE, son of Roswell, (172) was born in Granville, Mass., March 16, 1814. He is a carpenter and farmer in Gates, Monroe Co., N. Y.

He married, Sept. 14, 1841, MARY E. SHEDD.

CHILDREN.

1. *John.*   3. *George.*
2. *Randolph.*   4. *Mary.*

345. JOHN BIRGE WHITE, son of Roswell, (172) was born in Granville, Mass., Oct. 30, 1817. He is a farmer in Spencer, Medina Co., Ohio.

He married, Aug. 6, 1848, HANNAH LUCE of Spencer, dau. of Aaron Luce and Sally M. Grandy.

CHILDREN.

1. *Mary Elizabeth,* b. June 16, 1850.
2. *Lucy Maria,* b. Nov. 9, 1851.
3. *Franklin Aaron,* b. Sept. 23, 1855.
4. *Orrin,* b. Aug. 19, 1858.

346. CHARLES PLUMB WHITE, son of Chauncey, (173) was born in Winchester, Conn., Aug. 4, 1809. He is a shoemaker; has lived in Lenox and Marcellus, Onondaga Co., N. Y.; removed in 1857 to Belvidere, Boone Co., Ill.

He married, Oct. 10, 1833, MERCY A. WILCOX of Granville, Mass.

CHILDREN.

1. *Almira B.,*   b. May 2, 1834 ; d. March 5, 1857, æ. 23.
2. *Sarah M.,*   b. Aug. 31, 1835 ; m. June 11, 1854, Thomas Chryster of
    Marcellus, N. Y.
3. *William Chauncey,* b. May 22, 1837.
4. *Charlotte S.,*   b. Sept. 20,   ; m. March 5, 1859, John Coffin of Bel-
    videre, Ill.
5. *Philena C.,*   b. July 4, 1840.
6. *Imry Styles,*   b. Oct. 10, 1841.
7. *H.   E.,*   b. Oct. 16, 1843.
8. *Norman H.,*   b. Nov. 23, 1845.
9. *Orrin Charles,*   b. Sept. 16, 1847.
10. *James Orneldo,*   b. July 5, 1849.
11. *Leverett Alphonso,* b. Sept. 16, 1851.
12. *Martha Jane,*   b. Oct. 9, 1853 ; d. April 30, 1857.

347. ELIJAH BRAINARD WHITE, son of Brainard, (174) was
born in Torrington, Conn., Aug. 29, 1808. He was a mason,
resided in Winsted, Conn., and died March 16, 1859, æ. 50.

He married, Sept. 4, 1833, MARY CAMP of Winsted, born
Aug. 3, 1814, dau. of Moses Camp and Diadema Knowlton.

CHILDREN.

1. *Annie Elizabeth,* b. July 1, 1836.
2. *Mary Adelaide,* b. July 16, 1840; d. May 4, 1844.
3. *Julia Emorette,* b. Jan. 20, 1842; d. Aug. 21, 1842.
4. *Adeline Rosetta,* b. Sept. 9, 1845.

348. EDWIN RILEY WHITE, son of Brainard, (174) was born
Oct. 15, 1810. He is a merchant in Canastota, Madison Co.,
N. Y.

He married, April 26, 1836, JULIA WESTLAKE of Winsted,
Conn., dau. of John and Flora Westlake.

349. NATHAN CURTIS WHITE, Esq., son of Brainard, (174)
was born Sept. 24, 1820. He is a lawyer in Utica, N. Y.

He married, 1st, July 30, 1850, JANE CHEESBRO STANTON, of
Trenton, N. Y., who died Dec. 31, 1853.

He married, 2d, May 12, 1858, DELIA DANA of Utica.

350. WILLIAM WHITE, son of Joel, Jun., (176) was born in
Russia, Herkimer Co., N. Y., Nov. 9, 1805. He is a farmer
in Edwards, St. Lawrence Co., N. Y.

He married, 1st, March, 1832, MARGARET MORGAN of Gouverneur, N. Y., who died Sept., 1838.

He married, 2d, 1839, MARIAM CASTLE of Edwards, who died Feb., 1847.

He married, 3d, Aug. 5, 1847, MARIETT CASTLE.

CHILD ;—BY THE FIRST MARRIAGE.

1. *Mary,*   b. March, 1835.

CHILDREN ;—BY THE SECOND MARRIAGE.

2. *Margaret,* b. Dec., 1840; d. March, 1856, æ. 15.
3. *Henry,*   b. Sept., 1842.

351. ALBERT WHITE, son of Joel, Jun., (176) was born in Russia, N. Y., April 16, 1811. He is a farmer in Edwards, St. Lawrence Co., N. Y.

He married, 1st, Sept. 16, 1841, LUCY SLOPER of Pitcairn, St. L. Co. She was born June 4, 1817, and died Nov. 26, 1842, æ. 25.

He married, 2d, Sept. 14, 1843, MELVINA CAROLINE MITCHELL of Fowler, St. L. Co., born Dec. 14, 1817.

CHILDREN ;—ONE BY EACH MARRIAGE.

1. *Albert S.,* b. Nov. 24, 1842.   2. *Lucy,* b. Sept. 14, 1845.

352. FREDERIC WHITE, son of Joel, Jun., (176) was born in Edwards, N. Y., April 21, 1823, and is a farmer on the homestead there.

He married, Oct., 1851, NANCY SNOW of Pitcairn, N. Y., and has one son,

Harvey, b. Feb., 1853.

353. JOHN WHITE, son of John, (177) was born in Upper Middletown, Conn., June 26, 1790. He was a ship-carpenter; resided in Albany, N. Y., and died Feb. 10, 1846, æ. 55.

He married, 1st, Sept. 6, 1808, EMILY SAVAGE of Upper Middletown, dau. of Capt. Abijah Savage. She was born Feb. 12, 1792, and died June 11, 1826, æ. 34.

He married, 2d, Dec. 16, 1830, Mrs. SARAH JONES, widow of Ezekiel Jones of Up. Mid. She was the dau. of William and Ellen Belcher, and was born Oct. 31, 1797.

CHILDREN ;—BY THE FIRST MARRIAGE.

1. *John,*   b. Nov. 15, 1809; is a stove dealer in Wellsville, N. Y.
2. *Emma,* b. July 28, 1811; d. Oct. 2, 1825, æ. 14.

30

3. *Caroline,* b. Aug. 18, 1813; d. Feb. 15, 1818.
4. *George Henry,* b. July 5, 1815; m. Mary Sophia Tobey. . . (520)
5. *Nehemiah Bassett,* b. Dec. 24, 1816; m. Mrs. A. H. Newman, and another. (521)
6. *Russell M.,* b. March 31, 1819; m. Caroline B. Farnsworth. . (522)
7. *Caroline,* b. Dec. 5, 1820; m. June 21, 1847, George D. Jones of Fredonia, N. Y., a carpenter. She has had, John Leverett, b. Sept. 25, 1848, d. Aug. 2, 1849.
8. *Grace Savage,* b. Nov. 14, 1822; m. May 16, 1848, Joel H. Whitlock, a merchant in Galway, N. Y., who d. Nov. 5, 1853.
9. *Lucius,* } b. July 29, 1824; a merchant in Monticello, Ga.
10. *Linus,* } Twins. m. Mary Server. . . . (523)
11. *Emma,* b. March 24, 1826; m. Oct. 21, 1846, Wilson J. Hubbard of Wellsville, N. Y., and has had, 1. Charles H., b. Jan. 16, 1848, d. Aug. 1, 1848; 2. Edward L., b. Aug. 7, 1852; 3. Grace W., b. Feb. 18, 1855; 4. Lucius W., b. Oct. 2, 1858.

CHILDREN;—BY THE SECOND MARRIAGE.

12. *Josephine,* b. Sept. 16, 1831; d. Dec. 26, 1832.
13. *Josephine,* b. March 20, 1834; m. July 7, 1850, John Shaver, and has had, 1. Josephine, b. Oct. 19, 1851, d. Nov. 3, 1851; 2. Nellie, b. Sept. 11, 1852.
14. *Mary,* b. May 22, 1836.
15. *Charles,* b. May 25, 1839.

---

354. JACOB WHITE, son of John, (177) was born in Upper Middletown, April 27, 1792. He was a tanner and shoemaker, and in 1819 removed to Sandisfield, Mass., where he carried on the business of tanning for twelve years. He returned to Upper Middletown, and chiefly resided there until his death, Jan. 13, 1849, æ. 56.

He married, Nov. 22, 1815, SUSAN SAGE, born March 28, 1796, dau. of Capt. William Sage. She married, 2d, May, 1854, James Goodrich of Cromwell.

CHILDREN.

1. *William Sage,* b. July 22, 1816; m. Mary Savage. . . (524)
2. *Henry S.,* b. Feb. 12, 1818; m. Catharine Chandler. . . . (525)
3. *Luther Chapin,* b. Dec. 25, 1821; m. Jane A. Moses. . . (526)
4. *Harriet M.,* b. Oct. 3, 1825; m. May 16, 1850, Joseph Edwards, of Cromwell, and has had, 1. Catharine Augusta, b. Feb. 11, 1851, d. Aug. 1, 1854; 2. Mary Louisa, b. Feb. 11, 1853; 3. Susan Sage, b. March 10, 1855; 4. Joseph Wells, b. Jan. 3, 1857.
5. *Jacob Watson,* b. Sept. 19, 1827; m. Anna E. Wells. . (527)
6. *Abigail Eells,* b. Oct. 23, 1831; d. Sept. 24, 1833.
7. *Orrin Sage,* b. Aug. 10, 1834; d. Dec. 6, 1841, æ. 7.
8. *Jane Augusta,* b. Dec. 27, 1837; d. Dec. 19, 1841.

---

355. LUTHER WHITE, son of John, (177) was born in Upper Middletown, Jan. 11, 1799. He was a joiner, and resided in Hartford, where he died, Nov. 21, 1836, æ. 37.

He married, Jan. 6, 1831, MARIA HAYDEN of Hartford, dau. of Gen. William and Martha Hayden. She is now Mrs. Pease.

CHILDREN.

1. *Leverett*, b. Jan. 3, 1833; d. July 23, 1839.
2. *Eveline*, b. Sept. 19, 1834.

356. LEMUEL WHITE, Jun., son of Lemuel, (179) was born in Middletown, Conn., April 11, 1802. He was a steam-boat captain, and died at Charleston, S. C., March, 1848, æ. 46. He married, Oct. 6, 1824, ALMIRA HIGBY.

CHILDREN.

1. *Charles,* b. Aug., 1825.   2. *William*, b. Oct., 1827.
3. *A daughter*, b.   ; d. in infancy.

357. AARON J. WHITE, son of Lemuel, (179) was born in Middletown, Sept. 7, 1829. He lives in Rockford, Ill. He married, 1852, JANE CHAPMAN, and has one son,

George, b. 1853, and perhaps other children.

IN THE LINE OF JOSEPH WHITE, OF MIDDLETOWN.

358. Dr. WILLIAM MORELL WHITE, son of Joseph, (182) was born July 29, 1822. He is a physician in Fair Haven, Conn. He married, 1844, EMILY F. COOLEY.

CHILDREN.

1. *Franklin C.*
2. *Estella.*

DESCENDANTS OF JOHN WHITE, JUNIOR.

359. DAN WHITE, son of Capt. John, (186) was born in Windham, Conn., Oct. 21, 1789. He resided in Rome, N. Y., but now lives in Kenosha, Wis.

He married, Nov. 28, 1810, POLLY JONES of Rome, born 1794, dau. of Gideon and Lydia Jones.

CHILDREN.

1. *Benjamin,* b.   1811; m. Esther Noyes. .   .   .   .   (528)
2. *Mary Ann,* b. Feb. 3, 1814; m. Feb. 19, 1834, James N. Husted, now a merchant in New York, and had John White, b. Dec. 24, 1834, d. Oct. 1, 1839.
3. *Alonzo,* b.   1816; m. Lydia B. Leonard. .   .   .   (529)
4. *Francis,* b.   1818; m. 1st, Sarah Whitmore ; 2d, J. Moore. (530)
5. *Caroline M.,* b.   1821; m. Dr. Charles Frazier of Lee, Oneida Co., N. Y., and has, Elizabeth, Mary A., Charles, and Caroline.
6. *Eliza,* b. July, 1823; m. July, 1847, Cornelius Pell, a merchant-tailor

in Lyons, Wayne Co., N. Y. She has, 1. James Husted, b. July 11, 1848 ;
2. Mary Josephine, b. June, 1851.

7. *Merion,*   b.   1827 ; d. 1827.
8. *Edward,* ⎱ b.   1830 ; d. 1847 ?
9. *Joshua,* ⎰   Twins.   m. Margarette Worth.   (531)
10. *Martha,*   b.   1833 ; d. 1851.
11. *June,*   b.   1837 ; m. John B. Warner, a music-teacher in Kenosha,
    Wis., and has one son, Ole Bull.
12. *James,*   b.   1837 ; is a carpenter at Kenosha, Wis.

---

360. GURDON WHITE, son of Capt. John, (186) was born
June 24, 1791. He lived in Rome, N. Y., and removed to
Martinsburg, Lewis Co., N. Y., where he now resides.

He married, Aug. 28, 1811, BETSEY JONES, born in Conn.,
Dec. 27, 1791, dau. of Gideon and Lydia Jones.

CHILDREN.

1. *Harriet E.*, b. June 11, 1812 ; m. Edwin Pitcher, a farmer in Martinsburg, and
   has, Louisa, Lydia, Charles, Henry, Frank, Howard, Mary, and Nellie.
2. *Emily A.*, b. Nov. 7, 1813 ; m. Abner P. Conkey of Canton, St. Lawrence
   Co., N. Y., a farmer. She has, Caroline P., Gilbert H., Charles M., and
   John G.
3. *Albert A.*, b. April 2, 1816 ; is a carriage-maker. He m. Emeline McClene-
   then, of Norfolk, St. L. Co., and has Gurdon.
4. *Julia A.*, b. Aug. 6, 1818 ; m. Oliver Salmons of Turin, Lewis Co., a
   farmer. She has had six children, two of whom d. young.
5. *June,*   b. Jan. 1, 1821 ; m. Harvey Pitcher of Martinsburg, a farmer, and
   has, Helen, Julia, Martha, Herman, Alfred, and Caroline.
6. *Alfred,* ⎱ b. April 23, 1824 ; m. and has two children.
7. *Ambrose,* ⎰   Twins.   has four children.
8. *Harry,* b. April 7, 1830 ; a tinner in Ogdensburg, N. Y. Has 3 children.
9. *John,* b. April 5, 1832 ; lives with his father.

---

361. ASA WHITE, son of Capt. John, (186) was born in
Rome, N. Y., Oct. 13, 1796. He was a carpenter, and lived
chiefly in St. Lawrence and Monroe Counties, N. Y. He died
in Rochester, N. Y., April 16, 1830, æ. 33.

He married, 1817, ELECTA SLAYTON of Potsdam, born in
Chelsea, Mass., Feb. 5, 1797.

CHILDREN.

1. *Asa J.*, b. Sept. 13, 1818 ; m. Prudence Gallop.   .   .   .   (532)
2. *Harriet,* b. Feb. 7, 1820 ; d. in Potsdam, Feb. 12, 1849, æ. 29.
3. *Susan,* b. Jan. 20, 1822 ; m. Nov. 29, 1843, David Lewis of Potsdam, N. Y.,
   and has had, 1. George, b. Sept. 7, 1844 ; 2. Frances D., b. Aug. 8, 1846 ;
   3. Emeline, b. Nov. 16, 1848 ; 4. Abigail Adeline, b. Feb. 7, 1850, d. Sept.

13, 1853; 5. Mary E., b. Aug. 24, 1853; 6. John W., b. Jan. 27, 1856, d.
Sept. 29, 1857; 7. Charles W., b. July 18, 1858.

4. *George W.*, b. Feb. 3, 1824; m. Susan Boody. . . . . (533)
5. *Mary,* b. April 18, 1825; d. in Potsdam, March 28, 1844, æ. 19.
6. *Jane,* b. May 13, 1827; m. Nov. 13, 1856, James Putnam of Potsdam,
and has William, b. Sept. 5, 1857.
7. *Delia,* b. June 15, 1830; d. in Potsdam, Feb. 20, 1850, æ. 19.

362. Rev. HARRY WHITE, son of Capt. John, (186) was
born in Rome, N. Y., Feb. 23, 1801. He was a carriage
maker, and afterwards a civil engineer. In 1844 he was
ordained as a Baptist minister, and has since that time been
chiefly engaged in preaching. He resides at Oneida Castle,
Oneida Co., N. Y.

He married, Feb. 10, 1831, DEBORAH T. JENNE, of Shafts-
bury, Vt.

CHILDREN.

1. *Henry S.*, b. Nov. 25, 1831; was a civil engineer, and d. Aug. 28, 1852, æ. 20.
2. *Mary S.*, b. Aug. 16, 1834.
3. *Jenne L.*, b. April 8, 1836.

363. DAVID WHITE, son of Capt. John, (186) was born in
Rome, N. Y., Jan. 30, 1803. He is a merchant and farmer,
in Annsville, Oneida Co., N. Y.

He married, 1st, Aug. 20, 1830, CAROLINE SEYMOUR. She
was born Aug. 13, 1810, and died Jan. 17, 1837, æ. 26.

He married, 2d, Aug. 28, 1838, LAURA L. BARNUM, born
March 2, 1815.

CHILD ;—BY THE FIRST MARRIAGE.

1. *Collins Seymour,* b. April 28, 1836.

CHILD ;—BY THE SECOND MARRIAGE.

2. *Harrison Ezra,* b. Dec. 24, 1840.
3. *Martha Jennett,* b. June 27, 1851.

364. JOSEPH WHITE, son of Capt. John, (186) was born in
Rome, N. Y., in 1808. He is a carpenter, and lives in Kenosha, Wis.

He married, Sept., 1835, PHILENA TOPLIFF of Norfolk, St.
Lawrence Co., N. Y., born 1811, dau. of Moses and Zilpha Topliff.

CHILDREN.

1. *Jerome,* b. 1837.
2. *Jay,* b. 1839.
3. *Josephine,* b. 1841; d. 1845.
4. *Jenette,* b. 1844; d. 1846.
5. *Charles,* } b. 1849; d. 1850.
6. *Henry,* } Twins.
7. *Judson,* b. 1853.

365. Dea. Asa White, son of Dea. David, (188) was born in Barnard, Vt., July 20, 1797. He was a house joiner, but settled as a farmer in Windsor, Morgan Co., Ohio. He was a justice of the peace, and a deacon of the Presbyterian Church in Windsor. In 1853 he removed to Marion, Linn Co., Iowa, where he died, March 13, 1858, æ. 60.

He married, 1824, Cynthia Keyes, dau. of Jotham Keyes. She lives in Marion, Iowa.

CHILDREN.

1. *Addison Everett*, b. May 23, 1825; is a farmer in Marion. He m. March 18, 1847, Mary Evans, dau. of Samuel M. Evans and Polly White. (See in Family 189.)
2. *Patta Melissa*,   b. Aug. 9, 1828; d. 1847, æ. 19.
3. *David*,   b. Dec. 1, 1830; a farmer in Marion. He m. Lucy Ellis.
4. *Mary*,   b. Oct. 1, 1833; m. Charles Cooper, and d. July 1, 1857, æ. 23.
5. *Harriet*,   b. Sept. 2, 1835; d. Nov. 10, 1840.
6. *Cypron Keyes*,   b. Jan. 4, 1838.
7. *Charles Cory*,   b. Aug. 26, 1841.
8. *Justin Newel*,   b. Sept. 13, 1843.
9. *Martha Josephine*, b. July 6, 1848.

366. Wells White, son of Dea. David, (188) was born in Barnard, Vt., April, 1799. He was a farmer in Windsor, Morgan Co., O., and died June, 1846, æ. 47.

He married, 1819, Sarah Evans, dau. of Simeon Evans. She lives in Harrison Co., Mo.

CHILDREN.

1. *Jesse*,   b. April 2, 1821; d. April 11, 1843, æ. 22.
2. *Emily*,   b.   ; m. James McComas, and d. 1848.
3. *Elizabeth*, b. Oct. 31, 1826; d. March 19, 1845, æ. 18.
4. *Martha*,   b.   ; m. Leonard Muzzy, and d.
5. *Caroline*, b.   ; m.
6. *John*,   b.   ; m. —— Brooks.

367. David White, Jun., son of Dea. David, (188) was born July 4, 1804. He is a farmer in Belpre, Washington Co., Ohio. Has been a justice of the peace.

He married Nancy Ann Miller.

CHILDREN.

1. *Elizabeth R.*, b. Feb. 25, 1834.
2. *James L.*,   b. Oct. 11, 1835.
3. *Henry L.*,   b. Dec. 15, 1838.
4. *William W.*, b. Jan. 13, 1841.
5. *Erastus H.*, b. March 6, 1843.
6. *Sidney P.*, b. June 29, 1845.
7. *David R.*,   b. Dec. 5, 1847.
8. *Emma J.*,   b. Dec. 16, 1849.
9. *Charles C.*, b. March 13, 1854.

368. HARRIS WHITE, son of Dea. David, (188) was born Nov. 17, 1808. He lived in Waterford, Washington Co., Ohio, and was a steamboat pilot. He died Oct. 16, 1842, æ. 34.

He married FRANCES STEEL. She married, 2d, Amos Roberts of Waterford.

CHILDREN.

1. *Seneca Clark,*   b. Feb. 15, 1831 ; d. Dec. 4, 1849.
2. *Hiram,*   b. Aug. 9, 1833 ; m. Sarah Hoon.
3. *John Wickham,* b. Feb. 21, 1835 ; d. Aug. 13, 1841.
4. *Harris V.,*   b. Sept. 4, 1836 ; m. Jan. 7, 1858, Polly Cook Craig.
5. *Oscar F.,*   b. Feb. 20, 1839.

369. HENRY WHITE, son of Dea. David, (188) was born Nov. 12, 1811. He was a shoemaker, lived in Washington Co., Ohio, and died July 16, 1858, æ. 46.

He married, 1st, LOVISA COLEMAN, who died Aug. 1, 1843, æ. 31.

He married, 2d, ELIZABETH HINKLEY, who died March 10, 1856, æ. 27.

CHILDREN ;—BY THE SECOND MARRIAGE.

1. *Harris Winfield,* b. July 22, 1851.   2. *James,* b. May 22, 1853.

370. SAMSON KEYES WHITE, son of Thomas, Esq., (189) was born Aug. 21, 1796. He lives in Evansville, Ohio, and is a carpenter.

He married, Aug. 5, 1824, RHODA RICHMOND, who is dead.

CHILDREN.

1. *Austin,* b. May   6, 1825 ; d. July 26, 1825.
2. *Elias,* b. March 3, 1827 ; d. March 5, 1829.
3. *Thomas,* b. Dec. 15, 1829 ; lives in Ill.
4. *Jane,*   b. March 5, 1842 ; m. March 20, 1858, Charles Rollin of Marietta, Ohio.
5. *Hiram,* b.   ; d.
6. *Martha,* b. Nov. 11, 1844.

371. ELIAS WHITE, son of Thomas, Esq., (189) was born Nov. 29, 1798. He was a farmer in Windsor, Morgan Co., Ohio, and died Sept. 6, 1823, æ. 24.

He married, 1821, SARAH OLNEY, who married, 2d, Charles Davis of Windsor.

His only son,

Dexter, b. Nov. 17, 1821, lives in Windsor.

372. AUGUSTUS STONE WHITE, son of Thomas, Esq., (189) was born in Waterford, Ohio, May 5, 1818. He is a farmer in Kansas.

He married, 1840, LOCIA WEBSTER.

CHILDREN.

1. *Elias,*	b. Dec. 17, 1840.	4. *Mary Jane,*	b. April 11, 1847.
2. *Rebecca Hart,*	b. July 4, 1843.	5. *Rhoda,*	b. Dec. 30, 1849.
3. *Olcott,*	b. July 20, 1845.	6. *Florence Bell,*	b. May 6, 1857.

373. JOHN WRIGHT WHITE, son of Olcott, (191) was born in Middlebury, Vt., Oct. 19, 1814, and resides in Mt. Vernon, Knox Co., Ohio. He is a printer and telegraph operator.

He married, April 11, 1841, CATHERINE SPRINGER, born Nov. 11, 1822, dau. of Jacob P. and Catherine Springer.

CHILDREN.

1. *Caroline,*	b. Jan. 24, 1842.	4. *John Douglass,*	b. June 4, 1849.
2. *Oscar,*	b. May 28, 1844.	5. *Emma,*	b. Jan. 7, 1853.
3. *Edna,*	b. Nov. 24, 1846; d. Sept. 2, 1850.	6. *Frank Fremont,*	b. Jan. 15, 1856.
		7. *Jessie,*	b. Aug. 9, 1858.

374. HORATIO WHITE, son of Olcott, (191) was born in Windsor, Ohio, Nov. 5, 1823. He is a bookbinder, and lives in Zanesville, Ohio.

He married, Oct. 26, 1851, SUSAN CLOSSMAN of Zanesville, dau. of John Clossman and Hannah Kepler.

CHILDREN.

1. *Alfred,*   b. April 5, 1853; d. Sept. 6, 1853.
2. *John Olcott,*   b. Sept. 14, 1854.
3. *Caroline Augusta,* b. Oct. 12, 1856.

375. ASA GATES WHITE, son of Samuel, (192) was born in Windsor, Ohio, June 24, 1820. He is a farmer, near Marion, Linn Co., Iowa.

He married, 1st, April 4, 1846, AMANDA FITZALLEN DAVIDSON, of Mt. Vernon, Iowa, dau. of Robert and Sarah Davidson. She was born Feb. 4, 1825, and died Nov. 23, 1846, æ. 21.

He married, 2d, Feb. 22, 1848, ANN ELIZA STONE, born March 26, 1817, dau. of Harvey and Laura Stone.

CHILDREN;—BY THE SECOND MARRIAGE.

1. *Samuel Harvey,*   b. March 1, 1849.
2. *Calista Armenia,* b. Aug. 4, 1852.
3. *Glenn Wood,*   b. Sept. 1, 1857.

DESCENDANTS OF LIEUT. DANIEL WHITE.

376. JOHN WHITE, son of Elijah, (193) was born in Hatfield, Mass., Aug., 22, 1792. He is a farmer in Groton, Erie Co., Ohio.

He married, 1st, Jan. 27, 1820, SOPHIA WHITE, dau. of Ebenezer White. (See Fam. 197.) She was born Dec. 6, 1793, and died Jan. 10, 1853, æ. 59.

He married, 2d, March 13, 1854, ELIZABETH DRAKE of Groton.

CHILDREN ;—BY THE FIRST MARRIAGE.

1. *Ebenezer*, b. Aug. 5, 1822 ; m. March 11, 1855, Ellen Jones of Margaretta, Erie Co., O., and has two children.
2. *Elijah D.*, b. Dec. 15, 1824 ; m. Dec 15, 1852, Harriet Smith of Groton ; has one child.
3. *Mary S.*, b. Oct. 28, 1826 ; m. April 9, 1848, Erasmus Darwin Graves of Margaretta, and has four children.
4. *George*, b. July 28, 1828 ; m. Oct. 10, 1854, Emily Graves of Margaretta.
5. *John*, b. Jan. 27, 1831 ; m. March 2, 1858, Mary Rogers of Margaretta. These sons are all farmers in Erie Co., Ohio.

CHILD ;—BY THE SECOND MARRIAGE.

6. *Ida Elizabeth*, b. 1855.

---

377. GEORGE WHITE, son of Elijah, (193) was born in Hatfield, Dec. 28, 1799. He died July, 1837, æ. 37.

He married, Feb. 10, 1831, DELIA SHELDON of Rochester, N. Y., who married, 2d, David Patterson of Rochester.

CHILDREN.

1. *Julia*, b. ; d. æ. 6.
2. *Oliver*, b. April, 1836.

---

378. DANIEL WHITE, son of Elijah, (193) was born in Hatfield, Nov. 2, 1801, and resides there.

He married, Aug. 18, 1835, LUCY ELVIRA RICE, dau. of Josiah Rice of Conway, Mass. She died Dec. 22, 1837, æ. 28.

He has one daughter,

Frances Amelia, b. July 26, 1837.

---

379. QUARTUS WHITE, son of Elijah, (193) was born in Hatfield, Feb. 1, 1811, and resides there.

He married, April 1, 1840, JULIA ANN WILKEE, born Nov. 3, 1818, dau. of Henry Wilkee.

31

CHILDREN.

1. *Jerusha Williams*, b. Feb. 14, 1841.
2. *Mary Emeline*,   b. Oct. 10, 1846.

---

380. Dea. JUSTUS WHITE, son of Salmon, jun., (194) was born in Whately, Mass., in 1787, and was a farmer in that town. He was chosen a deacon of the Congregational Church in 1821. After the formation of the Second Church in Whately, he was a deacon of that Church, but subsequently returned to the First Church, and was again chosen to the same office. He died April 4, 1855, æ. 67.

He married, Jan. 17, 1809, RHODA FRARY of Whately, dau. of Phineas Frary and Rhoda Morton. She was born Sept. 11, 1788, and died Oct. 2, 1855, æ. 67.

CHILDREN.

1. *Cornelia*,   b. July 4, 1809; m. John White.   .   .   (Family 382)
2. *Salmon*,   b. Oct. 1, 1810; d. unm., Jan. 12, 1834, æ. 23.
3. *Lydia Amsden*, b. Jan. 1, 1814; d. Aug. 29, 1835, æ. 21.

---

381. LUKE BROWN WHITE, son of Dea. John, (195) was born in Whately, May 8, 1797. He was a farmer there, and was for several years a justice of the peace. He died Oct. 12, 1853, æ. 56.

He married, Oct. 21, 1830, MARY WELLS of Whately, dau. of Luke Wells and Polly Cooley. She was born May 7, 1810, and died June 15, 1839, æ. 29.

CHILDREN.

1. *Henry Kirke*,   b. Sept. 26, 1831.
2. *Theophilus Huntington*, b. Nov. 19, 1832; d. July 16, 1846, æ. 13.
3. *Mary Elizabeth*,   b. Aug. 2, 1834; m. May 21, 1856, Oliver D. Root of Conway.
4. *John Newton*,   b. Nov. 18, 1835; is a shoe dealer in Kingston, C. W.
   He m. Dec. 31, 1857, Mary L. Brown of Whately, dau. of Chester Brown.
5. *Sarah Wells*,   b. Sept. 14, 1837; d. April 14, 1838.
6. *Samuel Brooks*,   b. June 5, 1839.

---

382. JOHN WHITE, Jun., son of Dea. John, (195) was born in Whately, Aug. 2, 1804, and is a farmer in that place.

He married, Jan. 12, 1836, CORNELIA WHITE, born July 4, 1809, dau. of Dea. Justus White. (See Family 380.)

CHILDREN.

1. *Lydia Amsden*, b. Nov. 22, 1838.
2. *Salmon Phelps*, b. Feb. 1, 1841.
3. *Cornelia Maria*, b. Sept. 13, 1853.

383. SAMUEL BROOKS WHITE, son of Dea. John, (195) was born in Whately, Jan. 9, 1811. He is a merchant and farmer in that town; has held various offices, and has represented the town in the Legislature.

He married, Jan. 12, 1848, EXPERIENCE PHELPS WELLS of Whately, born Nov. 23, 1822, dau. of Luke Wells and Polly Cooley.

CHILDREN.

1. *Mary Elizabeth,* b. Aug. 11, 1850.
2. *Arthur,* b. Oct. 13, 1851.
3. *Sarah Almira,* b. Sept. 19, 1853.
4. *Fanny Huntington,* b. Oct. 28, 1856.
5. *Helen Phelps,* b. Aug. 31, 1858.

---

384. Rev. MORRIS E. WHITE, son of Thomas, Esq., (196) was born in Ashfield, Mass., April 27, 1803. He graduated at Dartmouth College in 1828, and at Andover Theological Seminary in 1831, and was for about twenty years pastor of the Congregational Church in Southampton, Mass. He now resides in Northampton.

He married, 1st, May 3, 1832, LOUISA CLIFFORD PAYSON, of Boston, dau. of Thomas Payson. She died Sept. 24, 1842, æ. 31.

He married, 2d, June 4, 1845, PENELOPE ROWE, of Milton, Mass., born June 26, 1804, dau. of John Rowe of Quincy.

CHILDREN;—BY THE FIRST MARRIAGE.

1. *Catharine Putnam,* b. Feb. 17, 1834.
2. *John Phillips Payson,* b. July 4, 1838; grad. Williams College, 1858, and is a medical student.

---

385. THOMAS WAIT WHITE, son of Thomas, Esq., (196) was born in Ashfield, Nov. 15, 1805. About 1836 he went with his two younger brothers to found a new settlement at the mouth of Grand River, Mich., and is now a lumber merchant at Grand Haven, Mich.

He married, Sept. 19, 1836, CAROLINE NORTON of Ashfield, dau. of Job Norton.

CHILDREN.

1. *Louisa H.,* b. Feb. 11, 1838.
2. *Thomas S.,* b. June 28, 1840.
3. *John B.,* b. June 14, 1843.

386. LUKE A. WHITE, son of Thomas, Esq., (196) was born in Ashfield, Oct. 17, 1808. He removed with his brothers to Michigan, but after a few years became a merchant in New York. He died at Grand Haven, Mich., Oct. 15, 1858, æ. 50.

He married, Sept., 1836, CLARISSA J. PERKINS, of Norwich, Conn., dau. of Jedediah Perkins. He had one son,

Thomas Perkins, b. June 3, 1844.

---

387. NATHAN HARWOOD WHITE, son of Thomas, Esq., (196) was born in Ashfield, April 13, 1811. He removed to Michigan in 1836, and is a lumber merchant at Grand Haven.

He married, June 28, 1840, SARAH B. BRITTON of Grandville, Mich.

CHILDREN.

1. *Francis H.,*   b. April   5, 1842.
2. *Clara V.,*   b. Dec.   4, 1844.
3. *Nathan B.,*   b. June 28, 1848.
4. *Luke W.,*   b. Dec.   9, 1852.
5. *Helen E.,*   b. April 17, 1857.

---

388. SILAS DICKINSON WHITE, son of Ebenezer, (197) was born in Hatfield, Mass., Dec. 25, 1810. He resides there.

He married, Sept. 16, 1840, Mrs. AMANDA CLAPP, widow of Samuel F. Clapp, and dau. of Albert Jones of Chesterfield, Mass. She was born March 11, 1817.

CHILDREN.

1. *Charles Edward*, b. Sept. 12, 1843; d. Sept. 11, 1844.
2. *Ebenezer,*   b. Feb. 15, 1845.

---

389. Hon. JABEZ LOOMIS WHITE, Jun., M. D., son of Jabez Loomis, Esq., (200) was born in Bolton, Conn., June 18, 1792. He was a physician in that place, having an extensive and successful practice. The honorary degree of M. D. was conferred on him by Yale College in 1828. He was a justice of the peace, several times represented Bolton in the Legislature, was twice a State Senator, and in 1842 and 1843 was chosen Treasurer of the State. He died Aug. 4, 1844, æ. 52.

He married, Nov. 21, 1816, EMILY HAMMOND of Bolton, born Oct. 9, 1799, dau. of Lemuel Hammond and Lora Kingsbury. She resides in Bolton.

CHILDREN.

1. *Lora Cornelia Kingsbury*, b. Oct. 4, 1817; m. June 11, 1835, Henry C. Woodbridge of Manchester, and d. Sept. 7, 1849, æ. 32. He d. Jan. 23, 1853, æ.
40. She had one son, Jabez Loomis, b. March 10, 1839.
2. *Jabez Loomis*,   b. Aug. 21, 1826; d. March 6, 1832.
3. *Jabez Loomis*,   b. Jan. 1, 1830; res. in Bolton. He was first called by
another name, but afterwards received that of his deceased brother.
4. *Emily Hammond*, b. July 29, 1835; d. Aug. 1, 1835.

390. Hon. JOEL WALES WHITE, son of Jabez Loomis, Esq.,
(200) was born in Bolton, April 24, 1795. He resided for
several years in Windham, Conn., and was a member of both
houses of the Legislature, and Judge of the Probate Court.
He subsequently removed to Norwich, Conn., where he was
Cashier of the Merchants Bank, and President of the Norwich
and Worcester Railroad. In 1844 and 1845 he was U. S.
Consul at Liverpool, England, and in 1857 was appointed Consul at Lyons, France, where he now resides, discharging the
duties of that office.

He married, 1st, June 24, 1824, SARAH Fox of Windham,
dau. of Jabez Fox and Jerusha Perkins. She was born June,
1784, and died Aug. 24, 1849, æ. 65.

He married, 2d, April 24, 1854, Mrs. ELIZABETH M. MOSELY,
of Boston, Mass., widow of David Mosely, and dau. of Capt.
Benjamin Pierce of Newburyport, Mass., and Elizabeth Gerrish.

391. THOMAS JEFFERSON WHITE, son of Jabez Loomis, Esq.,
(200) was born in Bolton, March 31, 1802. He is a farmer
in that town.

He married, Nov. 17, 1829, PHEBE ANN FARMER of Bolton,
born Oct. 31, 1809, dau. of Aaron Farmer, jun., and Lucretia
Phillips.

CHILDREN.

1. *Thomas Jefferson*, b. May 20, 1831; d. March 15, 1832.
2. *Josephine Maria*, b. July 6, 1834; m. Dec. 1, 1852, Dr. Charles F. Sumner,
a physician in Bolton, and has, 1. Cornelia Josephine, b. Sept. 6, 1853;
2. Elizabeth White, b. Aug. 7, 1858.

392. GEORGE CLINTON WHITE, son of Jabez Loomis, Esq.,
(200) was born in Bolton, Nov. 28, 1804. In 1836 he removed
to Buffalo, N. Y., and is President of White's Bank, in that
city.

He married, Sept. 23, 1841, Mrs. ELIZABETH B. MORGAN, widow of Gilbert Morgan of Colchester, Conn. She was born Sept. 23, 1817, and was dau. of James Tew and Sarah Briggs.

---

393. JAMES WELLS WHITE, son of Capt. Lemuel, (201) was born in East Hartford, Conn., Sept. 21, 1800. He has been a merchant in Hillsdale, Columbia Co., N. Y.; is now an insurance agent in Albany, N. Y.

He married, Oct. 21, 1828, CATHARINE REED GARNER of Hillsdale, born Dec. 21, 1808.

CHILDREN.

1. *James Reed,*   b. Sept. 22, 1829 ; d. Aug. 11, 1849, æ. 20.
2. *Wells Pitkin,*   b. May 10, 1831 ; d. June 24, 1834.
3. *Henry Garner,*   b. Oct. 12, 1832 ; d. Oct. 8, 1849, æ. 16.
4. *Sarah Bathsheba,* b. Nov. 19, 1835 ; d. Jan. 28, 1837.
5. *Thaddeus Reed,*   b. Nov. 24, 1837.
6. *Samuel Wells,*   b. April 22, 1841 ; d. April 2, 1842.
7. *Mary Elizabeth,* b. Jan. 30, 1843.
8. *Sarah Louisa,*   b. Feb. 5, 1849.

---

394. JOSEPH WOODBRIDGE WHITE, son of John J., (202) was born Aug. 7, 1818. He resides in Hartford.

He married, Dec. 15, 1852, MARY E. DOLLEN, of Worcester, Mass., born Oct. 15, 1832, dau. of John Dollen.

He has one son,

Charles Woodbridge, b. Jan. 22, 1854.

---

395. WILLIAM H. WHITE, son of John J., (202) was born Jan. 8, 1822. He resides in Hartford, on Governor Street, on a part of the original homelot of Elder John White.

He married, June 10, 1846, ELIZA DOLLEN, of Worcester, Mass., born March 10, 1826, dau. of John Dollen.

He has had one son,

Sheldon Woodbridge, b. Aug. 8, 1847 ; d. March 6, 1848.

---

396. JOHN TRUMBULL WHITE, son of Elihu, (203) was born in Hartford, Conn., Nov. 5, 1809. He was for many years a bookseller and type-founder in New York, but in 1854 retired from active business.

He married, Aug. 8, 1839, SARAH GRACE CARROLL of New York, born Oct. 17, 1821, dau. of Gabriel H. and Augusta N. Carroll.

CHILDREN.

1. *Emily C.,*   b. May   1, 1840.
2. *Charles Carroll,*   b. Jan.   22, 1842; d. May 3, 1847, æ. 5.
3. *John Atwood,*   b. Dec.   11, 1842; d. Sept. 27, 1849, æ. 6.
4. *Sarah Grace,*   b. March   6, 1844.
5. *Julia Lee,*   b. Feb.   20, 1846.
6. *Gabriel Carroll,*   b. March   8, 1847.
7. *Edward Trumbull,* b. June   27, 1848; d. July 18, 1858.
8. *Alfred Ludlow,*   b. Aug.   27, 1849.
9. *Ella,*   b. Feb.   24, 1851.
10. *Augusta,*   b. Oct.   15, 1852.
11. *Frederick Moritz,* b. Jan.   12, 1859; born in Dresden, Germany.

397. BENJAMIN DAY WHITE, son of Elijah, jun., (204) was born in Bolton, Conn., Oct. 11, 1819. He is a real estate and insurance agent, and resides in Delavan, Walworth Co., Wis.

He married, June 28, 1855, JULIA MARIA SHELDON, dau. of Nehemiah Sheldon and Maria Sanford. She was born at Glenn's Falls, Warren Co., N. Y., Aug. 20, 1829.

CHILDREN.

1. *Julia Seraphina,* b. Dec. 11, 1856.
2. *Charles Sheldon,* b. Nov. 2, 1858.

398. HENRY WHITE, son of Julius, (205) was born April 19, 1821. He resides in West Springfield, Mass., and is an insurance agent in Springfield.

He married, May 4, 1847, ELIZA HAZEN.

CHILDREN.

1. *Henry Day,* b. Jan.   17, 1849; d. July 12, 1853.
2. *Julius,*   b. June 14, 1851.   4. *John,* b. March 12, 1855.
3. *Edward,*   b. March 17, 1853.   5. *Lucy,* b. June 14, 1857.

399. WILLIAM WRIGHT WHITE, son of Asa, (207) was born in Bolton, Aug. 16, 1813. He lives in Norwich, Conn.

He married, 1st, Aug. 26, 1838, HARRIET E. LYMAN of Lebanon, who died July, 1852, æ. 40.

He married, 2d, Mrs. LUCY SEGUR of East Haddam, dau. of Abel Bingham.

CHILDREN;—BY THE FIRST MARRIAGE.

1. *Josephine Elizabeth,* b. Sept.,   1840.
2. *Abby Jane,*   b. June 16, 1843.

CHILD;—BY THE SECOND MARRIAGE.

3. *A daughter,*   b. March,   1858.

400. THEODORE HALE WHITE, son of Asa, (207) was born in Bolton, Sept. 19, 1819. He lives at Mystic River, Conn., and is a house-painter.

He married, July 3, 1843, PRISCILLA KING of Mystic, born April 14, 1826, dau. of Grover G. King and Lydia M. Watrous.

CHILDREN.

1. *Stella L.,*   b. Dec. 12, 1845.
2. *Theodore B.,* b. Nov. 20, 1847.
3. *Frederic M.,* b. Sept. 13, 1849; d. Oct. 5, 1853.
4. *Grove K.,*   b. Dec. 13, 1851.   6. *Gertrude M.,* b.   1855.
5. *Joel W.,*   b. Nov. 25, 1853.   7. *Jessie,*   b.   1857.

---

401. EDWARD ELIJAH WHITE, son of Asa, (207) was born in Bolton, Sept. 16, 1820. He lives in Portland, Conn.

He married, June 18, 1849, CHARLOTTE ANN WELLS of Portland, born Jan. 7, 1820, dau. of Roswell Wells.

CHILDREN.

1. *Charlotte Ann,* b. June 12, 1851.
2. *Ella Jane,*   b. May 26, 1854.
3. *Earl Edmund,* b. March 3, 1856; d. Nov. 13, 1858.
4. *Eunice Almira,* b. March 7, 1858.

---

402. HENRY ASA WHITE, son of Asa, (207) was born in Bolton, June 18, 1834. He lives in Plainville, Conn.

He married, Jan. 8, 1856, SARAH J. HAMLIN of Plainville, dau. of John Hamlin. He has,

Frederick Clayton, b. Dec. 1, 1856.

---

403. STANLEY WHITE, son of Daniel, Esq., (208) was born in Coventry, Andover Society, Conn., Sept. 18, 1802. He was a farmer in Andover until 1844, when he removed to Rockville, Conn., where he engaged in mercantile business. He has been a representative in the Legislature, from the town of Coventry.

He married, 1st, Oct. 17, 1838, ROSANNA REED, of East Windsor, Conn., dau. of Dr. Elijah F. Reed and Hannah McLean. She was born May 14, 1810, and died May 20, 1839, æ. 29.

He married, 2d, Nov. 30, 1841, Mrs. ANNA ROOT ROSE, of Coventry, widow of Levi P. Rose, and dau. of Calvin Manning and Desire Gurley. She was born June 5, 1815.

404. NORMAN WHITE, son of Daniel, Esq., (208) was born in Andover, Conn., Aug. 8, 1805. He has been for more than thirty years a merchant in the city of New York. He is an elder in the Mercer Street Presbyterian Church, a Manager of the American Bible Society, and one of the Directors of Union Theological Seminary.

He married, Oct. 15, 1828, MARY ABIAH DODGE of New York, dau. of David L. Dodge and Sarah Cleveland. She was born in Hartford, Conn., Sept. 1, 1808, and died Jan. 5, 1857, æ. 48. A little volume, "In memory of a Mother's Love," prepared by her eldest daughter, for private use, is a pleasing tribute to a rare maternal fidelity, and a most exemplary Christian life.

CHILDREN.

1. *Mary Stuart*, b. Aug. 31, 1829 ; m. Nov. 14, 1849, Rev. Matson Meier Smith. He graduated at Columbia College in 1843, and at Union Theological Seminary in 1847. He has been a pastor at Ovid, N. Y., and at Brookline, Mass.; is now pastor of the First Congregational Church in Bridgeport, Conn. She has, 1. Norman White, b. Oct. 20, 1850 ; 2. Emily Stuart, b. Dec. 9, 1852.

2. *Frances Stanley*, b. May 23, 1831 ; d. Feb. 29, 1844, æ. 12.
3. *Erskine Norman*, b. May 31, 1833 ; m. Eliza T. Nelson.   . .   (534)
4. *Charles Trumbull*, b. Jan. 20, 1835 ; m. Georgianna Starin.   .   (535)
5. *Emma Hale*, b. Aug. 19, 1836 ; m. April 5, 1859, Dr. Benjamin Lee of New York ; (see Family 203.)
6. *Julia Cleveland*, b. May 22, 1838.
7. *Norman*, b. Feb. 26, 1840 ; d. May 15, 1840.
8. *William Stuart*, b. March 8, 1841 ; d. June 26, 1842.
9. *Helen Clement*, b. July 26, 1843.
10. *Grace Stanley*, b. April 4, 1845.

---

405. Dr. SAMUEL POMEROY WHITE, son of Dr. Samuel, (209) was born in Hudson, N. Y., Nov. 8, 1801. He graduated at Union College in 1822, and at the New York Medical College. He is a physician in New York, and has been Lecturer in the Berkshire Medical College, at Pittsfield, Mass. The honorary degree of M. D. was conferred on him by Williams College in 1832.

He married, June 29, 1825, CAROLINE M. JENKINS.

CHILDREN.

1. *Robert Jenkins*, b. Dec. 8, 1826 ; lives in New York.
2. *Julia Cabot*, b. Aug. 8, 1828 ; m. April 18, 1849, Edward M. Livermore, of Cambridge, Mass.
3. *Benjamin Ogden*, b. April 15, 1831 ; lives in New York.

4. *Frances Chester,* b. March 3, 1833 ; m. Marcellus Hartley of New York.
5. *Henry Kirke,*   b. April 12, 1837.
6. *Samuel Pomeroy,* b. Oct. 31, 1839 ; d. March 2, 1841.
7. *Caroline Jenkins,* b. Dec. 20, 1841.
8. *Cornelia,*   b. Jan. 5, 1846.

406. JOHN CHESTER WHITE, son of Dr. Samuel, (209) was born in Hudson, N. Y., Feb. 21, 1811. He died there, Jan. 3, 1843, æ. 32.

He married, May 1, 1838, LAVINIA MAXWELL, born in Adams Co., Pa., in 1813. She resides in Philadelphia, Pa.

CHILDREN.

1. *Howard Maxwell,* b. Aug. 25, 1839 ; d. Dec. 26, 1843.
2. *John Chester,*   b. March 8, 1841 ; is a student in the University of Pa.

407. HANFORD WHITE, son of William, (210) was born in Killingworth, Conn., July 3, 1797. About 1820 he settled as a farmer in Twinsburg, Summit Co., Ohio, and died there, April 28, 1855, æ. 57.

He married, 1st, April, 1822, HEPZIBAH PRATT, who died Oct. 20, 1837.

He married, 2d, July 3, 1838, MARY HERRICK, who is living in Aurora, Portage Co., O.

CHILDREN ;—BY THE FIRST MARRIAGE.

1. *William,* b. April 30, 1823 ; is a farmer in Twinsburg.
2. *Maria,*   b. Jan. 16, 1825 ; lives in Hopkins, Mich.
3. *Heman,*   b. March 23, 1827 ; m. Jane Buskirk.   .   .   .   .   (536)
4. *Chauncey,* b. April 19, 1829 ; is a mason ; rem. to the West in 1858.
5. *Catharine,* b. Dec. 22, 1830 ; m. March 23, 1858, James E. Parmelee, of Hopkins, Allegan Co., Mich.
6. *James H.,* b. May 9, 1833 ; lives in Hopkins, Mich.

CHILD ;—BY THE SECOND MARRIAGE.

7. *Elisha,*   b. June 29, 1839.

408. WILLIAM WHITE, son of Elisha, (211) was born Feb. 18, 1799. He lives in Haddam, Conn.

He married LAURA DICKINSON of H., born Dec. 18, 1805.

CHILDREN.

1. *Henry W.,* b. May 8, 1823 ; m. Drusilla Tyler, and has one dau., Eva.
2. *Joseph,*   b.   ; m. Harriet Grinnell of New Haven. Has had, Daniel Webster, b. 1852, and two sons who d. in infancy.
3. *Lillis,*   b. March 27, 1827 ; m. Uriah Otis.
4. *Nancy,*   b. Aug. 6, 1829 ; m. Elisha Jordan, and has Ellen, b. 1851.
5. *Stephen,*   b. Feb. 13, 1833.
6. *John Franklin,* b. Nov. 13, 1835.   7. *Ellen S.,* b. Nov. 23, 1838.

409. LYMAN WHITE, son of Benjamin, (212) was born in Conn., Nov. 7, 1796. He resides in Fairfield, Herkimer Co., N. Y. Was formerly a hatter; is now a stone-mason. He married, Jan. 17, 1819, LYDIA SALISBURY.

CHILDREN.

1. *Levina M.*, b. Feb. 28, 1820; m. May 30, 1837, Daniel N. Johnson, a farmer, of Martinsburg, Lewis Co., N. Y. Has had four children, three of whom are living.
2. *Maria L.*, b. May 30, 1822; m. 1st, Dec. 8, 1842, Levitt R. Houghton, who d. Dec. 7, 1850. She m. 2d, Jan. 22, 1857, Lafayette Pool, a farmer, of Belleville, Jefferson Co., N. Y. She has had two children, one by each marriage.
3. *Emily,* b. March 28, 1824; d. March 29, 1825.
4. *Adaline J.*, b. July 21, 1826; m. Sept. 11, 1854, Thomas Huckans, jun., a tailor, now of Newport, Herkimer Co. Has had two children.
5. *Louisa E.*, b. Sept. 15, 1828; m. June 4, 1849, Lovell Houghton, a carpenter, now of Winnebago Valley, Houston Co., Min. Has had four children.
6. *Augustus S.*, b. June 27, 1830; is a merchant in Fairfield. He m. May 25, 1854, Amelia W. Read of New Hartford, Oneida Co., N. Y.
7. *Anna N.*, b. Sept. 11, 1833; m. Dec. 28, 1852, Thomas E. Smith, a carpenter, now of Winnebago Valley, Min. Has had two children.
8. *Emma C.*, b. Dec. 23, 1837; d. March 17, 1839.
9. *Dwight W.*, b. Sept. 12, 1841.

---

410. HARLOW WHITE, son of Benjamin, (212) was born Dec. 14, 1802. He is a farmer in Lowville, Jefferson Co., N. Y.

He married, Jan. 12, 1832, LEVINA TALCOTT of Leyden, Lewis Co., N. Y.

CHILDREN.

1. *Parsons,* b.   .   4. *Rodney.*
2. *Eliza,* b.   ; d. 1853, æ. 16.   5. *Louis.*
3. *Handford,* b.   .

---

411. ALFRED WHITE, son of Benjamin, (212) was born Dec. 12, 1803. He is a farmer at Middleville, Herkimer Co., N. Y. He married, Jan. 3, 1827, FLORILLA STEVENS of Fairfield.

CHILDREN.

1. *Elizabeth,* b.   ; m. Joseph Kelley of Newport, N. Y., and has four children.
2. *Larned,* b.   ; d. Jan., 1854.
3. *Delia,* b.   ; m. Dec. 29, 1852, Freeman Enos of Fairfield, and has four children.
4. *George H.*, b.
5. *Helen R.*, b.   .   7. *Mary.*
6. *Charles,* b.   .   8. *Harriet J.*

412. CHARLES WHITE, son of Benjamin, (212) was born July 17, 1810. He is a farmer in Russia, Herkimer Co., N. Y.

He married, Sept. 20, 1837, JANE M. CARTER of Russia, born Nov. 29, 1817, dau. of Hubbell and Sarah Carter.

CHILDREN.

1. *Maria S.*, b. Dec. 25, 1839.
2. *Emma E.*, b. July 12, 1845.
3. *Eudora J.*, b. Jan. 4, 1848.

---

413. HENRY WHITE, son of Henry, (214) is a brick maker in Athens, Greene Co., N. Y.

He married MARY ELISABETH AKIN, and has one daughter and one son. Record not furnished.

---

414. STEPHEN WHITE, son of Hon. George, (215) was born April 17, 1799. He resided in Watertown, Jefferson Co., N. Y., and died Nov. 12, 1857, æ. 58.

He married, July 10, 1833, CALISTA KEYES. His only child,

Mary, b.   ; m. John C. Streeter of Watertown.

415. LYMAN WHITE, son of Hon. George, (215) was born Sept. 14, 1800. He died in Joliet, Ill., Aug. 22, 1846, æ. 46.

He married, March 4, 1824, ABBY M. FISK.

CHILDREN.

1. *George C.*, b.   ; m. in Ill., and went to California.
2. *Hiram*, b.   ; d. in Cal., unm.
3. *Eybert*, b.   ; a land broker in Joliet, Ill.; is m.
4. *Cornelia*, b.   ; m. Dr. Chapel, now of Nebraska.
5. *John*, b.   ; lives in Cal.

---

416. FREDERICK W. WHITE, son of Hon. George, (215) was born May 6, 1806. He died Oct. 14, 1852, æ. 46.

He married, Jan. 27, 1825, ELVIRA P. FOSTER of Watertown.

CHILDREN.

1. *Vincent*, b.   ; m., is a painter.
2. *Frances*, b.   ; m. William Martin, and res. in Ind.
3. *Delia*, b.   ; m. Stukeley W. Henderson of Milwaukee, Wis., a broker.
4. *Celia*, b.   ; m. Curtis Wicks.
5. *George*, b.   .

---

417. WILLIAM H. WHITE, son of Hon. George, (215) was born Dec. 13, 1808. He died at Cold Spring, Suffolk Co., N. Y., Feb. 19, 1856, æ. 45.

He married Dec. 6, 1838, ABBY M. HARRISON of New York.

CHILDREN.

1. *Thomas H.*, b.   ·
2. *William,*   b.   ·
3. *Cameron,*   b.   ; is a student in College.

418. ALBERT L. WHITE, son of Hon. George, (215) was born Oct. 11, 1810. He resides in Redwood, Jefferson Co., N. Y. He married, Dec. 23, 1835, ALMIRA WHITE, born Nov. 28, 1807, dau. of Henry White. (See Fam. 214.)

CHILDREN.

1. *Henry A.*
2. *George L.*
3. *Lucy A.*

419. EDWIN C. WHITE, son of Hon. George, (215) was born May 18, 1816. He resides in Watertown, N. Y. He married, Nov. 14, 1844, LAURA J. WILSON of Rutland, N. Y., and has one son,

George H.

420. OLIVER WHITE, Jun., son of Oliver, (221) was born Nov. 12, 1796. He was formerly a manufacturer; is now a farmer in Winsted, Conn.

He married, July 6, 1817, PAMELIA BACON, of Barkhamsted, Conn., born June 10, 1797, dau. of Nathaniel Bacon and Orrel Wilson.

CHILDREN.

1. *James,*   b. April 9, 1818; m. Charlotte Greene. .   .   (537)
2. *Luman,*   b. July 19, 1819; m. Sarepta Raynolds,   .   . (538)
3. *Orrin Washington,* b. April 5, 1821; m. L. S. Lovejoy and P. L. Pope. (539)
4. *Wilson B.,*   b. Jan. 24, 1823; m. Harriet Leach.   .   . (540)
5. *George,*   b. June 4, 1825; m. Ellen M. Kelsey. .   .   . (541)
6. *Julia A.,*   b. May 29, 1827; m. Jan. 16, 1848, Charles H. Wattles, now of Cal.
7. *Aurelia A.,*   b. July 18, 1830; m. May 5, 1851, Grove Stannard, now of Cal., and has, Oliver Grove.
8. *Susan P.,*   b. May 11, 1832; m. April 19, 1850, Hiram J. Norton of Norfolk, Conn.

421. DANIEL WHITE, son of Oliver, (221) was born in Barkhamsted, Conn. He is a carpenter, and lives at Burr Oak, St. Joseph Co., Michigan.

He married NANCY ———.

CHILDREN.

1. *George,*	b.	1828; is a carpenter.		
2. *Avis,*	b.	1830; m. Heman Martin.		
3. *Abigail,*	b.	1832; m. Palmer Lancaster.		
4. *Sarah J.,*	b. June 22, 1834.			
5. *Oliver,*	b.	1837.		
6. *Morgan,*	b. March 14, 1839.		9. *Edward,*	b. June 5, 1847.
7. *William Henry,* b.		1842.	10. *Edwin,*	Twins.
8. *Lucy Maria,*	b.	1844.	11. *Anna Mary,* b. May, 1849.	

422. HORACE CLEVELAND WHITE, son of Daniel, (222) was born Feb. 22, 1809. He is a joiner and farmer in Sandisfield, Mass.

He married, April 10, 1838, SUSAN AMELIA WOLCOTT of Sandisfield, born Jan. 20, 1814, dau. of Josiah Wolcott and Amelia Cowles.

CHILDREN.

1. *Salome Benton,* b. April 27, 1839.
2. *Mary Bissell,* b. May 11, 1841.
3. *A son,*   Twins.   ; d. May 13, 1841.
4. *Clarissa Amelia,* b. Nov. 21, 1843.
5. *Susan Adelaide,* b. Oct. 31, 1845; d. Feb. 15, 1846.
6. *Theresa Lavinia,* b. April 25, 1848.
7. *Horace Wolcott,* b. July 9, 1853.

423. GEORGE CALDWELL WHITE, son of George, (223) was born in Hartford, Conn., Aug. 11, 1807. He is a jeweler in New York.

He married, Oct. 21, 1835, SARAH DUNN, born Feb. 22, 1809, dau. of Nathaniel Dunn of Poland, Me.

CHILDREN.

1. *Sarah D.,* b. July 2, 1839.
2. *George Caldwell,* b. Feb. 21, 1842.
3. *Mary Eliza,* b. March 8, 1844; d. Oct. 9, 1844.
4. *Julia Clarissa,* b. Aug. 6, 1848.
5. *Reginald Heber,* b. Dec. 2, 1852.

Eighth Generation and Descendants.

DESCENDANTS OF CAPT. NATHANIEL WHITE.

IN THE LINE OF DEA. NATHANIEL WHITE, OF HADLEY.

424. Rev. LORENZO WHITE, son of Ezra, (226) was born May 9, 1821. He is a Methodist minister, and resides in Wilbraham, Mass.

He married, July 5, 1849, ELIZABETH BABCOCK, of Chester, Mass., born Nov. 13, 1817, dau. of Abel Babcock and Sarah H. Cheney.

CHILDREN.

1. *Narcissa Amanda,* b. Sept. 25, 1850.
2. *Lucy Elizabeth,* b. April 22, 1852; d. Dec. 30, 1852.
3. *Charlotte E.,* b. April 10, 1854.

---

425. LUTHER WHITE, son of Lyman, (227) was born in South Hadley, Mass., Sept. 14, 1816. He is a shoemaker, and resides in Parish, Oswego Co., N. Y.

He married, April, 1857, Mrs. AMANDA DELVAN of Parish, born April 12, 1821, dau. of Frederick and Lucy Simmons.

He has one son,

Lyman A:, b. Dec. 21, 1857.

---

426. EDWIN WHITE, son of Lyman, (227) was born in Ludlow, Mass., Feb. 17, 1818. He resides in Athens, Bradford Co., Pa. Is a tinner.

He married, May 26, 1844, JERUSHA C. STEBBINS, dau. of Ralph and Laura Stebbins of South Hadley.

CHILDREN.

1. *Martha C.,* b. Feb. 26, 1845.
2. *Edwin L.,* b. June 2, 1854.

427. JAMES WHITE, son of Lyman, (227) was born in South Hadley, July 9, 1821. He was a mason in Brooklyn, N. Y., where he died, Feb. 27, 1858, æ. 36.

He married, Aug. 2, 1842, JULIET WASHBURN, of Belchertown, Mass., dau. of Maj. —— and Sabra Washburn.

CHILDREN.

1. *Adelaide L.*, b. Aug. 27, 1843.
2. *A child,*   b. Nov. 26, 1847; d. same day.
3. *William L.*, b.   ; d. at the age of two or three months.
4. *Charles L.*, b. May 8, 1851; d. Feb., 1854. *
5. *George L.*,   b. April 18, 1854.

---

428. WILLIAM WALLACE WHITE, Esq., son of Hon. Phineas, (230) was born in Putney, Vt., Aug. 31, 1816. He pursued a "Scientific Course" of study at the University of Vermont and at Union College, studied law, and practiced for a few years in New York and St. Louis. He now resides in Burlington, Iowa, is Mayor of the city, and President of the Des Moines County Savings Bank.

He married, April 14, 1846, FRANCES ANN ATHERTON, of Brooklyn, N. Y., born Aug. 9, 1822, dau. of George F. Atherton and Ruth Bartlett.

CHILDREN.

1. *Helen Esther Stevens*,   b. Dec. 16, 1846.
2. *Julia Ruth Bartlett,*   b. Dec. 31, 1848.
3. *Fanny Atherton,*   b. July 25, 1851; d. Oct. 26, 1852.
4. *Gertrude Goodman,*   b. March 6, 1854; d. Aug. 12, 1854.
5. *William George Atherton,* b. Feb. 8, 1856.
6. *Arthur Edward Chase,*   b. Nov. 10, 1858.

---

429. JONATHAN RIPLEY WHITE, Esq., son of Enoch, jun., (231) was born in South Hadley, Mass., Sept. 10, 1806. He is a lawyer, and resides in Lapeer, Lapeer Co., Mich.

He married LOUISA DEXTER. She was born April 11, 1808.

---

430. PHINEAS WHITE, son of Enoch, jun., (231) was born in South Hadley, May 1, 1810. He is a farmer in Lapeer, Mich.

He married, Oct. 23, 1837, FIDELIA DAY of South Hadley, who was born July 2, 1813. He has one son,

Austin Henry, b. May 7, 1851.

431. ENOCH J. WHITE, son of Enoch, jun., (231) was born in South Hadley, March 2, 1814. He is a surveyor and civil engineer, and resides in Lapeer, Mich.

He married, Oct. 16, 1839, ELIZABETH W. GAYLORD of Hadley, Mass., born Nov. 26, 1816, dau. of Chester Gaylord.

CHILDREN.

1. *Phineas G.,* b. Aug. 2, 1843.
2. *Chester G.,* b. Nov. 11, 1845.
3. *Abby F.,* b. Nov. 11, 1848.
4. *Martha L.,* b. Oct. 21, 1854.
5. *Enoch C.,* b. Jan. 9, 1857.
6. *Lucy H.,* b. Nov. 26, 1858.

432. OLIVER WHITE, son of David, (232) was born in Hadley, Mass., and resides there.

He married, 1849, SOPHIA S. PATTRILL of Enfield, Ms. Has,

1. *William Frederick,* b. Oct. 17, 1852.
2. *Ellen A.,* b. Jan. 19, 1854.

433. JAMES PORTER WHITE, son of David, (232) was born in Hadley, and lives in that place.

He married, 1849, CAROLINE A. JUDSON, and has,

1. *Charles Nelson,* b. June 30, 1851.
2. *James Judson,* b. Aug. 2, 1855.
3. *A daughter,* b. July 14, 1859.

434. REUBEN WHITE, son of David, (232) was born in Hadley, February, 1830.

He married, Jan. 10, 1849, HARRIET ——, and has had,

Clarence Eugene, b. Feb. 20, 1851 ; d. Sept., 1852.

435. DAVID WHITE, son of Elihu, (233) was born in Hadley. He married, Dec. 20, 1854, ANNA B. WARREN .of Enfield, Mass., and has,

1. *Carrie D.,* b. June 6, 1856.
2. *Anna Augusta,* b. Nov., 1857.

436. ELIJAH WHITE, son of Elihu, (233) was born in Hadley, Jan. 3, 1830.

He married, Aug., 1855, LUCY W. FITCH of Greenwich, Mass. He has,

1. *Henry Warner,* b. July 5, 1856.
2. *Laura Elizabeth,* b. Oct., 1857.

437. LEWIS CLAPP WHITE, son of Chester, (235) was born Oct. 9, 1809, and died Dec. 15, 1845, æ. 36. He was a harness maker.

He married, May 7, 1834, MARY ANN SMITH of Northampton, Mass.

33

CHILDREN.

1. *Lewis S.*, b. May 16, 1835.
2. *Charles E.*, b. June 17, 1839.
3. *Henry Goddard*, b. Jan. 17, 1841.
4. *Mary E.*,   b. May 3, 1844.

---

438. JAMES EDWARDS WHITE, son of Chester, (235) was born Jan. 14, 1812. He is a baker, in Greenbush, N. Y. He married, Aug. 27, 1833, JANE ANN PHISTY.

CHILDREN.

1. *Mary Elizabeth*, b. March 4, 1834.
2. *Theodore H.*,   b. June 3, 1836.
3. *Chester R.*,   b. Dec. 3, 1838.
4. *Cornelia M.*, b. Oct. 14, 1840.
5. *Eveline*,   b. Oct. 4, 1843.
6. *Eliza Jane*, b. Sept. 7, 1845.

---

439. WILLIAM CHESTER WHITE, son of Job, (236) was born Sept. 10, 1821. He is a hardware dealer in Port Byron, N. Y. He married, Jan., 1846, CATHARINE BRAMHALL.

CHILDREN.

1. *Frank Augusta*.
2. *Edmund Chester*.
3. *Charlotte Estelle*.
4. *Catharine May*.

---

440. HEMAN WHITE, Jun., son of Heman, (239) was born in South Hadley, Mass., July 2, 1820, and is a tailor there.

He married, June 25, 1845, CLARA N. BARTLETT of Hadley, born April 11, 1827, dau. of Levi Bartlett.

CHILDREN.

1. *Horace Clinton*, b. March 7, 1848; d. Aug. 24, 1849.
2. *Lizzie Mary*,   b. March 15, 1852.
3. *Hattie Annie*,   b. July 6, 1854.

---

441. EDWIN WHITE, son of Cyrus, (240) was born in South Hadley, May 21, 1817. He resides in New York, and is an artist. Two of his paintings have been engraved: "The Signing of the Compact in the Cabin of the Mayflower," and "The Evening Hymn of the Huguenot Refugees." He has recently completed a picture for the State of Maryland, to be placed in the Senate Chamber at Annapolis: "Washington resigning his Command of the American Army." The honorary degree of Master of Arts was conferred on him by Amherst College, in 1856.

He married, Dec. 7, 1841, HARRIET HINMAN ALLEN, of Bridgeport, Conn., born Oct. 15, 1817, dau. of James Allen and Harriet Hinman.

442. HORACE HOMER WHITE, son of Sewall, (242) was born in West Springfield, Mass., Jan. 1, 1810. He is Cashier of the Broadway Bank, in Boston, Mass.

He married, June 23, 1833, MARY JANE LORING of Boston, born March 31, 1811, dau. of John James Loring and Harriot Homans.

CHILDREN.

1. *John James,*   b. March 4, 1834; d. Nov. 6, 1836.
2. *Harriette Loring,*   } b. June 6, 1848.
3. *Catherine Frances,*   }   Twins.   d. Oct. 6, 1848, æ. 4 mos.

443. CHARLES WHITE, son of Sewall, (242) was born in West Springfield, Nov. 14, 1811. He is a farmer there, and has been town-clerk.

He married, Dec. 25, 1844, LOUISE BRADLEY of West Springfield, born Nov. 1, 1818, dau. of Ezra and Julia Bradley.

He has one daughter,

Alma Cooley, b. Oct. 12, 1851.

444. DANIEL H. WHITE, son of Gordon, (243) was born in Agawam, then a part of West Springfield, March 21, 1819. He is a farmer in Agawam.

He married, 1st, Oct. 16, 1842, THANKFUL LEONARD of W. S., dau. of Rufus and Anna Leonard. She died March 12, 1852, æ. 33.

He married, 2d, March 10, 1853, CELINA BILLS of Westfield, Mass., dau. of John Bills and Celina Allen. She was born Oct. 10, 1819, and died April 30, 1856, æ. 36.

He married, 3d, Aug. 16, 1857, SARAH B. COFFIN of New York, born Aug. 9, 1831, dau. of Benjamin Coffin and Sarah Rich.

CHILDREN;—BY THE FIRST MARRIAGE.

1. *Clara Nabby,*   b. June 23, 1843; d. Sept. 1, 1853, æ. 10.
2. *Jane T.,*   b. Jan. 19, 1845; d. Aug. 24, 1848.
3. *Gordon D.,*   b. July 2, 1847; d. March 19, 1849.
4. *Anna Leonard,* b. Nov. 1, 1849.
5. *Daniel,*   b. Feb. 29, 1852.

CHILD;—BY THE SECOND MARRIAGE.

6. *Celina J.,*   b. April 1, 1856.

CHILD ;—BY THE THIRD MARRIAGE.

7. *Clara N.,*   b. Sept. 29, 1858; d. Dec. 26, 1858.

445. JARED WHITE, son of Martin, (246) was born in Springfield, Sept. 9, 1800. He lives in West Springfield. He married ELECTA LOOMIS.

CHILDREN.

1. *Francis H.*, b. Jan. 11, 1827.   3. *Sarah M.*, b. Aug. 24, 1838.
2. *Joseph E.*, b. Dec. 8, 1830.

---

446. NORMAN STEBBINS WHITE, son of Luther, (247) was born in Springfield, Oct. 26, 1803. He is a carpenter there.

He married, Oct. 26, 1828, SUSAN NOYES, born in Winchendon, Mass., Dec. 10, 1802, dau. of James Noyes and Hannah Russell.

CHILDREN.

1. *Helen Marie*, b. Aug.,   1829; d. Sept., 1835, æ. 6.
2. *Adelaide*,   b. Jan. 21, 1831; d. Oct. 2, 1835, æ. 4.
3. *James Luther*, b. July 27, 1833.
4. *Daniel G.*,   b. Feb. 27, 1835.
5. *George A.*,   b. Nov. 5, 1837.
6. *John H.*,   b. July 11, 1843; d. Aug. 12, 1844.

---

447. ALFRED WHITE, son of Luther, (247) was born in Springfield, June 9, 1807. He is a carpenter in Chicopee.

He married, Sept. 25, 1833, EMILY CADY of South Wilbraham, Mass., born Feb. 7, 1812, dau. of Hezekiah Cady and Nancy Hale.

CHILDREN.

1. *Nancy Maria*, b. Oct. 8, 1838.
2. *Mary Frances*, b. Sept. 9, 1842; d. Feb. 1, 1843.
3. *Martha Emma*, b. Oct. 8, 1844; d. Aug. 18, 1845.
4. *Alfred Henry*, b. Oct. 11, 1846.
5. *Fannie Estelle*, b. April 20, 1850.

---

448. Dr. RODERICK ADAMS WHITE, son of Roderick, (248) was born in Enfield, Conn., Oct. 24, 1809. He graduated at the Medical Department of Yale College in 1832, and is a physician in Simsbury, Conn.

He married, Nov. 4, 1844, ELIZABETH W. HUNGERFORD, of Wolcottville, Conn., born in 1816, dau. of John Hungerford and Elizabeth Webster.

---

449. PRESERVED MERRITT WHITE, son of Preserved, (249) was born in Springfield, Mass., Oct. 10, 1816. He is a farmer in Farmersburgh, Clayton Co., Iowa.

He married, March 13, 1840, CATHARINE FINLAY, of Jersey City, N. J., born June 2, 1824, dau. of Robert and Sarah Finlay.

CHILDREN.

1. *Joseph Neill,*   b. Nov. 29, 1841; d. æ. 3 mos.
2. *Edward Chaffee,*   b. Dec. 28, 1843.
3. *Robert Finlay,*   b. Dec. 14, 1845; d. æ. 3. mos.
4. *William Finlay,*   b. March 28, 1846; d. æ. 1 yr. 4 mos.
5. *Alexander Finlay,*   b. Aug. 17, 1848.
6. *Sarah Wilhelmina,*   b. July 20, 1851.
7. *Preserved Merritt,*   b. April 27, 1857; d. æ. 6 mos.
8. *Mary Catharine,*   b. Dec. 27, 1858.

449a. ALBERT MILTON WHITE, son of Preserved, (249) was born in Springfield, June 18, 1824. He is a machinist in Hartford, Conn.

He married, April 1, 1846, LAURINDA CUTLER of Brookline, Vt., born March, 1828. He has one son,

Le Roy Albert, b. Sept. 27, 1859.

450. LEWIS WHITE, son of Preserved, (249) was born in Springfield, Dec. 22, 1825. He is a machinist, and resides in Hartford, Conn.

He married, Oct. 14, 1850, MARY WAKEFIELD, born Aug. 7, 1830, dau. of John Wakefield of Glastenbury, Conn.

CHILDREN.

1. *Charles Lewis,*   b. Aug. 26, 1851.
2. *Franklin Randolph,* b. Aug. 24, 1854.

451. LYMAN WHITE, son of Preserved, (249) was born in Springfield, Feb. 18, 1827. He is a machinist in Waterbury, Conn.

He married, Dec. 1, 1848, JULIA ANN BUSH, born July 17, 1829, dau. of Jonathan A. Bush of Enfield, Conn.

CHILDREN.

1. *Frederick Lyman,* b. June 29, 1850.
2. *Willie Howard,*   b. July 31, 1856; d. Feb. 16, 1857.

452. LE ROY SUNDERLAND WHITE, son of Preserved, (249) was born in Springfield, May 14, 1828. He is a machinist in Waterbury, Conn.

He married, April 24, 1852, SARAH JANE LANCEY, born Oct. 2, 1832, dau. of William Lancey of New Market, N. H.

He has one daughter,

Emma Almira, b. March 26, 1855.

453. WILLIAM WIRT WHITE, son of Preserved, (249) was born in Springfield, March 9, 1832. He is a machinist in Waterbury, Conn.

He married, Jan. 7, 1856, MARY JANE WASHBURN, born Sept. 13, 1839, dau. of Abiel Washburn of Springfield, Mass.

He has one son,

William Le Roy, b. May 27, 1857.

454. GEORGE HALL WHITE, son of David, jun., (250) was born in Longmeadow, Mass., March 30, 1815. He is a mechanic in Shelburne Falls, Mass.

He married, April 21, 1845, ELIZA MORGAN of Springfield, born Feb. 27, 1820, dau. of Jonathan Morgan and Ruth Loomis.

CHILDREN.

1. *Louisa Hall*,   b. June   4, 1846; d. Oct. 25, 1846.
2. *Henry Morgan*,   b. June 24, 1847.
3. *Robert Anderson*, b. March 14, 1853.
4. *Hattie Clarissa*, b. Feb. 18, 1855.

455. JOSEPH PYNCHON WHITE, son of David, jun., (250) was born in Longmeadow, Mass., June 14, 1822. He is a blacksmith, and resides in Gaines, Orleans Co., N. Y.

He married, Nov. 30, 1848, RUTH LOOMIS MORGAN, born March 13, 1822, dau. of Jonathan Morgan and Ruth Loomis.

CHILDREN.

1. *Clarence Hall*,   b. Nov. 5, 1851.   3. *Ella Augusta*, b. June 26, 1857.
2. *Willard Morgan*, b. July 12, 1853.   4. *Dora Elvira*, b. Aug. 27, 1859

456. WILLIAM PYNCHON WHITE, son of William, (251) was born in Longmeadow, Mass., Feb. 24, 1824. He graduated at Williams College in 1845, and is a merchant in Rising Sun, Indiana.

He married, Feb. 24, 1849, MARY A. JAMES of Rising Sun.

CHILDREN.

1. *William Clarence*, b. June,   1850.
2. *Charles*,   b. Oct. 18, 1854.
3. *Edward Dodd*,   b. Nov. 20, 1856.

IN THE LINE OF JOHN WHITE, OF HARTFORD.

457. JOHN WHITE, son of John, (260) was born in Hartford, Conn., and lives there.

He married, Dec. 3, 1830, SARAH HURLBURT of Wethersfield.

CHILDREN.

1. *Elizabeth*, b.	1833 ; m. George Ryer of New York, and has a son, Henry.
2. *Lucy Ann*, b.	; m. Milton Barber of Hartford.
3. *Laura* b.	1837 ; m. Gardner G. P. Otis of Saybrook, Conn.
4. *John*, b.	1839. 5. *Sarah*, b. Nov., 1842.

IN THE LINE OF ENSIGN DANIEL WHITE, OF MIDDLETOWN.

458. WILLIAM HENRY WHITE, son of Aaron, jun., (263) was born in Milton, Ky., Nov. 5, 1819. He is a farmer in Eaton Co., Mich.

He married, 1846, MARGARET HITCHCOCK, born in Granville, N. Y., 1830.

CHILDREN.

1. *Harriet Maria*, b. Dec. 17, 1847.
2. *Amanda Louisa*, b. April 14, 1849.
3. *William Henry*, b. April 20, 1851.
4. *Charles Augustus*, b.   1853 ; d. 1854.
5. *Royal Alphonso*, b. Feb. 10, 1856.
6. *Frances Lucretia*, b. May 14, 1858.

459. AARON WHITE, son of Aaron, jun., (263) was born in Medina, Ohio, Aug. 5, 1827. He is a stone mason, and lives in Battle Creek, Mich.

He married, July 2, 1856, LAURA J. BEMAN, of Verona, Calhoun Co., Mich., and has one daughter,

Emma A., b. May 28, 1857.

460. SAMUEL KELLOGG WHITE, son of Aaron, jun, (263) was born in Medina, Ohio, April 11, 1835.

He married, 1856, ANN REDFERN.

CHILDREN.

1. *Esther Jane*, b. Sept. 5, 1856.   2. *Frances Oliver*, b. March 8, 1858.

461. GEORGE CLINTON WHITE, son of Harold, (267) was born Aug. 27, 1828. He is a farmer in New Hudson, Alleghany Co., N. Y.

He married, March 4, 1852, EVALINE AUGUSTA COMSTOCK, of Fort Ann, N. Y., born June 18, 1829, dau. of Peter and Lucy Comstock.

CHILDREN.

1. *Marietta Lucy,*   b. March 31, 1854.
2. *Laura Comstock,* b. July   3, 1855.
3. *Clara Morley,*   b. Aug. 27, 1857.

462. WILLIAM HENRY WHITE, son of Amos, jun., (271) was born Aug. 15, 1815. He is a manufacturer, and resides in Baltimore, Md.

He married, 1844, MARY KING.

CHILDREN.

1. *William Augustus,* b. 1845.   3. *Charles,* b. 1857.
2. *George King,*   b. 1846.

463. JOHN ELIJAH WHITE, son of Elijah, jun., (272) was born in Granville, N. Y., Sept. 5, 1817. He studied law, but engaged in mercantile pursuits, in Detroit, Mich., and for twelve years in Cleveland, Ohio. He is now a flour merchant in New York, and resides there.

He married, June 6, 1844, EMMA LOUISA WALTER SHAW. She was born in New York, Nov. 1, 1825, and died at Newburgh, N. Y., May 29, 1857, æ. 31.

464. Rev. GIDEON STEBBINS WHITE, son of Wilson, (273) was born in Granville, N. Y., April 12, 1803. He completed his literary and theological studies in 1829, at the South Western Theological Seminary, now known as Maryville College, Tennessee, from which Institution he received the degree of Master of Arts in 1846. He resides near McMillan's Station, Knox Co., Tennessee, and has for more than twenty years had charge of the Presbyterian Churches of Washington, Knox Co., and Strawberry Plains, Jefferson Co. He has several times been a Commissioner to the General Assembly of the Presbyterian Church.

He married, Nov. 6, 1834, MARY ELIZA JARNAGIN, of New Port, Tenn., born July 16, 1819, dau. of Preston Bynum Jarnagin and Hester Shields.

CHILDREN.

1. *Mary Hester,*   b. Aug. 1, 1835; m. July 14, 1853, William E. A. Meek of Knox Co., a farmer, and has, 1. Theresia Luann, b. Sept. 11, 1854; 2. Joseph, b. Sept. 10, 1857.
2. *Martha Malvinah,* b. June 25, 1837; m. Oct. 2, 1855, James M. McCampbell, of Knox Co., a farmer, and has had, 1. Gideon Stebbins White, b. June, 1856; 2. Sarah Florence, b. March, 1858, d. May, 1859.

3. *Margaret Ellen,*   b. July 31, 1839.
4. *Elizabeth Meek,*   b. Jan. 26, 1842 ; d. March 23, 1842.
5. *Gideon Shields,*   b. Nov. 19, 1843.
6. *Cornelia Florence,*   b. May 27, 1850.
7. *Alice Jane Jarnagin,* b. May 13, 1852.
8. *Emily Eliza,*   b. Nov. 1, 1854.

465. ELIJAH WHITE, son of Wilson, (273) was born in Granville, N. Y., April 3, 1805. He resides in Ogdensburgh, St. Lawrence Co., N. Y., is a justice of the peace, and an elder in the Presbyterian church.

He married, 1st, Dec. 5, 1830, MARGARET SMITH of Ogdensburgh, who died Jan. 23, 1842.

He married, 2d, Oct. 5, 1843, JANE HAGGERT of Ogdensburgh, who died Sept. 12, 1844.

He married, 3d, May 31, 1846, PHILENA B. BROWN of Castleton, Vt.

CHILDREN ;—BY THE FIRST MARRIAGE.

1. *Gideon S.,*   b.   ; d. æ. 10 mos.
2. *Mary Adelia,* b. July 4, 1838 ; m. Oct. 6, 1858, William Stilwell of Ogdensburgh.

466. JOSIAH A. WHITE, son of Wilson, (273) was born in Granville, N. Y., June 13, 1807. He is a farmer in Brooklyn, Jackson Co., Mich., and has held town offices.

He married, 1st, Feb. 2, 1832, JULIA ANN WARREN, dau. of William and Mahala Warren. She was born in Hartford, N. Y., March 23, 1809, and died in Whitehall, N. Y., April 15, 1835, æ. 26.

He married, 2d, Aug. 28, 1846, JANE R. HUNGERFORD, of Van Buren, Onondaga Co., N. Y., born March 27, 1808, dau. of Asahel and Fanny Hungerford.

By the second marriage he has had one child,

Julia Ann, b. Aug. 12, 1847 ; d. Sept. 27, 1849.

467. CHARLES A. WHITE, son of Charles, (274) was born in Sandy Hill, Washington Co., N. Y., Dec. 14, 1823. He resides there, and is an artist.

He married DEBORAH BURCH of Easton, N. Y., and has,

Robert Edward, b. Sept. 30, 1855.

468. MILO EVERTS WHITE, son of William, (275) was born October, 1814. He is a hat and fur dealer in New York.

34

He married, 1841, JANETTE PADDOCK, and has one daughter, *Rose Clara.*

469. CORAL CASE WHITE, Jun., son of Coral Case, (276) was born Jan. 21, 1823. He is a farmer.

He married, Feb. 19, 1846, CORNELIA MORGAN.

CHILDREN.

1. *William Brainard,* b. Jan. 17, 1848.
2. *Frances Cornelia,* b. Feb. 18, 1849.
3. *Charles Sanford,* b. May 5, 1852.

470. WADE WHITE, son of Noadiah, (278) was born in Hartford, Vt., Aug. 21, 1805. In 1830 he removed to Garrettsville, Portage Co., Ohio, the region being then mostly unsettled. He is a farmer, and a deacon of the Congregational church.

He married, 1830, EMILY HUNT of Pomfret, Vt. She was born in Coventry, Conn., in 1809, and was the dau. of Eliphaz Hunt and Anna Phelps.

CHILDREN.

1. *John,* b. 1833; m. 1856, Martha Mousehunt.
2. *Emily A.,* b. 1837; m. 1857, Jerome B. Carman.
3. *Eliphaz W.,* b. 1838.

471. WILLARD STANLEY WHITE, son of Noadiah, (278) was born in Hartford, Vt., Dec. 4, 1807. He removed to Garrettsville, Ohio, in 1832, and is a farmer there.

He married, 1st, 1831, MARY NEWTON, who died in 1836.

He married, 2d, 1837, ELIZABETH DEAN.

CHILDREN;—BY THE FIRST MARRIAGE.

1. *Emeline,* b. 1833; m. 1851, Charles Landfear; has two children.
2. *Caroline,* b. 1835.

CHILDREN;—BY THE SECOND MARRIAGE.

3. *Mary E.,* b. 1839.
4. *Ann E.,* b. 1841.
5. *Elvira E.,* b. 1846.

472. JOSHUA HAZEN WHITE, son of Noadiah, (278) was born in Hartford, Vt., March 26, 1810. He was a farmer, and in 1853 removed to Lockport, Ill., where he died in 1854, æ. 44.

He married, 1st, 1833, HELEN BEMAN, of Hiram, Portage Co., O., who died in 1849.

He married, 2d, 1849, Sophronia Daily.

CHILDREN;—BY THE FIRST MARRIAGE.

1. *Wealthy J.*, b.   1834 ; m. 1854, Ephraim W. Moss, and has one son and one daughter.
2. *Harriet H.*, b.   1837 ; m. 1854, Edward Kirkham.
3. *Noadiah E.*, b.   1839.
4. *Emily C.*, } b.   1841.
5. *Eunice P.*, }   Twins.

CHILD;—BY THE SECOND MARRIAGE.

6. *Mary*,   b.   1850.

---

473. **John D. White**, son of Noadiah, (278) was born in Hartford, Vt., Oct. 15, 1813. In 1845 he settled in Whitesville, Andrew Co., Mo., and in 1857 removed to San Jose, Santa Clara Co., Cal., where he now resides. He is a farmer.

He married, April 24, 1834, Charlotte Hunt, of Hiram, Ohio, born Jan. 9, 1816, dau. of Lyman Hunt and Laura Loveland.

CHILDREN.

1. *Lyman A.*, b. Dec. 27, 1835 ; m. Feb. 5, 1857.
2. *Laura M.*, b. May 23, 1839 ; m. Aug. 31, 1854.
3. *Amelia A.*, b. Feb. 16, 1844.
4. *Francis I.*, b. Jan.   7, 1849 ; d. Sept. 30, 1851.
5. *Cora R.*, b. April 12, 1850 ; d. Aug. 16, 1852.
6. *Sanders A.*, b. Feb. 14, 1853.
7. *Amos O.*, b. Jan. 16, 1857.

---

474. **Richard W. White**, son of Noadiah, (278) was born in Hartford, Vt., in 1820. He is a farmer in Garrettsville, Ohio.

He married, 1845, Elizabeth Heath.

CHILDREN.

1. *Azubah*,   b.   1846.   5. *Lydia P.*,   b.   1855.
2. *Richard Noadiah*,   b.   1849.   6. *John C. Fremont*, b.   1856.
3. *Wealthy Sophronia*, b.   1851.   7. *Albert H.*,   b.   1858.
4. *Frank A.*,   b.   1853.

---

475. **Amos White**, son of Noadiah, (278) was born in Hartford, Vt., April 11, 1823. He is a farmer in San Jose, Santa Clara Co., Cal.

He married, July 30, 1846, Laura Hunt, of Hiram, O., born Jan. 4, 1824, dau. of Lyman Hunt and Laura Loveland.

CHILDREN.

1. *Ella Jane,* b. May 25, 1850.
2. *Frances Ann,* b. March 21, 1855.
3. *Clara Louisa,* b. July 2, 1856.
4. *Laura Eunice,* b. Dec. 2, 1857.
5. *Lydia Martena,* b. Jan. 10, 1859.

---

476. SYLVESTER WHITE, son of Amos, (279) was born in Williamson, Wayne Co., N. Y., Dec. 18, 1813. He is a farmer in Wheatland, Hillsdale Co., Mich.

He married, Jan., 1841, ROXANA RICE, and has,

1. *Sarah Eunice,* b. Jan., 1842.
2. *Lois Emma,* b. May, 1844.

---

477. ABIJAH WHITE, son of Amos, (279) was born in Williamson, N. Y., Dec. 3, 1818, and resides there.

He married, MARIETTE SNYDER, and has,

1. *Merret D.*
2. *Harriet Elizabeth.*

---

478. EVELYN WHITE, son of David, jun., (285) was born in Chatham, in the present town of Portland, Conn., July 13, 1806. He resides in Portland, and is master of a propeller.

He married, Nov. 26, 1828, FRANCES E. PENFIELD.

CHILDREN.

1. *Delia Maria,* b. Feb. 21, 1830.
2. *Frances Emma,* b. Sept. 8, 1832; m. May 18, 1851, Knowles H. Taylor of Portland, and has Emma White, b. Oct. 17, 1853.
3. *Arabella,* b. July 2, 1835; m. Dec. 31, 1856, Joseph Oliver Willcox of Portland, and has, 1. Frances Elizabeth, b. Sept. 17, 1857; 2. Charles Oliver, b. July 27, 1859.
4. *Abigail,* b. July 28, 1840.
5. *Charles Homer,* b. Oct. 4, 1842.

---

479. GEORGE COSSITT WHITE, son of Stephen, (288) was born in Granby, Conn., Aug. 10, 1816. He was formerly connected in business with his brother, in Rome, N. Y.; is now a merchant in Milwaukee, Wis.

He married, June 19, 1849, SARAH MARIA COSSITT, of Granby, Conn., dau. of Asa Cossitt, jun., and Rachel Steel.

CHILDREN.

1. *Frederic Henry,* b. June 16, 1850.
2. *George Cossitt,* b. Aug. 14, 1852.
3. *Sarah Lavinia,* b. Aug. 14, 1854.
4. *Stephen,* b. Jan. 4, 1858.
5. *William Pearl,* b. Jan. 26, 1859.

480. Matthew H. White, son of William Czar, (289) was born Aug. 24, 1819. He is a farmer in Sheridan, Mich.

He married, March, 1849, Victoria Lyman, and has,

1. *Junius,* b. Sept.,   1850.   2. *Lucretia,* b. Jan. 17, 1853.

---

481. Luther White, son of Samuel, (293) was born in Upper Middletown, Conn., April 5, 1807. He is a blacksmith, and is said to be living in Dover, Ohio.

He married Emily Phelps of Rocky Hill, Conn., and has,

1. *Edward.*   2. *Eugene.*

---

482. Heman White, son of Samuel, (293) was born in Upper Middletown, March 5, 1811. He was a merchant in Montgomery, Ala., until about three years previous to his death. He died April 8, 1852, æ. 41.

He married, 1st, July 7, 1835, Caroline Atwood of Berlin, Conn., who died July 18, 1841, æ. 28.

He married, 2d, Oct. 17, 1842, Catharine C. Mallory of Bristol, Conn., dau. of Ransom and Lucy Mallory.

CHILDREN ;—BY THE FIRST MARRIAGE.

1. *Caroline A.,*   b. June 8, 1837 ; d. in Meriden, Conn., June 1, 1856, æ. 19.
2. *Heman Montgomery,* b. Aug. 17, 1840.

CHILDREN ;—BY THE SECOND MARRIAGE.

3. *Ransom S.,*   b. Aug. 14, 1843 ; d. June 4, 1844.
4. *Ransom M.,*   b. Nov. 4, 1844 ; d. Aug. 29, 1845.
5. *Lucy J.,*   b. July 24, 1846.
6. *Emma N.,*   b. April 3, 1850 ; d. Nov. 24, 1850.

---

483. Samuel White, Jun., son of Samuel, (293) was born in Sharon, Conn., May 8, 1813. He is a farmer in Wolcott, Wayne Co., N. Y.

He married Almira Brooks, of Romulus, N. Y.

CHILDREN.

1. *Charles A.,* b.   1835.   3. *Emily.*
2. *Henry H.,* b. Nov., 1836.   4. *Ellagene.*

---

484. Henry S. White, son of Samuel, (293) was born in Upper Middletown, July 17, 1822. He is a mechanic in Wallingford, Conn.

He married, Oct. 17, 1844, Susan M. Couch of Meriden, Conn., dau. of Beri and Susan M. Couch.

CHILDREN.

1. *Susan E.*, b. March 9, 1846.   3. *Emma R.*, b. Feb. 10, 1855.
2. *Elbridge H.*, b. Jan. 16, 1848.

---

485. TIMOTHY WHITE, son of Samuel, (293) was born in Upper Middletown, Nov. 2, 1824. He is a mechanic in Forestville, Conn.

He married, Aug. 2, 1847, CAROLINE E. COWLES, of Cheshire, Conn., dau. of Juba Cowles.

CHILDREN.

1. *Cornelia E.*, b. Dec. 23, 1848.
2. *Garry H.*, b. Aug. 31, 1852.
3. *Flora E.*, b. July 31, 1845.

---

486. EDGAR WHITE, son of Hon. Fortune Clark, (297) was born in Whitestown, N. Y., Oct. 3, 1820. He is a farmer in Port Huron, St. Clair Co., Mich., and is Mayor of the city.

He married, Aug. 20, 1850, ADELIA JONES, of Ann Arbor, Mich., born Sept. 24, 1831, dau. of James Jones and Eliza Benham.

CHILDREN.

1. *Charles Patten*, b. May   4, 1852.
2. *Carrie Esther*, b. March 30, 1857.

---

487. JAMES HILLHOUSE WHITE, son of Hon. Fortune Clark, (297) was born in Whitestown, April 28, 1822. He is a farmer in Port Huron, Mich., and is sheriff of St. Clair County.

He married, 1st, April 6, 1843, ALICE M. WETMORE, who died May 4, 1844.

He married, 2d, May 25, 1847, CHARLOTTE H. TOMPKINS, of Wolcott, Wayne Co., N. Y., dau. of Nathaniel W. Tompkins and Bethiah Hubbard.

By the second marriage he has one son,

Nathaniel C., b. April 2, 1848.

---

488. Dr. HENRY RANDOLPH WHITE, son of Hon. Fortune Clark, (297) was born in Whitestown, April 23, 1824. He is a physician in Utica, N. Y.

He married, April 16, 1856, SARAH BRUCE CLARK, of Madison, N. Y.

489. Jonas Autle White, son of Jonas, (302) was born in Whitestown, N. Y., July 25, 1815, and is a farmer there.

He married, May 27, 1843, Almira H. Foote, of Sherburne, Chenango Co., N. Y., born Feb. 22, 1819, dau. of Asa and Elizabeth Foote.

CHILDREN.

1. *Louisa Amelia*,   b. Jan.   7, 1845; d. April 24, 1849.
2. *Louisa Amelia*,   b. March 22, 1850.
3. *William Stratton*, b. Nov.   18, 1855.
4. *Elizabeth Foote*,   b. July   13, 1857.

490. Morris Pratt White, son of Jonas, (302) was born in Whitestown, April 26, 1817. He is a farmer in Columbus, Chenango Co., N. Y.

He married, Feb. 17, 1847, Julia A. Jones of Columbus, dau. of Isaac Jones. He has one child,

Mary Frances, b. Nov. 30, 1847.

491. Lewis White, son of Jonas, (302) was born in Whitestown, April 30, 1819. He is a machinist, and resides in New Hartford, Oneida Co., N. Y.

He married May 16, 1848, Ambrosia Lamb of Columbus, N. Y., dau. of Joshua Lamb.

492. George Manchester White, son of Jonas, (302) was born in Whitestown, July 30, 1825, and died there, May 27, 1851, æ. 25. He was a machinist.

He married, Sept. 6, 1849, Submit Bliss of Whitestown, dau. of Nathan Bliss, and had one daughter,   .

Esther, b. Dec. 12, 1850.

493. Henry H. White, son of Capt. Aaron Clark, (308) was born in New Haven, Conn., April 19, 1821. He is a bookseller in that place.

He married, Dec. 24, 1844, Nannie Gerard, and has,

1. *James.*   2. *William.*   3. *Henry.*

494. Joel White, son of John, jun., (310) was born April 8, 1803. He is a farmer in Oxford, Conn. He has been for several years a justice of the peace, has held town offices, was a Representative from Oxford in 1846, and a member of the State Senate in 1851.

He married, Dec. 8, 1825, EMMA FRENCH of Bethany, dau. of David and Anna French.

CHILDREN.

1. *Mary*, b. Nov. 15, 1829; m. Nov. 26, 1846, S. W. S. Skilton of Watertown, Conn., now of Morris, Conn. She has had, 1. William S., b. Aug., 1847, d. Oct., 1849; 2. Joel W., b. Feb., 1851, d. æ. 8 days; 3. Truman Smith, b. June 6, 1853; 4. Joel White, b. Nov. 16, 1858.
2. *Emma*, b. Feb. 5, 1834; m. April 23, 1850, Milo D. Northrup of Tyringham, Mass., now of Oxford, Conn. She has Mary, b. Oct. 22, 1857.

---

495. ELISHA WHITE, son of John, jun., (310) was born in Woodbridge, Conn., April 5, 1805. He resides in Auburn, Cayuga Co., N. Y., where he has held offices of trust. Is a carpenter and builder.

He married, March 4, 1830, EMELINE CHAPMAN, of Marcellus, Onondaga Co., N. Y., dau. of Dr. Elisha Chapman and Phebe Gates.

CHILDREN.

1. *Herbert*, b. Aug. 14, 1835; d. Dec. 16, 1849, æ. 14.
2. *John E.*, b. Aug. 30, 1837.   4. *Arthur*, b. Dec. 12, 1843.
3. *William C.*, b. Aug. 17, 1839.   5. *Elisha*, b. Feb. 3, 1846.

---

496. WILLIAM C. WHITE, son of John, jun., (310) was born Nov. 15, 1817. He is a farmer in Bethany, Conn.

He married, Dec. 24, 1844, HARRIET PRINCE of Bethany, dau. of Abel and Fanny Prince. He has one daughter,

H. May, b. 1845.

496a. ISAAC WHITE, son of Daniel, (311) was born in Derby, Conn., Sept. 25, 1811. He is a farmer in Easton, Conn.

He married, Jan. 11, 1835, SARAH GRACE KENNEY of Derby, born May 13, 1814, dau. of William Kenney and Anna Smith.

CHILDREN.

1. *Helen M.*, b. Dec. 27, 1835.   4. *William E.*, b. Nov. 12, 1843.
2. *Elizabeth A.*, b. May 4, 1838.   5. *George M.*, b. May 20, 1848.
3. *Frances J.*, b. Dec. 19, 1840.

---

497. EDWARD WHITE, son of Raymond B., (313) was born in Plymouth, Conn., in 1824. He is a shoemaker there.

He married, 1847, MARY ANN SWEET of New Haven, Conn.

CHILDREN.

1. *William Raymond*, b.   1848.
2. *Eva Estella*,   b. April,   1854 ; d. June, 1855.
3. *Ella Louisa*,   b. July 2, 1856.
4. *Mary Isabel*,   b. May,   1859.

498. GEORGE WHITE, son of Raymond B., (313) was born in Plymouth, Conn., Sept. 8, 1833. He is a carpenter, and resides in Winsted, Conn.

He married, Sept. 25, 1855, LOVINA AMELIA DOWNES, born in Plymouth, Oct. 14, 1830, dau. of Samuel Downes and Harriet Andrews.

CHILDREN.

1. *Harriet Andrews*, b. Sept. 2, 1856.
2. *Frances Adelaide*, b. Jan. 26, 1859 ; d. March 28, 1859.

499. DANIEL D. TOMPKINS WHITE, son of Truman, (315) was born March 22, 1807. He is a farmer.

He married, 1831, ALMA WILBUR.

CHILDREN.

1. *Jane.*   4. *Truman.*
2. *Paulina.*   5. *Erwin.*
3. *Adeline.*   Five others died young.

500. JOEL CLARK WHITE, son of Truman, (315) was born Jan. 31, 1817, and died Sept. 11, 1850, æ. 33.

He married, 1st, 1841, MARY E. LAKE.

He married, 2d, MARY A. DE FOREST.

CHILDREN.

1. *Wesley.*   3. *A daughter*, d. æ. 4 yrs.
2. *Manley.*

501. HUBBARD TUTHILL WHITE, son of Truman, (315) was born June 7, 1819. He is a boot and shoe dealer in Buffalo, N. Y.

He married, March 24, 1846, CATHARINE TRUMBULL.

CHILDREN.

1. *A child*, b.   ; d. in infancy.   3. *Mary*, b.   1854.
2. *Eliza*, b.   1849.

502. CHARLES BURT WHITE, son of Truman, (315) was born Aug. 30, 1826. He resides in Illinois.

He married, March 23, 1851, MARIETTE CANADA, and has,

Hubbard.

503. BALDWIN T. WHITE, son of Truman, (315) was born Jan. 15, 1828.

He married LOUISA MACE, and has had,

1. *Charles.*
2. *Harriet.*
3. *Mary,* d. in infancy.
4. *Caroline,* d. in infancy.

504. ISAAC WHITE, son of Francis, (316) was born Feb. 7, 1810. He resides in Machias, Cattaraugus Co., N. Y.

He married ANNA SMITH of Brantford, C. W.

CHILDREN.

1. *Lucinda.*
2. *James.*
3. *Marava.*
4. *Chauncey.*
5. *Samuel.*

505. JACOB WHITE, son of Francis, (316) was born Feb. 6, 1812. He resides in Otto, Cattaraugus Co., N. Y.

He married ALVIRA TARBOX, and has,

1. *Francis.*
2. *Martha.*
3. *Alvira.*

506. RODERICK WHITE, Esq., son of Francis, (316) was born June 23, 1814. He was a lawyer in Olean, Cattaraugus Co., N. Y., and was elected a Representative in the Legislature in 1845, and a Senator in 1855. He died May 26, 1856, æ. 42.

He married SARAH NICHOLS.

CHILDREN.

1. *Emma.*
2. *Henry.*
3. *Ella.*
4. *Willis.*
5. *George.*
6. *Anna.*

507. JUSTUS WHITE, Esq., son of Francis, (316) was born Aug. 6, 1827. He is a lawyer in Olean, N. Y.

He married MARY J. HILL, and has a daughter,

Mary, b. Oct., 1858.

508. HIRAM W. WHITE, son of Moses, (317) is a gunsmith and hardware dealer in Jackson, Jackson Co., Ohio.

He married, March 27, 1840, ROSE ANN STEWART.

CHILDREN.

1. *Sarah Frances,* b. March 28, 1841.
2. *Almira,*   b. Feb. 28, 1844 ; d. April 25, 1846.
3. *Henry Kirke,* b. June   2, 1847 ; d. Jan. 10, 1849.
4. *Avon Lafayette,* b. Oct. 30, 1849 ; d. April 25, 1853.
5. *Hiram Wallace,* b. Oct. 12, 1853.
6. *A daughter,*   b. June   1, 1858.

509. LEONARD WHITE, son of Roderick, (318) was born in Paris, (now Kirkland,) Oneida Co., N. Y., May 30, 1817. He is a carpenter, and resides in Cazenovia, Madison Co., N. Y.

He married, Oct. 10, 1838, CLARISSA CONE of Paris, N. Y., born Aug. 19, 1817, dau. of Caleb Cone.

CHILDREN.

1. *Clarissa*, b. Jan. 17, 1840.
2. *Roderick*, b. Dec. 14, 1841.
3. *Huldah*, b. Oct. 12, 1843.
4. *Oscar*, b. July 20, 1845.
5. *Ossian*, b. June 7, 1847.

510. Rev. MOSES CLARK WHITE, M. D., son of Roderick, (318) was born in Paris, N. Y., July 24, 1819. He graduated at Wesleyan University, Middletown, Conn., in 1845, and from 1847 to 1852 was a Missionary of the Methodist Episcopal Church, in Fuhchau, China, where he labored both as a preacher and as a physician. In 1853 he returned to the United States, on account of impaired health, and is now a physician in New Haven, Conn. He received the degree of M. D. at Yale College in 1854.

He married, 1st, March 13, 1847, JANE ISABEL ATWATER, of Homer, Cortland Co., N. Y., dau. of Ezra Atwater. She died in Fuhchau, China, May 25, 1848, æ. 25.

He married, 2d, at Fuhchau, July 14, 1851, MARY SEELY, born May 13, 1821, dau. of Joseph Owen Seely of Onondaga, N. Y.

CHILDREN ;—BY THE SECOND MARRIAGE.

1. *George,* b. May 24, 1852; d. May, 25, 1852.
2. *Caryl Fenelon Seely,* b. April 5, 1856.

510a. AARON WHITE, son of Roderick, (318) was born in Paris, N. Y., Sept. 18, 1824. He graduated at Wesleyan University in 1852, and is Professor of Mathematics in Oneida Conference Seminary, at Cazenovia, N. Y.

He married, April 6, 1859, ISADORE MARIA HAIGHT of Cazenovia, dau. of William Henry Haight.

511. JOSEPH WHITE, son of Roderick, (318) was born in Paris, N. Y., April 10, 1827, and resides there. He is a joiner.

He married, April, 1853, SUSAN E. BEEBE, and has,

1. *Andrew Curtis*, b. Nov. 25, 1854.
2. *Albert Terry*, b. July 10, 1856.

512. WILLIAM WHITE, son of Almer, (320) was born April
5, 1828.

He married, July 3, 1853, CORDELIA HAMMOND, and has,

1. *Almer,* b. Aug. 11, 1854.   2. *Clark,* b. Aug. 25, 1856.

---

513. ALVERSE L. WHITE, son of James, jun., (321) was born
in Newport, N. H., July 31, 1811. He is a merchant in Boston, Mass.

He married, May, 1844, MARY COLE of Biddeford, Me.

CHILDREN.

1. *Mary Alice,*   b.   ; d. æ. 18 mos.
2. *George Alverse,* b. Jan. 22, 1849.

---

514. ROBERT CORNELL WHITE, son of Robert, (324) was
born in Birmingham, Eng., Nov. 1, 1823. He is a crockery
merchant in New York; resides in Brooklyn.

He married, Nov. 4, 1847, HANNAH D. BAKER, born Jan.
17, 1826, dau. of Dobel Baker and Mary Corlies.

CHILDREN.

1. *Henry Haydock,* b. Sept. 13, 1848.
2. *Sara Baker,*   b. June 2, 1851.
3. *Joseph Baker,*   b. June 15, 1854.
4. *Cornelia,*   b. Feb. 1, 1859.

---

515. RICHARD GRANT WHITE, Esq., son of Richard Mansfield, (325) was born in New York, May 23, 1821. He graduated at the University of New York in 1839, studied med-
icine and law, and was admitted to the bar in 1845. He
soon abandoned law for letters, and was connected with the
New York Courier and Enquirer, from 1845 to 1858, with a
brief interval, at first as critic of art and literature, but for
the last five years as editor. He is also an author, and a regular contributor to the Atlantic Magazine. Besides other
works, he has published "Shakespeare's Scholar," in 1854;
his edition of Shakespeare, 1857-9; and an Essay upon Henry
the Sixth, in 1859. He is now living, temporarily, at Ravens-
wood, L. I.

· He married, Oct. 16, 1850, ALEXINA BLACK MAESE of New
York, dau. of Charles Bruton Maese and Sarah Graham.

CHILDREN.

1. *Richard Mansfield,* b. Dec. 25, 1851.
2. *Stanford,*   b. Nov. 9, 1853.

515*a.* CARLETON WHITE, son of Moses, (326) was born May 11, 1834.

He married, Nov. 11, 1857, LIZZIE H. DUNN, and has a son,

Denton Dunn, b. May 6, 1859.

516. SAMUEL HOWES WHITE, son of Henry Champlin, (332) was born April 21, 1836. He resides in Hartford, Conn.

He married, Sept. 3, 1857, CECILIA AUGUSTA STILLMAN of Hartford, dau. of Allyn S. Stillman and Cecilia Andrus.

He has one daughter,

Mary Cecilia, b. Aug. 23, 1858.

IN THE LINE OF JACOB WHITE, OF MIDDLETOWN.

517. NORMAN BRIGHAM WHITE, son of Jonathan Porter, (335) lives in New York.

He married EVELINE GILBERT of Hartford, Conn., and has,

1. *Samuel P.*   2. *Norman B.*   3. *A daughter.*

518. HARRISON WHITE, son of Chester, (336) was born Sept. 21, 1816. He is a merchant in Albion, Mich.

He married SARAH DUNN, and has,

1. *William.*   2. *Thomas.*   3. *Emma.*   4. *Caroline.*

519. ALONZO WHITE, son of Ransom Coe, (341) was born in Burke, Vt., Nov. 2, 1830.

He married, Nov. 9, 1851, HULDAH L. HOSFORD of East Haven, Vt., and has,

1. *Herbert A.,* b. April 10, 1857.   2. *Helen A.,* b. Feb. 23, 1859.

520. GEORGE HENRY WHITE, son of John, (353) was born July 5, 1815. He is a carpenter in Fredonia, N. Y.

He married, Oct. 15, 1846, MARY SOPHIA TOBEY, of Hudson, N. Y., born Sept. 9, 1826, dau. of Henry Tobey and Sophia Hulburt.

CHILDREN.

1. *Emily S.,* b. Feb 18, 1848.   3. *Nehemiah B.,* b. Dec. 29, 1855.
2. *George H.,* b. July 14, 1850.   4. *Caroline J.,* b. Sept. 29, 1858.

521. NEHEMIAH BASSETT WHITE, son of John, (353) was born Dec. 24, 1816. He is a merchant in Monticello, Ga.

He married, 1st, Dec. 22, 1854, Mrs. ANN H. NEWMAN, widow of Joseph Newman; originally Ann H. Catlin, of Harwinton, Conn. She died July 10, 1856.

He married, 2d, Oct. 28, 1858, HARRIET N. SCOVEL of Albany, N. Y., dau. of Ashley Scovel and Ann L. Leland.

By the second marriage he has one son,

Ashley S., b. July 13, 1859.

---

522. RUSSELL M. WHITE, son of John, (353) was born March 31, 1819. He is a carpenter in Albany, N. Y.

He married, Jan. 20, 1842, CAROLINE B. FARNSWORTH of Albany, dau. of Rufus Farnsworth and Lavina Blanchard. He has,

1. *Addison F.*, b. June 3, 1844.   2. *Russell M.*, b. Sept. 30, 1853.

---

523. LINUS WHITE, son of John, (353) was born July 29, 1824. He is a merchant in Atalanta, Ga.

He married, Feb. 13, 1855, MARY SERVER of Albany, N. Y., dau. of Robert Server and Mary Ann Buckbee. He has had,

1. *Mary Grace*, b. Jan. 18, 1856; d. Nov. 5, 1857.
2. *Emma S.*,   b. July 8, 1858.

---

524. WILLIAM SAGE WHITE, son of Jacob, (354) was born in Upper Middletown, now Cromwell, Conn., July 22, 1816. He is a lumber merchant in Hartford, Conn.

He married MARY SAVAGE of Middletown, born July 17, 1819, dau. of Samuel Savage and Mary Haling.

CHILDREN.

1. *Frederick William*, b. July 1, 1838; m. Jan. 6, 1859, Sarah E. Adams of Wethersfield, Conn., b. 1839, dau. of William Adams and Sarah Crane.
2. *Leverett Henry*,   b. May 5, 1840; is in the U. S. Navy.
3. *Charles Austin*,   b. Aug. 24, 1843.
4. *Edward Emerick*,   b. Oct. 6, 1846; d. Nov. 16, 1847.
5. *Albert*,   b. Jan. 28, 1852; d. March 11, 1852.
6. *Isabel Gertrude*,   b. Oct. 8, 1858.

---

525. HENRY S. WHITE, son of Jacob, (354) was born in Cromwell, Feb. 12, 1818. He is a manufacturer in Middletown.

He married, Dec. 31, 1848, CATHARINE CHANDLER, of Montgomery, N. Y., born April 4, 1822, dau. of Charles Chandler.

He has one son,

Henry Chandler, b. Sept. 28, 1853.

---

526. LUTHER CHAPIN WHITE, son of Jacob, (354) was born in Sandisfield, Mass., Dec. 25, 1821. He is a manufacturer in Waterbury, Conn.

He married, Nov. 28, 1844, JANE AMELIA MOSES, born in Waterbury, July 19, 1825, dau. of Joseph and Mary Moses.

CHILDREN.

1. *William Henry*, b. May   7, 1847.
2. *George Luther*, b. July   15, 1852.
3. *Harriet Susan*, b. March 4, 1854.

---

527. JACOB WATSON WHITE, son of Jacob, (354) was born in Sandisfield, Mass., Sept. 19, 1827. He is a manufacturer in Waterbury, Conn.

He married, Sept. 19, 1850, ANNA ELIZA WELLS of Hartford, born May 7, 1828, dau. of Chauncey and Hannah K. Wells.

CHILDREN.

1. *Chauncey Wells*,   b. May   12, 1852 ; d. Dec. 11, 1852.
2. *Edward Luther*,   b. Dec.   12, 1853.
3. *Chauncey Howard*,   b. March 24, 1856.
4. *Anna Sophia*,   b. Sept. 20, 1858.

DESCENDANTS OF JOHN WHITE, JUNIOR.

528. BENJAMIN WHITE, son of Dan, (359) was born in 1811. He was a carriage maker; lived in Michigan, and died Dec. 18, 1853, æ. 43.

He married ESTHER NOYES of Michigan.

CHILDREN.

1. *James.*   3. *Ellen.*
2. *Miron.*   4. *Edward.*

---

529. ALONZO WHITE, son of Dan, (359) was born in Rome, N. Y., in 1816. He is a carpenter in Kenosha, Wis.

He married, 1844, LYDIA B. LEONARD.

CHILDREN.

1. *Edward*,   b. 1845 ; d. 1848.   3. *Edgar*,   b. 1848.
2. *Charles B.*, b. 1846 ; d. 1856.   4. *Florence H.*, b. 1857.

---

530. FRANCIS WHITE, son of Dan, (359) was born in Rome, N. Y., in 1818. He is a carpenter in Kenosha, Wis.

He married, 1st, 1846, SARAH WHITMORE, who died in 1848.
He married, 2d, 1849, JENETTE MOORE, and has one son,
Francis, b. 1858.

---

531. JOSHUA WHITE, son of Dan, (359) was born in Rome,
N. Y., in 1830. Is a carpenter in Kenosha, Wis.
He married, 1854, MARGARETTE WORTH, and has,
Caroline M., b. 1856.

---

532. ASA J. WHITE, son of Asa, (361) was born Sept. 13,
1818. He is a farmer, and has lived in Brookfield, Mass.
He married, July 4, 1846, PRUDENCE GALLOP of Brookfield,
born in 1819.

CHILDREN.

1. *Hannah*, b. July 9, 1847.	4. *Joseph G.*, b. 1853.
2. *Ira B.*, b. 1849.	5. *Myron Munson*, b. 1858.
3. *Frances*, b. 1851.	

---

533. GEORGE W. WHITE, son of Asa, (361) was born Feb.
3, 1824. He is a farmer in Potsdam, N. Y.
He married, March 4, 1846, SUSAN BOODY, of Pierpont, St.
Lawrence, Co., N. Y., born May 29, 1824. He has,
1. *Charles A.*, b. March 25, 1848.   2. *Mary Jane*, b. Feb. 1, 1854.

DESCENDANTS OF LIEUT. DANIEL WHITE.

534. Rev. ERSKINE NORMAN WHITE, son of Norman, (404)
was born in New York, May 31, 1833. He graduated at Yale
College in 1854, and at Union Theological Seminary in 1857,
and was ordained pastor of the Reformed Dutch Church at
Richmond, Staten Island, N. Y., June 9, 1859.
He married, May 24, 1859, ELIZA TRACY NELSON, of New
York, born Oct. 5, 1836, dau. of John G. Nelson and Eunice
Ripley.

---

535. CHARLES TRUMBULL WHITE, son of Norman, (404) was
born in New York, Jan. 20, 1835. He is a merchant in New
York.
He married, Sept. 30, 1857, GEORGIANNA STARIN, of Auburn,
N. Y., born Sept. 25, 1837, dau. of Josiah N. Starin and Anda-
lusia Henry. He has one son,
Norman, b. July 10, 1858.

536. HEMAN WHITE, son of Hanford, (407) was born in Twinsburg, Ohio, March 23, 1827. He is a farmer in Hopkins, Allegan Co., Mich.

He married, Jan. 1, 1855, JANE BUSKIRK, and has,

Franklin Fremont, b. March, 1858.

---

537. JAMES WHITE, son of Oliver, jun., (420) was born April 9, 1818. He lives in Winsted, Conn.

He married CHARLOTTE ANN GREENE of Cornwall, Conn., born Dec. 20, 1824, dau. of William Greene and Mary Wentworth.

CHILDREN.

1. *Ann Janette*, b. Jan. 1, 1841; d. April 18, 1841.
2. *Sarah Amelia*, b. March, 1844.
3. *Mary Pamelia*, b. Aug. 21, 1855.

---

538. LUMAN WHITE, son of Oliver, jun., (420) was born July 19, 1819, and lives in Winsted, Conn.

He married, July 5, 1841, SAREPTA JANE REYNOLDS, of Chatham, Columbia Co., N. Y., born Jan. 23, 1822, dau. of Jacob Reynolds and Polly Olds.

CHILDREN.

1. *Henrietta*, b. Jan. 23, 1843.
2. *Henry Clay*, b. Jan. 29, 1845.
3. *A child*, b. Aug. 29, 1849; d. Sept. 18, 1849.

---

539. Rev. ORRIN WASHINGTON WHITE, son of Oliver, jun., (420) was born April 5, 1821. He graduated at Oberlin College in 1848, and at the Theological Seminary in Oberlin, in 1854, and is a Congregational minister at Strongsville, Cuyahoga Co., Ohio.

He married, 1st, Aug. 23, 1848, LUCY STRONG LOVEJOY, of Oberlin, O., dau. of W. Lovejoy and Lydia Strong. She died Sept. 25, 1856.

He married, 2d, Sept. 6, 1857, PERLINA L. POPE, born July 16, 1834, dau. of Philander Pope and Lucy Pomeroy.

CHILDREN;—BY THE FIRST MARRIAGE.

1. *Orrin Kendal*, b. Feb. 23, 1854; d. Sept. 27, 1855.
2. *A child*, b. Sept. 14, 1856; d. Sept. 23, 1856.

36

540. WILSON BACON WHITE, son of Oliver, jun., (420) was born Jan. 24, 1823, and lives in Winsted, Conn.

He married, Dec. 26, 1847, HARRIET LEACH.

CHILDREN.

1. *Josephine,* b. April 18, 1850.
2. *Wilbur,* b. May 4, 1854.

---

541. GEORGE WHITE, son of Oliver, jun., (420) was born June 4, 1825. He is a mechanic in West Winsted, Conn.

He married, Aug. 5, 1850, ELLEN MARIA KELSEY of Winsted, born Jan. 15, 1831, dau. of Joseph Kelsey and Lucy Marsh.

CHILDREN.

1. *Mary Elizabeth,* b. Jan. 15, 1853.
2. *Ellen Augusta,* b. May 28, 1857.

APPENDIX.

J. Extracts from Records at Chelmsford, England.*

THE Registers of Wills, and the Parish Registers of births, marriages and deaths, in England, about the time of the first settlement of this country, are the principal sources of information respecting the pedigree of such American families as are descended from the middle classes of the mother country. Every extract from these Registers has, therefore, a value to the American genealogist, and is worth preserving in a permanent form. With this view, the following extracts from the Registers of Chelmsford, in Essex County, in old England, are here inserted. They were obtained by H. G. SOMERBY, Esq., the well-known and successful investigator of the English genealogies of American families, with the hope of finding in them some trace of the lineage of the patriarch, John White, who is commemorated in the preceding pages. Although the effort was not successful for this object, yet it is hoped that these materials may be valuable to other families of the name of White.

FROM THE REGISTRY OF WILLS, AT CHELMSFORD.

Thomas White of Chelmsford, vintner. Will dated January 28, 160⅘: proved March 16, 160⅘. He gives to his eldest son, Thomas, £40, when 24 years of age: to his daughter, Anne, £30, when 21 years of age. His son John to be bound apprentice to brother Bartholomew White, tailor. He had brothers John and George; a sister Elizabeth; an uncle George Solme.

---

* This part of the Appendix has been prepared and furnished by HENRY WHITE, Esq., of New Haven, Conn., who procured the examination of these records to be made.

FROM THE PARISH REGISTER OF CHELMSFORD.

The Register begins in 1538. Occasional chasms occur, of whole years, before 1600.

BAPTISMS.

1540, May 12.	John,	son of William and Agnes White.
1542, Aug. 2.	Mary,	dau. of William and Agnes White.
1545, July 10.	William,	son of Nicholas White.
$154\frac{5}{6}$, Mar. 22.	Thomas,	son of Edmund White.
$154\frac{4}{5}\frac{9}{0}$, Mar. 23.	Jesper,	son of Edmund White.
$155\frac{1}{2}$, Jan. 17.	Ione,	dau. of Edmund White.
1555, April 2.	Bridget,	dau. of Edmund White.
1565, April 23.	Agnes,	dau. of Edmund White.
1579, July 11.	John,	son of William White.
$15\frac{8}{8}\frac{0}{1}$, —— —.	Susan,	dau. of William White.
1582, Nov. 18.	Marion,	dau. of William White.
1584, Nov. 10.	Richard,	son of William White.
$158\frac{5}{6}$, Feb. 20.	Joan,	dau. of William White.
$158\frac{6}{7}$, Mar. 6.	Thomas,	son of William White.
1588, June 17.	Joan,	dau. of John White.
$158\frac{7}{8}$, Mar. 8.	William,	son of William White.
1589, July 29.	George,	son of John White.
1590, Sept. 29.	Thomas,	son of John White.
1594, Aug. 13.	Joan,	dau. of Thomas White.
1595, Dec. 13.	Thomas White.	
$159\frac{5}{6}$, Mar. 14.	Elizabeth White.	
$159\frac{6}{7}$, Feb. 6.	John,	son of Thomas White.
1599, Oct. 21.	Anne,	dau. of Thomas White.
1609, Aug 13.	Mary,	dau. of William White, cooper.
$16\frac{11}{12}$, Jan. 12.	John,	son of William White, cooper.
$16\frac{13}{14}$, Jan. 1.	Elizabeth,	dau. of William White, cooper.
1616, July 28.	Thomas,	son of Thomas White.
1616, Sept. 8.	William,	son of William White, cooper.
1619, Nov. 21.	Isaac,	son of Thomas White of Chelmsford, matmaker, and Anne his wife.
1621, Nov. 12.	Jane,	dau. of Thomas White of Chelmsford, matmaker, and Anne his wife.
1622, July 16.	Clemence,	dau. of Francis White of Moulsham, tailor, and Clements his wife.
1624, Oct. 28.	Helen,	dau. of Thomas White of Chelmsford, and Anne his wife.
1630, Nov. 19.	Thomas,	son of Thomas White of Chelmsford, vintner, and Joan his wife.

MARRIAGES.

1542, Nov. 12. William White, grocer, to Anne Harris.
1559, Jan. 19. Edmund White to Mary Lamb: (both strangers.)
1561, Nov. 19. John White to Bridget Johnson.
1573, May 17. William White to Margaret Pease.
1587, July 3. Thomas White to Ellen Mendbam.
1592, Sept. 3. John White to Agnes Scraston.
1593, Sept. 23. Thomas White to Anne Bachelor.
1595, May 5. William White to Anne Dinglie.
1595, July 15. Thomas White to Alice Dump of London.
1598, June 6. Thomas White to Elizabeth Smith: (strangers.)

II. Corrections and Additions.

Page 101, line 1, for Josiah Allis, read Elijah Allis.
Page 101, line 2, for (see Fam. 174), read (see Fam. 194.)
Page 162, line 37, for (376), read (375).
Page 259, line 33, for *Frances Oliver*, read *Francis Oliver*.

The errors above noticed are such as were overlooked in the proof-reading.

The following list of corrections and additions is prepared from information received since the pages referred to were printed.

P. 13. The ship Lyon sailed from London.—*Letter of Hon. James Savage.*

P. 36, l. 42. Elizabeth, dau. of Ebenezer Benton, was bap. Aug. 17, 1735.

P. 37, l. 4. Ezra, son of William Andrews, was bap. Jan. 2, 1732.

P. 37, l. 5. *Anna White*, m. June 4, 1731, Daniel Rust.

P. 49, l. 1, for Dec. 2, 1714, read Aug. 27, 1714. *Mary*, dau. of John White, bap. Nov. 5, 1727, was perhaps the one who m. John Baxter.

P. 67. The wife of SIMEON WHITE was not JERUSHA WAIT, but JERUSHA SMITH, of Hatfield.

P. 81, l. 1, for Jan., 1764, read June 19, 1764.

P. 84, l. 2, for 1847, æ. 60, read 1843, æ. 56.

P. 84, l. 23, for Brown Univ., read University of Vermont.

P. 86, l. 12. James and Lydia Cary removed in 1839 from Mexico, Oswego Co., N. Y., to Illinois. They both d. at Waukegan, Lake Co., Ill. He d. in 1846; she d. in 1848. They had no children.

P. 91, l. 15, for Killingworth, read Middletown.

P. 93, l. 16. ANNAR LOTHROP b. Apr. 5, 1742.—l. 24. *Lucinda* d. Apr. 22, 1836.

P. 96. ELIZUR WHITE died in Granville, N. Y., Oct., 1823, æ. 73. He m. June 26, 1769, HANNAH COOPER, who died Jan., 1828, æ. 79. He had,

1. *Elizur*, b. July 1, 1770; m. Hannah Savage. . . . (183)

2. *Hannah*, b. March 1, 1772; d. March 12, 1772.

3. *Joseph*, b. June 8, 1773; d. unm., Dec. 28, 1812, æ. 39.

4. *Hannah*, b. March 12, 1775; m. Joseph Ballory, and rem. to Grand Isle, Vt., where she d. about 1815, leaving five children ; Joseph, Eliza Ann, William, Fanny, and Deborah. The family afterwards rem. to Canada.

5. *Elizabeth*, b. March 29, 1777; m. Col. Nathaniel Frank, and d. May 3, 1823,

∘. 46. He d. Dec. 31, 1823. She had, Shipman, Hannah, Nathaniel, Elizur White, Andrew, Joseph White, and Eliza Ann.

6. *William*, b. Jan. 29, 1779; m. 1st, Grace Savage; 2d, F. Stocking. (184)

7. *Ebenezer*, b. June 19, 1781; m. Elizabeth Sage. . . .   (185)

P. 104, l. 6, read, He marched to New York, &c.

P. 108, l. 15, for east part of Rockville, read north-east part of Vernon.

P. 114, l. 16. Helen A. Henry m. Feb. 14, 1859, Harrie T. A. Smith, of New York.

P. 114, l. 23. Theodore W. Lyman m. 2d, Feb., 1859, Henrietta Wares of New York, where he now resides.

P. 114, l. 24. Wm. W. Lyman m. March 8, 1859, Lucy J. Snow of South Hadley.

P. 123, l. 13, for M. D. Van Hise, read M. S. Van Hise.

P. 125, l. 23, add, 7. James, d. in youth.

P. 127, **Family 131.** Correct the names and dates by the following:

DANIEL WHITE was born June 19, 1764, and died April 11, 1837, æ. 72. He m. Oct. 27, 1793, SALLY MERRIMAN of Richmond, Mass., b. June 1, 1772, and d. June 27, 1856. He had,

1. *Ruth Merriman*, b. Sept. 11, 1795.

2. *Lucia,*   b. April 27, 1797, m. Jan. 14, 1818, William Page, a farmer and magistrate in Stockbridge, Madison Co., N. Y. He d. Feb. 15, 1857, æ. 65. She has, 1. Sarah Samantha, b. Mar. 1, 1819, m. June 11, 1836, L. Johnson of Stockbridge; 2. Lucia Celestia, b. Sept. 7, 1821, m. Dec. 26, 1839, James Harris Ransom of Stockbridge; 3. Montgomery Hunt, b. Feb. 16, 1826, m. Dec. 23, 1848, Sophia A. Hinman of Augusta, N. Y.; 4. William K., b. July 10, 1828, m. Feb. 24, 1853, Mary Ann Wheeler of Chagrin Falls, Ohio; 5. Maryette, b. Nov. 7, 1830, m. Nov. 8, 1848, James H. Faulkner of Vernon, N. Y.; 6. Genevra L., b. May 14, 1833, m. Dec. 31, 1852, Hiram Van Swall of Augusta, N. Y.; 7. Melinda Jennette, b. Oct. 18, 1837, m. Nov. 30, 1858, James Horth of Oneida, N. Y.

3. *Abram,*   b. July 13, 1800; m. Dolly Gleason. . .   (268)

4. *Daniel,*   b. Sept. 1, 1802; m. Anna Hubbard. . . . (269)

5. *Eli Evarts,* b. March 29, 1808.

P. 143, l. 5, for Sally Sharp, read Sally Thorp.—l. 20, for 1803, read 1804.

P. 145, l. 10, for —— Sumner, read Elizabeth Sumner.

P. 147, l. 3, for 2. *Maria,* &c., read as follows:

2. *Maria,* b. June 4, 1794, m. Jan. 11, 1819, James N. Willard of North Hartland, Vt., a farmer. She has had, 1. James N., b. June 5, 1821, a farmer in N. Hartland. He m. Feb. 26, 1844, Mary G. Thayer; 2. Maria, b. April 23, 1823, d. May 13, 1823; 3. Phinehas K., b. Aug. 21, 1825, lives in N. Hartland. He m. Sept. 18, 1848, Ellen R. Pierce; 4. Louisa Maria, b. March 29, 1828, d. Sept. 10, 1829; 5. Allen H., b. Jan. 24, 1830, is a civil engineer in Davenport, Iowa. He m. Jan., 1857, Susan Collins; 6. Daniel S., b. Aug. 16, 1832; 7. George E. W., b. April 19, 1837.

P. 147, l. 26, for Oct., read Sept. 4. Insert Frances before Lucinda.

P. 147, for section 163, substitute the following:

ELIAS WHITE, Jun., son of Elias, (73) was born in Upper Middletown, Dec. 7, 1775. He was a shoemaker, and settled in Cornwall, Conn., where he died, Aug. 12, 1811, æ. 35. He m. Jan. 2, 1800, CYNTHIA ROGERS of Cornwall, dau. of Capt. Edward Rogers and Hannah Jackson. She was b. Dec. 8, 1782, and d. Sept. 12, 1813, æ. 31. Children—see Families 331a—331d.

P. 149, l. 31, for *Lemuel*, b. 1796, read b. 1795.

P. 152, Fam. 173. CHAUNCEY WHITE was a tailor: lived in Granville, Mass., till 1840. Mrs. MELINDA TAYLOR was wid. of George Taylor of Granville. For *Charles Plumb*, b. Aug. 5, 1809, read b. Aug. 4, 1809.

P. 157, Fam. 184. WILLIAM WHITE was born Jan. 29, 1779. He had one daughter by the first marriage ; *Grace Savage*, b. April 25, 1806, m. April 22, 1829, Andrew S. McPherson, and now resides in Galway, Saratoga Co., N. Y. She has had, 1, Catharine A., b. Sept. 1, 1835, d. Sept. 28, 1836 ; 2. Fannie G., b. July 26, 1843.

P. 157, Fam. 185. Capt. EBENEZER WHITE was born June 19, 1781. For 1. *Elizabeth Wells*, &c., read thus :
1. *Elizabeth Wells*, b. April 25, 1807 ; m. Dec. 4, 1833, Stephen S. Holmes of Springfield, Mass. She has had, 1. Emily Leavens, b. July 19, 1836 ; 2. Anna Elizabeth, b. Sept. 7, 1850, d. Jan. 28, 1859.

P. 167, l. 17, for Jabez Loomis, m. Oct., 1849, read Jabez White, m. Feb. 7, 1850.

P. 172, l. 19. Rev. Martin Kellogg has recently been elected a Professor in the College of California, at Oakland, Contra Costa Co., Cal.

P. 192, l. 13, read, 3. *Albert Milton*, b. June 18, 1824 ; m. Laurinda Cutler. (449a)

P. 202, Family 278, for 5. *John D.*, b. 1812, read b. 1813.

P. 213, l. 26, for *Willard Wetmore*, b. Feb. 7, 1835, read Feb. 7, 1836.

P. 215, l. 2, for Grace Keeney, read Sarah Grace Kenny.

P. 218, l. 1, read, 1. *Aaron*, b. Sept. 18, 1824 ; m. Isadore M. Haight.   (510a)

P. 218, l. 11, for *Sampson*, read *Frederick Sampson*.

P. 221, l. 4, read, 1. *Carleton*, b. May 11, 1834 ; m. Lizzie H. Dunn. .   (515a)

P. 245, l. 19, for Norman W., b. Oct. 20, 1850, read Oct. 29, 1850.

III. Summary.

THE following Summary and Tables include those persons only whose *names* appear in the preceding pages, or of whom some other definite information is given. A few descendants of Elder John White, but who derive the *name*, by intermarriage, from some other family of Whites, are classed with the descendants of other names.

The whole number of persons enumerated in this volume, belonging to the Family of Elder John White, is 5,074. Of this number, 2,850 bear the name of White, and 2,224 bear other names. The following Table shows the whole number of descendants in each generation, and also the number belonging to the line of each son of John White.

WHOLE NUMBER OF DESCENDANTS.

	1st Gen.	2d Gen.	3d Gen.	4th Gen.	5th Gen.	6th Gen.	7th Gen.	8th Gen.	9th Gen.	10th Gen.	Totals.
JOHN,	6	32	168	317	660	1353	1836	688	13		5074
Nathaniel,	8	71	208	473	924	1292	613	13			3603
John,	2	20	46	39	88	184	52	..			432
Daniel,	11	⌊ 46	60	145	339	360	23	..			985

The following Table shows the number of descendants named White, in each generation. Also, the number in the line of each son, and each grandson, of John White.

DESCENDANTS NAMED WHITE.

1st Gen.	2d Gen.		3d Gen.	4th Gen.	5th Gen.	6th Gen.	7th Gen.	8th Gen.	9th Gen.	Totals.
JOHN,˙	6		21	70	173	403	814	997	365	2850
	Nathaniel,	8	49	121	294	555	699	331		2058
		Nathaniel,	11	40	106	177	210	103		648
		John,	10	7	5	9	8	5		45
		Daniel,	11	43	123	249	377	188		992
		Jacob,	10	24	51	103	102	35		326
		Joseph,	7	7	9	17	2	..		43
	John,	2	10	18	19	59	98	18		225
		John,	10	18	19	59	98	18		223
	Daniel,	11	11	34	90	200	200	16		563
		Daniel,	11	34	90	200	200	16		552

Some interesting comparative results may be obtained from this Table. Of the descendants bearing the name of White, those of Nathaniel are nearly three-fourths of the whole number, while those of Daniel are more than twice as many as those of his brother John. There are still greater inequalities in the numbers descended from the several sons of Nathaniel. Two of these sons, Daniel and Joseph, married sisters. The descendants of Daniel are twenty-three times as many as those of Joseph, although the list of Daniel's descendants is quite imperfect, while that of Joseph's is supposed to be complete. In the line of Joseph, there are but two males of the seventh generation, to perpetuate the name. It should be observed, however, that the grandchildren of Nathaniel, having *other names* than White, were fewer than those of Daniel; and, in the next generation, those of Daniel were fewer than those of Joseph. So that if all the descendants were traced out, in the families of every name, the inequality in each case would be much less than it appears above. Other lines of the Family may be readily compared, by the aid of the Tables here given.

The number of descendants of other names than White, enumerated in this volume, appears below. This Table shows the number in each generation, and the number in the line of each son and grandson of John White.

DESCENDANTS BEARING OTHER NAMES THAN WHITE.

			3d Gen.	4th Gen.	5th Gen.	6th Gen.	7th Gen.	8th Gen.	9th Gen.	10th Gen.	Totals.
JOHN,			11	98	144	257	539	839	323	13	2224
	Nathaniel,		22	87	179	360	593	282	13		1545
		Nathaniel,		10	39	168	201	78	..		496
		John,		4	1	..	7	12	1		25
		Daniel,		30	100	154	264	160	12		720
		Jacob,		10	15	33	102	32	..		192
		Joseph,		33	24	14	19	..	..		90
	John,		10	28	20	29	86	34	..		207
		John,		28	20	29	86	34	..		197
	Daniel,		35	26	55	139	160	7	..		422
		Daniel,		25	55	139	160	7	..		386

In the 4th generation there were only *twenty-three* who perpetuated the name. Each one of these 23 is represented in the foregoing pages by descendants belonging to the 8th or 9th generation.

The volume contains some definite account of the children belonging to 1,000 families; 542 families of Whites, and 458 families of which the mothers were Whites. Those families of which a remoter female ancestor was named White, are not included in this enumeration. The two following Tables show the number of families in each generation, and in the line of each son of John White. The families are counted in the generations to which the parents belong.

FAMILIES OF WHITES.

	1st Gen.	2d Gen.	3d Gen.	4th Gen.	5th Gen.	6th Gen.	7th Gen.	8th Gen.	Totals.
JOHN,	3	7	27	54	127	203	120		542
Nathaniel,		5	18	40	90	141	104		399
John,		1	3	2	7	17	7		38
Daniel,		1	6	12	30	45	9		104

FAMILIES OF WHICH THE MOTHERS WERE WHITES.

	2d Gen.	3d Gen.	4th Gen.	5th Gen.	6th Gen.	7th Gen.	8th Gen.	9th Gen.	Totals.
JOHN,	2	9	19	44	88	184	105	7	458
Nathaniel,	3	12	31	58	127	91	7		329
John,	1	4	3	6	13	9	..		36
Daniel,	5	3	10	24	44	5	..		91

The following comparative Statement shows the *interval between the births of the oldest and youngest persons* of each generation.

Gen.	Eldest.	Date of Birth.	Youngest.	Date of Birth.	Years Difference.
2d.	Mary,	(p. 20,) b. about 1627.	Jacob,	(p. 20,) b. Oct. 8, 1645.	18
3d.	Nathaniel,	(p. 27,) b. July 7, 1652.	Mehitable,	(p. 32,) b. Mar. 14, 1683.	31
4th.	Elizabeth,	(p. 35,) b. Jan. 13, 1679.	Oliver,	(p. 44,) b. Mar. 26, 1720.	41
5th.	Moses,	(p. 46,) b. Feb. 7, 1710.	Joseph,	(p. 68,) b. Sept. 2, 1764.	54
6th.	Joel,	(p. 72,) b. about 1738.	Addison H.,	(p. 108,) b. Aug. 23, 1803.	65
7th.	Elijah,	(p. 129,) b. June 12, 1767.	John Jay,	(p. 178,) b. Sept. 7, 1854.	87
8th.	Theodore,	(p. 191,) b. Feb. 1, 1794.	Annie M.,	(p. 207,) b. Mar. 23, 1859.	65
9th.	Francis H.,	(p. 256,) b. Jan. 11, 1827.	Le Roy A.,	(p. 257,) b. Sept. 27, 1859.	32

It should be observed that very many of the 8th generation, and most of the 9th, are not yet born. There are doubtless a few descendants of the name, who belong to the 10th generation, but none have been reported. Of the descendants of other names, the first belonging to the 10th generation was William S. Skilton, (p. 268,) born August, 1847.

It appears from the above statement, that seven generations were added to the Family in two hundred years. Also, that the persons of the same generation were not all cotemporaries. The youngest child of the 5th generation was born less than three years before the oldest child of the 7th; while the youngest of the 7th generation was born 27 years later than the oldest of the 9th.

37

The *duration of each generation* is shown by the following Statement.

Gen.		Date of earliest Birth.		Latest known date of Death.		Years Duration.
1st.	JOHN,	(p. 13,)	b. about 1600.	JOHN,	(p. 20,) d. Jan.,	1684.	84
2d.	Mary,	(p. 20,)	b. about 1627.	Daniel,	(p. 29,) d. July 27,	1713.	86
3d.	Nathaniel,	(p. 27,)	b. July 7, 1652.	Esther,	(p. 31,) d. Sept. 7,	1766.	114
4th.	Elizabeth,	(p. 35,)	b. Jan. 13, 1679.	Oliver,	(p. 68,) d. Sept. 13,	1801.	122
5th.	Moses,	(p. 46,)	b. Feb. 7, 1710.	Jerusha,	(p. 67,) d. Dec. 1,	1839.	129

From a comparison of the foregoing Statements, it appears that John White lived five years after the birth of his oldest great-grandchild, and that each succeeding generation reached unto the third or fourth below it. Different members of the 4th generation were cotemporary with parts of each generation from the 1st to the 8th, and members of the 5th generation were cotemporary with parts of each generation from the 2d to the 9th. A considerable number of the 6th generation are still living, but nearly all of the persons now in active life belong to the 7th and 8th generations.

The *whole number of descendants named White* may be estimated from the foregoing data. The history of a large number of families shows that the ratio of increase in the early generations was nearly the same with that upon which are based similar estimates in the "Shattuck Memorials;" assuming seven as the average number of children in each family, and that two-thirds of the whole number live to be married. There were probably about 140 families of which the parents belonged to the 6th generation. Upon the above ratio of increase, there would be 980 descendants (named White) of the 7th generation, 2,289 of the 8th generation, and 5,341 of the 9th generation. The whole number in the first 8 generations would thus appear to be about 4,000. The descendants now living, with those of past generations, are probably more than that number. It will be seen by the first Table, on page 284, that the ratio of increase varies greatly in different branches of the Family.

A similar estimate may be made of the *whole number of descendants of every name.* The 170 great-grandchildren of John White would thus be multiplied to 17,213 in the 7th generation, to 80,325 in the 8th generation, and to 374,850 in the 9th generation. Perhaps one-fourth should be deducted from these numbers, to allow for intermarriages between descendants. There would still remain about 75,000 as the number of descendants in the first 8 generations, or the whole number of persons that may be supposed to have sprung from Elder John White, down to the present time.

These estimates are presented as only an approximation to the truth. The ratio of increase in the later generations is doubtless much smaller than that here employed.

The Third Part of the Index contains references to the names of about 2,200 persons connected with the Family by marriage.

INDEX.

PART First of this Index contains the christian names of descendants surnamed White. Part Second, the whole names of descendants having other names than White, with a few of that name, who derive the name from some other ancestor than Elder John White. Part Third contains the whole names of persons who have married into the Family. Part Fourth, the surnames of other persons mentioned in this volume. The names of descendants who are supposed to have died before reaching the age of ten years are omitted.

The number on the right of a name refers to the page. References to the name of the same person are connected by a hyphen. In Parts First and Second, the figure on the left of a name denotes the generation to which the person belonged.

PART I. DESCENDANTS NAMED WHITE.

PART II.   DESCENDANTS HAVING OTHER NAMES THAN WHITE.

9 Elizabeth, 231.
9 Mary A., 231.

French.

5 Daniel, 44.
5 Elizabeth, 44.
5 Eunice, 44.
5 Lucy, 44.
5 Samuel, 44.

Gage.

8 Calista, 151.

Gardner.

8 Austin A., 133.
8 Cynthia A., 133.
8 Dwight F., 133.
7 Emily, 95.
8 Esther, 133.
7 Franklin, 95.
7 Harriet, 95.
8 Harriet, 133.
7 Joel, 95.
7 Lucinda, 95.
8 Lucinda, 133.
8 Marinda, 133.
7 Orrilla, 95.
7 Permelia, 95.
7 Sally, 95.
8 Susan, 133.

Gates.

8 Francis, 119.
8 Lydia E., 119.
8 Sarah P., 119.

Gaylord.

7 Amanda, 92.
7 Cynthia, 92.
7 Lucy, 92.
7 Mary, 92.
7 Milly, 92.
7 Nancy, 92.
7 Sally, 92.
7 Vester, 92.

Gifford.

9 Abby F., 202.
9 Ann Eliza, 202.

Gilbert.

8 Caroline A., 168.
8 Charles M., 168.
4 Ebenezer, 24.
8 Eunice, 142.
8 Fanny C., 168.
8 Isaac, 142.
4 John, 24.
3 Jonathan, 24.
8 Julia M., 168.
8 Marcus A., 168.
8 Martha E., 168.
4 Mary, 24.
4 Mehetable, 24.
4 Nathaniel, 24.
4 Sarah, 24.

Goddard.

8 Charlotte M., 113.

8 Edward L., 113.
8 Evelina P., 112.
8 Harriet M., 113.
8 Nathan C., 113.
8 Nichols White, 113.

Goodman.

7 Cleopas, 70.
7 Cynthia, 70.
8 Edmund O., 115.
7 Enos, 70.
7 Erastus, 70.
7 Esther, 70.
8 Helen M., 115.
8 Henry M., 115.
8 Josiah White, 115.
7 Phineas, 70.
7 Sophia, 70.
7 Thomas, 70.
7 Tryphosa, 70.

Goodrich.

7 Abigail P., 78.
7 Butler, 78.
7 Caleb, 78.
8 Cordelia, 140.
7 Daniel, 78.
8 Dwight, 140.
7 Ebenezer W., 78.
8 Edmond C., 140.
7 Edward, 78.
7 Elizabeth, 78.
8 Ellen, 171.
7 George W., 78.
8 Gustavus, 140.
8 Henrietta, 140.
7 Huldah, 78.
8 Julia Ann, 171.
7 Lydia M., 78.
7 William, 78.

Gorton.

8 Helen M., 147.
8 Jane E., 147.
8 Laura A., 147.
8 Mary A., 147.
8 Melissa A., 147.
8 Roderick W., 147.
8 William B., 147.

Grandy.

8 Martin J., 152.
8 Mary L., 152.

Graves.

4 Abigail, 28.
4 Daniel, 28.
7 Daniel H., 77.
7 Emily, 77.
7 Fidelia U., 77.
7 Jane, 77.
4 John, 28.
7 John Judd, 77.
7 Julia, 77.
4 Martha, 28.
4 Mary, 28.
4 Rebecca, 28.

4 Sarah, 28-27.
7 Sarah Ann G., 77.
4 Thomas, 28.

Green.

9 Cornelia, 196.
8 Laura R., 162.
9 Oscar F., 196.
8 Philip M., 162.

Greenman.

8 Adaline, 160.
8 Amanda M., 160.
8 David White, 160.
8 Emily C. W., 160.
8 Esck E., 160.
8 Jeremiah, 160.
8 John, 160.
8 Lydia E., 160.
8 Mary D., 160.
8 William D., 160.

Grey.

9 Charles, 198.
9 Relland, 198.

Gridley.

7 Addison, 84.
7 Harry White, 84.
7 Laura White, 84.
7 Ralph Wells, 84.

Griswold.

5 Ann, 43.
5 Bathsheba, 43.
6 Chloe, 67.
6 Clarissa, 67.
5 Daniel, 43.
5 George, 43.
5 Hannah, 43.
6 Julia, 67.
5 Mindwell, 43.
5 Reuben, 44.
6 Sally, 67.
5 Sarah, 43.
5 Seth, 43.
6 Walter Price, 67.
5 White, 43.

Hager.

8 Edward A., 124.
8 Justina, 124.
8 Mary I., 124.

Hale.

6 Amelia, 56.
6 Anna, 56.
6 Ebenezer, 56.
6 Elias White, 56.
6 Esther, 56.
6 Gideon, 56.
6 Hannah, 56.
6 Hezekiah, 57.
6 Mary, 57.
6 Nancy, 57.
6 Reuben, 56.

Hall.

6 Alice, 50.

39

Johnson.
6 Abigail, 50.
8 Albert, 155.
5 Amos, 37.
8 Charles D., 165.
6 Comfort, 50.
5 Daniel, 37.
5 Desire, 37.
6 Henry, 50.
5 Hepzibah, 37.
6 Jesse, 50.
6 Levi, 50.
6 Ozias, 50.
5 Ruth, 37.
5 Stephen, 37.
5 Susannah, 37.
5 Thankful, 37.
5 Thomas, 37.
8 William, 155.
Jones.
8 Amelia D., 120.
8 Charles S., 120.
8 Henry White, 120.
8 William, 120.
Jordan.
9 Ellen, 246.
Judd.
7 Achsah, 71.
9 Lilian, 198.
7 Lydia, 71.
9 Mary A., 187.
7 Reuben, 71.
6 Submit, 45.
Keeney.
8 Julia Ann, 149.
8 Mary Ann, 149.
8 Samuel W., 149.
Keith.
8 Harriet S., 154.
Kellogg.
8 Allyn Stanley, 172.
8 Charles White, 127.
9 George, 194.
8 Martin, 172-283.
Kelsey.
8 Oscar O., 174.
Kennedy.
8 Arthur Sidney, 140.
8 Cornelia, 140.
8 Esther Elizabeth, 140.
8 Harriet White, 140.
8 Isaac Eugene, 140.
8 Norman Hulbert, 140.
Kimball.
9 Charles White, 184.
9 John D., 185.
Kimberly.
6 Anson, 66.
6 Electa, 66.
Kirby.
8 Catharine W., 157.
8 Fanny E., 157.

8 Sarah G., 157.
Lansing.
9 Arthur L., 209.
9 Henry White, 209.
Latham.
9 Alanson W., 182.
9 Augustus B., 182.
9 Benjamin F., 182.
9 Caroline A., 182.
9 Charlotte W., 182.
9 Francis E., 182.
Lathrop.
9 Harriet, 215.
9 Lillie, 215.
9 Nellie, 215.
Lawrence.
8 Henderson, 161.
8 Lydia M., 160.
8 Sarah White, 161.
Leach.
9 Carrie O., 183.
9 Ella, 183.
9 Eugene W., 183.
Leake.
8 Catherine Q., 173.
8 Charles P., 173.
8 Frances C., 173.
8 Henry D., 173.
Leavens.
8 Benjamin F., 157.
8 Edward, 157.
8 Emily W., 157.
8 Frederick, 157.
8 James B., 157.
Lee.
8 Alfred, 169.
8 Benjamin, 169-245.
8 Clementina S., 169.
8 Julia T., 169.
8 Leighton, 169.
Leete.
9 Ella Louisa, 193.
9 Theodore W., 193.
9 William W., 193.
Leonard.
8 Frances, 126.
8 Joseph W., 126.
Lewis.
9 Charles W., 233.
9 Emeline, 232.
9 Frances D., 232.
9 George, 232.
9 Mary E., 233.
Lindsley.
8 Abby Ann, 128.
8 Edward J., 128.
8 George White, 128.
8 Sarah White, 128.
8 Sylvester B., 128.
Lohnes.
9 Jenny, 218.

Looman.
7 Eunice, 72.
Loomis.
4 Azariah, 31.
4 Caleb, 31.
7 Chester, 105.
4 Daniel, 31.
4 Elizabeth, 31.
4 Isaac, 31.
4 Jacob, 31.
4 John, 30.
7 Russell, 105.
4 Samuel, 31.
7 Samuel, 86.
4 Sarah, 31.
4 Thomas, 30.
Lord.
7 Abigail, 82.
7 Epaphras, 82.
7 George, 82.
7 Hope, 82.
7 Rachel, 82.
7 Richard, 82.
7 Samuel P., 82.
7 Sophia, 82.
7 William, 82.
Lounsbury.
8 Amelia, 155.
8 Charles, 155.
8 Marion, 155.
Lyman.
7 Anna, 101.
7 Charles, 102.
7 Clementine, 102.
7 Elias, 102.
7 Fanny, 101.
7 George, 102.
7 Hannah, 102.
7 Horace, 102.
7 Jane, 102.
8 Joseph A., 114.
7 Lewis, 101.
8 Mary A., 114.
7 Normand, 101.
7 Simeon, 102.
8 Theodore W., 114-282.
8 William W., 114-282.
7 Wyllys, 101.
Lyon.
8 Charlotte, 110.
8 Christian, 110.
8 Ebenezer, 110.
8 Josiah, 110.
8 Lucy, 110.
8 Ruth, 110.
8 Solon, 110.
Malsom.
9 Anna, 209.
9 Julia, 209.
Mann.
9 Ellen, 225.
9 Harrison, 225.

Olmsted.

5 Asa, 41.
5 David, 41.
5 Elijah, 41.
8 Eveline J., 180.
5 Hannah, 41.
6 James, 52.
5 John, 41.
5 Joseph, 41.
5 Martha, 41.
6 Mary, 52.
6 Rachel, 52.
5 Simeon, 41.
6 Thankful, 52.
6 Timothy, 52.
6 Tryphena, 52.

Olney.

8 Alice C., 161.
8 Anna S., 161.
8 Elizabeth N., 161.
8 Franklin, 161.
8 Harriet N., 161.
8 John White, 161.
8 Louisiana, 161.
8 Mary E., 161.
8 Willard D., 161.

Orvis.

9 Clarkson F., 202.
9 Gurney M., 202.

Osborne.

6 Dolly, 54.
6 John Chevers, 54.
6 Joseph, 54.
6 Ruth, 54.
6 Samuel, 54.
6 William Franklin, 54.

Overton.

7 Augustine, 83.
7 Charlotte, 83.
7 Oliver, 83.
7 Prudence, 83.
7 Seth, 83.

Page.

7 Albert, 81.
7 Benjamin, 81.
7 Daniel, 81.
8 Elam C., 151.
7 Eli, 81.
7 Elvira, 81.
8 Flora E., 151.
8 Genevra L., 282.
7 Herman L., 81.
7 Louisa, 81.
8 Lucia C., 282.
8 Maryette, 282.
8 Melinda J., 282.
8 Montgomery H., 282.
7 Pamela, 81.
8 Sarah S., 282.
8 William K., 282.

Paine.

6 Electa, 61.
6 Elijah, 61.
7 Elijah, 61.
8 Eliza, 116.
6 Elizabeth, 60.
6 Hannah, 61.
6 Jerusha, 61.
6 John, 61.
7 John C., 61.
6 Mary, 61.
8 Melissa, 116.
6 Seth, 61.
7 William P., 61.

Palmer.

8 Abijah, 130.
8 Amos, 130.
8 Anna M., 130.
8 Charles W., 130.
8 Clarissa, 130.
8 Eliza D., 130.
8 Francis, 117.
8 Hannah, 130.
8 Henry W., 130.
8 Loren, 117.
8 Mary, 117.
8 Mary W., 130.
8 Nathan, 130.
8 Samuel, 117.
8 Sarah J. S., 130.
8 William E., 130.

Parker.

8 Harriet E., 115.
8 John H., 115.

Parmele.

8 Erastus, 150.
8 Hiram W., 150.
8 Mary S., 150.

Patterson.

9 Alexander J. L., 205.
9 Margaret W., 205.

Pease.

8 Delia S., 120.
8 Franklin W., 120.
8 Maria E., 120.
8 Mary C., 120.
8 William E., 120.

Peckham.

9 Charles, 209.
9 Edward B., 209.
9 Fanny, 209.
9 Julia B., 209.

Pell.

9 James H., 232.
9 Mary J., 232.

Pepper.

8 Hervey W., 114.
8 Simeon W., 114.

Perry.

8 Auguste Belmont, 168.
8 Edwin R., 179.

8 Frederick K., 179.
8 Jennett, 179.
8 Lavinia, 179.
8 Philenda, 179.
8 Philo, 179.
8 Samuel E., 168.

Phelps.

6 Mrs. Almira Lincoln, 33.

Pitcher.

9 Alfred, 232.
9 Caroline, 232.
9 Charles, 232.
9 Frank, 232.
9 Helen, 232.
9 Henry, 232.
9 Herman, 232.
9 Howard, 232.
9 Julia, 232.
9 Louisa, 232.
9 Lydia, 232.
9 Martha, 232.
9 Mary, 232.
9 Nellie, 232.

Pitkin.

6 Calvin, 62.
6 Elizabeth, 62.
6 Jerusha, 62.
6 Lucy, 62.
6 Martha, 62.
6 Paul, 62.
6 Samuel, 62.
6 Thomas White, 62.

Plumb.

6 Abraham, 56.
6 Amy, 56.
6 Anna, 56.
6 Frederick, 56.
6 Isaac, 56.
6 Joseph, 56.
7 Ovid, 56.
6 William, 56.

Pomeroy.

9 Ella L., 181.
9 Herbert W., 181.
9 Miriam W., 181.

Poss.

9 Elizabeth, 185.
9 Jonathan W., 185.
9 Tirza W., 185.

Powell.

6 Rebecca, 52.
6 William, 52.

Powers.

8 Abijah, 145.
8 Albina H., 145.
8 Elias F., 145.
8 Myra A., 145.
9 Orianna, 183.
8 Wilbur H., 145.

7 Perez, 72.
7 Pliny, 72.
7 Prudence, 70.
7 Rodney, 72.
7 Samuel, 98.
8 Samuel E., 132.
4 Sarah, 28.
7 Sarah, 98.
7 Sophia, 101.
7 Sylvester, 70.
7 Tamesin W., 70.
4 Thankful, 28.
7 Tirzah, 70.
8 Ursula P., 117.
8 Volney, 151.
7 William, 98.
8 William H., 135.

Soule.

9 Eugene, 196.
9 Frank, 196.
9 Henry C., 196.
9 Lizzie, 196.
9 Sarah F. P., 196.

Spencer.

9 Celia I., 206.
9 Harriet, 206.
7 John, 85.
7 Molly, 85.
7 Oliver, 85.
7 Samuel White, 85.
7 Susannah, 85.

Sprague.

8 Lydia Ann, 139.

Stall.

8 Ellen, 124.
8 Fanny W., 124.
8 Frederick E., 124.
8 Jane, 124.
8 Margaret E., 124.
8 Mary Ann, 124.
8 Samuel, 124.

Stanley.

8 Almira, 138.
8 Margaret, 138.
8 Oliver C., 138.

Stannard.

9 Oliver G., 249.

Stebbins.

8 Dwight, 149.
8 Edward, 149.
8 Theodore, 149.

Stocking.

9 George, 186.
9 Mariette, 186.

Stokely.

8 Benjamin O., 162.
8 Edwin, 162.
8 Rufus, 162.

Stone.

5 Aaron, 38.
5 Elihu, 38.
5 Isaac, 38.

5 John, 38.
5 Noah, 38.
5 Ruth, 38.
5 Sarah, 38.
5 Thomas, 37.
5 William, 38.

Storrs.

8 Eliza, 137.
8 Fortune K., 137.
8 Henry L., 137.
8 Peyton R., 137.
8 William C., 137.

Stow.

5 Bethiah, 39.
5 Freelove, 39.
5 Hannah, 39.
5 Jerusha, 39.
5 Martha, 39.
5 Mary, 39.

Strickland.

8 Julia Ann, 167.

Strong.

7 Amelia, 84, 105.
7 Charles, 84.
8 Charles C., 84.
7 Elnathan, 84.
8 Elnathan, 84.
7 Erastus, 84.
8 Harriet E., 84.
8 Henry White, 148.
8 Jane C., 84.
8 John E., 84.
7 Julia White, 105.
7 Lovina, 105.
8 Mary A., 84.
7 Nathan H., 105.
7 Theodore, 105.
8 William C., 84.

Sumner.

9 Cornelia Josephine, 241.
9 Elizabeth White, 241.
7 Margaret, 78.
7 Susan, 78.

Swift.

7 Charles, 98.
7 Eunice, 98.
7 Fanny, 98.
7 Guy, 98.
7 Ira, 98.
7 Lyman, 98.
7 Mary, 98.
7 Phebe, 98.
7 Rufus, 98.
7 Whitfield, 98.

Talcott.

7 Amelia, 105.
7 Asa, 105.
7 Polly, 105.
7 Southmayd S., 105.

Taylor.

10 Emma White, 264.

4 Mercy, 32.
3 Stephen, 32.
4 Stephen, 32.

Terry.

9 Cleveland, 225.
9 Harriet, 225.
9 Jenny, 225.
9 John, 225.

Thompson.

8 Almira, 109.
7 Eliza, 76.
8 Erasmus D., 109.
8 Luther, 109.
8 Milton, 109.

Tooley.

9 Charlotte E., 216.
9 Francis E., 216.
9 George A., 217.
9 Harriet L., 216.
9 Lucy J., 217.
9 Martha E., 217.
9 Mary L., 217.
9 Oscar P., 216.

Tower.

8 Charles, 124.
8 Lewis C., 124.
8 Lucy F., 124.
8 Pamela, 124.

Townsend.

7 Amos, 90.
7 Betsey, 90.
7 Eli, 90.
7 Hannah, 90.
7 Larmon, 90.
7 Nancy, 90.
7 Polly, 90.
7 William, 90.

Townson.

9 George E., 201.
9 Harriet C., 201.
9 Joseph N., 201.
9 Mary E., 201.

Tuttle.

8 Lucy A., 176.
8 Mary L., 176.

Ufford.

6 Jerusha, 56.

Villers.

8 Joseph J., 175.
8 Laura M., 175.
8 Mary V., 175.

Wadsworth.

7 Charles, 85.
7 Hezekiah, 85.
7 Mabel, 85.
7 Oliver, 85.
7 Polly, 85.
7 Samuel, 85.
7 Titus, 85.

Walcott.

8 Ann, 139.

PART III. PERSONS CONNECTED WITH THE FAMILY BY MARRIAGE.

40

Rogers, Mary, 237.
Rollin, Charles, 235.
Rood, Daniel, 46.
  Miranda, 222.
Roosevelt, Washington, 88.
Root, Anna, 139.
  Oliver D., 238.
  Stephen, 91.
Rose, Anna R. (Manning), 244.
Roseboom, Marietta, 203.
Ross, Dunbar, 226.
  Isaac, 98.
  Reuben, 149.
Rowe, Lucretia A., 195.
  Penelope, 239.
Rowell, Jonathan E., 219.
Ruffner, Joseph, 106.
Rugg, Edward A., 179.
  Lydia, 69.
Ruggles, Benjamin, 167.
Rushmore, Emma, 217.
Russell, Ambrose S., 173.
  Lucy, 77.
Rust, Daniel, 281-37.
Ryer, George, 259.

Sabin, Charles, 53.
  John, 91.
Sackrider, Norman, 200.
  Robert, 199.
Sage, Almina (Ingraham), 103.
  Elias, 176.
  Elizabeth, 157.
  Gideon, 52.
  Luther, 207.
  Mary, 81.
  Noah, 85.
  Roxy, 208.
  Susan, 230.
Salisbury, Lydia, 247.
Salmons, Oliver, 232.
Salter, Harriet, 65.
Samson, Joanna, 160.
Sanderson, Abigail, 145.
Sanford, David, 143.
  Elisha, 90.
Sarvant, Anna, 195.
  James, 79.
Savage, Edward, 204.
  Elisha, 37.
  Elizabeth, 35.
  Emily, 229.
  Gideon, 86.
  Grace, 157.
  Hannah, 156.
  Jonathan, 38.
  Lucy, 95.
  Martha, 54.
  Mary, 274.
  Prudence, 92.
Sawin, Louisa, 225.
Sawyer, Mary, 151.
Saxton, J. A., 100.
Scovel, Harriet N., 274.
Scovil, Eleazer, 129.
Scoville, Eunice, 171.

Scoville, Hannah, 94.
Scranton, Dennis, 130.
  Mary, 174.
Scripture, Abigail, 224.
Scrugham, Elizabeth, 114.
Searl, Harriet, 118.
Seeley, Samuel, 76.
Seely, Mary, 271.
Segur, Lucy (Bingham), 243.
Selden, Abigail, 70.
  Ebenezer, 27.
  Richard Ely, 82.
Sellew, Philip H., 131-204.
  Thomas, 55.
Sellon, William F., 114.
Sergeant, John, 81.
Server, Mary, 274.
Sewall, Esther, 120.
Seymour, Caroline, 233.
  Emily, 197.
  Hannah, 33.
  Henry, 105.
Sharp, Thompson, 161.
Shaver, John, 230.
Shaw, Emma L. W., 260.
Shayler, Mrs. Judith, 43.
Shedd, Mary E., 227.
Sheldon, Aaron B., 130.
  Delia, 170, 237.
  Elizabeth, 181.
  Julia Maria, 243.
Shelton, Elizabeth, 168.
Shepard, Deborah, 38.
  John, 27.
  Mary, 133.
  Rebecca, 75.
  Silas, 133.
Sherman, Martha, 213.
  Ruth, 121.
  Wealthy T., 167.
Shirtliff, Susannah, 44.
Shrader, John C., 161.
Sikes, Eleanor, 47.
  Silas, 76.
Sill, Zachariah, 129.
Simms, Benjamin, 97.
Skilton, S. W. S., 268.
Skinner, Hannah, 32.
  Jerusha, 112.
  Joseph, 33.
  Richard, 105.
  Sylvester T., 167.
  Thomas H., 80.
Slayton, Electa, 232.
Sloper, Lucy, 229.
  Ursula, 136.
Smead, Rachel, 71.
Smith, 92.
  Aaron, 84.
  Almon, 151.
  Alvah, 191.
  Amasa, 117.
  Angeline, 162.
  Anna, 270.
  Benjamin, 43.
  Benjamin B., 135.
  Betsey, 207.
  Chloe, 158.

Smith, Clarissa, 188.
  Cornelia A., 184.
  Darius, 70.
  Edward, 132.
  Elijah, 98.
  Emily, 70.
  Ephraim, 113.
  Erasmus D., 170.
  Frinda, 227.
  George, 175.
  Hannah, 72.
  Harrie T. A., 282.
  Harriet, 237.
  Henry C., 190.
  James L., 140.
  Jerusha, 281-67.
  John, 27, 213.
  John L., 219.
  Jonathan, 112.
  Joseph, 99, 101, 161.
  Mabel, 41.
  Margaret, 261.
  Martha, 32.
  Mary, 73, 162.
  Mary Ann, 253.
  Matson Meier, 245.
  Mehitable, 136.
  Orrin, 125.
  Patty, 113.
  Perez, 72.
  Philip, 41.
  Phineas, 73.
  Rufus, 70.
  Samuel, 27, 98.
  Sarah, 166.
  Susan, 138.
  Thomas E., 247.
Snow, Emeline M., 187.
  James H., 204.
  Jane N., 114.
  Lucy, 189.
  Lucy J., 282.
  Nancy, 229.
Snyder, Mariette, 264.
Soule, Henry B., 196.
Southworth, Mary, 201.
Spaulding, Celestia E., 186.
  James, 102.
  Levi, 102.
  Maria, 102.
Spencer, Clarissa W., 177.
  Hannah E., 151.
  Henry G., 206.
  John, 86.
  Lois, 119.
  S., 139.
  Samuel, 143.
Sperry, 90, 90.
  Jared, 90.
Spicer, Cyrus, 135.
Sprague, 139.
Springer, Catherine, 236.
St. John, Samuel H., 157.
Stacey, 124.
Stall, Isaac, 124.
Stamps, Thomas, 173.
Standish, Mary (Scott), 199.
Staniford, Timothy, 89.

41

The following name was omitted from page 315.

PART IV. PERSONS NOT CONNECTED WITH THE FAMILY.

The names of men whose daughters married men named White, are to be sought in connection with the names of their daughters, which appear in Part Third.

☞ The attention of those who consult this volume is directed to the list of *Corrections and Additions*, pages 281-283. That list was printed in the Appendix, rather than in its appropriate place, at the close of the volume, in order that the necessary references might be made to it, in the Index.

The following corrections have been received since the foregoing list was printed.

Page 36, Family 9. The wife of this John White (son of Capt. Nathaniel) was probably MARY REEVE of Hartford, b. July 31, 1665, dau. of Robert Reeve and Elizabeth Nott.

Page 222, Family 330, read thus: 3. *Calvin*, b. March 18, 1845; 4. *Thomas Ewing*, b. April 23, 1847; 5. *George B.*, b. Jan. 28, 1850; 6. *Clara*, b. Jan. 14, 1852.

LIBRARY OF THE UNIVERSITY OF

NOTE.

THE results of the efforts formerly made to trace the English ancestry of Elder John White have been given in the Appendix. Since the printing of this volume was commenced, some new interest in the inquiry has been awakened, by the discovery of an old coat of arms, engraved some time during the last century, and used for a book-label by one of his descendants. This coat of arms is that of a Mayor of the City of London, in Queen Elizabeth's time, whose name was *John White*, and whose pedigree can be traced several generations further back. Researches now in progress, with a view to ascertain whether any connection exists between our Patriarch, John, and the family of the Mayor, have not yet yielded any decisive results. The John White who was Mayor in 1563, was cotemporary, if not identical, with the grandfather of our Patriarch. Nothing has yet been discovered inconsistent with the conjecture that they were identical; and those of the descendants of our John who are not satisfied to derive their origin from so good and useful a man as he was, but must have an English pedigree, may adopt this conjecture, for want of one supported by better evidence.

One great difficulty in the way of discovering the English origin of the family is found in the fact that the name of *White* was a common one, in England. This fact appears not only from an examination of English records, but also from the number of persons bearing that name, who early emigrated to New England. Mr. Savage, the well-known genealogist, finds that there were about twenty-seven men named White, who came to New England before 1692, of whom it is probable that at least twenty became heads of distinct families in this country. The name has been so common in Massachusetts and Connecticut as to have much increased the labor and perplexity of preparing these Memorials. In numerous instances, persons named White, descended from some other ancestor, and not unfrequently, those bearing the same christian names, have lived in the same towns with those descended from Elder John White, and at the same time with them. The following are some of the heads of families of that name, who have lived in the same towns with Elder John's descendants, named in the preceding pages. In Massachusetts, *Henry* was living in Hadley in 1684. *Thomas*, from Lancaster, married a daughter of Thomas of South Hadley; (p. 72.) *John* was living in West Springfield soon after the death of the John named on page 57. In Connecticut, the multiplicity of families has been still more perplexing. In Lebanon there were *Nathaniel*, from Norwich in 1705, or later; *James*, who is found again in Coventry, in 1732; and *Jonathan*, from Weymouth, Mass., about 1751. In Hebron there are found, *Joseph*, who came from Oxford, Mass., in 1722; *Ebenezer*, from Lebanon about 1727; and *Obadiah, Samuel*, and *James*, who married in 1746, 1747, and 1748. In Chatham, (East Hampton Society,) *Joseph*, cotemporary with Dea. Joseph of Chatham, (p. 51,) had a son of the same name, and also a grandson *Joseph*, who married Ruth Churchill; (p. 50.) There was also a *Jedediah* of Chatham, at the same time that the Jedediah named on page 80 was living in Upper Middletown, on the opposite side of the river. Similar cases since the period of the Revolution are too numerous to be specified.

www.ingramcontent.com/pod-product-compliance
Lightning Source LLC
Chambersburg PA
CBHW030923050726
47498CB00003BA/872